IND

SERIES

1-3

Debt Inheritance

First Debt

Second Debt

by

New York Times, Wall Street Journal, & USA Today Bestselling Author

PEPPER WINTERS

Published: Pepper Winters 2014&2015: **pepperwinters@gmail.com**
Cover Design: by Ari at Cover it! Designs: **http://salon.io/#coveritdesigns**
Cover Design: Kellie Design Book Cover by Design:
http://www.bookcoverbydesign.co.uk/
Proofreading by: Jenny Sims: http://www.editing4indies.com
Proofreading by: Kayla the Bibliophile
Proofreading by: Erica Russikoff: http://www.ericaedits.com/
Proofreading by: Ellen Blackwell: http://www.blackwellproofreading.com/
Images in Manuscript from Canstock Photos:
http://www.canstockphoto.com

For every reader, blogger, reviewer, and friend who made my dreams come true.
I write for you.
…
Forever.

OTHER WORK BY PEPPER WINTERS

Pepper Winters is a New York Times, Wall Street Journal, and USA Today International Bestseller.

Her Dark Romance books include:

Monsters in the Dark Trilogy
Tears of Tess (Monsters in the Dark #1)
Quintessentially Q (Monsters in the Dark #2)
Twisted Together (Monsters in the Dark #3)

Indebted Series
Debt Inheritance (Indebted #1)
First Debt (Indebted Series #2)
Second Debt (Indebted Series #3)
Third Debt (Indebted Series #4)
Fourth Debt (Indebted Series #5)
Final Debt (Indebted Series #6)
Indebted Epilogue (Indebted Series #7)

Her Grey Romance books include:
Destroyed
Ruin & Rule (Pure Corruption MC #1)
Sin & Suffer (Pure Corruption MC #2)

Her Upcoming Releases include:
2016: Indebted Beginnings
2016: Je Suis a Toi (Monsters in the Dark Novella)
January 2016: Sin & Suffer (Pure Corruption MC #2)
2016: Super Secret Series to be announced
2016: Unseen Messages (Standalone Romance)

Follow her on her website
Pepper Winters

This story isn't suitable for those who don't enjoy dark romance, uncomfortable situations, and dubious consent. It's sexy, it's twisty, there's colour as well as darkness, but it's a rollercoaster not a carrousel.

Warning heeded…enter the world of debts and payments.

(As an additional warning please note, this is a cliffhanger, answers will not be answered, the storyline won't be resolved, and character motivations won't be revealed until further on. It's a complex story that will unfold over a few volumes.)

If you would like to read this book with like-minded readers, and be in to win advance copies of other books in the series, along with Q&A sessions with Pepper Winters, please join the Facebook group below:

Indebted Series Group Read

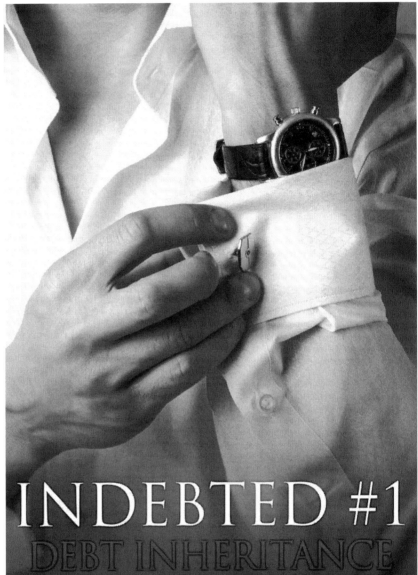

INDEBTED #1
DEBT INHERITANCE

INTERNATIONAL BESTSELLING AUTHOR
PEPPER WINTERS

Jethro

THE WORLD WAS a dangerous place, but I was worse.

The human race left the dark ages behind—technology improved and ruined our lives in equal measure, and the devils in society hid with better camouflage.

As the years rolled by, and we left our barbaric ways behind, people forgot about the shadows lurking in plain sight. Men like me morphed into predators in sheep's clothing. We preyed on the weak with no apology, and everything landed in our fucking laps. Civilization cloaked us, hiding the animals at heart.

We traded caveman mentality and murder for suits and softly spoken curses. I hid my true temper beneath a veil of decorum. I mastered the art of suave.

People who knew me said I was a gentleman. They called me distinguished, accomplished, and shrewd.

I was all of those things, but none of them. We might live in a civilized world, but rules and laws didn't apply to me. I was a rule-breaker, curse-maker, life-stealer.

The projection was a farce—but even the worst of us had someone who owned us. Whether family, honour, or duty.

I'd embraced my inner barbarian, yet was governed by a hierarchy and when the Hawk matriarch snapped her fingers, we all came running.

Including my arsehole of a father, Bryan Hawk.

There, in the cigar and cognac laced library, I learned a truth that forever changed my life.

And *hers*.

My family owned another.

An IOU on their entire existence.

Who gave a shit why a wealthy family called the Weavers were indebted to us? Who gave a damn that they'd royally fucked off my family and earned the wrath of my ancestors?

All I cared about was the news I'd inherited something more than just money, possessions, or titles.

My twenty-ninth birthday gave me a pet. A toy.

A responsibility I didn't want.

Debts I had to extract from unwilling flesh.

A job to uphold our family honour.

Nila Weaver.

One mistake six hundred years ago put a curse on her entire family.

One mistake sold her life to me in a mountain of unpayable debt.

I inherited her.

I preyed on her.

I owned her life and had the piece of paper to prove it.

Nila Weaver.

Mine.

And my task…

…

…

devour her.

"TOLD YOU THIS collection would be your break, Threads."

I smiled, not taking my eyes off the model prancing down the runway. My stomach churned like an overworked loom with stress and adrenaline.

"Don't jinx it. There's still the couture collection to go." I flinched as the model sashayed too much, wobbling in the insanely high heels I'd buckled to her feet.

My cell-phone buzzed in the only place I had available in this dress—my cleavage.

No, no. Not now.

I'd been waiting to hear from him for two days. Lying in bed in the fancy hotel, willing my phone to chime, granting me the intoxicating rush of flirtation. But nothing. Not a peep.

A month of this…*what was this?* It wasn't a relationship. Liaison? Nameless courtship? I had no name for the craziness I indulged in. I panted for scraps of communication like a high-school wallflower.

It's time to end it.

Another message vibrated, shattering my willpower to ignore him with his impeccable timing—as usual.

"You know the couture line will raise the roof. Stop being modest." Vaughn nudged my shoulder with his.

Ignoring my brother and the suddenly heavy cell-phone, I winced as the model flicked her hair pirouetting at the end of the runway, before flouncing away in a whirl of pink silk.

Too much attitude for that dress. I shook my head, stopping the inner monologue that never shut up when it came to models flaunting my creations.

"I don't know anything anymore. Stop nettling me, V. Let me focus."

Vaughn scowled. "I don't know why you're so worried. Cheque books are already open. You'll see."

Another message arrived, sending my phone into throbbing excitement. Even my phone got excited when he texted.

My heart fluttered. A hot flush covered my body remembering the last sentence I'd received from Kite007. I'd made the mistake of reading it just as I boarded the short flight from England to Spain.

Kite007: *I don't need to know what you look like to get hard—guess where my hand is.*

Of course I couldn't help myself. Because I was a sex-starved woman surrounded by over-protective men.

I replied: *I don't need to hear what you sound like to get wet—guess where my hand wants to be?*

I'd never been so blatant. With anyone. The moment I sent it I freaked out, wishing I could unsend.

I'd spent the trip in a confused state of arousal and denial. And never received a reply.

Until now.

I hid my flush, pretending nothing enticing taunted me on my phone. I loved my father and brother—so damn much—but if they knew…the proverbial shit would hit the fan.

"Oh, God." I clutched my heart as another stick-thin model paraded down the catwalk, failing to show off the intricate peacock-blue dress to its advantage. "No one will buy it if they can't see the potential of the design."

Vaughn sighed. "You worry too much. It's stunning. Anyone can see that." His dark eyes landed on mine. "Allow a thrill of pride—just once, Threads. It's going perfectly, and I couldn't be prouder of you." My twin brother draped his arm over my shoulders, tucking me against him. Considering the word 'twin' meant mirror image, Vaughn was taller, better looking, and overall more vibrant than me. He made others envious with his natural beauty, while I made others feel beautiful with dresses sewn with twenty-four carat gold and dyed with exclusive inks costing a small fortune.

I supposed that was my talent: making others feel worthy while he sold products thanks to his allure. Mirror image alright—the direct opposite.

"You're a model. Why aren't you showcasing my clothes?"

Vaughn laughed. "My figure doesn't look good squashed into some sequinned frock. Create some decent clothes for males, then I might stoop and be your headline act."

I thumped his arm. "You know I don't have the drive to stitch suits and boxer-shorts. I keep telling you to go into business with me and create a men's line. There'd be no stopping—"

Vaughn rolled his eyes. "Can't afford me."

I scowled. "Afford you? I've heard a perky pair of boobs and sex will buy your attention for at least a weekend."

He pointed at my small chest with a glint in his eye. "I see no perky pair and…gross, Nila. You're my sister. Why the hell are we talking about sex? You know we were raised better than that."

I didn't want to laugh. I didn't want to lose the wound-up tension from my collection, but Vaughn never failed to earn a lip-twitch.

I sighed, shaking my head. "Sex, shmex. You'd be lucky if I hired your scrawny ass."

He smirked. "Who're you calling scrawny?" He waved at his tall frame. "My skills are on the other end of the camera. As my track record states." His perfectly straight teeth flashed—daring anyone to deny the truth.

I used to be jealous of his deliciously good looks. My brother was rich brocade while I was boring calico. But now, I was proud. I might be graced with a body requiring embellishment by other means than fate, but I knew the secrets of illusion. I'd spun magic with a sewing machine since I was a little girl, stepping from the shadow of my family's name, carving a small slice of greatness for myself.

"Well if the show tonight flops, at least you can bail me out with all that cash you've earned thanks to your god-like looks."

A laugh barrelled from his mouth, loud but still hidden by the sultry fashion show music. The dark room hid the large crowd but couldn't disguise the heavy press and body heat of numerous buyers, shoppers, and catalogue procurers.

Vaughn squeezed me tighter. "Nila, I'm warning you. I want a smile. You've worked on this for months. Stop being so damn pessimistic and celebrate."

"I can't celebrate until the last model has shown their garment and not tripped over their arse in a seven thousand dollar dress."

My phone buzzed again.

I froze, cursing my twisting stomach and the fire-bolt to my core. Kite007. The nameless teasing male who had more power over me than any other man. A stupid secret crush. With a stranger no less.

It's a sad day when I'm emotionally invested in a fantasy. I should never have replied to the incorrectly sent message a month ago. Then I might've directed the small energy I had left after working so hard and find a real man. One I could kiss and flirt with in person.

The jagged pain lashed again. Rejection. I'd asked Kite, after a late night volley of messages, if he'd be interested in meeting.

Needle&Thread: *So…I was wondering…I'm sitting here drinking a glass of wine and thought you might like to do that sometime? Go out for a drink, in person, together?*

I'd pressed send on the jumbled, awkward sentence before I lost my nerve. I'd never asked anyone on a date before—it nearly gave me a heart attack.

He'd never replied. Silence was his usual reaction to dealing with something he didn't want to discuss—only to message a few days later on a completely different subject.

Where sexual innuendoes were hard for me, Kite007 was a master. He used it as a weapon, making me forget we had no depth to our conversations…not that they *were* conversations.

When he did reply, it'd been a clever mix of teasing and emptiness—reminding me not to read into this shallow form of communication.

Kite007: *I'm in a meeting and all I can think about is your nun outfit. You wearing underwear today?*

Yep. That stopped my wishful thinking of meeting him in person.

Untangling myself from Vaughn, I pretended to scrutinize the remaining models while I indulged in the very first text I received.

The one that began it all.

Kite007: *Tonight won't work for me, but waiting will only make you wetter. Be a good girl and don't argue. I'll make sure to reward your patience.*

A shiver worked its way under my expensive gown. I'd never received a message like that. Ever. And it wasn't meant for me. I imagined some lucky woman looking forward to her reward. I tried to delete the message—I really did. But after twenty-four years of being hidden away from boys, I couldn't help myself.

My reply was utterly ridiculous.

Needle&Thread: *I'm afraid you're talking to a nun who understands nothing of sexual hints and not-so-subtle suggestions. Patience to me is payment after waiting for a microwaved chocolate pudding. Wet to me is the brief enjoyment of a shower before the slave labour of my job. If your intention was to make me (an unknown stranger who could be your mother-in-law or an arthritic eighty-year-old) wet and impatient, perhaps you could bribe me with sugar, a hot bath, and a night off from work—then perhaps I'll obey and 'deserve' your veiled insinuation of pleasure. (By the way…if you haven't guessed, wrong number.)*

And so began a mistake that I had no intention of stopping.

I groaned under my breath, never failing to suffer a wash of embarrassment. I had no idea where the flippancy came from. I wasn't a nun—but I wasn't far off. Thanks to the two permanent men in my life, dating was a rare event.

A curvy model coasted down the runway in my favourite creation of cream lace, Victorian collar, and external bustle. I intended to head the trend of a historical fashion comeback.

"That would look better on you." Vaughn's husky voice cut through the graceful music.

I shook my head. "No chance." Looking down at my small cup size and overly trim frame, thanks to my obsessive running, I added, "You need femininity to pull off a corset like that. I'm a rake."

"Only because you exercise too damn much."

Only because I have you and father stopping me from getting exercise in sexual form. I didn't believe in self-pleasuring…running was my only hope at a release.

The model spun in place, swirling her train before disappearing up the catwalk. I suffered a moment of envy. It would be nice to have boobs and hips.

Vaughn's strong fingers caught my chin, breaking the unlockable stare I had on the strutting model, guiding my non-descript black eyes to his vibrant chocolate ones. "We're going out tonight. Hitting the Milan night clubs." The low lights around the runway made his skin glow with a natural dusky tan. His blue-black hair was the one beautiful thing I shared. Thick, dead straight, and so glossy people said it was like looking into black glass.

My one saving grace.

Oh, and my ability to sew.

And flirt with a stranger on an impersonal device.

My phone buzzed—a reminder my inbox had something delicious for me to read. And it would be delicious.

Dammit. The urge to look almost broke my self-control. What the hell was he doing messaging me? We knew nothing about each other. We shared nothing but dirty fantasies. My mind once again jumped back to the first relay of texts.

Kite007: *Shit, you're a nun? Sorry…what's the correct term of address…sister? I apologise for the incorrectly sent message. Despite your Godly perfection and sheltering, you deduced correctly. It was in fact very sexual. The woman in mind would never be welcomed into a sanctity such as yours.*

I'd had no reply to that, but he'd sent another twenty minutes later.

Kite007: *Sister…I need absolution. I find myself consumed with the image of a sexy nun stripping and sliding into a hot bath with chocolate sauce on her lips. Does that make me the devil, or are you for making me lust for someone I shouldn't?*

For the first time in my life, I'd felt the rush of power and need. This unknown man lusted for me. He'd replied based on what I'd sent. He'd been right about the blushing, but only because I was sheltered, not because I'd decided to dress in black and white garb for the rest of my life. I came from rainbow fabric; I drank textile ink as mothers' milk. I learned to sew before I could walk. I could never become a nun, purely because of the boring fashion choices.

My fingers shook as I messaged him back.

Needle&Thread: *I'm blushing but happen to be wearing something a lot more interesting than black and white or a boring shift.*

I had no idea what made me reply. I'd never been so bold and he was taken—obviously. He'd been messaging a girl.

Kite007: *Oh, see…you can't say things like that to a complete stranger who mistakenly messaged a hot nun who doesn't conform to the dress code picked out by God. Tell me.*

Needle&Thread: *Tell you what?*

Kite007: *What are you wearing?*

And that was where I freaked. He could be a ninety-year-old pervert who'd tracked down my number from one of my runway shows to stalk me. Nothing was as it seemed in today's world.

Needle&Thread: *I hope you find the person you were trying to contact. Enjoy your night of sexual torture. Goodbye.*

I'd closed my phone and done exactly what I'd said. Microwaved a chocolate pudding and slid into a hot bath. Only to be interrupted by a reply.

And another.

And another.

I lost count of how many messages I received. I managed to ignore him for five hours, but then my innocent soul became corrupted by a man I'd never met.

"What do you say?" Vaughn pursed his lips, accenting his well-formed jaw and rounded cheekbones.

I blinked, shattering memories of phone flirting.

"Huh?"

"Tonight. You. Me. A bottle of tequila and some bad decisions." My brother rolled his eyes. "I'm not having you holed away in your hotel room on your own—not after a show like this." Vaughn's voice cajoled, his face—a cross between a cherub-faced youth and heartbreaker man—implored. I could never say no to him. Just like countless other women. It didn't help he was heir to a textile business that'd been in our family since the thirteenth century and a seriously good catch.

We had pedigree.

History.

The bond between past and present. Dreams and requirements. Freedom and obligation. We had plenty of it, and the weight of what was expected of me hammered me further and further into the ground.

"No tequila. No night clubs. Let me unwind in peace. I need some quiet after the hectic day I've had."

"All the more to get messy on a dance floor." Vaughn grabbed my elbow, attempting to swing me around in a complicated dance move.

I stumbled. "Get your grubby hands off me, V." Vaughn was the only one who didn't inherit a nickname based on the industry that consumed not only our lives but our ancestors, too.

"That's no way to speak to your brother, Threads." V laughed.

"What's this? My two offspring fighting?"

I rolled my eyes as the distinguished silhouette of my father appeared from the crowd of buyers, designers, and movie starlets all there to witness the new season of fashion in Milan. His dark brown eyes crinkled as he smiled. "Congratulations, sweetheart."

Vaughn let me go, relinquishing his sibling hug for a paternal squeeze. My arms slinked around the toned middle of my father.

Archibald Weaver still had the Weaver signature thick black hair with a straight spine, sharp mind, and ruggedly handsome face. He only became more fetching the older he got.

"Hey. I didn't think you'd arrive in time." Pulling away, I inhaled his strong cologne. I wished mum was still around to see him evolve from distracted parent to fantastic support system. I never knew why we weren't close when I was young. He'd been sour, grumpy, and…lost. But he'd never burdened Vaughn or me with what troubled him. He remained a strict single parent, raising us motherless from eleven years old.

"I managed to get an earlier flight. Couldn't miss your headline show."

Another message came through, the vibration particularly violent. I shuddered and blocked all thoughts of the nameless man trying to get my attention.

"I'm glad. However, all you're going to see is your daughter shuffle down the runway, overshadowed by gorgeous models, and then trip off the end."

My father laughed, his critical eye perusing my gown. "Corset, tulle, and the new midnight-galaxy material—I doubt anyone will overshadow you."

"Help me convince her to join me tonight. We could all go out together," Vaughn said.

Great. Another night with two men—neither of whom I can avoid to acquire a real relationship.

I often felt like a kitten brought up by two tigers. They never let me grow up. Never permitted my own claws to form or teeth to sharpen.

My father nodded. "Your brother is right. It's been a few months since we were together. Let's make a night of it. Some of your best work is on display. You've made me very proud, Nila, and it's time to celebrate."

I sighed. Looking over his shoulder, I saw the last model disappearing into the wings, her train of silver stars and organza looking as if she'd fallen from heaven.

That's my cue.

"Fine. Sounds wonderful. I can never say no to you. Let me wrap this up and then I'll relax. Promise." I reached up and kissed him on his papery cheek. "Keep your fingers crossed that I don't trip and ruin my career."

He grinned, slipping into the much loved and well known persona of Tex—short for Textile—a nickname he'd had all my life.

"You don't need luck. Knock 'em dead." His brown eyes faded. The melancholy I was so used to seeing swallowed him whole, hiding his jovial spirit. It was his curse. Ours. All of us.

Ever since mum divorced him and disappeared we'd never been the same.

Vaughn pecked my cheek. "I'll help you get through the crowd."

I nodded and weaved through the crush of bodies to the small staircase at the side of the runway.

The organiser, with her headset, frantic blonde curls, and dog-eared notebook, squealed when her eyes landed on mine. "Ah! I'd sent out ninjas to find you. You're up. Like right now."

Vaughn chuckled. "I'll wait here for you." He faded into the living organism that was the fashion hungry crowd, leaving me at the mercy of Blonde Curls.

Bunching the overflowing train of my dress, I climbed the steps, hoping against all odds that I wouldn't faint. "Yes. I know. That's why I'm here."

"Thank God. Okay, stand there." She manhandled me until I stood just so. "I'll give you the cue in thirty seconds."

The girl couldn't have been much younger than me. I'd just celebrated my twenty-fourth birthday, but after leaving school at sixteen to follow in my family's footsteps and nurture my skills as a designer, I felt much older, grumpier, and less eager to please.

I love my job. I love my job.

And it was true. I *did* love my job. I loved transforming plain fabric, sourced by my father, into works of art thanks to the accessories, silks, and diamantes my brother imported when he wasn't modelling. We were a true family business. Which I loved and would never change.

It was the public eye I hated. I'd always been a homebody. Partly out of choice—partly because my father never let me date.

Talking of dates…

My fingers itched to grab my phone.

The girl nodded, pressing her headset hard to her ear. "Gotcha. Sending on now." Holding her hand out, she added, "Come. Your final model is ready. Get onto the runway."

I nodded, gathering the thick black material of the feather and gemstone dress I wore. Completely impractical. Completely couture. A bloody nightmare to wear, but the effect of soft wispy feathers and the glint of black diamantes set my hair off better than any other colour.

Some said colour was what made your mood.

I said black protects.

It gave me strength and boldness where I had none. It granted sexuality to a woman who'd been sheltered all her life by a severely overprotective father and insanely possessive brother.

If it hadn't been for Darren and the one night where I'd drunk too much, I would still be a virgin.

Taking my place in the middle of the runway, I smiled tightly at the model chosen to wear my centrepiece.

My heart fluttered, falling in love—just like I always did—with the garment I'd adoringly, intimately created. Wrapped around the girl's zero-size frame and shimmering in the low lights of the packed room, the dress was revolutionary. My career would reach new heights. It wasn't pride glowing in my heart—it was relief. Relief that I hadn't let anyone down—including myself.

I'd done it.

Despite my nerves, I'd done what I'd always needed and carved a name for myself despite the huge inheritance of the Weaver name and empire.

My collection was mine.

Every item from handbags to shoes and scarfs was mine.

Nila.

Just my first name. I hadn't wanted to use the power of our legacy. I hadn't wanted to let anyone down in case I failed. But now I wanted to sequester my success and hoard it.

The room hushed with anticipation as the music changed from Latin to symphony. A large spotlight drenched us in golden rays.

My heart rate exploded as I took the model's hand, flashing her a quick smile. Her cascading blonde hair glittered with gold plaited in the strands.

We matched perfectly in height—deliberately placed together for ultimate impact. Gliding forward in thousand dollar shoes, we walked the final stretch.

My black ensemble set off the gold, yellow, and burnt orange of her layers upon layers. She looked like crackling embers and fire where

I was the coal from which she sprang. We were the sunset of the show. The darlings of Milan.

Hushed silence. Bright lights. Immense concentration to stay on my feet.

The rest became a blur. There were no trips, or wobbles, or rushes of horror. Cameras clicked, praise murmured, and then it was over.

A year of hard work wrapped up in a two hour runway show.

The end of the platform became a sea of petals and strewn flowers full of accolades. Our coal and fire presence swallowed camera flashes, welcoming greedy eyes to stare.

Ten minutes I stood and drowned in praise. Vertigo hobbled my body as my gaze landed on my father and brother. They knew this part was the hardest for me. They knew my heart strummed fast and sickness rolled. Stress never sat well with my system.

Vertigo was hard to diagnose, but moments like these—where the madness of the past year culminated with yet more deadlines on the horizon—I recognised every symptom of wobbliness and fading vision. I felt drunk…I *wanted* to be drunk—even though I hadn't had liquor in seven years.

Swallowing the lightheadedness, I waved and bowed before hitting my limit. Gritting my teeth, I almost fell down the steps at the front of the runway right into Vaughn's arms.

He scooped me up, giving me a firm balanced form to clutch to. "Breathe through it. It'll pass."

Shaking my head, I blinked, chasing away the fear in my blood and weakness of an incurable illness. "I'm okay. Just let me go for a second."

He did as I asked, giving me space. The crowd stayed behind their small barricade letting me suck in much needed oxygen. My phone buzzed again and this time…I couldn't ignore it.

Pulling it from my ruffled, feathered cleavage, I unlocked the screen and indulged.

Kite007: *Haven't had a message from you in a couple of days. If you don't send one immediately, I might have to track down your name and location and come and spank you.*

My stomach flipped at the threat. He'd never insinuated a meeting…not after my bungle of asking him out and his blatant refusal.

Kite007: *Still no reply. If threats of physical harm won't make you respond, perhaps the mental visualisation of me stroking myself while reading some of your old messages will persuade you to.*

My core clenched. He'd pleasured himself while thinking of me? A stranger touching himself shouldn't give me such a thrill.

Kite007: *My Naughty Nun, I don't know what you're doing, but I've disgraced myself by coming all over my hand at the thought of you naked and smeared in chocolate. Hope you're happy.*

"What are you reading?" Vaughn peered over my shoulder.

My cheeks flamed and I wiped the screen of evidence that despite his and my father's best intentions, I'd managed to find a man interested in talking sex with me. I couldn't wait to be in private to respond. Kite seemed more…open. Maybe we could talk about real things and not just dirt.

"Nothing."

Vaughn scowled, then a large grin brightened his face. "Guess how many orders?"

My brain couldn't switch from wanting desperately to respond to Kite to normal conversation. "Orders?"

He threw his hands up. "Seriously! Your collection. Sometimes I worry about you, Threads." Still grinning, he added, "Your Fire and Coal collection has orders from all major retail chains in Europe and America, and the couture line is currently in a bidding war for exclusivity between a London boutique and Paris." He bounced with happiness—infecting me with energy. "I told you this was your break. You've cemented your name. *Nila* will be worn by celebrities around the world at their red-carpet premieres."

He lowered his voice. "You're your own, sister. You're more than just a Weaver. You're *you*, and I'm so damn proud of what you've achieved." Twin intuition had always been strong—showing just how much he understood without me ever having to voice it.

Tears sprang to my eyes. Vaughn didn't get sentimental often, so his praise was a well-placed dagger in my self-control. This time I couldn't stop the smile breaking through my defences or my heart glowing with accomplishment. "Thank you, V. That means—"

"Nila."

I spun around to face my father. Instead of the grin and look of love I expected, he stood cold and fierce. My stomach tensed, sensing something was wrong. So, so wrong. It was the same look he got whenever he thought of Mum. The same look I'd grown accustomed to hating and running from.

"Dad…what—" He wasn't alone. My eyes trailed from my father's pressed tux toward the tall, svelte man beside him.

Holy hell, who on earth…

Thoughts died like windless kites, littering my mind with silent dumbness. He was a stranger. But I felt as if I'd seen him before. He was a mystery. But I sensed I already knew everything about him. Two extremes…two confusions.

"Nila, I want to introduce you to someone." My father's jaw ticked, hands clenching into white-knuckled fists. "This is Jethro Hawk. He's a big fan of your work and would like to take you out tonight to celebrate your success."

I wanted to rub my eyes and have my hearing checked. Since the day of my birth, my father had never introduced me to a man. *Never.* And he'd never lied so obviously. This man wasn't a fan of my work—although he did have incredible fashion sense. He had to be a male model with his height, envious cheekbones, and perfectly styled salt-and-pepper hair. His white skin was flawless—no wrinkles or blemishes. He looked ageless, but I guessed he was late twenties despite his greying hair speaking of wisdom far beyond his years.

His hands were concealed in pockets of a dark charcoal suit with a cream shirt open at the throat and a diamond pin piercing his jacket lapel.

"Tex, what are you—" Vaughn's voice was quiet but possessive. Eyeing up Jethro, he stayed polite by offering his hand. "Nice to meet you, Mr. Hawk. I appreciate your interest in my sister's talent, but my father has it wrong. Tonight she is unavailable due to a family commitment."

I would've smiled if my stomach wasn't knotted as the two men assessed each other.

Jethro slowly took my brother's hand, shaking once. "Pleasure, I'm sure. And I, in turn, can appreciate your interest in keeping your prior agreement with your sister, but alas. Your generous father has allowed me the enjoyment of ruining your plans and stealing her away." His voice whispered through my gown, sending goosebumps down my spine. His accent was English, same as mine, but slightly more clipped. He sounded posh but rogue at the same time. Refined but uncouth.

My brother wasn't impressed. His forehead furrowed.

"I hope that isn't going to be an issue, Mr. Weaver. I've heard a lot about you and your family and would hate to upset you." Mr. Hawk's eyes landed on mine, capturing me in a cage of golden irises and effortless power. "However, I've heard the most about your sister. And I have no doubt it will be a pleasure knowing her."

I gulped. No one had spoken to me like that—especially in front of my *father*. Who was this man? Why did his very existence fill me with hot and cold and awareness and fear?

"Listen here," my father blustered. I tensed, ready for the outrage I knew he was capable of, but his lips snapped closed and the fire in his gaze didn't erupt. Swallowing hard, he finished, "I presume my obligations are complete?"

Jethro nodded, a lock of hair brushing his forehead. "You presume correctly."

Fear evolved to panic. Obligations? *My God, is my father in some sort of trouble?* I clutched his sleeve. "Dad. The show's over. Let's go for that drink." I glanced at Vaughn, cursing my fluttering heart and the mix-match of emotions colliding inside.

My father pulled me close, pressing a single kiss on my cheek. "I love you, Nila, but I've kept you to myself for long enough. Mr. Hawk has asked if he can take you out tonight. I agreed. Vaughn and I can wait till another time."

He didn't say—*only if you want to, of course*. It sounded more like a sentencing rather than freedom to date. Why this man? Why now?

Vaughn moved closer. "Tex, we already had plans. We can't just—"

My father glared at my brother, his gaze weighty with unsaid anger. "Plans change, V. Now give your sister a kiss goodbye. She's leaving."

"I am?" I took a step backward, clutching my phone. There was no denying Jethro Hawk was good looking and seemed to be successful judging by his attire, but if I was allowed to date, I wanted Kite007, not this cold outlander.

"You are." Jethro held out his hand, his gaze noosing me tighter in their golden cage. "I'm taking you somewhere special."

"She isn't going anywhere with you unless she wants to, dickhead." Vaughn puffed out his chest, placing a hand on my lower back. "Tex—tell him."

My eyes flew to my father. What existed in his gaze sent frost crackling through my blood. His lips were tight, eyes bright and slightly glassy. But his cheeks were dark with rage. He glowered at Mr. Hawk.

"I've changed my mind. Not tonight."

Vaughn huffed, nodding in agreement. The thick soup of male testosterone choked my lungs.

Jethro smiled coolly. "You've given me your word, Mr. Weaver. There are no rain checks." Aiming his sharp smile my way, he purred, "Besides, Ms. Weaver and I have a lot to discuss. It's time we got acquainted and tonight is the night."

"Excuse me while you all fight over me. But what about what I want?" I crossed my arms. "I'm tired, overworked, and not in the mood to entertain. Thank you for your interest, but—"

"No buts, Ms. Weaver. It's been arranged and discussed. You will come with me because it's the only way your night will end." Jethro lowered his head, watching me from beneath his brow. "I promise you'll have a good time. And I mean you no harm…do you really think your father would permit me to take you out otherwise?"

Coldness etched his gaze.

Aloofness whispered from his posture.

Calculation radiated from his every pore.

I'd never been so intimidated or so intimately challenged.

My father might have permitted this, but he didn't condone it. Somehow Jethro had achieved the unachievable and convinced my father he was dateable material. If he could manipulate Archibald 'Tex' Weaver, I didn't stand a chance…and yet…despite the arrogance and chilly façade, he intrigued me.

My father had kept me captive my whole life. This was the first man to stand up to him and grant a glimmer of freedom.

The fear disappeared, leaving a flicker of interest. If this was the only man I could spend an evening alone with, I would take it. I would practice my non-existent flirting skills and grow my confidence so I could ask Kite007 out again. And next time, I wouldn't take no for an answer.

Sucking in a gulp, I placed my hand gently into Mr. Hawk's. His touch was as cold as his demeanour and just as strong. I froze as his fingers tightened around mine, tugging me forward. "Good decision, Ms. Weaver. I look forward to getting to know you better."

My lungs dragged in his scent of leather and woods. Words deserted me.

The show disappeared along with my worry and thoughts of Kite007. Gone was the urge to return to an empty hotel room. This man was pure danger, and I'd never sampled anything but safety. "And you, Mr. Hawk," I murmured.

My date smiled, transforming his face from handsome to ruthless. "Please, call me Jethro." Changing our grip from handshake to handhold, he pulled me forward—away from my family, away from the men I'd known all my life, and toward a future I had no understanding of.

Vaughn's hand fell from my lower back.

I didn't look back.

I should've looked back.

I should never have placed my hand into that of a monster's.

That was the last day of freedom. The last day that was my own.

Individuality and uniqueness—those two words were so precious once upon a time. I'd been brought up with a gruff but fair father and a brother who I would marry if it wasn't incest, believing I was unique, different, never before created.

I hated being lied to.

I hated even more believing those lies until the truth decided to come for me.

Turned out, I was never an individual; I was a possession to trade.

I was never unique; someone had lived my life many times before, never free, never whole.

My life was never mine.

My destiny was already written.

My story began the night he came for me.

Jethro

IT WAS TOO easy.

I'd stolen her right before her father and brother. I'd taken her with no blood shed or bones broken.

Power wasn't threats or uncivilised fighting. It wasn't brawn or hard-won arguments.

Power was holding something so absolute, a man would do what he was told—all the while cursing your very soul. True power wasn't wielded by gangs or even loudly-spoken governments.

True power. *Limitless* power—only graced a fair few. It gave those lucky ones the ability—the nobility, to be courteous and polite. All while holding their fucking balls in their hands.

Archibald Weaver was one such example.

I shook my head, disbelieving how the so-called enemy of my family handed over his only daughter. The same daughter I'd seen in tabloids as a rising star of designers. The same offspring who was never photographed with a man on her arm or seen sneaking out of a restaurant with a hidden lover. He'd wanted to kill me. I had no doubt he would *try* to kill me.

But he would fail.

Just like he failed to protect her.

Because he had no fucking power.

All it had taken was two sentences and Nila went from his to mine. A thrill ran down my spine, remembering the rush of sensation when I'd tapped him on the shoulder. His dark eyes had been cool but welcoming, believing I was a stranger there to congratulate. That all changed when I handed over a black-flocked business card and said,

"The time is nigh to pay your debts. Your past has found you, and there will be no peace until she's ours."

His eyes went from cool to glinting with horror and rebellion. He knew everything I did. He knew there was only one thing he could do—no matter that it would break his heart.

This was his fate. Her fate. *Their* fate. It'd been written and understood the moment he'd knocked up his wife.

He knew the consequences, and he also knew the power we controlled. No matter his unwillingness and terror, there was no other course of action.

Without a single word, he'd marched me to his daughter and placed her life in my hands. I hadn't believed my father when he said it would go so smoothly. After all—none of this made sense. But it had. And it did. And now…it was all on me.

My education had begun a month ago. I'd been told of my upcoming duties, given history lessons of past debt collections. But I was as new to this as her.

We came from generations interlocked in the same untieable way.

Now, it was our turn.

And we would have to learn together.

I glared at my conquest. Letting her hand go, she glided beside me wrapped in darkness. I didn't need a physical claim on her now that she was outside—alone. Was it trust in her father's judgement guiding her feet or stupidity?

Either way, I would be the last person she would ever see.

I BREATHED A lungful of crisp Milan air as we left the ornate
building where the fashion show was held. For late summer, the
temperature danced with chill rather than heat. The night had finally
claimed the day. It didn't get dark until ten p.m., so it was late for me.
This time of evening, I would normally be buried under a mound of
cotton with a chalk pen and scissors deciding what my next creation
would be.

Coldness darted through my blood—not from the cool breeze but
from *him*. The silent, foreboding man walking soundlessly beside me.

Who is he? And why don't I trust a thing about him?

Studying him in my peripheral vision, he seemed to give off two
personas. One, a cordial, well-dressed gentleman who looked as though
he'd stepped through a wormhole from some ancient century. And
two, an assassin who moved like a dancer only because he'd been
taught the art of war and murder from the crib.

No words were spoken. No dalliance or small talk. His silence was
strangely welcomed and hated. Welcomed because it meant I could
focus on my vertigo and not let stress topple me over, hated because I
wanted to *know* him. I wanted to know why my father had vouched for
him and just where the hell he was taking me.

"I don't believe you," I said, my voice slicing through the crisp
evening.

Even in the gloom, with only street lights for illumination, his eyes
were bright and such a light brown they seemed otherworldly. His
eyebrow rose, but no other interest showed on his face. "What don't
you believe?" He fanned his arm to the left, indicating for me to travel

that way.

My feet behaved, tottering obediently in the black velvet heels, but my brain swam with a sudden gyroscope of vertigo. I focused hard on the diamond glinting on Jethro's lapel. *Find an anchor. Hold on tight. Do this and you'll be alright.* The stupid rhyme echoed in my brain. My brother had made it up when we were eight after I'd broken my arm falling off the bottom step of our porch.

"That you convinced my father that you're dateable material." I bunched the front of my skirt, wishing I could've changed before traipsing through Milan in a couture dress. "You either bribed him or threatened."

Just like you're threatening me with your silence and imposing attributes.

"Threatened….interesting word." His voice positively purred. Placing his hands into his pockets, he added, "And if I did? What difference does it make? You're still here—with me—alone. Dangerous, really."

The footpath decided to roll beneath my suddenly unsure feet. *Breathe. Get it together.*

Heroines in books were portrayed as quaint and lovable if they were clumsy. I had more bruises and scrapes from falling and slamming into things than I would ever admit, and there was nothing quaint about it. I was a hazard. Especially if I had a pair of wickedly sharp dress scissors in my hands and stood up too fast. Anyone in a two metre radius was in danger if my brain decided to throw me helter-skelter into a wall.

It was also a huge inconvenience when faced with an overbearing stranger who just used the words *alone* and *dangerous.*

"Dangerous isn't a good word," I muttered, allowing a little physical distance to grow between us.

"Stupid isn't a good word either, but it's been echoing in my head."

I slammed to a halt. "Stupid?"

Jethro glided to a stop, looking so cultured and sharp I had a terrible urge to rip his jacket or ruffle his hair. He was too perfect. Too collected. Too *restrained.* My heart stuttered. *What exactly is he restraining?*

"You say I threatened your father as there's no other explanation as to why you're standing here with me. I say if you feel that way, then you're stupid for agreeing. It was *you* who took my hand, you who followed me from the crowd to empty streets." Leaning down, his eyes narrowed. "Stupid, Ms. Weaver. Very stupid indeed."

I should've been insulted. Beyond livid at being ridiculed and slandered, but I couldn't deny the idiocy of my situation. I'd meant it as a joke, sort of, but how could I ignore the truth blazing bright in his dark words?

"I'm twenty-four, Mr. Hawk, and you were the first man my father agreed I could spend an evening alone with. If it makes me stupid to want something I've been denied all my life, then yes, I guess I'm incredibly stupid. But you've just proven that no matter how much I wanted freedom, I love my family more, and I didn't say a proper goodbye."

The sudden need to see V and my dad overwhelmed me. Something morbid inside taunted with the horrible thought I would never see them again.

Glaring at Jethro and his imposing silence, I sucked in a breath. "This was a mistake. I'm sorry."

Gathering my train, I spun on my heels and stalked toward the huge portico and arched doorway. Blessedly my head remained clear and my feet suffered no stumbles or falls. The heaviness of my train billowed in the rush. I had no logical explanation why I suddenly needed to be around people again, but I couldn't deny the strong pull toward family.

Jethro didn't say a word. He stayed statuesque and proud in the evening darkness.

With every step I took, I expected him to call out or find some way to stop me. He didn't seem like a man who accepted no for an answer. But only silence followed, pushing me faster toward the door.

The moment I stepped through the polished entry and into the hive of heat and voices, I plucked my phone from my cleavage. There was one person in particular I wanted to speak to. A stranger I'd never heard or seen. My father had allowed me one night of freedom. I didn't want it with Jethro, but I did want it with someone else.

Maybe Kite lived close by? His number prefix said he dwelled in the United Kingdom. Like me. It wasn't a long flight to get back home.

I'd lived in London all my life, moving from the outskirts to downtown five years ago. The Weaver empire had always been based in London—right from conception. And probably always would be—if business continued to boom.

I opened a message to Kite007.

Needle&Thread: *Sorry I didn't reply before, I was busy cementing my career and ensuring I have a lifetime of servitude and sewing.*

I sighed, staring at the words. They sounded whiny and ungrateful, which I wasn't. Plus, the unsaid rule between us was no personal information. I didn't know what he did for a living or his real name or favourite food. Sex messaging was a void with no depth.

Which shows how lonely you are.

I scowled, deleting what I'd typed. I wasn't lonely. I had the best family and support in the world. I was just…tired. *Maybe I should book a holiday somewhere hot? Somewhere where I can't sew or design or get sucked back into work.* It sounded great—but one problem. I didn't want to be the loner around a pool on some tropical island. I didn't want to eat on my own by candlelight on the beach.

Take Vaughn.

I smiled. People already whispered that our relationship was too close. Going on an island getaway? That would definitely get the gossip columns buzzing.

My heart panged for the only relationship I had and how shallow it was. There was so much I wanted to say:

I want to meet you.

Please, can we skip the innuendoes and just talk?

I'm at the Nila Coal and Fire Exclusive *in the heart of Milan. I want to go for a drink with you.*

I want to get to know you.

I couldn't type any of that as it was against the rules. The unsaid rules hinted at by Kite. No personal details. No over-sharing. No information of any kind but sex.

Damn rules.

Damn life.

Damn men.

My fingers flew over the screen.

Needle&Thread: *All I can think about is you and your wandering hand. I'm mad at you for coming without me, but not mad because you came while thinking of me. I've had a long night and plan on releasing my tension the moment I'm alone.*

A cynical smile twitched my lips. Kite would think I meant self-pleasuring. I really meant hitting the treadmill and running until my legs turned to jelly.

My phone came alive in my hands.

Kite007: *Me and my wandering hand missed you. By a long night I'll take it you mean on your knees servicing God in prayer. (let a man indulge in the dirty thought) Message me when you're alone. I can help with your tension.*

I looked up. Couples mingled; groups gathered. Fashion was the celebrated highlight of the evening with guests dressing in their absolute best. But it was smiles and genuine happiness that made the evening glow. I missed being happy. I hadn't laughed or smiled properly since Mum left. I could never understand how she could love us as much as she claimed, then switch off her heart…just like that.

When she'd returned from her disappearance to file for divorce from my father, she'd ruined him. Completely and utterly stole his heart and shot it to pieces on the lobby floor.

I remembered that day. I remembered thinking she'd returned with such a pretty necklace. So sparkly, it'd blinded me when she blew kisses as she walked out the door the final time.

Ever since that day, I'd been afraid of love. Afraid of the pain it could cause and how easily something so pure could turn into something so filthy.

Anger filled me. Anger I rarely let myself indulge in. I would never admit the pain my mother caused, but it was the driving force behind my workaholic nature. It was the catalyst of my life that turned me into the woman I was.

Alone. Afraid. Angry. So damn angry.

Sliding my fingers across the keypad, I sent an impulsive message.

Needle&Thread: *What if I don't want to be alone? What if I wanted help physically rather than a meaningless text? Would you help then?*

I probably shouldn't have sent it. I already knew his response. But what was so wrong with me that no man wanted to face the wrath of my father and take me for a drink?

Jethro stood up to him.

I frowned, clutching my phone. That man didn't count. He was as terrifying as my father, and his motives weren't genuine. He didn't want to listen to my tales of woe over dinner. He wasn't there to woo me. He wanted something more. And it was the more I was petrified of.

Kite007: *Okay…whose balls did you steal to write that? You know that doesn't work with me. I'm not some boy you can snap your fingers at and I'll come running.*

Pain lacerated my chest but I already expected it. Before I could reply, another message vibrated.

Kite007: *You just had to fucking do that didn't you? What do you want from me? A commitment? A relationship? You knew what this was. I thought you were having fun getting off—same as me. Why ruin what we have?*

My heart, the same useless organ that'd never been in love, cracked with agony. His anger bled from my phone, poisoning my hand. Fantastic. The only outside interaction I'd had, and it was over. But why his sudden viciousness?

Needle&Thread: *All I asked was a simple question, but you jumped down my throat. What's your deal? Don't tell me. I can guess. You're only happy when you're in charge. But guess what? I can simply delete your number and never reply to you again. You were the one who found me, remember?*

I breathed hard, huddling over my phone. I wasn't done. It was refreshing to finally allow myself to be angry. I wanted to pour it all out before I could swallow it back down again.

Needle&Thread: *I think you need to come again, Kite. Your temper is completely uncalled for and misdirected. All I implied was a meeting. One phone call. A kiss maybe if we hit it off in person. Why is that so hard for you? I'll tell you why. Because you're commitment phobic and a cheater.*

"Congratulations on your collection, Nila. I'm sure—"

I looked up into the eyes of a stranger. The woman had plump lips and wore black eyeshadow.

She paused mid-sentence. "Are you okay?"

I hated her concern. I hated that I came across as some stupid girl who could make exquisite clothing but never grace someone's arm.

I don't want to be here anymore.

I needed fresh air. I needed silence.

Him.

The silent masculinity of Jethro Hawk suddenly called to me like a cooling balm after a burning fire. He might scare me, but he had a body to touch and a mind to explore. Motives or not—he wanted me for the evening. And I was feeling reckless.

"Yes, I'm fine. Excuse me." Bunching my skirts, I dodged groups of people, heading for the exit. My phone buzzed as I reached the door.

Kite007: *Don't call me that. You lost the right to call me anything the moment you changed from tempting to annoying. I'm not a cheater or commitment phobic. And it's not hard for me to deny a meeting with you, because I already have women to fuck. I already have enough physical connections and stupid girls making demands of me. You just broke something that wasn't broken. Congratu-fucking-*

---

lations.

My nostrils flared. *I broke it?* There was nothing to break! This whole thing had been a mistake. Unknowingly he'd taken advantage of some loser gasping for friendship. I was done being that girl.

I was done living life in black and white.

I wanted colour. I wanted passion. And there was only one man who could give me what I wanted tonight. I would use him and throw him away—just like Kite did to me.

Kite007: *If you didn't know—that was me cutting you loose. You're acting like a brat. Go and get laid. That's what I'm about to do. You want to know things about me? How about this? The woman I meant to text when I mistakenly messaged you is coming over for her long overdue reward. Don't message me again. The jerking off to your timid replies has bored me. Whoops, I just lost your number....*

My teeth gritted. My heart thundered. Pain was swamped by livid rage. How *dare* he break up with me? How dare he hurt me! How dare I let myself be hurt by a fucking arsehole who I'd never met?

I didn't care. *I don't care.*

But I did care.

I'm so stupid!

Stopping in the entrance way, my hands shook, jiggling my glowing screen. People mingled around, skirting the huge puddle of black material from my dress. I stood surrounded, yet I was all alone.

Tears pricked my eyes, but I swallowed them back. It was my own stupid fault. *I'm so stupid. Stupid...*

I sent my final message.

Needle&Thread: *When you end up alone and unloved, I hope you remember this moment. You aren't breaking up with me. I'm breaking up with* you. *Thank God I'm not a nun so I can curse the very ground you walk upon. You don't want to meet me? Fine. You just got your wish. I'm done. (hope you wank so much your dick falls off)*

Whirling around, I faced the doorway—the same doorway leading to a man who was scary and cold and silent but he was *real*. He had fingers to touch me with and a mouth to kiss. Who cared who he was? I could be stupid and use him for my own release.

Tonight I wouldn't be draining a treadmill of life. Tonight I would be riding a man who terrified me in some recess of my soul. Tonight I would be selfish and wicked and cruel.

Tonight...I would be Jethro's.

I SAT ON my newest purchase, resting like a mechanical shadow by the curb. It didn't glint or gleam. It didn't entice or welcome. It waited in black silence ready to charge into the night.

Give her options. Don't make her suspect. Threaten only when necessary. Above all, take her without causing attention.

The rules my father told me the morning I left to fly to Milan, repeated in my head. I was obeying. Even though it was fucking hard. I struggled to balance my true nature with that of a polite gentleman, coaxing a skittish woman out for dinner.

As if I would be interested in a girl like her. Meek. Skinny. Beyond fucking sheltered it was insane.

Grabbing the throttle of my bike, I waged with ignoring my father's rules and stalking into the venue and stealing Nila Weaver in front of everyone. She could scream, shout—it wouldn't make a difference. But that wasn't *allowed*.

The other option was I could just fuck off and kidnap her from her hotel room.

She has to come willingly.

My father's voice again. Kidnapping was the last resort.

I growled under my breath.

I'd let her go, not because of some decency, or concern of what would happen to her family's happiness, or even the upcoming pain in her future. No, I let her go, because I was my father's son and followed a plan.

I was a hunter. Skilled with both bow and arrow and gun.

The chase was the best part. And knowing I had the power to

snuff out Nila Weaver's life the moment I caught her gave me a certain…thrill.

That was the only reason I restrained myself and followed the rules.

I had no secrets of why I would stain my hands with her blood. I had no misplaced vendettas or agendas. Everything that would come to pass was for one simple and undisputable fact.

There was a debt to be paid. And I was the method of extraction. Plain and simple.

I'm a Hawk. She's a Weaver.

That was all I needed to know.

In the library a week ago, while sipping on a ten thousand pound bottle of cognac, my father proceeded to tell me a little of our history. He told me gruesome things. Dastardly things. Tears shed. Blood spilled. He told me what happened to Nila's mother.

He also told me why every firstborn Weaver girl had a stain upon her life. I understood it. I accepted it. I was given the task to uphold my family's honour. And I fully intended to extract payment as meticulously and as painfully as possible.

Because it was my task.

It wasn't often I was given the opportunity to make my bastard of a father proud. I didn't intend to let him down.

Even though I wouldn't enjoy it.

Nila Weaver would be my greatest trophy.

Oh, yes. I would enjoy ruining her. I liked playing with the inner mechanics of people. I liked to break them smoothly, gently, ruthlessly. I liked to think I transformed creatures from their present to their potential.

Pity once Nila was transformed she wouldn't be allowed to enjoy her evolution. She would be dead. That was the final toll. That was her future.

To kill something so naïvely pretty…

It made me angry to think of such delicate perfection snuffed out. But there was no point thinking of the end when the chase had just begun.

"Nice bike."

My head snapped up, eyes locking onto my prey. The same prey who'd run yet returned.

She'd returned? *I was right before. She truly is stupid.*

Nila drifted forward, threading and unthreading her fingers. I didn't move or utter a sound. She responded to my silence—like everything. I'd learned that cursing and yelling could be frightening—but silence…it was the empty void where enemies' fears polluted. Stay quiet long enough and horror would be struck with one whisper instead of a multitude of profanities.

She waved at my bike, her eyes wider than before…darker than before.

Deciding to grant her a reply, I said, "It's my version of accessorising." The sleek Harley-Davidson was a new purchase.

Stroking the throttle, I tilted my head. Her dusky skin had colour. Her pronounced cheekbones were flushed, trailing residual temper down her neck. Something had happened. Something had upset her.

Did she find her father, only for him to disown her and send her back to me?

I frowned. Could Archibald Weaver truly send his only daughter not once, but twice, to her death? He knew what awaited her. He knew what would happen if he didn't give her up. But was family honour that strong? Or was there more to this debt than I'd been told?

Either way, it was time to go. Time to begin her nightmare.

"You returned."

She nodded. "I returned. I want something from you. And I'm not going to be shy about asking."

A flicker of surprise caught me unaware. She came across shy and timid, but there lurked steel in her voice. Little did she know what I wanted from her in return.

"Fair enough. I have something to discuss with you."

Don't make her suspect.

"What?"

Your future. Your death.

"Nothing important, but we need to go."

Time to begin. The time is nigh to pay your debts.

Nila came closer, shedding the tameness, and embracing courage. I would've been intrigued if I didn't already know everything about her.

Such a silly girl. A silly toy.

Whatever she wanted from me, I'd oblige. After all, she'd been given to me to do as I pleased.

And everyone knows you don't give a pet to a killer.

"GET ON."

I blinked. "Excuse me?"

Jethro didn't move. He didn't look condescending or annoyed or anything other than cold and collected. Nothing seemed to interest him. I thought I could use him for sex? He didn't look like he knew what a smile was, let alone passion.

His legs bunched beneath the dark charcoal of his trousers, steadying the heavy motorcycle between them. "I said, get on. We're leaving."

I laughed. What a ludicrous suggestion. Waving down my front, I hoped he wasn't blind, because no one could ignore the kilograms worth of black diamantes or acres of material I wore. "I struggled to get here in a limousine. There's no way I can perch on the back of a stupid motorcycle."

Jethro's lips quirked. "Come closer. I'll fix that."

My heart jumped; I clutched my phone tighter. No response from Kite. *Which is a* good *thing.* I just had to keep telling myself that. I never wanted to hear from him again. "Fix it how?"

"Come here and I'll show you." His eyes drifted down the front of my dress.

I'd been around powerful, attractive men all my life. Both my father and brother were well known for being eligible bachelors, but they lacked something that Jethro held in abundance.

Mystery.

Everything about him spoke of trickery and wile. He'd barely spoken, yet I *felt* his requests. For some stupid reason, it felt as if he'd trained me with his silence to be alert, ready, eager to please.

I hated his effortless power.

Backing away, I shook my head. "I won't."

A small smile graced his lips, golden eyes flashing. "That wasn't very polite. I gave you a request, kindly delivered, respectfully even." His fingers tightened around the handle bars. "Should I ask again, or will you rethink your reply?"

A trickle of fear blustered down my neck. I knew that glint in his eye. Vaughn would get it when we were younger. It meant destruction. It meant getting their own way. It meant a world of pain if I didn't obey. And for some reason, I didn't think a wedgie and being tickled until I couldn't breathe counted as pain in Jethro's dimension.

Clutching the bodice that'd taken me weeks to hand-sew, I took another step backward. "I'm not being impolite; I'm stating the obvious. If you wish to leave, we need a different method of transportation." Speaking so formally sounded odd after screaming via text message to Kite. "And besides, I don't want to leave yet. I promised myself I'd ask you something, and I'm not going anywhere until I do."

God, Nila. What are you doing?

Nerves attacked my stomach, but I kept my stance. I wouldn't back down. Not this time.

Jethro shook his head, displacing his longish salt-and-pepper hair. His smooth face remained expressionless with patience, but it didn't relieve—it terrified. With precision born of wealth and confidence, he kicked the stand down and placed the bike into a resting position. Swinging his leg over the machine, he climbed the curb and hunted.

No. Don't let him touch you.

I stumbled backward, a slight edge of dizziness catching me off guard.

Jethro caught me, placing his large, cold hands on my waist.

I froze, breathing shallowly. Shoving away the moment of wobbliness, I fixated on his strong jaw and glinting diamond pin.

The temperature of his touch seeped through the ruffles on my hips, bringing with it fear manifesting like icicles over an innocent dawn.

"What's wrong with you?" Jethro jerked me closer, peering into my eyes. The first sign of animation lurked in their golden depths. It wasn't concern though, merely annoyance. "Are you ill?" Annoyance turned to carefully hidden anger.

I swallowed hard, hating my condition all over again. To him, I would come across as weak. He wouldn't understand the strength it took to live a normal life while shackled to an improperly balanced form. If anything, it made me stronger.

"No, I'm not ill. Not that you're worried for my health." Twitching in his hold, I searched for a way free. But his touch only tightened. Blowing a blue-black strand from my eye, I added, "It's not contagious. I suffer from vertigo. That's all. Google it."

That's all. I scrape my knees if I get out of bed too fast and faint if I swivel my head too quick, but that's all.

Jethro scowled. "Perhaps you shouldn't wear such heavy clothing." He plucked the dense material and delicate stitching on my waist. "It's a hindrance and delaying my night's activities."

My eyes flared. Night's activities?

Perhaps he had the same conclusion of where we'd end up? Captive in his strong hands, I stared up. I wasn't short for a woman, but Jethro had at least half a foot on me. He didn't move, only watched as if I were an interesting specimen he couldn't decide to enjoy or throw away.

My breathing grew shallow the longer he held me. Dropping my gaze to his lips, it didn't help my anxiety at having them so close. *It's now or never.*

I knew nothing about him. He scared me. But he was a man. I was a woman. And once, just once, I wanted pleasure.

"I want something from you," I murmured.

He stilled. "What exactly makes you think you're in a position to ask something of me?"

I shook my head. "I'm not asking."

A moment thickened between us. His nostrils twitched. "Go on…"

"Take me for a drink. I want to get to know you."

Not quite what I wanted to ask, but I couldn't be so bold.

He laughed once. "Believe me, Ms. Weaver, I'll save you from a mundane conversation. The most you'll ever know about me is my name. Everything else…let's just say, ignorance is bliss."

His aftershave of woods and leather came over me again. The chilliness in his gaze warned not to push, but I couldn't help myself.

Not after the way Kite treated me.

"Bliss…that's a word I don't understand."

Jethro cocked his head, the trace of annoyance coming again. "What exactly are you trying to do?"

A rush of wobbliness hit me. I looked over my shoulder at the café across the street. "Have a nightcap with me. Over there." I motioned with my head. I didn't care in the least I wore a huge gown or that the coffee shop was empty. The couch in the window looked comfy, and I wasn't ready to have this small freedom destroyed.

He looked to the small venue, a flicker of confusion filling his eyes. "You—" Cutting himself off, he straightened and let me go. "Fine. If that's all you want, I see no reason why I can't prolong our true agenda for thirty minutes." Capturing my elbow, he half-dragged, half-marched me across the street.

My heart sank at the lack of romance and anticipation. I'd hoped he'd relax a little—knowing I was interested—and drop the chilly façade.

What if it's not a façade? His demeanour was steadfast and engrained. I doubted he'd ever been carefree or impulsive.

The propulsion was fast, too fast for someone like me with the balance of a damn butterfly, but his hold was firm and granted a certain safety.

Striding over the curb, Jethro yanked open the glass door, scowling at the bell jingling above. A young Italian girl looked up, smiling in welcome.

The rich aroma of coffee and warmth instantly stole the stress from my blood from Kite, the show, and Jethro's company.

"Sit." Jethro let me go, pointing toward the faded yellow settee with purple and orange throw cushions. "And don't move."

I stood frozen. Jethro had no wish to be here, especially with me. What the hell was going on? First my father pushed me on him, then Jethro barely tolerated my company. *Am I that repulsive?*

"Wait," I said. "Aren't you going to ask what I want?"

Jethro raised an eyebrow. "No. Want to know why?"

I did. But I didn't want to play his ridiculous game. The night had turned from promising to disastrous.

When I didn't reply, Jethro waved his hand. "It doesn't matter what you prefer in beverages. You only get one request and you got it. I'm here against my plans; therefore, you'll drink what I give you."

My mouth parted, amazement stealing my ability to shout the incomprehensible phrases jumbled inside. *Seriously?* Who was this man?

Jethro strode away, leaving me gawking at his powerful back dressed in an immaculate, tailored suit. He completely ignored me while he ordered.

Not wanting to stand like a dismissed damsel, I moved to the couch and sat in a cloud of midnight-galaxy material. The underwire and other tricks to keep my dress buoyant argued against sitting, but my feet breathed a sigh of gratefulness.

Jethro returned with two cups of coffee. Espresso. Tiny cups, no biscotti, or anything to prolong something he obviously didn't want to do. Placing the hot drink in front of me on the low table, he sipped his own, glaring at me over the rim.

I broke eye contact, collecting the cup of black liquid. Truth be told, I hated coffee. I'd only suggested the café to delay whatever he'd planned that was so urgent.

Inhaling the strong caffeine, I pretended to sip while sneaking glimpses at the mystery beside me. Did it matter he was an arrogant arse who didn't know the difference between cruel and polite? He had a killer body, distinguished good looks, and a presence that screamed domination in the bedroom. I could choose worse for a night of guilt-free sex.

Sitting taller, I said, "So…the thing I wanted to ask you…"

What are you doing? He's not a nice person. And he's got the patience of a Doberman.

Jethro clenched his jaw, swirling his coffee. "I won't answer, do, or respond to any more requests. Drink your coffee. We're running late."

I ignored that and tried to break the ice between us. "You seem to know my father. What obligations—"

"No questions." Jethro tossed his head back, swallowing the double shot in one go. Licking his lips, he carefully placed his cup on the table, eyeing my untouched one.

The unease of why my father had permitted me to go out with such an insensitive bastard came back. I feared there was a lot I wasn't aware of.

Running a hand through his greying hair, Jethro suddenly shoved my overflowing skirts off the couch and slid closer. So close his body heat seared my naked arms, prickling me with intensity.

I gulped, curling my hands in my lap.

Jethro bristled. "Whatever you think you're doing, it won't work. I will neither make small talk nor enter into meaningful conversation. You request to visit a coffee shop, yet don't touch what I bought you." He sighed, tension tightening his eyes. "I'm done playing silly games. Tell me what I need to do to make you come without making a fuss, and I'll do it."

My heart stopped. Anxiety roared back into existence. Why had I thought I could seduce this man? I had no hope, especially when he was obviously pissed off rather than intrigued. Linking my fingers together, I said quietly, "Why would I make a fuss? Where exactly do you want to take me?"

Please say a hotel and admit your attitude is all an act. Please say my brother hired you to play the horrible arsehole only to sweep me off my feet in a night of escorted bliss.

I should've known better than to wish for such things.

Jethro frowned. "What did I just say? No questions." Grabbing my wrist, he tugged me closer, crushing my dress between us. "I don't have time for games. Tell me what you want." His mouth was so close, his brooding temper filling a bubble around us.

My eyes dropped to his lips. All I could picture was one kiss. One beautifully gentle, romantic kiss that turned my insides molten and my mind to stars.

I breathed shallowly, unable to raise my gaze to his.

He half-smiled. "*That's* what you want?"

I blinked, dispelling the haze of intoxication he'd placed me under. "I didn't say anything."

Letting my wrist go, he trailed his fingertips up my arm. I shivered, loving and hating his masterful touch. "You didn't have to. I should've known this would happen."

My eyes flared. "Known?" Embarrassment came swift and hot. Was I so obvious? So needy?

"No questions," he snapped. Sighing heavily, he added, "You forget your life is rather public, Ms. Weaver. And I happen to know you're not…experienced." Cupping my chin, he ran the pad of his thumb over my bottom lip.

I froze.

Jethro's face didn't soften or beguile, but his voice dropped to a murmur. His masculine scent threaded around me transporting me from the coffee shop and into his control. "What is it you want? A kiss? A caress?" His voice echoed like a deep baritone until I felt his question in my bones.

Leaning closer, his mouth hovered over mine. He smelled decadently of coffee. "Do you *ache* for something? Do you lie in bed at night and crave a man's touch?" His breath feathered over my lips, drugging me. "How wet do you get? Answer my questions, Ms. Weaver. Tell me how you pleasure yourself while fantasising about a man fucking you."

I couldn't feel any part of my body apart from the firm hold he had on my chin and the tingling of my lips. I couldn't think apart from the dark visions he coaxed in my head of nakedness and fingers and stolen caresses.

"Tell me. Convince me," Jethro tormented, bringing his mouth closer. Only a feather breadth away—a phantom kiss, but it made every inch throb.

"Yes," I whispered. "Yes, I fantasise. Yes, I ache." Wishing I could pull away and hide my vulnerability, I added, "That's what I wanted. From you."

Everything you painted and more.

"When you imagine a nameless male taking you, do you picture champagne, massages, and soul-shattering sex?" His nose nudged mine.

I nodded, eyelids drooping, begging him to kiss me.

His head tilted, grazing the corner of my mouth with his. A tease. A half-kiss. A promise. His mouth trailed to my ear. "You naïve little girl. If I took you, you wouldn't be adored or worshipped. You'd be used and *fucked*. I have no patience for sweet."

I opened my eyes, fighting against the thick lust in my blood.

Jethro sneered. "Pity you didn't say you fantasised about a man using you, abusing you. Pity you didn't admit to darker desires such as bondage and pain. Then perhaps I might've granted your wish." He trailed his lips over my cheekbone. His touch was condescending rather than erotic. "Now tell me, Ms. Weaver. Knowing my certain appetites, are you still wet for me? Is that what you're asking for? My tongue. My attention. My…" He nuzzled away my hair, biting painfully on the shell of my ear. "…cock."

I wanted to deny the flutter in my heart and the intense heat billowing in my core. I wanted to be outraged at his crudeness and blatant sexual thrill. But I couldn't. Because despite never entertaining the idea of violence with sex, I couldn't stop the undeniable allure.

Pulling back, Jethro whispered, "Don't turn timid on me. Say it. Say what you want."

I was no longer human; I was liquid. Hot, pliable liquid just waiting for some force to reshape me. Everything he'd said flared a need inside until a fever broke across my brow.

Dropping my eyes, I whispered, "I want…I want…"

Jethro tightened his fingers on my jaw. "Say it." His eyes flashed and the misconception that he didn't know passion dissolved. He knew it. He wielded it. He hid it beneath layers and layers of mystery I would never hope to unravel.

Taking a shaky breath, cursing the damn corset, I said, "I want your mouth."

He nodded. "Fine. But I'll have yours first." His thumb stroked my lips again, breaking the seal of my red lipstick, and penetrating my mouth.

I froze, eyes wide and locked on his. "Where do you want it?" His voice dropped to a barely murmured curse—impossible to ignore, deadly to my ears and body.

He didn't care about the waitress or that anyone on the darkened street could see us. He just pinned me with unswerving golden eyes and hooked his thumb against my tongue.

I couldn't speak. His large palm held me immobile while his finger rendered me silent. I didn't know what to do. Should I suck? Bite? Do nothing?

Jethro smiled, it wasn't his usual icy edge, but it wasn't soft either. "Follow your instincts. You want to suck, so suck." He forced his thumb deeper into my mouth, eyes darkening.

He so easily placed me into a position of submission, but I'd never felt so powerful. Closing my lips, I sucked. Once.

His jaw clenched, but nothing more.

I did it again, licking his finger with an eager tongue. My mouth filled with liquid, tasting him. Wanting him. Every suck sent a wave of insatiable need to my core, making me wet.

Jethro's shoulders tensed. "See? You didn't need to tell me what you wanted. Your body does that for you. You've surprised me, and that isn't an easy thing to do." My dress rustled as he wrapped an arm around my waist, dragging me against his hard body.

I went willingly, trapped in so many ways. My mind was consumed with only him. There was peace in that moment. Lust yes, feverishness definitely, but also serenity at the complete attention he demanded. I didn't have to think of my family, my company, my endless work schedule.

I was nothing but flesh and blood and bone.

I was need personified, and only Jethro could put out the fire he'd cajoled.

His lips brushed against my ear again. I tensed for the bite of teeth. "Know what else your body tells me?"

I shook my head, swirling my tongue around his thumb. My core clenched; my mind blanked.

"You need something. You want something that you're not ready to understand." Jethro placed a delicate kiss against my jaw. "You need it so bad you'd allow me to run my hand up your knee, between your legs, and sink my fingers deep inside you this very second. You'd open your innocent thighs, even with witnesses, and moan as I sank my cock deeper than anyone."

A bubble formed in my chest, twisting and glistening with a mixture of denial and agreement.

His thumb pressed hard, pinning my tongue below.

I jerked, eyes tearing wide.

"You'd let me drag you into some sleazy alley, tear off your dress, and…"

I didn't want to hear the rest. But I did. Oh, how I did. He'd taken the power of speech away. I couldn't deny anything he said. And I didn't want to. For the first time in my life, I had something real. Cheap and shallow, just like Kite, but hot-blooded and absolute.

I would willingly trade my flawless reputation for one night of sordid incredibleness. *What does that make me?*

I flinched, answering my own question. *Lonely.* I hated that word more than any other in the dictionary.

Jethro's thumb slinked slowly from my mouth, holding me firm. "You'd let me make you scream, Ms. Weaver, and because of that willingness, I would never bow to what you want."

The heat generated from the intense conversation dispersed, faster and faster. He curled his lips. "Whatever would your father say if he knew his daughter secretly wanted to be *fucked* against an alley wall by a stranger?"

The crudeness of his words slammed me back to reality.

He dropped his hand, and plucked a napkin from the table. Imprisoning my gaze, he slowly wiped his glistening thumb, before tossing the tissue into his empty coffee cup. "I dare you to deny any of that. Or pretend you didn't want every inch of me." He smirked at the double entendre.

The flush of mortification crested over my breasts to my cheeks. My tongue bruised from his rough handling, my mouth empty from tasting him. I couldn't sit there and be ridiculed any longer.

This was karma, and it stung like hell.

Grabbing the mountains of fabric wedged around me, I tried to stand—unsuccessfully. "I'm leaving. I can't—"

"If you can't speak the truth, I don't want to hear your other excuses or reasons on why you suddenly need to run. You're not permitted to leave my side, so be a good girl and fucking listen and obey." His voice whipped me, but his body remained immaculate and collected. The two dynamics of temper and poise pierced my stupid haze, slamming me back into fear.

Who *was* this man?

And why didn't I run the moment I set eyes upon him? Something wasn't right. Something was building, rushing toward a conclusion I wanted no part in.

Jethro stood upright, jerking me to my feet. "I take by your silence you've made a sensible decision and acquiesced. I'm also assuming that this—whatever this was—is over?" His fingers bit into my bicep, shaking me. "Stop acting the fool and realize what is happening."

Anger replaced my embarrassment. It was like Kite all over again, only worse, because this was real and I had nowhere to hide. "I have no idea what's happening, and I'm not going anywhere with you. You've proved that you find me gullible, stupid, and unworthy of your precious time, so leave. I'm not keeping you here." Twisting my elbow, I tried to get free. "I don't want to do this anymore."

Jethro smiled coldly. "Ah, there's the conundrum, Ms. Weaver. You're not keeping me. But *I'm* keeping *you*."

I stopped with my hand over his, unsuccessfully trying to pry his fingers off my arm. "What?" The dreaded drunkenness of vertigo took that moment to tilt my world.

Jethro took my weakness as an opportunity, pulling me toward the door. He didn't give me any support other than the harsh hold on my upper arm, leaving my untouched coffee on the table. "I'm leaving.

And you're coming with me."

The door jangled as we exited in a flurry of bustle and feathers. I gasped as a frosty gust cut through the warmth lingering on my skin, decimating all remainders of the café.

Slamming my heels into the pavement, I snarled, "You seem to have the wrong information. I'm not going anywhere with you."

Jethro didn't reply, dragging me effortlessly across the road to the shadowy entrance of an alley and his bike.

An alley?

He couldn't mean what he'd threatened...could he?

You want me to make you scream.

I fought harder. But no matter how much I struggled, he didn't break his stride or look back.

Tripping forward, I winced as my flesh bruised beneath his hold. I angled my nails, preparing to drag them over his forearm, but he stepped onto the curb and yanked me forward. The inertia propelled me into a spin, slamming me painfully against his motorcycle.

My black hair whirled over my shoulder, sticking to the fear perspiring on my chest. I struggled to keep up—to believe how stupid I'd been. I prided myself on being smart, but I'd allowed the temptation of sex to cloud my judgement.

Jethro glowered; his suit as crisp as his unflappable control. "My information is perfectly correct. And you *are* going somewhere with me. Climb on."

I tore my elbow from his hold and shoved his chest. "Wrong. Let me go."

He growled under his breath. "Stop, before you get hurt."

I pushed him again, focusing on the ridiculousness of my night, rather than the rapidly expanding terror in my heart. "I told you. I came in a limo; there is no way I can travel on a two-wheeled death machine."

Jethro rolled his shoulders, maintaining his cool. "I gave you one rule—never ask questions. I'm giving you another—don't ever argue with me."

My heart raced. Glancing around, I searched for late night stragglers, party goers, moon-light walkers—anyone who could intervene and save me. The roads were empty. No one. Not even a scurrying rodent.

"Please, I don't know what game you're playing—"

He shook his head, exasperation in his eyes. "Game? This isn't a fucking game." Glaring at my dress, he encroached on my space. Pressing his lips together briefly, he muttered, "I hope you're wearing something beneath this."

My lungs stuck together. "What? Why?"

"Because you're going to be indecent if you're not." With a savage jerk, he tore the endless seams, stitching, and hard work of my dress. The rip sounded like a scream to my ears. Horror swarmed as the outer layer fluttered to the ground, followed by organza, feathers, and beadwork.

My jaw hung open. "No—"

Jethro spun me around, his hands skating over my lower back. "You're like a damn pass the parcel." With strong fingers, he tore the second layer of heavy ebony silk.

The sound of shredding broke my heart. All that work! My father would be pissed to see his expensive material littering the dirty pavement. My blood existed in the needlepoint from pricking my fingers. My tears soaked the train from overworking. He couldn't do this!

I couldn't speak—struck mute by shock.

"Good God, another?" Jethro spun me back to face him. I swished in the remaining starchy petticoats—the tool beneath the dress that granted such volume.

I can't do this anymore.

I plastered my hands down my front, seizing the remainder of my gown. "No, pleas—"

Jethro ignored me. With one last brutal tug, he tore the petticoat off, disposing it on top of the already ruined layers.

Tears glassed my eyes. "Oh, my God. What did you do?" The cool Milan air swirled around my naked legs, disappearing up the thigh-length satin skirt I wore to prevent chafing from the petticoat underwire. My entire ensemble—destroyed. I'd been the only female in a household of men. I'd spent an entire lifetime covering up my girlish body with lace and camisoles and tulle. Femininity was something I created rather than lived. To see it demolished on a filthy sidewalk enraged me to the point of tyranny.

Gone were my tears. I embraced furiousness. "How *could* you?!"

Shoving him away, I fell to my knees, trying to gather the rhinestones and swatches of handmade lace. "You—you ruined it!" All around scattered couture fashion. Diamantes glittered on bland concrete. Feathers twitched, dancing away on the breeze.

"I'll ruin a lot more before I'm through." Jethro's barely uttered words existed, then…didn't, snatched by a gust of wind.

I glared up at the man I'd stupidly returned for—all because a stranger hurt my feelings. A man I'd allowed to manipulate me and make me heinously wet in a coffee shop. "Does it make you feel better? Destroying other's things? Don't you care that you just ruined something that took hours upon hours to create? What sort of cruel—"

"Stop." He held up a finger, scolding me like a little child. "Rule number three. I don't like raised voices. So shut up and stand."

We glared; silence was a heavy entity between us.

He was right. I was so, so stupid. He'd successfully hurt me more than anyone since my mother left. His callousness gave no room for hope or tears. And I knew it all along. I'd seen his coldness. I'd felt his hardened will. Yet it didn't stop me from being an utter fool.

Grabbing a puddle of cloth, I yelled, "Leave me alone!"

"Goddammit, you're testing me." He ducked suddenly, grabbing my bicep and hauling me to my feet. He shook me—hard. My corset dug into my hipbones now that it had no bustle or layers to rest upon.

"You don't get to ask any more questions. You don't get to yell or act ridiculous. This is happening. This is your future. Nothing you say or do will change that—it will only change the level of pain you receive." He shoved me backward against his bike. "Your dress is conveniently no longer an issue. Get on. We're leaving."

Fury exploded through my heart, thankfully keeping my terror at bay.

Don't think about his threat. Focus on making him yell. Loudness. I needed commotion to garner attention and safety.

"You just ruined my showpiece. That dress was already sold to a high-end boutique in Berlin! You think I want to go anywhere with you after you ruined over two months' worth of work? You're insane. I'll tell you how this is going to go—"

"Ms. Weaver, shut the fuck up. I'm done with this charade." His face remained impassive, but the muscles beneath his suit bristled. Moving horribly fast, he tugged my long, unfettered hair, crowding me against his bike. Wincing against the pain in my scalp, I tripped, splaying over the leather seat.

Looking around quickly, he relaxed when he noticed we were still alone. "If you knew me, you'd know how I react to incorrect statements about my mental health. If you were smart, you would know never to raise your voice and to maintain proper conduct in public."

He bowed his head, brushing his nose threateningly against my ear. "But seeing as you *don't* know me, I'll withhold the punishment—for now. But a word of warning, Ms. Weaver. Just because I don't lower myself to the unattractive use of volume, doesn't mean I'm not pissed. I'm very fucking pissed. I gave you an order, and you've disobeyed numerous times already. This is the last time I'll ask politely."

Pulling away, he grabbed my middle and with strength that terrified, plucked me from the ground and plonked me on the back of his bike, side-saddle.

Giving a mock salute, Jethro said, "Thank you for obliging me. I'm so glad you decided to climb aboard." With a scowl, he noticed my high heels. Dropping to one knee, he tore them off my feet, throwing them over his shoulder. They disappeared in the clouds of decimated fabric behind him.

I truly was Cinderella, only my prince threw away the glass slipper and stole me away before midnight struck. My prince was evil. My prince was the villain.

I couldn't breathe.

Run. Kick him. Do not let him take you.

All manner of horrible situations ran wild in my head. I'd been brought up in a safe neighbourhood, instilled with common-sense and morals. Yet nothing had prepared me to fight for my life against a lunatic who came across as sane.

"You can't do this. I don't want to go with you." I tried to jump off, but Jethro's sleek bulk prevented me from moving. He loomed upright like a terrible sentence—a judgement of my past and present. "You have no choice. You're coming with me. Your wishes have no relevance."

Stabbing him in the chest with my fingertip, I shouted, "My wishes are completely relevant. You can't take me against my will. That's called kidnapping." My body flushed with hot anger. "Let. Me. Go. Before I scream."

Vaughn. Shit, I wanted my brother. The amount of times he protected me growing up from bees, and badgers, and boys who picked on me at school.

Vaughn!

Jethro shook his head. "It's too late. For any of that. And don't scream. I don't do well with screamers." He chuckled mirthlessly. "Unless I'm the reason for said scream and we're in private."

I ignored the 'scream topic' and focused on the horrible ultimatum. Too late? *What's too late?* I wasn't on some countdown where my life ended as I knew it. I didn't agree to any of this!

I didn't, but maybe father did.

The thought stopped me like a knitting needle to the heart. He'd introduced me to Jethro—over any other man. He'd encouraged me to go with him—against my brother's wishes.

Jethro might've been able to hoodwink my father, but I saw his true colours, and I wasn't going to tolerate it any longer. This fiasco had gone on long enough.

I opened my mouth to scream. My lungs expanded with a plea. "Help—"

Jethro lashed out, slapping a cool palm over my lips. The first sign of uncontrollable emotion blazed in his eyes. He sighed heavily, shaking his head. "I'd hoped you'd be more intelligent than that."

I slapped him.

The sharp ringing of flesh against flesh froze time. I didn't move or breathe or blink. Neither did Jethro.

We stared at each other until all I knew was gold from his eyes. The air dropped from autumn to blustery winter the longer we glowered, freezing over with his temper. It could've been a second or ten, but it was Jethro who broke the brittleness between us.

His cold fingers trailed from my mouth to my throat. Wrapping tight. Unforgiving. The action showed the truth—the inhuman truth. This man was fastidiously groomed and softly spoken, but beneath it all raged a devil in disguise. His touch told endless information of the man he tried to hide. He was the ultimate in camouflage.

He was iron-fisted and remorseless.

Tilting my neck with bruising fingers, he murmured, "Obey and I won't hurt you. Fight me and I'll make you scream."

Every muscle in my body jolted. The decimation of my dress no longer mattered. All I cared about was running as far and as fast as I could. Tears bubbled in my chest; I bit my lip to stop the rapidly building sob from escaping.

Jethro never let go of my throat. "I'm not here to kidnap you. I'm not here to knock you out or drug you. Call me old-fashioned, but I'd hoped you'd come willingly and prevent both of us an inconvenience." Stroking my hair with his free hand, he cupped the back of my skull. "You're probably wondering why I said you have no choice but to come with me. Because I'm a fair man and believe in equality—even between hunter and prey—I'll tell you."

His breath was the only warm thing about him, scalding my skin with words I didn't want to hear. "I'm here to extract a debt. The reason for that debt will be revealed when I'm good and ready. The method of payment for that debt is entirely up to you."

My brain swam, trying to understand. "What—"

His fingers tightened, cutting off my air supply. Choking, the instinct to fight overrode my frozen terror. I squirmed, scratching my nails over his wrists.

My nails didn't affect him—if anything, it made him calmer. Tutting under his breath, he said, "The first thing you should know about me is I *never* forget. If you draw blood trying to get free, I'll only repay in kind. It's worth remembering, Ms. Weaver."

His gaze fell to my clawing fingers, tightening his own until I fought against what I truly wanted and let them slide from his wrists.

"Good girl," he murmured. Pulling back, he unwound his digits one at a time from my throat. Meticulous in slowness. Terrifying in control.

I only repay in kind. His voice echoed in my head. I balled my hands in my lap, hoping I wouldn't lash out or do anything he might deem repayable. I wanted to hurt him so much I trembled. I wanted him bleeding on the pavement so I could *run.*

Standing tall, Jethro glared, waiting to see what I would do.

I was half his size—and without witnesses, I was helpless. I'd never taken self-defence or thought I'd be in a situation that required it. The treadmill trimmed my figure, but didn't give me muscle to fight.

What could I do but obey? I didn't move. I couldn't. Even my vertigo didn't dare make me queasy when I was trapped in his savage golden eyes.

A moment ticked past before he nodded curtly. "I'm glad you're acting with more decorum. To ensure that behaviour, I'll share one piece of information about the debt with you." He ran a finger along his bottom lip. "You are the only one who can repay. You must come of your own free will. You are the sacrifice."

I swallowed, flinching at the bruising around my larynx. His level voice lulled me into thinking I had a chance at escape. *Keep him talking. Get him to care.* "Sacrifice?" I instantly hated the word.

His eyes narrowed. "A sacrifice is something you do or give up for the greater good. All of this could stop…you have the power."

It could? The promise of freedom hung in the night-sky, taunting me.

I shifted on the seat, shivering from the cold. "If I have the power, why do I feel as if you're laughing behind my back?" Steeling myself, I snapped, "Whatever you might think of me, I can read between the lines of what you're not saying. What are the consequences if I don't go with you?"

I felt ridiculous talking of debts and consequences. None of this made sense, but a horrible sensation slithered up my back. A memory that I'd buried…from a long time ago.

"You have no choice, Arch. I can't explain it, but you, me, no one can stop this. My only regret is meeting you."

My father huffed, whirling around in the drawing room of our eight bedroom manor. "Your only regret? What about V and Nila? What should I tell them? What should I say when they ask why their mother abandoned them?"

My mother, with her glossy ebony hair and dusky skin, stood tall and fearless, but from my hidden spot by the stairs I knew the truth. She wasn't fearless—far from it. She was petrified. "You tell them I loved them but I should never have given them life. Especially Nila. Hide her, Arch. Don't let them know. Change your name. Run. Don't let the debt get her, too."

The memory had ended abruptly thanks to Vaughn throwing a soccer ball at my head and shattering the final moments my parents had together. That had been the last time I ever saw her.

I rubbed my palm against my chest, cursing the tightness around my heart. Confusion weighed heavily, equally as pressing as despair.

Jethro smiled. "I'm glad you're being more reasonable. That is one question I will answer. The consequences of not coming with me are Vaughn and Archibald Weaver, amongst other things."

My whole world flipped upside down—and this time it wasn't vertigo.

"Your life for theirs." He shrugged. "Simple really. But don't worry about the details. There's the fine print and endless history lessons to explain."

My heart stopped. My life for theirs? *He has to be joking.* I didn't know if I should be screaming in terror or laughing with amazement. This couldn't be real. It had to be a farce.

"You can't be serious. You expect me to believe you?"

Jethro lost his ice, sliding straight into arctic winter. "You think I *care* if you don't believe me? Do you think all of this is bullshit and you can somehow argue with me?"

My heart jack-knifed. He was so sure. So resolute. No hint of worry that his scam might be revealed.

It isn't a joke.

Jethro lowered his voice. "I'll let you in on another secret about me. I never do things by half. I never take chances. And I never hunt alone." Leaning closer, he finished, "Ever since I set eyes on you, your family has been watched. They're being judged. And if you so much as sneeze wrong, that judgement will turn into something a lot more invasive. Do you understand?"

I couldn't reply. All I could picture was Vaughn and my father being exterminated like vermin.

"Say another word and I'll end them, Ms. Weaver." With a glacial glare, Jethro grabbed the handle bars and swung his leg over the black powder-coated machine. Every inch was black. No chrome or colour anywhere.

Shit, what do I do? I had to run. *Run!*

But I couldn't. Not now he'd threatened my family. Not now my brain had unlocked a memory adding weight to Jethro's lunatic suggestions. Not now I *believed.*

A debt.

I didn't know what it was. It could've been code for something I didn't understand or literal and requiring payback. But one thing I knew, I couldn't risk not obeying.

I loved my family. I adored my brother. I wouldn't chance their lives.

I jumped as the ignition growled to life, tearing through the silence, and somehow granting me strength in its ferocity. Kicking the stand away, Jethro took the weight of the bike.

He didn't wear a helmet or offer me one. I expected him to turn around and deliver more information or demands, but all he did was reach behind, steal my arm, and place it around his hips. The moment my hand rested on him, he let me go, unknowingly giving me a safe harbour but with an anchor I already despised.

I looked longingly at the building where my brother and father mingled with fashionistas and the only world I knew. I silently begged them to come running out and laugh at my stunned, fear-filled face yelling 'we fooled you.'

But nothing. The doors remained closed. Answers hidden. Future unknown.

I'm alone.

I'm being stolen for a debt only I can repay. A debt I know nothing about.

I was idiotic to wish for more than what I had.

Now, I had nothing.

With a twist of his wrist, Jethro fed gas to his mechanical beast and we shot forward into darkness.

The Milan airport welcomed me back.

It felt like an eternity since I flew in, though in reality it'd only been two days. My skin was icy, and despite my repellent dislike for Jethro, I hadn't been able to stop huddling against him while he broke speed limits and took corners at hyper-speed on his death machine. My tiny skirt and sleeveless corset weren't meant for gallivanting around Milan so late.

Pulling into a short term parking bay, he killed the engine and kicked down the stand. I immediately sat back, unwinding my arms from around his waist.

The fear remained in my heart, growing thicker with every beat. I couldn't look at the so-called gentleman without swallowing a cocktail of murderous rage and teary terror.

His profile showed a man with a five o' clock shadow, windswept thick hair, and an edge that catapulted him from sexy to dangerous. He stood out from a crowd. He drew need and desire effortlessly. But there was nothing tame or kind or normal. He reeked of manipulation and control.

He's an iceberg.

The car park wasn't empty, but it wasn't rush hour either. Despite the clunking echo of a couple dragging suitcases toward the terminal, the night was quiet.

Jethro climbed off the bike. Once standing, he rolled his neck, rubbing the cord of muscle with a strong hand. His eyes latched onto mine. They looked darker, more autumn leaf than precious metal, but still as cold.

I glowered back, hoping my hatred was visible.

His face remained closed off—not rising to the challenge of a staring war. Holding out his palm, he waited. The way he watched spoke volumes. He didn't wonder if I'd take his hand. He *knew*. He believed in himself so damn much everything other than his wish was dismissed as ludicrous.

Too bad for him, I didn't do well with the silent treatment. V had trained that out of me. Having a boisterous twin armed me with certain skills. And ignoring moody males was one of them.

Swatting his hand, I pushed off from the black leather and landed on bare feet. The brisk concrete bit into my soles. Wrapping my arms around my shivering torso, I muttered, "As if I'd accept your help. After everything you've done so far."

Dropping his arm, he chuckled. "So far?" He leaned closer. "I've done nothing. Not yet. Wait until you're in my domain and behind closed doors. Then you might have something worthy of being melodramatic about."

My skills at coping with the future rested on being able to ignore his threats and focus on the now. Standing tall, I said, "I could ask something stupid like why are we at the airport, but I can guess why. However, you failed to think about my schedule—"

"Schedules change."

"I don't travel alone, Mr. Hawk. I had tickets booked for my brother, assistant, and wardrobe organiser. Not to mention the excess luggage. They'll be expecting me. Hell, my assistant will be expecting me back at the hotel tonight. All of this—it's a waste of time. It's a waste because the police will be told and if you think my father won't come for me, you're mistaken."

Even as I said it doubt crept over my soul. Tex Weaver shoved me into this nightmare. Why did I think he'd come and bring me home?

Jethro crossed his arms, lips in a tight smile as if I were amusing and not pointing out valid facts. "There were a multitude of mistakes in that paragraph, but I'll focus only on the relevant points." Tilting his head, he continued, "Your father is fully aware of everything. Your loyalty to the man who gave you away with no fight is misplaced. His hands are tied and he damn well knows it. As for the police, they have no relevance in your future. Forget about them, your family, *hope*. It's over."

His voice dropped to a growl. "Do you know *why* it's over? It's over because your *life* is over. There's so much you don't know, and so much I can't wait to tell you."

He shed his icy exterior, grabbing my hair and jerking my head back. "You'll learn about your peerage. Your rotten family tree. And you'll pay. So shut up, give up, and appreciate my kindness thus far because I'm running low on decency, Ms. Weaver, and you won't like me when I hit my limit."

My shivers evolved to full blown tremors. "I don't like you now, let alone in the future. Let me go."

He surprised me by stepping away, releasing me. My scalp smarted, but I refused to rub my head.

"You're testing me. But lucky for you, I know how to deal with troublesome pets."

Pets?

My hands balled.

How did I ever think I wanted him? The fact his lips had been on my face and his thumb in my mouth repulsed me.

Jethro's gaze drifted down my state of undress. "You're shaking. I don't want you getting sick." His eyebrow quirked. "I'd offer you my jacket, like the chivalrous man I am, but I doubt you'd accept it. However, I have something better."

Spinning around, he drifted toward a deep shadow cast by one of the large pillars. "Flaw? Get out here. You damn well better be—"

"I'm here." A man appeared from the shadows. Dressed in black jeans, shirt, and black leather jacket, the only glint of colour came from a simple silver outline of a diamond engraved on the front pocket. He looked like a thief waiting for a victim. "Been here for forty-five minutes. You're late." He tossed Jethro a duffel, running a hand through long dark hair. "Lucky for you the flight's delayed."

Jethro caught the bag, glaring at the man. "Don't forget your place. I'm not late according to my rules—not yours." Manhandling the duffel, he said, "You did as I asked?"

The man nodded. "Everything. Including photographic evidence. It all went smoothly, and the tickets are inside. I'll take care of the bike, just leave it there. Cushion and Fracture are tracking the Weaver men until you tell them otherwise."

Jethro pulled out an envelope, then flicked through the contents. He looked up, something resembling a smile gracing his lips. "Good work. I'll see you back at Hawksridge."

My ears pricked at the name. It sounded familiar—reeking of old money.

He's from nobility? The concept of Jethro being a duke or an earl was preposterous, and yet…uncannily perfect. Everything about him was deceptive and…bored. Was that all this was? A game to pass the time for some rich brat who got sick of killing puppies?

I couldn't stop my teeth from chattering—both from disgust and cold. The man named Flaw glanced my way. His eyes narrowed. "He's expecting you and the woman. I'll message and let him know it's gone well."

"Don't," Jethro snapped. His English accent thickened with the demand. "He doesn't need to know. He'll see us soon enough." Dismissing the man as if he was the hired help and no longer required, Jethro stalked toward me, holding out the bag.

Flaw dissolved back into the shadows like a scary apparition.

"This is yours. Get dressed. You won't be allowed in the building half-naked and shoeless."

Taking the duffel, I muttered under my breath, "I was dressed in an outfit worth thousands of pounds before you tore it off me."

I had two wishes—one, that he'd heard me and knew just how pissed I was. And two, that he didn't hear, because I was afraid of his reaction.

Jethro smirked before turning to his bike.

I opened the bag and promptly dropped it.

Oh, my God. I had to be dreaming. *Wake up, Nila. Please, wake up.*

My knees buckled, following the bag to the floor. Shaking, I collected the photos sitting on top of a mound of clothes. *My* clothes. Everything I'd brought to Milan—minus the fashion show apparel and my work tools—running gear, a bikini, sweat pants, pyjamas, and a simple collection of blouses, jeans, and maxi dresses.

But on top of it all rested strewn photographs.

Photo-shopped images that never happened.

Doctored snap-shots of lies. Such horrible, horrible lies.

No one will come.

Jethro was right. The police would laugh if anyone asked for their help. What I held cemented my new life being Jethro's plaything.

Shuffling through the deck, I couldn't stop a hot tear searing down my cheek.

There was me—smiling, glowing. I remembered the day. V and I had headed to Paris for a local mid-season show a few years ago. He'd beaten me at poker in a silly pub tournament and a patron snapped an image of us. Laughing, overly warm, arms wrapped around each other in sibling affection, we'd been so happy.

Only Vaughn didn't exist in this photo. The background had been amended to show a fancy restaurant while the man who clutched me was Jethro.

The smile on his face was the warmest I'd seen. His attire of open-neck black shirt and jeans made him look young, in love, and dashing.

I couldn't study it anymore. Flicking to another one, I slapped a hand over my mouth.

This one pictured my father and me. Or *had*. He'd splashed out for the annual staff retreat, and we'd gone on a one week cruise around the Mediterranean. We'd stood with the setting sun dancing on the orange tinted waves, dressed in loose fitting 'cruise wear' that I'd created only days before. I'd planted an adoring daughterly kiss on his scratchy face.

That kiss now belonged to Jethro.

The ship had been tweaked to show a luxury yacht rather than commercial liner. The sunset cast a different glow. Jethro stood broodily, staring into the camera with such an intense glare of sexual power, no one would disagree that there was chemistry and need between us. The way my body curved into his, the sweetness and trust I displayed, only helped confirm the illusion of a couple besotted with each other.

The photos wobbled in my hands; another tear stained the glossy deception.

I looked up, not caring my heart was ripped out and beating coldly on the car park floor. "How—" Gritting my teeth, I tried again. "Destroying my dress wasn't enough? You had to steal my past, too?" I held up a photograph of a half-naked Jethro holding my chin as he kissed me. That wasn't based on my dateless life, but it was so lifelike, so true, so incontestable.

How did they make it so realistic?

Jethro shook his head, rolling his eyes. Locking the bike, he pocketed the keys before turning to face me. Dropping to his haunches, he whispered, "I not only stole your past. I've already stolen your future." Never breaking eye contact, he tapped the photographs in my hands. "You didn't see them all. Flick to the back. They're especially for you."

I couldn't unglue my lungs. I didn't think I'd ever be able to breathe without pain again. Splitting the tower of pictures, I glanced at the last ones. Immediately, I looked up. All sense of decency and pride gone.

"Please, you can't. This—it will break their hearts."

Tears scalded the back of my throat. My eyes burned, glancing down again. This one showed my empty hotel room—exactly as I left it with last minute ribbon and feathers littering the bed before rushing to the show—but now my toiletries from my nightstand, my laptop, and belongs were gone. Including my carry on and suitcase.

The room was abandoned. It looked as if I'd packed up and left my dreams, livelihood, and family without so much as a backward glance.

This would break my brother and father's heart, because it was the exact same way of how my mother, Emma Weaver, left us.

But unlike my mother, there was a simple note placed upon the dresser.

"Turn it over. I took the liberty of asking for a close-up, so you can read what you wrote as your final goodbye," Jethro murmured, stealing the photo from my fingers and tapping the fresh one revealed beneath it.

I curled over my knees, cradling the glossy replica of a goodbye letter penned in my hand. The writing was exactly like mine, even I couldn't tell the forged sweeps and cursive from reality.

It's time I came clean.
I've been lying to you for a while now.
I've fallen in love and decided that my life is better with him. I'm done with the deadlines and unachievable pressure placed on me by this family.
I know what I'm doing.
Don't try and find me.
Nila.

I looked up. My heart collided with my ribcage, bruising, hurting. So much pain. I couldn't contain the sorrow when I thought of V reading this. To be left behind by both his mother and sister....

"They won't believe this. They know me better than anyone. They know I wasn't in a relationship. You said Tex knows all about you and why you're doing this. Please—"

Jethro laughed. "It's not for your family, Ms. Weaver. It's for the press. It's for the world stage who will make this fiction a reality. Your brother will find out the truth from your father, I'm sure. And if they behave, they'll both remain untouched. Believe me, this isn't to hurt them—if I wanted that, I have much better means." He cupped my cheek, brushing away long strands of my hair. "No. This was just an insurance policy."

"For what?" I breathed.

"So no one believes your family when they break and try to find you. They'll be all alone. Just like you. Controlled by the Hawks who've owned the Weavers for almost six hundred years."

Six hundred years?

"But..."

Jethro sniffed, his temper building like a ghost around us. "Stop crying. The images portray the truth. It proves you did what you did and no one can be angry or distrustful."

"What did I do?"

"Ah, Ms. Weaver, don't let shock steal your intelligence. You. Left. Voluntarily." He waved at the photo. "This confirms it."

"But I didn't," I whimpered. "I didn't leave—"

Jethro tensed. "Don't forget so soon what I taught you. You are the *sacrifice* and you..." His eyes dared me to finish his sentence, to admit to everything I'd done by protecting my family. His fingers twitched between his legs, looking like he wanted to strike.

I'd never been good at confrontation—not that my father yelled often or Vaughn and I argued. I'd grown up with no need to fight. I knew how precious my family was. My mother left, proving just how heartless someone could be if they didn't hold onto love. So I'd held on with both hands, feet, every part of me. Only to have it torn away so easily.

You'd rather they lived and never saw them again than die because of you.

Hanging my head, I murmured, "A sacrifice comes of their own free will. Therefore, I left voluntarily."

Jethro nodded, patting my thigh like the pet he thought I was. Covering the photos with his large hand, he pressed down until my elbows gave out and I lowered them. "Good girl. Keep behaving and the next part won't be too hard to bear."

Another rush of tears suffocated me, but I swallowed them back. He'd told me to stop crying. So I would.

Jethro stood, reaching down to scoop up the awful photos and duffel bag of belongings. "Come. We have to go." He didn't offer me his hand to climb to my feet.

The simple act of raising myself from cold concrete to freezing air taxed my already fractured world. Rolling vertigo pitched my balance, sending me reeling backward. My arms shot out, searching for something to grab hold of.

With drunken eyes, I begged Jethro to catch me, but he just stood there. Silent. Exasperated. He let me trip and fall.

I cried out as I collapsed on the ground. My fingernails dug into the rough flooring, holding on while the parking garage danced around like a nightmarish carrousel. Pain radiated from my hipbone, but it was nothing compared to the overwhelming nausea.

Stress.

It wouldn't be Jethro who ended up killing me, but the inability to deal with a gauntlet of emotions.

Closing my eyes, I repeated Vaughn's silly nursery rhyme. *Find an anchor. Hold on tight. Do this and you'll be alright.*

"Get up, goddammit. Stop acting the victim." A pinching hand grabbed under my arm, jerking me to my feet.

I doubled over, holding my stomach as another wave of sickness threatened to evict the only food I'd had today—a luncheon prior to the rehearsal of the runway show.

"You're useless."

When the debilitating wave left, I glared up. "I'm not useless. I can't control it." Breathing hard, I begged, "Please, let me talk to my brother. Let me tell him—"

"Tell him what? That you're being taken against your will?" Jethro chuckled. "By the look on your face you seem to think I'll forbid you having any outside communication—cut you off from everything you hold dear." Letting me go, he scooped my heavy hair from my neck, giving me a reprieve from the sticky heat of not feeling well. "Contrary to what you think, I have no desire to dictate what you can and can't do."

Twisting my hair, tugging lightly, he added, "This may surprise you, seeing as you have such a low opinion of me, but you can go online, keep your mobile—even continue to work if you wish. I told you before—this is not a kidnapping. It's a debt. And until you understand the full complications of the debt, I suggest you keep what's happening to yourself."

I couldn't understand. I was being stolen, yet was allowed access to avenues that could bring me safety. It didn't make sense.

"You've made a decision to come with me, and it's irreversible. You can't change your mind, and you can't change the payments required, so why make others worry on your behalf?" His eyes glinted. "I suggest you become good at pretending if you wish to maintain the pretence of freedom. But I won't stop you from creating extra worry and strain for yourself." Bowing over me, he smiled. "It only makes my job easier."

Grabbing the black rope he'd made from my hair, I stepped away from him. "You're insane."

He gave me a sideways look, rummaging in the duffel to grab a handful of clothes. Closing the distance between us, he shoved the balled items into my stomach.

Oxygen exploded from my lungs from the force.

Jethro pulsed with anger. "That's twice you've questioned my mental state, Ms. Weaver. Do. Not. Do. It. Again." Running a hand through his hair, he growled, "Now get dressed. Time to go home."

I COULDN'T DO it.

It was like looking after a needy, sickly, disobedient child. Bryan Hawk, my father and orchestrator of this mess, assured me it would be a simple matter of a few threats and blackmail.

She'll come easy if you threaten the ones she loves.

Bullshit.

The so-called inexperienced dressmaker had her own agenda. Beneath the chaste little girl, lurked a devious woman who was so tangled and confused she was fucking dangerous.

Dangerous because she was unpredictable. Unpredictable because she didn't know herself.

I was clueless on how to control her. I didn't understand her.

For instance, what the fuck happened at the coffee shop? She'd gravitated toward me. She'd licked my thumb like she imagined it was my dick. She'd *surprised* me. And I didn't do well with surprises.

My structured world—my rules and agendas—were not something that had room for twists and turns. Unless I was the one creating them. And I definitely didn't have time for my cock to twitch and show an interest in the woman I meant to torture and defile.

I would get hard when she was alone on my estate. I would come with her gagged and subdued, hating me with the intensity of her forefathers.

Her pain was my reward. The fact she got me hard by being shy but so bloody tempting was completely unpermitted.

I checked my watch. The plane was due to leave in thirty minutes.

Do it. You know you want to.

I couldn't stomach her presence any longer. I couldn't answer any more of her idiotic questions, or pretend I wasn't raging to teach her a lesson. Her tripping and stumbling got on my nerves. Not to mention her blind love toward a family that no longer had any right to her.

She needed discipline, and she needed it now. *Your hands are bound until you get her home.*

If I had to listen to one more beg or witness another tear, I'd end up killing her just to shut up her loud emotions.

Nila craned her neck, trying to read the boarding passes in my hands. Flaw, my right hand man and secretary to the Black Diamonds brotherhood, had already checked us in. Along with dealing with shipping my new purchase, the Harley-Davidson, and staging the runaway scene at Nila's hotel.

In precisely six hours, a housekeeper would find the photos, notes, and abandoned items, then the gossip columns would spread the story like a well incubated disease.

Nila Weaver's found love.

Nila dispels rumours she's in love with her twin by running off with some unknown English aristocrat.

My lips quirked at that. Me? An aristocrat?

If only they knew my upbringing. My history. If only Nila's father had spent the years he'd had with her preparing her for this day— informing her of our shared heritage, then perhaps she wouldn't look so fucking ill.

I'd told her the truth. Vaughn and Archibald Weaver were under strict monitoring. If they obeyed and went along with the ruse of Nila leaving for love, all would be harmonious.

If they didn't—well, the Weaver line would be snuffed out with the aid of a silenced pistol. And we didn't want that. After all, if there were no more Weavers, who would the Hawks rein over? Who would continue to pay the debt?

I looked at the woman destined to die for the mistakes of her ancestors.

She caught my eye. "Where are you taking me?" Her cheeks were colourless even though she had to be warm with the amount of layers she'd put on.

"I told you. Home." The word scratched across her face like carving knives. Home to me would be hell to her. I should've been more understanding—I could practically hear her heart shatter—but

I'd been born into a family where emotion was a weakness. I prided myself on being strong, unbreakable. Empathy was the downfall of any human.

The ability to *feel* their pain. The nuisance of *living* their trauma.

That inconvenient ability had been beaten out of me as a child. Lesson after lesson until I embraced the cold.

The cold was emotionless. The cold was power.

Nila sniffed, striding a few steps away. Her curves were hidden in her new wardrobe of dark purple dress that came to her ankles, and a denim jacket. I hadn't permitted myself to truly look at her. She was skinny. Too skinny. But her black hair was thick and begged to be fisted.

Watching her dress in the parking garage irritated me. Her unsureness came across as coyness. Pulling the dress over her skirt was a reversed striptease. Her shaking fingertips had turned the ice in my blood into a lust I hadn't felt before.

It wouldn't take much to snap her petite frame. But despite her breakable body, her eyes gave a different story.

She ran deep.

I didn't bother caring how deep. But it did tempt in a way I hadn't expected.

A girl like Nila…well, that wasn't something to be broken lightly.

Her complexities, subtleties, depths, and secrets.

Each layer begged to be unwrapped and enjoyed.

Only once she stood before me, stripped bare of sanity and dreams, would she be ready.

Ready to pay her final debt.

Nila rubbed her cheek, displacing another silent tear. That single fucking tear stopped everything, freezing over the unwanted feeling of excitement at what my future held. Her sniffle gave me a layer of obligation rather than anticipation.

I wasn't going to, but she's given me no choice. Fuck it.

Moving closer, my hands opened to throttle her—to give her something to truly cry about, but I restrained myself.

She looked up, eyes glassy.

I forced a smile—a half-smile, letting her believe her tears affected me, offering false humanity. I let her believe I had a soul and didn't punish her for hoping. Hoping I was redeemable.

She bought it. Stupid girl. Allowing me to offer my arm as if it were some sort of consolation and guide her from purgatory into hell.

THE AIRPORT BAR reeked of sad goodbyes and tears. *Just like my soul.*

I rolled my eyes. I didn't like the sort of person Jethro made me. Someone who only saw the negative and was ruled by fear. *I'm an award winning designer. I'm wealthy in my own right.*

The unknown future crushed my heart, but it was the thought of losing myself while it happened that scared me the most.

"I need a drink. I'll get you one, too," Jethro muttered.

I spun to face him. Big mistake. I stumbled to the left, cursing the suddenly tilting room. My vertigo wasn't normally this bad. An episode a day was my norm, not every time I tried to move.

A cold hand grasped my elbow. "That condition you have—it's really getting on my nerves."

The floor steadied beneath my feet; I tore my arm from his hold. "Leave me alone then. Get on the plane and let me fall over in peace."

He shook his head, gold eyes darkening with impatience. "I have a much better idea."

I looked away, taking in the low square-line sofas, sad plastic plants, and dirty carpeting. *This can't be happening.* Everything seemed surreal. I was at the airport with a man who'd threatened the lives of my brother and father. I was about to climb on a plane with him. I was about to *disappear.*

And probably never be found.

It wasn't rational. It was completely nonsensical.

Suddenly, a drink sounded perfect. Alcohol and vertigo didn't mix, but damned if I wanted to exist full of grief and horror.

Jethro motioned toward a booth by the window where large spotlights turned the black sea of tarmac into false daylight, casting a warm glow on sleeping jumbo jets ready to depart.

Not giving me a chance to say anything else, or to even relay my preference, he stalked away, beelining for the bar.

Quick. Now.

The moment he had his back to me, I pulled my cell phone from my jacket pocket. He said I could keep it. He said I could talk to anyone I chose. He hadn't said when—now or when we got to his 'home', but I desperately needed Vaughn.

My eyes burned as I unlocked the screen. Hunching over the glowing device, I did as my captor ordered and made my way to the booth.

Typing in the number I knew by heart and practically the only number I ever called, I sucked in a breath.

A wall planted itself in my way.

A cold, unforgiving wall.

My head snapped up. Jethro crossed his arms, anger radiating from every inch. "What are you doing?"

I swallowed hard; my palms grew slippery with nervousness. "You said I could keep my phone. You said—"

"I know what I *said*. I may not stop you, but you still need permission. I am, after all, in control of your life from now on." Peering into my eyes, he added, "Don't make a rash decision you can't undo, Ms. Weaver." His English accent clipped my name in an unfamiliar way. He spoke it as if it were dirt. A filthy word contaminating his mouth.

My finger hovered over the call button for my twin. The one man who I could say anything to and he would understand. Summoning what useless power I had, I said, "Please, may I make a phone call? I won't be stupid. I know what's on the line."

Jethro tutted under his breath. "That's the problem. You *don't* know. You think you do. You think all of this is a joke. You're not grasping the depth of what this means, nor will you until you've been educated."

Taking a step, closing the distance between us, he breathed, "But you do know one thing. You know what I will tolerate. Lying to me is another offence that comes with swift punishment. Stay honest, polite, and obedient and your heart will remain beating."

I wanted to scream at him. His quiet voice was worse than being yelled at. It was so…decent…so eloquent. It made all of this seem normal. And it so wasn't. So not normal.

"I understand. Do I have your permission?" My jaw ached I gritted so hard, refraining from what I really wanted to say. If I wasn't so afraid of this psycho I would hit him. I would leap onto his back and pummel him until he bled. Just to see if he *did* bleed, because a part of me expected him to be nothing but stone.

He frowned. "Fine. But I'll remain in earshot for this first conversation."

I shook my head. "No. I need privacy."

He smiled—a thin ribbon of emotion. "You need to realize privacy is a luxury you'll no longer have. Everything you do from now on will be monitored. Nothing will be hidden. Everything must be approved."

Everything? A horrible image of me begging to go to the bathroom only to be refused filled my mind. Not only had he taken me for something I didn't understand, he'd stolen my basic rights as a human.

I truly am a pet.

Jethro's hand whipped out, stealing my phone.

No! Being separated from it made all of this far too real. The starkness of my situation hammered at my soul.

Staring at the screen, he scrolled rudely through my contacts. My very limited contacts. His eye twitched, handing the device back. "You seem to live in a world dominated by males. The only names in your preferred lists are men, aside from a mysterious entry Kite007." He stiffened. "Care to tell me if that person is female? I somehow doubt it, seeing as it's clearly a reference to the ridiculous James Bond Franchise."

Snatching the phone, I said, "I don't care to tell you anything. Leave me alone. I'm calling my brother. I gave you my word I wouldn't jeopardise whatever you're planning until I know the full story."

Jethro placed his hands into his pockets. His cream shirt and diamond pin were the epitome of class. In an ordinary circumstance, I would've been honoured and thrilled to have a date with a man with deliciously thick greying hair and a handsome face. I'd always preferred men over boys.

But he had to ruin it.

He ruined everything.

Jethro didn't move. Just stood there. Silently.

There was no winning. He wouldn't raise his voice or strike me to get his way—not in public anyway—but his posture intimidated me until I gave in.

Staring at the awaiting number, I deliberated against calling V. What did I hope to achieve? It would kill me to hear his voice. *But what if it's a lie and the moment he's got you where no one can see, he takes the only thing you have left?*

I couldn't risk it. Not if I could speak to V one last time.

Locking eyes with my gorgeously-groomed nemesis, I pressed the 'call' button and held the phone to my ear.

Being granted no privacy was horrid. My back stayed straight and all feelings of weakness were buried beneath false strength.

Do not cry. Do. Not. Cry.

The call connected on the first ring.

Vaughn never kept me waiting, almost as if he sensed it was me calling—twin empathy connecting us once again.

Shit, what if he hears? What if he sensed my unhappiness? How would I stop him from coming for me—wherever I was going.

Vaughn's husky voice came down the line. "Nila. Tell me where you are. I'm coming to get you. Tex is acting really strange, and I'm done not being able to get a straight answer."

I sighed, turning my back on Jethro, staring at the airplanes below. So many things ran through my head. I wanted to ask how Dad was acting strange. What all of this meant. But I kept it all bottled up. For him. For them.

"I'm fine, V. I'm…"

I need you. Come get me. Save me please.

"You don't sound fine. Where are you?"

In hell with a monster.

Looking around the bar, I shrugged. "I'm exactly where I need to be."

To keep you safe.

"Stop with the bullshit, Threads. What's really going on?"

Sighing hard, I pressed a palm against my feverish forehead. I sucked at lying. Especially to V. "Something's come up. I'm going away for a little while. A holiday where I can unwind. I should be able to contact you—if the Wi-Fi and phone lines are good." I couldn't stop rambling. "Tonight really put a strain on me, you know? It came together so well, but it wasn't easy—you saw how bad it got toward the end. I just need—"

"What you need is a fucking spanking. You don't just leave without talking this through!" Vaughn paused, a disbelieving huff coming down the line. "You can't be serious. We had plans. You said you'd come with me when I went to Bangkok next week for more merchandise. We've booked the flights and everything."

I didn't want to be reminded of everything I was walking away from.

"I'm sorry, but I can't go. You have to trust me and not push. Just accept what I'm telling you and that I need some alone time, okay? You'll be able to contact me by phone and email."

"This is bullshit."

"V, please. Be supportive, like you always are."

Don't make this ten times harder to say goodbye.

"Skype? I need to see you, Threads. Something doesn't feel right. You're keeping things from me."

A firm fingertip prodded my shoulder. Jethro whispered, "No Skype."

I didn't know how he heard V and didn't want to ask why Skype wasn't permitted. Why doesn't he want my family to see me? *Because who knows what you'll look like when he's finished.*

The fear I'd been able to keep leashed suddenly swamped me. I moved forward, collapsing into an uncomfortable booth.

"Threads. Threads?" Vaughn's voice echoed down the line. "Goddammit, Nila. What the fuck is going on?"

Sighing, I rested my elbows on the table. The weight of aloneness and depression settled heavily. "I don't know," I whispered.

The phone disappeared from my fingertips. "Hello, Mr. Weaver. We met earlier. Jethro Hawk." Jethro glowered, making me wish the seat would devour me.

A loud stream of curses came through the phone. Jethro pinched the bridge of his nose. "No, see that's where you're wrong. If you have an issue with me enjoying your sister for a time, speak to your father. For now, Nila is mine, and I won't have anyone saying differently."

He held the mobile away from his ear for a second while Vaughn exploded. A furious shadow darkened his face.

Jethro gripped the phone, growling like a rabid wolf. "That's none of your concern. I'm taking her. I've *already* taken her. And there's nothing you can do. Goodbye, Mr. Weaver. Don't make me regret my kind generosity toward your sister so soon."

He hung up, tossing me the useless phone. "If you want a piece of advice on how to survive the coming months, don't talk to your brother again unless you want to pay a serious price. He's detrimental to your willingness to obey, and a fuckwit."

Tears welled. I didn't want to cry. Damned if I'd shed anymore useless liquid over this bastard.

"Don't call him a—" I stopped mid-sentence. There really wasn't any point in arguing. He'd win. Just like he'd won up till now without a curse uttered or shout yelled.

I'm meek. He was controlling me with no ropes or chains or curses. I was under his horrible spell, threatened by the illusion of him murdering the people I held most dear.

My eyes flickered toward the exit behind him. Jethro followed my gaze. He side-stepped, waving his arm toward the temptation of running. "You want to leave? Go. If you're so selfish to let others die for you, I'm not going to stop you. One phone call from me, Ms. Weaver, and it all ends for them."

I didn't move, deliberation a heavy cross on my shoulders. How could I sit there and let him take control of my life? But how could I ever live with myself if I ran?

He'd kill my family and there'd be nothing to run toward.

I hunched, deliberately looking away from the exit.

Jethro came closer, crowding me into the booth. "Good choice. Now sit there, don't move, and I'll get you something that'll make this easier." He turned away, but not before I heard his murmured, "For me at least."

I waited until he stood at the bar, smiling at the barmaid, before I opened a new message.

My hands shook, jiggling the phone, but I wouldn't stop. He might not let me talk to people I love, but people I hated didn't matter. The one person who drove me into this mess might be my only hope at surviving it.

If he forgave me.

Needle&Thread: *Kite, I don't do this lightly, but my life has taken a certain change and…well, I would like to be able to message you if it gets too much.*

I'm sorry I overstepped. I'm not going to say any more than…please. I need to be able to talk to you if I need to.

I pressed send, hating myself and how weak I sounded. He wouldn't understand the strength and courage it'd taken to write that or bow into the meeker role. But I needed someone—a friend. And the sad part of my life was—I had none.

Resting my phone on the table, I stared unseeingly out of the window. Tears tried to take me hostage again, but I curled my hands, digging long nails into my palms. The pain gave me a distraction, letting me stay outwardly calm.

Jethro took his time, talking softly to the botoxed waitress. I wished he'd forget all about me so I could sneak out the door and never return.

My phone buzzed.

I'd never hoped for anything more in my life as I read the new message.

Kite007: *Understand me too when I say I don't forgive or forget lightly. But I appreciate your message and can't deny you've got me intrigued. You've almost got me wanting to know what changed in your life to send you grovelling back to me. I'm not an idiot to know it must've been pretty big after what we said to each other. I'll let you message me and reply on one condition.*

There was nothing else. Glancing over at Jethro, he had his back to me waiting for his order. Still time. Still hope.

I swiftly messaged Kite back.

Needle&Thread: *I accept. Whatever your condition.*

Please just give me someone to talk to. No matter how cryptic and shallow he was, I needed it. So much.

Kite007: *No details. I'll reply as long as your messages don't make me care. You've got the wrong man if you want sympathy.*

I wanted to tell him to piss off. That he wasn't worth it. But I swallowed my pride just as Jethro placed a single shot of white liquor in front of me. "Whoever you're messaging, stop."

Glaring into his light, unfeeling eyes, I flicked a curtain of hair over my shoulder.

In my first, but definitely not my last act of defiance, I typed a single word.

One word that gave me a shallow friend who didn't care if I lived or died.

The only person I had left.

Needle&Thread: *Deal.*

I TRIED.

If anyone asked, I could tell the truth. I did *try* to stay a gentleman.

But who the fuck was I kidding? My manners had an expiration date, and Nila pushed me too far.

I guided her from the dismal excuse of a bar, through the terminal, and past security. Her arm stayed looped with mine, following submissively, obediently—like a good pet. Her feet glided in flat shoes, her dark eyes glazed but aware.

It'd been too easy. Both breaking my word and dissolving the tablet into her drink. I said I wouldn't kidnap or drug her—that was before she showed some backbone in the coffee shop, and had the fucking audacity to ask me for something.

Sex? She willingly wanted some sort of meaningless connection with me? That pissed me off.

I'd been too soft. Too gentile. It was time to make my prey fully understand the nightmare she'd walked into and put a stop to the stupid fantasises she entertained.

And I couldn't think about her brother without wanting to fucking punch something. I shouldn't have been so lenient. I didn't care who she talked to as long as she remained mine to torment. But him—he could ruin everything. The Weaver men had been a constant pain in the arse since the Hawks started taking their women.

War had broken out. Lives were lost on both sides.

But we won. And would continue to win, because they were pussies and we were strong.

Nila didn't say a word as I guided her down the airbridge and onto the plane. To an outsider she looked perfectly normal. Perhaps a little tired and spaced out, but content and not in any way distressed.

That was the wonder of this particular drug.

Externally, she acted the perfect part. Internally, well....

It wasn't my problem if she saw everything that happened. Her mind was unhindered—loud and shouting—but all motor control was stolen. And there was nothing she could do about it. She dealt with vertigo on a daily basis—this was no different. I'd taken her ability with the help of a simple chemical. In fact, I was kinder than vertigo, because I gave her something to hold onto.

Patting her hand that rested on my forearm, I guided her into business class. Pointing at the window seat, I waited till she sat heavily, then buckled her in. Her breathing remained low and regular, but when I sat beside her, took her hand, and guided her face to mine, I saw the truth.

She knew.

Everything.

Perfect. It's time to begin.

Brushing black hair from her neck, I whispered, "I should warn you of something." Running my fingers down the silky strands, I moved closer so I could breathe the threat. Silence was terrifying. Whispers petrifying. But barely spoken threats were the worst.

"Be afraid of me, Ms. Weaver. Be afraid because your life is now mine and I'm the master of everything that happens to you. But know this...it's not just me you'll have to fear."

Her chest continued to rise and fall, no hiccup or flinch. But her eyes fought against the glass of unwilling intoxication, struggling to break the surface and no longer drown.

"There are others. Many others who have the right to help me ensure the debt is fully repaid. Ultimately they have to ask permission from me. But there are exceptions to every rule."

Settling back into the leather seat, I smiled. "Remember what I told you and you might survive."

My mouth said one thing, my eyes another.

Remember that and you'll still die.

She heard the truth as well as my lie. Her fingers twitched, mouth parted, but the drugs were stronger than her terror.

She was inert while inside she was screaming.

The silence was a screeching-symphony to my ears.

THE BLACK SUV that I'd been stuffed into at the airport rolled to a stop beneath a humongous archway. A gatehouse, so typical of large wealthy estates in England, soared above us. Through the glass roof of the car, I made out the same crest that emblazed the door panels of the vehicle I sat in. The up lighting made it glow like a rare monument—an over emblazed welcome doormat.

A huge filigree design with four hawks circling a nest of fallen women welcomed, complete with a large diamond glinting in the centre. It screamed of hunting and violence and winning.

I would've shuddered if I had the ability to move. How many of the fallen women lived through what I was about to? How many survived?

None of them.

I knew that now. I knew what my future held.

I'd screamed and raged and howled beside Jethro on the plane. My throat bled from shouting. My heart burst from begging. But he hadn't heard a whimper, because of the magic he'd used to subdue me.

The journey had torn my heart into shreds. Every step I took, I battled to break whatever spell he'd placed me under. Every breath I took, I fought to speak.

If I had the power of speech, I would've screamed that I had a bomb. I would've taken detainment and a full body strip search to flee from Jethro's undeniable, possessive hold.

My entire undoing and decimation was done in utter silence. And the bastard just sat there, holding my hand, nodding at the air-hostess when she said what an elegant couple we were.

He let me dissolve into misery. He lapped up my unshed tears, and I'd seen a glimpse of the monster I'd given my life to. Thousands of feet above the earth, I'd witnessed the cold gentleman mellow into something resembling a happy lover. Someone who'd won and got their way.

"Welcome home, Ms. Weaver," Jethro whispered against my ear.

I tried to cringe from his mouth, to huddle against the door, but the damn drug kept me locked beside him.

I blinked, inwardly sobbing, outwardly a perfect porcelain doll.

Everything had been stolen. My sense of touch, ability to speak, muscles needed to run.

A man in his early twenties appeared from a large pillar of the archway. Manifesting from the dark like a ghoul on Halloween. Jethro stiffened.

The new arrival opened the front door, sliding into the seat and nodding at the elderly man driving us. "Clive."

The driver nodded in return, gripping the gear stick with an arthritic hand, and engaging the car once again. He hadn't said a word since picking us up at Heathrow. *Perhaps he doesn't have a tongue? Jethro and his family probably ripped it out to protect their sadistic secrets.*

We inched forward, trading the soft lighting of a hawk engraved logo for the deep darkness of forest. I stared out the window into pitch black. From Italy to England, from night to night. The engine purred, following a quaint road slicing through dense woodland.

I wanted to run. And scream. I wanted so much to scream.

Jethro scowled as the newcomer twisted in his seat, awkwardly facing us. I struggled to make out his features thanks to the dark, but the high beams of the SUV cast shadows enough to see.

"Jet." He gave a mock salute.

Jethro sniffed. "Daniel."

"This her?" The man trailed his eyes from my lips to my breasts to my demurely placed hands in my lap. "She looks like a Weaver."

Jethro sighed, sounding bored and annoyed. "Obviously."

Daniel reached over, grabbing my knee. His touch sent shivers of repulsion over me, even through the cotton of my dress.

I felt that.

I held my breath. Sense of touch was the first sign of the drug wearing off. I knew when Jethro touched me, because of the pressure of his fingers. They acted like a punishment, a leash, and a reminder that my life was his. But up till now I hadn't been able to feel temperature or texture. Neither hot nor cold. Gentle or soft.

But now I could.

It's fading.

I hoped joy didn't show on my face. If I could move, I could escape. *Oh, Nila. Don't be so stupid.*

My joy fizzled out as fast as it'd arrived. There would be no escaping. It was yet another thing I knew just by what Jethro *wasn't* saying. I'd learned something in the short flight here. His silence told me more than any part of him. His silence shouted too loudly to be ignored.

I was dead already. My last breath hinged only on how quickly he tired of his new toy.

Keeping my emotions buried, I stared blankly at the man who dared touch me. His lips pulled into a cruel smile; his fingers tightened until every inch of me wanted to jerk away.

Jethro sat still, letting him touch me.

Daniel's nose was slightly crooked from a bad break, face fuller, body softer than Jethro's, but there was no denying the family resemblance. Jethro was cold stone with sharp contours, gravelly voice, and imposing personality while the younger brother had more animation.

If it wasn't for the greed glowing in his eyes, I would've preferred him. But despite Jethro's granite exterior and sharpness, I knew in my heart I was better off being his plaything than this new Hawk.

There was something missing inside him.

A soul.

With a sneer, the man ran his palm up my inner thigh, bunching the material of my dress. "I must say you're very well behaved." He dug his nails into my delicate flesh, only a hand distance from my crotch. "You don't flinch." His hand suddenly left my thigh, connecting with a loud, stinging slap on my cheek. The force of his strike sent my useless body falling into Jethro. "You don't cry."

My face smarted and throbbed, making my heart race. I squeezed my eyes, wishing the sense of touch hadn't returned. I didn't want pain. I didn't want any of this.

Jethro grunted, pushing me upright with a rough shove to my shoulder. "She's not normally like this. Couldn't shut her up, or stop her endless questions. So I drugged her."

The man's eyebrow rose. "With what?" Eyes slithering over my chest, he planted his hand back on my leg. Pushing my dress out of the way, he inched higher and higher and *higher* on naked skin.

I wanted to curl into a ball and cry until I drowned from tears. I wanted oblivion from this nightmare. But the drugs kept me sitting prim and willing, a perfect toy to play with.

There are others. Many others who have the right to help me ensure the debt is fully repaid. The sentence had been on repeat in my head ever since Jethro whispered it on the plane. Was that why he permitted his brother to manhandle me? Would I be given to him to do as he pleased?

Please, God. Please don't let that happen.

I had enough strength to stay true to myself and survive one man. But multiple? They'd tear me into smithereens and ruin me even for death.

Jethro placed his hand—slightly larger and far more scary—on my other leg, pressing me hard against the leather. His touch hurt—burning my exposed skin like dry-ice. "I gave her Diamond Dust."

Daniel's vile touch stopped just as the tips of his fingers brushed the crotch of my knickers. I sat frozen, every part of me humming with horror.

"Diamond Dust? Shit, Jet, that stuff hasn't finished testing. You know Cut didn't authorise it to be sold yet—let alone be used in public. What if she had a seizure? How would you have explained she's nothing and deserved to die? You couldn't. You'd end up in fucking prison."

My heart hammered. Not only had he stolen my mobility, he'd run the risk of killing me. The fear crested again, burning through the drugs bit by bit. Even with the knowledge that I'd have to live through countless horrors before my time was up, I was glad I hadn't had a seizure. Death was so final. As long as I breathed, I *might* find some way to survive.

You say that now. My pain threshold hadn't been tested. I had no guide on how strong I'd remain or how precious my life would be when I no longer wished to live it.

Jethro shrugged. "If she died then the final debt would've been paid sooner rather than later." Glancing at me, he added, "I admit it's taking longer than I thought to leave her system. But it did a nice job shutting her up."

His fingers turned to pincers. "See how enjoyable silence is, Ms. Weaver?"

I stayed immobile beneath his touch, but my heart flew with terror, burning off the residual frozenness, leaving me at the mercy of reactions. Every second the drug weakened only meant I had to work extra hard to maintain the deception I was still its prisoner.

Daniel's fingers inched further. His eyes locked on mine as he touched my clit through my knickers. His touch was horribly warm, invasive, and gross.

I wanted to kick him in the damn nose.

But I just sat there.

And died a little.

I sat there, because I had no damn choice.

Don't. I swallowed, drinking the tears fighting so hard to be shed. *Don't spiral.* I couldn't let myself be sucked into useless sadness. I'd never claw my way out. I'd never be ready to fight.

And I mean to.

My life might be earmarked for extinction, but I meant to be the last Weaver the Hawks ever took.

At least I don't have children. Once they killed me, there'd be no more Weaver women.

Oh, my God. Until Vaughn has children.

The fist around my heart squeezed until lightheadedness made the car swim.

Daniel yanked me from my horror, rubbing my clit. He grinned. "She looks younger than twenty-four. Sure you didn't get the younger sister instead?"

What!?

I jolted, sucking in a breath. I forgot to pretend the drugs still held me prisoner. A sister? Impossible.

She left us. Could my mother have had another life—a whole other existence that I didn't know about?

The thought pulverized my heart. Not only did she have a family—tearing us apart when the debt came for her—but she'd thoughtlessly given life to another girl?

Jethro's head snapped toward me, his light-brown eyes flashing in the darkness. I stayed as statuesque as possible. My gasp was the first sound I'd made since the bar. Since I entered into an agreement with

Kite not to make him care, and the last conversation I had with my brother for who knew how long.

Jethro leaned into my neck. "I see you fighting it. I see you winning. You can't hide anything from me." Pulling away, his eyes narrowed. "You'd do well to remember that. Don't give me a reason to hurt you so soon."

Looking to his brother, he muttered, "She's the right one." His fingers clenched and unclenched on my thigh. In a lightning move, he snatched Daniel's wrist and jerked his probing fingers from my core. "She's the right one and *mine*. Enough."

I couldn't stop the sigh of relief. Only one other man had touched me there. Only one boy had seen me naked and taken my virginity. I never thought I'd be in a situation where I'd be forced, and for a fraction of a second I was grateful toward Jethro for stopping it.

"I can touch her if I want. Shit, I can fuck her too."

"I didn't say you couldn't. I just said…enough." He bit the word into pieces. Sharp, deadly, unforgiving.

Daniel tore his arm from Jethro's grip. "Fine. But don't climb up your arse thinking she's just yours. She's not. She belongs to all of us."

There are others. Many others who have the right to help me ensure the debt is fully repaid.

"No. But she's mine until I say you can have her. Hierarchy, little brother. You know how receiving charity works."

"Fuck off, Jet." Pointing a finger at Jethro's face, he said, "Cut changed a few things tonight at the Gemstone. He's named me VP— given me your role."

Jethro settled into the seat, his broad shoulders brushing mine. "If you think he did that behind my back, you're mistaken. I asked for time. Cut was more than happy to grant it. After all, I'm the firstborn son of a Hawk. She's the firstborn daughter of a Weaver. There are more important things on my agenda for the foreseeable future."

My brain swam. Everything they said sounded cryptic and layered in code. Cut? Was that a name? Gemstone? It sounded like a place, but that didn't make sense.

"You've always thought you're better than me. But you'll see who extracts a debt from flesh better when I get my turn." Daniel sneered, his gaze bouncing from his brother to me.

I gritted my teeth against dropping my eyes or trying to turn invisible. As much as I hated Jethro, I would make sure to remain in his good graces as long as possible.

Daniel reached out and patted my knee, ignoring Jethro's icy look. "Enjoy your time with my brother, because when you're mine…enjoyment won't be something you'll be feeling."

Jethro sat forward, his suit rustling against the leather upholstery. In his signature terrifying quietness, he said, "You disturb my work before I'm through, blood or not, you'll pay the price."

The two men glowered. I didn't know either of them, but the air shimmered with past conflict and animosity—hinting that this standoff was nothing new.

"You're not untouchable," Daniel hissed. "You better—"

Jethro shook his head, eyes dark as amber. "Stop. There's nothing I better do. Father didn't pick you. He didn't *choose* you." His hand came up, casually checking his fingernails. "Life rewards those who deserve it. And you—don't."

Jethro was calm, made worse with the swirling ferocious temper existing just below the surface. The atmosphere thickened, changing the breathability of the car's interior until I choked with the urge to flee.

Clive, the driver, never slowed, continuing through the night as if brother rivalry and debts extracted from human misery was common. The gentle rocking of the vehicle did nothing to relieve the anger between Jethro and Daniel, but every wheel spin helped shed the fogginess I'd existed in for the past few hours.

The fact I was trapped between two males who might explode at any second helped drench my system in adrenaline, kick-starting my heart, dragging me to the surface of being master of my own body once again. The heavy drug-ocean receded.

I didn't witness what made Daniel concede—Jethro never moved—but he growled a curse, then spun in his seat to glare out the windscreen. I followed his attention, holding my breath at the soft glow in the distance. If that was our destination, it was giant. A looming residence breaking the darkness with false warmth and welcome.

My new home.

My new hell.

My end.

"It's called Hawksridge Hall. Take a good look, because it's the last place you'll ever live." Grabbing a handful of my hair, Jethro tugged me closer. His hot breath disappeared down my dress, making me tremble. "Hawksridge has been in our family for countless generations. A fortune we built from nothing. Unlike you, we weren't born into privilege. We earned our wealth. We deserved the titles bestowed, and it's time to show you what we had to do to achieve that."

His fingers wrapped tighter, burning my scalp. "To dispel any thought of running, there's over one thousand hectares of land. You'd never find your way to the boundary. You're trapped." His lips grazed over my jaw. "You're mine." Keeping his fingers tangled in my hair, he reclined, pulling my neck into an uncomfortable angle.

The sadness I'd done so well at battling crested again. There wouldn't be bars on my cage—or at least I didn't think so—but there was a fortified moat in the design of woodland and lakes and hills. I wasn't outdoorsy. I didn't know north from south.

But you do run.

I was fast. I had stamina. If the opportunity came, I wouldn't hesitate to put my obsession with running to use.

Until you fall and break your leg thanks to an episode.

My shoulders rolled. Not only was I trapped by a maniac family, but I was vertigo's favourite stumbler.

The car continued deeper and deeper. Every turn, I lost all sense of direction and knew I would never find the gatehouse without a miracle.

Taking a deep breath, I looked at my hands in my lap. I willed sensation to come back. They twitched, returning to life with a wash of pins and needles.

They fell off my lap involuntary as we bounced over a cattle grate. Jethro pursed his lips, looking at my offending limb on the seat beside him. His gaze trailed up my arm to my chest.

I breathed faster at the calculating look in his eyes. Unwinding his fingers from my hair, he trailed them down my neck, along my clavicle, across my shoulder, and down my arm. "My brother was the first to touch you below, but I'm going to be the first to touch you here." His hand skated across to my breast, clamping around the sensitive tissue.

The soft cotton of my dress did nothing to protect me from the coldness of his grip.

"You seemed to want my attention at the café. Don't say I never give you anything." His finger pinched my nipple, rolling it painfully. There was nothing sexual about his hold—only punishment.

Giving up pretence of being under the influence of whatever he'd given me, I squeezed my eyes, swallowing back a whimper.

He twisted my nipple again, shifting from demeaning to the edge of painful, but what made it worse was I'd *wanted* him to touch me there. I would've willingly slept with him only hours before. Before I knew the animal inside the cultivated man.

"You're too skinny. I prefer women with more…assets than you," he whispered, cupping my other small breast. "However, your tiny stature might prove to be a blessing with some of the things I have planned." He pinched me again, turning my nipple like a corkscrew.

I flinched, forehead furrowing against the pain.

He chuckled. "I knew it was wearing off." His touch turned from painful to excruciating. I bit my lip, barely holding back a cry.

"Just in time." Letting my breast go, he captured my hand, linking his icy fingers through mine. There was nothing romantic or caring about Jethro holding my hand—it was a pure reminder that I had no chance in hell of getting free.

Vaughn. Tex.

I wanted so badly to talk to them. To beg for rescue. But I could no longer be the woman I'd been. I couldn't be the workaholic who blamed others for my unhappiness. I'd accepted my father's old-fashioned law about not being permitted to date, because in all honesty, I wasn't ready. I would never be ready. Because meeting someone meant the possibility of falling in love. Which meant the worst pain imaginable when they left.

If anything, Jethro had done me a favour. I never wanted male company again. If I could return to my sewing machines with no other companionship but my twin, I'd be happy, eternally grateful, and would live the rest of my life in peace.

Tugging my hand into his lap, Jethro murmured, "I meant what I said on the plane. Play your part and you'll live to see another sunrise."

Something snapped inside as if the drug suddenly gave up its hold on me, along with everything I'd been trying to avoid. The tears, the fears, the constant worrying of what was to come.

It all disappeared.

I couldn't afford to drain my energy with useless wonderings. Jethro said I could work. I intended to drown myself in fabric and continue designing my next runway show. I would pretend my world hadn't become a monster-filled nightmare, and lock my mind in a place where it was safe. Mundane was safe. Routine was safe.

I would create a sewing room deep in my soul and ensure no one—including the numerous activities Jethro had planned—could ever ruin me.

And talk to Kite.

My heart thumped. He wasn't kind or a sympathetic ear to cry to. But I was glad. I didn't want someone to pat my back and make me feel worse with commiseration. I needed someone to tell me to buck up, keep going, and never wallow in darkness.

Kite didn't know it yet, but I planned to use him as my barometer of liveliness. If I could muster up the energy to flirt and chat and pretend everything was okay, I had the strength to continue. The moment I used him as an outlet to purge whatever Jethro did to me, I would know I needed to re-centre myself and dig deeper to stay true.

Jethro let my hand go, tossing it away almost violently.

I breathed a sigh of relief, then stiffened as his fingers latched around my upper thigh.

Whispering harshly, he said, "Keep watching the horizon, Ms. Weaver. You're about to see your new home." His hand crept up my leg, following the same path his brother had—freezing my exposed skin with his icicle-like fingers. "Don't take your eyes off the windscreen. You behave and I'll make sure you have somewhere warm to sleep tonight. You disappoint me and you'll sleep with the dogs."

I bit my lip, eyes flaring wide.

Sleep in a kennel? *Shit, Nila. You couldn't be any more stupid.*

All this time I'd braced myself for sexual payments—bodily taxes and unwanted attention—but in reality I hadn't stopped to think about the bare essentials of living. There was so much more Jethro could do to me than torment my body.

He could deprive me of nutrition.

He could prevent me from sleeping.

He could make me live in squalor and suffer illness after illness.

Daniel stayed facing the front, ignoring us. I risked my first question since the airport bar.

"You aren't just going to use me. Are you?" My voice sounded strange after not speaking for so long.

Jethro stilled, his fingers twitching on my inner thigh. "So naïve. You're worse than a pet. You're like a child. A loveless girl who knows nothing of the big, bad world." Breathing shallow, his hand moved higher and higher. "Pity I'm not turned on by little girls. Pity you don't get me hard, my loveless, clueless Weaver. Then you might've been prisoner in my bed."

In front of us, the car's headlights illuminated a driveway. The woodland stopped, giving way from thicket to a huge expanse of manicured lawn and a large oval fountain. Birds of prey replaced angels and fair maidens, their talons dancing on top of water spray.

Jethro's hand burned, never stopping his slow assault. My heart jack-knifed, pain shooting in my chest as panic replaced my blood. I'd wanted sexual contact for so long but not like this. Not taken. Not even wanted.

The car slowed, skirting around the fountain. We turned left, following the sweeping driveway.

And that was when I saw it.

The monstrosity that was my so-called new home.

The rising monolithic, French turreted, tower fortified, sweeping, soaring mansion. Tarmac turned to gravel beneath the tyres, pinging against the metal panels below. Jethro's fingers crept higher, demanding I pay attention to everything he did.

"Welcome to Hawksridge Hall, Ms. Weaver. It's going to be a pleasure entertaining you as my guest." The sentence wrapped around me like a noose; my eyes snapped closed as his fingers brushed my core. Firm, unyielding, he cupped me through my knickers, sending snow to my womb with his vile fingers.

I bit my tongue, hating him. Hating myself. Hating everything to do with debts and vendettas and family feuds.

"This is what you wanted, isn't it?" Jethro whispered, pressing harder.

Everything clenched, repelling against his awful ministrations.

I tore my eyes open. "Not like this." Dropping my voice, I locked eyes with him. "Please, not like this."

The car rocked to a stop.

Daniel looked over his shoulder, his gaze dropping to the blatant position of Jethro's hand between my legs. He smirked. "Welcome to the family. Don't know how much you've been told about us, but forget everything." His teeth glinted in the pooling light from the mansion. "We're much worse."

Jethro stroked me, drifting down to where the silk of my underwear gave a little, pressing against my entrance. "He's right. Much worse."

I shuddered as his finger bit into me. The unhurried, controlled way he touched me twisted with my mind. His violation was different than his brother's. Still not wanted, but at least more easily tolerated.

He was the devil I knew. Not the devil I didn't. In a morbid way, that made Jethro my ally rather than tormentor.

"I'll look forward till we meet again, Weaver." With another smirk, Daniel shoved open his door and disappeared.

Jethro's fingers rocked into me, but I refused to give him any reaction—neither upset nor regret. Sitting with my hands balled, I asked, "Why are you doing this?"

Jethro chuckled. "The ultimate question. And now that we're home, you're about to be told." Removing his hand, he opened the car door and climbed out.

All the blood in my body rushed between my legs—almost as if every molecule needed a cleansing—searching for relief from the hot, cold, tempting, *vile* way he'd touched me.

He looked so elegant in his dark grey suit, so refined with the glint of diamond on his lapel. Why did someone so horrid look so beautiful? It wasn't fair. Nature's cruel irony. In jungles, birds died from being attracted to the gleam of cavernous flowers. In rainforests, snakes and omnivores succumbed to toxin-riddled-jewelled frogs.

Beauty was the ultimate arsenal. Beauty was meant to deceive. It was meant to trick and beguile so their prey never saw death coming.

It worked.

And to a woman who made her life creating beauty for others and never being granted the ease of naturally acquiring it, Jethro was a double threat, both to my ego and lifespan.

Turning back to offer me his palm, Jethro waited for me to accept his token of help.

I ignored him.

I wasn't naturally a defiant person, but there was something about him that made me become a brat. Pushing off the seat, I propelled myself awkwardly and stiffly to the open door. The moment I was in grabbing distance, Jethro snatched my wrist and jerked me from the vehicle.

Of course, standing for me was already a careful affair, mixed with an unknown substance that'd hijacked my motor controls, I didn't land on my feet.

With a cry, I tripped out of the SUV, sprawling face first on the gravel below. The car suddenly cranked into gear and drove off. Leaving me alone and bruised before a manor worth millions.

"What on earth?" The gruff exclamation came from above—different from Jethro's deep timbre, but powerful and full of supple authority.

"Goddammit, this is getting ridiculous," Jethro muttered. "Are you going to be like this all the time?"

His strong hands lassoed around my waist, yanking me to my feet. The moment I was vertical I blinked, trying my hardest to find an anchor and remain standing. The world steadied and I shook Jethro's lingering hold off my hipbone. "Yes, I'm ridiculous. Yes, I've suffered all my life. Yes, I know it's a *huge* inconvenience for someone who wants to kill me that I'm already a little bit damaged, but did you stop to think—just once—that the reason I'm struggling more than normal is because of the stress you're loading my system with?

"Have you never dealt with an upset stomach or a tension headache?" Waving my hand in his face, I snapped, "It's the same thing. My body doesn't handle upsetting circumstances well. Get over it or let me the hell go!"

It felt wonderful to let go of the anger bubbling inside. It purged me a little, giving me room to breathe.

Jethro remained steadfast, his eyes wide, mouth thin and unamused.

"Well, she has fight. All the fun ones did."

The man who'd spoken stood on the second-to-last step of a humongous portico. The house loomed overhead, blotting out the moon and stars as if it were a living entity. Burnished copper gilded the many roofs and turrets, criss-crossing flowerbeds lived beneath soaring lead-light windows, and lattice planted grass grew on the side of the turrets. It wasn't just a building—it was alive. Maintained, proud, a piece of impressive architecture that had weathered centuries, but been so well cared for.

I craned my neck left and right. The building continued on and on, at least ten stories high, with intricate alcoves, sweeping doorways, and a hawk embellishing every keystone.

It's a work of art. I was a creator. My passion didn't just lie in textiles, but in everything where a level of skill blared from every inch.

And Hawksridge Hall was majestic.

I wanted to hate it. I despised the family who owned it. But I'd always been a lover of history. I'd always pictured myself as a lady of a manor, with horses and gardens and refined dinner parties. I loved exploring stately homes, not for the furniture or statues, but for the drapery, hand-stitched wallpaper, and massive hanging tapestries.

Jethro took a step toward the older gentleman. "You said it would be easy. I can assure you, it wasn't." Throwing a cold look over his shoulder, Jethro motioned me forward. "Come here and pay your respects."

I didn't move.

The older man chuckled. He wore all black, and just like the man who brought my belongings in the parking garage in Milan, he wore a black leather jacket with a silhouette of a diamond on the pocket.

His hair was fully white, yet his face wasn't too weathered. He had a goatee, which was more dirty grey than snow, and eyes were as light and unnerving as Jethro's.

Instantly my back stiffened; my heart bucked in refusal. This man didn't deserve respect. I wanted nothing to do with him.

Just as I knew the younger man in the car was Jethro's brother, I knew without a doubt this was his father. This man was responsible for upholding the evil pastime of torturing innocence for something that should stay in the past. He was ultimately responsible for my demise.

Jethro stalked back, stole my arm, and marched me forward. Under his breath, he said, "Don't annoy me. I'm warning you."

Jerking me to a halt in front of his father, he spoke louder. "Ms. Weaver, let me introduce you to Bryan Hawk. Head of our family, President to his fellow riders, and current man in a long line of succession to wear the family name."

He glared at me, making sure I listened. "He's also known as Cut amongst his brotherhood. But to you, he will always be addressed as Mr. Hawk."

Mr. Hawk grinned, holding out his hand. "Welcome to my humble abode."

I shied away, not wanting to touch him, be close to him, or even have to tolerate talking to him.

Jethro growled under his breath, grabbing my elbow and holding me firm. "You're one infraction away from sleeping with the hounds, Ms. Weaver. Try me. Disobey once more."

His father laughed. "Ah, I remember those days. The fun, the discipline." Climbing down the final step, he closed the space between us. His aftershave reeked of sadism and old money—if that had a smell. A horrid mix of spice and musk that gave me an instant headache, whilst his eyes stole everything about me from my reflection to my dismal future.

He cupped my cheek.

I flinched, expecting the brutality and roughness I'd come to expect from a Hawk, but he ran his thumb gently over my cheekbone. "Hello, Nila. It's a pleasure to once again entertain a Weaver in our modest home."

Hearing my name repulsed me. Jethro hadn't used it yet—sticking to the impersonal address of my last-name. I hated that Mr. Hawk thought he had the authority to speak it.

Wanting to spit in his face, I focused on the house behind him—swallowing the urge. My gaze soared to the stained glass windows, the imposing spires, and impressive stonework. There was nothing modest about this dwelling, and he knew it.

I kept my lips clamped. I had a whole novel of horrible things I wanted to say, but Jethro's seething bulk beside me kept my tongue in check.

Jethro let me go, pushing me into his father. "She's been nothing but trouble. I can't deny I'm looking forward to tomorrow."

My heart leapt into my throat at the dark promise in his voice. *What's going to happen tomorrow?*

Mr. Hawk dropped his palm from my cheek, wrapping his arm around my waist. With his free hand, he brushed wayward strands from my eye. "You look just like your mother. It's a pity I'm not the one extracting in this particular instance, but rest assured, I will enjoy you once or twice."

My stomach latched onto my heart, making me sick. *Don't ask.* The question blared in my head. *What did you do to my mother?*

I'd been so young and full of righteous anger at her leaving my father. I thought she was the villain—the heartbreaker.

But she was the one who paid an unpayable price. And never returned.

Mr. Hawk's eyes glinted. "I see Jethro hasn't told you anything yet." Trailing his hand from my hair to my lips, he stroked me gently. "That's going to be a fun conversation, but for now I'll let you in on a little family secret." Crushing me against him, he whispered, "I'm the

96

one who stole her. I'm the one who took debt after debt from her unwilling skin. And do you know what she begged for in her final minutes of life?"

My head swam. My world roared. Life as I knew it ended.

I hated him.

I loathed him.

I'll kill you.

I'd never felt such heat, such insanely burning desire to cause harm. My teeth ached from clenching; my nails drew blood from my palms.

"She begged for your life. To end it with her and to let you live in peace." His hand left my waist, grabbing my arse with a vicious grip. "Know what I told her?" His breath smelled of liquor and cigars, making me swallow his words. "I told her you were born a Weaver, you'll die a Weaver. And that's the simplistic way of our world."

Shoving me away, I ping-ponged from father to son, coming to an abrupt halt in Jethro's arms. The relief at being away from the man who'd murdered my mother made my limbs weak and jittery, but I couldn't stop the hatred from gnawing a gaping hole in my soul. I needed it out. I needed it spoken so he would know the debt might not have ended with my mother but it would end with me.

It will.

"I pity you. I knew nothing about you, your sons, your warped perception of life until tonight. I may not know why you're doing this but I do know one thing. I know that it's the last time you'll ever do it."

"Quiet!" Jethro shook me. But I wasn't scared of him. I wasn't scared of any of them anymore. They were bullies. Sadistic bastards who'd met their match.

Struggling in his arms, I freed my hand, pointing a livid finger at Mr. Hawk. I lost my rage, tilting head first into lunacy. My temper gave me power over everything. My cursed balance. My sheltered beginnings. In that one moment of brazenness, I found a nucleus of strength I didn't know I had.

My voice pitched as I yelled, "I'll kill you! I'll watch you die just like you watched my mother—I'll kill you! You don't deserve to live. I'll kill you and—" I launched myself at him, only to stumble and go slamming back against a powerful form.

Jethro grabbed my shaking arm, pinning it to my side. His strong hold crashed me against his body, moulding my wiggling behind against his rigid front.

His body was hard and firm—exactly like the stone I thought he was. The bulge in his trousers pressed against my lower spine.

"You've pushed me too far. You just had to fucking push. No one threatens my family, least of all a girl who can barely stand without support. And a Weaver." He spat on my feet. "Fucking filth."

"Remove her from my sight." Mr. Hawk sniffed. "Teach her her place, Jethro. I won't put up with such stupid behaviour." His eyes landed on me. "As for you. I'd hoped you'd show more promise. Think what you want of us, Ms. Weaver, but this isn't a simple matter that will end quickly. You're ours for however long we wish to keep you and you'll learn proper manners if we have to beat it into you."

Nodding at Jethro, he climbed the steps to the two-story-sized front door and disappeared.

The moment he vanished, my spine rolled and I wanted nothing more than to fall to my knees and cry.

What was I thinking?

My rage and hatred snuffed out like a candle in a storm. I'd never been so out of control. My emotions had held me hostage and I'd snapped—for the first time since my mother left—I'd succumbed to the intense freedom of bitterness.

Jethro dragged me backward, his dress shoes crunching against gravel. He didn't wait for me to back-peddle, just clutched me hard, dragging me like a corpse. "You've surprised me twice tonight, and I haven't liked either of them. You've pissed me off. So much so that—"

Slamming to a halt, he shoved my shoulder blades. "Get on your knees."

I wheeled forward, crashing from standing to landing on all fours. *No!*

I winced as the driveway bit into my palms; my knees throbbed as sharp pebbles cut into my skin. I looked up, my face swollen and achy from unpermitted tears welling as deep as a bottomless lake.

This was the truth. This humiliation and admittance of power, not the farce he'd painted.

Jethro towered above, his legs planted wide, face etched in livid anger. "I'm a firm advocator of rewarding good behaviour but after tonight you've proven there is nothing to reward. You're wild, unwilling, and a spoiled brat who *will* learn her place."

Leaning down, he grabbed my long hair, jerking it hard. "Did you honestly think, after an outburst like that, that you'd deserve the comfort of a bed? Why do it, Ms. Weaver, when you knew what was on the line?"

I couldn't speak. My throat was pulled back, the pressure stopping all sounds and swallows.

"I have a good mind to fuck you right here. To smash whatever sense of entitlement or hope you're holding onto." He shook me.

My eyes watered at the pain.

"You're not hearing me. This is your life now. I am your only friend. Stop. Pissing. Me. Off."

You're not my friend. I have one, and his name isn't Jethro.

Kite.

I didn't think I'd want to message him so soon, but I needed someone from the outside world. I needed reminding that the universe hadn't entered an alternate dimension and there was still hope.

When I remained silent, Jethro snarled, "You're sleeping with the dogs. They have better obedience than you, perhaps you can learn from them on what we expect."

I sniffed, fighting so hard against tears.

I didn't even care that I wouldn't sleep in a bed. I was past worrying about sanitary conditions or nutritious food. All I wanted was freedom.

"Move," Jethro breathed, his beloved silence smoothing his outburst from before. "Don't make me show you how a good dog moves."

He wants you to crawl.

It had begun.

This was the beginning. And I'd brought it upon myself.

He wants to destroy you.

Using my hair as the leash, Jethro paced beside me as I went from stationary to crawling. I crawled like an animal. I crawled like a pet. I crawled through manicured gardens, past ponds, and statues, all the way from manor to kennel.

I STRETCHED, LOOKING up at my ceiling. The plasterwork around the huge chandelier never failed to let me know who I was.

A Hawk.

The intricate rosettes and architraving was a testament to my namesake. Birds of prey swooped, hunted, and devoured small animals from above.

My hard cock lay heavily against my stomach. My hands clenched beneath my head. I was so fucking close to breaking the rules and taking Nila last night. She'd pushed me too far. I'd wanted to see how smart her mouth could be with my dick jammed down her throat.

I should've taken her.

Removing my hand from beneath my pillow, I grasped my morning wood and stroked. My eyes snapped closed as I imagined a different outcome to last night.

Nila's pink plump lips opening. Me sliding inside her mouth. My balls tightening as her timid tongue welcomed my cock. She'd lick me just like she'd done my thumb. Eager, inexperienced—a novice with so much to give.

I'd rock forward, holding her head, giving her no choice but to take more of my length.

I'd thrust harder, driving her from accepting to choking.

Fuck.

My hand worked tight and fast. The large bed creaked as I arched my back, giving into the fantasy of blowing down Nila Weaver's throat.

Fuck, yes. Take it. Yes.

My quads tightened, and I groaned as the first spasm of release shot from my balls, creating a sticky mess on my stomach.

Fantasy Nila kept sucking me, drawing another wave of pleasure. I liked her a lot more with my cock in her mouth. She was silent. Incapacitated.

I shivered as the last spurt of my orgasm joined the mess. I opened my eyes.

"Goddammit." I hadn't meant to do that. *Fuck it. It was a long night.* I deserved a little…unwinding.

It's going to be an even longer day.

I might've blown my load with an imaginary vision of Nila on her knees, but it would soon become real. Today, Nila would be initiated. She'd be welcomed. And not just by me.

Swinging my legs out of bed, I prowled across the thick red carpet toward my private bathroom.

I smiled, perversely happy with the day's upcoming activities. The next few weeks weren't about debt repaying or vengeance, they were about hospitality and welcoming a new Weaver into the Hawk household. She had much to learn, her place to recognise, and all thoughts of who she was torn from her soul and burned.

I'd use her. My father would use her. My two younger brothers would use her. If I let myself, I would feel sorry for her.

But that permission had long since been beaten out of me.

After spending some time alone with her, I knew the handful she was. Despite her disobedience, I rather liked her fire. Pity that fire would snuff out almost instantly.

I paused, searching inside to see how strong my barricades were. To see if I had enough ice inside to do everything expected of me. She was pretty, I had to admit. She had a certain intrigue. But she was just a woman.

A woman who confuses you.

Scowling, I shoved the thought away. She confused me which wasn't a good thing. It was almost as bad as surprising me.

One moment she seemed so sure and strong. The next she was brittle and breakable. And her bloody vertigo was getting on my goddamn nerves.

No. I was more than happy to let my fellow brothers share the work in ruining her. It would be over faster, and I could go back to my life before I knew of the stupid scroll stained with the blood of the first

Weaver debts.

The sun spilled like a golden carpet, leading the way from bed to shower. My room was vacant of personal touches but reeked in history of past owners. Rococo style dressers, Victorian designed chairs. The wallpaper was embossed maroon leather with gold accents.

The entire space was brooding and temperamental. I would've preferred clean lines. White—which was the silence of the colour palette—with stone furniture and metal chairs. I liked to be surrounded by an unfeeling atmosphere but I'd never be permitted to change this area.

It was sacred.

All because it'd been the bedroom of all Hawk men who'd inherited a Weaver woman. Their last breath was taken in this mansion. It held the ghosts of Nila's ancestors and would one day absorb hers, too.

The birthday present of new spurs and a heinously wicked whip glinted on the eighteenth century sideboard. At the time, I'd thought it was a piss poor present for turning twenty-nine, but the best present was due next year. The true inheritance I'd been waiting for. One much better than a woman or her tears. When I turned thirty, I would own it all.

Everything. All mine.

The fantastic ruling of Primogeniture meant as firstborn son, I inherited the lot. My brothers wouldn't get penny. My sister not a single diamond. They would survive by my charity. Just like my father.

The brotherhood. The mines. The yachts. The cars. Hawksridge. And every property overseas.

Mine.

Bryan Hawk, Cut to those in the Black Diamond brotherhood, would be second to me. The way of our ancestors ensured young authority remained in control of an estate that'd spilled enough blood to fill a moat around our gates.

My father would retire, and I would be king.

I'd upgrade from living in the bachelor wing with its pool room, theatre, office, weaponry, solarium, six bedrooms, and six bathrooms to having the pick of a fifty room, two ballroom, and a dungeon-equipped house to play in.

And by play, I meant *rule*.

Collecting new clothing from my walk-in wardrobe, I glimpsed myself in the mirror. My lips curled in disgust at the sticky mess on my stomach. I had a good mind to get Nila and make her lick me clean.

That was her fault.

My mind drifted back to her—against my will. She'd not only taken up valuable space in my head, but my day's structure as well. There would be no hunting today or inspecting the latest diamond shipment.

There'd be no business or travel.

All my energy and focus belonged to the woman who was a waste of my time.

Another daydream of forcing her to her knees stopped me on the outskirts of the bathroom. Would she cry or scream as I fucked her from behind? Perhaps she'd surprise me again and moan in ecstasy. I planned on taking her that way—the animalistic way. After all, she did spend the night with the dogs. It would only be fitting.

Dumping my clothes on the vanity, I strode into the four-headed quartz shower. I had no need to strip. I slept naked.

Always did.

It was part of the rules.

Living at Hawksridge, the grandest and most exclusive motorcycle club compound in all of England, came with strict unbreakable rules. Our brotherhood was different. We were smart, cunning, focused.

Any man found sleeping with clothes on was in for a night of pain. We might have left the dark ages behind but my family upheld strictness.

We made our fortune in the most transferable precious item there was. And we'd learned a lot from past mistakes on how to treat those who tried to steal them.

No clothes at night and random cavity searches by day.

All to protect our legacy. The way we made our money. The way we rose from penniless thieves at the beck and call of the Weavers to gathering a wealth that morphed to obscene a few centuries ago.

Stepping into the shower, I turned on the hot spray. Smiling at the mirrored wall, I cupped my cock, washing the residue of my indiscretion.

The next time I come, I'll be inside the woman I inherited.

With my cock in my hand, I nodded at my reflection.

I'm a Hawk but blood doesn't flow in my veins. I'm born of a substance unbeatable by any other—diamonds.

I'm a smuggler.
I'm a dealer.
And I'm about to become…a killer.

NEEDLE&THREAD: *I'm warm and in bed. Surprisingly I slept better than I thought I would. Did you have a good night? Did you lie in your bed and picture me pleasuring you? What did I do to you? Tell me, Kite. I want you to transport me from reality and give me a fantasy stronger than my present humdrum life.*

Kite007: *Forward this morning, aren't we? You're that desperate to talk about my cock? Not that I'd ever say no—but I'm rather impressed. Tell me more...beg.*

Needle&Thread: *Beg? How does one beg for something they need rather than want? Would you prefer me on my knees? Or perhaps on my back ready for whatever you wanted to give me?*

Kite007: *Fuck. What's got into you? Beg. Imagine I'm standing over you with my hard cock in my hand. I'm throttling it—my fist working so fucking hard at the thought of you spread-eagled and fingering yourself. Give me a visual. Now. Then I might reward you.*

Needle&Thread: *I'm exactly as you said. Begging, whimpering, touching myself until my whimpers turn to pants and my begs turn to moans. I'm wet for you. I'm hot for you. Please, Kite. Give me my fantasy. Give me something warm to hold onto.*

Kite007: *What the fuck is this about? How can I come when you sound weird?*

Needle&Thread: *Weird? I'm not. I'm giving you what you want in return for what I need.*

Kite007: *Is that supposed to make sense, 'cause I don't understand bullshit code. Fuck, you're seriously making me do it.*

Needle&Thread: *Do what?*

Kite007: *Ask you! Okay, fine. What's got your panties so bunched that you're coming onto me so strong. What happened to my timid naughty nun? Why the fuck do you sound so different?*

I stared at my phone, heart rate skyrocketing. I'd tried to play it coy and courageous. I thought I'd pulled off the pantomime that I was still myself, still living my content but uninspiring life.

Obviously not.

I re-read my past replies, unable to see the difference. Had I changed that much already?

There was nothing soft about Kite. There was no reason for me to seek him out when I had enough bastard in my life thanks to Jethro. It made no sense to let him use me—but it did in a strange way. It made sense because I *willingly* gave him control over me—something I needed in my rapidly spinning out of control life. While Jethro was determined to undermine, throw away, and rule every inch of whatever little power I had left, Kite gave it back in some strange, wonderful way.

He's the monster I know. He's not sweetness and light—but he's mine because I choose *him to be.* The defiance was yet another stupid score against the beast called Jethro Hawk.

Straightening my back, I tried to figure out a way to possibly get Kite to soften—just a little.

Kite007: *Tell me, then make me come. You've got two jobs to do. Do them.*

Taking a deep breath, I opened a fresh message.

Needle&Thread: *Tell me if this is out of bounds, but in answer to your question—why do I sound different—I suppose it's because I* feel *different. Everything is different. I thought I'd always fight against different. I like normal. I like routine. I thought different would ruin me. But...then...I changed.*

Kite007: *Changed? You really going to make me drag this out? My cock is hard and balls want to come. Spill it, so we can get to the second part of your to-do list.*

Needle&Thread: *I'm the one who's different now. It's as if everything I've been dealing with suddenly doesn't matter. It's just gone....*

Kite007: *Gone?*

Needle&Thread: *Yes. It's liberating, scary as hell, and confusing. But something's changing inside—it feels as if I'm...growing up.*

I sighed. He'd send something horrible back—my response had been too personal. I knew that. But I'd sent it anyway.

Kite007: *Out of bounds. Get back to the subject. Let's try this, here's something you obviously want: I'm happy you're growing up—makes me feel a lot fucking easier knowing I'm not jerking off to a kinky fourteen-year-old. And now for want I want: I'm done with the cryptic crap. Pay attention, because I'm sliding my cock into your mouth. You try to talk but you choke on my length, your voice is humming against my balls. Stop trying to communicate and settle in to your task. Suck me.*

I sighed. Two emotions swirled inside—exasperation and gratefulness. He'd replied to my overshare. He hadn't shot me down or been the pillock he usually was. Progress.

The tentative softness inside was enough to get me through the next few hours.

Shouldn't you want more?

My heart hardened.

Kite had replied to my veiled hints for encouragement but I'd hoped…

It doesn't matter what I hoped.

It seemed everything I wanted in this world wasn't available—including more than one kind word from Kite. We'd been so close to a normal conversation. Learning, sharing, building a connection despite the complications of sexting.

He'd let me in for a microsecond then shut me out once again, using sex as a tool to keep me in my place and remind me I didn't factor in his life. I was the unseen whore. The unpaid prostitute who lived in his phone.

I couldn't let him hurt me. I couldn't let him weaken me.

He'd done what I needed—reminding me I was strong enough. There was nothing else to do but finish the conversation, so I could leave the soul-sucking fantasy and return to the tragedy of my new world.

Kite007: *You're not sucking. Fine, I'll give you some encouragement. If you blow me, I'll return the favour. I'll flip you onto your back, spread your legs, and bury my face between your legs. I'd bite you, fucking you with my tongue until you forgot everything and came.*

My stomach attempted a small swoop. It wasn't romantic, but it did give me a tiny bit more warmth I needed.

Before I could reply, another message vibrated.

Kite007: *Tell me where you are right now. Are you naked? Finger yourself for me. Take a photo if you're brave.*

I laughed. The sound shredded the space that Jethro had so kindly given me for the night. Laughing was the only thing I could do. Take a photo? Of *what?* The bruises on my palms from crawling to the kennels last night? How about the cuts on my knees?

Maybe he wants a picture of my elegant bedroom and wonderful bedfellows.

Looking up for the first time since I woke, I let the uselessness of my situation get the better of me. The bravery I'd been clutching to like a raft in a rolling ocean, splintered and drowned. Painful despair saturated my heart, weighing me down like the anchors I so often clung to.

By all standards, the kennel was sheer luxury. The roof was watertight. The floor clean and sanitary. It was even draft free.

But it wasn't just mine. I had to share.

Squirrel, my favourite of the eleven canines I'd spent the night with, nudged my arm. I'd named him after the tree-climbing rodent thanks to his slightly bushy tail. With a doggy smile, he wheedled his way under my arm, leaning heavily against my torso.

I'd never had pets growing up. As a family, we were too busy working or travelling to exotic places to source more material and merchandise. Until last night, I'd had an adolescent fear of dogs.

That had evolved to terror when Jethro threw me inside.

I shuddered, hugging Squirrel closer to me, stealing his gentle warmth. Last night Jethro had tried to destroy me. Not through fists or rape or even harsh words. No, he tried to destroy me by removing any entitlement I had as a human. Marking me as no better than the dogs he kept.

He would've succeeded if my terror hadn't mellowed into bewilderment then gratefulness. He'd done me a favour—I preferred the company of his hounds. They not only tolerated my intrusion but welcomed me into the pack.

Squirrel licked my pebble-indented palm, letting me know he understood my aches. I still suffered from crawling from the manor, past immaculate flower beds, over precision mowed grass, and cutting through shadows cast by imposing hedges.

Everything throbbed when I finally crawled the last metre and sat waiting beside a large roller door. My dress was torn, my knees bleeding—not that he'd cared.

The estate was bigger than I could contemplate, but even in the darkness, I'd made out the buildings around us. The stables were across the cobblestone yard. A granary let its soft grainy fragrance permeate the air. The gentle huffing of horses broke the silence along with wuffles and snuffles from dogs.

Jethro left me sitting on my knees while he disappeared into what I assumed was a tack room. He returned with a large scratchy blanket and a bucket, before unlocking the roller door and beckoning me inside.

Throwing the items into the dark interior, he bowed. "Your boudoir, my lady." Leaning down, he swatted my behind. "Go to bed like a good little pet. You have a big day ahead of you."

When I didn't move, his foot landed on my arse, shoving me forward, giving me no choice but to crawl quickly into darkness.

The moment I'd traded starlight for no light, I panicked.

Jethro threw the bolt home, locking me inside a room that thrived with moving bodies, claws on cobblestones, and soft growls of ownership.

The first brush of a wet nose on my cheek ripped a small scream from my lips. I curled tight into a ball, hugging my knees, squeezing my eyes against being eaten alive.

I waited for sharp teeth.

But they hadn't eaten me.

Far from it. I'd been licked and nuzzled and welcomed into a pack.

I was a stranger in their domain, but when I finally overrode my fear and looked into their eyes, they were bright with curiosity rather than territorial anger.

The rest of the night was spent making a semi-comfortable bed out of a loosely packed hay bale, and wrapping myself tight in the scratchy blanket. I'd aimed to sleep alone with my new friends scattered in their usual spaces, but they had other ideas.

Once I was settled, they'd crowded around me, squeezing close, curling around each other until I was the epicentre in a nest of canines.

The moment they'd quietened, I took out my phone.

Five missed calls, three messages from my twin, and one from my father.

Biting my lip to retain what composure I could, I'd read my father's first.

ArchTextile: *Nila, I know you'll have questions. I know you'll hate me. But please, my wonderful girl, know I didn't want any of this. I was stupid not to heed your mother's warning. I thought—well, it doesn't matter what I thought. I hope we can talk—when you're ready. I understand if you can never forgive me. I don't know how much of this they'll see, but I'll never stop searching, never stop hoping. Please don't think I gave you up lightly. They have…ways. They have you but they'll keep you in good health. We have time. Love you, sweetheart.*

I didn't want to focus on what time meant. The slow plod of time intertwined with the fast tick, tick, ticking of my final heartbeats.

My fingers hovered on the reply button. But I couldn't. Not yet.

Instead, I opened my brother's messages.

VtheMan: *Threads, pick up your goddamn phone.*

VtheMan: *Threads. I'm warning you. You're not happy. I sense it. I'm worried shitless and Tex is being a secretive arsehole. Call me immediately, sister. Or I'll make your life a living hell.*

VtheMan: *Please, Nila. Talk to me. Put me out of my misery. I miss you. Love you so fucking much.*

My teary gasp in the darkness pricked a few hounds' ears. I'd wanted so much to reply. But I didn't dare. I didn't trust myself not to beg him to get me out of this. I was there of my own free will to *protect* him. I wouldn't be protecting him if I was weak.

I wanted hard facts on why the Hawks' could do this. And I wouldn't stop until I knew everything.

Closing my messages, I opened up a picture of Vaughn and me that'd been taken right before the doors opened to the show last night. The tiny bit of strength I had left deserted me and I let go of my tight control.

I sobbed.

My heart expunged its grief through my eyes, drenching my cheeks, blurring the last photo I had of my brother . I cried until dehydration throbbed my head and my neck was sticky with salt.

A low battery reminder beeped. It was the hardest thing I'd done to shut down the picture of V and turn it off.

More tears trickled and a hound raised his head, looking at me with wise understanding. He inched forward on his belly, crossing the hay until his claws tugged at my blanket.

His canine concern produced another torrent, but I opened my arms, and with a wagging tail, he fitted himself around me like a living shield. His doggy heart thudded against mine as I hugged his silky coat.

I went from the Darling of Milan with needle pricks on her fingers to huddled on the floor with only hunting dogs for company.

A soppy tongue had licked my cheek, stealing the endless stream. And that was when it happened. The change I'd told Kite about. The ending. The beginning. The freedom of just letting go.

All my life, I'd been stressed with making a name for myself, building my career, loving my brother, being a worthy daughter. Bills. Deadlines. Reputations. *Expectations.* It all balanced precariously on my shoulders, moulding me into a quiet workaholic.

But at four a.m., in the kennels of the man who meant to kill me, I let it all go.

I said goodbye to control. I waved farewell to everything that made me live, but had also suffocated me, too. I didn't have photo shoots to worry about anymore. I didn't have concerns on what to wear, where to be, how to act.

All of that had been stolen. And there was no point crying or fighting against it.

The moment I embraced the freedom of nothing, I stopped crying. My headache left, and I drifted to sleep wrapped in the four legs of my new best friend.

Squirrel nudged my hand, bringing me back to the present and the waiting message from Kite. The past struggled to let me go, but I blinked, dispelling my forlornness.

"He wants to know where I am. What should I tell him?" I asked my entourage of hounds.

Foxhounds to be exact. Their black, tan, and white coats became visible as the sun rose, glinting off their glossy fur. Their silky ears slapped their pretty heads as they lopped around the enclosure, waking up as the sun grew brighter.

They didn't give me an answer.

Needle&Thread: *Where I am right now doesn't matter because I'm in a fantasy with you. I'm in your bed. Naked.*

It was much better than the truth. I focused on the huge roller door. I'd checked last night to see if there was a way out, but of course, there wasn't.

Kite007: *You took a while to reply. Did you pleasure yourself?*

Throwing myself back into Kite's sexual world, I replied.

Needle&Thread: *I'm coming now. Both hands are between my legs, feeling how wet I am. I'm crying out your name over and over. The neighbours might hear me I'm so loud.*

"Don't tell him I released my tension by crying myself to sleep with you in my arms." Rubbing the head of Squirrel, I smiled. "And don't tell him I've never had an orgasm."

The dog cocked his head, an expression of confusion on his face.

Kite007: *I like it when you talk dirty. Keep going. I have my cock in my hand and want you to make me come.*

My heart sped up. Reclining against the hay bale, I bit my lip. I'd never made anyone come. The drunken night of losing my virginity didn't count because we were both so intoxicated it was a miracle he found the right place to stick it in. After a few half-hearted thrusts, he'd rolled off me to throw up, and I'd pulled up my knickers. I'd been silently horrified at the blood on the sheets.

The copious amounts of alcohol had stolen any pain I might've felt when he penetrated me. It'd also stolen the rush of entering womanhood, swapping it with age-old regret.

The night definitely hadn't been a success. Or the next day. Because no matter how hard V tried to hide my hangover from Tex, he couldn't prevent me from vomiting on my dad's shoes when he plucked me from my bed and took me to the doctor.

I groaned in remembered embarrassment. "He found out, you know." I scratched Squirrel behind his large ear. "The doctor told him I'd been taken advantage of. We'd used protection but it didn't stop the endless STI tests or pregnancy exams." Another hound slinked closer, plopping next to me, looking for a scratch. "That was the last time I was alone with a man other than my dad or brother. Sad isn't it?"

The dog panted, looking as if I'd told the world's best joke.

Maybe Tex prevented you from dating, so when they came for you it was only his *heart you broke—not a husband or children.*

The sudden thought stole my vision with horror.

Was the overprotectiveness to shield *others*? Had he kept me locked up like some princess in a tower, all to stop me being my mother?

He'd fallen in love with my mother.

They'd had children young.

They'd come for her.

I rubbed my chest, unable to stop the epiphany shedding my father in a new light. Was it selfish of him to protect me from living, knowing I was destined an early grave? Or merely a tragedy that he prevented others enduring heartbreak by loving me.

Vaughn.

He would sense the moment my life was snuffed out. We were linked more than spiritually—but soul-glued and breath-bound. I'd known when he broke his collarbone from kayaking. He'd known when I'd dropped my heavy Singer sewing machine onto my foot.

Linked.

Don't think about it. It hurt too damn much. Tears pricked my eyes but I blinked them back, trying to remain in my false bubble of sexting. This was all I had. I could flirt with Kite with complete safety, knowing I would never be able to break his heart when the time came.

In a way, his fastidious request for distance protected him. And for that, I was oddly grateful.

I smiled softly at Squirrel. "If a drunken whoopsy daisy was my only attempt at making a man come, how the hell am I supposed to do it via a faceless message?"

Be someone you're not. Pretend.

"Fine."

Swiping at the dirty mixture of hay, dog hair, and dust from the blanket Jethro had given me, I prepared to embrace my inner sex-kitten.

Needle&Thread: *Imagine your hand is my hand. I'm holding you firm, tight. I'm kneeling at your feet while you sit on a large chair. A throne. Your hand wraps in my hair, pulling me forward. I obey because I know what you're asking me to do. Your eyes don't ask, they tell, and I lower my head into your lap. You're big. Smooth. Begging for my mouth.*

My breath came faster; my mind playing out the fantasy in crystal detail. The warmth I'd been looking for spread from my core like a tentative sunrise.

Kite007: *Fuck me, woman. Why haven't you been talking to me like that all along? What was with the shy bullshit? Keep going. I'm so damn hard. I want your mouth so fucking much.*

My skin broke out in goosebumps. The power. The *approval.* Kite was a wanker, an arsehole, and a complete shallow prick, but he approved of me. He *wanted* me.

Needle&Thread: *You're holding your cock while I lick you once at the very tip. You want me to swallow you, but you don't force me. Because you know I'm going to swallow every drop.*

Kite007: *Did you taste it?*

I frowned.

Needle&Thread: *Taste what?*

Kite007: *My precum. Fuck, I'm so close. I'm in your mouth. I'm fucking your lips. I'm holding your hair as I drive so deep down your throat. What do I taste like to you?*

Needle&Thread: *You taste...*

"Hell, I don't know." Looking at the cluster of dogs, all watching me as if they knew what I was up to, I swiped a hand over my face. "What the hell does a man taste like?"

Needle&Thread: *You taste of expensive liquor, making me drunk as you come. Spilling over my lips, dripping down my chin. You don't want me wasting a drop, so you capture the liquid on your thumb and push it back into my mouth.*

The instant I sent it, a chill darted in my blood.

Thumb. Mouths. Sucking.

Him.

My taste buds brought back the crisp taste of Jethro. His unyielding hold on my chin as I licked his finger. He hadn't really had a taste. Just the cold precision of stone. But having him dominate had given me the permission to feel a flutter in my core, to not be embarrassed of wanting more. Of becoming wet.

Kite007: *Fuck me. I haven't come like that in a while. It's all over me— splashed up my chest, sticking to me like glue. I like you like this, naughty nun. You're more...relaxed.*

My voice was soft. "That's what happens when your life is no longer your own and there's nothing you can do to control your future."

Squirrel yipped in agreement.

"That's also what you do to survive. You become different. You change."

As much as I hated the Hawks, they'd given me something I'd been searching for all my life.

My little kitten claws were growing, prickling. Still too new to scratch with—but there.

My battery flashed again and I knew this would be the last time I'd have the luxury of using it until Jethro let me charge.

Ignoring the emptiness inside and the sharp twinge of letting Kite use me, I sent my last message.

Needle&Thread: *I'm glad. I'm licking you clean. I'm drunk on everything you've given me. I'll be here for you when you next need a release, but please...don't call me naughty nun anymore. Call me Needle.*

114

Jethro came for me at eleven a.m.

The horses across the yard were gone—to do what, I had no clue. I'd spent an hour or so listening to the grooms prepare them and the comforting *clack* of their metal shoes disappearing into the distance on cobblestones.

I pictured myself commandeering one and galloping away. Not that I knew how to ride. I'd never had time. Sewing had been my one obsession.

Squirrel and his gang of hounds had left not long after I finished messaging Kite. A piercing whistle summoned and they'd charged from the kennel through a small dog-size exit down the back. I'd tried to follow—to get free—but it only opened if a coded collar was in range. A password programmed to every dog allowing them access.

So, I'd spent the remainder of my morning alone. Alone with thoughts I flatly ignored.

It was odd to sit and do nothing. I had nowhere to rush off to. No emails to reply to. No to-do list to attack. I was in limbo, just waiting for the man I loathed to appear.

My stomach was a ball of knots wanting him to get it over with, whilst my jangled heart wanted him to stay away forever. I'd never felt so jumbled inside.

Hunger pangs growled for food—the empty ache only grew worse.

Jethro swung open the top partition of the barn door, leaving the bottom closed. Resting his arms on the top, he nodded. "Ms. Weaver."

The sun took the liberty of bouncing into the gloomy kennel, silhouetting Jethro. His face remained in shadow but his thick hair was wet and messy from a shower.

He'd shed his charcoal suit for a more casual grey shirt, the diamond pin twinkling in his lapel. I'd grown to recognize it as his signature piece, linking him to whatever organisation his father ran.

Is it a gang? Did they rob and cheat and kill?

It wasn't my issue. I didn't care. I was the innocent party—their hostage.

I didn't return his greeting, deciding to stay bundled in my blanket and glower.

Jethro sniffed impatiently, removing his arms from the door. He unlocked the bottom partition, swinging it wide.

More sunshine entered, illuminating the bottom half of his wardrobe. Dark jeans. Well-fitted jeans. Jeans that made him seem young and approachable and *normal*.

My hands balled. *Don't buy into the projection.* There was nothing normal about this man. Nothing sane or kind. I learned that last night—many times over. There would be no more begging from me. No more pleading. It fell on deaf ears, and I was done.

Jethro snapped his fingers as if expecting me to heel. "Get up. It's time to begin." Taking a threatening step into the kennel, he pursed his lips. "Shit, what did you do in your sleep? Roll around like the dogs?"

I kept my lips pressed together, watching him in the silence he so seemed to enjoy. When I didn't move, his face twisted, taking in my hay-riddled hair and dirt-covered blanket. "I won't tell you again. Get. Up."

I shrugged. It was liberating to no longer care. To no longer be captive by the need to obey and jump to attention for fear of retribution. I meant what I said to Kite. Everything inside me was gone. Locked down, bunkered inside, ready to weather whatever war was coming.

Standing slowly, I placed my dead phone into my jacket pocket. Letting the blanket fall off my hips, I brushed lingering lint off my clothes.

Jethro snapped his fingers again, and I moved willingly—coasting to his side exactly as he wanted.

He scowled, his gaze full of suspicion.

I gave him an empty smile. I'd found salvation in not caring. It didn't mean I had to pretend to like him. He wouldn't know that by trying to break me last night, he only gave me a new avenue of strength.

I'm ready.

For whatever he threw at me.

I'll survive.

Until I no longer needed to try.

Running my hands through my hair, I quickly gave up with the tangles and focused on pinching some colour into my cheeks instead.

"You think that will save you? Looking presentable?" His voice was blizzard and snow.

I didn't say a word.

Jethro gritted his jaw. His hands curled beside his spread legs.

My muscles braced for punishment. The air shimmered with violence.

Jethro's hand suddenly shot out, capturing my throat. Without a sound, he spun me around and marched me backward out of the kennel. The sun kissed my skin, fanning the warmth I'd tried so hard to keep hold of from talking to Kite. I embraced it, hugging it close, so Jethro's ice didn't slice me into pieces.

His fingers tightened around my neck, but I refused to claw at his hold. *I repay in kind.* Whatever I did to him in self-defence, I'd get back ten times worse. But none of that mattered now, because I knew how to survive.

By being above them. By being untouchable on the inside, even while they broke me on the outside.

"You think you've got it all figured out, don't you?" His arm hoisted me onto the tips of my toes. Breathing was difficult, not fighting was impossible, but I permitted it. All I did was stare silently into his golden eyes.

"I understand what you're doing." He smiled. "But mark my words. You won't win." Shaking me, he unwound his fingers, then smoothed the front of his jeans. The sun gleamed on the gold buckle of his belt.

My stomach clenched, but I held my ground. "Mark *my* words. I will win. Because I am right and you are wrong."

Jethro seethed, silence thick between us.

"You're so high and mighty, aren't you, Ms. Weaver? So sure you're the one in the right. What if I told you, your ancestors were scum? What if I showed you proof of their corruptibility and eagerness to hurt others in their chase for wealth?"

Lies. All lies.

My family tree was impeccable. I came from honest and good and hardworking stock. Didn't I?

I ignored my rushing heartbeat.

Jethro stepped closer, crowding me. "The things your family did to mine sicken me. So continue on your quest believing you're pure, because in a few hours you'll know the truth. In a few hours, you'll realise we aren't the bad guys—it's you."

My throat closed up. I didn't think he could say anything to crumble my fortress so soon, but every word was a carefully planted spade, digging at my foundation until I stood on crumbling ground.

My eyes danced over his, trying to decipher the truth.

Were my bloodlines tarnished with crimes I didn't know about? My father hadn't exactly been forthcoming with our history, apart from telling us our family had always been involved in weaving and textiles. It was how we were granted the last name Weaver. Just like the Bakers, and the Butlers, and every other trade that dictated their last names.

Jethro chuckled. "Don't believe me?" His hands landed on my shoulders, pushing me backward. I stumbled, wincing as my spine collided with the bricked wall of the kennel.

"Don't believe your forefathers were sentenced to death by hanging for what they did to mine?" His gaze latched onto my mouth. "Don't believe you're alive because the Hawks granted them mercy in return for a few signatures on a few debts?"

His voice dropped, sending a constellation of warning over my skin. "Don't believe I'm fully within my right to do whatever I damn well please to you?"

His touch seared through my jacket and maxi dress, sending unwanted intensity down my arms.

Do I believe it? Could I believe it? That everything I understood of this situation was reversed?

Mind games. Illusions. All designed to trip me up.

Shaking my head, I snapped, "No. I don't believe it." My blood pressure exploded, thundering in my ears. His focus was absolute, and it burned, oh how it burned. "Nothing you say will make you the victim in this situation. Nothing you show me will make this permissible. You think I believe a ludicrous debt that you say is over six hundred years old. Wake up! Nothing like that would hold up in a court of law these days. I don't care that you've staged my disappearance, or following my family with a loaded pistol. I don't believe any of this, and I certainly don't believe you have anything law abiding on your side."

Jethro scowled, but I continued my tyrant.

"All I believe is you're a bunch of sick and twisted men who made up some bullshit excuse to make themselves feel justified while tearing other's lives apart. Show me where you have the right to own me. No one has that right. No one!"

He chuckled, gold eyes growing dark. His body language switched from stand-offish to oozing with sexual innuendo. It was like watching a glacier melt, shedding winter for volcanic heat.

"I like it when you're feisty. Your whole perception of the world is warped. You live in a fairytale, princess, and I'm about to destroy it."

His shoulders softened, lips parting; his gaze caressed my face to land on my mouth. "You think we don't have men in high places? Men who make what we say absolute law? You think we got to the level of standing in society or the obscene amount of wealth we have by not using the very same law you think will protect you for our gain?"

His voice whispered over me, threading with his heady scent of woods and leather. "So stupid, Ms. Weaver. We own more than your family. We own everything and everyone. Our word is unbreakable. And we have proof."

He leaned in; the violence he emitted switched to dangerous lust, buffeting me harder against the wall. His eyes were rivers of fire, annihilating my argument, dragging me under his spell. "You think I can't make you do what I want?"

I sucked in a breath.

He'd never looked at me like that. Never given any hint he might find anything about me exciting. He treated me like a leper. He looked at me as if I were a different species—a species not evolved enough to warrant his sexual attention.

But that'd changed.

His interest trapped me, consuming me better than threats and tightly restrained anger. This was unexplored territory. Lust and attraction and flirting were terrifying, because I was the novice and he was the expert.

I couldn't fight against something that made me *feel*.

Jethro's nostrils flared, fingers twitching on my shoulders. His voice lowered to a husky whisper—a whisper best suited for seduction. "You think you deserve a life built on other's blood? You think you're worthy?" The rhythm and volume turned the horrible questions into a poem rather than curse.

Don't fall for it. Don't let him win.

He was already winning. He spun a tale of a lethal, unstoppable force. His family's legacy somehow granted him police approval, government blind-eyes, and the right over life and death.

Who *gave* him that right?

I still couldn't believe it. But it didn't stop my legs shifting, pressing together, trying to alleviate the strange ache building with every moment.

Our fighting coaxed my unseen claws to grow a little more. My temper made my legs firmer; my vision clearer. My body unknowingly found a cure from dreaded vertigo, all while embracing anger and rage.

Jethro noticed my tension, stroking my shoulders as if I were a skittish prey. "We're simple creatures, Ms. Weaver. I know what's happening to you." He smiled gently, his gold eyes attempting to look soft, but unable to hide the steel beneath. "Your skin is hot. You're breathing faster."

He ducked his head, murmuring, "You like this. You like being pushed past your limits."

I shook my head. "You're wrong. There's nothing about you that I like."

He sighed, his gaze whispering over my mouth. "Lying won't work. I know you're growing wet for me, wanting me." His touch morphed from menacing to lightning, sending a rain of sparks through my blood. "Want to know how I know? Because I taste it in the air. I smell it all around you. I *feel* it."

My lips parted. My chest rose and fell, increasing faster and faster. I couldn't look away; I couldn't push him away. I couldn't do anything but revel in the intoxicating, melting, glowing, sparking need building rapidly in my core.

Closing my eyes, I swallowed hard, trying so hard to dispel the sick and twisted desire he conjured. "I'm—I'm not."

He ran his thumbs over my shoulders, following my collarbone with infinite softness. "You're not?" he breathed. "You're not feeling the rush of lust or the knowledge you'd throw all your rules away for just…one…little…taste?" His lips came so close to mine, pulling away in the ultimate tease.

Yes. No. I don't know.

I'd lost control of my body, hurtling straight for a cataclysm where everything was hot and sharp and intense.

I didn't have an answer. I didn't know what he wanted.

He's fucking with your mind. That's all he's doing.

His thumbs stroked higher, smoothing away the bruises he'd caused on my neck. "Tell me you're not wet for me. Say it."

I shook my head, willing the words to come. "I'm not. I'm…"

"What?" Jethro murmured.

The ache grew stronger, sending a rush of dampness against my knickers. My body didn't care this was a monster. My body didn't care about the future. All it cared about was curbing the intolerable need.

Opening my heavy eyes, I said, "I'm not wet. Not for you."

My hands balled, fighting against the thick intoxication. I couldn't let him steal the warmth from Kite. He'd already turned the small flame into an out of control inferno, cindering my morals, turning my hatred to ash. I couldn't fall into his web—he'd eat me alive.

But, one kiss…would it be so wrong?

To take something from him when he'd already taken so much from me?

I swayed closer, unconsciously seeking everything he dangled before me. I wasn't equipped to play these games. I was naïve and woefully unprepared for combat where lust was used as the weapon.

"You're a little liar, Ms. Weaver." He dropped one hand from my shoulders, tracing my contours until he captured my hip, the other skated upward, cupping my cheek. Every millimetre he travelled sent sparks along my skin unlike anything I'd ever felt before.

His tongue appeared, licking his lips. "You want this." His knee nudged against mine, forcing my legs to spread. "You want something you know you shouldn't." With seamless authority, he pressed against me, tilting his hips into mine.

I shivered. Hating him. Lusting for him. Hating myself. Loving the forbidden rush.

The reasons for our fight flew away on soundless wings, leaving me with no argument against the swelling swollen ache.

"All that separates my cock from your pussy is a few fragile pieces of clothing." He drove upward, grinding himself punishingly. "You won't stop me." There was no space, no secrets—our bodies glued together.

My mind went blank with sheer-numbing pleasure. I felt every ridge and contour of him. From the pressure of his shoe against mine to the hot heat in his jeans growing larger every second.

You know what he intends to do. Stop this, I screamed at my betraying body. But it replied in force with a clenching ripple, turning my legs to jelly.

I held my breath. His hard body was as unmovable as the wall I stood trapped against. His ripped stomach pressed against mine.

I wasn't cushy or curvy. I had no feminine attributes—I'd exercised away any hope at softness.

But it only amplified the intensity.

There was nothing to cushion the firmness of bones and sinew and craving flesh. It was visceral. All consuming.

"Tell me again you're not wet for me." His hooded eyes imprisoned mine. "Tell me another lie."

I tried to look away, but he thrust again, enticing another ripple of pleasure. I hadn't planned on being the innocent girl. The stuck-up princess who never self-pleasured or enjoyed men. I hated that I came across priggish, uptight, and repressed. Those traits were a hazard of my upbringing, and I desperately wanted to turn them into weapons.

I wanted to use them as effortlessly as Jethro wielded his wintery charisma.

My body knew what it wanted. It wanted a release. It wanted to satiate and be sated. And it didn't give a flying arse who granted the freedom of the mysterious orgasm. I knew who Jethro was—I knew this was all a game to him. But why couldn't two people play? Why did I have to justify his touch as bad when it was so amazingly *good?*

Death was coming. Shouldn't I try to *live* before I died?

For once in my life.

Be true and honest and raw.

Why can't I use him? Just once be the bad girl and use the monster. Win by not fighting. Be stronger by giving in.

My pussy grew bolder, taking my unvoiced permission and growing wet, greedy, eager to experience the cock pressed firmly against me.

I…can't.

You can.

I…won't.

You will.

Jethro ducked, nipping my jaw with sharp teeth.

I unlocked my chastity belt, and melted into him. I arched my back, deliberately pressing my breasts against his chest.

His seduction lost the calculating edge, his breath went from calm to uneven.

Something new broke free inside. Some level of embarrassment of sex—the unapproved thoughts of being used—disappeared. I was a business woman. A daughter. A sister. The fantasies inside weren't the thoughts of a puritan.

Deep inside, where I never let myself go, a sexual deviant lurked.

A woman who was bold and angry. A woman beyond ready to admit she'd hidden so much of herself—even from herself.

Jethro's hand moved to grab the back of my neck. His hips pulsed; his heart thudded hard, vibrating our tightly pressed forms.

I shivered in his hold, giving in completely to the clench between my legs.

"Answer me. Tell me the truth." His mint-fresh breath fluttered my eyelashes as he hovered possessively over my lips. Only a tiny space between a tease and a kiss. Only a fraction between right and wrong.

Do it. Accept it.

He paused, murmuring into my mouth, "Tell me a secret. A dirty, dark secret. Admit you want me. Admit you want your mortal enemy."

I admit it.

"I won't." My heartbeat switched from thumping to humming; my skin prickled with heat.

I hated him. I wanted to kill him before he killed me. But I couldn't ignore the overwhelming attraction he'd created. And it wasn't just me affected. His breathing turned ragged; his fingers dug deeper with need. Every pulse of his hips drew a quickening in my core. I couldn't control it. I didn't *want* to control it. I was done controlling my life.

I'm free.

The longer we stood, the further we blurred the lines between debtor and debtee. Weaver and Hawk. In that tiny moment, we were each other's answer to freedom. A mind-blistering coupling that would surely ruin me for life. But at least I would've *lived*.

I looked deep into Jethro's burning eyes, transmitting everything I suffered. *I hate you for making me acknowledge this part of myself.*

His face tightened; his body slammed harder against mine. Whispering his lips over my cheek, bringing them low, lower, lower, the tip of his tongue tasted the corner of my mouth.

My world disintegrated with an ecliptic *bang*.

I trembled, eyes snapping closed on their own accord.

His hand on my hip shot downward, disappearing between our bodies.

I gasped, jolting in his hold as his fingers scrunched up my dress, shoving it out of the way as if it were nothing. My gasp turned to a ragged moan as he cupped me bold and strong. My gaze flew wide, locking onto his.

Never had something felt so good. So bad. So intensely delicious.

His gold eyes turned to a burnt sunset, filling with fire as he fingered my knickers. "Do you think you're so perfect you wouldn't scream my name? Do you think you'd be able to say no if I dragged you into the kennel and fucked you?" His fingers bit into my pussy, hot and punishing. "Because I want to. Fuck, how I want to. I want your screams. I want you begging."

I lost myself completely, throwing myself into this new creation. The one who had the power to do this and still retain her heart. The one who would give Jethro her body because *she* wanted it. Not him.

His fingers scattered my thoughts, probing against the thin satin of my underwear. His touch was electrifying. I wanted more. I wanted everything.

I stepped off the cliff. "No. I'm not so perfect. And yes, I would scream." Clawing at his shoulders, I forced myself deeper onto his hand. "You think I'm immune? You think I'm dry and repulsed by you?" Dragging him closer, I murmured, "You couldn't be more wrong."

Jethro's nostrils flared. His fingers twitched as he narrowed his eyes. "You think you can confuse me?"

I pressed a finger against his mouth. "Shut up."

His eyes popped wide; he growled low in his chest. His lips pulled back, revealing sharp teeth.

I didn't remove my finger. *I* was in charge. *I* was the one taking. "My heart hates you, but my body….I'm drenched. I'm begging. So stop your endless questions. Stop taunting me and deliver."

Kite flew into my mind, then was gone. I'd surpassed awkward sexting, embracing physical coyness.

The world paused for a millisecond.

Jethro sucked in a shocked breath. Then his hand left my pussy, tore the small stitches holding my knickers in place, and drove one finger so damn deep inside me, I did what I said I would.

I screamed.

My head fell back, smashing against the wall. My heart exploded into a mess of passion and rage.

Oh, God. Oh, *God.*

My mouth sucked in air, but it didn't stop the swirling, blinding need stealing my remaining sanity, giving me completely and utterly to Jethro. I cried inside. I wailed inside. I wished I could be different.

Someone not so deprived of her animalistic needs. Someone who could scream and call for help. Not someone who tilted their hips and moaned at the curses spilling from Jethro's lips. Not someone who gripped the man who tore her from her world and opened her legs wider.

But then Jethro touched a spot that made my muscles lock and a need so violent to seize. I grabbed his wrist, forcing him to take me harder. My tears turned to joy, writhing on Jethro's hand.

"Fuck. Me." His voice was sex-gruffed and so low it echoed over cobblestones. "Who the hell are you?" His finger worked me, pulsating deep inside.

I opened my legs as wide as I could. I gave up on everything, embracing the simplicity of being a sexually starved creature.

This wasn't making love. This wasn't even fucking. This was war. And hell it felt good.

Digging my fingernails into his shoulders, I jerked him closer. "Harder."

Jethro groaned, and in a twist of fate—obeyed. His finger drove so deep his knuckles nudged against my swollen flesh. His thumb swirled around my clit, smearing wetness, taking me to ever new heights.

I turned to stone before detonating into tiny pieces. Every inch of my thoughts, emotions, and reactions were stolen by his mind-blowing touch. I hadn't felt anything like it.

Guilt tried to claim me, reminding me this was the man who ruined my life. But lust quickly devoured the guilt, turning it to raging passion.

"You're so fucking tight," he growled, thrusting his finger harder.

I felt as if I'd not been living. As if my world was dark and Jethro was the sun bringing me nutrition I never knew I needed.

A painful pressure burned as he tried to fit two fingers inside me. I flinched, rocking my hips away. "Stop—"

He paused, then removed the second digit, driving a single finger deep, dragging me back to willing. "You're a virgin. The rumours were true."

I shook my head. "No."

"No?" He grabbed my chin, holding me firm, driving his finger harder. I cried out, letting my head loll on my useless neck with bliss. "How are you this tight and not a virgin?"

"Once. I only—" I stopped, consumed with every pulse of Jethro's finger. "I'm—"

I gave up.

I was completely illiterate.

"If you're not a virgin, prove it." His fingers tightened around my chin. "Pull out my cock."

My mind blanked out. I hung onto the precipice of my good girl ways before throwing myself head first into a woman who would do anything to feel alive.

"Pull out my cock, Ms. Weaver." He thrust against me, battering me with the hardness in his jeans.

My eyes flared wide. My stomach hollowed out at the same time it swooped upright as he thrust his finger.

"Goddammit," he growled. "Do it. I'm not going to come in my jeans like an idiot."

Would he fuck me? If I took out his cock, would he take me? Sex? With him?

I…

I couldn't have sex with him. This cold-hearted monster. But my raging heart and bubbling blood said *yes*. God, yes.

Shutting off my thoughts, I dropped my hands from his shoulders and fumbled with the buckle of his belt.

The hardness of his erection burned my fingertips. Jethro didn't help my concentration, driving his touch deeper. "Hurry up. I need your sweet fingers jerking me off. Goddammit, I don't know—" His voice cut off as I undid his button and zipper.

I gasped as his cock sprang out, escaping the top of his grey boxer-briefs. He shuddered, groaning in relief. The tip glistened with wetness, slightly red, slightly swollen.

My eyes grew wide, fear chasing away the lust in my veins. I looked up, swallowing hard. "You're…I can't—"

He scowled. "Too late to back out now, woman." Grabbing my hand, he placed it roughly around his thick, hard *massive* cock. I had no experience to go on, but he would *never* fit inside me. He wouldn't fit inside any woman.

"Shut up and stroke me."

I opened my mouth, unable to form words. "It can't—there's no way—"

In a lightning fast move, he jerked his finger from my core, smearing my dampness on my cheek as he pinched me hard. "You're out of excuses, Ms. Weaver. You were the one who started this. You're the one who rode my finger as if you'd never come before." His voice dropped to a dark whisper. "So shut up, wrap those little fingers around my cock and stroke me; otherwise, I swear to God I'll throw you on your hands and knees and fuck your tight little cunt right here."

My heart lurched. There wouldn't be anything erotic about that. It would hurt. He would split me in two.

Biting my lip, I cupped the exposed head, spreading the sticky residue at the top down his hot shaft. Locking eyes with Jethro, I pushed my hand into his boxers, following his long, long length.

His eyes snapped closed as my timid fingers latched round him. "Fuuuuck," he groaned. His forehead smashed against mine, hips pulsating into my hand. "Stop taunting me. Harder, goddammit."

That was asking for the impossible. I couldn't get my fingers to connect around his girth. My grip was useless around the throbbing heat—the only hot part of him. Holding my breath, I wrapped my hold as hard as I could.

Jethro grunted. "Squeeze it. Stop being a fucking tease. Was I teasing you?" His hand suddenly disappeared up my dress again, his middle finger thrusting so hard and quick inside me, he sent a galaxy of stars exploding behind my eyes.

Then he glided upward, smearing the wetness around my clit. My legs tried to scissor closed; all my attention shot between my legs.

I went rigid. Having him touch me was amazing. Having him rub that small bundle of nerves was *incredible*.

"Return the favour, Ms. Weaver. Make me come. Right here. Right now. And I'll drive you so wild, you'll beg and never want anyone else."

Coming. The blissful end of sex. Was that what the sharp sensation was? Growing tighter and tighter in my core? If it was, I wanted to come.

Badly.

Winding my fingers as tight as possible around his girth, I squeezed until a jagged pain erupted down my palm. I didn't have the strength. I didn't know what to do. Did I just squeeze and let him thrust into my hand? What else was expected?

With a low growl, Jethro stopped stroking my clit. He turned to granite. "*That's* your idea of making me come?"

I swallowed, jerking my hand away. The thrill of being touched and touching faded, rapidly replaced with despair. "I'm—yes…uh."

"For fuck's sake." Rolling his eyes, he removed his hand from between my legs and stepped back. With a grunt, he yanked his trousers back into place, but not before I caught a glimpse of just how huge his cock was. It was flawlessly straight, veiny, silky, so proud and rigid—just like its owner.

It terrified me.

"Fuck, what was I thinking? You're useless. Completely useless." Buckling his belt, he ran his hands through his hair, smearing the lingering wetness from me through his silvering strands. "*Huge* disappointment, Ms. Weaver." His cold glare sent a snowstorm wiping away the bonfire in my belly. "I'm done playing games, so cut the bullshit. Time to begin the day." His voice gave no room for interpretation. A cold draft shot down my back.

My brief reprieve from debts and horrible Hawks was over. I'd been shown something I desperately wanted, but was denied it because I failed to please him.

"You could teach me…show me how…" I couldn't make eye contact with him. Mortification painted my cheeks for both admitting I was clueless and asking a monster to coach me.

Jethro laughed. "You think that will save you from what's coming? Was that your little plan? To make me fuck you in the hopes I might *feel* something for you?" He shook his head. "I'm not teaching you anything—especially how to jerk me off. As you told me once—Google that shit—but it won't do you any good, because next time…I won't need your hand to come."

My breath caught in my throat.

My heart hung heavy and I shivered. The sun crept behind a cloud, leaving us in haunting shadows.

Jethro stood glaring, the outline of his erection visible in his jeans. But there was no hint of the lust he'd suffered, or the passion that blazed between us only seconds before. His unfeeling eyes burned a hole straight into my soul, condemning me for my past treasons and present failures. The longer he stared, the more he undermined my carefully built fortress.

I couldn't stand the intensity any longer. The humiliation of standing there unwanted, slightly used, and entirely frustrated. With shaking hands, I smoothed down my dress and pushed away from the wall. Without a word, I flicked my hair over my shoulder and skirted around him. With confident steps, I left him behind, heading toward the manor.

He'll chase. He'll hunt.

I expected to land on my face from a carefully planned strike. I waited for vertigo to steal my quiet assurance and spiral me to the ground. But nothing happened.

Jethro didn't pounce, and I didn't fall.

I was steady for the first time in my life.

My world continued even though I'd been thrown off my axis and into a brand new realm. A realm where sex beckoned like the Holy Grail and my self-hatred magnified a thousand fold.

My empty stomach threatened to steal the remaining strength in my limbs, but I kept going, ignoring my body's protests, walking like a good little animal to the slaughter.

I didn't think I was about to enjoy my penance of being a Weaver.

Balling my hands, I made a promise. A promise I hoped would grant me strength for the coming days.

They can't touch me. I'm not Nila or Threads. I'm done being weak.

My heart swelled as I crested the hill, staring at Hawksridge Hall in all its glory. I shed my kitten baby-fur and embraced a new pelt. One that filled me with fight. One that embraced the elongating claws I'd begun to grow.

I was no longer protected by tigers but forced to become one.

I'm Needle, and I will survive.

CONTROL.

I loved it.

I wielded it.

I *owned* it.

But that little Weaver broke my control, turning me into nothing more than a sex-driven idiot. She'd made me throw my decorum, calmness, and carefully laid plans out the goddamn window.

Her timid fingers. Her fluttering breaths. They'd been more of a turn on than the most experienced of lovers. She was so fucking pure she choked on a halo.

And to ask me to *teach* her? Granting me power by evolving this virginal creature into anything I damn well wanted?

It was temptation.

It was not fucking permitted.

She was mine to take from. Mine to share.

I refused to train her, because in the end *I* would be the one delivering the killing blow. She wouldn't succeed in dragging me into whatever game she played.

I breathed hard, even now struggling to find my beloved coldness. I needed an icy shower. *I need to teach her a fucking lesson—that's what I need.*

A knock snapped my head up. I spun in place, trading the view of the front gardens to glare at my father. The man who'd taught me how to be the master of my emotions. How to rein in the uncouth part of ourselves and be ruthless with silence. He'd taught me the most—

beaten me the most—and I was his favourite.

Thank God there were no cameras by the stables—if he saw how far I fell, his disappointment would bring repercussions. Big repercussions.

My father popped his head into the 'Buzzard Room' named for the hand-stencilled wallpaper of hunting buzzards and the mounted carcasses of ducks, swans, and small birds.

It was also the room I'd picked for Nila. This would be her quarters—a room stinking of death and decay.

She'd somehow won the lesson I wanted to teach her at the kennels. She'd managed to make me trade control for the promise of sex. It had worked.

It. Would. Not. Work. Again.

I pitied her really. She'd shown me so much in that brief moment. She was hungry. She was hidden. And she was so damn vulnerable it made me smile to think of her illusions. She thought she could outsmart us.

Us?

Diamond merchants, biker royalty, and proven masters of the Weaver's fate.

Stupid, *stupid* girl.

I nodded at my father. "Cut."

His grey goatee bristled. "Bring her into the dining room when she's ready. Everyone's gathered." He puffed on a giant cigar, wearing a tweed waistcoat and trousers complete with a leather jacket from the Black Diamonds. He looked an enigma of motorcycle world and English aristocracy.

I nodded again.

He left without a goodbye, and I moved to sit on the seventeenth century hand-carved brooding chair. A chair made for men and only men. Complete with ashtray, newspaper stand, and heavy, dark brocade designed with our family crest.

Ten minutes later, the door to the ensuite bathroom opened, revealing a freshly showered Nila. Her long black hair draped like ink on her naked shoulders. She looked younger, innocent without the heavy makeup smeared from last night. Her eyes were bigger, like black unhappy pools whilst her skin glowed a natural dusky tan.

I'd seen her in magazines. I'd run a fingertip over her snapshot in the fashion columns, but never found her attractive. She didn't have breasts. She always stood like a fading shadow next to her brother and looked too prim and stuck up.

She was nothing to me.

Then why did I almost come while fingering her?

My mouth watered, remembering the wildness lurking beneath that up-tight-virgin bluff.

I swallowed, battling the blood rushing to my dick. The way she rode my hand—fuck.

Then I laughed. Out loud.

Waving at her tiny hands clutching the towel, I said, "I see your fingers are capable of holding something." My head cocked. "Do I need to remind you what a disappointment earlier was?"

She was nothing to me before, and she would remain nothing to me. And after this afternoon, there would be no way in hell she'd ever let me touch her again.

Which was perfect, because the next time wouldn't be for pleasure. It would be for pain. And permission would take the control away.

She froze, locking her knees. The heavy cloud when she suffered a stupid balance attack swirled in her eyes. Sucking in a breath, she said quietly, "No, you don't. You've told me countless of times. You've made me very aware of what you think of me, and I'm sick of hearing it."

I took my time glancing down her body.

She didn't fidget or blush, which pissed me off. I wanted her nervous. I wanted her terrified of what was to come.

I stood up slowly, clicking my tongue. "Ah, ah, ah, Ms. Weaver. Don't take that tone with me. You're the failure. *You're* the prisoner. You take what I give you. You do not assume to have any say or authority. That includes listening to everything I deem important to tell you." Ghosting to a stop in front of her, I murmured, "Is that quite understood?"

I flexed my muscles, welcoming back the soothing chillness of control. I hadn't liked stepping outside my confines of civility. Things got messy when silence was disrupted. Things got rushed when tempers rose and curses flowed.

And I couldn't handle that.

Running a fingertip along her damp shoulder, I smiled at her flinch. "Did you do as I asked and wash your filth away?"

Her lips pursed, anger glowing in her eyes. But she swallowed it down, muting the light. "Yes."

"Did you leave your pussy alone? No trying to finish what I started?"

Her head hung a little lower. "Yes."

My finger followed the contour of her shoulder, tracing down her arm. She stood silently, hiding the wild creature from before, depicting quiet sexuality and vulnerability. My mouth watered again, but it wasn't with need to shove her against the wall and drive my dick inside her. No, it was because I'd never made someone with her skin colour bleed. Would her blood be darker? Would it be a rich chocolate like her eyes?

I knew her family tree. I'd studied it in preparation. Her bloodlines weren't pure—there was mixed race in her past. A blend of Spanish and English. Another reason why Hawks were better. We were one hundred percent English stock. Unsullied.

Nila looked into my eyes. Her skin broke out in goosebumps. "Stop whatever you're doing and let me get dressed. Where are my clothes?" She clutched the silver towel harder, hiding everything but her longer than average legs and tiny feet. "I need to charge my phone. I want my suitcase."

I didn't bother caring who'd she'd texted last night to drain her battery. There would be no cavalry coming to her rescue—of that I was completely sure. "You'll receive your belongings if you please us."

"Us?"

Stepping back, I smoothed my shirt, taking my time in delivering the truth. I hoped she'd move away—run even. But she locked her knees again, standing firm on the thick mahogany carpet.

"Yes. Us." Holding out my palm, I waited. "Take my hand."

She hesitated, hoisting her towel higher, her tiny fist jammed against her small breasts.

I looked forward to making her obey, but then the aloofness I'd briefly witnessed in the kennels came over her features—blotting out the fire, turning her into an obedient robot.

Slowly she did as I requested, placing her slightly damp hand in mine.

The moment I had her, I marched across the bedroom floor. She gasped, jerked into motion, her legs darting to keep up. Silently, I wrenched open the door and stalked down the huge corridor, past shields and lances and crossbows, to the end of the bachelor wing where the Black Diamond brotherhood met once a week in a club meeting called the Gemstone.

This afternoon, it wasn't business being discussed. It was Nila. This was her welcome luncheon.

A tradition unbroken for hundreds of years. An esteemed event that all our brethren knew.

The day they all sample a Weaver.

Slamming my palm against the double doors, I jerked Nila into the room. She wheeled to a stop, her face losing its colour in favour of snowy white. I searched her features for fear. I hunted for terror, but I only witnessed blank resignation.

Turning away from her, I focused on what she couldn't look away from.

Men.

Some smooth faced and young, others bearded and old. But they all had something in common. They belonged to the Diamonds and were our most trusted employees. Flaw, Fracture, and Cushion weren't present. Their task was to watch Vaughn and Archibald Weaver from doing anything…reckless.

Nila struggled, trying to take her hand back. I clamped my fingers around her, not giving an inch. "Don't be rude, Ms. Weaver. Say hello and be courteous. This is, after all, your welcome lunch."

She jolted, shying backward, testing my hold.

My father sat at the end of the extremely long table. The room was huge. Decorated with gold-spun drapery and massive oil paintings of my ancestors, it glittered with crystal chandeliers and silverware.

The paintings were of male Hawks only. The women of my family tree were designated to another room. Still celebrated, but not nearly as important.

Each artwork showed a man of distinguished wealth and intolerable power. I'd studied them in great length this past month, preparing for Nila's arrival. My favourite was Owen Hawk.

I looked just like him.

Snapping his fingers, my father called the small murmurs of masculine voices to attention. Pointing at Nila trembling beside me, he said, "Brothers, this woman will be our guest for the foreseeable future, and in honour of her company, we have something special planned."

The men grinned, reclining in their chairs, ready for the show to begin. The hiss and crackle of the log fire added a cheery background noise as well as welcome heat to the cavernous room.

"Jet, if you would be so kind as to make sure our guest is appropriately attired."

Pleasure.

Tradition had begun.

Dropping Nila's hand, I moved toward the large side table that held crockery, wine glasses, and decanters. The food that'd been prepared by the full kitchen in the other wing of the house waited on the matching sideboard across the room. There were countless dishes, at least seven courses, but no wait staff to present it.

I smiled.

That was where Ms. Weaver came in. Along with…other duties.

Gathering the items that were meant for Nila, I returned to her side. She hadn't moved, but not from obedience. Two large men in leather cuts blocked her way out. The moment I came back, she looked pleadingly into my eyes.

"I can't—Jethro, don't make me." She swallowed. "Not so many. I can't do—"

Snatching her arm, I spun her to the corner of the room, away from hungry onlookers. "You dare say no? Do you *want* this to be over?"

She nodded rapidly. "Yes. More than anything yes."

"Fine. It's over. But you're sentenced to watch your father and brother be slaughtered, along with the decimation of your family's business and assets. It will be obliterated. Gone. Is that what you're willing to pay?"

She squeezed her eyes in horror.

Didn't think so.

I never wanted to be that weak. That driven by compassion. I obeyed my family. I accepted my position. But I would *never* let love dictate my actions.

That wasn't what a Hawk did.

We were untouchable.

Taking the liberty of her lack of vision, I placed the first item on her head. A sexy, frilly maid's cap. It perched on her head, gracing her damp black hair like a sad crown.

Her head dipped, shielding her eyes. Her body convulsed, trying hard to maintain the blankness she thought would be her salvation.

Tugging her hands, I muttered, "Let go of the towel."

She cowered away.

Growling under my breath, I wrapped an arm around her waist, holding her firm. "Don't make me ask again. You're not new to this game. Let go of the towel."

Her eyes flew wide, fighting my hold. "No!"

Goddammit, she tested me. A headache brewed behind my eyes. I sighed. "Make me ask you one more time. Go on…"

She froze, breathing hard. A battle broke out between us. I should never have let her get away with what she pulled at the stables. She thought I'd softened. She thought I'd be lenient. If anything, she'd proven my errors and I'd go above and beyond to ensure I didn't falter again.

Ever.

She had to learn that the day granted hope and happiness, but I stole it. She had to face that the night hid evil and darkness, but my soul was blacker.

There would be no winning. None.

We didn't speak, but our eyes shouted, wrapping us tight with unsaid tension.

Finally, she lowered her chin in defeat. Her death grip on the fluffy material loosened, allowing it to flutter to the floor.

Ordinarily, I would've rewarded her. A kind word. A gentle gesture. But that was before I learned I couldn't give her any softness. She needed a firm, masterful hand. Otherwise, she'd make my life a living hell until I stole hers.

My eyes latched onto her naked body.

I paused.

Fuck.

Nila Weaver was like the needle she used to make her livelihood. Long, sculptured. Muscle tone so defined, her hips defied her supple skin, almost piercing her. Her breasts were small but high with perfect dark nipples.

My gaze dropped between her legs. The part of her I'd intimately explored already. I expected an inexperienced girl to not maintain her pussy, but there was only a strip of black hair, hiding and teasing at the same time.

My heartbeat thickened.

And then I noticed the bruises.

Everywhere. On her ribcage, hips, thighs, and arms.

I prodded at a particularly large purple one. "Who did this?"

She crossed her knees, clamping a hand over her breasts.

I swallowed hard, hating that my cock twitched.

Her mouth parted, then understanding flared. "Not who. What." Looking down at herself, she whispered, "The perils of vertigo."

I had no reply to that. She already had a condition that hurt her.

I hated that I understand that…more than she knew.

"Put your arm down." I slapped it away from her breasts. She stiffened, but left it by her side, standing taller than before.

Holding out the tiny excuse of an apron, I placed it over her head. It was black with white lacy trim, low enough to show the tops of her breasts and nipples, short enough to show the trimmed delight between her legs.

Spinning her around, I tied the strings at her neck and lower spine. When she faced me again, she choked, "Why?"

"Why?" I raised an eyebrow.

"Is this all a game to you?"

I smiled. "No game. We're deadly serious. As you should know by now." Leaving her, I returned to the table and collected the final item. The Weaver heirloom.

Prowling back to her, I held up the collar.

Her eyes popped wide. She gawked at the solid encrusted diamond collar made from our very own imports. Two hundred carats, valued at over three million pounds—it'd been in my family since the first debt had been claimed.

"Do you know what this is?" I dangled it in front of her face.

She clamped her lips, eyes deathly cold.

I didn't need a reply. She'd know soon enough.

Unlocking the collar, I held the two ends and bent over her. Wrapping it around her throat, I moved from front to back, positioning myself to fasten it. I kept my voice low and soothing, embracing my cold ruthlessness again. "It's affectionately known as the Weaver Wailer." Using the special clasp—an irreversible clasp—I murmured, "It's your gift from us. Jewels from the best of our mines. You should be proud to wear such wealth."

Nila shivered as the lock snapped into place.

My shoulders relaxed. It was on. It was done.

Her option to leave had just disappeared.

"You're ours now. Want to know why?"

She whimpered, shaking her head.

Gathering her thick black hair, I ignored her plea for ignorance. I'd told her ignorance was bliss—which was true. But my job was to torment her. She had to fully embrace her future.

Breathing gently on her neck, I whispered, "Because once the Weaver Wailer is in place...there's only one way to get it back off."

"ENOUGH PLAYING, JETHRO, bring her here."

The command burned my ears, turning my false belief I could survive into dirty soot. The fire I'd nursed inside was gone. All the stupid pretending that I could block the worst from damaging my soul disappeared. My little claws had fully retracted into nothing once again.

I was cold. Cold as *him*.

Shut down. Same as him.

Silent. Same as him.

Only one way to get it off.

I swallowed. My head pounded. My hands flew up to tug at the jewelled collar. It was heavy and lifeless and ice. Pure ice. The perfect clarity and flawless sparkle of the diamonds leached into my skin, claiming me, marking me.

Only one way to get it off.

I thought I'd come to terms with my mortality. I thought I'd face the end with my head held high and dry eyes—but that was before they told me the method of my execution. When I thought of death, I pictured…nothing…I had no image of how the end would come.

Now I did.

Only one way to get it off.

I was to be beheaded.

There'd be no sawing off the collar or picking the lock. The way the clasp snapped so resolutely hinted at a one way mechanism. The heavy noose was now mine…an accessory slowly strangling me by diamonds.

It wasn't breakable. But I was. So fragile really, when a single sharp blade could cast me from life into the nether. Diamonds were nature's hardest fortress—the quintessential marriage of unbreakable ice and power.

A new unwanted respect curdled in my stomach. Jethro said his mines. *Their* mines. Diamonds were pure, but the method of collection had a chequered history of death and violence.

They didn't just play the part of untouchables. They *were* untouchable.

No!

My tugging fingers turned frantic. I arched my neck, searching with an edge of insanity for a weakness in the soldered white gold and gemstones. It had to come off.

It has to.

I didn't have the strength to die. I didn't have the martyrdom to let them do this. Not for family. Not for fortune. Not for anything.

I'm weak. I don't want to die!

Jethro grabbed my wrists, effortlessly pulling my arms away from my throat. My eyes opened and all I saw was malevolent stone. There was no compassion in his light-brown eyes. No sympathy or even guilt. How did he have the power to be so close to me—to grow hard wanting me—and know all along my fate?

Only a special person could do that. A person who wasn't born of this world, but brimstone and fire. From *hell*.

I struggled in his hold. The collar settled heavily, spreading its heinous ice. "I was wrong about you."

Jethro placed my hands by my sides, then let me go. He shrugged, running a palm through his thick salt-and-pepper hair. "I've been nothing but forthright and honest from the beginning. You're the one who spun a lie from the truth. *You're* the one who ignored everything I was telling you."

Turning to face the table, he wrapped a cold arm around my waist. "And now it's time to face the reality of everything you tried to ignore."

Mr. Hawk, with his ridiculous tweed and leather outfit, stubbed out a smouldering cigar. "Did you tell her?"

Jethro stiffened. "I forgot."

His father reclined into the high-backed chair and folded his hands on his stomach. "You were meant to tell her when you put it on.

It's called the Weaver Wailer and it belonged to…"

A loud screeching sound exploded in my ears. My stomach rolled. Vertigo spread its nullifying tentacles through my brain.

It's the necklace. The one she wore when she came back the final time.

Jethro looked down, trying to capture my eyes, but I wouldn't do it. I *couldn't* do it. I kept my vision blank, looking resolutely over his shoulder. "I think you've already guessed who it belonged to." Lowering his voice, he whispered, "The last person to wear this collar was your mother. She wore it for two years and twenty-three days before it was…forcibly removed. It carries not only the diamonds of my bloodline, but also blood from yours. We, of course, clean it thoroughly after every owner, but if you look closely, I'm sure you'll see the tarnish of their lives given in return for their crimes."

"Nila, when you're a big girl, you can wear my clothes, shoes, and jewellery, but you have to grow a little taller before that day." My mother laughed, looking down at me on the floor of her walk-in wardrobe. I'd not only raided her jewellery box and draped myself in gemstones, but wore a feather boa with a baggy one piece swimming suit and giant high heels. I thought I looked incredible. For a seven-year-old.

Holding up the pearls around my neck, I said, "Promise? I can have these when I'm your size?"

She ducked, pulling me into a hug. "You can have everything of mine. Why?"

I smiled. I knew the answer to this. "Because you love me."

She nodded. "Because I love you."

The memory came and went, stealing the firm ground beneath my feet and sending me headfirst into nausea. Spirals, loop de loops, and spin-cycles all churned my brain until I didn't know up from down.

It wasn't vertigo this time, but grief.

Crushing, crashing grief. A grief I hadn't suffered, because all my happy memories of her had been blocked by the wall of hatred. She was supposed to be the bad guy for leaving my father. I'd been safe from hurting. Safe from reliving everything with the knowledge of how precious she was. How tragic her life became and for *two years* after she'd left. Two years we didn't try and save her.

The Hawks had stripped her from me and torn away any armour I had against missing her. She wasn't the bad guy. *They* were. They would all die for this. They would rot for eternity. I would find a way.

Please, let me find a way.

I wore a necklace every firstborn woman in my family wore before they were murdered—I was owed serious revenge. Disgusting, painful revenge.

A sob escaped my mouth. I couldn't fight the spinning anymore and doubled over. With a sickening splash, I threw up all over Jethro's shiny black shoes.

"Shit." He jumped back, not that there was much mess. It'd been almost twenty-four hours since I'd eaten—I had nothing to waste or purge. But the dry heaves wouldn't stop racking my frame.

"For fuck's sake, Jet. Get her under control. We don't have all day." Mr. Hawk's voice shouted across the room.

Cold hands grabbed my shoulders, jerking me from bowed to straight. I moaned as my head sloshed with pain.

"Stop embarrassing me," Jethro snarled.

Embarrassing him? Bastard. Arsehole. Son of Satan. I glowered with tear-swimming eyes into Jethro's cold uncompassionate gaze. Something flicked over his gold irises—a dark shadow. That was the only warning I received before his hand came up and struck me around the side of the head.

I thought I was brave. I thought I was strong. But I'd never been struck before. Daniel's slap in the car last night didn't count. This abuse had come from a black place—a place inside Jethro where unsurmountable anger boiled. And it was endless. He may be a glacier on the outside, but in there…in his heart…he steamed with pressuring rage.

Crashing to my knees, I curled my smarting head into my arms. I came from a family who loved each other so much a disappointed look or stern word was enough to break your heart. Physical abuse wasn't something I knew. It wasn't something I could prepare for.

Jethro grabbed my hair, pulling me upright. I held onto his wrists to prevent the tearing pain. My blurry gaze focused on his grey shirt and perfectly creased jeans.

He glared. "You'll clean that up, but for now you have other things to attend to."

Not letting go of my hair, he carted me toward his father. Every step I took, I tried to hide my exposed breasts and ignore the breeze between my naked legs. The pinafore Jethro had put on me barely covered my stomach let alone valuable places. Places I would give my entire design line to have covered. The stupid maid cap tilted to the side, clinging to my tangled hair.

I couldn't count how many men existed around the table, but their eyes never met mine. Most were glued to my chest or mesmerized lower down as I side-shuffled to hide as much of my decency as possible.

But it wasn't just their eyes sending spider legs scurrying over my flesh. It was the huge immaculate paintings of men wearing white wigs, elegant coat and tails, and hunting regalia glaring down from the dark red walls.

Their eyes weren't lifeless but full of disdain—somehow they knew a Weaver was in their midst and the crackling fireplace was useless to stop my chill.

My sentence was to be carried out with ancestors and family heirlooms as witnesses.

The moment we came to a stop beside Mr. Hawk, sitting in his ornate dining chair, Jethro jerked my neck back. His flawless face filled my vision. "You are no longer free. Look. See your future and understand there's no sweet talking, begging, or bargaining your way out of this. You wear the collar. You're ours completely." Jethro's voice was arctic, glittering with power.

The collar cut into my skin. I wanted to spit in his face.

Shoving me toward Mr. Hawk, the old man snaked an arm around my naked waist, tugging me onto his lap.

"Obey and make me proud, Ms. Weaver." Jethro crossed his arms. He shifted to stand behind his father's chair, removing himself from the role of authority, becoming merely a spectator.

He's never called me Nila.

The stupid thought came and went on a heartbeat. Jethro was yet to use my first name.

I shuddered, feeling overwhelmingly sick again.

Jethro was awful but being disowned and handed over to a room of men was worse. I would've given anything to avoid was what about to happen. I would willingly trade all my nights in a bed and return to the kennels. The hounds were loving, kind…warm.

I sat frozen on Mr. Hawk's lap.

His hand rested on my upper thigh, not violating but terrifying. "Now that we all understand each other, I want you to look at something for me, Nila. Then the festivities will begin. Every man you serve, you'll receive another snippet of your history. Only once you've completed your task will you know the entire story and will be free to spend the afternoon either in the steam baths below the house as a reward or in solitary confinement in the dungeons as punishment, depending on how well you please us."

I couldn't understand how my body still functioned. Shock turned my limbs to statues, fear made me mute—I died inside until there was no part of me left. But still my heart kept pumping; my blood kept flowing—staying alive only for their sick pleasure.

The weight of my mother's collar bit into my neck and a question came from no-where. My mother was a Weaver. Her mother before her was a Weaver. But wouldn't they have changed their names according to the surname of their husbands?

I blinked, trying to remember my father's last name.

I can't.

"You look confused. I'll permit you to ask a question before we proceed," Mr. Hawk said, settling me higher on his knee.

I fought my cringe, struggling to formulate the words. "My mother's maiden name was Weaver, but she would've changed it when she got married." I glanced at Jethro behind his father's chair. He tilted his chin, looking down his nose.

Mr. Hawk shook his head. "That son of mine hasn't explained anything has he." Twisting in the seat, he glanced at Jethro. "What exactly have you been doing? You know information is what grants us control. We're the ones in the right. How can she hope to accept her situation if you keep her in the dark?"

Jethro clenched his jaw but remained silent.

Rolling his eyes, Mr. Hawk faced me again and smiled. "I'll give you a brief history lesson, then you must begin your duties." Reaching up, he tugged the maid's cap on my head.

Every inch of me crawled, but I didn't move away. I was hungry for knowledge. Starving to know just how they continued to control my family with no fear of police interference or retribution.

Mr. Hawk reclined, his thumb drawing small circles on my upper thigh. "It all began with one man, who you'll find out about in a little bit. He had children, gracing them all with the Weaver name. Now, from that day on, the power of the family name travelled with the firstborn girl. No matter if she married, divorced, or suddenly wanted to change her name to something whimsical, she wasn't permitted. Whoever she married, it was a condition that the *man* change his name so that their offspring always bore the Weaver name and continued the line of succession of the debt."

Why did they do it? Why keep a name that only brought misery? My mind hurt trying to understand the Hawk's power.

"You, I believe, are the seventh woman to be taken. And the claiming can happen anywhere between the ages of eighteen and twenty-six."

"You have rules on ruining someone's life?"

His forehead furrowed. "What do you think we're doing, Nila? *Everything* we're doing is following a strict set of rules—laid out in utmost simplicity and must be followed."

"If you're following rules, then follow the rules of today's society. You think I accept what you're telling me? That all of this is *legal?*" I spat the last word. "You think its common place to threaten my family, steal me away, and imprison me with a collar of diamonds that won't come off until I die? You're completely insane. And wrong. And—"

"No one—especially a Weaver—has the right to speak to me like that." Mr. Hawk's fingernails bit into my thigh. "What part are you not understanding, girl? We haven't threatened your family—they are under observeillance to ensure their best behaviour. We didn't steal you away—you came voluntarily, remember? And as for the collar—you should be proud to wear it. It's the most treasured piece in the Hawks antiquities."

I bit my lip as his fingernails pierced harder.

His voice dropped the scholarly softness, sliding into strictness. "I see you need more concrete evidence. Fine. The diamonds you wear are worth millions. The diamonds we've sourced have been used to trade, buy services, bribe officials, own prime ministers, even control diplomats and royalty. No one is above the allure of a flawless diamond, Ms. Weaver. Everyone has a price. Lucky for us, we can *afford* any price."

His tone sharpened. "Does that answer your rude question?"

What response could I give? There was nothing I could say or do to ignore my entire situation. They might have some misplaced belief that they were in the right—but that didn't matter. Because they owned the very people I would need to save me.

My shoulders dipped.

Mr. Hawk grinned. "Glad you're coming to your senses. Don't under estimate us, Nila Weaver. We've had the law on our side for hundreds of years. We *still* have the law on our side and that won't change. You are nothing more than a single woman who left the world's spotlight because she fell in love. You are already consumed and forgotten."

His fingernails stopped slicing my leg; he patted me gently. "I apologise that my son didn't inform you of this. It's his job to be implicitly open with you. To ensure you accept your new standing quickly." He threw a glare at Jethro behind us.

Jethro locked his jaw, his eyes unreadable.

Mr. Hawk bounced me on his knee. "Now, no more questions. Serve my Diamond brothers and earn your right to more information."

My heart shot up my throat. "Serve them how?"

Mr. Hawk shook his head. "Ah, I just told you, no more questions. I have no doubt Jethro would've been rather firm on *that* instruction. Silence is the key to pleasing us." He pinched my lips together. "Don't say a word until we permit it, and you'll be rewarded."

I'm to be a blow-up doll with no voice or soul?

Looking down, I fought against the urge to tear my face from his grip.

He didn't let me go. And I couldn't keep fighting the urge. So I did the only thing I could. Slowly, I nodded, losing another battle against the trickling tears cascading silently down my cheeks. They continued their unhindered sad journey down my neck, through the collar, to my naked nipples below.

The sun glinted through the window, blinding me for a second on the diamond pin in Jethro's shirt. His eyes were tight and narrowed, glaring at the room of leather-jacketed men; his face resolute and frozen.

Freeing me, Mr. Hawk ordered, "Lean forward, and retrieve the first bit of parchment."

I sat unmoving. I didn't want to wriggle on his lap. I didn't want to give any reason for things to grow or hands to grope.

Jethro lashed out from behind, catching me by surprise. He didn't hit me, but grabbed my diamond collar and snapped a leash to the back. Tugging the restraint, he muttered, "Lesson one. You'll do as your told the *second* you're told it. Otherwise, you'll choke until you do."

He moved to the back of the chair, leaving my line of sight. The moment he was gone, the pressure on the collar increased, digging into my larynx, cutting off my air supply.

Just let him strangle you.

It would be easier.

But as my body crushed against Mr. Hawk from the pressure, and the natural instinct to fight took over, I knew I couldn't be so weak. There was no point in being stupid. If I was plane-wrecked in a jungle, I would obey the law of the wild—doing absolutely anything to survive.

Wasn't this the same thing?

I was in a den of beasts and they were trying to help me by teaching me their law. If I obeyed, I would live. Entirely simple. Stupidly simple.

No sound, Nila. Not one word. Switch off. Retreat into that spot inside and get through this.

I could do it by adapting, by learning. I refused to be hurt for punishments I could avoid.

Jethro sensed my acquiescence at the same time as his father. I didn't know what gave me away—the slouching of my shoulders, the soft puff of sadness? Regardless, they knew I wouldn't fight. They'd won.

Jethro released the pressure on my throat, removing the leash and dangling it over the back of the chair as he moved back to his position. Mr. Hawk angled my face, pressing a wet kiss on my cheek. "Good girl. You're learning."

I didn't even flinch. I was as cold as his son.

Embrace it.

Locking eyes with Jethro, I kept myself anchored while his father's hand slipped inside the stupid pinafore and found my breast.

Jethro gritted his teeth, but never stopped glaring into my blank gaze.

I tensed, willing every molecule to stay frigid and unattached. There was freedom in drifting—as I'd learned in the kennel—and I let my mind go.

I would be Jethro and remain stone cold on the outside. But inside I would be Kite and cut the strings of my soul—soaring where they'd never touch me.

No matter what they did.

My head bowed as Mr. Hawk pressed up, grinding a hard cock against my naked arse. "Read the parchment."

My hair fell in a thick black curtain, obscuring half of the men who watched with eager eyes.

My hands didn't shake as I reached for the parchment. I lowered my eyes to read. I was silently amazed at how collected and aloof I seemed. Shocked that I'd so easily turned off. What did that say about me? I'd just learned about my mother. Spent the night with a pack of dogs. *Am I really that adaptable?* Or was shock to blame?

The parchment used to be whole—it was age-stained, blood-marked, and torn. Glancing upright, I noticed the remaining pieces scattered around the table. A treasure hunt to read what would be my sentence.

Not every man had a piece, but at a quick count, I guessed four to five shards of secret-tarnished paper were out there, waiting for me to read.

Looking back to the parchment in my hands, my eyes landed on the crest I'd grown fast to recognise of hawks, women, and diamonds. It took pride of place at the top of the letter with intricate calligraphy and penmanship.

Taking a deep breath, I read.

On this date, the eighteenth day, of the eighth month, of the year of our Lord fourteen-seventy-two, we hereby convene to settle the unsightly claims and forthwith family disruptions between Percy Weaver and Bennett Hawk.

We call upon the royal sovereignty to grace this binding agreement upon the two houses, to put aside flagitious slander, and immoral actions, and settle this as gentlemen.

As esquire over this binding estate, I have mention Percy Weaver and family, including church-sanctified marriage to Mary Weaver, and his thrice offspring of two boys and one girl are also governed by the degree found today, or they shall hang by the neck until dead for heinous crimes found unjustifiable by the court of England so help me God.

It ended.

I stopped reading but didn't move. Not a breath. Not a fidget. It was true then. My family had done something to justify all of this.

But what could be so awful to earn a contract spanning generations of repayments?

Mr. Hawk bounced me again, tweaking my nipple. "Finished?"

My heart neither fluttered nor sank. I was flying free—escaped from this unfolding nightmare.

"Intrigued? Want to know the rest?" His fingers twisted harder, but I didn't care. All I cared about was finding out more.

Ignoring his touch, I breathed for the first time and nodded. As much as I didn't want to get close to the other men, curiosity burned. I was desperate to read more torn pages and solve the mystery of my lineage.

Why did father never say anything? Why did he raise me to think we were good people?

That question would probably never be answered.

Mr. Hawk placed his hands on my hips, hoisting me from his lap. I stood with my eyes cast downward. Silent and waiting.

He smiled in encouragement. "Behaving well so far. Let's see if you can keep it up." Waving toward the overladen sideboard full of hors d'oeuvres, fish dishes, meat dishes, roast vegetables, and desserts, he said, "You're our waitress for this little get together. Please be so kind as to serve our meal. You'll receive a token of thanks from each of the Black Diamond brothers and earn the right to finish your reading."

My legs moved before my brain registered. The primal part of me taking over to jump to the task. I might be a naïve woman who didn't know how to jerk a man off, but I was a businesswoman at heart. I'd been around strict shop buyers, ditzy models, and sulking catalogue owners. I'd learned how to adapt and sell my work.

This was no different.

I had to adapt and sell myself.

Make him care. Make him feel.

My eyes flew to Jethro. Was it possible? Could I break his ice and find a man deep inside—a man who I could seduce, beguile, and ultimately use to stay alive?

Am I that strong?

Mr. Hawk tapped my behind as I skirted the back of his chair. Jethro didn't move, granting a small space for me to pass.

I hunched into myself, preparing for whatever cruelty he had planned.

His body twitched. The perfect lines of muscle and masculinity once again making me despise his natural beauty. An unwilling rush shot through my system at the memory of him fingering me.

He'd wanted me in that moment and it had nothing to do with debts or pain. It'd been pleasurable, confusing, and awkward but…maybe there was something I could work with.

The idea to seduce Jethro flowered quickly. The bloom wasn't fresh like the bud of a rose but *black*. The unfurling petals dripped with filth, sprouting from a place I never wanted to acknowledge. He belonged to a family who ruined mine. He had no compassion. No heart.

How could I make him care when stone was utterly heartless? *I'll try, though.* I had nothing left to lose.

I could be their ward, to be tormented on a daily basis, for years. I would be his toy for however long he wanted. Time could change anything if the elements conspired with me. A mountain ultimately had to give way to the sea if hammered by its salty waves.

I'll be that wave.

Jethro cleared his throat, deliberately stepping forward. His large frame pressed against mine, causing my body to twist and brush my naked breasts against him.

"Oops," he breathed.

I didn't look into his eyes. I couldn't stand to look at him. All of this was his doing and I refused to let him unsettle me anymore. "Don't touch me," I whisper-hissed.

His hand lashed out, slinking up my pinafore and tweaking the same nipple his father had. "Silence." He bowed his head to mine. "And you loved me touching you. Stop being a little liar, Ms. Weaver."

Gritting my teeth, I darted away, tearing his fingers from my breast. I breathed hard when I reached the sideboard. So much food.

My stomach scrunched into a hunger ache.

So what I was naked? So what over twenty men waited to do who knew what to me? It didn't matter. Because my life hinged on throwing away normal and embracing the crazy I now lived with.

I would meet them in hell and play their horrid games. *I'll come out the victor.*

Grabbing a tiered platter of pâté, crusty bread, and pickled vegetables, my mouth watered.

I'm so hungry.

My stomach growled, sending spasms of pain. I'd never gone this long without food, and the lack of sugars and vitamins faded the edges of my vision. My fingers whispered over a piece of roasted potato. Just one little taste…

"Hurry up," Mr. Hawk ordered.

Shaking my head from the overwhelming need to shove a handful of delicious looking food into my mouth, I turned to face the table. I'd never waitressed before, but I guessed the man in charge would get first choice.

That means passing him again.

Holding tight to the platter, I held my head high, and made my way past Jethro. His mouth twitched as he once again blocked my path. I kept my lips tight together, not looking at the challenge in his eyes.

"Not interested in me anymore, Ms. Weaver?" he purred.

Mr. Hawk looked over his chair and pointed at me, then placed his finger over his lips in the universal 'hush' sign. A non-so-subtle reminder that I wasn't permitted to speak.

When I didn't respond. Jethro smiled. "I'm impressed."

He might terrify me, but he needed to know I wouldn't give up. I had plans for him, and I wouldn't be so easily cowed. Plus, he had my vomit on his shoes, he shouldn't be so smug.

I let myself glance into his golden eyes. *You don't scare me.*

His capricious demeanour shifted slightly, a silent message glowing in his gaze. *Give me time.*

He let me pass without another word.

Breathing shallowly, I came to a standstill beside Mr. Hawk. He nodded, choosing a selection from the platter. "Good girl. You may now serve the rest of the table. Left to right, if you please."

Straightening, I forced myself to truly look at the men before me—the gauntlet of masculinity I had to travel through to reach my destination.

My heart raced; a cold sweat broke out down my spine.

Stay cold. Stay free. And you'll get through this.

I placed one foot, then another. My heartbeat ratcheted as I came to a stop beside a large man. He had orange hair and a tattoo snaking up his neck.

My vision wobbled; I tottered to the left as a small wave of vertigo reminded me I'd been stable up to this point thanks to a miracle. Orange Tattoo shot out an arm, preventing me from slamming into the table.

He grinned. "Steady, I won't bite." He brought me close, smiling so deep a dimple formed. "I'll lick though."

Before I could move, his tongue landed on my thigh, licking long and slow like a giant animal.

What?!

I squirmed, almost dropping the tray. His grip was absolute, holding me firm until he'd tasted his full. The rush of vertigo turned to nausea. The sickly scent of my previous sickness didn't help my stomach from rolling like a shipwreck.

Letting me go, I stumbled and tried to rub away the glisten of wetness from his awful mouth. It only transferred to my naked elbow.

Orange Tattoo beamed, licked his lips, and took a selection of breads and pickles. "Thank you, Ms. Weaver."

I spun to face Mr. Hawk.

This couldn't be true. He expected me to let this happen. From *everyone?*

Mr. Hawk chewed thoughtfully, raising an eyebrow, daring me to speak.

My lips parted—to demand to know what happened. Was that the token of gratitude he spoke of? A *lick?*

My chest puffed, sending a wash of embarrassment through me. Not only was I naked but I had to permit them *licking* me!

Mr. Hawk pursed his lips, waiting for me to explode.

He'll punish you. Don't ask. Do. Not. Snap.

It took more courage and energy than I had. But I managed to suck in a breath and release the stress swirling in my system. I had too many other things to focus on to care about an unorthodox dinner soirée.

No speaking.

I had to pretend I had no tongue. Otherwise, waitressing would be the least of my problems.

Glancing back at the men, they grinned, knowing I had no choice but to continue.

Jethro's voice ghosted behind me like a dark cloud. "You're the main course, Ms. Weaver. Each brother gets a taste—anywhere he chooses. You'd be wise to allow it."

My heart thundered. *Anywhere?*

But if it was just a lick—was that so bad? Perhaps this dinner party might not be as awful as I'd feared. A lick I could tolerate. A touch I could handle. Full penetration would drive my mind from its sanctuary straight to an asylum.

It was as if Jethro knew that. Pushing me, little by little, past my comfort zone.

I moved to the next leather-jacketed man. This one was skinny but had an edge of violence. His shaved head shone as he helped himself to the food before placing his finger in the top of my pinafore and pulling me down to his level.

His tongue lashed out, tracing my cheekbone all the way to my ear.

Shuddering, I swallowed back my repulsion.

You can handle it.

The moment he'd finished, he said, "Thank you, Ms. Weaver."

What did they want for me—permission that it was okay? That I was *grateful?*

Standing upright, I struggled to move. Struggled to keep going when I knew how many more licks I'd have to earn before it was over.

"Proceed, Ms. Weaver. Don't disappoint me." Jethro's gravelly voice invaded my ears. Damn him. Damn all of this.

Swallowing hard, I moved to the next.

He was handsome. Quite like Jethro in a stockier, less devilish kind of way. He had dark hair with flecks of grey and a bird of prey tattooed on his forearm.

Never taking his eyes from mine, he took a few items, then hooked a strong arm around my waist and pushed up my maid's uniform. His lips pressed a kiss on my hipbone, the wet tease of a tongue hidden by the warm pressure of his mouth.

Every inch of me revolted but I didn't flinch.

Smirking, he let me go. "Thank you, Ms. Weaver."

It was the smirk that gave him away.

He's another Hawk.

The man nodded, sensing my connection to his pedigree. "I'm the second brother," he said softly. "I doubt you know my name seeing as Jethro gets to have all the fun—but I'll tell you—so you know who to scream for when my older brother goes too far." He crooked his finger, hinting for me to move closer.

Despite myself, I bent. There was something about this brother. Something different.

His light-brown eyes—a Hawk family trait it seemed—crinkled at the corners. "I'm Kestrel." Pointing at the tattoo on his arm, he added, "Like the bird."

"Leave her alone, Kes. Other brothers want a turn." Jethro's demand snapped from behind.

Kestrel chuckled. "Easy there, Jet. Only playing with my food." He sat back, motioning me to continue.

How many sons did Mr. Hawk have? How many must I submit to

when Jethro had had enough of me? I didn't have the mental protection to sleep with an entire family of evilness.

My eyes didn't linger on him and I wasn't permitted to speak, but I wanted to know more about him. I wanted to know why I had a sense of kinship—no matter how slight.

Tense, I darted around his chair, moving to my next customer.

The next man had piercings in his eyebrow and lower lip. Blue-black hair, so similar to Vaughn's, tore my heart out as he bent his head over my arm and dragged a pointed tongue toward my elbow.

V.

Tears threatened. V was everything to me. I couldn't stand to think of him while this happened. I should've messaged him back. I was cruel to leave him in distress.

Closing my eyes, I put one foot in front of the other, moving toward the next man.

And then the next.

And the next.

Each one thanked me once they'd tasted, acting like gentlemen rather the lair of monsters they truly were.

With every lick, I froze, standing tense and hating while they dragged their saliva all over my skin.

Thankfully, the lack of hunger tripped time, merging the men and tongues into a merry-go-round of nightmares. I lost track of who licked where, hiding myself away and focusing on the weight of my platter growing lighter and lighter.

But not one person tasted my breasts or pussy.

It sent me into a state of uncomfortable awareness. They were men. Taunting a woman who they'd been given permission to taste. Why hadn't they gone for the prized locations?

The unknowing and waiting sent my skin crawling more than their eager tongues.

The next man I served was older with a greying moustache and wispy hair. He licked my neck, nuzzling my hair before taking his fill of food.

I went to move, in a trance, to the next diner.

But the older man captured my hip and presented me with the next part of the parchment.

My trance evaporated, leaving me hungry for information. This was why I permitted this. I let myself be governed by history. The double meaning of the thought didn't escape me. *You were taken because of history. You're staying because of history.*

The diamonds of my collar bit into my neck in agreeance.

Placing the platter on the table, I removed myself from the twenty-first century and proceeded to be swept to 1472.

For actions committed by Percy Weaver and his entourage of well-to-do associates, he stands judged and wanting. His life is determined by the grace of Bennett Hawk who states the following comeuppance:
Monetary compensation
Public apology
And most of all, bodily retribution

What a bastard. He couldn't let some petty grievance go?

He did save the entire family from hanging. Somehow, he'd kept Percy Weaver and my ancestors from swinging on a rope, and in a way, I had to be grateful. Grateful to a man who'd saved my bloodline but stolen my future at the same time.

If this document had never been agreed upon, I would never have been born. No one past Percy and Mary would've existed. It was hard to hate someone who'd granted life, but easy to hate them for stealing countless of those lives generations later.

"Keep going, Ms. Weaver," Jethro purred.

My head snapped up.

He stood there, wrapped in his horrible silence.

I wanted to glower. I wanted to do something idiotic and stick my tongue out at him. But there was no point making him hate me more than he already did. The moment I could charge my phone, I would Google every enticing come-hithers a woman could make.

I'll seduce him.

I'd enjoyed seeing his impeccable control snap by the stables. I loved that I was the one to do it.

I'll make him care.

I would turn this travesty into a prophecy by weaving my Weaver magic over a Hawk.

With strength building in my heart, I grabbed my tray.

Moving forward on unsteady knees, I looked greedily at the next piece of paper. It sat coyly in the centre of the table, beckoning.

The next man to taste me was a young boy, barely out of his teens.

His touch was gentle, tongue barely licking. He was my favourite from the table.

After another two licks, I hoped I deserved the next scrap of parchment, but no one gave it to me. My heart sank as I completed a full rotation, squeezing my eyes as each tongue inched closer to the places I wished were covered.

I couldn't stop shivering when I placed the empty platter on the sideboard. Resting my palms on the hard surface, I breathed deep. Tears pressed on the back of my eyes, disgust rolled in my stomach growling with desperate hunger. This was torture on so many levels. Delivering food to well-fed men all the while they feasted on me, too.

"The main course, if you will, Nila," Mr. Hawk muttered.

I looked over my shoulder. He sat there, running his fingers through his goatee. His golden eyes, so like Jethro's, held no patience or tolerance but his lips tilted in mirth. He was enjoying this.

Of course he was. They *all* were.

Including my main tormentor.

Pushing off from the sideboard, I collected a large silver tray of chicken and asparagus. Keeping my eyes down, I deliberately kept the tray high and outstretched, giving me a shield in which to pass Jethro.

Not that it helped.

His arm shot out, stopping me. I cursed the familiarity of his touch. Screamed at the horrible way my body remembered the pleasure he'd granted by the stables. I wanted nothing from him. Especially the memory of his fingers.

I glared into his eyes. *Stay silent.*

It was hard.

I had so much I wanted to say. So much to yell. The side of my head still throbbed from his strike; my ego still hurt from not knowing how to jerk him off the way he desired. He made me feel like a rejected little girl.

Bowing close, he whispered in my ear, "I'm enjoying watching you be so obedient, Ms. Weaver. And your silence..." He brushed my hair away from my cheek, fingertips lingering on my neck. "...is making me hard."

I sucked in a gasp, looking to the front of his trousers despite myself. The outline of his massive cock that terrified me—more than his hands, temper, or god-awful silence—stood firm and bulging against his jeans.

He smiled. "Keep up the good work and you might get two rewards this evening." His eyes darkened. "Because we both know you want me to finish what I started."

My gasp turned to a growl. I couldn't fathom how my stomach swooped even while sickness swirled. Damn my traitorous body for finding his evil beauty attractive.

Are you sure you want to seduce him just for protection? I hated the question. I hated that I didn't have an answer.

Jerking away from him, I stalked toward my starting position. Standing beside Mr. Hawk, I served him first. The moment he'd taken a few morsels, I moved to leave, but he pinched my pinafore, keeping me still.

His eyes met mine and I knew, just *knew*, this serving round wouldn't be my arms, neck, or hips up for a taste. This would be worse. *Much* worse.

"Face me, girl," he ordered.

My teeth chattered, but I slowly did as he requested.

"Lean down."

Closing my eyes, I obeyed.

His hot breath clouded over my chest before a wet, warm mouth latched onto my nipple. A graze of teeth, a swipe of a tongue—it all drove me to the pinnacle. The pinnacle where I knew I would burn in hell for not only permitting it, but for the tiny flutter of need that had burst into life while his son drove his finger inside me.

My head pounded as I shoved the betrayal away. I was the one who betrayed myself. I was the one not strong enough to fight Jethro. He'd won the moment I saw him and let my need for touch consume me.

Tears tickled my spine and the moment Mr. Hawk pulled way, I ran.

I didn't get far.

Orange Tattoo, who sat next to Mr. Hawk caught me, holding me tight. "Now, now. You're doing so well. Don't ruin it." His large hand splayed on my shoulder blades, jerking me to his sitting level. With a tight smile, his mouth latched onto my other nipple.

I whimpered as his large soppy lips sucked. He took his time, swirling his tongue around the hard bud, before letting go in a loud slurp.

I stood shaking as he selected some chicken and sent me on my way.

I can't do this.

Self-pity filled my empty stomach, and I stood frozen to the thick burgundy carpet.

"Move, Ms. Weaver," Jethro murmured.

My body swayed to obey but everything inside rebelled. I didn't care Mr. Hawk had eloquently described my cage with the use of diamonds and debts. I didn't care that I had no choice but to do as I was told.

I just couldn't do it.

My eyes flew wide as Jethro's hands landed on my shoulders. He spun me to face him, breathing hard. "Do. It. Now." The force of his command buckled my knees. I dropped my head.

Silently, Jethro stormed me forward, presenting me to the next man. The platter wobbled in my hands but I stood upright while a vile mouth suckled on my breast.

Once it was over, Jethro manhandled me to the next, whispering in my ear, "Make me come back and show you how to behave, and I won't be nice. You still cling to the ideology that you're better than us. That any moment this will be over." His teeth nipped at my ear. "That's torture because it's false. It won't happen. Accept it and be done with the past. Accept it and embrace everything we're giving you."

Shoving me forward, he patted my backside. "I can be nice if you give me reason to be, Ms. Weaver. Try me by behaving for the rest of the luncheon."

I didn't watch as he left, resuming his standing position behind his father's chair.

I can be nice.

Bullshit he could be nice. But the sooner I obeyed, the sooner it was over.

So…I obeyed.

Mouths.

Fingers.

Tongues and teeth.

They all tasted. They all groped.

I thought the first course was hard. I'd clung to the morals of how wrong it was for so many men to treat one woman so unfairly.

This course did things to me I wished I could deny. Fat lips, thin lips, hot mouths, cool mouths. They all not only *took* from me but *gave* something in return.

A horrible realisation that my body was taking over.

My horror sank like a rock every time a man had a new taste. Slowly my stomach fluttered; my insides rebelling against the melting that occurred.

The men didn't care countless mouths had been on my skin. They took turns between my left and right nipples, nibbling, sucking. I wished they'd bite. I willed them to hurt me—*something* to prove how vile they were.

But each one—old, young, trim, overweight—they all loved me. They adoringly suckled. They moaned with such deep appreciation, I struggled to remember this was by force not by choice. I felt as if I granted them a gift.

A gift they truly appreciated.

Don't. Don't buy into the mindfuckery.

Even my inner voice turned slightly breathless, a lot confused, and edging toward acceptance.

I grew lightheaded as I trudged from man to man. I didn't make eye contact with any of them. I became listless. Numb. Apart from a tiny spark tugging on the invisible cord from my nipples to my core. I wished it wasn't so. I craved to remain unaffected.

But slowly they turned me from intellectual businesswoman to trembling plaything.

Slowly, I grew wet.

Sharp teeth dragged my attention through the blackness that'd become my soul, back to reality.

I looked into the eyes of Daniel.

The mellow trance I'd been lulled into snapped like a rubber band. I no longer found any acceptance or lusty appeal, only hollow rage.

"It's not much fun licking a woman when she isn't paying attention," he sneered.

My heartbeat flew terrorised around my chest. My nipple throbbed from where he'd bitten me.

Licking his lips, he added, "You taste good, Weaver, but I'm looking forward to the next course."

My heart promptly shot itself and splattered against the floor.

The next course.

No. No. No. No.

"Here. You earned this." Shoving another piece of parchment my way, I forced back my tears.

Moving awkwardly, I placed the empty tray on the sideboard, then returned to Daniel's side. My skin broke out in goosebumps being so close, but he dangled the parchment like a present I desperately wanted.

Taking it, I couldn't hide my shakes this time. My aloofness and spirit were gone, replaced by a brittle shaking leaf.

A leaf that was turned on and damp.

Upon reflection of his crimes, Percy Weaver hereby submits to this esquire's ruling and moves to action the latest degree formulated in this very chamber by Bennett Hawk. The death warrant upon the heads of the Weaver House will be eradicated and burned upon signature of this newly drafted document. Terms forthcoming...

That was it?

Tears spurted from my eyes. I'd let countless men suck on my breasts for no more than a tease?

How could they?

How could *I*?

How could I allow my body to react to their foul ministrations? I hated myself. I hated that I couldn't hide my weakness or the stupid hormones I'd spent my whole life ignoring.

My knees wobbled and I almost folded like an accordion to the floor.

"You pass out and you won't like what you find when you awake." Jethro's voice cut through my grief.

Anger battled away my tears, nursing a new warmth inside. A warmth born of rage rather than flimsy passion. This burned hotter; it licked with orange flames, abolishing my hunger and weakness.

I was fed by anger. I smouldered with hate. I became stronger because of it. It gave me power to continue, but also stole my safety of acceptance. I hissed and scalded with liveliness. I couldn't switch off.

"The next course, Ms. Weaver," Jethro commanded from his position at the head of the table. Balling my hands, I threw away the parchment and stalked to the sideboard.

Dessert.

I knew what would happen.

I can't do this.

You will *do this.*

In my rage, I made a reckless decision. I was at war with my body—why not step over the battle line and join them? Why not embrace it? It was yet another tool—another lesson. If I embraced the new feelings inside, I would be better equipped at chipping away at Jethro's cold exoskeleton of ice and burrowing my way into his warmth.

I would make him care.

I would pleasure him.

Then I would kill him.

My legs scissored together. Everything inside curled deeper into hiding. The moment I went near the table, I would lose all control. I didn't trust my body. It overpowered me every time. And it sucked to be in this mess with a traitor.

Get it over and done with.

Taking a deep breath, I collected my last course.

Passing Jethro with a gilded tray of mini éclairs, bon bons, and trifles, I kept my eyes down. He'd torment me, no doubt.

Sure enough, his arm wrapped around my shoulders, forcing me to face him. His breathing was slightly uneven; his voice lost a tiny shred of chilliness. "Get through this, and I'll reward you. I'll be kind, because you deserve it." Pressing a possessive kiss on my cheek, he whispered, "I'll wipe it all away."

I was struck dumb by the rare and scarily beautiful glimpse at a man I didn't know existed. But then I blinked as Jethro's ice slid back into place, a grim smirk on his lips. "My offer only stands as long as you don't speak, act out, or disappoint me."

Unwinding his arm, he shoved me toward his father.

Almost drunkenly, I moved toward Mr. Hawk. My stomach quivered with trepidation; my heart was prey running frantically for its life.

Mr. Hawk smiled, holding up another piece of paper. "Here. Your last one until you've completed this final service. I think you deserve it, don't you?" His eyes raked down the front of my ridiculous maid's uniform. The cap had stayed in place—how, I didn't know.

Patting my arse, he added, "I must admit you refrained beautifully, even your mother who was my favourite, didn't do so elegantly at her first dinner party."

I ignored that, latching onto the parchment.

Mr. Hawk motioned me to put the tray on the table, before handing over the small piece.

Percy Weaver and family hereby acknowledge his agreeance to the one and only term set forth by Bennett Hawk. In accordance with the law, both parties have agreed that the paperwork is binding, unbreakable, and incontestable from now and forever. Details and parties of both signatures are displayed on the enclosed verified document, henceforth known as the Debt Inheritance.

My eyes met his.

If only I had the rest. I would scream and give up the charade of obedience. I was done. I would take pain to avoid what was about to happen. I would take pain rather than pleasure because then I would still know myself. The longer this went on, the less in-tune I was with the girl I'd been.

Too many feelings. Too many sensors. Too many rabbit-holes with too many right and wrongs.

You're giving up so soon? They killed your mother! They've broken your father's heart. Could I not stomach some unpleasantness and confusion in order to find a way to repay them?

Disappointment weighed my heart. I thought I'd have more endurance.

No. I won't give in.

This is nothing. Be that kite. Cut your strings again.

Bracing my shoulders, I moved closer to Mr. Hawk without being asked.

His eyes widened, then a grin spread his lips. "Good girl, indeed." Bowing his head, his arm wrapped around my waist, tilting me back a little. "You're proving to be a testament to my son's training."

My waist height was almost perfect for a lowered mouth to latch onto the front part of my sex.

And that was when I felt the strangest, wettest, alluring, *disgusting* thing of my life.

His tongue slid along my clit, wriggling softly, drenching me in saliva.

My stomach clenched, my hands balled, and I wobbled in his arms.

The disgusting element didn't leave. I waited for my body to betray me, to *like* it, but all I felt was grotesque impatience for it to be over.

And then…it was.

My first experience with a tongue down below, and it'd been done by a man older than my father. If I didn't have an empty stomach, I would've thrown up all over again. There was nothing sexy or erotic about that.

Tapping my behind, he murmured, "Proceed."

Swallowing hard, I collected the dessert tray and crossed the small distance to Orange Tattoo. He crooked his finger, beckoning me closer. Locking my jaw, I held the desserts high and did as he requested. His orange hair tickled my thighs as he leaned down, running his tongue over the private bundle of nerves.

Luckily for me, I wasn't sensitive, nor did I enjoy it.

Once he'd taken his trifle and tasted his fill, I left to serve the next.

And the next.

And the next.

Some men forced my legs to spread, angling their faces deep. Some men barely touched me, their hot breath wafting between my thighs.

I would like to say I managed to turn my brain off—to do what I promised and fly free, but every tongue kept me locked in the world I lived in. Every lick made my body turn to stone while my tummy twisted and ached from clenching.

I delivered dessert, but I was the ultimate sweet. The men took their time, firm fingers holding my hips, dragging their foul tongues. And after every violation, they'd wipe their glistening mouths and say, "Thank you, Ms. Weaver."

Thank you.

As if their appreciation was enough to stop me from feeling like dirt. Their treatment never changed. They remained courteous and gentle. Obeying boundaries and not doing anything but licking me in a place they had no right.

Their pleasantness made all of this seem so normal. So terribly normal. And my hatred slowly switched back to acceptance. The small flutter I'd felt from my nipples being sucked returned—frightful, tentative, but softening my hate tongue by tongue.

They weren't hurting me. They weren't making me do anything that had the potential to shatter my mind.

They just tasted.

A little taste.

That's all.

And I didn't fight.

Not at all.

I'm wet.

By the time I came to Daniel, my legs were drenched and the trimmed hair I meticulously maintained was mattered with droplets of Diamond brotherhood.

My hands were balled around the tray; my jaw tight and aching. Because no matter my good intentions—they'd won. They'd caused my body to have a reaction, and I was soaking.

The strange ache that Jethro had conjured was back, pulsing deep in my core. The flicker of tongues and gentle tastes frustrated me and I hated, *positively hated*, that I had to fight my hips from pressing harder against them.

I'd begun the service uptight but now I was *wound* tight. Seeking something. Seeking relief.

Daniel pushed his chair back, angling me physically between his spread hips. With a malicious glint in his eyes, he pushed me back with a firm palm between my breasts. "Fuck the stupid rule."

I gasped as his mouth latched around my clit. The suction of his mouth made my body twist with oversensitivity. He wasn't playful or respectful like the rest of the men. He knew what he wanted and he took.

Hard.

The ache wound tighter and tighter, clawing its way toward relief.

I squeezed my eyes. I couldn't look at the men watching. I couldn't do anything but breathe and get through it. And I definitely couldn't look up where a small growl came, masked with silence.

It was nothing more than a growl.

But it resonated in my bones with knowledge.

Jethro.

The few seconds that each man had taken seemed much longer in Daniel's arms. Suddenly, I cried out, jerking hard.

The tip of his tongue probed my entrance, trying to enter me.

No one had done that. They'd behaved with some unspoken rule to taste but not devour.

Fuck the stupid rule.

Daniel's voice repeated in my head. Had there been guidelines on how I was to be treated?

Everything we're doing is following a strict set of rules—laid out in utmost simplicity and must be followed.

I recalled what Mr. Hawk had said.

He had rules meant to ruin me but also…protect me?

Daniel tried again, his fingers biting into me painfully.

Then, I was wrenched away.

Torn free of his grip with a slice of his fingernails and dragged to the end of the table. The empty dessert tray went flying, clanging against the floor.

My legs tripped, sending me colliding with a body I'd been so intimate with only hours before.

The crash of the tray cut through the room like a loud cymbal. But no one said a word.

The moment Jethro dragged me to the head of the table opposite Mr. Hawk, he shoved the largest of all parchments into my hands. His eyes were dark, face tight. "Here, read it."

Breathing fast, trying hard to forget about the sticky saliva between my legs and the sensation of having his brother's tongue trying to enter me, I took the tattered age-stained scroll.

Jethro scowled, keeping a small distance between us. His coldness buffeted me, sending ice scattering over my bare arms. He looked pissed off—furious, yet there was something there that made my stomach twist.

Whatever game we'd played, whatever war we'd started back at the stables, wasn't finished. He knew it. I knew it. And the knowledge sent power thrilling through my veins.

Leaning close, he hissed, "Stop staring at me, Ms. Weaver. I gave you a request." Tapping the scroll in my palm, he snapped, "Read. It."

Tearing my eyes from his, I obeyed.

The intricate border caught my attention first. Along with a design of vines and filigree, the words *bound, indebted, owned* were entwined in red ink.

The calligraphy of ancestors past sentenced me to a life worse than death. My rights had been taken. My life stolen. My body no longer mine.

18th August 1472

Signed and witness by Esq John Law
Matter between Weaver versus Hawk
Known forthwith as the Debt Inheritance

This hereby concludes all debate and conversation and puts forth a binding debt. Council has been provided along with sovereign approval for such an agreement.

As set in this chamber, I have witnessed the signatures of both parties of House Weaver and House Hawk, along with their significant entourage and companions.

The debt states as follows.

Percy Weaver hereby solemnly swears to present his firstborn girl-child, Sonya Weaver, to the firstborn son of Bennett Hawk, known as William Hawk. This will nullify all unrest and unpleasantries until such a time as a new generation comes to pass.

This debt will not only bind the current occupancies of the year of our Lord 1472 but every year thereafter. Every firstborn Weaver girl will be gifted as fair comeuppance to the firstborn Hawk boy to be claimed between the years of one and eight and six and twenty respectively. Both parties will be forever agreed on this day set forth.

The life and all attributes will be determined by the current Hawk, no rules or precedence will be set, and this agreement raises them above the law, operating within the grace of the royal decree.

Signed:

Bennett Hawk & Family

Percy Weaver & Family

I KNEW WHEN she'd read it.

I knew when the final sentence sank in.

We had a document signed, sealed, and delivered by the royal magistrate of England giving us carte blanche to do as we liked. There was nothing illegal about my actions. There was nothing anyone could find me guilty of.

It was the ultimate approval.

Not to mention, we had wealth to ensure no one would contest it. There was nothing to fight against. The sooner she accepted that, the easier this would be.

Nila's eyes bugged wide, looking up from the parchment.

Grabbing her shoulders, I backed her against the table. The horror living in her black gaze was enough to drag a tiny bit of humanness from my cold soul.

Watching her being tasted—I wouldn't deny—it fucked me off. She was *my* plaything. *Mine* to torment.

I was pissed at my father for permitting the entire brotherhood to use her. They weren't deserving of drinking someone's misery. That right was a Hawk's and only a fucking Hawk's. Excluding my younger cock of a brother.

He deserved shit.

Grinding my teeth, I placed my palm against her sternum, pressing her breakable chest. Her heart beat like a war drum beneath my fingers.

Her lips parted, but she didn't fight as I pushed her backward.

I didn't say a word—controlling her by sheer anger and will.

Her defined stomach muscles clenched as she gave in, sprawling backward onto the table. A small sound of pain came from her lips, catching her weight on her elbows.

She refused to lie down.

She would.

My cock fucking bruised itself, punching my belt time and time again. Only I knew how she tasted when she *wanted* to be tasted. Only I knew how she sounded when she wanted it so fucking bad. And only I knew how tight she was.

That tightness belonged to me.

I doubted I'd fit. I doubted I'd get half my dick inside her, but until I'd had the pleasure of trying, no one else was permitted near her. I had the scroll giving me power over everyone on that subject— including my father.

I swallowed hard. The anger watching my brother stick his fucking tongue inside her boiled. I teetered on a dangerous edge.

Pull back.

I couldn't.

I wanted what I wanted, and I'd take what was owed to me.

"You finally understand." My voice was thicker, deeper, overrun with the dark lust that'd been created this morning. She'd done this to me. It was her curse to fix me.

I couldn't look at her without feeling her thrust against my finger. I couldn't see past the challenge. The building strength in her skinny frame.

She was learning.

I was learning.

We were learning how to play this game together.

She shivered as I dragged my hand down her front, moving lower and lower. My cock ached for the wet temptation belonging to me. I was responsible for her.

She'd been through a lot. She'd obeyed even though she'd fought. She'd kept it together but now she was precariously close to losing it. I wasn't so heartless to ignore that craving in her eyes. The borderline insanity of needing a release. Combined with finally seeing proof that *we* were the good guys? Well, I owed her.

Just a little.

It was my job to take her to the edge, dangle her for a time, but then draw her back into safety. My purpose was to bridle everything she was, so she would do anything I asked.

Glaring into her eyes, I said, "You are mine. I am not your master or owner or boss. I am the man who controls your entire existence until you pay off your family's debts. You don't breathe unless I permit it. You don't move unless I request it. You live a simple life now. One with a single word you need remember…yes."

My touch skated from her belly to her hips.

She stiffened to a plank. Her gaze left mine, locking on the ornate ceiling.

"Look at me." My voice turned harsh, barbaric beneath its cultured refinement. "Has it sunk in yet? That I can do anything I want to you?"

She didn't respond—just like she'd been told not to. Silence. Blissful, blessed silence. She couldn't admonish or argue. She was pliant. Wondrously pliant.

She deserves a reward.

I tried to hold back.

I didn't want an audience.

But fuck it.

Shoving her higher on the table, I slapped away her position on her elbows, crashing her spine onto the wood. She cried out, then sucked in a harsh breath.

I grabbed her legs, forcing them wide.

Her pink flesh invited me, glistening, not from other men's tongues, but arousal. Arousal for me. Arousal that I intended to take advantage of.

Grabbing an untouched glass of water from a Diamond brother, I dumped the liquid all over Nila's pussy.

She cried out; legs trying to scissor. But I didn't let her move.

The water trickled through her dark hair, pooling beneath her. It wasn't enough, but it washed at least some of the men's spit away.

I only wanted to taste her.

Hooking my hands beneath her hips, I held her tight.

"No. Don't—"

Too fucking late.

With a fleeting smile, I captured her swollen cunt in my mouth.

The moment my tongue shot out, pressing firm and hard, she arched off the table.

"Ah!" Her mouth hung wide, her neck straining as every muscle shot into stark relief. Her black hair fanned out on the table, sliding against her shoulders as she writhed on the wood.

Snapping my fingers, I glared at two Diamond brothers. They leapt to attention, grabbing her wrists and holding her down.

She squirmed. She fought. But my fingers only bit harder into her arse, keeping her pinned wide and open.

My fucking brother didn't have the right to tongue-fuck her.

But I did.

I hadn't planned on giving her such a reward, but...it wasn't just her getting off on this.

The power. The submission. Her taste. Her damn fucking taste.

I showed too much. I let go of my tight restraint and drank.

She groaned as I shifted a hand, holding her hipbones hard on the table. Then she whimpered. My tongue became my weapon of choice as I licked downward. No hesitation. No teasing.

I was there for one goal.

Her goal.

My eyes rolled back as I plunged my tongue inside her tight hot warmth.

Fuck me.

"God!" Her hips tried to run from my invasion. Her mouth opened wide; her ribcage visible as her lungs strained to breathe.

I set a pace no one would be able to ignore.

I fucked her. There was no other word for how I drove my tongue in and out, fast and possessive. The muscles in her belly clenched. She panted, she moaned, then she screamed.

She gave up the fight, giving into me.

A spasm of pre-cum dampened my jeans as her hips shot upward, her clit brushing against my nose.

Her body twisted, trying to get her hands free, but the brothers wouldn't let her go.

She turned wild. Seeking. Demanding. The same sexual creature from the stables.

I couldn't breathe without dragging her scent into my lungs. I couldn't swallow without drinking her. And I couldn't fucking think without wanting to tear off my jeans and plunge deep inside her.

My tongue worked faster, the tips of my teeth gracing her pussy as I drove deeper than I'd ever gone before.

I ate her. I fucked her. I *owned* her.

Her tight pussy squeezed my tongue, begging for more.

I'll give you more.

I'd given her too much already.

Fuck.

Her legs suddenly latched around my ears, grinding herself onto my face.

She moaned hard; a breathless beg on her lips. I couldn't stop myself.

My tongue drove harder; my head bobbed faster.

She unravelled.

She combusted.

She screamed as she came on my tongue.

OH, MY GOD.

Oh, my *God*.

It didn't. It couldn't. He didn't. I couldn't.

What the *hell* did I just do?

Jethro stood straight, breathing hard. His eyes were tight; his mouth drenched and red.

My cheeks flamed, heart racing like I'd run ten kilometres.

What *was* that?

What magic did he possess that made me throw away self-consciousness, decorum, and hatred? How could I squirm that way? Sound that way? *Come* that way?

I came.

He made me come.

My captor shot me free for one blissful second, granting me something no one else had. The sparks and waves and mind-twisting delicious clenching. I wanted more. I wanted it *now*.

Jethro wiped his mouth, trying unsuccessfully to hide the lust glowing in his eyes. He'd given, not taken. He'd done what he said.

I'll wipe it all away.

The only thing I could focus on was him. The room of men didn't matter. Their tongues and touches and pleasantly whispered thank yous were gone. Burned to a crisp thanks to the nuclear explosion he'd set off. I was no longer at the mercy of the room. I *owned* the room.

Then everything came crashing back.

My first orgasm was given by a man whose father killed my

mother.

My privacy had been completely stripped by the man who'd stolen me from my family.

He'd made me sleep with dogs.

He played with my head.

He didn't give a damn about me.

Why was he so clever? So perfectly designed for this game?

I struggled to sit up. The two men holding my wrists let me go, and I shot into a sitting position, wrapping arms around my torso.

The hot sparkly burst that made everything so inconsequential faded with every rapid heartbeat. It was like being in the eye of the storm. Jethro granted me silence. He'd shared his heavenly silence and quieted my mind from everything I was feeling.

But now the storm gathered strength, howling, twisting, sucking me back up the funnel of horrors.

Eyes.

So many eyes upon me. Paintings and real. Men who'd seen me naked. Men who'd licked every inch. Men who didn't care if I lived or died.

You let him control you.

You let your body rule your mind.

You let yourself down.

Crushing grief swamped me. I couldn't be there another moment. I couldn't sit there with residual sparks shivering in my core. I couldn't pretend that everything was acceptable.

Jethro smirked, his breathing calmed as he dragged large hands through his hair. My heart broke into shards. How could he give me something so incredible all while hating me? His mercurial moods, his unreadable face—it confused me. Even worse, it *upset* me.

Visceral repulsion and horror howled through me as the storm grew in strength. The compliant prisoner disappeared under a tsunami of rage. This wasn't okay. None of this was okay.

This is not okay!

Balling my hands, I scooted off the table. Keeping my distance from Jethro, I bared my teeth at him—the first male to drive me up a mountain I'd never leapt off before.

Him.

He'd had no right to make me come. To give me a gift not out of kindness but control. He'd proven a valuable lesson. He could make me do anything he wanted, and there was nothing I could do about it.

His eyebrow quirked; chin tilted with arrogance. He didn't say a word, moving to lean against the door with his hands jammed in his pockets. He gave nothing away. No hint at how he felt watching other men use me. No clue as to what he was thinking when he made me come.

I was his to repay this horrible ludicrous debt. But he didn't seem to care.

And that was what broke my heart.

He didn't give an arse about what happened to me. Everything I'd hoped—the secret plan to make him care—was smashed to dust. There was no pleasing a rock like him. No appealing to his compassion.

He has none.

Tearing my eyes from his, I glowered at the table. Standing tall, I embraced my nakedness. I throbbed with righteousness. I trembled with indecency.

I hated what I wore. It covered nothing and was theirs. I wanted nothing to do with them. I wanted to refuse their food, spit out their water, and burn their clothes. Not that they'd offered me any.

With suddenly steady hands, I tore the French maid's cap off my head. I threw it down the table. The satin wood let it slide all the way to the centre where it rested like a stain, a sin—a simple innocuous thing screaming of wrongness.

The men didn't move.

Fumbling at the ties around my neck, I pulled the hated pinafore over my head and balled it up. Standing proud, naked—showing off my bruises from vertigo and tongue smears from bastards—I spoke. "Look at you. Look at how masculine and powerful you are." Pointing my finger around the table, I growled, "Look at how scary and dominating and strong you are. Look at how *proud* you must be. You proved you're invincible by taking advantage of a woman brought here against her will. You used a girl who has to live her worst nightmares to protect those she loves."

Stabbing myself in the chest, I whispered, "Wait…I got it wrong. *You're* not the strong ones. *I* am. You're weak and disgusting. By doing what you did, you gave me more power than I've ever had before. You gave me a new skill—a skill at ignoring you because you're nothing. Nothing. *Nothing!*"

"And you!" I swung my arm, gaze zeroing in on Jethro. The one man who held my life in the palm of his hand. He was nothing. Just like his brethren of bastards.

Jethro stood taller, a shadow darkening his face. His hands came out of his pockets, crossing in front of his large chest.

"You…" I seethed. "You think you're the baddest one here. You think I'll cower. You think I'll obey." Running both hands through my hair, I shouted, "I'll *never* cower. I'll *never* obey. You'll never break me, because you can't touch me."

Spanning my arms, I presented my naked form as a gift—the gift he'd hinted at wanting but hadn't taken. "I'll never be yours even though you own my life. I'll never bow to you because my knees don't recognise your so-called power. So do your worst. Hurt me. Rape me. Kill me. But you'll never ever own me."

Breathing hard, I waited.

The room had remained silent. But now it filled with rustling of leather as men shifted in their seats. The atmosphere went from shocked silence to heavy anticipation.

My overworked heart kicked into another gear, sending my vision a little grey, a little fuzzy. *Please, not now.*

Planting my legs, gripping the soft carpet beneath my toes, I locked my knees against a wave of vertigo.

Mr. Hawk was the first to move. He placed his elbows on the table, linking his fingers together. "I was wrong. You're nothing like your mother. She had a brain. She was smart." His voice dropped the chivalrous country man edge, deepening into violent snaps, "You, on the other hand, are wilful and stupid. You don't see that *we* are your family now. The moment you slept under my roof you became a Hawk by means of acquisition."

I laughed. "I'm still a Weaver then because I didn't sleep under your roof." My kitten claws sharpened. I'd never been a fighter, but something called to me. Something intoxicating and lethal.

He leaned forward, anger etching his face. "You *will* learn your place. Mark my words."

I wanted to fight. I'd listened to their damn history lessons, it was time they listened to mine. "I may not have records so perfectly kept as yours, but I do know my family is innocent. Whatever happened back then was between them—not us. Leave it in the past. My family created a business of making clothes. We dressed the royal court but also donated to the poor. I'm proud of where I've come from and for you to—"

"Jet!" Mr. Hawk pinched the bridge of his nose. "Shut her up."
Jethro immediately slammed a hand over my mouth.

I froze. I knew I'd brought whatever punishment was about to
happen upon myself. I couldn't blame anyone, but I wouldn't let myself
regret what I'd said. I believed I was a good person. So were my twin,
father, mother, and ancestors.

"You just had to push," Jethro hissed. "I'm going to draw blood
for this."

My heart rabbited but I forced myself to remember one important
fact.

They can't hurt you too much.

There would be pain. There would be agony. But they meant to
keep me alive. I had debts to repay before my life was stolen.

Never taking his eyes off mine, Mr. Hawk, ordered, "Jethro. Teach
this woman that Hawks are a forgiving family but there are times when
strictness is required in lieu of allowing little tantrums like this to
occur." His eyes switched from mine to his son's. "Take her. Deal with
her. I don't want to see her again until she's lost the misplaced
righteousness she seems to think she's owed."

Jethro nodded, jostling our bodies. His fingers unglued from
around my mouth and he grabbed my wrist. Every part of me shrank
from his overbearing body and granite golden eyes, but I forced myself
to stand tall.

I growled, "Whatever you do won't matter. What happened before
will *never* happen again." I would never let my body rule my mind no
matter what he did. "You may be able to hurt me but you should know
how pathetic it is for a man to hurt a woman. That isn't power. It's a
weakness!"

He grunted under his breath. "Motherfucking Christ." His temper
increased until the large room pulsed with it.

Another wave of vertigo grabbed my brain. But I managed the
impossible, fighting through the grey unsteady wave—staying on my
feet.

I fought the imbalance thanks to letting myself unlock so many
facets of who I truly was. I stood proud and naked, wearing only dried
saliva and bruises.

Jethro jerked me closer. He swallowed his anger until nothing
outward showed—no annoyance or amazement—he was as opaque as

a black iceberg and just as sharp.

"If you will, Ms. Weaver." Suddenly he let me go, waving toward the double doors behind me. They opened wide as if staff waited on the other side for his command.

When I didn't move, he snapped, "Now!"

My arms wanted to wind around my body. I wanted to hide from his intense gaze, but I fought every instinct and elegantly pirouetted on my toes. I left the room as demurely and proudly as possible. Without a backward glance.

The moment the doors slammed behind us, Jethro grabbed my elbow, prowling forward as if the flames of hell craved his soul. I went from walking to jogging to keep up with his pace.

My vision lost its clarity for a moment, fading in and out as another wash of unbalance tried to steal me, but Jethro didn't give me time to give in. He didn't give me time to care that he dragged me down a corridor so wide it could've been a hall. He didn't let me inspect the countless weapons—swords, bayonets, crossbows, and knives—or catch the eye of surprised staff.

I breathed hard when we finally crashed through one of the many exterior doors and were welcomed from brooding red corridor to bright early-autumn sun.

Jethro kept walking, not letting me catch my breath.

Dragging me down the four huge steps, I winced as the gravel bit into the soles of my feet. But he didn't care. He didn't even notice.

Our feet kicked up pebbles as he headed toward the treeline several metres from the house. I'd never seen this side of the property before. But the grounds were just as expansive and impressive as the other perimeters and just as dangerous.

This was my cage. Leaves and thorns and brambles.

And I'm naked.

The moment gravel was replaced by soft grass below my toes, Jethro tossed me away. I would've fallen if I wasn't malleable and given up fighting his momentum. I stumbled forward, arms soaring outward as if I could suddenly leave the world behind and fly. Fly away. Fly free.

The moment I came to a halt, I spun to face him.

Jethro was right behind me. He fisted my hair, twisting my neck.

I whimpered as he raised my head, higher and higher. My eyes coasted over his crisp grey shirt, and locked onto a pair of ferocious eyes.

"Tell me. What did you hope to achieve in there?" He didn't give me a chance to reply, tugging my hair in a painful jerk. "Did you honestly think before you opened your mouth? If you had stood there and been silent, it would've all been over. You earned an afternoon on your own in a hot steam bath. A maid to bring you whatever you wanted to eat." He shook me. "What part of a *gift* for good behaviour did you not understand?"

"I don't want your charity."

He groaned. "It's not fucking charity if you've earned it." Lowering his head, his nose pressed against mine.

I froze.

"You earned it today. You pleased me by letting those men sample you. You surprised me in a good way." The softness of his voice disappeared under a torrent of rage. "But then you fucked it all up by being *you*. And now…" He trailed off, ideas glowing in his eyes.

Letting me go, I backed away from him, grabbing my hair and quickly twisting it into a loose braid down my back. I hated the thickness, the length. It seemed to invite Jethro to use it anyway he pleased. My scalp had never been so bruised.

The diamond collar sent little rainbows of light bouncing from the sunlight. I would've laughed if I wasn't so tense. I was naked but wearing rainbows—I never would've thought to combine magic with fashion.

Ideas for a new design line came thick and fast. I craved a pencil to sketch before they disappeared.

Jethro placed both hands on his hips, watching me silently.

I didn't move. I didn't say a word. The fragile ceasefire between us stretched uncomfortably thin. It would either snap and ricochet onto me with terrible pain or fade away like a feather on a breeze.

"I see threats don't work on you. But perhaps a negotiation might."

Despite myself, curiosity and hope swelled in my heart. "A negotiation?"

"A one shot offer. You win, you're free. I win, you forget about your old life and give in. You say I'll never own you. If I win—you willingly give me that right." His lips pulled into a cold smile. "You sign not only the debt agreement but another—one that makes me your master until your last breath is taken. You do that, and I'll give you this."

"Give me what?" I asked breathlessly.

"A chance at freedom."

My eyes popped wide.

What?

He cocked his head at the forest behind me. "You wanted to be free—so go. Run. Go seek your freedom."

I twisted on the spot, looking over my shoulder. The sun dappled patches of leaf-strewn ground, looking like a fairy glen, but then it grew darker and thicker and scarier.

The diamond collar rested heavy and ruinously ominous on my throat. My spine ached from the short time I'd been made to wear it; the coldness still hadn't adapted to my skin. How could I run with such a deterrent?

How can you not?

It was the one chance I'd hoped for. The one chance I didn't think I'd get.

Squeezing my eyes, I let Jethro's ultimatum—his negotiation—seep into my brain. If I ran, I might make it. If I ran, I might get what I wanted. But if I lost…

Turning to face him again, the golden-light from the sun cast him with ghostly silhouette, blurring his outline, creating more than just a man. He looked as if he had one foot in this world and one in hell. A fallen angel who still burned with fire—yet it wasn't purity he burned with but hate.

Jethro raised an eyebrow. "What's it going to be?"

"I don't know what you're offering."

"Yes you do."

I did. *I do.*

He took a small step toward me. "You want to break the contract? You want to keep your brother and father safe? Fine. I'm giving you a one-time deal. Run. If you make it to the boundary, you're free. Your family will never be hunted by the Hawks again. You make it, and this is all over. Every last debt and ounce of history—disappears." His voice licked through the sunshine.

A small sparkle from my earlier orgasm rippled between my legs. "And if I don't?"

Jethro frowned. "What?"

"If I don't run…what happens then?"

"You wouldn't run? After I just offered you what you've wanted all along?"

I crossed my wrists over the junction of my thighs, hiding my pussy. "I didn't say I wanted the chance to run naked through a thousand hectares. I said I wanted this to be over."

Jethro smirked. "It's not over until it's over." His eyes fell to my collar, glinting with darkness. "And we both know how it will be over."

Moving closer, he said quietly, "There is no other option here, Ms. Weaver. I'm not giving you the choice to run. I'm *telling* you to run. You wanted it. You got it. One chance to save your family as well as your own life. One chance. You do not want to fuck it up by testing my patience."

My mind stumbled with everything that'd happened. There was no denying chemistry flew between us—but Jethro didn't respond. He was only interested in the chase. The hunt. The *sport*.

He stood so close, every time he breathed, his chest almost touched my nipples. He didn't seem to care I was naked or offer clothing for this one and only chance at freedom. He would make me run unprotected through a forest full of brambles, predators, and trip-worthy roots.

His arm raised and I clamped every muscle from cringing as he cupped my cheek. His heady scent of woods and leather settled over me. Tracing the pad of his thumb over my cheekbone, he bowed his head. "Run, Ms. Weaver. Run. But one thing you should know before you go."

Do not play his games. Do not rise to the bait.

My lips stayed pinched together. I stiffened in his hold.

His mouth tickled the soft skin below my ear. "While you're running, I'll be hunting. You not only have to get to the boundary but you have to do it before I catch you."

The tingle and horrible promise of hope evaporated. Cruel. Vicious. Evil.

I'm to be hunted.

There wouldn't be freedom. There would only be blood. Just like he said in the dining room.

Energy left my limbs. Who was I kidding? I hadn't eaten since I was stolen. I'd barely had a decent sleep. I existed like a junkie on adrenaline and fear. It was no combination for a long distance run through thickets and bush.

Jethro pulled away, dropping his hands. He smiled. "Your head start begins now, Ms. Weaver. I'd leave if I were you."

Now?

I backpeddled, heart bursting with terror. "How—how long do I have?"

Jethro carefully raised his cuff, looking sedately at the diamond and black watch on his wrist. "I'm a seasoned hunter. I have no doubt I'll find you. And when I do…what those men did to you will be nothing." Cocking his head, he said, "I think forty-five minutes is rather sporting, don't you?"

My mind was no longer there. It was leaping and flying over leaves and dodging ancient trunks.

Run. Go. Run.

"Make it and you're no longer mine…."

Freedom taunted me, making me believe I had a chance. A slim, barely non-existent chance—but still a chance. The muscles in my legs reacted, already poised to take off. I had to trust my body. It knew how to flee.

I could make it. If I did, I would no longer be his pet to torture. But if I didn't….

Don't ask. Don't ask.

"And if I don't?"

Jethro lowered his head, glaring at me beneath his brow. His eyes were tight and dark, glinting with excitement at the upcoming hunt. "Don't and the debt I'll make you repay will make you wish you *had* made it to the boundary." He stepped from the sun's glare, his teeth sparkling like diamonds. "Now…run."

. . .

. . .

I ran.

Continues in FIRST DEBT

"You say I'll never own you. If I win—you willingly give me that right. You sign not only the debt agreement, but another—one that makes me your master until your last breath is taken. You do that, and I'll give you this."

Nila Weaver's family is indebted. Stolen, taken, and bound not by monsters but by an agreement written over six hundred years ago, she has no way out.

She belongs to Jethro as much as she denies it.

Jethro Hawk's patience is running out. His inheritance gift tests, challenges, and surprises him—and not in good ways. He hasn't leashed her but he thinks he might've found a way to bind her forever.

Debts are mounting. Payment waiting.

THE ENTIRE SERIES IN THE INDEBTED SERIES ARE OUT NOW!

Playlist.

Leave out the rest by Linkin Park
In the end by Linkin Park
Yesterday by Fallout Boy
Butterflies and Hurricanes by Muse
Breath of Life by Florence and the Machine
The Lonely by Christina Perri
Titanium by David Guetta
Bittersweet Symphony by The Verve
Battlecry by Imagine Dragons
I know what you did in the dark by Fallout Boys
Copy of A by Nine Inch Nails
Strange Love by Depeche Mode
Precious by Depeche Mode
Louder by Lea Michele

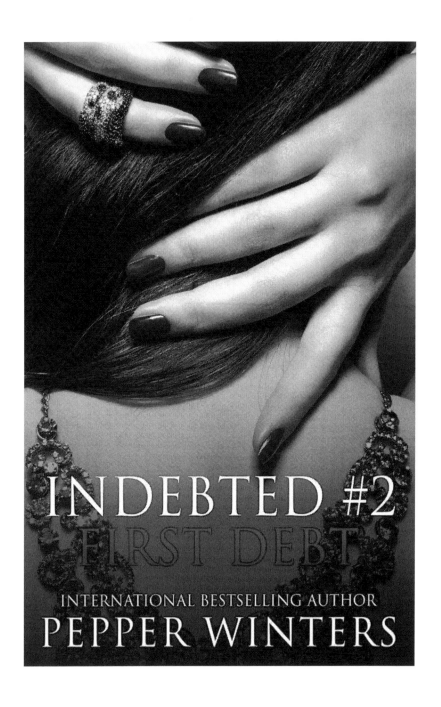

INDEBTED #2

FIRST DEBT

INTERNATIONAL BESTSELLING AUTHOR

PEPPER WINTERS

IF I HAD known my life would change so drastically, I might have planned a little better. Strategized a little smarter, researched a little deeper.

One moment I was the Darling of Milan, the next I was a Weaver Whore.

But despite my lack of skills and weapons, I wasn't ready to go down without a fight.

In fact, I prospered into a woman I'd always been too afraid to find.

I became more than Nila Weaver.

More than daughter, twin-sister, and seamstress.

I became the woman who would bring down a family's legacy.

I evolved into the woman who captured a Hawk.

I STALKED TOWARD the stables and the very lodgings Nila had inhabited the night before.

The image of her bounding away—pristine naked skin glowing in the sunshine and long hair flowing like black silk—played on a loop inside my head.

Everything I'd been prepared for—every argument, every hardship I'd been drilled to expect—hadn't prepared me for the complication that was Nila Weaver. How could I understand and keep my bearings when the bloody woman had more personalities than a Picasso painting?

Sometimes naïve. Sometimes coy. Smart, fearful, proud, *gullible*.

And above all, evolving.

And rapidly.

I wasn't used to…mess. The chaos of a human psyche or the overwhelming pull of emotions was not permitted in my world. In the short time I'd known her, she'd successfully made me feel something I had no fucking right to feel.

Don't admit it.

I balled my hands. No, I wouldn't admit it. I would never verbalize the slow burn of possession in my gut or the confusion in my mind when it came to understanding her.

Run, Nila. Run.

And she had.

Despite her nakedness, lack of sustenance, and the fact that my family had just finished abusing her, she'd glared into my eyes and bounded away like a deer bolting from a gun. A flash of vulnerability glowed on her face before she was swallowed by the forest.

I expected her to faint with her ridiculous condition—an experiment, as it were, to see what she would do when I pretended to give her what she wanted.

Run?

I never for a fucking moment thought she'd do it.

I expected her to cower. To beg. To cry for the men in her life who had let her down. But she'd done none of those things. I'd known her only briefly, yet she'd demanded more of me than any other woman ever had.

It wasn't permitted, and now that she'd run, she'd given away more of the disarray inside her. I'd glimpsed the perplexing woman who'd become my charge, prisoner, and plaything.

Someone who had successfully confused the shit out of me.

As much as you don't understand her, you want her. She came on your tongue, for fuck's sake.

I stopped in my tracks. She'd fought me on every turn, yet the moment I'd claimed her in front of my brothers, she'd given me ultimate control.

She'd spread her legs and forced her hips into my mouth, giving complete authority for me to lick and nibble and drive her high until she shattered, regardless if she meant to do it or not, she'd used me for pleasure.

She'd gotten off on me fingering her.

My cock stiffened.

The taste of her still lingered in my mouth—the phantom pressure of her cunt squeezing my tongue as she rocketed skyward and detonated. Her fingernails had scraped the table, hands spread thanks to the brothers holding her down. But she hadn't squirmed to get away from *me*.

No, she'd fought to get closer.

And I'd obliged.

Drowning myself in her scent, bruising my lips as I licked her harder and *harder*.

She'd squirmed and moaned and gasped. She'd delivered herself into my clutches, all because I knew how to make a woman come.

But she didn't just give me her pleasure.

Christ, no.

She'd given me the briefest taste of how divine it would be to own, not just her body, but her mind and soul, too.

It was addicting.

It was fucking twisting with my head.

I growled under my breath, striding onward. The bloody hard-on I'd sported since she walked into my life poisoned me, turning me against everything I knew, everything I'd embraced since I learned the meaning of survival and discipline.

Hot lust tumbled through my veins.

How could I stay the cold beast I'd been groomed to be when my blood raged for another little taste? Another little indulgence of her tight, wet heat.

Shit, I was going to make myself come if I didn't stop thinking about her.

My cock rippled, totally agreeing.

I shook my head, breaking into a jog toward the stables.

You will remain everything you are.

You will.

There was no other choice in the matter.

I'd been taught to be the master of my emotions. I prided myself on embracing all that he taught me. One little Weaver would not undermine me. This was the way of our world.

My world.

Her world.

No matter how she bewitched me, no matter how she turned my body and willpower against me, I wouldn't give in.

She'd learn that soon enough.

The moment I caught her, she'd learn her place. The moment I had her back in my arms, she'd never run again.

That was a fucking promise.

It's time to hunt.

The stables were empty apart from Kes's polo pony, my father's prized thoroughbred, Black Plague, and my ebony gelding, Fly Like The Wind. That was his show and hunting name. In private, I had another name for him.

Wings.

Because riding him allowed me to fly the fuck away from here and find a small sliver of freedom.

Nila wasn't the only one who wanted to run. Unlike my prey, I faced my demons and embraced them. I made them work for me, rather than control me, and forced them to submit by bowing at my feet.

Just like I'd make her do the moment I found her.

The instant he saw me, Wings' velvet ears pricked, his metal shoes clicking against hay-strewn cobblestone.

A stable boy appeared from mucking out the stalls. "Sir?"

"Saddle him. I mean to leave in fifteen minutes."

You told her you'd give her forty-five.

I shrugged.

There was no point giving her any longer. Her feet would bleed from running barefoot. Her skin would bruise from whatever ludicrous illness she battled. And it would all be for nothing.

Contrary to what she thought of me, I wasn't a monster.

I needed her strong.

Plus, I could grant hours, days even for her to run—but she'd never make it to the boundary.

I knew that completely and utterly.

I knew, because I'd been in the exact same situation she was—only it hadn't been summer like it was now, but middle of winter. Training, he'd said. Masculine growth, he'd lectured. *Run in the snow, become the ice that drips from boughs and stems. Use the primal part of yourself to seek out the edge of our property, or pay the price.*

Three days I'd run, jogged, and crawled. Three days I didn't find the boundary.

I was found the same way I would find Nila. Not through tracking or GPS or even the cameras dotted sparsely over the grounds.

No. I have much better means.

My lips twisted into a smile as I traversed the courtyard from stable to kennel. I whistled, listening to the scrabble of claws and excited yips inside. Then the hounds bounded from their home, bumping into each other, wriggling like they'd been electrocuted.

I stood tall, letting the sea of canines wash around my knees. Eleven in total, all with keen ears, sensitive smell, and the training of a hunter.

Leaving them to sniff manically around the yard, I headed into the tack room where supplies, medicines, and feed were stored for the horses.

My hands drifted over the blanket Nila had used.

My cock lurched, remembering how lost and young she'd looked with hay in her hair and eyes raw from tears. Yet she'd writhed on my fingers like a fucking minx. Her hips had tilted, seeking more as if she were born to be pleasured.

My balls ached for a release. Goddammit, I needed to come. Twice now she'd brought me to the edge, only to ruin the ending.

This wasn't me—I was never this sex-driven or clouded. I couldn't think straight.

The second I caught her, I was taking her. Rules be damned.

You think she wants you, knowing what you're going to do to her?

The question caught me in a trap with sharp teeth.

I froze.

What the hell sort of question was that?

One I'd never had before or even contemplated. My hands curled. I wasn't allowed to consider someone else's wellbeing. Never allowed to be…compassionate. The closest thing I had to a friend was my younger brother, Kestrel. He somehow escaped the conditioning by Bryan Hawk. Kes took after our mother. God rest her soul.

And Daniel.

He took after the fucking psychopath who'd been our uncle until my father killed him for almost exposing us all those years ago.

Not for the first time, I wondered if my entire family tree was batshit crazy.

In the end, none of it mattered. Not heritage, or destinies, or debts.

The moment Nila came on my tongue, she owed me. Not my family. *Me.*

The least she could do was reciprocate.

Shaking my head, I gathered up a saddlebag and stuffed everything I would need inside. With each item I picked up, my heart thawed then refroze. A blanket of snow grew thicker with every heartbeat. As ice glittered and crept over my soul, the silence from my colliding thoughts deepened until all weakness, ideas of running, and traitorous concepts of betraying my family disappeared.

I sighed in relief as I slipped back into my icicle-barred cage.

You're tired, overworked, and dealing with a runaway. Keep your head in the game.

I knew what would happen if I lost control. I could *not* let that happen.

I checked my watch.

Twenty minutes.

Long enough. To her it would feel as if she'd run for miles. She would never know the difference.

Turning to go, I brushed past the shelf where my extra whips and spurs were stored. I grabbed one, sticking a whip through my belt.

It would come in handy if she disobeyed.

Taking a pair of sunglasses, I quickly traded my dress shoes for knee-high riding boots, and checked inventory. Pity I didn't have time to change. Jeans were a bitch to ride in—terrible chafing on long excursions.

But this isn't going to be a long ride.

A smile stretched my lips. No, it wasn't going to be long. *But it will be fun.* And fun wasn't something I got to indulge in very often.

Exiting the gloomy tack room, I squinted in the bright sunlight and slipped the silver-tinted aviators over my eyes. Wings stood obediently by his hobbling post, his equine coat gleaming like the rare black diamonds we mined.

The foxhounds barked and threaded around each other like an organism, never taking their eyes off me as I gathered my reins and placed a foot into the stirrup. Swinging my leg over the massive animal, the rush of being on something so powerful whipped through my bones.

Wings was eighteen hands of pure fucking muscle. He was the fastest horse the Hawks' owned, excluding my father's race horse, Black Plague, and he hadn't been hunting in days.

He pranced in place, his large lungs huffing with anticipation.

The energy vibrating from his bulk infected me, reminding me who I was and the life of privilege I lived.

Twisting his head toward the open grounds of Hawksridge Hall, I dug my spurs into Wings' side.

An insane surge of power detonated through the animal's muscles. Wings went from stationary to flying, his hooves clattering with speed. With a sharp whistle, I summoned my canine companions.

The sharp scent of dug-up turf hit my nostrils as we tore across the grass.

I'm coming for you, Nila Weaver.
I'm coming.
Over the roar of galloping thunder, I commanded, "Chase her."

MY LUNGS BURNED.

My feet stung.

My legs ached.

Every inch of me screamed with fear.

Run. Run. *Run.*

I lowered my head, pushing harder, forcing my body to find non-existent energy and propel myself from hell toward salvation.

How long did I run? I didn't know. How far did I get? Probably not very.

But no matter the stitches in my side or the spasms in my lungs, I kept going. Kept running. I thanked God for my endless nights of pounding the treadmill, and for the first time in my life, was thankful for my small chest size.

Shadows chased my every step. The sun remained blocked by the tree canopy. The yellow glow was still light, still bright, coaxing me on, screaming at me to get up when I stumbled, and ordering my tears to stop as I gasped for breath.

I kept running—zigzagging as much as I could, cutting through a stream, and almost rolling my ankle on the slippery rocks below. I did everything I'd ever seen survivalists do when being hunted.

With my heart whizzing, I bypassed woodland trails, avoided muddy paths, and obscured my scent as much as possible.

But I knew in my heart, it wouldn't be good enough.

He'll find you.

My body begged to stop and let the inevitable happen. To stop punishing myself for no purpose. My mind howled in frustration as lactic acid burned in my limbs.

It won't work. Give up.

Go on, just…stop.

I shook my head, driving myself harder.

He'll catch you.

It wasn't a matter of if, but when.

I could run for years, and he would still find me. How did I know? I didn't trust him.

I didn't believe he'd let me get away so easily. Everything about him was a carefully scripted lie. Why should his word be any different?

I had no doubt if he *didn't* find me, something else would—a snare, a trap—something just waiting to ambush its prey.

Every footfall I tensed, waiting for death—wondering if that last step would trigger a net or an arrow to my heart.

Stop running.

Just…stop, Nila.

My breathless inner voice was tired and hungry and completely worn out. My muscles cramped. My mind seized with too many questions.

At least it was summer, and I didn't have to combat the cold on top of everything else. My skin glistened with sweat from exercising so hard.

But I hated the defeat in my soul—the rapidly spilling courage and hope.

This wasn't about the chase. We all knew who would win. It was about defiance. The word that I never knew or put into practice until last night, but now I lived and breathed it. I would be the most defiant thorn, stabbing holes in Jethro's carefully made plans.

I would never be able to win. The only way I had a chance at surviving long enough to reap vengeance on the men who ruined my ancestors was to fight his ice with fire.

I had to burn.

I had to blaze.

I had to cinder his beliefs and control to the ground. And smear his soul with the ashes of his sins.

A loud howl came on the breeze.

My knees locked, slamming me to a standstill.

No. Please, no.

My heart squeezed. I should've guessed. He wouldn't run after me like a typical chase. Why would he waste his energy hunting in the wrong direction?

He was smarter than that. Colder than that. He'd use the tools he had to make sure this little inconvenience was over and dealt with. Of course, he would use the very animals who'd become my friends last night.

Teaching me not one but two lessons in quick succession. One, the animals currently tracking me, currently hunting me, were not my friends, no matter how warm and cosy they'd been last night. And two, everything here, no matter human or animal, would not hesitate to kill me.

The thought depressed then infected me with strength I'd only just become acquainted with. There was no hope at making Jethro feel. The only hope I had was to fight ruthlessness with ruthlessness.

I had to contest him on every step and ignite that spark buried deep within.

Another howl and a bark.

Energy shot through my body, hot and bullet-fierce.

I took off again, sprinting down a small hill, holding onto branches as a rush of vertigo threatened to spill me into nettles and brambles.

The collar on my throat was heavy, but at least it had warmed. The diamonds no longer felt alien but a part of me. The courage of my ancestors. The spirit-strength of women I'd never met, living in a piece of jewellery throbbing with their guidance and energy.

The hatred and repulsion I felt toward the collar disappeared. Yes, the Hawks had given it to me, sentencing me to death with an action I couldn't think about, but they'd given me a piece of my family. A piece of history I could use to my advantage.

Another bark, followed by a loud whistle.

You can't outrun him.

I scowled at my pessimism.

But you can hide.

I shook my head, fighting tears as a twig dug into the sole of my foot.

I wouldn't be able to hide. He came with foxhounds. Their noses were legendary.

Up high. Get up high.

I skidded to a stop. My neck craned as I peered up the length of a knobbly-looking tree. The branches were symmetrically placed, the leaves not exactly thick but its trunk strong enough to take me from earth to sky.

I'd never climbed anything in my life. I could fall to my death. I could cripple myself when I suffered a vertigo wave. I'd never been stupid enough to try.

You've never had to run for survival, either.

Shoving useless fears away, I moved toward the tree with outstretched hands. It didn't matter I'd never climbed one. It didn't matter I'd avoided all gym games and apparatuses, because I only ended up getting hurt.

I would climb the damn thing and conquer it.

I have no choice.

Either stay on the ground and sit quietly for him to arrive, run blindly through woodland, or climb.

I'll climb.

My toes gripped the base of the tree as I reached for the first branch. I put my weight on it.

It snapped.

Shit!

Another bark—loud and clear, just over the ridge.

I moved.

Scrabbling at the tree, I hugged the rough bark and hurled myself up, reaching like a crazed, climb-retarded monkey for a branch just out of grabbing distance. I didn't think I'd make it. I closed my eyes in preparation for a painful fall, but by some miracle, my fingers latched around the bough, clinging harder than ever before.

Go. *Go!*

I gave myself over to a skill I'd never used but hoped remained dormant in some part of my human evolution. I placed my foot against the bark, pulling upward with my hands. I reached for the next.

And the next.

And the next.

My breath came hard and ragged, my heart an overworking drum.

I used the tree as my own personal stepladder to freedom, climbing higher and higher until I daren't look down in case I blacked out and tumbled from heaven to hell.

A large thundering came, overshadowing the yips and excited

barks of dogs. The leaves around me shuddered as footfalls of a bigger beast came closer.

Had Jethro come with others? Would Daniel be with him? Or even his father?

My skin rippled with hatred. I meant what I'd said. I would find a way to kill them all before this was over. I wouldn't let them spill any more Weaver blood. It was the Hawks' turn.

I'll make them pay.

Turning slowly, cursing my shaking legs and suddenly nervous hands, I faced the forest floor from which I'd climbed. I was at least two and half stories up.

I closed my eyes, swallowing hard.

Don't fall. Don't even think about falling.

Faintness existed on my outer vision, teasing me with the awfulness of what could happen. I dug my fingernails into the bark, lowering myself slowly onto the branch. The minute I was sitting, with the roughness of the tree biting into my unprotected behind, I wrapped an arm around the trunk and sat wedged against the wood.

I looked around for weapons, but there were none. No pine cones. No easily snappable branches to stab him with. All I had was the element of disappearing. A naked girl vanishing into the green haze of the forest.

My heart lodged in my throat as the first dog appeared. I didn't recognise him from the night spent in the kennels. He whirled around and around, sniffing the spot where I'd stood.

Another dog appeared, then another and another, pouring from the woods like ants, growling in delight at the strength of my trail.

Distress gripped my stomach.

Go away, damn you.

Then, *he* arrived.

Sitting proudly astride a black horse, so big it looked like a beast from the underworld, he cantered into being. His polished boots soaked up the dappling sunlight; a whip with a diamond wedged on the handle glinted menacingly.

He looked in his element.

A gentleman out hunting with his faithful steed and gallant party of dogs. His silvering hair sparkled like tinsel in the sun. His ageless face the epitome of ferocity and winning.

In his late twenties, Jethro wore command like one would wear cologne. His strong jaw, pursed lips, and sculptured brow shouted power—*true* power. And there was nothing anyone could do about it.

Sitting with his back ramrod straight and hands fisted in the horse's reins, he was...majestic. It didn't matter if I hated him or wanted him. That fact would always be true.

Excitement blazed in his eyes as he scanned the undergrowth, a smile teasing his lips.

How long had this farce been going on? An hour? Maybe two? Had he kept his word and given me the full forty-five minutes? Somehow, I doubted it.

"Find her, goddammit," he snapped, losing his smile and glaring at the dogs.

The canines wove around his horse's legs, sniffing, darting into bushes only to come back to try all over again.

Jethro spun in his saddle, planting a hand on the rump of his horse, glowering into the dense foliage. "Have you stopped running, Ms. Weaver, or have you somehow managed to trick my companions?" His voice caused the leaves to shiver, almost as if they wished to hide me further.

I held my breath, hoping to God he didn't look up.

A foxhound with a large black ear barked and took off down the path I would've continued on if I hadn't decided to prolong my freedom by hiding.

Jethro shook his head. "No. She's around here. Find her."

The dog licked its muzzle, baying in the direction its wriggling body wanted to go. The rest of the dogs, either brainwashed by their leader or picking up on the scent of rabbit, all joined in the urge to leave.

My heart galloped. *Please, let him go.*

I might have a chance, after all.

The horse pranced—hyped up on the dogs' energy, wanting to chase after them.

Jethro stayed steadfast, his hand expertly holding the reins so tight the poor beast had no choice but to tread on the spot. His long legs wrapped hard around the animal, sticking glinting silver spurs into its sides. "Wait," he growled.

The horse huffed, tossing its head, fighting the tight possession of its mouth. It cantered in place, puffing hard through velvet nostrils.

The dogs disobeyed.

Their patience was done and with a loud howl, they took off in a cloud of tan, white, and black.

"Christ's sake," Jethro muttered. "Fine." Digging his heels hard, the horse broke into a gallop, disappearing in a whirl of black through the undergrowth.

Shakes. They attacked me hard and fast the second he'd disappeared.

Hope attacked me second.

Unbelievable hope hijacked my limbs turning me into shivering jelly until I was sure the entire tree vibrated. Did I actually stand a chance at making it to freedom? Could I make it to the boundary and escape their clutches?

I could save all of us—my father, brother, future daughters.

"Life is complicated, Threads. You don't know the half of it." My father's voice popped into my head. Anger filled me. Dreadful, terrible anger toward the man who was supposed to keep me safe. If he knew this would happen, why hadn't he protected me? I'd always trusted him. Always followed his rule explicitly. To see him as human who made a mistake—*many* mistakes—hurt.

A lot.

A wave of sickness had me clutching the tree; I swallowed back the misfortune of having vertigo along with the emotional upheaval of what I'd lived through.

The foreignness of dried saliva on my body made my skin crawl. The memory of shattering beneath Jethro's tongue totally blasphemous.

The sun glinted through the canopy—highlighting trails of where men had licked me.

My stomach threatened to evict the emptiness inside. I was hungry, dehydrated, and cracked out on adrenaline. But beneath it all, my soul ached with growing pains. My claws were forming, my tail twitching with annoyance.

It didn't escape my knowledge that, as a kitten, I'd stayed on the ground. But now I was in a tree—did that make me a panther? A feline predator that hunted from above, unseen?

I liked that idea.

Forcing myself to concentrate on the trees surrounding me, I strained my ears to hear.

Only insects and birds. No Jethro.

How far was it to the boundary? What direction should I go?

Time seemed to slow, braiding with the fluffy white clouds above as if there were no cares in the world.

It was hypnotic.

The lack of sustenance in my stomach made me tired; I needed a rest.

Just a little one.

The screech of a crow snapped me awake.

Shit!

How could I have faded out like that?

How long had passed? It could've been hours or just minutes.

I have no idea.

My heart rabbited, energy heating my limbs. *Move. Run again.*

Jethro was far away. I couldn't hear him or the howls of hounds.

Looking at the ground, my lungs crawled into my mouth. Down there, I didn't feel safe...up here, I did.

Move!

I couldn't move.

I would probably cling to my sanctuary until I died of hunger and became fossilized. To be found like a mosquito wrapped in amber a thousand years from now.

The thought made me smile.

Would they be able to bring me back to life like in *Jurassic Park*, outliving the Hawks by thousands of years to finally have the last laugh?

A twig snapped below, wrenching my attention back to the forest floor.

Oh, shit.

Squirrel stood below, looking directly into my eyes. His bristle tail wagged back and forth, his tongue lolling happily. He yipped, scrabbling at the tree.

Tears.

I couldn't hold them back.

The one dog that'd granted such comfort last night was the one to ruin my future today.

How could you?

I wanted to scream at him for destroying me.

Jethro stepped silently from the shadows like a glacial ghost. His horse was hidden, along with the pack of dogs. In his hand, he held the whip and a saddlebag.

He touched the end of the whip to his temple in a salute. "Well played, Ms. Weaver. I didn't think you'd have the coordination to climb. I must admit, foolhardy of me not to think of all avenues." A smile crept across his lips. "I suppose desperation will make one do things they might not ordinarily be able to achieve."

Stepping forward, he nudged Squirrel out of the way. "What I would like to know is how did you manage to stay up there? Did you not have another one of your annoying fainting incidents?"

The oxygen in my lungs turned into spikes and spurs, digging painfully into my sides. I held tighter to the tree, wondering if I could kill him from up here.

When I didn't respond, he smirked. "You look positively wild up there. My own little forest creature, caught in my web."

My arms lashed tighter around the trunk.

Jethro shifted, his movements quiet even with the leaf matter littering the earth. The happiness from his victory dissolved. "Come down. It's over. I've won." He smiled, but it didn't reach his eyes. "Or do me a favour and fall out. That vertigo has to be useful for something." Spreading his arms, he muttered, "Go on, I'll catch you."

The strength that seemed to feed off Jethro's cruelty churned hot in my stomach. "You should know me by now. I won't obey you. You or the rest of your family."

He chuckled. "Found a backbone up there, did you?"

I bared my teeth. "I found it the moment you stole me from my family and showed me what a monster you are."

He held up the whip, a shadow falling over his features. "I didn't *steal* you—you belong to us. I only took what was rightfully mine. And I'm no monster."

My heart raced. "You don't know the meaning of the word, so how can you define yourself?"

He narrowed his eyes. "I think the height of the tree is giving you false confidence. I doubt you'd be talking to me that way if you were down here." He twitched the whip. "Where I could reach you, hit you, make you behave like you ought to."

He's testing you.

I tilted my chin, looking down my nose. "You're right. I probably wouldn't, but right now I have the advantage, and I mean to use it."

He laughed, absently stroking Squirrel's head as the dog plonked himself by Jethro's feet. "Advantage? I wouldn't go that far, Ms. Weaver."

My skin crawled at the use of my last name. He didn't use it out of consideration or even because the address was my identity—he used it to keep the barrier between us cold and impenetrable.

What is he so afraid of? That my first name will make him waver in his ludicrous family's goals?

"Why don't you call me Nila?" I leaned forward, not caring I was naked or stuck in a tree. I had the power for however long I kept him talking. "Are you afraid using my first name is too personal? That you'll start to feel something for me?"

He sneered. "You're doing it again."

"Doing what?"

"What you did at the stables. Showing me sides of you that you've kept hidden, in the hopes it will spark some sort of humanness in me." He shook his head. "I'm not someone you can manipulate."

A small smile stretched my lips. "I already did." Gathering my leaf-tangled hair, I draped it over my shoulder. The last dregs of sunshine disappeared behind a cloud, leaving us in green shadows.

"What?" His nostrils flared, his temper sparking like an uncontrolled blaze.

I smiled, enjoying his annoyance. He claimed he was cold-hearted and impervious. He lied.

I'll show him. I'll prove he's as ill-equipped to play this charade as I am.

"Do you want me to paint it out for you? To show you how hypocritical you are?"

He grabbed Squirrel's ear, making the dog flinch. Squirrel moved away, an angry reproof in his black eyes. "Careful, Ms. Weaver," Jethro whispered. "Everything you say up there will have consequences when you get down here."

I refused to let fear quiet me. Not when I had the freedom to speak—no matter how brief.

"Nila. My name is *Nila.* Say it. It seems we're going to be spending a lot of time together, so you might as well save yourself breath when you need to summon me. Or do you like reminding yourself that I'm a Weaver? Your so-called hated enemy. Do you need to reinforce that knowledge every time? How about that beloved silence you keep claiming you wield? You think you hide so well. Listen up. You don't."

Jethro backed away, crossing his arms. A dark, unreadable expression etched his face. "I call you by your last name out of *respect*." He spat the last word. "We aren't friends. We aren't even acquaintances. We've been thrown into this together, and it's up to me to make the fucking rules on how you'll be treated."

We both froze, breathing hard.

Oh, my God.

He's been thrown into this. My mind charged ahead with questions. Did he not want this?

Was he forced, same as me?

Jethro hissed, "Get out of the fucking tree. I want to be home before dark."

Hoarding my questions and the small furl of hope, I pointed at the sky. "It's already dusk. How long did you hunt me, Jethro? How long did you search for a vulnerable, weak, little Weaver?"

He ignored my questions, focusing on the last part of my sentence. "You think you're weak?"

"No, *you* think I'm weak."

"How so?"

I straightened my shoulders. There was a...genuineness in his tone. The animosity between us suddenly...disappeared. It took me a few seconds to answer. My voice was quieter, less abrasive. "You think I'll put up with what you plan to do with me—that I won't fight? That I won't do everything in my power to stop you from killing me?"

His face battled with a smirk and understanding. He settled on a frosty grimace. "Of course, I expect it. If you didn't, I'd say you were already dead inside. No one wants to die."

I had no reply to that. A chill darted over my skin. For the first time, we were talking. So much had happened since we met. There was so much between us that it felt as if we'd been fighting this war for years—which maybe we had, and we just didn't know it.

"What do you mean to do with me?" I whispered, dropping all pretence and opting for truth.

He jerked, his eyes tightening at the softness in my tone. "I've told you."

I shook my head. "No, you haven't." I looked away. "You've threatened me. You've made me come in a room full of men, and you've told me the method of my death. None of that—"

"You're saying that isn't being honest about your future?"

I glared. "I wasn't finished. I was going to say, before you rudely interrupted, what *else* is there?"

His mouth parted in surprise. "Else? You're asking what else there is to this debt?"

"Forget the debt. Tell me what to expect. Give me that at least, so I can prepare myself."

He cocked his hip, trailing the whip through the rotten leaves by his feet. "Why?"

"Why?"

He nodded. "Why should I give you what you want? This isn't a power exchange, Ms. Weaver."

I bit my lip, wincing at the sudden hunger pains in my stomach. What did I have that he wanted? What could I hope to bribe him with or entice some feeling of protectiveness and kindness?

I have nothing.

I hung my head.

Silence existed, thick and heavy like the rolling dusk.

Amazingly, Jethro murmured, "Come down, and I'll answer three questions."

My head shot up. "Give me answers now, before I come down."

He planted his boots deeper into the mulch-covered dirt. "Don't push me, woman. You've already gotten more conversation out of me than my family. Don't make me hate you for causing me to feel weak."

"*You* feel weak?"

"Ms. fucking Weaver. Climb down here, right now." His temper exploded, smashing through his iceberg shell, giving me a hint at the man I knew existed.

A man with blood as hot as any other.

A man with so many unresolved issues, he'd tied himself into untieable knots.

My heartbeat clamoured as Jethro's ice fell back into place, blocking everything I just glimpsed.

I sucked in a breath. "Hypocrite."

He seethed. "*What* did you just say?"

"You heard me." Standing on awkward legs, I hugged the tree. "Three questions? I want five."

"Three."

"Five."

Jethro moved suddenly, stomping to the base of the tree, gripping the bottom branch. "If you make me climb up there to get you, you'll be fucking sorry."

"Fine!" I moved carefully, wondering how the hell I would climb down. "Call me Nila and I'll obey."

He growled under his breath. "Goddammit, you push me."

Someone has to. Someone has to smash that hypocritical shell.

I waited, face pressed against knobbly bark, fighting against the weakness in my limbs from exhaustion and hunger.

The mere thought of climbing down terrified me.

Jethro paced, crunching the undergrowth beneath his black boots. He snapped, "I will *never* say your first name. I will never be controlled into doing something I don't want to do ever fucking again—*especially* by you. So, go ahead, stay in your tree. I'll just camp down here until you either fall or wither away. I don't revel in the thought of you dying in such a fashion. I don't relish the conversation I would have when I returned empty-handed with just a diamond collar sliced from your lifeless neck, but never think you can make me do something I don't want to do. You'll lose."

He smashed the whip against the tree trunk, making me jump. "Is that *quite* understood?"

His temper seethed from below, covering me like a horrible quilt of scorn. I pressed my forehead against the bark, cursing myself.

For a moment, he'd seemed normal.

For one fraction of time, I didn't fear him because I saw something in him that might, just might, be my salvation.

But he'd been pushed too far by others. He'd reached his limit and had nothing else to give. He'd shut down, and the brief glimpses I saw weren't hope—they were historic glints at the man he might've been before he'd been turned into…this.

I climbed.

It was a lot harder going down than going up. My eyesight danced with grey, my knees wobbled, and sweat broke out on my skin, even though I was freezing now the night had claimed the day.

I battled with him and lost.

Time to face my future.

The closer I came to the ground, the more fear swallowed me.

I cried out as Jethro's cold hands latched around my waist,

plucking me from the tree as if I were a dead flower, and spinning me to face him.

His beautiful face of sharp lines and five o'clock shadow was shaded with darkness. The hoots of owls and trills of roosting birds surrounded us.

"I have a good mind to whip you." His voice licked over me with frost.

I dropped my eyes. I had no more energy. It was depleted. Gone.

When I didn't retaliate, he shook me. "What? No reply from the famous Weaver who swore at my father and brotherhood and earned the right to run for her freedom?"

I looked up, stealing myself against his golden eyes. "Yes and what was the point?"

"There's a point to everything we do. If you've forgotten it, then you're blinded by self-pity."

A ball of fire rekindled in my belly. "Self-pity? You think I *pity* myself?"

He shook his head. "I don't think. I know." Letting me go, he grabbed the saddlebag resting against another tree and pulled out a blanket. Spreading it over roots and crinkly leaves, he ordered, "Sit, before you fall."

I blinked. "We're not—we're not leaving for the Hall?"

He glowered. "We'll leave when I'm damn well ready. Sit."

I sat.

WHAT THE FUCK are you doing?

I couldn't answer that. I had no clue.

I should throw her over my shoulder and escort her back to Hawksridge. Instead, I made her sit. In the middle of a forest. At dusk. What the fuck?

Nila sat by my feet smiling sadly as Bolly, the top foxhound, nuzzled into her naked side—his wet nose nudged against her breast as he whined for attention.

She sighed, hugging him close, pressing a kiss into the ruff of his neck. "You outted me, you rascal." Her voice wobbled, even though a tight smile stayed locked on her face. "I want to hate you for it, but I can't."

Bolly yipped, hanging his head, almost as if he understood exactly what she jabbered on about.

I stood staring at the odd woman—the woman who, even now, surprised me.

Something twisted deep inside. Something I had no fucking intention of analysing.

Everywhere I looked, she was scratched and bruised. New bruises on top of old bruises, shallow lacerations that'd scabbed over and deeper ones still oozing blood. My eyes fell to her feet. They were covered in cuts with a puncture on the fleshy part of her large toe.

I waited for a twinge of guilt—for that humanness I told her I didn't possess. The only emotion I got was annoyance at her hurting herself. She'd marred herself, and that reflected badly on me.

"You would rather slice yourself to pieces while running away from me, than suffer a few debts by my side?"

Her head snapped up, dark eyes arresting mine. "I would gladly hurt myself to gain my freedom."

"And why is that pain any different from the pain I might give you?"

So much feeling existed in her gaze as she whispered, "Because it's *my* choice." She let Bolly go, dropping her hands into her naked lap. "It's what I've been saying all along. You've stripped me of any rights. You've planted photographs ruining the only life I've ever known. You've destroyed—"

Something cold and angry slithered in my heart. "You talk of hurt and pain—as if I've treated you so unfairly." Leaning over her, I hissed, "Tell me one instance in which I've hurt you."

She frowned, her body neither flinching nor curling away from my encroachment. "Pain comes in many appearances, Jethro. Just because you haven't raised your hand to me—apart from a slap in the dining room—doesn't mean you haven't hurt me more than anyone else before. You degraded me."

"I've been nothing but civil. I wiped it all away for you. I did what I promised."

She shook her head, sadness glassing her eyes. "You think that by taking me at the end, everything that happened is forgotten?" She laughed; it was full of brittle anger. "You say I belong to you—that I'm yours—custom-made and born for your torment." A single tear fled her gaze. "Then why didn't you stop them? Why let them have me if I'm meant to be yours?"

I stumbled backward. "*That's* what hurt you the most? The fact that I let my father welcome you the way it's always been done? That I'm obeying *tradition*? You're hurt because I'm following the rules—the same rules which you don't seem to comprehend?"

My brain hurt. I'd never talked so much in my life. Never argued a subject or permitted myself to understand another's point of view. That wasn't my world.

Shut her up.

I hated her questions and accusations. They didn't just stop at one but dragged a whole caravan of inquiry and slurs behind it. She made me second guess everything I knew and was.

I hated it. I hated *her*.

She said, "Those rules aren't mine. I'm not yours or theirs. I'm telling you how wrong all of this is, yet you shut down the minute I see something normal inside you."

Growling under my breath, I grabbed the saddlebag and turfed the supplies onto the blanket.

Bolly moved in front of Nila, sniffing at the items as if they were a danger to the woman he'd helped hunt down.

I was a hypocrite?

Look at the bloody dog.

Nila glanced at the packets strewn on the plaid. I shoved the damn dog out of the way, reaching for her.

She ducked, unable to disguise her flash of terror.

My stomach twisted. I bared my teeth. "What? You think I'm going to hurt you?" Breathing hard, I grabbed a blister packet and threw it at her. "I'm not going to hurt you, even though my whip would like to strike something more than just my horse after the issues you've caused."

Her dark eyes met mine, rebellion bright. Then her eyebrow rose as she glanced at what I'd tossed her. "You—"

I snatched the packet and popped out two high-strength painkillers. Stealing her hand, I placed both into her palm. She cupped them instantly.

"You're hurt. I told you I'm not a monster, Ms. Weaver. Would a beast give you something to mute your pain? The same pain, I might add, that you brought on by yourself?"

Her face went white, her fingers unlocking to peer at the two white tablets. Her face twisted with a mixture of disbelief and utter confusion.

Another dagger to my gut. There was something about her injuries and vulnerabilities that were the perfect chisel to my iron-clad resolve.

The resolve that'd saved me from myself. The lifestyle that I'd been taught when nothing else had worked.

Fuck.

Looking away, I tossed a water bottle at her. She caught it clumsily. Unscrewing the lid, she placed the tablets on her tongue, and drained the contents in three seconds flat. She wiped her mouth, eyeing up the bag by my feet.

Silence existed for a heartbeat. Then two.

Her eyes met mine, granting me something I hadn't sought to

gain. Her gratefulness. The fight and future was forgotten—her bodily needs overtaking everything else. And I was the one who could give her what she needed.

"If you're looking for food, I have some."

She swallowed hard.

I forced myself to shove aside my tangled emotions, grabbing my icy persona with both hands. "I need something from you first."

She grabbed the damn dog again.

I hated how her arms lashed around him, seeking something else she needed—something I couldn't give her.

I whistled.

Bolly instantly heeled, leaving Nila rejected on the tartan blanket.

She rolled her shoulders, looking longingly at the dog. Slowly, the strength I grew to recognise cloaked her; her eyes met mine. "Fine. What do you want?"

Everything.

The parts of myself I kept hidden, driven so far inside I'd forgotten they'd even existed, sparked with possession.

"You owe me something."

Her gaze popped wide. "Excuse me?"

I fell to my haunches, balancing myself with a fingertip placed on the ground. My heart beat thickly. "I gave you something in that dining room…remember?"

Her lips curled in disgust. "You gave me to your father and your so-called brothers."

I shook my head. "More than that. I gave you freedom. I took their memory and made it mine…" I devoured her with my gaze, saliva filling my mouth remembering her taste.

Realization slammed into her. "You can't be serious. You expect me to repay the *favour*?"

I balled my hands.

She shook her head. "No way. You're insane."

Insane?

I couldn't do it.

I'd done my best to be civil. I'd spoken calmly, rationally. I'd been perfectly cordial and fought everything I was to become something I knew I had to be.

I was the exact opposite of insane.

"You really shouldn't have said that," I muttered.

She knew what I expected. I'd told her. It wasn't my fault she was totally stupid. I'd warned her never to question my mental state. And I wouldn't permit such ridicule from a girl who didn't recognise the entire world was fucking nuts.

Punish her.

I stood, towering over her. Moving forward, I grabbed the whip from the top of the bag, slapping it against my palm. "On your knees."

She scurried backward, slamming into a tree behind her. "Jethro. Please—"

I pinched the brow of my nose. "You insulted my mental state again, Ms. Weaver. I told you what would happen the next time you did." Bending over, I grabbed her shoulder. "On your damn knees." With a sharp push, I shoved her from sitting to kneeling.

Tears streaked her dirty face. "I didn't mean—I'm—"

I cocked my head.

If she apologised, I'd stop. Just one little word. A sign that she was permitting my power over her.

It wobbled unsaid between us. *Sorry. I'm sorry. Please, forgive me.*

Her lips tasted the words, the syllables echoed silently in my ears.

But then she ruined it by sucking in a breath and clamping her lips together. With a glare that shot heat straight into my heart, she planted her hands on the blanket, and cocked her hips.

Fuck. Me.

My cock immediately sprang to attention. The perfect lines of her overly skinny body. The pert breasts and hard muscles of her back and thighs.

Shit.

I squeezed my eyes. *What the fuck is going on with me?*

Sure, I wanted her. Sure, I wanted to use her and come so deep inside her, she'd taste me for days. But lust had never made me see things like this. Never made me lose the fine frost of control. Every second spent with her undid all my hard work.

She was my pet. Her wellbeing and happiness hinged on me. Just like Bolly, Wings, and all the other hounds tethered in the forest just out of ear reach. I'd left them there so I could sneak upon her silently.

I'd known she was up there. I'd felt her eyes boring into me.

But this was all a game.

What was the fun in reaching the destination when the chase was the best part?

Nila looked over her shoulder, daring me with flames in her eyes. "I hate you."

Her words slammed me back to earth, her fire somehow giving me back my ice. I smiled. "You don't know the meaning of hate. Not yet."

Hair fell over her shoulder, hanging thick and enticing. "You're wrong again, Mr. Hawk. I know the meaning of it. It's becoming a favourite emotion of mine. I told you before you'll never own me. And you never will."

That reminds me.

"I caught you. You agreed you'd willingly sign that nonsense away."

"What nonsense?"

I fell to my knees, positioning myself behind her. Grasping her hips, I dragged her against my front. My jaw locked as my erection dug into her firm arse.

She cried out, trying to squirm away—not that it did any good.

I hissed between my teeth at the delicious friction she caused.

"You're mine. You ran and failed. I'll have the papers drawn up to ensure you know your place, and we can put this idiocy of you not believing this is your future behind us."

She gasped as I rocked into her, pressing punishingly hard.

Fuck, who was I kidding? She owned *me*. Her laughable rage, her stupid sense of fairness. Somehow, she'd ensorcelled me.

Fuck.

Forcing my terrifying thoughts away, I said, "I've made you come. I gave you a gift, which you took wholeheartedly. It's your turn to do the same for me."

The whip grew slippery in my grip as I pulled back. "You have three questions, and I have a point to make. You ask, and I'll make it. We both get what we want. Then, when it's all over, we'll go home and start our lives together."

"Until you kill me."

I sighed. Really? She was so repetitive. "Yes, until I kill you. Now, ask your first question."

She smashed her lips together, thoughts skittering over her face. Fine, if she needed prompting, I would oblige.

The whip was firm—plaited black leather and two supple ends made for shocking with noise rather than pain. Wings was so obedient, he didn't need it most of the time. It was fitting to use the equipment on something else that needed breaking in.

I stroked her lower back, ignoring her whimper. "You're green and unbroken, Ms. Weaver. Don't think I won't tame you before this game is through."

I struck.

The sound of the two leather ends snapping together ricocheted through the woods.

She cried out, rolling her hips.

"Question, Ms. Weaver. I'll keep striking until you ask."

To prove my point, I hit her again. "That's for your smart mouth undermining my control in front of my father and brothers."

Her skin pinked as I struck again. "That's for riding my hand like I'd given you everything you ever dreamed of, then looking at me as if I was a piece of shit."

"How long? How long will you keep me alive?" she screamed, staying my hand.

I paused. In all honesty, I didn't know. Her mother had been my father's charge for over two years. She'd known her place enough to permit a brief visit to her old family to sever ties once and for all.

I doubted Nila would ever be so well trained, but I didn't want to rush what we had. After all, once we reached the final debt, it would be over.

And that...didn't sit well in my gut.

"It depends," I murmured, stroking her burning skin.

I waited to see if she'd ask another question, but she remained silent. Pliant and listening. Her quietness soothed my nerves, and I allowed myself to give her a little of what she needed.

You're doing that far too often.

I shot the voice in my head.

"Years, Ms. Weaver. We have years ahead of us."

Her head sagged, lolling forward. Quietly, another question came. "And the debts? How bad are they? What do I need to prepare for?"

"Ah, ah, ah, I said you could have three questions in total. That was three in one breath. Pick one or forfeit anymore."

Nila sighed, a small hiccup jolted her frame. "How bad are they?"

I struck her. Short and fast. The noise was worse that the bite. I knew. I'd been on the receiving end myself.

"They start easy. Simple really."

She sucked in a breath, already knowing what I would add. "Then they get worse."

I struck her again, loving the bloom of red and the way every muscle in her sinewy body twitched. Throwing the whip to the ground, I murmured, "One more. Don't be shy."

Her breath was ragged. "Will—will you ever be nice to me?"

The question hung between us, so at odds to the scene of her on her hands and knees and me positioned behind her. It wrapped around us with sadness, digging the newly placed dagger deeper into my heart.

"I am nice. Once you get to know me."

Her small laugh surprised both of us. "You're a lot of things, but nice is not one of them."

Anger boiled in my stomach. "You pissed me off before I had the opportunity to be nice. Didn't I say you deserved to be rewarded after this afternoon? I have many things to lavish you with, Ms. Weaver. You only have to give in. Grant me the power. Give up and stop fighting me." I stroked her spine, gritting my teeth against the ripple of pre-cum shooting up my cock. Goddammit, she was too delicious. Too strong. Too much.

She's a Weaver.

I shook my head, dispelling everything until only silence remained.

"You must know I can't do that. I've given up power to men all my life. I stupidly let my father control me, believing he knew what was best for me. And you know what that got me? A one-way ticket to hell to play with a devil I never knew existed." She looked over her shoulder, making eye contact. "Why should I give you that courtesy? Why should I let you rule the remaining shortness of my sad, little life?"

For once, I was speechless.

Nila murmured, "You can't reply, because you know this is wrong. On some level, you know the only right thing to do is to let me go and forget about this madness, but you won't. Just like I won't give you the power you seek. Just like I will never stop fighting you."

She suddenly shot forward, breaking my hold on her hips.

My heart raced at the thought of her running again, but she turned to face me, kneeling upright so we were eye-to-eye. The muscles in her stomach shadowed in the rapidly gathering darkness, her white skin glowing with interspersed cuts and bruises.

"You said I owe you. I agree. You gave me something in that

dining room. As much as you think you were only helping save my mental state, you showed me more than you probably wanted. I *see* you, Jethro Hawk. I see what you're trying to hide, so don't delude yourself into thinking I buy your hypocritical bullshit."

Crawling forward, her tiny hands landed on my belt, releasing the button and zipper in one short second. It was my turn to blink in shock.

She's a seamstress, idiot.

She dealt with buttons and zippers every day—they were her forte. Dealing with what lived behind them however was entirely another.

I hated, positively hated, that she'd stolen my power again. She'd drugged me with her witch potion, making me think only with my dick.

Fisting her hair, I growled, "You're on thin ground, Ms. Weaver."

Her temper exploded like a firework. She snarled, "Wrong. I'm on Hawk ground, and I'm still standing. You want me to pay you back? Fine. Tell me what to do, then feed me and take me back to your vile home. I'm ready for this day to end."

My mind went numb as her hand disappeared into my jeans, cupping me boldly.

"Or better yet, take what I damn well give you."

I HAD NO words for what I was doing.

Seriously, no words.

Part of me hated myself for being drawn to Jethro even now—especially after he'd hunted me down and punished me like some animal. But the other part—the bigger part—loved the woman I was becoming. I didn't have anyone to rely on. I had no one saying what was right or wrong. The rules of everyday life had no place in this new existence, and if Jethro thought I would play by *his* rules, he was a fucking idiot.

His erection leapt in my hands, hot and scalding—the only part of him warm.

His golden eyes were blank of all feeling, and for one blessed moment, he stared at me with lust. Only lust.

Then anger saturated him, his fingers latching around my invading wrist. "What the fuck do you think you're doing?"

I tugged the waistband of his boxer-briefs with my free hand, twisting my other from his grip, and sliding my fingers into the dark heat of his underwear. He locked his jaw as I traced the length of his cock.

"I'm paying you back. This is what you had in mind, right? An orgasm for an orgasm?"

He growled low in his chest, his eyes narrowing with hate and need.

Don't lie to me, you bastard.

He opened his mouth, but no words came out. I squeezed him

hard—hard enough to cause shooting pains in my palm.

He jerked in my hold. "*Jesus.*"

That one word switched the rage splashing my insides into lust-blazing gasoline. The hardness of him sent electricity humming in my fingertips. The anger brimming below the surface turned my insides into hot liquid.

This.

This power.

This body-consuming connection.

It was pure.

Simple.

Intoxicating.

The whipping he'd given me hadn't made me wet. I'd never associated pain with pleasure. Sure, I'd read the books and heard rumours about how exciting a BDSM relationship could be with someone you trusted implicitly, but that was the key difference.

I didn't trust Jethro.

At all.

This was a battle.

Every time we touched, licked, and eventually fucked, it would be war.

And only one victor would come out alive.

I have every intention of winning.

Sex to me didn't come with past perceptions or notions. Sex wasn't wrapped up with love or sweetness in my brain. In a way, I had my father to thank for keeping me secluded and untouched. I'd uncovered an aptitude for delivering pleasure—an affinity for the basest of need.

I trembled, glowing so damn bright inside, I felt as if I'd swallowed the stars.

Jethro wanted me.

He couldn't deny it. He didn't want to deny it.

And I wasn't above using my body to make him *feel*. Make the cold-hearted, untouchable bastard come apart beneath my touch.

Holding a man by his most precious body part and making him bow to my commands.

That was true power.

This was true power.

Testing my theory, I jerked my hand up and down, thinking of every text Kite had sent me. Every dirty innuendo he'd replied.

I'm stroking my cock.

I'm jerking hard.

Stroking. Jerking. Made sense. In a way the motion would be the crude action of fucking. Jethro would be forced to make love to my palm all while my fingers squeezed him to death.

With determination strong in my heart, I stroked.

Jethro wobbled on his knees, his eyes snapping closed. "Fuuuck," he groaned as I squeezed hard, stroked even harder. There was no build up. No tease.

This is war.

Two sides. Two players. He'd made me come; now it was my turn to learn everything about him, so I could make him unravel.

Pushing his shoulder, I barely hid my victory smile as Jethro toppled backward. His eyes flared wide. "What—"

I didn't speak. Instead, I clambered closer, never stopping the mind-crippling stroke of his cock. Up and down. Twist and around.

His sharp gaze turned hazy, his lips parting as his breath grew heavy.

His hips thrust, just once. Surprise battling for supremacy over his need. I didn't let him overthink it or realize I was winning. I crawled on top of him, spreading my legs, straddling his large, powerful bulk.

My heart strummed; my blood grew thick and cloying as every stroke I gave caused my inner muscles to clench. Giving him pleasure—*taking* his pleasure—was the headiest aphrodisiac.

I was a goddess. An accomplished geisha.

I lost track of lust versus vengeance. I didn't care about last names or futures. All I wanted, all I focused on, was the sweetly plaited emotion where the rush between my legs took control.

My touch turned frantic, jerking rather than stroking.

His icy hands clamped around my hips, grinding himself hard against my grip. Our eyes locked, our breathing synced, we became two animals in the forest.

More.

I wanted more.

Yanking at his boxer-briefs, I tried to push them down. Jethro raised his hips, taking my weight with him as he gave me room to wrench his jeans and boxers to mid-thigh.

The moment his cock sprung free, thudding against his muscular stomach, he lashed out, fisting my hair and dragging my mouth to his.

My tongue tingled to taste him—to indulge in a kiss. But he held me firm, millimetres away from his lips. "You're playing a dangerous game," he groaned as my fingers encircled the large girth of my enemy.

I didn't reply, my mouth watering for his so temptingly close.

Dropping my hand to the base of him, I cupped his balls in my palm.

His back bowed as I rolled the heavy, delicate flesh. "Christ!"

My tummy twisted, my heart thundered, and my nakedness couldn't hide how much his need turned me on.

His fingers went slack in my hair and I sprawled over him, unashamedly rubbing my throbbing core on his thigh. "You called me a disappointment. You said my hands were good for nothing but holding up my towel." I squashed my breasts against his chest, snapping at his lips with the threat of a kiss. "Do you still believe that?"

I jerked my wrist, stroking the velvety flesh of his erection.

His eyes rolled back, his entire body vibrating.

"I'm proving you wrong." I sat up, my gaze latching onto his hot cock. Smiling sweetly, I murmured, "Isn't this what you wanted?"

His eyes stole mine. "There's nothing about this that I want."

I laughed—it sounded a little demented. "Who's the liar now, Mr. Hawk?"

His hand snaked up to cup my throat, the other captured my hip. His face darkened. "You want the truth? I'll give you the fucking truth." His muscles contracted as he braced himself against my touch. "I want you begging me. I want you so damn hot—you'll let me do anything to you."

His raspy voice tore away my past, throwing me headfirst into sex.

I squeezed harder, riding his cock with my fingers, driving blood to blaze in the tip.

He'd gotten what he wanted. By letting me touch him, he'd made me seduce myself. I'd never craved to be filled before. But now…every inch of me felt empty and greedy and needful.

I'm fucking your mouth. I want to blow down your throat.

The text from Kite suddenly popped into my head as if his ghost watched over me, giving me instructions on how to destroy the man glowering into my eyes with a mix of rage and lust.

Fear wrapped around my heart as I looked at the angry erection in my hand. I doubted my jaw would accommodate it, but I'd try. I would try my hardest and give it my all to make him come.

Not to please him. But to *ruin* him. To prove I could control him as easily as he could control me.

I moaned as a delicious throb worked its way from my womb. I was hungry for another orgasm. Instead of sucking him, I toyed with the idea of impaling myself on his huge size, wanting so much to chase my own pleasure.

My eyes couldn't look away from Jethro's parted lips. I would've given anything to kiss him. To be devoured the way my body craved.

You can't.

I shook my head, dispelling the connection. A kiss was too intimate. A kiss would destroy me.

Squirrel nuzzled closer, wondering what the hell we were doing, sniffing at the violent war taking place in the dark forest on a plaid blanket.

Jethro snarled, shoving him away.

In the same movement, he spread his legs, clenched his hands by his sides, and wordlessly gave himself to me.

My heart leapt, blazing with sunshine and happiness, before plummeting back into the tar pits my life had become.

"Suck me. Fucking suck me," he growled, thrusting his cock harder into my hand. The command sent a ripple through my core.

I didn't hesitate.

Bowing over his body, I straddled his knees and in one swift move, slid his silky, salty steel into my mouth.

He bucked, his entire body going rigid. "Fuck…me." His lips clamped shut as his eyes rolled back.

I moaned, adoring the power I wielded.

My nipples tightened. I stopped looking at him. Closing my eyes, I pictured another time, another place. I pictured my lonely existence in some repetitive hotel suite sewing tulle and silk. I pictured my life as it was—a slave to my craft with no peaks or valleys of living.

Then I pictured myself naked and spread over the man who meant to kill me, while my head bobbed furiously over his cock. I relished in how dirty and wrong and primal it was.

I preferred it.

Every inch of me screamed for a release. Every atom thirsted for blood and violence. My teeth ached to sever Jethro's body—horrible images of killing him in the worst pain imaginable consumed my mind.

The other part of me wanted to give him the most pleasurable, erotic blowjob he'd ever experienced, with the hope I would smash his walls, liquefy his ice, and melt him into the man I *knew* was inside.

His hands fisted my hair, grunting low in his chest. He drove into me, forcing himself deeper. "Take it."

I gagged; spit ran from my lips. I struggled to maintain the furious rhythm he set, but he didn't stop using me.

And more importantly, I didn't falter.

I forced him high. I forced him fast.

I stroked and licked and sucked and swirled until everything bellowed with pain. My jaw, my neck, my shoulder, my wrist.

All in the name of winning.

Jethro's stomach tensed, his balls tightened, and the musky smell of him shot up my nostrils, drenching my soul in his flavour.

His hands dug harder into my hair, fucking me just as surely as I fucked him. Our weapons were different, but we were duelling hard and fast.

Jethro groaned long and low as I cupped his balls and squeezed.

I'm winning.

I'm coming. I came down your throat. Kite's message burned my brain; I threw in every last reserve I had. My eyes swam, my brain swirled, and the world tipped upside down.

But still I sucked, and in some far off dimension, where sanity no longer existed, I tasted the first splash of cum on my tongue.

Jethro cried out, his body bowstring tight as his hips drove his erection past my gag reflex and emptied himself inside me.

I had no choice but to swallow. My stomach rolled as his salty release disappeared down my throat. I felt sick. I felt empowered.

He shivered as the last wave of his orgasm finished, a soft groan coming from his parted lips.

Despite the abhorrent dislike I felt toward him, something luminous dazzled in my heart as I sat up. I smiled, victory burning brilliant and sweet.

Jethro's light brown eyes met mine, wide with shock, pupils black with sated pleasure. He breathed hard and fast.

We didn't say a word.

We didn't have to.

We both knew who'd won.

And he was fucking pissed about it.

FUCK.

Fuck her. Fuck me. Fuck everything.

For the first time in my life, I felt a stirring inside my frozen-over heart.

Not gratefulness or humaneness or tenderness.

No.

I felt...*undone.*

I should've known then that it was the beginning of the end.

I should've guessed how badly she would ruin me.

But all I could manage was dumbstruck desire.

I stared into the eyes of a worthy opponent.

I stared at Nila Weaver with awe.

CLIMBING TO MY wobbly feet, I ignored Jethro and beelined straight for the saddlebag. Inside, I found my running shorts, t-shirt, jumper, and summer sandals.

The instinct to turn around and make sure I was permitted to dress came sharp and strong. How had he worked his wizardry to make me second-guess my right to dress?

I would put a stop to that nonsense that very instant.

Slipping into the clothing, I winced as the shoes brushed against cuts and punctures. The painkillers he'd given me hadn't worked their magic just yet.

The second I was dressed, I snagged a waxpaper-wrapped sandwich from the almost empty bag.

Striding away a little, I inhaled the sandwich like an urchin or homeless vagabond. Food. Glorious food. I'd never been so grateful for something as simple as a sandwich before.

It tasted unbelievably good. Roast chicken, crisp salad, and creamy mayo on fresh white bread. I wanted another. Hell, I wanted ten.

"Here." Something landed by my feet. I ducked to pick it up, throwing a look over my shoulder. Jethro had stood and buckled his trousers. He ran a hand through his silvery hair, watching me with a livid expression.

I looked at the green apple in my hand then inhaled that, too. I didn't care what I looked like. My body demanded I eat. I obliged as fast as humanly possible.

But no matter what I chewed, all I could taste was Jethro.

The apple core was the only thing left of my piranha-speed eating.

It was gone too quickly and still I was starving.

Jethro prowled toward me.

My muscles moved, retreating from the anger wisping off him.

Don't move away. It's a weakness.

Stand up to him. Make him see you.

Tensing my muscles, I locked my knees. I'd won. If I backed down now, everything I had done would be for nothing.

Here and now—with no other Hawks or Weavers—it was just us; us in this game where the rules were unknown. The only way to win was to maintain the ground I'd gained.

If he wanted to control me with violence and softly spoken curses, fine. Then I would control him with sex.

The one thing I knew nothing about, but seemed to have a great aptitude for.

My lips twisted at the irony. I'd gone from untouched designer to depraved prisoner.

I only did it to prove a point—to extend my life by however long possible.

Liar. You're wet.

You enjoyed giving as much as you enjoyed his tongue between your legs.

I gritted my teeth.

Jethro didn't say a word, just stood there seething.

My body itched with need; I couldn't stop thinking of his mouth on my pussy or the exquisite sensation of exploding into pieces.

I wanted to come again. And soon.

Finally, he clicked his fingers. "Come. We're leaving."

Ducking, he scooped up the blanket and bag, before stalking to me and grabbing my wrist. He whistled for Squirrel to come galloping from the undergrowth and dragged me through the now almost pitch-black forest.

At least I had shoes, so twigs were no longer a painful foe. The food I'd eaten sat in my stomach like a gift, spreading its energy, while the clothing granted me warmth.

My eyes widened.

I'm…content.

Somehow, amongst the stress and fears, I'd found a small slither of serenity. How long it would last, I didn't know, but even Jethro couldn't take it from me.

We didn't walk far. My ears understood where we were going

before my eyes did. The gentle snuffles of dogs drifted between the branches, followed by a soft huff of a horse.

Stepping into a small clearing, Jethro let me go, moving toward the huge black beast.

He murmured to the animal while securing the saddlebag to the pommel. His large hands were white flashes in the moon-starved night.

I stood silently as Jethro untied the foxhounds, patting them in greeting. The dogs couldn't contain their wriggling behinds, excitement sparking between them.

Squirrel joined his comrades, but he was never far from my side; his intelligent eyes always on mine no matter when I looked at him.

Jethro grabbed the reins of his horse, bringing the animal closer. He stopped in front of me. His body had shut down, face impassive. His chilly façade was back in place as if we were total strangers who happened to meet in the forest on some mystical night.

I've tasted you.

You've tasted me.

We weren't strangers anymore.

"Get on. I don't want you falling over."

I stepped back. "I've survived running through the woodland, climbing trees, and bringing you to an orgasm. I think I can manage walking back to Hawksridge."

"Don't, Ms. Weaver. Just don't." He ran a hand over his face, his mask slipping just a little, showing the strain around his eyes.

My heart clenched in joy. I was happy to see him tired. I was happy to see such an egotistical arsehole suffer from dealing with the girl who everyone thought was weak.

His gaze found mine. Something passed between us. This wasn't a challenge or threat. This was…softer.

"Get on the horse," Jethro ordered, but the unspoken word dangled behind his angry sentence.

Please.

I moved forward, eyeing up the giant beast. The horse swung its head to inspect me, its huge nostrils inhaling my scent.

Do I smell of your master?

Even though I'd eaten a sandwich and apple, Jethro's heady flavour still laced my tongue, saturating me with his essence.

In some horrible way, I felt as if I'd consumed a part of him— giving him power over me.

That's not possible. He didn't give you that willingly.

I'd taken pleasure from him. I'd forced him to give into me, even though his intention all along was to make me repay.

I couldn't stop my small smile this time.

Jethro muttered, "Smugness is not becoming on you, Ms. Weaver."

I shot back, "No, but vulnerability is such a fetching result on you, Mr. Hawk."

His eyes narrowed. In a whiplash, he grabbed my waist and hurled me up over his head. "Get on the fucking horse, before I lose my temper."

Not being given a choice, I grabbed the pommel and swung my leg over the saddle. The horse was a solid mass between my legs, the polished smoothness of the saddle sticking to my bare knees.

Jethro grabbed the reins, placed his foot in the stirrup, and swung up behind me. His hard body wedged against mine.

There wasn't enough room for both of us, but that didn't seem to matter. Digging his heels into the poor creature, we shot forward as his right arm lassoed around my waist, pressing me tight against his chest.

The night silence became awash with dogs and thundering hooves as he carted me back toward the torturous existence at Hawksridge Hall.

Morning.

The sun shone through the lead light windows, highlighting the embossed leather walls and maroon brocade of my four-poster bed.

All around me rested stuffed birds. Swans and swallows. Finches and thrushes. I knew Jethro had chosen this room for me because of the beautiful creatures all shot, murdered, and stuffed by fellow man. I knew because he'd told me.

He also told me I slept in the bed my mother had and her ancestors before her. All carefully designed to tear away my strength and send me hurtling back to the woman I'd been when we first met.

Pity for him, I had no intention of ever being that woman again.

It was early. The sunshine was still new and tentatively shooing away the night. I'd slept—deep and dreamless and awoken full of energy. A night alone. A night warm and unmolested.

There was something to be said for finding solace in one's company.

Shoving back the covers, I dashed to my suitcase that rested in the corner of the room. The bellhops of the Black Diamonds had been kind enough to deliver my belongings, including the maxi dress and jacket Jethro had confiscated from me in favour of the ridiculous maid's uniform I wore to serve the brotherhood's lunch.

I shivered, shoving away the memory of men and tongues.

Falling to my knees, I searched in the jacket pocket until my fingers found what I was after.

My phone.

I quickly located my charger in my suitcase and took both back to bed. Plugging the charger in, I allowed the wonder of electricity to grant new life to the dead machine.

As I waited for the phone to reboot, I smiled at the minor accomplishment I'd achieved last night.

The moment we'd arrived back at Hawksridge, Jethro had marched me to my room and thrown me inside.

Not a single word or lingering look.

The lock clicked into place, and he left me to shower in peace—to dress in a comfortable, baggy t-shirt and curl up beneath fine Egyptian cotton.

The time alone, coupled with the knowledge I'd stolen something from him in the forest, allowed me to relax for a few welcome hours.

Holding my phone—the link to the outside world—filled me with yet more strength. It was the key to finding a balance in this strange existence. My past wasn't gone, just hidden.

The moment the connection synced, the device went bonkers in my hands.

Messages flew into my inbox. Missed calls. Emails.

The emails I ignored: my assistant and designers. Requests for more patterns. Deposits from successful bidders on the collection from Milan.

None of that mattered—not anymore. The freedom I felt at ignoring the pressure of my career shouldn't please me so much.

Three messages from my father glowed on the screen.

My heart lurched, but I neglected them. I wasn't ready to deal with him. The mixture of despair and betrayal had yet to be unbraided and understood. For now, I needed some space.

I clicked on the latest message, sent early last night.

VtheMan: *Nila. Fucking call me.*

Vaughn's message reeked of desperation.

My heart hurt to think of him missing me. I couldn't stomach his loneliness or confusion. I shouldn't have rejected him. It was unfair, and I couldn't do it anymore.

Jethro could jump off a bridge, telling me not to contact my twin and best friend. V needed me.

Needle&Thread: *V, I'm fine. I'm so sorry I made you worry. I don't know how much Dad has told you, but I'm alive and doing everything I can to come home. Please know that I love you, and I wouldn't have gone if I didn't have reason to.*

I pressed send.

A reason like trying to keep you alive.

The melancholy from thinking about my brother threatened to sink my newfound hope. Quickly, I opened the messages I'd been eager to read since my battery died.

Kite007: *Had a pretty fantastic daydream about you, Needle. You let me tie you up and spank the living daylights out of you. Tell me…does that make you wet, 'cause it sure as fuck makes me hard.*

The familiar tug in my core was happiness on this bleak day. So much had changed but not this. Not him.

Careful, Nila.

I paused, tracing the keys with worry. Kite was the one constant in this mess. The only one not involved in some way or another. He wasn't a Hawk. He wasn't a Weaver. He was neutral territory where I wanted to camp and never leave.

You think *he's not a Hawk.*

The sudden thought stopped me, sucking up my oxygen with terror.

What?

My mind skipped back to the luncheon. To the strange connection I'd shared with the brother whose golden eyes weren't cold or full of malice but playful. My heart raced, recalling the inexplicable kinship we'd shared—no matter how brief.

He looked at me as if he *knew* me.

Kestrel.

I dropped the phone.

Could it be?

Shaking, I picked up the device and typed a response.

Needle&Thread: *I had a similar daydream. You spanked me in the woods with a whip. You kneeled behind me and struck just enough to burn but not bite. I'd never been hit before, but you...you made it seem all right.*

Send.

Only, it wasn't a daydream, and it was with my mortal enemy.

I settled back into the covers, breathing shallowly. I flip-flopped with fear, hope, and anger. If Kite *was* Kestrel, what did that mean? Why had he been so cruel to me yet considerate in the dining room? Why had he messaged me a month ago?

The text.

It was never a wrong number.

My hands fisted around my phone. Could I have been manipulated?

Angry tears shot up my spine. All my life, everyone I'd ever known had manipulated me behind the scenes, moving me around at their whim, tugging my skirts until I stood in the right place, while I smiled stupidly and so damn naïve.

I wanted to scream.

You're making something out of nothing.

It could very well be a wrong number and nothing sinister at all.

My anger was too hot—I couldn't reason with myself.

Kite007: *Fuck, that sounds hot. Did you come?*

I stared at the message with fire burning in my soul. I wanted to confront him. I needed to know the truth.

Needle&Thread: *Did you come after you licked me yesterday? Did you jerk off to the thought of me being tormented by your family, you sick bastard?*

My finger hovered on the send key, my breathing harsh in the silent room.

If I asked and I was right—what then? Where did that leave me? Was it better to play them at their own rules? Hide my tentative conclusion and finally learn how to play this secretive, devious game?

I deleted the message.

Needle&Thread: *No, but I made you come. You shot your release so deep down my throat, I can still taste you.*

I grinned, feeling a little psychotic.

If Kite was an innocent party in all of this, then he could continue to be my escape. Meanwhile, Jethro would give me answers that I hadn't had before. Such as granting me knowledge to Kite's previous question. *What do I taste like?*

If he tasted anything like Jethro, it was an overpowering mix of no taste at all and too much taste all at once. An oyster mixed with caviar infused with the strongest shot of vodka. Not entirely pleasant, but not disgusting either.

I had experience now. Experience garnered by blowing a man who may or may not be related to my tormentor.

You might have it totally wrong. You're jumping to conclusions.

I paused, fingers stroking the screen. It was entirely possible I was clutching at straws, looking for connections to make sense of this catastrophe. But I couldn't ignore the tug inside—the sixth sense burning stronger with every second.

My lips twisted at how disgusting all of this was. How the unsaid lies made me endlessly suspicious.

Kite007: *Fuck, do you hear yourself? Something's changed. Again. I can't believe I'm asking this, but spill. I need to know how you've gone from shy little nun to confident tease.*

He wanted to know. As if he didn't know. As if the entire Hawk family weren't laughing behind my back.

You don't know it's him!

I knew I should calm down, seek out clues, and formulate the truth before tearing into the most-likely innocent Kite. But after being through a transformation from meek to fierce, I couldn't bottle myself up. I refused to corset my emotions any longer.

I would take back control message by message.

Needle&Thread: *You want to know? You want to hear personal details of my life? What happened to you, Kite? Someone drop you on your head?*

Kite007: *Careful. I'm one push away from deletion and walking away from this. You're the one who begged me to stay in contact. Remember?*

Needle&Thread: *You have a short temper.*

Kind of like someone else I know.

Kite007: *Want me to stay a fucking arsehole? Got it. Don't ever say I never tried to help you.*

My heart lurched.

If he *was* Kestrel, then he might be my only ally. I couldn't afford to piss him off—not while I lived in a nest of reptiles. If I could befriend him—make him care—he might be my ticket to freedom.

What better way for a Weaver to escape than for a Hawk to open her cage?

Back in the dining room, Kes had been the only one who'd looked at me with…compassion. He'd seen my struggle, and even though he'd treated me the same as all the rest, he'd been chivalrous in a strange, fucked-up way. Unlike his brother, who'd made me come—who'd stripped me of my rights and privacy and given me a gift I'd never been given before.

Bloody Jethro.

Needle&Thread: *I'm sorry. I've been through a rather big change in the past few days. My temper is a little short.*

Kite007: *I've noticed. So…you going to tell me how you found a pair of balls?*

Needle&Thread: *No, I don't think so. You wanted no personal details…remember?*

I sat biting my lip, my fingers poised to cast my first web. How could I phrase a question to make him give away his identity: do you live in the country? Do you ride motorbikes? Did you happen to taste a woman yesterday along with twenty of your gang brothers?

Kite007: *Shoot me down, then. See if I care. Enough talking. Let's get back to a subject we both enjoy. Touch yourself. Tell me how wet you are at the thought of me spanking you. Because you deserve a spanking. A fucking hard one.*

Needle&Thread: *I don't believe I've been anything but good. I don't deserve anything of the sort, seeing as you whipped me last night.*

Kite007: *What's with the whip fantasy? Why not my hand? I want to feel your skin burn while I punish you. I want equal pain in my palm as you scream and beg for my cock.*

I stopped.

My heart switched from burning to frozen. What sort of response was that? Equal pain? Shared pain? Was that what pleasure-pain was all about? Equal measure of obedience and trust?

Kite007: *You've gone quiet. Fine. You want a whip. I'm hitting you with a whip.*

Needle&Thread: *No. Actually…I would prefer your hand. I want to feel you touch me. I want to be stroked, caressed by you, all while you do whatever you want to me.*

I swallowed the tiny thrill at the thought of Kes spanking me and quickly sent another message before he could reply.

Needle&Thread: *Where are we while you hit me? Bedroom? Forest? Countryside? Across your motorcycle?*

His response was instant.

Kite007: *How the fuck do you know I have a motorcycle?*

I threw my phone away as if it had electrocuted me.

I couldn't breathe.

Oh, God. It had to be. The strange connection. The glint and secretive smirk on Kestrel's face. Even the two words were similar. *They're both birds of prey.*

I'm so stupid!

All this time, I thought Kite stood for the winged paper craft decorated with bows and string, when in reality it was another bird of prey.

Don't believe it until you can prove it!

My internal dialogue went unheard.

I couldn't shake the overwhelming *knowing*.

My world ended again, and the one person who I trusted to be impartial and grant me strength to get through this was the vilest liar of them all.

Kite was Kestrel.

Kestrel was Kite.

He's a Hawk.

I DIDN'T GO to Nila for two days.

Two long fucking days.

She'd successfully done what I'd sworn never to let happen again. She'd made me lose control. Bad things happened when I lost my ice. People got hurt. Possessions got broken.

Things did *not* go to plan when I stepped from the comfort of my arctic shell.

There was a reason people called me distinguished and shrewd—a carefully groomed perception. To be cruel but firm was the ultimate calmness—the persona that smoothed out my violent life.

I'd lived in the cold for so long, it'd become a part of who I was, yet all it'd taken was a silly little girl to burn cracks in my carefully designed control.

Those two days were a reprieve. Not for me, but for her. For my family. For every goddamn soul who had to live with me.

She thought I was a monster? Ice wasn't a monster—it was unyielding and inviolable—a perfect cage for something like me.

She thought she understood me?

I laughed.

She would *never* understand. I would never permit her to.

I made sure food was sent to her morning, noon, and night. I spied on her with the bedroom cameras to make sure she didn't do anything idiotic like break through a window or try to slit her wrists with a piece of crockery.

Two days I left her in the room of death, only to see the girl I'd taken evolve into a sexual creature who glowed like a beacon.

She spent most of the day on her phone—texting, reading, surfing

God knows what. Sometimes, her face would fall. Sometimes, her lips would tilt into a smile. Sometimes, she'd pant, her small chest rising and falling. The flush of sex on her skin drove me fucking insane with jealousy.

Jealousy.

An emotion not permitted in my snowy world.

The second day I abandoned her, I went for a hunt. I let loose the hounds and thundered after a herd of deer. I stalked the poor creatures, and shot a quivering arrow through some feeble herbivore's heart. Some things still functioned correctly in my world, even if most of it had been bulldozed into ruins.

The cracks that'd formed froze over.

Rationality and tranquillity returned.

That night, my father and brothers had a family dinner—just the four of us. The deer I'd shot graced a stew, roulade, and roast.

Dinner talk was sparse, but an undercurrent of anger hummed between us. Daniel smirked with his insane arrogance. Kes smiled occasionally for no good goddamn reason, and my father...

Shit, my father.

I was a fucking twenty-nine-year old man. I had blood beneath my nails and ice around my heart, but still I wasn't good enough. Still, I *lacked*. I had something inside me that he'd tried to kill, but despite his best efforts, it survived.

I'd learned how to hide it.

But Nila...*fuck*.

She had the power to expose it.

I wanted to rage. To step into the truth and show my father who I truly was.

But I wouldn't. Not yet. That would be weak.

And I wasn't fucking weak.

I was one year away from inheriting it all. I had my own Weaver to play with. The power shift had begun—all the brothers of the Black Diamond knew it. My relatives knew it. The world fucking knew it, but my father...he wasn't happy with the change.

His gaze ensnared me; I glowered back.

The animosity between us was rife tonight, unable to be buried beneath the rotting veneer of respect and mutual alliance to never challenge each other again.

The last time we did, one of us walked away broken and the other almost didn't walk away at all.

Dessert was brought in, some raspberry soufflé affair. The matriarch of our family finally decided to show her face from her private wing at Hawksridge.

Bonnie Hawk might've looked bonny in her day, but she was well past her prime. At ninety-one, she moved painfully and with difficulty—the stubborn cow refusing to use a wheelchair or even a cane to get around.

"Hello, my son." She nodded at Bryan Hawk then looked to Kes, Dan, and me. "Hello, my grandbabies."

Daniel rolled his eyes, Kes shot up to help her into a chair, and I smiled the signature 'warm-but-not-too-warm' smile I'd perfected since I was ten. "Hello, Grandmamma," the three well-trained Hawk boys said in unison.

Bonnie sat, snapping her fingers for the unobtrusive staff to ladle her plate with the raspberry sweet. She placed an over-piled spoon into her mouth.

Her brown eyes landed on mine. "Tell me, Jet. How are things going with the latest Weaver?"

My back straightened as my cock twitched unbidden. That damn witch had ruined me. I only had to hear the word *Weaver* and I became fucking hard.

That's why you're avoiding her.

Another reason, I admitted.

I scowled.

Swallowing my one and only mouthful of soufflé, I smiled tightly. "She's a work in progress, Grandmamma."

My father jumped in. "The little brat had the audacity to speak back after her welcome luncheon. The cheek of her. If she was mine to discipline, she would be missing a body part by now."

He spoke the truth. I'd seen what he'd done to Nila's mother, and I fucking *hated* him for it.

The venison in my stomach rolled as a wash of ferocious rage exploded through my blood. I stabbed my butter knife into the table. "Thank fuck she's not yours to torment, then. It so happens I like my women whole."

The moment the words were out of my mouth, I froze.

The table froze.

The fucking candles flickering on the sideboards froze.

236

Shit.

Bryan Hawk steepled his fingers, his eyes narrowed and dark. "That was a rather uncalled for outburst. Do you want to rephrase that, perhaps?" He never looked away.

My palms grew slick with sweat. I hadn't meant to show what I'd kept hidden successfully for years. My true nature was not tolerated in the Hawk family—even by my grandmother, who by all rights should encourage us to be gentle and forgiving—not keeping alive a ridiculous debt over a family that made a few mistakes hundreds of years ago.

Fuck, I need time alone.

I needed to get myself under control, before I dug a grave worse than the one I just did.

When my jaw refused to unlock, my father muttered, "Maybe I've put too much responsibility on you, Jet. Are you taxed already? Maybe I overestimated you, and Kes or Daniel should share your workload?"

Something slithered across my soul.

Daniel snickered. "Give her to me, Pop. I'll make sure I don't let you down." His eyes danced with evil. "Unlike some."

We glowered at each other; he tried to intimidate me but didn't succeed. He never succeeded. *Fucking twat.*

Tension crackled around the table. Kestrel stopped shovelling food into his mouth long enough to say, "You know Jet is the best man for the job. I've never seen him fail you yet, Pop. Give the bloke a chance." Giving me a conspiring look, he added, "She's highly strung and goddamn beautiful. Can't blame a man for wanting to enjoy the chance to break such a filly."

Goddammit, what the hell does that mean?

My temper raged beneath my thin exterior of ice. Lately, I was a fraud. A hypocrite, just like Nila said. The coldness inside was mysteriously missing. The blissful uncaring, the emotional detachment I'd been forced to live with since my father taught me how to behave was gone—almost as if someone had flicked a switch.

Before, I felt nothing. I permitted my senses to neither care, nor feel hate, nor feel happiness. I was blank, blessedly blank and strong. Now, I felt *everything*. I overthought *everything*. I wanted to murder every man I lived with purely because I wasn't what they'd groomed me to be.

I fucking hated it.

And I hated that Kestrel—my one ally who knew the truth about me—was pushing my damn buttons. "If you think a speech like that will get you near her, think again. Good try, brother, but I'm watching you."

Kes grinned. "We'll see. After all, she's *ours*. Not just yours. Our adoptive pet, if you will. Can't help it if the pet prefers someone else than the original owner."

My hand clenched around the butter knife.

"Enough," my father snapped. It echoed around the room, bouncing off the images of our forefathers.

"I expect you to do the First Debt before the week is out, Jet," my grandmother said, her lips covered in clotted cream.

I swallowed in disgust. "Yes, Grandmamma."

Cut, my father, muttered, "Do what you think you need to do, Jethro. But mark my words…I'm judging your every move."

Judge me, you bastard. Watch me behave just as you've taught. Watch me be the perfect Hawk.

I would make sure to give him something to judge.

Tonight, I would 'fix' myself. Tonight, I would smooth away the chaos that Nila fucking Weaver had caused and find that saviour of snow.

Cut continued to watch me as he spooned dessert into his mouth. "Make me proud, son. You know what you need to show her and what needs to be done afterward."

Forcing my hand to uncurl around the knife, I placed it slowly on the table. Swallowing the overwhelming emotions that had no place in my world, I muttered, "I'll make you proud, father."

Cut relaxed into his chair.

Instantly, a wash of relief fell over me. It had always been the same. I lived with a family of devils. I was one year away from being emperor to them all, yet I still craved my elders' respect.

The kid inside never fully got over the need to impress—even though deep down he knew it was an impossibility.

"We'll be watching, Jethro. You don't want to disappoint your family."

My eyes snapped to Bonnie Hawk as she licked residual cream from her fingertip. Tilting her head, she quirked her lips into a secretive smile.

My muscles locked. Being the head of the family, she continued to hold the last say—the last piece of power over anything we did. She knew more about me than even my father. I might crave my father's respect, but I would never get over knowing I would never earn Bonnie's.

She would die and never grant me absolution of being satisfied with what I'd done.

I was the firstborn son.

I'd bowed to conformity and rules all my fucking life.

Yet, it was never enough.

Nodding stiffly, I muttered, "I won't let you down, Grandmamma. I won't let anyone down."

I'll make you see that your frailty only increases my power. I'll make you see that fire is better than ice, and I'll fucking show you how youth comes before wisdom.

I'll make you see.

Just you watch.

That night, I retreated to my wing at Hawksridge Hall.

I turned off the lights.

I sat in the dark and welcomed the shadows to claim me.

Before me rested my arsenal to 'fix' the things wrong inside me.

And just like my father had taught me—just like I'd done countless of times before—I found the frost deep inside and permitted it to chill me, calm me…

…

make me impenetrable.

I KNEW IT was too good to be true.

The last three nights and two days of being Jethro-free screeched to a bitter end when he came for me at daybreak.

I wasn't asleep but mid-text with Vaughn.

The early morning sun had a horrible habit of highlighting the stuffed birds around the room, sparkling on death and reminding me that my future only held carnage—no matter how alive I felt. No matter how strong I'd become from taking power from Jethro, in the end, it would all finish the same way.

With my head in a bloody basket.

I should've been petrified—wallowing in misery at the thought of how a successful career and life in the limelight had suddenly become so limited with options. But…strangely…I *wasn't.*

If anything, I was more focused now than I'd ever been. More aware of consequences of choice and the brutality of the world that'd been hidden from me. I'd been raised to believe in fairy tales—my father deliberately kept me young. Why? I hadn't figured that out yet, but now my eyes were open, and it was…refreshing to know the world wasn't pristine and taintless.

All my life, I'd pretended to be perfect. And all my life, I'd nursed the truth inside that I was far from it. The Hawks were crazy—there was no other explanation for their fixation on something so far in the past—but they were *passionate* about it.

Passion had trickled from my world as if every dress and collection had been vampiric—sucking my will to keep striving for greatness in my designs.

If you felt this strongly about it, maybe you should've gone on holiday. Had a break from being a Weaver.

But that was the thing. I would never have admitted it to myself, because I would never have recognised it. My vertigo spells, my lacklustre acquiescence of my father's wishes—I couldn't see how lost I was from my true self. I'd never been given the time to figure out who I was—only what was expected of a daughter born into the Weaver empire.

The beauty of distance meant I *saw* my life without being immersed in it. It all boiled down to the fact I'd never had anything of my own. I'd shared my life with a twin, who I positively adored, but who outshone me in every way. I'd been drowning with self-doubt and nervousness. I'd crippled my instincts and skills, terrified of letting others down.

Oh, my God.

I clutched the phone harder.

I'm a better person away from the people who love me most.

That meant I excelled while living with people who hated me.

It was fucked up.

It didn't make sense.

But how could I argue against something that was true?

VtheMan: *I know everything, Threads, and I'm coming for you. I'll bring the army. I'll kidnap the fucking Queen if it means I'll get you free. Just stay alive, sister. I'm coming.*

My attention reverted back to the current issue.

Vaughn.

Father must've told him what happened. I didn't know how much he shared—hell, I didn't really know how much he even knew himself—but I feared for my brother. I feared for myself.

Vaughn was volatile and likely to do anything to get me back. Every day since I was born, I let him baby me, protect me from life experiences I really should've faced rather than hide from. That protectiveness sometimes came across as too much, and before, I secretly loved it. I loved being so significant to someone—their entire reason for living.

But everything had changed.

I'm not the same person I was a few days ago.

If I was bluntly honest, our relationship seemed a little much now.

Blurring lines that had kept me firmly in my place as daughter and sister with no need to spread my wings and hurl myself from the nest.

"Get up." Jethro paced to the huge windows, wrenching open a sash pane letting the pretty English morning into the stuffy room. I breathed deeply as sunshine bounced around, merrily painting corpses of winged creatures.

Yesterday, I'd named some of the prettier ones. Snowdrop, Iceberg, and Glacier were all addressed in honour of their tormentor and mine.

I needed to reply to Vaughn, but I tucked the phone beneath the quilt, eyeing up my nemesis. "Nice to see you, too."

His nostrils flared. "Don't get uppity, Ms. Weaver. I don't have time for nonsense."

I stretched, deliberately taunting him. "Nonsense? You can't talk. All of this Weaver and Hawk charade is utter nonsense."

Jethro stomped over. Dressed in beige corduroys and black shirt, he looked as if he had a meeting with his local backgammon club. The requisite diamond pin glinted on his lapel. "Shut up and get out of bed. Now."

My heart thundered. His golden eyes were icy and steadfast.

The intensity and raw visceral desire I'd seen in the forest was gone. Hope fizzled into dirty bubbles in my chest. I'd thought we'd climbed to a new dimension with what happened in the woods. I thought I'd showed him that he couldn't undermine me without undermining himself.

How wrong I'd been.

Squinting in the sun, I whispered, "What did you do?"

He reared back as if I'd slapped him. "Excuse me?"

Shuffling in the covers, I eyed him closer, trying to figure out what had changed. Nothing outward looked different. He was the perfect resemblance of a country gentleman. But his tone was smooth as silk and just as unbreakable.

"You've done something. A few nights ago you looked human...now..."

"Now?"

I scowled. "Now you just look like the cold-hearted robot who came for me at my runway show."

Before he could answer, another vital question popped into my head. "Why now?"

"What?" His face twisted into a glower. "That doesn't even make sense. Your questions are really starting to grate on my nerves, Ms. Weaver." Running a hand through his hair, he said quietly, "If you rephrase that into a coherent sentence, I might answer, if it means you'll kindly get out of bed."

There he went all pomp and ceremony again. No curses. No snapping. No spikes of emotion of any kind.

He stayed away to distance himself, regroup.

I *had* affected him. So much so, he'd needed three nights to deal with it.

A hot douse of power shot through my veins.

"Why did you leave me on my own for days?" I held up a hand. "Don't get me wrong, I'm not complaining. The wait-staff did an impeccable job of keeping me fed, and the downtime was rather welcome after the manic few years I've had travelling and working non-stop, but it is a little odd."

He sedately placed his hands into his corduroy pockets. His eyes were completely unreadable—it was like trying to decipher a damn vault. "Please, tell me what you find so odd. Then perhaps I can help you."

If I hadn't seen the passionate man in the forest—if I hadn't wrapped my lips around his throbbing cock and swallowed his cum—I might've shrunk back in reprimand. I might've feared the silence more than his temper, because it heralded something terrible coming.

But now…now I saw it for what it was.

It's a coping mechanism.

We all had them. Mine was permitting my father and brother complete control over me. My only freedom from that was running until I passed out on my treadmill.

Jethro didn't run, but he did use something extremely effective to push aside the tangled emotions I knew he felt and embraced the glacier he pretended to be.

"Never mind," I whispered. "I understand."

Beneath the power in my veins, a small cloud of depression settled. I'd worked hard breaking his arctic exterior. I'd thrown my all into showing him pleasure that he could find by giving in to me. The fact he'd been so affected that he'd had to shut down and hide should've pleased me.

But really, it reset everything. I was back at the starting line.

For a second, I slouched in defeat. Did I have the energy to go through the arguing and battle of wills again?

Tilting my head, I stared at him. He clenched his jaw, not giving anything away.

My spine straightened as resolution fortified my defeat. So be it. I would do it all over again. And again. And again. Until he realized he couldn't win. Not against me.

I was strong enough to break him ten times, a hundred times. I was strong enough to kill him and his twisted family before he dispatched me. I meant to keep my vow that I was the last Weaver they would ever hurt.

Jethro crossed his arms. "Considering you no longer have any more frustrating questions, I presume you'll oblige and get up, like I ordered."

Without a word, I shoved back the covers and climbed from the warm sheets. "Where are we going?"

Jethro's eyes fell on my naked legs. I'd worn black and pink shorts with a matching camisole to bed.

"Did I say you could ask questions?" Moving smoothly, he stepped away. Roaming sleek and sharp around the room, he gathered mismatched clothes that were draped on chairs and a sixteenth-century dressing table then came back toward me. Dumping them at the end of the bed, he said, "Get dressed. I'm going to count to ten. If you aren't decent, I don't care. I'm dragging you out of here naked or clothed— it's entirely your choice."

I wrinkled my nose at the attire. I had more of an understanding about my enemy, but I still feared him. I didn't want to go anywhere. I didn't want to be commanded or dragged—

"One." His eyes glittered.

He couldn't be serious.

"Two…"

Quickly, I reached for a peach t-shirt with Victorian lace on the collar and denim shorts.

"Three."

Shit, how could I get dressed with him standing there? I couldn't strip so blatantly.

He's seen you naked. You ran through a forest with nothing on. He's tasted *you, for God's sake. Seriously, why are you suddenly precious about it?*

"Four."

244

Biting my lip, welcoming my rational common sense, I hastily tore off the camisole and let it flutter through the air.

Jethro sucked in a breath at my exposed breasts. "Five."

Tugging the t-shirt over my head, I dropped my hands to my hips. "Six."

Locking eyes with him, I shimmied out of the shorts, letting them puddle around my ankles. I had no underwear on.

I searched for the lust that'd burned in his gaze a few nights ago. I sought to witness just a hint of the Jethro who'd wrapped his fingers in my hair and driven his cock down my throat.

He merely cocked an eyebrow at my naked pussy and continued to count. "Seven."

Anger siphoned through my heart. Stepping into the shorts, I snatched them up and fastened the zipper.

"Eight."

Remembering Jethro's tendency to use my long hair as handle bars and worse, as a leash, I quickly smoothed the black thickness into a messy ponytail and secured it with a hair tie from my wrist.

"Nine."

The diamond collar sat around my neck—ridiculously expensive considering my understated outfit, making my breathing a little irregular. Slipping my feet into a pair of sparkly flip-flops on the floor, I was done.

I smirked. "Finished, oh impatient master."

Jethro stiffened. "Record speed, Ms. Weaver. I'm impressed." He held out his hand. "Give me your phone."

I blanched. "What? No!"

He leaned closer, his temper shimmering just beneath the surface of his cool exterior. "Yes. I won't ask again."

For a second, I wondered if I could hit him over the head and run. So many scenarios of running had entertained me these past few days. I'd tried to pry the diamond collar off. I'd tried to open the window. I'd tried to pick the lock on the door.

But nothing worked. Aside from death, I wasn't getting out of there.

I'm coming, Threads.

My heart seized at the thought of Vaughn charging in here trying to save me, only to be slaughtered by the men holding me captive. I couldn't let that happen.

Gritting my teeth, I turned and plucked my phone from the tangled sheets. Reluctantly, I passed it to his awaiting palm.

His fingers curled around the delicate device. "Thank you."

I couldn't tear my eyes from it. My only link to the outside world. My only avenue of freedom. I didn't realize until that moment how much I valued it and how stir-crazy I would go if deprived of the simple things, such as texting Kite.

Admit it, you're screwing yourself up over him.

The past few days Kite had been…different. The messages from the night before last came back to mind.

Kite007: *Have you ever noticed how things you've always been told were wrong are the only things that feel right?*

Needle&Thread: *That's rather deep coming from the man who only wants to sext and avoid personal subjects.*

Kite007: *If I said I wanted one night of blatant honesty, no douche-baggery, no bullshit of any kind, what would you say?*

Needle&Thread: *I'd say you'd completely lost it and wonder if someone with a heart had stolen your phone.*

Silence.

I'd been justified in not letting my guard down. After all, I'd tried many times to get him to be a little kinder, more human toward me, but he'd always shot me down. But as ten minutes turned into twenty and still no reply, I'd felt guilty for hurting someone who obviously needed to talk.

Why didn't he talk to others who knew him? Find solace in friends who would understand? My earlier conviction of him being Kestrel had faded a little after the initial panic attack. Since his vicious remark, asking how I knew about his owning a motorcycle, we'd both skirted the issue as if we were both afraid to pick at that particular wound.

It was best to let it scab over and not spew forth poison that wouldn't be able to heal.

This blindness—this naivety about our true agendas and names—was strangely hypnotic, and I didn't want it to change. I didn't want to let him go yet, and I would have to if I knew the truth.

Needle&Thread: *Kite, I'm sorry. No bullshit. No games. One night only to be ourselves and let the stark, painful truth come out. I'm here to listen if you want. If you've had second thoughts that's fine, too. Either way, I hope you have a great night.*

It'd taken a while, but finally he'd texted back.

Kite007: *Sometimes, it seems as if those who have nothing in life have everything, and those who have everything have nothing. Sometimes, I want to be the one who has nothing, so I can appreciate all the things I think I'd miss. But the scary thing is, I don't think I'd miss a single fucking thing.*

My heart fluttered. It was as if he'd pulled my fears straight from the darkness inside me.

Needle&Thread: *I understand completely. I love my family. I love their faults as well as their perfections, but I can't help being angry, too. By keeping me safe and sheltered, they made me become someone who was a lie. I now have the hardship of figuring out the truth.*

Kite007: *The truth of who you truly are?*

Needle&Thread: *Exactly.*

Kite007: *We're all a product of obligation. A carbon copy of what is permitted in the world we're born into. None of us are free—all raised with expectations to fulfil. And it fucking sucks when those expectations become a cage.*

I couldn't reply. Tears had spilled unbidden down my cheeks. I shook so much, I'd dropped the phone.

If Kite *was* Kestrel. He was hiding just as much as me. A man camouflaging everything real in order to protect himself in a family of monsters.

Jethro snapped his fingers in front of my nose, breaking my daydream.

My heart galloped at the thought of never being able to text Kite again, especially now we'd broken some barrier and admitted we had more in common than seeking sexual gratification.

"You're a thousand miles away. Pay attention."

I blinked, forcing myself to lock onto Jethro's golden gaze.

"I was giving you an idea of how today would go. You asked me to inform you, remember, back in the woods?"

Blinking again, I nodded. "Yes. Can you repeat?"

He chuckled coldly. "No, I will not repeat. I showed kindness in bracing you against today's events, yet you couldn't grant me the courtesy of listening. I refuse to reiterate myself."

Rolling my shoulders back, I tried not to worry about what my future held and only on what was important. "Please, I need my phone back."

Jethro shook his head. "No."

My heart sprinted. "But you said I could use it."

"I did." His lips twitched. "I also said you had to ask permission in order to do so. I want to check your history. Make sure you're not disobeying the rules."

Shit, why didn't I delete my inbox?

"The rules?"

His eyes narrowed. "Rules, Ms. Weaver. I don't have many, but I did request you didn't contact your brother. If you've obeyed, you have nothing to worry about, and I'll return the phone to you."

Shit.

Not only had I been texting V, I'd also shared more with Kite than I wanted Jethro to see.

If Kes was Kite, Jethro would know of the connection I had with his brother. He would use that knowledge. He would hurt me with it.

I can't let that happen.

I wanted to scream.

Standing as tall as I could, I said, "My brother knows."

Jethro went still, his face tightening. "I suppose I should thank you for your honesty. I thought he would by now. The Weaver men aren't ones for letting us take their women. Even with the correct paperwork."

I glared. "You knew he would come for me?"

Jethro nodded. "I suspected, and your father, too. It's been the case for hundreds of years. Do you really think your father didn't come and try to rescue your mother?" He laughed. "What sort of man do you think he is?"

A man I never knew.

Jethro smirked, seeing my answer flicker in my eyes. He reached out, tenderly tucking a stray strand of hair behind my ear. "To lose faith so soon in the ones you hold most dear is the worst crime of all, Ms. Weaver. I hope, for your sake, he never knows how you doubted him."

"Why are you telling me this? Isn't it better for you if I feel cut off and abandoned?"

He shook his head, his fingers dropping from my ear to cup the back of my neck. "No. Where's the fun in that? You were loved. You *are* loved. It's more bittersweet to know the men who tried to protect you are now on the outside trying to break in to free you. It's much more fun when there are more players in the game."

I whispered, "I don't understand you at all."

He grinned, looking positively light-hearted. "That's the nicest thing you've ever said to me."

"It wasn't a compliment."

He gripped my neck harder. "Regardless, I like it." His eyes drifted from mine to latch onto my mouth. The air between us went from sharp to lust-laden. His tongue came out, tracing his bottom lip.

My core warmed. I was too weak to ignore the masculine call of him, even while hating his guts.

His thumb caressed the column of my neck, both in a threat and a tease. "You won the other night. We both know that. But you won't win today. Today is mine. Today, you obey."

I couldn't breathe. His mouth came so close to mine, making me drunk on the anticipation of kissing.

He'd tormented me with the illusion of a kiss ever since we'd met: in the coffee shop, by the stables as I squirmed on his fingers, and now here. His lips were a fraction away from claiming mine. His breath smelled of mint and sin, and his fingers dug into my nape with everything he kept hidden.

A kiss could very well be the one thing that could shatter the icy wall he hid behind once and for all.

I swayed forward, trying to capture his mouth.

He reared back, clucking his tongue. "So eager, Ms. Weaver. If I didn't know any better, I'd say you like the taste of me." His brow lowered to darken his eyes. "You seemed to enjoy what I shot down your throat in the woods."

That was how he wanted to play? Fine. I would play dirty. I had nothing left but to tear away any illusion of being an innocent seamstress and embrace this nonsensical war. I wanted to roll in dirt and filth; I would meet him on the battlefield and never back down.

"I did enjoy it. But not as much as you enjoyed sticking your tongue inside me." Smiling coyly, I whispered, "Admit it, Jethro…admit that your mouth waters to have more of me. I bet your cock is hard right now, thinking of going where your lucky lips have been."

I quaked with an odd combination of fear and confidence. "You could do it, you know. I wouldn't stop you. In fact, if you want to know the truth—the deep, dark, bitter truth—I want you to fuck me. I want to feel you fill me, thrusting into me, stretching me to the point of pain. Want to know why?"

Somehow, I'd started this masquerade to get under his skin, but

I'd successfully gotten under my own. My breath became a pant. My skin sparked with need. My core twisted with wetness.

Jethro's lips parted, his fingers clutching harder and harder around my nape. "I know what you're doing, and no, I don't want to know why."

The air throbbed thick and hot, threading around us with blatant need. "I don't care. I'll tell you anyway." Licking my lips, I murmured, "I want you to fuck me, Jethro Hawk, so you can see that you may own my body, but you will never own my soul. By taking me, you'll finally realize that I'm the strongest one here. That I can manipulate you into wanting me."

Taking a huge risk and gambling with my life, I reached up to cup his cheek.

He flinched but didn't move away. "The moment when you fill me, you'll see. That moment when you douse me in your cum, you'll be completely in my power. I'll own you. A Weaver owning a pet Hawk."

And when I'd collared and blinded him, I would use my bird of prey to hunt on my behalf. I would teach him to tear out the hearts of my enemies and obey my every whim. Because I was done being controlled. I was done being a girl.

I'm unconquerable.

Silence fell thick and cloying. We both didn't move, our breathing ragged and torn.

Then Jethro released me, stepping back with unmeasured steps. "Confidence will only hurt you in the end."

The back of my neck tingled from where he'd held me. "I guess we'll see. Unless you plan never to sleep with me."

Ignoring that, he snatched my wrist and dragged me toward the door. "Enough. I'm done with your games."

I stumbled after him, following the muddy wake of his anger. "Where are we going?"

His voice dropped to a hiss. "First, you have a history lesson, and then…"

My heart fell into my toes as he wrenched open the door and tugged me into the corridor.

I couldn't help myself. I had to ask. "Then?"

Smiling cruelly, he said, "Then it's time for payment. Today is your First Debt, Ms. Weaver. The Debt Inheritance has begun."

FUCK IT ALL to hell.

It'd taken the longest session of my life to claw back my chilly shell. It'd taken more out of me than even the first lesson taught by my father.

But within ten minutes, Nila fucking Weaver had found the smallest of cracks and used a crowbar of words to snap it wider.

Too bad for her, I wasn't giving in today. I had a job to do—a mandate to fulfil—and I would carry it out to the best of my ability. If I didn't, everyone would see. And everyone would know that the firstborn son was weak.

I'd been watching Kestrel and his sneaky smiles. I'd been stalking Daniel and his maddening glares. They both wanted what I had. And I wouldn't give my father any reason to think I couldn't tame Nila like any self-respecting Hawk. Cameras around the house would report how I treated Nila to Cut and the Black Diamond brotherhood. Spies would be on the lookout, judging my final test to ensure the Hawk fortune was going to the right brother.

This was the ultimate test. The Debt Inheritance was more than history and payments—it was an important sequence of events that every firstborn Hawk had to complete in order to inherit his legacy.

If I failed…who knew if my father would let me live. A firstborn son didn't necessarily inherit everything—not if death stole him too soon.

And judging by family records, there had been a few that hadn't passed the examination.

I can't afford to fuck it up.

Not if I wanted to keep Nila as mine.

Not if I wanted to keep my own life intact.

And not if I wanted to...*protect*...her from men who would undoubtedly be worse than me.

Protect.

What a strange, horrible word. It came layered with responsibility and commitment. Both were fucking vile on my tongue.

As I dragged Nila down the corridor, I gritted my teeth at the flashes of light on hidden camera lenses. What Nila didn't know was this was all a charade and we were the main attraction, playing it up for the audience behind the curtain.

In a way, we were both controlled—her by love, me by...

Clenching my jaw, I shook my head. *Get out. You found that silence. Time to find it again. The cameras are rolling, the puppeteers are tugging, and it's show-time.*

Stalking past the corridor that led to the bachelor wing—my bachelor wing—I kept tugging my unwilling Weaver toward the first part of the debt.

I was lucky that so much of the house was segmented just for my use. My brothers shared with the Diamonds. Their quarters far exceeded any other compound, but they still had strict rules to follow.

My stomach tensed, thinking of last night's business. We always conducted the bulk of our work at night. Ten of us had fulfilled the brief, and I'd cranked up my newest Harley that'd arrived from Milan, thanks to Flaw, and thundered through the darkness to ensure a new diamond shipment made it intact to the cutters and dealers.

Diamond smuggling was fucking dangerous. Not only was the law out to prosecute, but every sticky-fingered arsehole wanted a piece. Diamonds were the easiest, most convenient way to move wealth— small but worth a fortune. The Black Diamonds had formed, not for the love of riding and a brotherhood of like-minded bikers, but purely to kick the shit out of anyone who managed to get close enough to rob us.

Before, we'd moved merchandise with armoured vans and suits in broad daylight. But vans were such easy targets—so damn obvious.

So, we'd evolved.

Ten bikers...six with diamond cargo, four without. We rode in formation with guns armed and ready to defend. Police scanners kept us off roads where roadblocks were prevalent, and our fierce notoriety steadily grew.

Robberies were still attempted—shit, they always would be. Opportunists would give anything to intercept even a small shipment. Who wouldn't for an easy catchment of over three million pounds' worth of stones?

But we never chose the same route twice, we never let thieves walk away with their lives, and we earned the reputation of ruthless murderers.

After dealing with Nila and the mess she caused inside me, I'd craved an ambush. I'd wanted some motherfuckers to pounce, so I could give myself to mayhem and teach them a lesson. I'd wanted a fight.

But the night remained silent apart from our grumbling machines, and the delivery went smoothly.

By the time I crawled into bed at four a.m., I suffered a knot of tension in my gut and no amount of fantasising about fucking Nila could stop it. I'd laid in bed going over what happened in the forest. I gripped my cock and imagined sliding inside her and showing her once and for fucking all she couldn't win—no matter that she had. I'd never had an orgasm so intense, so draining. Her mouth had been alchemy. The release she'd given left me silent inside...but different to the icy silence I'd been taught to wield.

I'd been sated enough to permit my barriers to drop, to relax for the first time in my life.

And I wanted to hurt her for making me feel that. To glimpse an alternative to the one I'd been taught. But no matter how much I wanted to teach her a lesson, I also wanted to drive her insane with pleasure, so she felt what I did.

"I can walk on my own, you know." Nila tugged her wrist, trying to free herself from my grip.

Our feet—mine in dress shoes, hers in flip-flops—whispered down the plush red-carpeted corridor. "I like knowing you have no choice but to follow my every footstep, Ms. Weaver."

She growled under her breath.

Turning a corner, I took her down a different route. I had no reason other than to confuse her. She would have no idea where we were going until the final second.

"Wow." Nila lagged behind, her eyes fixated on the perimeter and the huge wall hangings. The beautiful tapestries hung from brass rods two stories high. Depictions of hunting mythical creatures—blood spurting from unicorns and griffons impaled on spikes—were the cheery décor.

"Who did all these? Was it your ancestors?"

I chuckled. "You think we're skilled at arts and crafts?" Shaking my head, I said, "We aren't weavers or sewers. We have much more important things to do."

"Like hunt?"

I nodded. "Amongst other pastimes."

"So who did them?"

I scowled. "Why do you think there has to be a link between something appealing to the eye and history? Diamonds buy a lot of things, Ms. Weaver. There comes a time when wealth transforms, and purchasing works of art is one of them."

She shuddered, looking away.

Why the fuck did she shudder? It was the way of the world. Everybody knew that the rich grew richer, and the poor sold their souls for a piece of it.

Silence fell awkwardly between us as we traversed the distance to the other wing of the house. I'd spent an entire lifetime in this monolithic prison and still managed to get lost.

Turning the last corner, Nila slammed to a halt.

My lips twitched at the corners. "Recognise something?"

Her dark eyes widened with horror. "You can't take me in there."

"I can and I will."

Before us rested the huge double doors of the dining room.

Nila squirmed in my hold. "You said I was to pay the First Debt. I've already paid the one where your foul associates licked me. You can't mean to repeat it."

I growled, "What time is it?"

Her face went blank. "Excuse me?"

I pointed down the hall, where the sun beamed through the French doors at the end. "It's morning. I was out late last night working up an appetite, and it's that time when people typically eat."

"Breakfast?" she squeaked. "You're making me eat in the same room where your awful family—"

"No need to repeat the facts, Ms. Weaver. I'm fully aware of what happened to you in there. Unfortunately for you, I don't care. I'm hungry. You're hungry. We have a big day ahead of us, and it's time for fucking breakfast."

Her head tilted as the curse fell from my mouth.

Goddammit to fucking hell.

Why did I have to end up with a Weaver who seemed to tap into a never-ending well of strength and intelligence? Her question before hadn't stopped ringing in my ears: *"What did you do?"*

How had she seen my transformation so clearly, so shrewdly? Even my own family didn't notice things like that—only if I went too far did they ever intervene. I had to keep her at arm's length if I had any hope of hiding my true self.

I leaned down to her level, my eyes disobeying my command not to stray to her lips. So pink and full, just the memory of having them wrapped around my cock made me ripple with need.

You want to kiss her.

I crucified that thought immediately. A kiss was connection—a kiss could never happen, because I wanted no connection with this woman. I *couldn't.*

"I agree it's morning and we should eat, but please, Jethro, take me somewhere else. Hell, give me a picnic in the kennels. Just don't take me into that room."

The plea in her voice disgusted me. I preferred her when she remained defiant, rather than begging. "No arguing. Gemstone is always held in this room. We won't break tradition for anyone, especially you."

Her eyes narrowed. "Gemstone?"

"Our weekly meeting with the Diamond brothers. While you were relaxing the past few days, some of us were working. The meeting is a recap of dealings and revenue, and you're a Hawk now. You get to be privy to our inner empire. Lucky, wouldn't you say?"

She tried to jerk her wrist from my hold. It didn't work. "And if I don't want to be a part of it?"

I smirked. "Do you really think you have a choice?"

We glowered at each other.

Placing my palm on the doors, I pushed them open and pulled her into the room where her induction had taken place.

I looked over at Nila.

She sat wedged between Kestrel and Flaw. For the first twenty minutes of the meeting, she'd been jumpy, angry, and downright livid to be back in the room with the same men who'd seen and tasted every morsel of her.

Now, an hour into the meeting, she'd stopped hissing whenever a brother asked her a polite question, and had even eaten half of her salmon and poached eggs with hollandaise sauce. She'd refused coffee, which reminded me of how she didn't drink the one I bought her in Milan, and her body language was so fucking uptight, I expected her to pass out from muscle exhaustion any second.

For the past sixty minutes, we'd discussed the successful transaction last night, the rare delivery of a diamond over twenty-six carats next week, and the on-going politics in Sierra Leone. Boring stuff for an outsider.

She isn't an outsider. She's ours now.

More often than I wished, I caught myself watching her, my eyes seeming to land on her, regardless of who was speaking. She was the only splash of colour in the line-up of men on her side of the table—a peach fiesta smack in the middle of leather-jacketed bikers.

"Now that we've got the basics out of the way, Jethro, do you have anything to report?" Cut looked down the table, surveying his good disciples.

I stiffened in my chair as all eyes turned on me, including Nila's. Last night had been fucking boring. I had nothing to add. Now that I'd eaten, I just wanted to leave, get the debt over with, and go for a ride. I needed to get out of this place and away from these people.

"No, nothing to add. You've covered it."

Daniel snickered, his dark hair spiked with too much gel. "Yeah, Pop, you've gone over the boring shit. Let's get to the good part."

Nila froze; her dark eyes glared, shooting hatred across the table toward my younger brother.

Couldn't say I blamed her; the feeling was mutual.

Daniel sneered at Nila, licking his lips and blowing her a kiss. "I want to see how our guest reacts."

My fists clenched on the table.

Kestrel shifted beside her, nudging her shoulder with his. Loud enough for his voice to carry, he said, "It's okay, Nila. You're on the sane side of the table. I won't let him touch you."

Nila tensed as her head swivelled to look at him. Her eyes

searched his, her chin cocked in a strange mixture of defiance and curiosity.

The second turned into a drawn-out moment, and still they stared. *What the fuck?*

Finally, Nila nodded, her black ponytail draping over her shoulder. Never tearing her gaze from Kes, she said softly, "Thank you."

Kes beamed, his golden eyes, the trait all Hawk men carried, glowed. "You're welcome." Something passed between them. Something I fucking hated.

Running a hand through his dark, silver-flecked hair, Kes tore his eyes from Nila's to look directly into mine. "You only have to come to me if you ever feel overwhelmed."

That lowlife bastard.

My hands balled in my lap. "Enough."

Kes reclined in his chair, dropping his forearm—the one tattooed with a bird of prey—beneath the table.

Nila jumped a mile.

He'd touched her! That goddamn arsehole touched what was mine.

The instant Nila jolted, Kes pulled away, a smug smile on his lips. "Sorry."

"Don't touch me," Nila hissed.

Something warm sprang from nowhere in my chest. Warm? How was that possible when my heart was full of snow?

My lips twitched, smugness of my own unable to be hidden. Nila might be intrigued or even drawn to Kes, but it was my cock that'd been in her mouth, *my* tongue that'd been in that pretty cunt of hers.

Kestrel's suave smile dropped. He always did think too highly of himself. Just because the club whores preferred him, it didn't mean he was better than the rest of us. He was my favourite person; however, I would not tolerate him poaching my prey.

Kes hung his head, turning on the charm and magic puppy-dog eyes that twisted the knickers off many women. "I only meant to offer comfort. I'm sorry if I offended you."

Nila crossed her arms, breathing shallowly. Before she could respond, a Diamond brother muttered from across the table, "Yes, I'm sorry if we offended you the other day."

Nila's head shot up.

Daniel thumped him in the arm. "What the fuck, man?"

Stupid Daniel.

He didn't understand how unravelling a person's psyche went. First came cruelty—a stripping of every high and mighty concept that they were untouchable. Then came tenderness—an acknowledgement of going too far and promises of safety.

This was the second stage.

I'd seen it happen with Nila's mother. I'd witnessed the bewitchment as she fell under my father's spell.

That's going to happen to Nila.

My heart froze at the thought of her looking at me the way her mother looked at my father. Not with fear or panic or loathing but with trust and happiness and…affection.

"Excuse me?" she whispered, almost mute with shock.

The brother who'd spoken, an older man with a goatee, smiled gently. "You have to understand, it was our way of welcoming you into our midst. You do not need to be afraid of us."

She squared her shoulders. "I'm not afraid."

I swallowed hard as a foreign emotion crawled into my chest. Goddammit. *Jealousy.* Again. I was fucking jealous of the men around this table. I wanted to rip their heads off for tasting what was mine.

Don't go there, Jet.

My father was right to give her to the brotherhood the moment she arrived. If he demanded I strip and deliver her for a round of service again, I would draw a sword from the armoury on the walls and strike him down.

I would never be able to stand behind his chair now. Even though only a few days had passed, so much had happened. Nila had evolved into someone who drove me past rationality and straight into the chaos she wielded so well.

While Nila had been licked and tasted, I'd fought an unwinnable battle of possession. I'd said the words—I went along with the act of sharing her—but that was fucking bullshit now…

Now, I would never be able to share.

Never.

She was mine.

Not my brothers', not my father's, and definitely not the conclave of bikers, who by rights were my minions.

Mine.

Another brother broke through my tormenting thoughts, saying to

Nila, "It was a special circumstance to welcome you into our family. We were all honoured to have you become a part of us."

Nila's face twisted in disgust. "A *part* of you?"

I jumped in before anyone else could. Ingrates. There was a way of delivering this so it made sense, not repulsed. "We all tasted you. We all licked a part of you and absorbed your sweat, your tears, your fears. No other initiation could've broken the barriers between newcomers and old-timers better than stripping you bare."

Nila's mouth fell onto the table. The same table I'd spread her over and driven my tongue deep inside.

Fuck, shouldn't have thought about that.

My cock went from soft to hard in an instant. I shifted in my chair as memories of her blowing me in the forest came thick and fast. *I'd come thick and fast. All down that beautiful throat.*

I felt Cut watching me, the intensity of his gaze searing into my skin.

"*What* did you just say?" Nila whispered, her features strained.

Cut sat taller in his chair at the head of the table, steepling his hands in front of him. "Jethro's right, Nila."

Nila.

I hated that everyone called her Nila. They had no right to her first name. If and when anyone addressed her by it, it should be me.

Why don't you then? She wants you to. She asked strongly enough in the woods.

I didn't have an answer to that. And I didn't have the guts to search for one.

Nila shook her head, looking at my father. "Is this another one of your mind games?"

Cut smiled reservedly. "No games. I told you, you're a part of this family now. You'll be treated kindly and respectfully. You will come to care for us, just like you care for your own flesh and blood."

"Never," she spat.

Cut chuckled. "Your mother said the same thing, but by the end, she willingly paid the last debt. A pet can only hate its owner for so long. But ply it with warmth, safety, kindness, and good food, and soon…you'll have no choice but to let go of that hatred in your heart and embrace the life we're giving you."

"The life you mean to steal."

He nodded. "The life we mean to steal. But also the life we will continue to nurture as long as we have your strict obedience." His eyes landed on me. "Give me an update, Jet. How are things progressing? Have you followed my instructions?"

Not one.

Not a single fucking rule had I followed. And yet…what had happened in the woods after I'd hunted her down had taken something from her. We'd shared something. Something I never wanted to share with another human being, because it made me feel so damn weak.

Ignoring the question, I sat taller. "The First Debt will be paid this afternoon."

Nila sucked in a breath. Her fear of the unknown did a much better job than I ever could.

Cut relaxed into his chair. "Good."

A second passed.

Another ticked silently before Nila snapped, "Have you forgotten my promise so soon, Mr. Hawk?"

The table froze; men looked from the skinny seamstress to their leather-jacketed leader.

Cut tensed. "No, I haven't forgotten."

"I meant what I said," Nila growled. "I *will* kill you. You can pretend you're kind and keep me in good health, but I will never forget what you've done."

I stood up, slapping my palms loudly on the table. "Ms. Weaver!"

Her head snapped in my direction, her dark eyes blazing. "Was I talking to you? You're as bad as he is. I have a good mind to kill you, too."

My heart raced, shedding the glacier in favour of excitement.

Excitement? How the hell did she confuse me and draw out such lubricous reactions? "Oh, you can try. We'll see who wins. A seasoned hunter or a fumbling dressmaker? I know who I'd place money on."

Nila shoved her chair back, standing in one swift move. She looked as if she would hurl herself over the table to slap me.

Cut shouted, "Out! All of you."

Shit.

Tearing my eyes from the trembling, angry woman before me, I muttered, "Cut, let me—"

Punish her.

Fuck her.

Ruin her in my own way.

Anything to stop you from touching what's mine.

My father pursed his lips, pointing at the doors. "Out. I won't ask again."

The Diamond brothers stood up, their chairs sliding over thick carpet, before disappearing out the door in creaking leather and boots.

Daniel, Kes, and I didn't move.

Nila stood locked in place.

Cut raised his eyebrow. "I believe I just gave an order?"

"What? All of us?" Kestrel asked, disbelief in his voice.

Cut didn't reply, only glowered until the power of his rank, and the fact he was not only our father but our president, overrode our rebellion.

My brothers stood.

I gritted my teeth as Kes placed a hand on Nila's shoulder, sharing a look with her that made my stomach fucking shake off any pretence of ice and go nuclear with fury.

Nila smiled softly, standing and moving toward the exit.

"Not you, Ms. Weaver. You and I are going to have a little chat," Cut said quietly.

Nila closed her eyes briefly, blocking her panic. When she opened them again, all that remained was reckless confidence.

I wanted to say something, but my tongue tied into a useless piece of meat.

"Out, Jethro. I won't ask again."

Nodding once at my father, I moved stiffly. Nila refused to meet my eyes as I stalked out of the room, following my two siblings.

The last thing I heard as the doors closed was my father's voice. "Now that we're alone, my dear, I have something I want to share with you."

I COULDN'T MOVE.

My knees locked against buckling. My heart thundered from fighting with Jethro. I hated myself for *missing* him. The instant the door closed behind him, I couldn't stop the overwhelming urge to follow.

It's because you think you understand him enough to predict his next atrocity.

I supposed that was right. Locked in a room with the man who killed my mother was a lot worse than being with the son I began to see as more than just a cold piece of ice.

"Sit, Nila." Mr. Hawk smiled from the head of the table. I was grateful he didn't come toward me or request that I go to him. But it did nothing to stop fear, repulsion, and rage from saturating my heart.

Pouring himself some orange juice from the carafe beside him, he muttered, "You have such a low opinion of us."

Slowly, I sank back into my chair. Gripping the lip of the table, I forced myself to stay calm and ready to fight. "What do you expect? You stole me then let your men *lick* me."

"Did they hurt you?"

His question hung heavy between us.

I wanted to lie and say yes they'd hurt me. Mentally scarred me. But that wouldn't be the truth. If anything, they'd been the first step into finally embracing the strength I'd always been afraid of. Hurt me? Yes, they'd transformed me into a stranger.

I tilted my chin, looking down my nose. "It was wrong."

"Was it? You seemed to find it pleasurable."

I refused to let my cheeks pink.

"To give an unwilling woman to a room of men is wrong. Gross. Against the law."

He chuckled, sounding way too much like his son. "Let me lay this out for you, seeing as Jethro currently seems to be struggling with following orders and discipline." He placed his elbows on the table. "Obey, and you will have free reign of my home, go where you please, direct my staff as you see fit, and truly become one of us. I don't have the time nor the inclination to keep you trapped in a tower with only the occasional scraps to keep you alive. That, my dear, in my experience doesn't make a good pet, nor does it make a willing Weaver to pay back the debts owed."

There was so much information in that small speech, I grasped at each word with eager fingers.

Jethro struggled with discipline?

Free reign?

Willing?

I wanted answers to all my questions, but I focused on the one I needed most. Twisting the truth a little, I asked, "Why do you say that about Jethro? He's been nothing but freezing cold since we met."

Mr. Hawk smiled. "Yes, he's been doing well with that. I'm rather proud of him."

My heart seized. What did that mean?

He added, "You seem to think these debts will be monstrous. Shall I put your mind at rest, so you may relax and enjoy our hospitality?"

There's nothing you can say to make me relax while under your heinous roof.
"No. I'll never enjoy anything you offer me."

He scowled. "The First Debt will be the easiest. The simplest extraction of payment for something your ancestors did. The next will be slightly more taxing and so on and so forth, until all debts are accounted for."

I know that, arsehole. Your son told me.

Smirking, he added, "The timeframe for each debt will be decided by Jethro and myself, depending on your acceptance of your new life. And rewards will be given when you fully cooperate." Taking a sip of juice, he finished, "Don't worry about your future; we have it completely under control."

Ugh, I couldn't stand his egotistical attitude. "You do realise none of this is legal. The Human Rights Act abolished selling people into slavery. You can't keep me forever."

Mr. Hawk went deathly still. "I see you've been researching while cooped up in your room." Wiping his mouth, he muttered, "No amount of laws or rules will save you, Ms. Weaver. The debts between our two families trump all that."

Only in your sick, twisted mind.

Changing the subject, I crossed my arms and snapped, "Jethro already told me how the debts would be laid out. Tell me something new."

Mr. Hawk froze. "He did *what?*"

Oh, God. Jethro's weakness around me was to my advantage. Why did I say that? Why tip off his tyrannical father to his son's hidden softness?

Backtracking, I muttered, "He told me while dragging me back after hunting me down." Holding up my scratched arms from tree branches, I hoped the evidence of being mistreated at Jethro's hands would mollify him. "He hunted me with the same dogs he made me sleep with. You should be proud of your son, sir. He's a monster."

A monster with a heart buried deep beneath that snow you make him embrace.

Mr. Hawk smiled coldly. "I'm rather surprised and impressed by his initiative. That wasn't discussed, nor part of the planned activities, but perhaps I underestimated him."

Standing, he threw his napkin from his lap onto the table. "Now, if you'll excuse me. I'm late to another meeting. I'm sure Jethro will come collect you."

Bowing, as if I were the Lady of the Manor all set for a day of cross-stitch and sedate relaxation, he pressed his fingertips to his mouth and blew a gentle kiss. "Good day, Ms. Weaver."

My ingrained manners almost repeated the polite parting; I bit my tongue.

Don't you dare. He's the devil, not some kind-hearted father figure.

Keeping my lips glued together, I remained silent.

Mr. Hawk passed my chair, stopping briefly to run his hand through my ponytail.

I shivered as the soft tug of his fingers whispered through the black strands.

"Such a pretty thing. I can see I'll have to step up my lessons with my son to ensure you both behave."

My heart lurched, speeding around my chest.

What the hell did that mean?

Staying stiff and unyielding, I didn't mutter a sound as he tugged once on my ponytail, then disappeared from the room.

I was left alone in the cavernous space with the beady eyes of past Hawks watching my every move. The glittering chandeliers above twinkled with sunlight spilling in from leadlight windows.

Little rainbows danced across my knuckles, reminding me of the design that'd come to me when I stood naked and about to run for my life. Fractals from the diamond collar around my neck had inspired rather than repulsed.

That seemed like an age ago.

My old life had faded so fast; it seemed almost dreamlike. Had I really been heralded as the next star of London couture?

It seemed surreal and something I didn't even crave. I hated the limelight. So how did I think I could walk headfirst into a career where I would forever have to sell myself in order to peddle my creations? I would no longer be holed up in a room full of calico and satin with assistants. I would be the face of *Nila*—my brand.

The show in Milan had taken every reserve I had. And that had been the first one.

I would never have survived.

Yet another part of my life where the Hawks had meddled and granted me a reprieve. I hated that they'd shown me a different way of existing—one I was better suited to than my own heritage.

The longer I sat there, the more my mind skipped from subject to subject. My fingers itched to text my brother and Kite, but bloody Jethro had my phone.

I have to get it back.

I didn't know what I waited for. Someone to come and claim me? Jethro to ensnare me and cart me off to do whatever horrible things he planned next? But no one came to fetch me or demand I follow.

Staff, a mixture of men and women in smart black and white uniforms, entered the room to clear away breakfast.

They smiled kindly, going about their business as if life was normal. Completely fucking normal.

I deliberated staying in the dining room where it was moderately peaceful with the bustle of staff and gentle clinking of crockery, but I couldn't look at the table without flushing and suffering a dreadfully unwanted spasm of lust at the memory of Jethro's tongue.

My skin crawled to think that I found comfort in the very same room men had stripped me bare—not just my body, but my sanity, too—and delivered me into this new fate.

I have to leave.

Standing, I stumbled forward as the room went blank.

I groaned as I clutched frantically at the table, only just managing to stay on my feet as a heavy black wave of vertigo stole my vision and hijacked my limbs.

"Miss, are you okay?" a sweet maid asked. I couldn't see her as my vision remained blocked.

"Yes, I'm fine. Just stood up too fast, that's all."

I began counting down from ten silently. By the time I hit three, my vision suddenly shed the blackness, splashing colour and images onto my retinas.

I sighed in relief.

Swallowing back the small wash of sickness, I smiled at the maid and made my way to the double doors. I pushed them open, heading into the corridor.

The attack had been the first one today.

I didn't want to admit it, but the last two days of peace locked in my room had done me a world of good. I would never tell the truth to Jethro, but my episodes seemed to have relaxed their lunatic need to torture me. Either a mixture of my new strength or just the vacation from overworking…my body had found a sustainable equilibrium.

For now.

Looking around, I frowned.

No one.

The corridor was empty with only glittering polished weapons and immaculate tapestries for company.

Where is everyone?

Mr. Hawk did say I could roam free. Should I see if that was true?

Hesitantly, as if I expected someone to jump out from behind a suit of armour and attack me, I drifted left—the same direction where Jethro had dragged me toward the exit and given me my one and only chance for freedom.

Peculiarly, knowing that I'd had my shot and failed granted a sense of indulgent serenity. I lacked that drive to run, because I knew there would be no point. As much as I wanted to escape, it took away the obligation of *trying* to get free by knowing it was impossible.

I couldn't get it balanced in my head. But there it was.

Another truth I'd been made to face—another facet of myself I had to come to terms with.

Deciding not to go outside, despite the pleasant sunlight, I turned right down another corridor. Following the ribbons of pathways, I moved toward the bowels of the house.

After a few minutes, the rumble of voices came from an ajar door. I froze.

I didn't want to get caught doing something I wasn't supposed to, but I couldn't stop my abhorrent curiosity.

Tiptoeing closer, I peeked inside.

There were two men in leather jackets, laughing as they packed guns into a satchel. I leaned forward for a better vantage. *Guns?*

The floorboards creaked beneath my toes, whipping their heads up.

My heart sank. Kestrel and Flaw.

"Nila," Kes said, dropping the bag on a wingback chair. Striding quickly to the door, he dragged me into the room.

The décor was best described as old-world comfort. A saloon of sorts with glass cases full of antiquities and soaring shelves of leather-bound literature. The huge windows permitted sunshine to illuminate dust motes and drench the slightly faded geometric carpet.

My skin tingled beneath his touch.

I backpedalled, tugging on his hold. "Let me go."

Kes grinned. His broad jaw, dimple in one cheek, and muscular frame was so different to Jethro. Jethro was sleek, refined—a true diamond. Kes was more of a diamond in the rough.

His fingers squeezed mine in welcome. "A pleasure to see you again." He poked his head back into the corridor. "And wait…no brother to fight for your affections?"

I couldn't untwist my tongue to reply; my mind was otherwise occupied with all things deception. *Kite. Is he Kite?*

When I didn't reply, Kes let me go and moved deeper into the room. Smiling, he asked, "Exploring the place?"

My heart raced at the way he watched me. Eager, interested, and…inquisitively kind. The crude text messages and short temper of Kite all tripped and tangled in my mind. He was such an arrogant arse via text messaging, but he seemed open and…understanding in person.

Of course, he understands. He's been talking to you for a month. Having phone sex with you. Masturbating to the messages you sent.

I shuddered in disgust and embarrassment.

It'd been fun when we'd had the power of anonymity. Now, faced with what I'd said, it was downright mortifying.

How can I get you to admit what I know? Correct that—what I think I know.

How could I be so sure that the tall, strong Hawk before me was Kite?

"Cat got your tongue?" Kes cocked his head.

"I think she's bowled over by your welcoming charm," Flaw chuckled.

My attention diverted to him. To the biker who ruptured my life by planting false photographs and standing by as I fell prey to a heartless hellion.

I wanted to tell them what I really thought. I wanted to ask why they were being so nice to me all of a sudden, but the only word I could catch hold of was Kite.

Kite.

Kes.

Kite.

Get it together. Until you know for sure, don't let on.

Straightening my shoulders, I inched forward. "No one has caught my tongue, and I wouldn't kid yourself that I'm speechless thanks to a welcome from either of you."

"Oh, she has a backbone," Flaw said, grinning.

Kes's golden eyes, so like Jethro, Daniel, and Mr. Hawk, searched mine. "She has more than that. Her entire body is made up of steel."

My knees locked into place. I wanted to scream at him to speak the truth, then strike him down for lying to me.

What did that mean? Some cryptic clue that he knew I knew along with some vague acknowledgement that we weren't strangers? That he was my...*friend?*

No, he's not my friend.

He's my enemy in disguise.

I couldn't let myself be swayed by anyone's motives.

Sticking my nose in the air, fully embracing an uppity heiress, I said, "You're just like the rest of them."

Kes blinked. "Pardon?"

"Don't 'pardon' me. You know exactly what I'm talking about."

The messages, you idiot.

Flaw stepped forward, looking at both of us. Standing just outside my personal space, he extended his hand. "I think we got off on the wrong foot. I'm Flaw. Real name's Rhys, but we never go by birth names in this place."

I couldn't stop anger heating my cheeks. "You think I wish to shake your hand? The same hand that went into my room, packed up my belongings, and wrote a note to my father explaining my disappearance?"

Flaw held up a finger. "Technically, that wasn't for your father but for the paparazzi who followed you around. But I will take responsibility for breaking into your room and packing."

The way he talked and moved reminded me a little of my brother. Both were black-haired with lanky frames. A crippling pang of homesickness filled me. "Were you there?"

Flaw frowned. "There? Where there?"

I balled my hands. I didn't remember him being there, but then again my attention at that welcome luncheon was skewed. I'd been more focused on the pieces of parchment rather than tongues. "Were you one of the ones who...*licked* me?"

Flaw had the decency to blanch. "No. I was overseeing a shipment for Jet. I heard about it, though."

I laughed coldly. "*Heard* about it?" I shot a glower at Kes. His arms were crossed, looking pensive.

My voice ached with defiance. "If you've been told details of what happened, what is your opinion, from an outsider's perspective?"

What are you doing?

The whole conversation had no point. I didn't know why I pushed it. I just knew I couldn't breathe properly ensconced in a room with Kestrel. I was argumentative, jumpy, and completely on edge.

Flaw looked at Kes, shrugging as if asking for guidance. Kes nodded, chewing on the inside of his cheek, obviously just as lost as I was with where I was going with this.

Taking a deep breath, Flaw muttered, "I was told why they did it—it was an icebreaker. To remove barriers between you and the brotherhood. I was told it was a onetime thing and from now on to treat you as one of us."

"Better than one of us," Kes murmured. "You're our guest, first and foremost, and we're responsible for your wellbeing."

There were so many inconsistencies in that sentence; I didn't know where to begin.

Didn't he get it that I wasn't a guest but a woman destined to die? I was their captive!

Ignoring Kes for now, I glared at Flaw. "That was the reason you were told. What about what *you* believe? Tell me if you found it acceptable. Tell me how you would feel if all of this happened to your sister or wife."

Kes sucked in a breath beside me. "I see what you're doing, Nila."

I shuddered at the use of my first name. I'd been trying so long for Jethro to use it, yet his younger brother needed no such encouragement.

Abandoning my witch-hunt on Flaw, I turned to the man who made me itch with annoyance, intrigue, and temper. "What do you see, *Kestrel?*"

Kes's eyes tightened; something harsh and hot flowed between us. Some resemblance of the kinky, sexual man from our text messages flashed, then was hidden. "I know you're searching for validation of being debased in such a way. Regardless of what you think, it wasn't sexual. Those men weren't there to get off on tasting you. They were there to strip you."

I laughed. "Well, they certainly succeeded."

I was naked and had my first orgasm in front of them. *If that isn't the bare essentials of any human, I don't know what is.*

Kes continued, "What if I told you that whole thing wasn't just about you? What if I told you the men who witnessed your nakedness and were privileged enough to taste you were now indebted to you?"

"Don't talk to me about debts," I snarled.

Kes inched closer, encroaching on my mental safety. "By seeing you struggle, by witnessing the power that grew in you with each round of the table, you earned their respect. You earned their devotion. And you were welcomed into our world with no barriers. *That's* what the lunch was about. A power play where you gave up your power and gained theirs in return."

I couldn't stand his crisp, accented voice delivering something that shouldn't make sense, only for it to resonate perfectly inside.

Murmuring, he said, "You can't deny you feel different. Stronger. Braver. You were at your most vulnerable, but you survived." Reaching up, he captured the ends of my ponytail cascading over my shoulder. "We showed you your true worth, Nila Weaver, and now you'll have the strength to face the future intact and not break until it's time."

My heart stuttered then died. "You gave me all of that, just so I wouldn't be broken for the Final Debt?"

The cruelty. The *brutality*.

Locking eyes with me, Kes whispered, "I give you my word. You are strong enough to get through this."

The room faded until the only thing that existed was Kes and I. I didn't know if it was the possibility of him being Kite that drew me to him or the empathy deep in his gaze but *something* was undeniable. The longer we stared, the more he drained me of fight and fortified me with courage.

"Forgive me?" he whispered.

"*Forgive* you?"

My mind skipped. Was he asking for forgiveness for licking me like his brothers or for deceiving me with text messages?

Either way, I had no willpower to offer him absolution.

Did I take a wrong turn somewhere? Had I entered an alternate universe where I was no longer a prisoner, destined to be a plaything for bastards, and somehow became an...*equal*?

Kes moved closer, his body heat making me quiver. "I understand why you can't. I was selfish for asking something you can't give."

A crashing headache squeezed my temples. "I—I don't understand what's going on." I flinched as the words spilled from my mouth, raining confusion and vulnerability.

Kes didn't twitch or move away, only twirled his fingers in my hair. "You'll understand, soon enough." Closing his eyes briefly, he released my ponytail and took a step back.

Instantly, the real world swamped into being: sunlight, the feel of luxurious carpet beneath my flip-flops, and the crackle of wood burning in the large fireplace behind Flaw.

If this was another game orchestrated by the hellish Mr. Hawk, then he'd just won because Kestrel had drained me more successfully than anyone. He'd made me pliant and submissive. He'd done what no amount of fear or arguing with Jethro could achieve.

And that made Kestrel deadly.

My heart thrummed with true fear.

Another huge difference between the brothers: one used softness to control me; the other wielded frost and fury.

How naïve was I to believe Kes could ever be on my side. He was the polar opposite—the snake in the proverbial grass—just waiting for Jethro to fail, so he could sink his fangs of pity into me and bring me under his spell.

I knew without a doubt I had to understand my enemies, and quickly, before they manipulated my mind with falsities.

Taking a deep breath, I crossed my arms across my chest, wishing I had a jacket. The chill of my conclusions stole into my blood, making me shiver with trepidation.

What had just happened, and why did I feel as if I'd lost?

At least with Jethro, I *saw* him. We were evenly matched in will and temper. And we both conceded defeat with yet another challenge met head on.

Kestrel was dangerous.

Treacherous.

Skilled in manipulation so clever, my thoughts were enamoured and I had no hope of deciphering what truly occurred.

Flaw clapped his hands, completely dispelling the tense mood. "I'm glad that's all resolved."

Moving toward the wingback where a saddlebag revealed the muzzles of weapons, he plucked it off and patted the buttoned leather. "Sit. Hang out with us, if you don't have anything else to do." Shooting a look at Kes, he said to me, "Can I get a maid to bring you something? Coffee, tea, a snack?"

I looked into his dark eyes, utterly gobsmacked. "Is this a new strategy? Commiserate with the indebted girl—give her the illusion she has *friends*?"

Flaw shook his head. "Uh…"

"Everyone is to treat you with utmost civility, Nila. It isn't a trick," Kes's deep voice rumbled.

Trick?

This was beyond a trick. It was an entire *production* of tricks.

But what could I do? Nothing. I just had to play along and hope I could see the truth through the lies.

Flaw nodded at the door. "You found us—remember? We have nothing to gain by inviting you in here and talking."

Kes said, "He's right. We're not going to hurt you."

But you did if you're Kite. You hurt me by pretending.

I glared hard, hoping he'd get my unspoken message.

Kes looked away, hiding any hint he might've picked up on my temper. Stalking toward the groaning bookshelves lining the walls of the saloon, he cupped his chin, searching for something.

"Ah, ha." Snagging an oversized tome with tatty bindings, he brought it back toward me with a twinkle in his eyes. "I think this might interest you."

Beckoning me to take a seat, he pulled up an ottoman and sat beside the empty wingback. Quirking his eyebrow, he waited for me to deliberate.

Should I leave or stay? Should I continue to play whatever this was or go and hunt for the man who made me wet and terrified me?

Slowly, my feet moved toward the chair. Sinking down onto the firm leather, Kes placed the heavy book into my lap. "Relax and forget about this world for a while."

I couldn't take my eyes off the literature. A large gold filigree 'W' embossed the cover with what looked like an oak tree sprouting countless limbs of foliage.

"What is it?" I asked, tracing the majestic old-wealth of such a book.

Kes grinned, inching closer to open the first page. "It's your history."

My heart thrummed as his bulk seared my left side. My eyes devoured the beautifully scripted calligraphy.

"Every Weaver woman who's stayed with us has made notes and shared her journey, along with patterns and fashions created while living with us." He gently flipped a page, where faint sketches decorated along with the signature of one of my ancestors. Notes scribbled about what sort of fabric to source, along with diary-like entries of what life was like living in the nest of Hawks.

My hands shook. Leaning over, I couldn't read fast enough.

Today was a good day. Bonnie had the chiffon I requested delivered, and I spent the afternoon in her chambers, creating a new crinoline evening gown. She's a surly old bat, but when you get to know her...

The next paragraph had been scribbled out, so dark and determined, I had no hope of reading what was written. It continued:

The passion to create had disappeared. I lived in a void with no urge to sketch or pin or sew. I hate that I've found that passion here of all places, but at least...

As much as I do not wish to admit—I'm happy.

My eyes shot up to Kestrel's. "You're trying to prove that my family were *content* with their imprisonment?" My heart froze over at such atrocities. But how could I deny it when it was in black and white?

Kes smiled softly. "Happiness comes in many forms: sex, freedom, control. I think everyone has the capacity to find happiness in even the darkest of places."

Grabbing the majority of the pages, he flipped them over, revealing unmarred parchment.

Chills scattered down my back.

It's for me.

It's been waiting for me to fill with my journey.

"This is yours, Nila. If there aren't enough blank pages, we'll have a book binder add more." With gentle fingertips, he tucked a loose piece of hair behind my ear.

I jolted from his touch, my emotions going haywire.

"This is the first gift of many. You'll see."

My eyes locked with his; a ball lodged in my throat.

Awareness sparked between us; my lips parted as I sucked in a breath. Kes looked at me the exact same way Jethro had after our fight in the forest, after he'd blown down my throat, after I'd won. That same awe, same secretive amazement, now blazed in his brother's gaze.

Words deserted me as I fell into his soul, allowing him to spellbind me, despite everything that he was.

I gasped as his fingers clasped mine, squeezing hard. Dropping his voice to a soft whisper, he said, "Whatever you think of my family, don't let it taint what you think of me." Waving with his free hand, he continued, "These are my quarters. My bedroom is off this saloon. If it ever gets to be too much, if my brother ever goes too far, you're welcome to find sanctuary here."

Bowing his head, energy and connection poured from him. "You're *always* welcome."

My heart hurled itself against my ribcage, bruising itself in its urge to flee or perhaps surrender to the perfectly delivered offer of kinship.

I froze as he cupped my chin. My skin twinged as he held me firm. "Now, Nila Weaver, read. Forget us, and spend time with your true family."

THREE FUCKING HOURS, I looked for her.

I hunted through Hawksridge Hall, opened doors into rooms I never wanted to step foot into ever again, and stalked down corridors I'd long since forgotten about as I never explored that part of the house.

I bumped into Diamond Brothers and got caught up in a strategy meeting for the next shipment arriving in three days, but no matter how many bedrooms, bathrooms, and lounges I searched, I found nothing.

Nothing!

Had she run again? Could she be that fucking stupid to try and escape after I'd proven how useless that was?

Damn my father for dismissing us.

The moment I'd stepped outside the dining room, Kes had requested my help on a matter. Seeing as he was the only person I had time for, I reluctantly followed, even though I wanted to wait till Cut had finished with Nila. I fucking *hated* her being alone with him. My knuckles ached from fisting so hard, and I didn't know how I would survive when the time came to share.

I'd go fucking insane.

I'd have to make sure all loaded ammunition was barred from the house, so I didn't end up slaughtering my entire family.

Nila Weaver was mine, goddammit. I didn't want anyone talking, touching, or twisting her thoughts without my permission.

Calm the fuck down.

I slammed to a stop in the middle of a corridor. If I bumped into

Cut in this state, he'd know I wasn't coping. He'd take me so damn low, I wouldn't stand a chance of climbing out of the glacier so fast.

You shouldn't be thawing so quickly.

I agreed with my internal logic. I shouldn't be feeling this type of emotion. I shouldn't be letting my feelings get the better of me.

Breathing hard through my nose, I locked my jaw and recited the same thing I did every day, ten times a day, twenty even—all to remind myself of who I was meant to be and hide who I truly was.

My lips moved as I let the words trickle silently in my mind.

I'm a shadow lurking in plain sight.

A predator in sheep's clothing.

I prey on the weak with no apology.

I hide my true temper beneath a veil of decorum.

I've mastered the art of suave.

I'm a gentleman. Distinguished, accomplished, and shrewd.

I'm all of those things but none of them.

Rules and laws don't apply to me.

I'm a rule-breaker, curse-maker, life-stealer.

The minute I'd finished, my hands balled, and the devil's advocate whispered in my ear.

You're lying. It's a farce.

Clenching my jaw, I forced my heart rate to calm and for the ice to take me hostage. Repeating the mantra, I slowly fell under its hypnosis. My back relaxed, the knots in my muscles unthreading. My sweaty palms went paper dry and cold, while my face turned slack with uncaring.

Finally.

The calmness siphoning through my veins was welcome, turning everything frigid and controllable in its path.

Everything about my life since I was fifteen fucking years old was a carefully designed and executed illusion.

Up till now, I'd survived.

I'd buried the true me beneath a man so cold and perfect—even I believed—most of the time.

But every now and again, a hairline fracture would show in my glacier shell.

And my father would notice.

And he would...'fix' me.

Until I was old enough to fix myself, of course.

Which I'd done only the night before, so why was I having such difficulty now?

The thawing had happened too fast. Normally, I could pass a few weeks, sometimes more, before I ever needed to be fixed. But Nila Weaver was the sun upon my ice, turning me into a river that wanted to flow and change and *grow*. Not freeze and remain forever unmovable.

There was only one course of action to get through her invasion into my senses and survive her stay with us. I just didn't know if I had the strength to do it.

Shaking away that terrible thought, I prowled forward.

The sounds of men came and went as I passed rooms, and scents of fresh baking from the kitchens made my mouth water.

I almost walked right past her as I moved through the house lost in my thoughts. The sounds of conversation muted my attention, and if it hadn't have been for the strangest sound imaginable, I would've strode right by.

I slammed to a halt outside my brother's room.

Outside my *brother's* room.

The abominable sound came again.

Laughter.

Feminine laughter.

Nila's laughter.

And it wasn't cynical or full of contempt—it was light-hearted and relaxed.

The lyrical sound twisted my heart, turning my self-pity into fucking rage. I barged into Kestrel's apartment wing with no knock, no request, and slammed to a halt.

Flaw, Kes, and Nila sat in a grouping of wingbacks, smiling and sharing a good old fucking laugh.

What. The. Fuck?

Kes looked up, his mouth spread into a broad smile. "Jet! Nice of you to join us." His tone was a direct contradiction to his welcome.

I narrowed my eyes, trying to understand how my brother—my one ally who knew the truth about me—was antagonising me to the point of ruining everything. What was his deal?

I stupidly felt betrayed—worse than betrayed—*provoked*.

Nila's laugh cut off as she sat straighter in her chair. Her cheeks were flushed, annoyance at my interruption bright in her dark eyes.

She had the gall to be annoyed at me? When she *belonged* to me?

Flaw had the decency to stand. "Eh, I think I better go check on the…" Clearing his throat, he moved away from the small group. "Catch you guys later."

With a sideways look at me, he disappeared through the door, shutting it behind him.

The moment he'd gone, I seethed, "Care to explain what's going on?"

Kes stood up. "Calm down and no, I don't. You don't have to understand everything, Jet." Throwing a quick grin at Nila, he asked, "Unless you'd care to tell my brother what's so funny?"

Nila stared at me coldly. A second ticked past, then another, her temper shooting me cleanly through the chest.

"Well?" My heart pounded, once again shrugging out of the frosty shield in favour of rage.

Finally, she shook her head. "No. I don't think he deserves to know."

Okay…that was just plain rude.

Kes snickered. "Fair enough."

My teeth almost cracked from clenching. Why had I been worried about what I was about to do to her? She made me believe she cared—just a little—about me. She'd sucked me off for Christ's sake. She'd asked me to *fuck* her. She was attracted to me. I *knew* that.

Just like I was attracted to her.

So much.

Too much.

I was beyond fucking ready to slam inside her wet heat and finally show her the truth. That no matter her birth-right or mine, we were equals. And I'd never met anyone as challenging or intriguing.

But she'd manipulated me.

She'd used me, not once, but more times than I knew. All along I'd been fighting for the right to gain her trust, only for her to give it to my bloody brother.

Damn woman. Damn Weaver Whore.

Snapping my fingers, I hissed, "You've had your fun. Congratulations on winning once again, Ms. Weaver." Pointing at the ground by my shoes, I ordered coldly, "Come. It's time. You've wasted my day hiding. Now it's time to get this over with."

Nila tilted her chin insolently. "I didn't know we were fighting for something. Why exactly did I win?"

Goddammit.

Ignoring her question, I repeated. "Come. Now."

Kes crossed his arms, watching us as if we were his favourite volleyball match.

Nila rose gracefully from her seat. In her hands, she held the Weaver journal, which she stroked reverently, before transferring it from her lap and onto the chair she'd just vacated. Her actions were stiff, back ramrod straight. "Whatever you believe, I wasn't hiding, Jethro. Merely finding friends in the unlikely of places."

I froze as she moved toward Kestrel.

He opened his arms.

She walked into his embrace.

She walked into his *fucking* embrace.

I couldn't understand.

I didn't *want* to understand.

She prefers him over you, idiot. She can see you're different. She can sense you're screwed up.

The hug lasted far longer than my tolerance level. Who was I kidding—I *had* no tolerance level.

Kes was mine, and Nila was mine. They both belonged to me. They had no right to gang up against me.

"Kes…" I immediately snapped my lips together. I refused to be weak and ask him what the hell this meant. Instead, I embraced vulgarity. "I wouldn't get close to her, brother. Never know where her mouth has been." My tone was a viper ready to strike.

Kestrel let Nila go, eyeing me coldly. "If it's been anywhere on you, then I can guess. But you're forgetting, *brother*, I'm not the one with sharing issues. Am I?"

My mouth fell open. A pain shot deep inside my heart. In our entire lifetime together, he'd never provoked me that way. Never brought up something so painful or the crux of my whole issue.

"Fuck you," I growled.

Kes's eyes tightened, finally showing some sign of regret. Bastard.

Nila looked between us silently, crackling with energy. No doubt this family drama was hugely amusing to her. I never wanted her to see me like this. What was this? Had Kestrel finally had enough of being second best to the firstborn son, or had he seen something he truly wanted in Nila?

Either way, it didn't matter. He couldn't have her. No one could.

"Jet, let's forget it, okay?" Holding up his hands, he added, "Bygones, yeah?"

"Bygones? What the hell are you doing?"

Kes shook his head. "We'll talk about it later. Right now, you have things to do."

"Things like extract a debt from me?" Nila snapped.

My attention flew to her, just in time to see her topple sideways as one of her stupid episodes rendered her incompetent.

"Shit." Kes ducked at inhuman speed, catching her before she hit the ground.

My stomach twisted with jealousy.

Moaning, Nila crumbled into Kes's arms.

"You all right?" Kes slowly guided her onto her feet.

That—right there. *That* was the true difference between my brother and me. He caught those who needed to be caught, while I stood by and watched. The memory of Nila falling to the parking garage floor at the Milan airport showed me just how true that statement was.

I have no choice.

Empathy and softness weren't permitted. They were the root of all evil for a person like me.

Taking a deep breath, Nila pushed Kes gently. "I'm fine. Thanks for your help."

Kes nodded, shoving his hands into his jeans pockets. "You're welcome. You should probably have that looked at."

"It's not a disease," I jumped in. "Besides, she's better than when I first collected her."

Nila's cheeks blazed with colour. She wobbled a little as another wave hit her. "Do you know why that is? I was thinking about it before actually."

No one spoke, waiting for her to continue.

"I get them when I'm stressed. I probably suffered five or six a day when I was working so hard and presenting my new season to buyers and reporters. And yet, here...I only seem to suffer them around *you*." Cocking her head, she placed her fists on her hips. "What does that tell you, Jethro?"

What did it tell me? Apart from the fact she was weak-minded and needed professional help for a counter imbalance? "That I stress you out."

"Exactly."

Another wave crippled her. Kes was the convenient arsehole who captured her elbow giving her an anchor. "There you go again. You okay?"

She nodded, rubbing her temples. "Sorry. Damn vertigo. Can't control it."

Kes smiled, his body curved into hers. "Don't apologise. We all have flaws, and sometimes they're not something we have the power to change."

He's talking about me again. Fuckwit.

Nila's lips popped open, her eyes searching his. "You're nothing like your phone messages."

My muscles instantly locked.

Her voice was barely a whisper. I wouldn't have caught it unless my ears weren't already straining for every nuance in her tone.

She knows.

Kes cocked his head, his eyes blocking all clues and answers. Laughing self-consciously, he quickly pressed a kiss on her cheek and released her. "If that's a good thing, I'll take the credit."

That's it.

I was fucking done.

Stalking forward, I plucked Nila from the carpet and threw her over my shoulder. Kes's mouth fell open. "Um…"

"Don't say another word, *brother*." I transmitted everything I couldn't say with one glare. "Stay out of this. All of it."

Nila squealed, hitting my back with tiny fists. "Put me down, you arsehole."

"No chance," I growled. "I'm not letting you go until I have you exactly where I want you."

Preferably naked with my cock driving between your legs.

But because I was the perfect son, I would have to save that for another day.

There was a small matter of a debt. A debt that had to be repaid before the day turned into dusk—for no other reason but tradition. We'd run out of time.

Kes stared at me, his eyes waging with an apology and confrontation. If Nila wasn't here, I had no doubt we'd either pummel each other or have the deepest, longest conversation of our lives. This one incident had brought everything we'd avoided to a head.

Kes and I were friends—more than I could say for the rest of the people inside this house—but despite our friendship, there was still a thick rivalry between us. Not just because of primogeniture and the fact I would inherit everything, but because we'd both been hurt by the same incident in our pasts.

We just dealt with it differently.

He'd played a good game where Nila was concerned. A game I'd never been able to master—the art of wielding kindness. My kindness came with too many conditions and more pain than if I remained cruel. But Kes, he was…better than me.

I knew the real him. And despite my agony at him wanting Nila's attention, he was a good guy.

Silently, he raised a finger, pointing it in my face. Nila couldn't see him as he mouthed, "I know it's not working. We need to find other methods."

Shit, if he could see, Cut wouldn't be too far behind.

"Dammit, Jethro, put me down." Nila hammered on my lower back.

Ignoring her, I shifted her higher over my shoulder and nodded once.

Then I put every worry and thought in the vault deep inside me and lashed the chains tight. I had work to do.

Not giving Kes the satisfaction of seeing me ruffled, I spun around and left without a word with my prize slung over my shoulder.

"Let me go!" Nila continued to pummel my back with every step.

"I won't put you down until we get there. I've wasted three hours of my life wondering where you were. I'm not going to release you just so you can escape again."

"We've already solved the 'what if I ran game.' I know you'd hunt me down. I wouldn't waste the energy trying to escape."

I grunted. "At least you've learned one thing that's valuable."

"I've learned a lot more than that," she muttered quietly.

Yes, like who Kite007 is.

My arm squeezed tighter around her. Bloody brother. The minute I had time, I would confront him with all the shit he'd caused.

Swallowing hard, I forced myself to slip back into the ice and embrace everything that I ought to be.

I had a debt to extract.

This was what was expected of me.

And I meant to do it fucking well.

It didn't take long to arrive in the room where the First Debt would take place.

Tradition dictated where each one was to be carried out. And this one was the nicest location of them all.

As the debts progressed, witnesses would be called, but as this was the first, it was just me and Nila. Blessed silence and no critical eyes on my deliverance. Only the hidden video camera would document everything and go on file.

Entering the solarium, I locked the large glass doors and pocketed the key before gripping Nila's waist and placing her on the ground. She immediately stepped backward, her chest heaving with fear.

If she passed out again, my brother wasn't there to catch her. She'd fall, and I'd use her unconsciousness to place her exactly where she was needed.

"Where have you brought me?" She glanced around the space, taking in the palm trees, exotic ferns, orchids, and soaring three-story glass roof. The room was big, shaped like an octagon, made entirely from glass. It was hot, humid, and stuffy.

Perfect for being naked and encouraging skin to flush. To react to something painful and bloom.

"Be grateful it's not the dungeon or the ballroom—both of those will be used, and both will be a far sight worse than this."

Nila swallowed, the column of muscle of her throat contracting with nervousness. "You really are insane."

I stepped forward, secretly pleased when she reeled backward. After spending time in my brother's company, she had to remember who she truly liked. As much as she'd vehemently deny it, she enjoyed sparring with me.

And fuck, I enjoyed it, too.

"Mental health, Ms. Weaver. Need I remind you I'm in perfect capacity?"

Her head swivelled to a large post in the centre of the room. It was used mainly for fern seedlings and vines, before being replanted once their root system was strong enough. I wasn't a gardener, but my grandmother often brought me and my sister in here to teach us about decorum and what was expected of us. She'd prattle on, all while tending to her beloved greenery.

283

Nila drifted forward, noticing what was hidden amongst the cleaned post and silk flowers that were there purely for morbid decoration.

Cuffs were chained to the top of the post, dangling down the sides. There was a winch and pulley so as to tighten the length of chain. It was simple, entirely in keeping with how they would've used a whipping post six-hundred-years ago.

She shook her head, swivelling to face me. "Whatever you're about to do, stop."

"Stop?" *As if I have a choice. Smile for the cameras. We're both on show.*

"Yes. Just—find that morality I know is inside you. Show some compassion, for God's sake." She staggered to the side, another small vertigo spell.

I'd hated her weakness before, but now it could be used as an aid. Whenever she stumbled or fell, it meant I was getting to her. It meant I'd made my way beneath her skin and stressed her just enough for her mind to try and flee.

It was a symbol of power over her.

I liked it more than I should.

"Compassion isn't in my repertoire, Ms. Weaver. I have no remorse, no pity. The unnecessary emotion of affinity for victims is the worst kind of betrayal." My father's words came out smoothly, stroking my raw nerves, granting a strange kind of peace.

"You can sprout bullshit all you want, but no matter your lies, you *feel*, Jethro. You felt something for me in the forest. You felt something for me when your brother held me in his arms. And if you can't see that, then I feel sorry for you."

I prowled forward, chasing her slowly around the post like a hawk chases a sparrow. "You're mistaken. I've told you on numerous occasions—please me, and you'll be rewarded. You pleased me by making me come, and you pleased me by showing how affected and scared of me you truly are by seeking comfort from my brother. Both will be rewarded."

I hoped to God she didn't hear my lies.

She stopped moving, holding her ground. "Fine. Have it your way. Your father repeated what you told me about the varying degree of each debt. This whole thing is completely ludicrous, but I'm done playing your game."

I cocked my head. "This isn't a game."

She sneered. "It's the worst game of all, don't kid yourself." Spreading her stance and opening her arms wide, she murmured, "Do your worst, Jethro Hawk. I'm ready to pay your First Debt."

I WANTED TO hyperventilate; my heart winged with such terror.

But I wouldn't give him the satisfaction. He already knew he affected me by my stupid vertigo spells. He didn't need to know the complex fear and fascination bubbling in my blood.

Why hadn't I seen it sooner? Why hadn't I seen past what he projected and looked deeper into his golden eyes? He was so tangled up in what he *thought* he was, he had no clue what he might be.

And that was a pitiful shame, not to mention dangerous for all involved. I could predict how he would react, based on what values he pretended to follow, but he could easily snap and do something completely the opposite.

Damn man.

Damn Hawk.

Jethro lowered his chin, glaring at me from beneath his brow. His hands opened and closed by his thighs. "You're ready to pay the First Debt? Just like that?"

I nodded. "No point in dragging it out. I want it over with."

Something flashed over his face, but he didn't retaliate. Instead, he gritted his teeth and moved toward the post in the centre of the octagonal greenhouse.

My vision wouldn't stop hazing in and out, tugging on the strings of my brain, threatening to throw me into the wall or shove me to the ground.

This is the First Debt.

Mr. Hawk's and Jethro's words echoed in my head. *The debts start off easy.* It was the later ones I had to worry about. The ones I didn't know of. The ones that would ultimately deliver my head.

Don't think about that.

I turned my mind to Kestrel and the surprising kinship I'd begun to feel, before Jethro rudely stole me away. For almost three hours, I'd found something I didn't think I'd ever find—in my old life or new.

A friend.

Kes had been witty and kind, sharing anecdotes of his childhood, Jethro's childhood, and even some details he remembered of my mother. For some reason, having him talk about her didn't upset me nearly as much as hearing it from Jethro or his father.

I knew I had to stay on my guard after what Cut had said: *I'm to be treated with kindness and compassion.* I could easily fall into the trap of thinking their concern was genuine. But…if Kes *was* Kite, we had a connection that went past family obligations.

Don't we?

Regardless, we'd spent a couple of hours sharing things that'd transported me away from Hawksridge Hall and to a place filled with softness. A connection formed, dusting my tummy with tentative bubbles of attraction.

He was nice…despite my healthy suspicion of his motives.

But one thing niggled me.

One thing I hadn't been able to figure out.

He was completely different from the man who cursed and acted so crude via text messages. His arrogant way of demanding sexual gratification when not face-to-face was a direct contradiction to his kindness in person.

It didn't make sense—almost as if he had split personas—once again proving my theory that all Hawks were daft.

"What did my father tell you?" Jethro asked.

I blinked, forcing myself to pay attention to the mad man currently circling me like a vulture. "What?"

Jethro balled his hands. "When he kept you back, what did he say?"

I shrugged. "Same thing as you. I learned nothing new." The way he watched me hinted that he had secrets he didn't want spilled. Narrowing my eyes, I asked, "Why?"

He shook his head. "No reason." Clearing his throat, he added, "So, you were told you're now the obedient family dog, correct? To be treated kindly and receive everything you want."

My heart squeezed. Anger flowed thick and cloying. "Something like that." *And just like a mistreated pet, I'll shred the fingers that feed me.*

Jethro huffed, returning to the post again. With competent hands, he tugged on the hanging cuffs and kicked something covered by a towel at the foot of the wooden structure.

His eyes locked on mine. "Tell me, Ms. Weaver. Are you sure you're ready?"

My heart bucked into panic mode. I'd taunted him and said I was, but now faced with willingly handing myself over and letting him do whatever he wanted, it was entirely different.

When I didn't move, he murmured, "No tears. No screams. Own this just like my ancestors did when it was done to them."

The Debt Inheritance came back to mind. What had my family done that was so heinous that it called for such horrendous payback?

Swallowing hard, I inched closer to the post. "I need to understand why."

"Why?" His forehead furrowed. "Where exactly is the fun in that?"

"Fun?" Oh, my God, he would enjoy this? *What did you expect?* I supposed I kept seeing the man who was human beneath the icy robot. It led me to false conclusions, which Jethro seemed to love to smash.

"I suppose that is the wrong word." Jethro stilled, his eyes filling with things I couldn't decipher. He stood still for a long moment, before visibly shaking off whatever held him hostage. "Come here. Let's begin."

My stomach fell into my toes. Making me come on my own made all of this worse. I was the sacrificial lamb willingly walking toward the pyre.

Goosebumps broke out over my body as my feet whispered slowly toward Jethro.

He sucked in a breath.

The air went from humid to sharp with awareness. I hated that he had the power to tingle my skin and twist my belly. It wasn't fair. It wasn't right that I found him so attractive when I ought to be abhorred.

My eyes fell on the cuffs dangling between fake flowers. I didn't need to ask what he had planned. It was obvious, and I wouldn't give him the enjoyment of dragging out the suspense and toying with me.

Gritting my jaw, I pressed closer, holding my wrists up to the leather cuffs.

Jethro quirked an eyebrow, his tongue darting out to lick his bottom lip. "What are you doing?"

Gathering as much courage as I had, and hoping to God my vertigo would stay away, I smiled diabeticly sweet. "The cuffs are obviously there for a reason; I'm just saving you the trouble of instructing me."

Silence fell, rippling around us.

His jaw worked. "Just like smugness, cockiness is not becoming on you, Ms. Weaver." Leaning forward, his torso turned the already sharp awareness into biting attraction. His scent of woods and leather enveloped me. Against my wishes, my stomach clenched, and I breathed deeply.

His nostrils flared, but he didn't say another word as his strong, cold fingers latched around my wrist, tugging it higher to wrap the supple cuff around me.

The chemistry between us—or was it just blind hate—crackled and fizzed, sending the hair on the back of my neck bristling.

I couldn't deny I was drawn to Kes—partly because I thought he was Kite and partly because he had an ease about him, a generosity that made me want to know more—but it was nothing, *nothing*, compared to the fierce hunger I felt when Jethro touched me.

His lips parted as he buckled the cuff. Refusing to make eye contact, he remained focused as he cinched it tight.

Moving stiffly, he captured my other wrist.

A small gasp fell from my lips as his fingers kissed the paper-thin skin. His eyes held me hostage. The golden brown was now a swirling bronze, raging with the same demanding hunger I knew reflected in mine.

"This sort of reminds me of the forest," I whispered. "The trees around us—no one else." My words fell like petals, waiting for Jethro to crush them beneath his glossy shoe.

But…he didn't.

Tracing one hand from my wrist, along the inside of my arm, and right to my throat, he fisted my ponytail. With intensity that stripped my soul to the very essence of who I was, he pulled my head back slowly, sensually, full of sexual power.

His eyes dropped to my mouth. "I'll let you in on a little secret,

Ms. Weaver."

I panted, my neck straining against his hold, but I made no move to break the poignant awareness.

"You won that night, but I lied when I said it pissed me off." His mouth dropped, his tongue licked my bottom lip with the barest of grazes. "I've never enjoyed coming in someone's mouth as much as I did in yours." He licked me again, quaking my frame. "In fact, I would willingly let you win again, if I received the same ball-shattering release."

My lips begged to connect with his. This single-minded lust between us was sacred. The only place where we were both equal, and heritage had no authority. I'd made a promise to use sex against him, but now I added to my promise.

I will use him to make me stronger, better—invincible.

I wanted to become a woman whose arsenal included lust and sensuality, regardless of my slight frame and inexperience.

"Kiss me," I murmured, tugging my hair gently in his hold.

Jethro shook his head, his fingers tightening around my ponytail. Tracing the tip of his tongue once more on my bottom lip, he whispered, "I don't kiss my enemies."

My heart became an inferno, sending flames blazing with every beat. "You just fuck them?"

His mouth twitched into a roguish smile. "Only if they beg."

His body pressed against mine, his thigh going purposely between my legs.

My eyes snapped closed as he rocked against my throbbing clit. "Would you beg, Ms. Weaver? How hot and frustrated do I have to make you before you'll beg me to drive my cock inside you?"

My brain spasmed at the thought. The answer? Not long. I would beg right now if it meant he would forget about the debt and take me back to his room. I wanted to see where he slept. I wanted to infiltrate the home ground of my opponent and undermine him right at the source.

"You're all talk. You won't even kiss me, let alone fuck me."

Jethro yanked my head back. Pain shot down my spine. "How wrong you are, Ms. Weaver." Then a vindictive smile replaced the black desire. "Very clever, though, I must admit."

I blinked, trying to dispel the fog of lust and keep up with him. "Why?"

His thigh slid out from between my legs; his fingers untwined from my hair. "Very clever to make me focus on other things than the true reason of why we're here." Stepping back and sucking in a deep breath, he dragged a hand through his hair. "You keep on surprising me, and I keep on despising what you show me."

I laughed tightly. "Doesn't look like you despise me." I cocked my chin at the straining erection in his trousers. "I think you like me, and despite what you're going to do and who you are, I still find you attractive."

And believe me, if I had a cure for that insanity, I'd take it without hesitation.

Cruelly, he snatched my free wrist, wrapping the remaining cuff tightly. Quickly securing the buckle, he muttered, "The way you threw yourself into my brother's arms hints you might have a desire for all Hawks." His breath was hot in my ear as he spun me to face the post. "You're just a conniving manipulator."

I cried out as he disappeared behind the post and hoisted my arms high with the aid of a hidden winch. Another jerk and my wrists burned in the supple leather. My torso smashed against the damp wood as my body weight transferred from my toes to my arms.

"How does that feel?" Jethro asked, coming back around.

My shoulders screamed; my blood throbbed with effort to reach my raised fingertips. I dangled with no chance at escape.

How does it feel?

It fucking hurt! It made my previous thoughts of lust seem ridiculous.

All concepts of seducing him disappeared. I only wanted this over fast, so I could admit defeat and lick my wounds in private.

"I asked you a question," Jethro growled, his hand stroking my spine.

I flinched at his touch. It was sacrilegious, because even now it *still* made my core clench with want. "It hurts. Is that what you want to hear?"

Jethro's torso pressed against my back, squashing my cheek against the damp wood of the post. The crispness of plants and the musky scent of earth overpowered his smell, giving me a welcome reprieve from the man who drove me mad.

"You look rather tempting like this, Ms. Weaver. Perhaps it will be *me* begging before this is done."

I couldn't stop my skin shivering with awareness or my heart seizing with anxiety and desire.

"Don't touch me," I hissed.

With a small laugh, he pushed away, ceasing contact.

I twisted my neck, never letting him from my sight. I hated having him so close. I hated that I had no power to stop him. I hated how he stood there, wrapped in silence, watching me like some mystery he had yet to solve.

We didn't speak, waiting to see who would break first.

Finally, after a minute, he said softly, "I'm going to give you a history lesson, Ms. Weaver. You'll listen closely and understand why you're repaying this certain debt." Pacing, he added, "Every debt will begin this way. The history will be told, then the debt repaid. You'll be informed of what your ancestors did to mine. You will apologise and repent for their past sins, and only then will the extraction take place."

Coming close, his body heat burned me. His words were tiny whips lashing my ear. "If you do not repent and permit the debt to be paid, you will be beaten. If you do not accept why a debt has to be paid, the extraction will be taken twice. Do you understand?"

Twice?

Double horror.

Double terror.

Then…I laughed. Morbid, yes, but the image in my head was comical.

"You mean to tell me, you'll behead me twice?" I smiled. "Are you necromancers as well as lunatics? Please, inform me on how that will work."

His hand lashed out, spanking my denim-clad behind.

I groaned, jolting in the binds. I couldn't unravel the painful smarting from his strike and the throbbing in my nipples and clit.

Shit. Don't let him see that he's broken my mind already. If he touched me, felt how drenched I was, I would never live with myself again.

"I've had enough of your mouth, Ms. Weaver."

"Are you sure? Didn't seem that way in the forest with my lips around you. Did you know that was my first ever blowjob?"

He sucked in a breath. His hand landed in my hair, fisting the thickness and burning my scalp. His lips tickled my ear as he whispered, "You keep taunting me with what happened in the forest. Do you think just because you swallowed that I'm what…*grateful?*

Sentimental? In *love?*" He shook me. "What, Ms. Weaver? Shall I not remind you it was *you* who clenched around my tongue so hard you almost fucking bruised me? Every lick and fucking taste I had of your pussy, I drove you wild." He trailed the tip of his tongue from my ear to my cheek.

I trembled, every part of me tightening.

"We're on even ground. Orgasm for an orgasm. Don't think it gives you power, because it doesn't."

I breathed hard, trying to find some resemblance of the hatred I'd nursed. But he pressed his body flush against mine, grinding his erection into the small of my back.

He groaned under his breath. "What I wouldn't give to fuck you. To stop your teasing and use you like you want me to."

Everything inside me charged, ignited, spindled out of control.

The thought of having him inside me both repulsed and enticed. The mental image of us fighting this unknown battle while our naked bodies fought for domination sent scorching thrills through me.

My breathing turned to pants. "Why haven't you?"

Damn, the words fell from my lips before I had time to censor them.

Jethro's hips twitched harder against me. He didn't reply.

The question hung like a flag fluttering in the lust-thick breeze. I couldn't take it back, and Jethro wouldn't answer it.

Pulling his body heat away, he shoved his hands through his hair and paced the room. "Time for your history lesson."

I wriggled against the pole, dreadfully uncomfortable and vibrating with anger and desire.

I hated the wetness between my legs. I hated that whenever he touched me, I would rather kiss *then* kill him, rather than flat-out destroy him.

My body was hot and confused. Desperate for freedom. Ravenous for lust.

"In 1460, the Hawks were nobodies. We had no land, no titles, no money of any kind. We were the lowest of the low and survived on the generosity of others. Luckily, after years of begging and living on the streets, my ancestor and his family managed to find employment in a household who were the opposite of everything they were.

"At the beginning, it seemed like luck had finally shone upon them, and their days of thievery and struggles were at an end. What they didn't know was it marked the end of their freedom, and, ultimately, their lives. They became slaves—available at the Weavers' every beck and call for every frivolous demand. Not only did my ancestor work for the family, but his wife became their kitchen maid, his son their stable boy, and his daughter their scullery underling. A family of Hawks working for a family of Weavers."

Jethro's voice was hypnotic, whisking me away from the greenhouse to a time where sewage flowed in busy streets and rat meat was as common as chicken in the slums of London.

Jethro never stopped his tale. "They worked every hour—cooking, cleaning, fetching—ensuring the Weavers lived a life of well-tended luxury. Nothing was too much for them—they were the cogs that made the household run."

"So they were employees," I butted in. "They were hired to look after my forefathers and no doubt given room and board as well as food and clothing."

Jethro stalked toward me. Fisting my hair, he snarled, "You'd think that, wouldn't you? A fair trade for the amount of hours they slaved. But no. The Weavers didn't believe in fairness of employment. They didn't pay a cent—not to those who came from the gutter. But you're right—they did provide board and lodging, but they taxed it so heavily, my family existed in the Weavers' cellar with scraps from their table. Every year their unpayable taxes grew higher."

Sickness swirled in my stomach. "How do you mean?"

Jethro let me go, continuing his stroll around the room. "I mean that every year they were worse off, not only working but *paying* their employers for the chance. Every year at Christmas, they were ordered to pay back their taxes of being privileged enough to live in the graces of the Weavers, and every year they couldn't pay it back."

That's awful.

My heart hurt for such unfairness, of such unnecessary brutality. *It can't be true. No one could be that horrid.* Then again, it happened so long ago. It was still insanity to make me pay for it.

I gritted my teeth, fortifying myself against Jethro's brainwashing. I couldn't believe my forefathers were tyrannical employers. There would've been rules—even then. Surely?

It's sad, but it's also hundreds and hundreds of years ago. Get over it.

I said with half-hearted conviction, "They could've left and found other work. They didn't have to put up with that treatment, even if it was true."

Jethro laughed coldly. "Seems so simple to you, doesn't it, Ms. Weaver? Inhumane treatment, so leave." He glowered. "Not so easy when *your* ancestor was raping *my* ancestor's wife every night, and the mistress of the house had turned every law enforcer in the county against them. She spun such an elegant tale of espionage and thievery; no one would listen to the truth. Everyone believed the Hawks were cold-hearted criminals who were unappreciative of the generosity of the upstanding Weavers."

Jethro crossed his arms. "Can you believe the Weavers even managed to coerce the police to issue a standing warrant, stating if ever a Hawk stopped working for the Weavers, they would be punished? The law said they'd be thrown into the keep and tortured for their crimes, then murdered as an example to other misbehaving working class."

My stomach twisted into knots. I wished my hands were untied so I could clamp them over my ears and not listen to Jethro's lies.

This was sick. Terrible. Woefully unjust.

Jethro moved closer, no sound, just like his beloved silence. "Needless to say, they were very unhappy. The wife tried to commit suicide, only for her daughter to find her and the Weavers' best physician to bring her back from the dead. She couldn't escape the nightly exploits of the man of the house, and day by day, her children starved from lack of proper care and nutrition.

"So, one day Frank Hawk waited until the Weaver bastard had raped his wife for the second time that night and put her to bed with her ailing offspring. He waited until the house was quiet and everyone rested, before sneaking from the cellar and into the kitchens."

The image Jethro painted drove needles deep and painful into my heart. I couldn't think of such horrible people or such a sorry existence. How could my ancestors have done such a thing?

"He should've snuck up the stairs and slaughtered his employer while he slept, but his inner fire had been well and truly beaten out after years of abuse. He had no other drive but to stay alive in the hope redemption would save him.

"That night, he only took enough to keep them alive, because no matter their rancid living conditions, he wasn't ready to die. He wasn't ready to permit his children to fade away. He was ready to find his self-worth again and fight. To find the rage to commit murder. And to do that, he needed strength.

"Tiptoeing back to the basement, he and his family had their first good meal in years. Scotch eggs, crusty bread, and anything else he managed to pillage." Jethro smiled, before continuing, "Of course, their meal didn't go unnoticed."

I gulped, completely wrapped up in his tale.

"The next day, the cook announced someone had been in her kitchen and stole. Mr. Weaver immediately turfed my family from their beds, finding evidence of misdeeds in the way of crumbs and hastily devoured food. He announced a crime had been committed; therefore, punishment must be paid.

"He dragged Frank Hawk to the village square where he strung him up on the whipping post and left him to hang by his wrists for a day and a night in the dead of winter." Jethro's hands suddenly clasped mine, straining above me to thread his fingers through my digits—his touch cold and threatening.

I shivered, biting my cheek.

His lips brushed against my ear as his cock twitched against my lower back. "Do you know what they did to thieves back in the 1400s, Ms. Weaver?"

I closed my eyes, bile scalding my throat.

Yes, I knew. The methods of law enforcement were a hot subject at school. The Tower of London had extreme inventions for dishing out pain to those who didn't deserve it.

"Yes," I breathed.

Jethro tugged my fingers. "Care to share?"

Swallowing, I whispered, "The usual punishment for stealing was hands being cut off, ears nailed to spikes, flogging…all manner of beastly things."

My fingers ached beneath his as he squeezed hard.

Then he stepped back, letting me go. "Can you empathize with my ancestor? Can you tap into the panic he must've felt to lose a hand or other body part?"

I squeezed my eyes, nodding. It would've been awful and even worse for the wife as she stood by and watched the love of her life— the same man who had no power to protect her—accept punishment, all for just keeping her alive. A life she probably didn't even want with rape and destitution as the highlights.

Jethro said, "This is the easiest debt to endure, Ms. Weaver. But back then, it was one of the worst." Moving behind me again, his fingers fumbled at the hem of my t-shirt. Pulling it from my skin, he tore it in half with one vicious tug. The crack of the material ripping echoed in the octagonal space.

I jerked as humid air kissed my naked spine.

A moan escaped my lips as I finally understood what he would do.

I wanted to beg for mercy. For him to stop this ridiculous ancient tally and let bygones be bygones, but no sound came as he shoved my tattered t-shirt to my shoulders, exposing my back. His fingers were firm and unyielding as he reached in front and undid the button on my shorts.

"Please," I moaned as he undid them and shoved them to my ankles.

Jethro didn't reply, nor did he ask me to kick the discarded shorts away. I let them stay—imprisoning my ankles, just like the cuffs imprisoned my wrists.

Leaving me naked and quivering with fear, Jethro disappeared.

I didn't try to follow him with my eyes. I kept them squeezed tight, shivering and trembling, wishing I was anywhere but here.

Jethro tapped me on the shoulder a few moments later, his touch harsh and demanding. "Open your eyes."

I reluctantly obeyed, focusing on his flawless face and cold, unforgiving gaze.

He dangled a flogger in front of my vision. It held a multitude of leather strips with knots in regular intervals down the strands. "Have you seen one of these?"

I nodded.

I was a designer. I garnered inspiration from everything and anything, including different lifestyle choices, eras, and kinks. However, there was nothing sexually playful about this one. It was mean and meant to hurt.

I balled my hands, cursing the pins and needles in my fingertips as blood rushed faster. "Yes."

"And do you think it was a just punishment for stealing something, all to keep his family alive?"

I shook my head. "No."

Jethro agreed, "No. Especially in the dead of winter where his body was frozen and brittle, and the slightest touch would've been agony." He ran his finger down my shoulder blades. "You're warm, in a

297

humid room. Your skin is supple and flushed. Pain won't register as badly as if I'd placed you inside a freezer or dumped you in ice water before we started."

He dropped his voice. "Want to know another secret, Ms. Weaver? Want to know something that could potentially get me into a lot of trouble?"

My eyes flared. The way he asked…he was serious. I twisted, trying to catch his eye, but he remained just out of looking distance. "What?" I breathed.

Jethro pressed his body against mine again, digging his belt buckle painfully into my lower back, sandwiching my naked skin harder against the post. "I was supposed to do that. Supposed to make you so cold, I could snap your arm with one touch. You were supposed to be numb and chattering with chill so that every lash would make you scream in endless agony."

I swallowed hard, fear lacing my blood. "Why—why didn't you?" Even my heart stopped beating in fear of missing his answer. I needed to find a way to understand this man, before it was too late.

He dropped his voice to barely a whisper, "Because no one should have to be as cold as I've been taught." He suddenly stepped back, letting the flogger hang down in his grip.

He snapped, "I suggest you hug the post, Ms. Weaver. This is going to hurt."

NILA IMMEDIATELY DID as I said.

With no hesitation, she pressed her body harder against the post, doing her best to hold on despite the restricting cuffs.

Every muscle in her back stood out: every ridge and valley from her trim arse to her taut shoulders. Bruises from vertigo stained the flawless white. Scratches from trees and nature marred her with violence. Every rib stood out as she stopped breathing and locked her knees.

I couldn't have her passing out from lack of oxygen. She had to stay with me. We were in this together.

Gathering the knotted torture device, I murmured, "Do you repent? Do you take ownership of your family's sins and agree to pay the debt?"

Nila pressed even harder against the post, as if she could morph into the wood and disappear.

When she didn't reply, I coaxed, "I asked you a question, Ms. Weaver." Running the flogger through my hands, I stepped closer. "Do you?"

She sucked in a breath, her ribcage straining against her blemished skin. "Ye—yes." Her head bowed, and her lips went white.

I nodded. It was on record. I'd asked and she'd agreed—that was all I needed.

Taking my place for deliverance, I murmured, "I want you to count."

Her eyes shot wide, her cheek squished against the bark of the post. "Count?"

I smiled. "I want to hear you acknowledge every lash."

With my heart in my throat, I spread my thighs and jerked my arm back. I told her the truth about disobeying the order to lock her in the chiller. If my father found out, I could be in serious shit.

We both could.

I hadn't found the balls to delve into the reasons why I hadn't obeyed the procedure. All I could focus on was delivering the First Debt. Then I could get out of here. Then I could get some peace.

"Don't stop counting," I grunted. My arm sailed forward, sending the four-stranded flogger whistling through the air.

For a split second, I suffered an out-of-body experience. I *saw* myself. I witnessed the anger and power on my face. I watched as if I wasn't the one wielding pain but an outsider. And I wondered what it would be like to belong to a different family. To have a different upbringing.

But then the experience stopped, slamming me back into my body.

The flogger sliced through the thick silence.

Nila screamed.

I jolted.

Raw redness bloomed as the lash licked across flesh.

Her skin was so delicate; blood welled instantly.

I stumbled at the sight. My heart shot from my chest and lay beating and mangled on the floor. Images of hunting and killing flurried in my mind. Drawing blood was not new to me. But drawing it from a woman I'd developed feelings for was.

It felt…

…

Fuck, I don't know.

Strange. Exotic. Not entirely distasteful but not fully delectable either.

A realm of uncertainty.

Nila slouched against the post as pain washed through her system. She panted, moans ragged in her chest.

I'd done my part, but she'd yet to do hers.

"Count!" I roared.

Flinching, she stood taller. Sniffing back unshed tears, she yelled, "One!"

Her voice hijacked my body; my cock throbbed.

I'd been prepared to do everything that I'd been ordered. After all, I *wanted* to. I'd been taught to crave this control. To hurt others.

But in that second, I craved something entirely different. I wanted to feel the heat of her whipped back against my front as I slid into her tightness and fucked her. I wanted her to scream for an entirely different reason.

Goddammit, what the hell is happening to me?

I struck again, sending the flogger flying. The soft leather bit into her back. "Count!" I snapped. Causing her pain helped ease a little of mine. This woman had the power to ruin me. That would never be permitted. *I have to ruin her first.*

She screamed again. "Two!"

My muscles already ached from being tense and on edge. My balls disappeared inside my body with the urge to come.

How the fuck will I get through this?

Two down.

Nineteen to go.

The number was written in the logbook of the county enforcer. Twenty-one lashings for Frank Hawk on account of thievery. His son, Bennett Hawk, was the stable boy who wrote up the Debt Inheritance.

Frank had been bleeding and left to freeze. Twenty-one oozing cuts turning to red frost before being deemed repentant for providing for his family.

Like for like.

Debt for debt.

That was my purpose.

That was the madness of my family. Not so much for principle or honouring our ancestor's hardships—but to embrace the power we once lacked. Power we now wielded in perfect precision. The Weavers weren't our agenda—it was the convenience of having an exclusive family tree destined to let us torment and torture, to keep our fangs dripping and claws sharp.

I raised my arm, sailing the knotted strands, tearing across Nila's skin.

"Ah!" Her body shuddered with agony.

My cock stabbed painfully against my belt as Nila writhed on the pole. Dropping my hand, I grabbed the rock hard piece of flesh, rearranging its position so it didn't snap itself in two in my trousers. "I don't hear counting," I growled.

"Three," she cried.

Another lash.

"Four."

Another.

"Five!"

With each one her back blistered, turning from un-whipped perfection to weeping rawness. The humidity of the conservatory drenched my shirt until liquid salt covered my skin. Every lash, savage hunger built inside, feeding off Nila's pain and my own for wanting her.

My mouth watered to kiss her spine, to lick at the mess I'd caused. I wanted to nuzzle her tears and whisper the truth of who I was.

You never can.

Just the mere thought of being honest petrified me. If I spoke it, how would I keep it hidden?

I should never have done this in such a hot place. I should never have attempted something so barbaric without shielding my mind properly. Every strike hurt Nila externally, but she couldn't see what it did to my soul.

I struck again, breathing hard through my nose.

"Six," Nila moaned.

The heat of the room seeped through my pores, twisting my heart, melting any frost I might've conjured. Every cold shard melted, turning into a cascade of warmth.

I swallowed as I drank in Nila's exquisite form. The way she trembled but refused to let her knees buckle. The way her cheeks flushed and dark eyes sucked power from the room.

She was...magnificent.

I cocked my arm, sending the flogger to claw at her lower back. Nila groaned loudly. "Seven."

My arm ached as I struck again.

"Eight."

And again.

"Nine."

Nine down.

Twelve to go.

Shit, I was ready to collapse. I was ready to crawl to her feet and beg for her to forgive me.

Forgive me?

There was nothing to forgive. She deserved this!

I struck hard, forcing myself to stay ruthless.

"Ten!" she screeched.

My ears rang with her pain.

I gave up trying to control my emotions and surrendered.

The sooner I delivered her penance, the sooner I could undo the wrong I'd done.

Gritting my teeth, I picked up my pace. Delivering blow after blow, quicker and quicker.

"Eleven," Nila sobbed.

"Twelve."

"Thirteen." Her voice broke and a glistening tear slicked down her cheek.

It cleaved my fucking heart.

"Fourteen!"

Sweat poured down my face as I hit again and again. My breathing matched hers. I'd never been so turned on in all my life or so fucking disgusted.

It made me face things I'd hidden deep, deep inside. It drew ghosts and terrors all into confrontation. I needed to run. Before I lost myself.

But I couldn't leave. I knew in my heart, I wouldn't be able to walk away from this without fucking her. There was nothing on this earth that would stop me from taking her the moment I'd finished the last lash. I didn't care I wasn't supposed to touch her until the Third Debt.

I don't fucking care.

Everything was on the line. Everything that before had been enough to keep me subservient and in my father's pocket, now wasn't.

I'd been obedient. Loyal. Done everything he ever asked of me.

But that was before I found something I wanted more than what my future held.

My cock rippled with pre-cum as I struck.

"Fifteen!"

Nila was mine.

I wanted her.

I'd take her.

I grunted as I swung again, throwing my body weight into the strike.

"Sixteen." She shifted, pressing her forehead against the post. Her hair stuck to the blood oozing on her shoulders. She gasped, dragging in air as if she drowned.

"Seventeen!" she screamed as I drew forth more crimson agony. Her abused, glowing skin split, sprinkling rusty droplets down her ribcage.

My eyes glazed; I stumbled closer.

I'm sorry.

You're not sorry.

I needed to touch her. Heal her. Fuck her.

My arm bellowed as I delivered three in quick succession.

"Eighteen."

"Nineteen."

"Twenty!" Nila collapsed, her knees buckling. Her weight transferred entirely to the cuffs.

My arm fell by my side. I could barely stand. My lungs sucked in air as if I were dying; my heartbeat existed everywhere, vibrating in the plants around us, roaring in my ears.

One more.

Do it.

I looked to the camera hidden in the ferns. My father would watch this later and reprimand me for being affected. He would see the glaze in my eyes, the desire on my face. He would make me pay for not freezing her first. He would destroy all the warmth that now existed in my heart and take me back to the person I hated.

That was my future.

But this was our present.

This was *ours.*

I struck. Hard. Too hard. Too fucking hard. My mind couldn't free itself from things Nila would never understand. Her world was black and white. Betrayal versus love. Truth versus deception.

My world was different. So very, very different.

"Twenty-one!" Nila let go of her frayed self-control. Sobs broke through her lips, tears cascading down ghost-white cheeks. "Please— no more. Stop." She tried to stand but couldn't find the strength. "Please! No—I can't—"

Twenty-one.

The lucky number.

Her tears dragged dangerous compassion from my arctic soul, hauling me into humanness.

Bad things happened when I let myself get this way.

Terrible things that I couldn't control.

But Nila was my undoing.

I think I'd known that the moment I tore her dress off in Milan. I had no strength to pretend—not after this. Not now.

I needed to take her. To fully claim her, so I could give in completely to the one thing I'd run from all my life.

If I took her now, there would be no turning back for me. Damn the fucking consequences.

Groaning, I threw away the flogger. "It's over."

Nila sobbed harder, gratefulness a sharp tang in the air.

With shaky fingers, I unbuttoned my jeans, moving forward into destruction and disrepair.

She was my prize.

Nothing would stop me from taking it.

I COULDN'T MOVE.

I couldn't stand up, breathe, think, or feel without being bombarded by agony. I'd never hurt so much. Not even after a tortuous fifteen-hour day huddled over a sewing machine, or twelve hours on my feet in stilettos.

I'd never been subjected to pain such as this.

To a *beating* such as this.

And this was the easiest of the debts?

Terror clogged my throat at the thought of what the others entailed.

Movement caught my attention. I forced my tear-stained vision to focus on Jethro as he prowled to the ferns and reached into the foliage. What was he doing?

A second later he moved toward me, every step full of temper and thick, thick lust.

Shit.

I squirmed, tugging on the cuffs. Before the whipping, I would've willingly let him take me. I *wanted* him to.

But not like this.

Not like this!

Not when my brain wept with agony and my emotions were completely screwed up.

"No," I groaned.

Jethro gritted his jaw, his hand disappearing into his jeans.

A keening wail clawed up my throat. I couldn't let him fuck me. I hurt. So damn much. I wasn't turned on or interested in the slightest. I couldn't stomach being molested further.

You don't have a choice.

My heart cracked at the thought. No, I didn't have a choice. He would take me. There was nothing I could do about it.

Apart from…

Appeal to the warmth you know is inside him. Make him listen. Make him see.

Jethro's hands landed on my hips, yanking me away from the post. My body was jelly, my skin slick with sweat and blood.

Shaking my head, I moaned, "Please don't touch me."

Jethro's only response was rubbing his thumbs in slippery circles on my damp hips.

Clamping my thighs together, I forced my depleted body to obey. My ankles crossed awkwardly, my breathing tattered. "Jethro— please…don't do this."

He froze, panting harshly in my ear. "You want me. You've toyed with me and offered yourself up every time we fight." His forehead rested against my nape, his breath scattering down my spine. "Yet, now that I'm willing to throw away the fucking rule book, you decide you don't want me?" His voice dripped with venom. "Make up your damn mind, woman."

His knee tried to wedge between my legs, working its way to widen my thighs. I used every ounce of remaining strength to lock my knees tighter.

"Let me give it to you. Don't take it. Not by force. Don't make me ha—hate you more than I already do." Tears torrented from the corners of my eyes.

Jethro sucked in a breath. "Goddammit." His voice was alive and full of need. More alive than I'd ever heard him. Gone was the cold precision and careful calculation. He was hot-blooded and raging, and some part of me was flattered by his desire.

He wanted me.

A lot.

That power turned the burning fire on my back into something twisty and wrong. But I didn't succumb. I couldn't.

If I did, there would be no hope for me. No chance at ever redeeming myself if I let him take me like this.

I wanted to seduce him.

I wanted the power of winning.

This…this would be rape, and it would reinforce in his head that he could take whatever he damn well wanted and suffer no repercussions.

"Stop it!" I screamed as his hands drifted down my front. The fight inside intensified, blotting out the awful radiating pain in my back.

Something hot and silky nudged against the small of my spine. "Christ's sake, woman. You have no idea what you're doing to me."

What is that?

All senses shot to where he stroked me with a hard throbbing…

It's his erection.

My heart leapt into my throat.

Jethro rocked harder, his body heat scalding every inch. His naked cock lurched against my bloody back.

I hissed as pain intensified.

He grunted as I jolted in the bindings. "Please—" I begged.

The tips of my fingers scrabbled at the post as I tried to keep my balance. His knee worked harder to unlock my thighs.

"You can't stop this. Neither of us can."

The truth in his voice daggered my heart.

If we did this, we would slip from humanity and turn over our souls. We'd become animals, forever fighting and cursing each other.

My back flared with flames as his arm wrapped around my waist, pulling me from the post and into his twisted embrace. I wriggled against him, blocking out the agony. "Jethro!"

His cock nudged me again, bruising me with his need.

"Shit, let me—"

"I won't! Not like this."

He groaned, a savage mixture of a growl of frustration and grunt of regret.

My vision blacked out then returned, masking the pain and encouraging me to drift. I expected a longer war. In complete truthfulness, I expected to lose and be taken like a common slave against the whipping post with my blood smearing between us.

It was better to give in—get it over with.

Then I could rest.

Yes, rest. Sleep…

Fight siphoned from my limbs, succumbing to the inevitable.

But Jethro…the moment I submitted, he stiffened.

He…he let me go.

His body heat stayed blistering and all-consuming behind, but he didn't touch me.

Neither of us moved. I was too shocked to ask why.

Then, a noise hit my ears. A noise I wasn't familiar with yet knew *exactly* what it was. Some primal part of me needed no confirmation, painting a vivid scene in my head of what Jethro was doing.

My heart sped up as the rhythmic sound grew louder. His breathing came short and sharp, sending my skin prickling with knowledge.

My mind filled with images of him. I pictured his head tossed back, his chest rising and falling, and legs spread for balance. I bit my lip as I let my imagination wander, bringing into focus his strong fingers wrapped around his cock, punishing himself with a grip that worked up and down, up and down. Faster and faster.

His breathing matched my sick daydream. My tummy clenched at the thought of him masturbating while I stood there prone, bleeding, and silent.

A soft groan decorated his harsh breathing as something hot and stinging splashed across my lower back.

Did he just—?

He moaned louder as another stream lacerated the cuts on my spine.

He grunted one last time as a torrid spurt marked my skin, seeping into my wounds like acid.

My eyes shot wide as my lips thinned in repugnance. Like some crazed beast, he'd marked me with his cum. He'd respected my plea and not taken me, but he'd had to service himself.

I shuddered in the cuffs as Jethro's forehead landed on the base of my skull. "Fuck, you're ruining me."

The atmosphere changed instantaneously. It switched from abuse and debt payments to fragile and perplexed.

I couldn't calm my heart or ignore the fiery sting of his cum on my wounds.

Wordlessly, Jethro stepped away. The faint sound of a zipper being refastened was the only sound apart from our tattered breathing.

Awareness slowly came back—I wished it wouldn't.

Inch by inch, pain on top of pain made itself known. My muscles bellowed; my back hummed like a hundred bee stings. And the questions that bombarded me made nausea swirl with confusion.

Tears stole my vision as everything became too much.

The whipping.

Jethro's desecration and confession.

It felt as if my skeleton had been ripped into view, hanging bony and stripped bare with every colliding thought on display. The licking flames of whiplashes stole the remainder of my energy.

I buckled, giving up all control to the cuffs.

I didn't want to cry again.

I didn't want to seem weak in front of the monster who'd not only hurt me but gotten off on it. He'd been turned on so much, he had to mark me with ownership. Like I was his territory—his possession.

No matter how much I wished I were stronger, I wasn't. I couldn't stop the tears rivering from my eyes or the hiccupping sobs building in my chest.

Softly, silently, the winch released, dropping my arms so I only remained standing by leaning against the post.

The buckles on my wrists were removed, cuffs no longer imprisoning.

Jethro's touch was infinitely gentle and kind.

My legs gave a second warning before they collapsed from beneath me.

I braced myself for the fall. I gritted my teeth against more agony.

But I didn't tumble to the travertine floor.

I landed in strong arms.

And the only thing that registered was shock.

The arms weren't cold.

But hot.

I came to being placed gently on my stomach.

Whatever I lay upon was soft as a cloud and smelled just as fresh.

I snuggled deeper into the fluffiness, wishing for oblivion once again, but the agonizing pain from my shredded back wouldn't let me fade.

My hands balled the sheets beneath me as I struggled to stay still and not squirm.

It hurts. Crap, it hurts.

I would've murdered for a painkiller—something to dull the mind-numbing agony.

A cool hand pressed against my naked behind, holding me against the mattress.

My mattress?

Where am I?

I couldn't tell without raising my eyes. I would have to tense my spine to look, and no way in hell was I moving.

"Stay still," Jethro ordered, his voice calm but lacking the usual icy edge.

I froze, just waiting for more torture or horrible mind games. I was at my weakest, most vulnerable. I had no defence—mental or physical—if he decided to hurt me more.

His touch drifted over a particularly violent lash mark.

I hissed, biting my lip.

I wanted to moan—to see if vocalizing the agony would help release it. Coupled with the cuts on my feet from running and my bruises from vertigo, I'd never been so banged up.

Vaughn would kill him for this. My brother could never stand to see me hurt.

The bed shifted as Jethro disappeared. Vaguely, the sound of a tap being turned on and the groan of old pipes expanding with water drifted to my ears.

I didn't know how much time passed; I drifted in and out of pain, wishing I could transplant a pair of wings from the stuffed birds around the room and fly away.

Then the mattress dipped again, my skin crackling with awareness as Jethro hovered beside me.

Something clanked onto the bedside table, smelling sharply of antiseptic.

I flinched, turning my head to see what it was.

At least we have drugs to stop infection. Back in the 1400s they wouldn't have been so lucky.

Jethro's fingers landed on my hair, stroking softly. "I'm going to fix you. Don't move."

"Fix me?" My voice came out scratching and sore from previous screaming. "You can't fix me."

He didn't reply.

Instead, he dipped a soft white cloth into the bowl of clear brown liquid and wrung it out.

His eyes met mine then locked onto the mess that was my back. The moment he pressed the warm dampness against a cut, I burst into tears. The lashes roared with everlasting brimstone. "Stop! Ah, it hurts."

His other hand held me down, petting my head as if I would endanger myself further. "I know it hurts, but I have to clean your wounds before I can bandage them."

My mind twisted, trying to make sense of this. "Why—why are you the one tending to me?"

He took a while to reply, dipping the now hated rag into the disinfectant concoction and once again searing my skin with purgatory.

"Because you're mine."

I hated that reason. "I'm not yours."

His voice came softly. "There are a lot worse things than being mine, Ms. Weaver. Being under my control means I'll do anything to keep you safe. Keep you from other's cruelty. Don't throw my offer in my face without fully realising what I'm giving you."

His touch dropped lower, gently dabbing my open sores.

My hands fisted the sheet, breathing hard through my nose. My head ached from tensing, and tears leaked unbidden from my eyes.

"I do know what you're offering, and I don't want it."

The moment I said it, I wanted to snatch the words back.

I *wanted* him on my side.

I wanted him to care for me, so I could use him to exterminate his family like vermin.

"Are you sure?" he murmured. "Are you sure you want to throw away whatever's building between us?"

I flinched, bracing myself to deny it. *There's nothing building between us.*

You always were a hopeless liar, Nila.

How could I admit to an emerging connection between hunter and prey?

Jethro caressed my hair again. "I know what you're thinking—I know you feel it, too." He dropped his voice, whispering, "Don't lie, Ms. Weaver. Not when we both know the truth. Do you deny we're drawn to each other? Fighting more with ourselves than what we know we shouldn't feel?"

Silence.

I had no reply. Nothing that wouldn't give me away.

Jethro continued to rinse and dab, slowly but tenderly cleaning my smarting back.

"You're strong. Stronger than anyone I've met. But still so naïve, which makes you incredibly dangerous." His touch pulled me deeper into his icy charm.

"What are you trying to do?" I pinched my lips together as a particular sharp lance of pain caught me by surprise. "Why are you saying all of this?"

A minute ticked past.

For the longest moment, I worried he would never reply, just like so many of my questions.

"I don't know." His answer ached with confession, cleaving open my chest.

Memories of what happened at the end of the debt repayment took my mind prisoner. "How could you do that? How could you come after hurting me so much?" I pressed my cheek harder against the bed as agony bonfired down my spine. "To get off on drawing blood makes you sadistic. It makes you twisted."

Jethro paused, letting me go completely to swirl the cloth in the bowl. The brown liquid turned rusty from my blood. "Sadistic?"

I swallowed back a groan as I arched my neck, making eye contact with his turbulent golden gaze. "Yes. You enjoyed seeing me hurt from running in the woods. You like seeing me uncomfortable. Sadistic fits you perfectly."

He sighed, looking at the dripping cloth in his hands. It stained his trousers, not that he seemed to care. "I'm many things but not a sadist."

I scoffed, tearing my gaze away.

He didn't deserve a reply when he blatantly lied.

Silence fell between us as he slowly continued to wash my back.

His hands dropped lower—to where he'd branded me with his orgasm.

I flinched. He sucked in a harsh breath as he reached the base of my spine. The residue stickiness felt foreign and unwanted. I wanted his pleasure gone. I didn't want to wear evidence of his toxic mind games.

I whispered, "See the evidence? You came in seconds. You were so caught up in needing a release, you couldn't even wait to subdue me to rape me." I sighed. "Who needs to come so badly they'll throw their

313

dignity away and come like a little boy caught looking at *Playboy* for the first time?"

The memory of walking in on Vaughn doing exactly that was seared into my brain. I'd been scarred for life after that. Terrified of what it meant. Unable to understand what my brother was doing hurting himself in such a manner.

I'd bolted the moment I'd seen, and to this day, we'd never discussed it.

"You're right," Jethro whispered. "I disgraced myself. But I had no alternative. I couldn't do what I wanted without hurting you more, and you'd already been hurt enough. It was the only way to see straight—to let the poison out of my system."

"Poison?"

He chuckled sadly. "It's one word for it."

His touch landed on my spine again, wiping away the leftovers of his transgression. "If you want an apology, I won't give it."

"So I'm to accept you smearing your cum into my flayed back?"

I'm to accept that I belong to you, because I have no other choice?

He didn't reply. Tossing the rag into the bowl, he grabbed a tube of cream beside it. Silently, he smeared the lotion onto my cuts.

I hissed as the cream stung before fading to a gentle throb. Every hair on my body bristled with how tenderly he cared for me. My heart raced for an entirely different reason as he meticulously smeared my entire back in balm.

The moment I was covered, he stood.

"Sit up," he ordered.

Sit up? That was asking for the impossible. I couldn't.

When I tried half-heartedly and swallowed a moan of agony, Jethro moved closer. "Let me help."

He hovered, his scent of woods and leather scrambling my heart until I suffered a bad case of arrhythmia.

He didn't touch me, only waited.

He's waiting for your permission—transferring power back to you.

I frowned. What tricks was he playing? Who was this silent attentive man, and what the hell happened to the bastard I wanted to murder?

Jethro continued to watch me, his face tight and unreadable.

I nodded once.

With powerful hands, he helped me sit up and swing my legs over the side of the bed.

Squeezing my eyes, I almost succumbed to pain-induced vertigo as I swayed in his grip.

"Trust me," he murmured, reaching beneath my arms to scoop my weight, helping me stand.

I moaned as a few of the shallower cuts reopened, oozing painfully.

"Can you stand on your own?"

I wanted to berate him. Ridicule his kindness with what he'd done. But something in his eyes implored me to relax—to not fight him on this particular subject.

I blinked, completely lost as to his motives or plans.

Slowly, I nodded.

Leaving me to wobble in place, he pulled free a large bandage from a first-aid kit on the floor.

Between my teeth, I muttered, "You always intended to patch me up…afterwards?"

His eyebrow rose, locking me in his stare. "You still don't understand."

I struggled to suck in a decent breath with the intensity in his gaze. "I understand plenty."

He shook his head. "No, you don't. You think we're going to torture and maim you for the next few years. Yes, your future is set in stone, and yes, it will hang over your head until it's finished. But you have to keep living, keep experiencing. You're part of our family now. You'll be treated as such."

My brain whirled.

"In answer to your question, I always intended to tend to your wounds, just like I will do with every debt. You're mine." His lips twitched. "In sickness and in health."

Temper flared through my blood. "Don't twist the vows of matrimony. This isn't a marriage. This is the worst kind of kidnapping."

His eyes hooded, hiding his thoughts. "A marriage *is* a kidnapping. After all, it's a contract between two people." He came closer, unravelling the end of the bandage and holding it against my side. My arms wrapped around my naked chest hating that even now, even after everything he'd done, my skin still rippled with want.

His face tightened and he grabbed my wrists, placing them forcibly by my sides. "Arms down." His attention turned to holding the bandage against my ribcage. Once in place, he moved in a circle around me, wrapping my torso caringly in gauze. The soft fabric granted needed relief.

I bit the inside of my cheek. How was it that the gentlest of his touches killed me the most? I'd never been this light-headed without the curse of vertigo. Never been this confused by one person.

Jethro kept his eyes down as he waltzed around, slowly binding me with more of the bandage.

On his second rotation, he murmured, "In a way, we *are* married."

I rolled my eyes, cursing my taut nipples. "In no universe would this be called a marriage."

He sighed. "How do you explain the similarities then? The fact we were raised to be a part of each other's lives, groomed by families, governed by dictators, and forced into a binding agreement against our wishes."

The air solidified, turning from unseen substance to heavy bricks of truth. My head snapped up, eyes latching onto Jethro's golden ones. "*What* did you just say?"

The man he kept hidden blazed bright.

Against both our wishes.

That was the second time he'd said it.

Go on. Admit it. Say that all along you've been acting. That this is as repulsive to you as it is to me.

We stood silent, neither of us willing to look away in case it was interpreted as defeat. Slowly, the concern in his eyes shifted to glittering frost—the chill I knew so well giving him somewhere to hide. "You misunderstood me, Ms. Weaver. I meant to say *your* not *our*—slip of the tongue." He continued wrapping the bandage around my middle, covering my breasts with the length of softness, protecting the seeping cuts on my back.

I wanted to yell at him. To find the crack I'd just witnessed and force it to turn from hairline into crevice. But I stood silently, breathing hard as he finished wrapping me like a priceless present, securing the bandage with a small clip.

He stepped back, admiring his handiwork. "You did perfectly, Ms. Weaver. You repaid the First Debt with strength, and you've earned a reward." He moved closer, wrapping his arms around me. His embrace scalded, heating the lash marks to a boil.

I froze in his arms, completely dumbfounded.

To an outsider, it would've looked like an embrace—tender, sweet, the coupling of two people crackling with anger and unwanted lust. To me, it was a torment—a farce.

Pulling back, he whispered, "Do you know we met when we were young? I barely remember, and I'm a few years older than you, so I doubt you will recall."

"What?" My mind flew backward, trying to remember a fiendish little boy with icy winds in his soul. "When?"

He reached up, undoing my ponytail and running his strong fingers through the strands. "Back in London. We met for ten minutes. My grandmother escorted me. They made us sign something—you used a crayon that you'd been drawing a bright pink dress with."

My heart stormed with denial. How could that be?

Jethro bared his teeth, his eyes locking onto my lips. "That was the first document they made us sign—the beginning of our entwined fate. However, soon you'll be signing something else."

Oh, God. My stomach revolted at giving him any more rights over me.

It wouldn't happen. The only thing I'd sign when it came to the Hawks was their death certificates.

His thumb traced my bottom lip. "You can't say no. You promised."

I shook my head. "When?"

"When you ran. We agreed if you didn't make it to the boundary, you would sign another document—one just between us that trumps everything else." The tips of his cool, no longer warm, fingers trailed along my collarbone. He leaned in and placed the slightest of kisses on my cheek. "I've been rather busy, so haven't had time to draw it up, but once I do, that's the one I'll treasure. That's the one that will contain your soul."

I tore from his grip.

I couldn't stand it any longer.

I slapped him.

Hard.

Viciously hard and firm and so full of *anger*. I wanted to smite him into the ground.

He hissed between his teeth as my palm print glowed instantly on his shaven cheek.

I seethed, "You're forgetting that no matter how many contracts you make me sign, none of them will own my soul. I own that. Me! And I'll make you watch, before this is over, while I burn your house to the ground and bury your family."

Jethro turned to a rock.

Grabbing the diamond collar around my neck, I hissed, "And this. I'll find a way to remove it. I'll tear every single diamond from the setting and donate it to victims of bastards like you."

Jethro's anger dissolved, almost as if he shed it in one swoop. His smile was forced, but the passion in his eyes was fire not frost. "Bastards like me? I don't think there *are* other bastards like me."

Suddenly he lashed out, grabbing the diamond choker and dragging me forward.

My hands flew to cover his, cursing the huge flare of agony down my spine.

His lips hovered over mine, instantly igniting my overwhelming need to be kissed. How many times would he tease me and not deliver? How many times must he jerk me close, whisper his taste across my lips, and renege on following through? "I told you, you can't get it off." His finger trailed to the back of the necklace, tugging gently. "There is no possible way to get this off once it's on. No key. No trick."

I gasped, stumbling a little as vertigo played on the outskirts of my vision. "There has to be a way to undo it."

After all, you took it from my mother's corpse.

Jethro smiled grimly. "Oh yes, it comes undone when it's no longer fastened tightly around something as impeccable as your neck." His beautiful face twisted with something hideously evil. "Think of an old-fashioned handcuff, Ms. Weaver." He forced two fingers down the collar, effectively strangling me. "It has to get tighter and tighter..." He tried to fit a third finger but it wouldn't work. Dark spots danced in front of my eyes.

My heart bucked and collided.

"It has to revolve on itself to open, only then will the latch snap free and be ready to be fastened again."

The horror I'd been locking deep inside took that moment to crest. My knees gave out, hopelessly giving into rage and terror. If I failed in my quest to make the Hawks pay, who would wear it next?

Who?

Vaughn's unborn daughter? The sister Daniel had hinted at in the car but I didn't know was real or fiction?

Jethro caught me, placing me back on the bed.

My life switched. My path, my destiny no longer belonged to creativity, design, or couture.

It had never been that clear-cut.

My fate—the very reason why I'd been put on this earth—was to stop these men. To end them. Once and for all.

There will be no more wearers of the Weaver Wailer collar. No more victims of such a ludicrous, sadistic debt.

The ice that lived in Jethro's soul seeped into mine, and this time…it stayed. There was no Kite to help me soar or hopeful naivety of the girl I used to be. I embraced the chill, letting it permeate and consume.

I will make him care.

My stomach churned with the promise.

I will make him love me.

My conviction wasn't flimsy or half-hearted.

And then I'll destroy him.

My vow was unbinding and unbreakable, just like my diamond imprisonment.

"Kiss me, Jethro."

Jethro froze, eyes wide.

He tried to stand tall after leaning over to plant me safely on the bed. But I lashed out, grabbing his shirt and keeping him folded. "Kiss me."

His eyes flared wider, panic filling their depths. "Let me go."

"If we're effectively married with contracts, carefully designed futures, and interlocking pasts, why are we fighting our attraction? Why not give in to it?" Yanking his shirt, I forced him to stumble closer. "We have years together before the end. Years of fucking and taking and pleasure." Licking my lips, I purred, "Why wait?"

Ripping my fingers from his clothing, he backed away, ferocity and confusion equal bedfellows in his eyes. "Shut up. You're hurt. You need to rest."

I laughed, unable to hide the mania in my tone. "You wanted to take me in the greenhouse. I'm not saying no now." I spread my thighs; apart from the bandage wrapped around my chest, I was naked.

Jethro's gaze dropped to my exposed core, his jaw twitching.

"Kiss me. Take me. Show me you're a man by being the first Hawk to claim me." My stomach rolled with the filth I spoke.

But I'd made a vow; I intended to see it through.

Dropping my head, I let a curtain of black hair obscure one eye. "Let's draw our battle lines right here, right now. We'll fight. We'll hate each other. But it doesn't mean we have to let family dictate every action we do."

Fire filled my belly. He wanted me. I knew that much. He wouldn't have come all over my back if he didn't. And there was something inside me—some all-knowing part that not everything was as it seemed. Sometimes he was so sure—so resolute and unswerving in the belief of what he said—and other times, it was a lie. A big, fat, obnoxious lie that even he struggled to hide.

"I told you at the coffee shop. If and when I take you, it will be on my terms. Fucking hard and nasty. I won't kiss you, touch you— because I *don't care*. I'll just fucking take, and you'll wish you hadn't taunted me."

"You'll take me against my will?"

Liar—you stopped before.

He froze, a cold veneer creeping over his features. "Exactly. You begged me to take you. Well, keep begging because I'm not ready to grant you my cock just yet."

I tilted my head. "You'll give in. I'll win."

He laughed loudly, the tension dispersing. He looked at me as if I were a feral puppy who he'd been temporarily wary of but now thought was ridiculous. "Back to winning. Always winning with you, Ms. Weaver."

I nodded. "If there is no winner or loser, what else is there?"

Partnership.

The thought appeared from nowhere. Partnership. I tasted the word, wondering just how likely an alliance could be between this law-bound Hawk and me—his victim.

Could I not only seduce him but use him against his family? I'd thought it before, but it'd been frivolous, something I said to make myself feel powerful...but what if...

The idea was absurd...*but*...

Jethro moved, placing his palm squarely on my bandage-bound chest and pushing me backward onto the bed.

I hissed at the pressure of the mattress on my whipped flesh.

"Stop your silly games, Ms. Weaver. It's time to rest."

His eyes glinted. "You'll need it for tomorrow."

DAMN HER.

Fuck her.

She was worse than my fucking father with her manipulation and guile.

I needed a session.

For the first time since I'd turned eighteen, I needed help. I wouldn't be able to fix myself on my own. I hated to do it to her. It was the epitome of cruel.

But the only person who could help me remember why I couldn't let go of the ice in my veins was my sister.

Jasmine.

I'm a Hawk. Remember that fucking fact and own it.

Stalking through the house, I tried to find my father. I didn't want to do this. I hated that we used our own flesh and blood this way. But I had no *choice.*

Not if I wanted to remain strong.

Not if I wanted to remain true.

A child was the product of his upbringing. They had certain obligations to live up to, expectations to obey, and scripts to follow. Elders knew better.

It was time to embrace my life path completely, rather than fight against it.

I was done fighting against it.

It was too fucking hard.

He'd told me it would only bring confusion and pain.

He was right.

Time to stop fighting and become my father's son.

Once and for fucking all.

TWO WEEKS PASSED.

Fourteen days where I didn't see a hint of Jethro.

Where he'd gone and why was a mystery, and I'd like to say I didn't care.

But…I'd never been a good liar.

No matter the itch of curiosity, I continued to live and didn't let his disappearance undermine my resolve.

I didn't mope in my room. I formulated my attack plan and executed it.

The first three days were hell. My back cracked and bled whenever I moved. I stayed confined to my bed with only the ceiling for entertainment and food delivered by softly smiling maids.

I craved my phone. I missed the freedom of conversing with the outside world.

By the fourth day, I risked a shower and unwound the bandage from my back to twist and stare in the mirror.

As much as the pain crippled me, my skin had knitted together and scabbed nicely. The shallower cuts were nothing more than a pink mark. And the deeper wounds were well on the road to recovery.

I would always bear the scars. A new wardrobe of silver lashes marking me firmly with ancient scandals. However, the body was a miraculous thing—healing itself from crimes of hate and unpayable debts.

I just hope my soul is as curable.

The hot water had killed to begin with, but slowly I grew used to the pain and washed away the whipping and turbulence Jethro had left me with.

On the fifth day, I dressed in a floaty black dress that had no elastic or grabby material that would irritate my back and stepped from my room. I had cabin fever, and as much as I didn't want company, I needed a change of scenery.

Drifting toward the dining room, I jumped whenever I heard the slightest noise. I felt guilty for wandering, even though I'd been told I could. And as much as I wanted to see Jethro, to demand my phone was returned, I didn't have the strength to fight with him yet.

It was well past breakfast, which was fine because I'd had mine in bed, and there were no Black Diamond men around.

Where is everyone?

Hawksridge Hall had an eerie way of hiding people from view. The huge spaces making it seem as if I were all alone. I might not want to suffer through Jethro's company, but his younger brother wasn't blacklisted.

Turning down the corridor leading to Kes's quarters, I found him with four men discussing some sort of strategy at the large table in the saloon.

The moment I entered, Kes's golden eyes lit up. He bounced from his chair and came to offer his hand, tugging me closer to the bikers. "Nila. What a pleasant surprise." His gaze went to my back, spinning me around a little to see. The lash marks were on display, having left the bandage off to help with healing. My dress was a scoop back, permitting my flesh to breathe.

"Ouch. I'd heard he hadn't held back."

"You heard?" I frowned. "He told you what happened?"

Kes swallowed, running a hand nervously through his hair. "Um, not quite. Anyway, that's beside the point. I'm just glad you're well and on the mend." Grabbing my elbow, he carted me closer to the table and beaming men. "You know Flaw."

I nodded briefly at the black-haired man who moved like Vaughn, before inspecting the two other accomplices—one with dirty blond hair, the other with long brown hair in a ponytail down his back. "That's Grade and Colour."

What the hell sort of names are those?

It didn't escape my attention that these were the same men who'd had their tongues on every part of me. But there was no awkwardness—no side glances or intimidation.

I snorted. "Ah, I get it now. I couldn't work out your names before. Flaw, Cut…you name yourselves after diamond properties."

Kes grinned. "Yep. Apart from the Hawk boys, of course. The Black Diamond brothers picked a name based on the gemstone and the properties in which they can be transformed."

Grade—the man with dirty blond hair and a snub nose—grinned. "Happy to meet you, Nila."

I didn't bother saying he'd already met me, or at least his tongue had.

Colour, with his brown ponytail and broad grin, leaned the small distance between us and placed a chaste kiss on my cheek. "Hello, Ms. Weaver. Lovely to see you again."

The other day, Kes had said I was to be treated with kindness and respect, but a part of me hadn't believed him. However, faced with men who had helped strip me of everything, it seemed as if they genuinely liked and wanted me in their company.

I couldn't get my head around it.

Or they're just perfect actors in the pantomime put on by Mr. Hawk.

Waving away the proprietary of my title, I shivered slightly. "Please, call me Nila." I couldn't stomach anyone else calling me by my surname and hated that Jethro continued to use it. I didn't want to be reminded of the man who'd disappeared without a trace.

Kes pulled up an extra chair. "Sit and stay a while. We're just discussing another diamond shipment due in tonight. It will be boring, but we'd be honoured if you'd share your opinions."

I couldn't stop staring at him. How much had Jethro told him of making me pay the First Debt? Did he know the battle that waged between his brother and me?

But most importantly, did he wonder, if he *was* Kite, why I hadn't texted him in so long?

Damn Jethro for taking my phone.

Arsehole.

Flaw disappeared as the men fell back into conversation. He returned a few minutes later with a huge basket overflowing with items.

The bikers laughed, pushing back from the table to give Flaw space to present the basket to me. I strained forward, very aware that my raw back would be on display despite my long, unsecured hair hiding some of the evidence.

"What's this?" I asked, eyeing up the pink concoction of crepe paper, chocolate bars, sweeties, magazines, and a brand new Kindle. "For you," Kes murmured, moving forward to rummage in the gift basket. "I wanted to come to your room yesterday and give it to you, but…well, Jethro has banned anyone from stepping into your quarters."

Why am I not surprised?

Tentatively, I plucked the Kindle from the basket and turned it on. A stocked library full of romance greeted me.

"Wow," I murmured. Then I looked at the name given to the device in the top right corner. *Weaver Wailer.* That would have to change straight away.

Kes shrugged, standing tall and running a hand through his messy hair. "Figured you must be going stir-crazy in this house. It will keep you occupied."

And, it did.

For the next five days, I spent my mornings relaxing in bed with fresh pastries reading about alpha males and swooning heroines, while my afternoons were spent with Kes and the boys in his quarters.

My strange world settled into routine, and although I craved my phone and the ability to talk to Kite, I valued the reprieve—the preciousness of a secretive smile from Kes and the gentle touch of a fatherly biker.

They all doted on me.

They all smiled when I walked into the room and listened attentively to anything I had to say.

I felt valued.

I felt *appreciated.*

Which was the oddest thing to admit as I'd never felt cherished, even when delivering fashion-changing designs and bringing the Weaver name to even greater heights. No, that wasn't true. I felt beyond loved and adored by my father and brother, but it'd been the everyday reporters, models, and shop owners that'd made my career a hardship.

Away from the toil of work, I found no drive to return. No urge to create.

It was scary to have that part of my identity taken away but refreshing and almost medicinal, too.

Bizarre to say, the same men who'd licked me had somehow become my…friends. I didn't know how, but I did know I healed faster because of their friendship and found sanctuary for my heart.

Just like Kestrel had said I would.

Just like Cut had said I'd be welcomed into his house. I should've been colder, less easy to win over, but I was tired of overthinking everything and peering around corners for the next trick.

There was only so much fear a person could live with before the brain gave up and accepted.

The days stretched unnervingly…normal. If I wasn't in Kes's saloon, I was wandering down pristine corridors full of priceless artwork and tapestries. I strolled in gardens surrounded by manicured hedges and even took a nap beneath the dappling leaves of an apple tree in the orchard.

Not one person stopped me from entering a room or leaving. Not one person raised their voice or gave me any reason to fear.

If I bumped into a man dressed in leather and stomping in fierce-looking boots, he would smile and ask after my health. If I bumped into Cut heading to a meeting, he would bow and smile cordially, continuing on his way as if I had total right to be sneaking about his home.

The only person I didn't bump into was Jethro.

It was as if he'd disappeared, and with his disappearance went my torment.

I began to wonder if I'd been forgotten.

Not forgotten.

Just *forgiven*…

They'll never forgive.

I had to admit the Hawks were diabolically clever. With their welcome came a relaxation I would never have found if I wasn't permitted to explore on my own. A self-centred acceptance that only came from settling into a new environment with no duress.

I truly felt a part of their household. As sick and as twisted as it seemed.

By the end of fourteen days, with nothing to keep me occupied but reading and exploring, inevitably, my mind turned to what it had always known.

Sewing.

Not designing under pressure or rushing to deliver the next big thing.

Just sewing.

The epicentre of my craft.

I commandeered a writing pad, thanks to interrupting a business meeting. The lined paper only lasted me a day before I hunted Kes down and requested a sketchpad with no lines. The moment he'd given me one, I couldn't stop the drive to draw, to pluck the rapidly forming ensembles from my mind and transcribe to paper.

That evening, Kes had four additional sketchpads delivered to my room.

I found the passion I'd lost with overworking and stress. Enjoyment and creativity came back with a vengeance. My hands turned black with lead from sketching well into the night. The pages became littered with rainbows and the barbaric sensuality of diamonds. I embraced a carnal wardrobe of want and inhibitions, creating my most daring collection to date, pulling ideas from my imagination like silver threads, splashing them onto the paper thanks to my trusty pencil.

When my mind was blank of artistic drive, I would turn to the large volume of Weaver history and read my ancestors' scattered thoughts and notations. I wasn't gullible enough to write things of importance—the Hawks would only read it. A diary was the window into someone's soul, and I had no intention of them seeing into mine.

But I did scribble two questions.

Where the hell is Jethro?

What weapons are best used against ice? A chisel or a candle?

It was on the sixteenth night of being Jethro-free that I stumbled upon the official library. Drifting down dark corridors, unable to sleep, I felt as if I'd fallen through a wormhole into ancient literature and knowledge. The ceiling was a dome, painted with a navy sky and glittering yellow stars. The walls were three stories high with swirling ladders leading onto brass walkways to peruse each shelf with ease.

The moment I walked into the hushed world, I knew I'd found home.

That night, I'd spent hours reading by low light, fingering leather-bound limited editions, before curling up in the most comfy of beanbags and falling asleep.

Kes found me the next morning, nudging me awake with an amused grin. "Hi." He threw himself into the chaise lounge that was decorated with bamboo leaves, cranes, and Chinese symbols, not far from my commandeered beanbag.

I sat up, rubbing sleep from my eyes and stretching my stiff but mostly healed back. "How did you find me?"

Kes pointed upward, smiling. "Cameras."

My heart leapt into my throat. "Of course." *That* was why I was given free reign. Why no one tried to stop me. Everything I did was on show.

I was stupid not to realize it sooner.

I frowned. Was that what Jethro had switched off after he'd whipped me? Did he not wish his family to see him come all over my back—to show he had a *weakness* for me?

And if so…*why* didn't he want his family to see? He was only doing what he was told…wasn't he?

The past two weeks had delivered far too many questions where Jethro was concerned, and I still had no answers.

I did have one scary conclusion, though. As much as I detested Jethro's mind games and sick control…I missed the spark he conjured inside. I missed the clench when he touched me, and I craved the addictive fear of duelling.

As much as I enjoyed Kes's company, and as fond as I'd grown of him, I didn't grow wet at the thought of winning him over or dream of his lips kissing mine.

"Do you like the library?" Kes asked, craning his neck, trying to catch a glimpse at the open sketchpad beside me. The pages depicted a flowing silk cape that would be a mixture of air and thread.

Forcing Jethro from my mind, I nodded. "Yes. I love the silence and smell."

He smiled. "Bet you'll like what Jethro has to show you then."

I very much doubt that.

I stiffened slightly, hearing Kes talk about his brother. I'd picked up on a strange edge in his tone whenever he mentioned him. And I couldn't understand the dynamic between the two. They cared deeply for each other—that was undeniable—but there was something else, too. Something deeper and more complex than just sibling rivalry.

Hang on.

My ears pricked. "What does Jethro have to show me?"

"You mean, he hasn't shown you yet?"

"Shown me what?"

Kes shook his head. "He hasn't come to find you? Hasn't explained?" Dropping his voice, he asked, "How long has it been, since he's come for you?"

My forehead furrowed. Shouldn't he know that? Wasn't he privy to Jethro's convoluted inner thoughts?

Dropping my eyes, I said, "I haven't seen him since the First Debt was repaid."

Kes sucked in a breath. Rubbing a hand over his face, he stood quickly. "Look, forget I said anything. I have to go."

He strode from the library in a rustle of leather and denim, most likely going in search of his wayward brother.

Forget I said anything. Kes's words repeated inside my head.

I would like to forget everything that'd happened since the Hawks had come for me, but that was an impossibility.

Just like obeying Kes was.

From that moment on, I couldn't think of anything else.

What does Jethro have to show me?

And why hasn't he come to torment me?

THE NIGHT SKY exploded with a blue and gold firework. It rained through the blackness, dazzling through the skylight of the stable.

Goddammit, they'd started early.

Wings stomped his hoof against the cobblestone at the explosion. He didn't do well with fireworks—almost bucked me off last year when I'd gone for a midnight ride, rather than smile and be merry with my father.

Today was his birthday.

The joyous occasion of Cut being one step closer to a coffin.

Wasn't my fault that I preferred to celebrate for different reasons than his. He would be basking in toasts, counting the obscene amount of wealth gushing in, and patting himself on his back for a lifetime well spent.

Meanwhile, I would be sulking in the shadows just waiting for my turn to reign.

Was it despicable for a son to wish his father to die so he could inherit everything sooner rather than later, or was it merely a coping mechanism at surviving yet more years under his thumb?

Either way, it no longer mattered.

I was thirty next year.

And the fireworks would be bigger, louder, and more extravagant than my father's, because I would be the new owner of Hawksridge and hold all the power. That day had seemed like an eternity away when I was eighteen, but now it was within grasping distance.

I've almost made it.

Wings stomped his metal shoe as another firework detonated. All day the festivities had continued—starting with a hunt for pheasant, which began immediately after breakfast, followed by trout fishing in the fully stocked lake. The staff worked furiously and meticulously, making sure each element of his magical day was better than the one before.

I might secretly enjoy the news that my father inched closer to demise, but I hated celebrating my own birthday. Why rejoice another year passing, another year closer to death? I preferred to pretend I was immortal.

That way, I would never have to pay for my sins or fall from earth to hell.

Another firework boomed over the estate.

Wings huffed, nudging his velvet nose against my tweed jacket.

"You're greedy tonight," I said, fishing out a handful of oats and handing them to the gelding.

In perfect late summer tradition, England had put on a gorgeous day. No wind, no clouds. Endless yellow sunshine drenched Hawksridge Hall, granting perfect conditions for Cut and his Black Diamond brothers to hunt, fish, gamble, and drink all on the front lawn. Gazebos had been erected, and the dinner had been a banquet of roast pheasant, grilled trout, and venison stew.

My mind skipped back to watching Nila. I'd avoided her for two weeks.

Two weeks that I needed to screw my head back on fucking straight and stop allowing my stupid emotions to get the better of me.

Today was the first time I let her see me, but I hadn't gone close enough to talk.

What could I say? Sorry for whipping you? Sorry for coming on you? Sorry for my fucked-up soul that can only be controlled by a regiment of 'fixing myself?

There was nothing I could say and nothing I wanted to explain.

I sighed.

Jasmine had worked her magic, and I was back. I'd found my way into the cold shell that protected me and spent the last week cold, remote, *unfeeling*.

I was eternally relieved.

The messiness of life no longer affected me, and I trusted myself not to boil over with no provocation. Even *with* provocation, it would take a lot for me to snap. I wasn't just glacial; I was a continent of blizzards and perma-ice.

The moment my brothers, father, and I returned from the pheasant shoot, Nila had been sitting on the front terrace, sketching. She wore a long pale blue skirt with a slight train that rippled over the black tiles of the patio and a cream blouse with a ruffled collar and big buttons.

She'd looked content...centred.

The time apart had given us both much needed space, and the fiery emotion she'd conjured inside was a distant memory.

I didn't even hate her. I didn't have any drive to torment her, fuck her, or fight in any way. All emotions came from the same place.

That was what I'd forgotten.

Hate and love...they were the same thing. I'd tried to harness only one—hate. I tried to be my father's son, full of mistrust for others, while asserting dominance and fear.

And I'd succeeded for a while.

But with hate comes passion—either for those I loathed or circumstances I couldn't stand. Every spike of emotion permitted more awareness to steal my indifference and make me care.

Caring was my problem.

Caring was what got me into messes I couldn't repair.

Caring was what would kill me in the end.

But that was fixed now.

Resting my head on Wings' muscular neck, I breathed in the scent of equine and hay. "Suppose I better get it over with."

Just the thought of confronting Nila made my skin prickle. I'd shown her too much, and now she thought she understood me. She would *never* understand me.

Shit, I didn't understand me.

Then again, there was nothing left to understand. It was all...gone.

Wings huffed, searching my pockets for more oats.

Another boom of a purple and yellow firework shook the stable walls. The dogs howled in the kennels across the courtyard. Seemed everyone was on edge tonight.

Giving the horse one last handful, I left the stables and made my way reluctantly toward the Hall.

Nila's black eyes found mine the moment I joined the milling men and families of Black Diamonds. Women weaved, giggling and tipsy with our own brew and vintage. No children ran around—they weren't allowed on the estate—but the atmosphere of happiness scratched painful nails across my skin.

Nila never looked away as I was congratulated for being the winner at poker this afternoon and for losing the bet that I could catch more trout than my father.

It took ten minutes to cross the lawn with brothers detaining me and gossiping. Kes was in charge of the large bonfire roaring in the corner, burning off boughs and branches that had been trimmed from the forest closest to the house. Daniel—as was typical for my younger, psychotic brother—was nowhere to be seen. And Cut sat like a king on a throne, watching the staff set off dangerous fireworks.

The large box of pinwheels, squealers, and sunbursts waited to die in an extravagance of gunpowder and brilliance.

Stopping a few metres from Nila, I ignored her and watched the swarm of festivities. I hoped she would stay away.

But of course, that wish went unanswered.

"Hello," Nila said, appearing by my side. She still wore the long skirt with blouse and large buttons. Her hair was down, thick and glossy, mirroring the flames from the bonfire. Her cheeks were flushed from being out in the sun all day, but her eyes were clear from intoxication.

"I was beginning to forget what you looked like," she prompted when I didn't move or acknowledge.

Looking at her quickly, I touched my temple in greeting. Taking a sip of the elderberry and thistle beer that had been a trial brew last year, I deliberately refrained from talking. I wouldn't let her sucker me into another fight.

I was done fighting.

I would extract the debts, bide my time until all of this was mine, then get the final requirement out of the way.

Final requirement?

Her death, you mean?

Scowling, I took another sip. The concoction actually wasn't too bad. Standing stiff and remote, I stared at nothing, wishing she'd just leave.

Her presence gave no hint of how she felt about me. I couldn't tell if she hated me, desired me, or nursed vengeance deep in her heart.

I expected all of that and more. I expected to be slapped and told to never go near her again. I tensed for a spark in the tinderbox of emotions we stood in, just waiting for this crumbling truce to annihilate both of us.

What Nila didn't know was, if she struck me, I wouldn't retaliate. I would permit the slap with no spike of heartbeat or temper and walk away. I would stay my distance until the next debt was ready to be paid.

Because I was done.

I'd found peace, and I didn't want to enter the chaos of fighting with her again. It was too fucking dangerous.

"Where have you been?" she asked, moving closer and watching the staff drive a large firework peg into the ground. They fumbled around trying to set the fuse alight.

I didn't say anything. Just took another sip of my beverage.

The hiss and fizzle of the fuse was the only warning before the firework shot into the sky and rained over us with sparks and thunder.

Nila's face lit up with the glowing atoms, dark eyes wide with appreciation.

Once the night sky was no longer polluted by fake sunshine and the cloud of smoke disappeared, Nila frowned in my direction. "Are you going to say something?"

I shrugged. Why? What was there to say? Nothing of importance and I'd done enough talking. Enough fighting. Enough fucking masturbating over the girl I was destined to kill.

Why was she talking to me? Shouldn't she be avoiding me at all costs?

I stilled as Nila placed her hand on my forearm. Her feminine heat seeped through my tweed, reminding me of the last time we'd been together and what I'd done.

I stepped sideways, breaking her hold.

"Jethro—I—" Her voice tugged at my unbeating heart. I risked a glance at her. Her eyes glowed with onyx intelligence.

"Is this a different kind of torture? You no longer deem me important enough to even talk to?" The hurt in her voice dove under my skin, igniting my blood despite my will.

Locking every muscle, I said, "Don't flatter yourself. I have nothing to say, and you have nothing I wish to hear." Turning my attention back to the fireworks, another explosion wracked the atmosphere, disintegrating into not one but three different sunbursts of colour.

"You are the most confusing man I've ever met." Irritation twisted her voice.

A small smile twitched my lips. "Thank you. That's the second nicest thing you've ever said to me."

"What was the first?"

That you don't understand me.

My secrets were safe as long as I confounded her.

I sipped my beer, deliberately ignoring her.

Masculine laughter suddenly rose as one drunken club member fell face first into the punch bowl. His woman kept slapping him with the ladle as he proceeded to slurp up the spilled alcoholic liquid.

Nila smiled, sighing. "I'd like to say I've missed you, but that would be a lie."

My back stiffened, but I forced myself to relax. Good for her.

I suppose.

"Seriously? What happened to you? Two weeks ago, you would've jumped down my throat and growled like a demented wildebeest. Now…nothing." Nila placed her hands on her hips, glaring.

I drained my beer, placing the empty cup on the food-strewn table to our right.

She huffed, running her fingers through her hair. "Fine. Keep your freaky silence. I'm sure Kes would love to talk to me."

Gathering the front of her skirt, she pranced away.

Kestrel.

Images of her spending so much time with him bombarded me. Despite the success of the conditioning session I'd had with Jasmine, I couldn't seem to stop myself watching the footage of Nila drifting around the Hall and laughing with my brother.

They were close.

She didn't trust him—the look of wariness never fully left her face—but she tolerated and enjoyed his company.

Unlike mine.

She accepted his gifts without suspicion, and never tried to antagonise him to the point of showing his true self.

Why did she accept his friendship yet go out of her way to rip me to shreds?

I gritted my teeth. Stupid question. The answer was plain and simple. I was her tormentor; Kes was her saviour. That was how this was always orchestrated. I should be happy it was working so flawlessly.

Plus, she was drawn to him because of the messages. The ruse of Kite007.

My hands curled. She'd let Kes waltz into her life, because she believed they had history. She might even believe he was ultimately on her side.

Silly, silly Weaver.

She hadn't asked him outright yet. I knew that for a fact. Everything would change when she did.

I stood frozen as Nila traversed the small distance across the lawn toward Kes. He reclined in a deck chair, a cigar dangling from his fingers, his shirt open and showing his muscular stomach. Kes had always been stronger than me—more brawn than brains—but he'd also never used it against me unless it was in play.

Now, though, he played a dangerous game, deliberately drawing Nila away from me.

My teeth clenched as Kes opened his arms and Nila perched on the arm of his deckchair. He said something to her, and she giggled.

My stomach churned; elderberry and thistle flavoured bile crawled up my throat.

Every second I stood and witnessed the friendship that'd blossomed between my captive and brother sent my gut convulsing.

Every moment I watched, my ice steamed until I billowed with smoke.

I didn't give myself permission to stomp across the garden.

I didn't even notice I'd gone from standing to stalking.

And I definitely didn't permit my body to bend and grab her wrist.

But that was what I did.

Somehow, I'd gone from standing to yanking Nila Weaver from my brother's embrace and dragging her like a hunted deer toward the Hall.

"Hey!" Nila dragged her nails over my wrist. It didn't do any good. Pain was another emotion I'd managed to shut off. "Let me go."

"No," I muttered. "There's something I need to show you." The party was left behind, and Kes had the sense of mind to stay where the fuck he was.

No one intervened or glanced our way as I carted her closer to the Hall. Once we entered the huge mansion, I let her wrist go and moved behind her to splay a guiding hand on her lower back. She stiffened but didn't shy away. Silently, I propelled her down the corridor.

What are you doing?

This was important.

You agreed you wouldn't go through with it.

That was before my brother stepped over the line.

Fuck trying to keep myself removed.

Nila was mine, and she would never be permitted to forget it.

At the time, I'd drafted it purely to keep myself busy while staying my distance. But I think I always knew in my heart I would make her sign.

After all, it would ensure Nila would stay mine, even if she fell for my brother. Even if Kes won.

A binding agreement.

Something that trumped even the Debt Inheritance.

An agreement my father would disintegrate if he ever found out.

My study.

My sanctuary.

The one place no one else was permitted to go.

What are you doing bringing her in here?

I hadn't thought this through. But I couldn't turn back now.

Unlocking the thick carved door, I pushed Nila through the entrance. Once inside, I locked it, letting her drift forward on her own accord. Her eyes moved around the space quickly, expertly going to the exits of bathroom, balcony sash window, and the doorway in which we'd come.

Poor girl.

She'd changed so much already. A true survivalist. A puritan who only wanted to live.

But you'll die. Just like the rest of them.

I searched for the cold smugness drilled into me by my father. I was supposed to enjoy this—to love the hunt and dispatching of

Weavers.

It was a family hobby. A trade passed down, linking our forefathers and ensuring our lineage had common ground.

So why did the thought of beheading her twist my gut?

Why did the very notion of watching her fuck my brother churn my heart in a blender?

My entire body rebelled at the thought of an axe detaching her long black hair, slicing through the vulnerable cord of muscle, shutting her dark eyes forever.

My cock twitched as she spun to face me, her hands flying to her hips. She seemed out of place in the rotund room with its six windows, lush Chinese sewn carpet, and treasure trove of small lead figurines from Indian and Cowboy child play-sets.

The wealth of history and monetary value of the things in this room would make a museum weep.

"What are we doing in here?"

I stalked to my desk. Unlocking a secret drawer beneath the jumble of stationery, I pulled forth a drafted document that no one else knew about but me. There were no cameras in this room. No one spying on what I was about to do.

Just us.

Only we would know what we'd done.

"Come here," I said, snapping my fingers.

Nila narrowed her eyes. "You do that often."

"Do what?"

She snapped her fingers. "Summon me like your pet; like your dogs."

I placed both hands flat on the desk. "You *are* my pet. I thought we'd discussed that."

She stomped forward, a conundrum of bright temper in the drab world of my study. Her sandaled feet padded on the thick carpet, planting herself in front of my desk. Her head tilted, long hair cascading over her shoulder, completely free and glossy as the midnight sky. "Funny, I thought we'd established I was something more."

My back stiffened. "Since when?"

Her lips stretched, baring her teeth in an evil little grin. "Since I made you come. Since you showed me you were human. Since you ran from me for the past fortnight, all because you're not dealing with whatever is going on between us."

She moved closer.

I stood ramrod straight, clenching every muscle against her advance.

"Tell me, Jethro Hawk. Would a *pet* be able to suck you? Would a *pet* swallow your cum? Would a pet *pleasure* you?" Her voice dropped to a seduction. "Would a pet admit to missing its owner, because it'd become addicted to the desire it felt in its master's presence?"

My mind exploded.

I swallowed hard, hating the swirl of lust and temper that had no right to build. I'd barricaded emotions from my life, so why did the mere hint of an argument with Nila completely undo everything I'd tried so hard to fix?

I couldn't breathe.

Needing a distraction, I pulled her phone that I'd confiscated from my pocket and held it up.

Instantly, her mouth fell open. Greed and excitement glowed on her face. "You still have it."

"Of course, I still have it." Swiping my finger over the screen, I muttered, "There are some extremely interesting messages on here."

Nila froze. Her cheeks lost all colour. "I told you that I'd been in touch with my brother. I told you he knew."

I nodded. "You did."

She tried to hide her nervousness but didn't succeed. "So what's interesting? I told you the truth."

What was interesting?

How about the fucking messages reeking of smut and combustible need? I'd spent many an evening sorting through the unsent drafts to Kite007. She'd deleted more messages than she'd actually sent, hiding so much.

By reading the messages she didn't want seen, I saw right into her soul. I finally got a clue of who Nila Weaver was. And she was no longer the heartbreakingly timid woman who'd been a plaything for her brother and a slave for her father.

She was so, so much more.

Every draft she'd typed but never sent rested in her phone like a perfect calendar of her growth from gullible daughter to fierce opponent.

Every single message she'd typed to *him*—to the man she knew as Kite—further showed the truth of who she really was.

Her emails had been nothing but work related.

Her brother nothing but demanding and dominant.

Her father nothing but pleading and clinging.

But Kite...

He brought out the best in Nila. And I brought out the fucking worst.

I shook my head, unable to stop the chuckle breaking through my lips. Why hadn't I seen it? Why hadn't I understood it before now? I was a fucking idiot.

Nila crossed her arms, glaring pure death. "Are you done laughing at my personal life?"

I stopped chuckling, embracing vacancy once again. "What makes you think I'm laughing *at* you, Ms. Weaver?"

The moment I spoke her name, the fight, the intoxicating addictive need to battle with her broke free from the prison inside.

Goddammit, it seemed the only time I could be free was to stay away from her. But the only time I was alive was to provoke and drink in her kitten-like wrath like an elixir of life.

Fuck, I'm screwed.

For the first time, I acknowledged it. Not with hatred or fear or frustration—just accepted that Nila Weaver was a force I couldn't control, and as much as I would like to deny it, she had a power over me.

Jasmine had seen it.

That was what my sister meant.

But I'd been too much of an arsehole to listen.

Tomorrow, you're going back to your sister and talking this through.

I needed answers. And she was the only one who I trusted enough to give me unbiased, pure direction. We were the black sheep of the Hawk family, and for that one reason, we'd become close. Kes was my best friend—until recently, of course—but my sister was my rescuer.

Not that my father knew, or even my grandmother, who kept Jasmine far away from us men and our contamination.

No one knew the bond my sister and I shared.

Just like no one knew the bond Nila and I shared.

Both were secret.

And both meant more to me than any other relationship I'd ever had.

Shit.

Running a hand through my hair, I placed her phone on my desk.

Nila never took her gaze from the device. "You seem to laugh at everything I do, so it's only rational to think my messages entertained you to no end."

I had to do what I came in here to do before I lost all focus and allowed Nila to drag forth everything I'd worked so hard to swallow.

I murmured, "You're tempting destruction, Ms. Weaver." My breathing turned shallow as I moved around the desk and captured the ends of her long hair, twirling them around my fingertips.

There was something about her hair. Something that called to the feral part of me that wanted the strands on my cock as she sucked me, or better yet, stuck to my sweaty chest after I'd come deep inside her.

Those fantasies had not helped clear my head. The past fortnight, they'd only gotten worse.

Just like I had Nila's hair wrapped around my little finger, she had me wrapped around hers.

"Nila. My name is *Nila*. You might as well call me that, seeing as I've had your cock in my mouth and your tongue between my legs. Nothing like tasting each other to be on a first-name basis, huh, *Jethro?*"

I tugged her hair. "Quiet."

"No chance."

My eyes widened. Who was this woman? Taunting me, provoking me while her body trembled with anger. It was almost as if she *wanted* me to explode. To hurt her. To retaliate.

Maybe she does?

Perhaps she felt the same way I did—a connection in our arguments, a freedom to give into the overwhelming emotions that didn't need to make sense when in the heat of a fight.

How did I think I could maintain this persona I'd created? This suave sophistication that I'd successfully worn for so many years?

My time was up.

And it would remain up until Nila was gone.

I swallowed hard at the thought of her disappearing.

My eyes fell on the diamond collar. "I could make you, but I think you'd just like it."

As long as the collar remained around her neck, she was alive. As long as the diamonds glinted and drenched her in rainbows, she would be there to torment me.

And day by day, she would make me weaker.

And weaker.

Until one day, I would lose it all.

It can't happen.

But what could I do to prevent it?

Make her hate you. Make her despise you.

Then it would be against my will, even if I suddenly wanted a change of heart.

"Everything you do to me I hate," she hissed.

Crowding her against the desk, I murmured, "Everything?" My eyes fell to her lips. What I wouldn't give to just fucking kiss her. I'd wanted to kiss her for weeks.

Her mouth parted, breath turning soft and quick. "Yes, everything."

Temper swirled in the room, heating the space. "You seem to enjoy the anticipation of me kissing you."

She snorted. "Don't flatter yourself."

Capturing her chin, I dug my fingers into her cheeks. "If I kissed you right now, you'd let me do whatever the hell I wanted."

She struggled, eyes sparkling with black ferocity. "Kiss me and I'll bite you."

I wanted to laugh at the absurdity of our fight, but fuck if it didn't make me feel more alive than I had in two weeks.

I couldn't let it continue, though.

It has to stop.

Letting her chin go, I slapped her.

A puff of surprise and pain escaped her lips.

The ring in my palm reminded me of the man I'd been groomed to be, and I threw myself headfirst into it. The bright flush on her cheek as her face snapped sideways begged me to lick her.

So, I did.

Dragging her close, I lapped my tongue over her hot, punished flesh, whispering, "You would like me too much if I gave into your goading, Ms. Weaver. I warned you before—if you insist on playing this game, you won't win."

She breathed hard. "Funny, I thought the score was pretty even."

I pressed my cold lips against her smarting cheek. "Funny, I thought you lost the day you were born."

She sucked in a breath, her dark eyes swimming with tears.

Strike for me.

I'd won that argument, so why did my stomach feel like fucking lead?

Letting her go, I grabbed the newly drafted contract from the desk and shoved it in her face. "You agreed to this. Sign it."

Her mouth popped wide, taking in the freshly inked document. I'd spent many nights carefully penning it in the way of our custom with quill and ink, rather than computer and printer. It wasn't perfect, but it was binding, and that was all that fucking mattered.

Grabbing the same swan feather I'd used to scratch out the paperwork, I stole Nila's hand and hooked her fingers around the quill.

"What is this?"

"The agreement owed from your disastrous attempt at running." Tapping the page, I said, "Sign it."

"I'm not signing anything until I've read it." Her gaze glowed black, her cheek still pink from my slap.

Taking a step back, I splayed my hands, presenting the contract. "By all means, Ms. Weaver. Read away."

She scowled, her hands shaking as she snatched it from my grip.

Her lips parted as she read.

I didn't need to see it to know what it said. It was ingrained on my soul.

Date: 5th September 2014

Jethro Hawk, firstborn son of Bryan Hawk, and Nila Weaver, firstborn daughter of Emma Weaver, hereby solemnly swear this is a law-abiding and incontestable contract.

Nila Weaver revokes all ownership of her freewill, thoughts, and body and grants them into the sole custody of Jethro Hawk, as per the agreement made the morning of the 19th of August when Nila Weaver took up the offer from Jethro Hawk to run in exchange for her freedom.

The previous incontestable document named the Debt Inheritance falls into second right of claimant and will remain void as long as this new agreement is in effect.

The terms brokered were for Nila's freedom and release of the Debt Inheritance if she won, and her willing signature revoking everything that she is to Jethro Hawk if she lost.

On the 19th of August, Nila Weaver lost; therefore, this agreement is complete and binding.

Both Nila Weaver and Jethro Hawk promise neither circumstance, nor

change of heart will alter this vow.
   In sickness and in health.
   Two houses.
   One contract.

I'd already signed, taking up half the page below.

Nila looked up, completely horrified. "You can't be serious. You—you—"

I tensed. "Careful what you say. Think about how painful it will be for you if you insult my mental health again."

She swallowed back the words dying to spew forth. "I'm not signing this, you bastard."

I tilted my head. "Bastard? Interesting choice of words."

"Don't like that one? How about fuckwit? Murderer? Rapist?"

I slapped her again, revelling in the equal burn we shared.

Pain to deliver pain. Pleasure to deliver pleasure.

Funny how the two were correlated.

"I'll accept 'bastard' and 'fuckwit,' but under no circumstances will I accept 'rapist.' Have I tried to take you? Have I forced you? And, I'm no murderer."

Her eyes glittered, fingers rubbing her cheek. "Are you deliberately blocking out what happened after the First Debt was repaid, or are you that much of a lunatic to remember only the things convenient to you?"

Lunatic.

I ran a hand infinitely slowly through my hair. I had full grounds to punish her. I'd warned her time and time again.

"Tell me, Jethro, you say you're not a murderer—*yet*. But it will be you who delivers the killing blow, won't it? You admitted as much in the past. Unless you're too chicken and make your father do it. Or even maybe poor Kes. Will he kill me? Is he the bigger man than you? To kill off the family pet when it's no longer wanted?"

My jaw ached from clenching so hard. "You really want to know?"

You've already guessed the truth.

The thought blazed bright, almost as bright as her cheek.

"No need, I already know. What will you use? A butchers block? A sharp blade or dull?" The strength and fight in her voice suddenly dissolved into sobs. "How will you live with yourself when my blood pours over your perfect shoes?"

The room shattered with sadness; the walls trampled us with appalling futures.

With a horrified wail, she curled into herself, holding her stomach as if her very soul tried to claw its way out. "Tell me, Jethro, if I only have a limited amount of time left, why go through the charade of making me sign this?!" She shook the parchment in front of my face. "What is this anyway? Does it have a name? 'Weaver Vexation,' perhaps?"

Her sanity quickly unravelled with every syllable.

I stood stiff, frantically clutching at my beloved ice. But in that moment, I felt her pain. I tasted her tears. I lived her grief.

My hands balled. The title I'd given it had been flippant at the time, but now I could see how it could shatter her.

Don't say it.

The air in the office turned stagnant, waiting for me to speak.

Finally, I admitted, "Sacramental Pledge."

She half-cackled, half-giggled, before everything seemed to fold in and crush her. "You made this our vows?! Sacramental, holy matrimony *vows?*"

Before I could answer, she shook her head and collapsed to her knees before me. Rocking, hot tears splashed onto the contract, mixing with ink and staining it with large swirls of black.

She was the one who gave me the idea. After all, we *were* technically married. Groomed for one another, destined to drive each other to insanity. This was our fate. Our motherfucking *destiny.*

Her laughs interspersed with sobs. The sound was utterly heart-crushing. I locked my body from moving as she curled tighter on the floor.

"This is real. This…it's not a nightmare. *This is real!*"

Tears rivered from her eyes, tracking faster and faster as her breath caught and she choked. She choked and sobbed and choked again. "It's not fair. I w—want to go h—home."

I'd never seen anyone come apart so completely.

This wasn't just about the deed. This was about everything she hadn't let herself feel. She hadn't let go of her past. She hadn't faced the reality that this was her future, and there would be no going back—no matter how much she thought it was possible.

Was this how she'd survived—by pretending it wasn't real, that everything would somehow disappear?

Everything crested and breached, shuddering her small frame with grief.

I stood over her, hating to see such weakness. Despising that I'd driven her to break. But at the same time, I stood protective over her vulnerability, standing guard, making sure she had the peace in which to purge.

In a way, I knew exactly how she felt. We were both chained to a future we didn't want, and there was no way out—for either of us.

I didn't touch her. I didn't torment her.

I let her spew her worries and cleanse herself.

I just let her cry.

As each droplet splashed onto the carpet, I found myself growing fucking jealous. I was jealous that finding a release was so easy for her. So easy to come undone, knowing she'd have the power to stitch herself together again.

Half an hour passed, or maybe it was only ten minutes, but slowly Nila's tears stopped, and her wracking frame fell into a deep, eternal silence.

The night was entirely tainted. I had no drive to make her sign anymore or to wage war. And I definitely had no more energy to be cruel.

There was no need. I didn't have to break her—not after she'd broken herself.

I sighed heavily. "Get up."

Slowly, quietly, and obediently, she climbed to her feet. She stood swaying, white as a fucking ghost. In her hands, she still clutched the quill and parchment having drenched it in her tears.

Without a word, she placed the soggy document onto the desk, dipped the swan feather into the ink well, and signed her name.

My stomach swooped in the wrong direction. I should've been happy, but instead my joy was filthy oil, corrupting my insides.

Avoiding eye contact, she whispered, "I want to go back to my room. If you have any soul inside you, Jethro, you will do this one thing for me."

My heart squeezed, cracking its glacier frost, melting drop by drop.

My hands itched to touch her, to grant solace…comfort.

She hates you, you arsehole.

There was no way she would want to be touched. Especially by me.

The least I could do was release her.

With infinitesimal slowness, I turned to the desk and retrieved her phone. "Here." I pressed it into her lax palm.

She didn't even acknowledge me.

With nothing else to say, I guided her back to her room.

NEEDLE&THREAD: *I wish you'd answer me, Vaughn. Please tell me you're not about to blow something up, charge in here with God knows what, and get yourself arrested or worse… killed. Please…reply. I miss you.*

I swiped at the sticky salt on my cheeks. My heart hung heavy like a charred piece of meat. Last night was a distant memory, rather foggy and blurred. I remembered the fireworks, I recalled the relaxed day of reading and helping the staff set up the garden buffet, but I struggled to remember what happened in Jethro's office.

All I knew was I'd finally snapped.

The cry I'd had in the kennels the day I arrived was nothing to how undone I'd become.

I should care that Jethro had seen me at my absolute weakest, but I couldn't get up the energy. I felt strangely aloof, removed from everything.

He let you cry.

He didn't torment me or make it worse by delivering yet more horror. He'd stood like an ice statue, completely unyielding and not melting at all, towering over me while I wept into his carpet.

But in that arctic silence, there'd been something…something different.

His silence had throbbed with regret…of understanding and even mutual anguish.

The moon and stars had given way to another stunning day, miraculously cancelling the horrible ending to a nice party.

The best thing? I'd slept like the dead after Jethro had left me alone. The cry had drained me of everything, leaving me with a thick headache that sent me slamming into unconsciousness.

My phone buzzed.

Shaking my head, I dispelled last night and looked at the glowing screen. I wanted a reply from my twin. But what I got was better.

My heart soared as I read the first message from Kite007 in two weeks.

Kite007: *Don't know why I keep hoping you'll reply, seeing as you've been quiet for two weeks, but I had a shit of a night and need to talk to someone who won't judge.*

He'd been trying to message me?

I quickly scrolled through the inbox but found nothing. My stomach rolled at the thought of Jethro deleting Kite's messages. What an arsehole.

I'd gone from a secluded seamstress, whose only contact was her father and brother, to being torn in three directions. As much as I wanted to deny it, I had feelings for Kite. He'd been a bastard to me, but he'd granted me the strength to stand up to him, which then led me to develop feelings for Kestrel. *Because he's the same person; I know it.*

I still hadn't gotten up the guts to ask him, but sometimes I'd catch him watching me with secrets in his eyes.

I didn't care that it might all be a ruse to get inside my head. I didn't care I was nothing more than a marionette being told what to think and who to trust. I had to forget about all that and follow my heart—because, ultimately, that was the only thing that might save me.

Then, of course, there was Jethro. He confused me, perplexed me, and completely befuddled me. One minute I would gladly pour gasoline over his wintry shell and see if I could burn him into the person I saw rare glimpses of, the next he did things like last night and ruined all the softness I had for him.

How could I understand someone who didn't even understand himself?

You can't talk. One second you're trying to seduce him, the next you're trying to make him bleed.

We were as bad as each other.

Looking at the text again, I clicked reply. Biting my lip, I wondered why Kes/Kite had had a bad night. What had happened when Jethro tugged me away? And why hadn't Kes tried to talk to me when he realised I wasn't replying to his messages?

We saw each other every day. All he had to do was whisper something in my ear. Something that would confirm this labyrinthine mystery once and for all.

Perhaps Jethro showed the new contract to Kes—rubbed it in his face that no matter how Kes felt about me, he could never have me?

Ugh. The headache from last night came back with a heavy cloud.

Needle&Thread: *I'm here now. And you're right, I won't judge. What happened last night?*

It was odd to have nothing sexual included in the message, but our 'friendship' had more depth now.

I settled deeper into the pillows. The diamond collar bruised my neck, throbbing with heat; it wasn't exactly comfortable to sleep in.

Kite007: *I stooped to an all-new low. Remember when I said we're all products of our upbringing? Well, I keep blaming everything wrong inside me on that. I use it as an excuse, but what if it isn't good enough anymore?*

Oh, my God.

I'd never heard Kite sound so melancholy. My heartbeat increased as my fingers flew over the keyboard.

Needle&Thread: *There's nothing wrong inside you.*

I paused before pressing send. If I did this, he would know I suspected. If he read between the lines and didn't see it as a blasé comment, the truth would be out and the choice of how to proceed would be in his court. Did I want him to have that power?

Gritting my teeth, I pressed send.

Immediately, I got a reply.

Kite007: *You don't know anything about me.*

Needle&Thread: *We can keep pretending if you'd like, but it's just another excuse. It sounds like you're ready to face the truth. So…it's your call if you want to or not.*

Minutes ticked past.

My mind skipped back to the day I'd arrived. The welcome luncheon, the night in the kennels, and the strange degrading encounters with Jethro. How was it the Hawks had everything, yet everyone seemed to be hiding the truth? Jethro was hiding. Kes was hiding. Daniel had disappeared—the little creep—and Cut walked around with an air of mystique.

There was so much beneath the surface that no one dared discuss.

And, if I was honest, they'd transformed me into the same kind of creature. Someone who had evolved from a single dimension and now lived with so many avenues of personalities.

I was still the quiet, vertigo-stricken girl from London, but I was also the woman who *liked* being tormented, who thrived on a fight, and who thirsted for sex.

And that stupefied me even more, because I wanted sex with *Jethro*, not Kestrel.

What does that mean?

Jethro had made me come totally and spectacularly in front of witnesses. He'd manipulated me—given me a reward. It was both sick and…sweet.

No, never sweet, Nila.

Yes, sweet.

Beneath the mask, he was so many things, and sweet *was* one of them.

Kite007: *My call? You're so sure I'll be honest?*

Needle&Thread: *Why wouldn't you be? You know who I am. I want to know who you are. I'm trustworthy.*

Kite007: *You're wrong. I don't know who you are. Every day I think I do, but then you do something that changes my perception. You're a complexity.*

My heart exploded.

Finally. Confirmation.

Every day you do…

Not say, or text, or imply. Do—as in action—*physical.*

My hands shook as I replied.

Needle&Thread: *Perhaps you need to drop your guard, in order to see in to others. You're just as complex, just as confounding.*

The second I pressed send, I panicked. He'd admitted we knew each other. I'd admitted it, too. This anonymous freedom was now a knowledgeable cage.

Kite007: *Tell me one thing you've lied about. Tell me the truth. Let me see what you're hiding.*

My brain smarted. There were so many secrets, too many puzzles. I'd changed so much; I no longer knew what I should hide. The little kitten who didn't have claws would've curled into a ball at such a revealing question, but that was no longer an option, and I didn't want it to be.

I was no longer afraid of diving deep and finding out who I truly was.

Needle&Thread: *You want something real? I've only come once in my life, and it was just a few days ago.*

It seemed like a small confession, but it was huge after all my fibbing of releases and kinky messages.

Kite007: *How is that even possible? What was with all the other releases you had? I thought you were a master at self-pleasure.*

Needle&Thread: *You're asking questions that will lead to finding out who I am. Are you ready for that, Kite? Truly? No turning back once you do.*

Radio silence.

Typical.

He'd run again.

My fingers hovered over the keys, determined not to end this. Not when we were so close to admitting this charade.

Needle&Thread: *I could continue pretending I'm the masturbating minx you think I am or be honest with you. Again, your choice.*

I rolled my eyes. *He's a Hawk.* Maybe he already knew everything about me? They'd probably had my family under surveillance for years. Maybe that was the whole reason why Kes messaged me on a wrong number—to drip-feed Jethro information on how pathetic and hopeless I was.

I slumped against my pillows. It made sense. And hurt far too much.

Kite007: *Masturbating minx? I like that title.*

My eyes flared; my stomach twisted with eagerness.

Kite007: *I need to know more. Stick to the subject and give me the truth. Nothing more. Nothing less. What were you doing when you said you came?*

My heart raced.

Needle&Thread: *Releases for me were found either on my treadmill or from working until my brain was numb.*

Five minutes passed.

Kite007: *And the only time you came? How did that happen? As if you don't know.*

Suddenly, I was over it all. Over the fibs, the half-truths, the veiled secrets. He knew how it happened. He'd watched his damn brother stick his tongue between my legs and make me combust.

Needle&Thread: *I came with the tongue of my enemy between my legs. He drove me so damn high and hard that I gave him a piece of myself no one else ever had, and he used it as a weapon against me. There, you happy?*

My chest rose and fell. Arguing via faceless messages wasn't enough. I wanted to strike and hurt and scream.

Kite007: *If you were here with me, I'd give you your second release. I'd finger you until you were soaking, then I'd do what I've wanted to fucking do since I set eyes on you.*

My mouth went terribly dry.

Needle&Thread: *What have you wanted to do?*

Kite007: *I want to feel how tight you are. I want to experience your wet heat as I fill you. I want to give you my cock, Needle. Would you let me?*

Oh, my God. My body turned boneless with desire.

Another message from a different sender arrived.

Textile: *Nila? I understand why you haven't replied to me, but I thought you should know that V and I are closer to figuring a way to end this ridiculous nightmare. Don't lose hope, sweetheart. I love you so much.*

Oh, bad timing, father. *Seriously* bad timing.

My lust turned to smouldering rage.

Ridiculous? He thought this was *ridiculous*? This debt that killed my mother and all the firstborn women in my family tree was ridiculous?

I laughed at his choice of words. This wasn't ridiculous; it was insane.

Needle&Thread: *Father, you let them take me. You knew all along they were coming, yet you did nothing to protect me. You handed me over like a fattened calf with no tears or violence. How can you say you're coming for me? How can you say you love me? I'm not losing hope. I'm building my own brand of hope, and for the first time in my life, it doesn't hinge on you. Leave me the hell alone.*

I shook hard when I pressed send. I'd never spoken to my father that way before. Never been so disrespectful. It made me feel sick but also free. Free from the fear of disappointing him.

Because he'd disappointed me first.

Kite007: *Would you let me fuck you? Would you break the rules and give me what I need so fucking much?*

My mind swarmed with images of sleeping with Kestrel, but try as I might, all I could see was Jethro. All I could feel was Jethro. All I wanted was Jethro.

Shit.

I wanted to throw my damn phone against the wall.

Needle&Thread: *Answer me one question before I give you an answer.*

Kite007: *What?*

Taking a deep breath, I typed:

Needle&Thread: *Would you kiss me first? Or is that against the rules?*

A minute. Then two.

Kite007: *I wouldn't just kiss you. I would hold your cheeks and worship your mouth. I would devour your lips and make drunken love to your tongue. I would fucking inhale you, so you would live forever in my lungs.*

I couldn't move.

Yet another difference between the Hawk brothers. One would kiss me, and one went out of his way to avoid it. One would adore me until the day of my death, and one would probably dance upon my grave because it meant his obligations were complete.

My heart crumbled into dust.

I couldn't—I couldn't do this anymore.

Turning my phone around, I undid the case, tore the battery out, and dumped the dismantled device into the drawer of the bedside table.

I didn't care about replying.

I didn't care if my silence hurt his feelings.

All I cared about was nursing the cyclonic pain inside me.

And trying to forget all about Jethro fucking Hawk.

The next morning, I was showered and clothed in a black maxi dress with a sequined orchid on the chest and purple ballet slippers.

I needed some space and planned to go for a walk around the estate. I still hadn't turned my phone on and had no desire to do so. It was still in pieces in the drawer. For now, I didn't care about the outside world or even Kite's reply.

I didn't *care*.

It was liberating.

Sitting on the end of my bed, I quickly plaited my hair and draped the long rope over my shoulder.

My head wrenched up as the door to my room slammed open.

"What the—"

Jethro stood breathing hard in the doorway. My cold-hearted nemesis wore black jeans and a grey t-shirt—seriously, didn't he own any other colours?

"Where do you think you're going?" His voice was gravel and granite and ice.

I stood up, planting my hands on my hips. "Good morning to you, too. If you must know, *master*, it's time for my walk. I'm a good little pet, you see. Making sure I have my daily exercise."

I knew I played with fire, or ice as the case might be, but I really didn't give a damn.

The previous night in his office had broken something inside me and Kes/Kite had finished me off with talks of wanting me.

I couldn't decipher my panic last night when Kite said he would kiss me—my sudden terror hadn't made sense. But now it did.

If I let myself fall into Kes's/Kite's trap of kindness, I would lose everything I'd fought to gain. And I wasn't willing to give that up. I was selfish and liked this new Nila. And if that meant I had to keep my distance from kind-hearted people and only surround myself with bastards, then so be it.

Jethro would be the only one permitted to spike my heart and draw reluctant wetness. No one else.

"Careful, Ms. Weaver," Jethro murmured. Stalking into the room, he kicked the door closed behind him.

His presence was a challenge, and I was prepared to meet it. Crossing the small distance between us, we met in the middle of the carpet; every muscle tense and ready to fight.

His nostrils flared, golden eyes delving deeply into mine. "I thought you'd be hiding under your bed after your debacle in my office."

I shrugged. "Everyone has a limit, and I crossed mine. Unluckily for you, my limit has now increased, so don't expect me to break again anytime soon." I smiled, thinking of my reply to my father. I'd finally had the balls to tell him to leave me alone. Jethro would be no different.

I was prepared to unplug him, just like I'd unplugged my phone.

Taking another step, my fingertips landed on his chest, dipping coyly to his belt. His eyes flared, but he held his ground. "Thank you for pushing me, Jethro. Without you, I would still be terrified. But now I feel surprisingly…calm."

A calm where I'd stopped fretting over the future. A calm where I was just as volatile and just as unhinged as they were.

"I can't keep up with you." His voice was dark with a trace of anger. He cocked his head, his salt-and-pepper hair catching the morning sun glinting through the window. "You've surprised me again, Ms. Weaver, and once again, I don't like it." He leaned forward, his lips so close to mine. "I'm beginning to wonder if everything I know about you is a lie."

I stood firm. "You don't know a thing about me."

Why does this conversation sound like the one I had yesterday by phone?

He chuckled. "We Hawks have our ways. I know more than you think."

His cryptic comment didn't derail me. He'd read Kite's messages. He knew everything about me that I'd meant for a perfect stranger.

I stared harder, trying to uncover his many, many layers. But it was pointless—like staring into a black lake with no reflection other than myself.

"Come. It's time for Gemstone and breakfast." He smiled coldly. "I have no doubt you'll be starving after your…what was that? Would you prefer the word *breakdown* or *hysterics?*"

I straightened my shoulders. "Neither."

"You have to pick one."

"No, I don't. If you want me to define it, I'll call it my way of saying goodbye."

He jerked. "Goodbye?" His knuckles went white as his hands clenched into fists. "To whom?"

My eyes tightened, trying to read him. He played the perfect part. If he knew Kestrel messaged me, he hid his deception so well—too well. The perfect liar.

"To my past, to who I used to be, to a friend called Kite."

The reaction was subtle.

The small intake of breath. The slight whitening of his face. The indiscernible flinch of his muscles.

Then it was gone, hidden beneath the snowy exterior he held so well. "Ah yes, the James Bond idiot, 007. The same idiot who just can't seem to stop messaging you." Moving quickly, he grabbed my elbow, dragging me toward the door. "Well, I'm glad you said your goodbyes. Nothing worse than dying with unfinished business." His smile sent gale-force winds howling through my suddenly torn-open chest.

I slammed to a halt. "You can't help yourself, can you?"

He paused, forehead furrowed.

"You just have to be so damn cruel."

He sighed dramatically, backing me away from the door and toward the centre of the room again. "I'm not cruel."

I laughed. "Says the heartless human who probably doesn't have a reflection when he stares in the mirror."

He took another threatening step. I took one, too. Backing away from him, waltzing slowly around the room as hunter and prey.

"You're saying I'm soulless?"

I nodded. "Completely soulless."

He smirked. "Okay, try me. Ask me to do something. Make me prove to you that I have a soul."

I frowned. "Like what?"

He took another step, pressing me closer to the bed. The anger throbbing around him switched to sexual interest. My breathing picked up as his golden eyes darkened. "You're the one who needs proof, Ms. Weaver. You make the choice."

What could I make him do?

What would prove he had a heart and my resolution to seduce him would actually work?

I know.

The one thing that seemed to be the epicentre of whatever I was trying to do.

I stopped retreating, locking my knees to prevent myself from losing confidence and running. "I have something. A test. It will prove you're not the monster I think you are."

He came closer, a slow smile spreading his lips. "Go on."

I balled my hands, taking a deep breath. The precipice opened wide. I took a leap of faith. "Kiss me."

The oxygen in the room disappeared. My heart erupted into flurries.

Jethro froze. "Excuse me?"

Standing tall, I said, "You've come so close to kissing me. By the stables, in the forest, when you made me pay the First Debt, even in your office. I'm done with your teasing, Jethro. I'm done with you pulling away whenever things get interesting. I want to know why."

Jethro's hands clenched by his sides. "And you think a stupid kiss will prove—what will it prove?"

I narrowed my eyes. "That you're not as cold as you think you are. That you do care—care enough to be affected by kissing your arch enemy."

Jethro laughed, but it was laced with uncertainty and…was that fear? "I'm not kissing you to prove such a ridiculous point."

I splayed my hands, mocking him. "You said you'd do anything I asked."

He chuckled softly. "I said something worthwhile."

"Kissing me isn't worthwhile?"

His gaze latched onto mine. A second ticked past. Another. Then he lost his icy shell. "What the fuck do you want from me, Nila?"

My heart stopped.

Nila.

He'd called me *Nila*.

I'd won. I'd somehow made him say my name.

My heart winged just as surely as my core flickered with desire.

Say it again.

Let me hear the bliss of winning.

Jethro's eyes widened, noticing his slip, then furious temper etched his face. He stormed forward, threading his fingers around my throat. The smooth edges of his control were now jagged with temper.

I backed up until the bed stopped my escape. Jethro followed, his fingers tightening around my neck. "Tell me, goddammit. What the fuck are you trying to do?"

My heart hurt at the indecipherable expression in his gaze. He hid himself so well. The brief flashes of truth I'd gleaned didn't add up. I was fishing for something that didn't exist.

It does exist. Keep pushing.

My eyes were heavy, body pulsing with rapidly building lust. "I just want...."

There was no point to this argument. It was over before it began. "I need..."

To know you are capable of caring, just a little.

For you to want me, just a little.

For you to find something inside me that prevents you from killing me.

It was like wishing for Pegasus to fly in and whisk me away. I wouldn't get anything I wished for. Whatever I felt for Jethro was misplaced, ill-advised, and false. I'd seen him hunt me. I'd seen his cold enjoyment of talking about taking my life. Everything else that I thought I'd seen had been a lie.

He breathed hard, his scent of woods and leather surrounding me.

My hands flew up to hold his, trying to pry his fingers off. "Just...forget it. Let me go. Forget I was stupid enough to say anything."

Jethro dropped his hands, pacing away. "Forget it? You're the one bringing it up. Time and time again, you bring it up. I'm fucking sick of you asking me to kiss you." Dragging a hand through his hair, he added, "*You're* the one ruining the agreement between us."

"What agreement?"

"The debts, Ms. Weaver! That's all we're meant to do. I don't care about your wellbeing or emotional satisfaction. Sex between us is meant to be a punishment, yet you keep making it seem like a reward. A fucking delicious reward."

His jaw clenched at another slip, his features blackening. "You ruined a straight-forward obligation by trying to fucking kiss me in that coffee shop! This is all your fault. If you'd just been fucking petrified of me, then this would've been easy!"

My head shot up. Jethro was close to losing it. His eloquence became littered with curses.

"*Easy?* You think this would've been *easy?* None of this would've been easy, Jethro—for either of us. Even if I'd been crying in the corner every time you came to harass me, it wouldn't have been better. It would've just been *different.*"

Jethro exploded. "It would've been better than me fighting a fucking battle every damn day with how much I want to fuck you!"

My heart swooped, nipples pebbling with the tormented need in his voice.

"Don't you think I have the same problem? How can I live with the knowledge that I hate you, that you're my future killer, yet I can't stop my body from craving you? Don't you think I hate the fact that you make me wet against my wishes?"

Shit, I shouldn't have said that.

Jethro froze, panting hard.

The silence was deafening.

Sighing, I tugged my plait. "Look, I tried to kiss you that night in the coffee shop because for the first time in my life, my father gave me freedom. Can I help it I found you attractive? We're suffering the same pain. Our bodies want what the mind knows it shouldn't. It's the law of chemistry, and I refuse to let you put this disaster on me. *You're* the one who stole me. *You're* the one in control of my fate. If this is anyone's fault—it's yours!"

The atmosphere changed, shedding its brittle battle for heavy heat and intoxication.

His lips twitched. "You found me attractive?"

God, he was so obtuse.

I couldn't stop the insane laugh bubbling from my mouth. "Do you honestly think I would've sucked you in the forest? Do you think I would've writhed on someone else's fingers the way I did yours? I'm sexually starving but I'm not so desperate to allow someone to touch me unless I want them to!"

I clamped a hand over my lips. Shit. Another thing I hadn't meant to say. That was a lie I was hiding unsuccessfully, even from myself. Sex with Jethro was supposed to be a weapon. Whenever I thought of him touching me, it was to win—not to give in to my overpowering urges.

I wanted to *take* from him. Not enjoy what he'd give me.

Jethro prowled closer, pinning me against the pole of the four-poster bed. His body heat sparked hot and dangerously close to mine. His hands opened and closed at his side. So close. So temptingly close.

"This is getting interesting, Ms. Weaver. You mean to tell me you want my cock? You want me to…fuck you?"

My stomach twisted. Wetness built in my core as the argument switched from exposing his weaknesses to exposing mine.

I bit my lip, refusing to answer.

He smirked, his eyes dropping to my mouth. His lips parted as his breathing turned heavy and ragged. "Tell me what you want from me. You have my undivided attention."

All the frustration from dealing with Kite came back. Despite the crudeness of our sexting, I missed messaging. Talking dirty fanned the need inside, amplifying the sexual burn. I had no reprieve from living an endless torture with a man who meant to kill me. A man my body wanted more than anything. A man who gave me the gift of pleasure—who would always be wrapped up in some twisted way in my soul.

I embraced the heat of anger, glaring into Jethro's golden eyes.

Don't do this.

You'll get hurt. Terribly hurt.

I couldn't stop myself.

"I told you what I want. Kiss me." My arms swooped up, looping around his neck.

He reared back, breaking my hold. His chest rose and fell as he breathed hard. His eyes were almost black with need. Need I was sure reflected in mine. "Stop asking that, damn you." He snapped, "Why would I stoop to kissing you? A kiss is emotion. A kiss is a weakness." Placing his hands on either side of me, he grabbed the post and murmured, "I've told you time and time again; a kiss is not something you'll get from me."

I moved forward, pressing my chest against his until he broke away. He stepped backward; it was my turn to stalk him for a change. "A kiss is nothing. What are you so afraid of?"

What am I doing?

What were *we* doing?

Rules were being broken. Houses were being betrayed.

Consequences would come. Pain would be endured. But in that moment, I didn't care.

All I cared about was Jethro's lips on mine.

He dodged my grasp, then forced himself to stand tall and unmovable. I pressed myself against him, looking up into his gaze. His lips were so close. My heart fluttered like a dying hummingbird, my stomach twisted. So…close.

I couldn't move.

Jethro didn't shift back, he stood there, his hips flush against mine. Suddenly, his hands came up, grabbing my waist, holding me in place.

We didn't speak, only breathed. The truth crackled around us. We knew how dangerous this fight was, how frayed our self-control had become.

We'd been dancing this tango for weeks, and the electricity between us was a lightning storm threatening to incinerate everything in its path.

"Stop. Stop playing me. What did you hope to achieve? That I'd kiss you? Fuck you? Come to care for you? That I'd fall in *love* with you." Jethro dropped his voice to a whisper. "That I wouldn't kill you?" He shook his head. "You're still as clueless as the day I stole you."

You don't believe that.

"Prove it."

His nostrils flared. "I will not."

Cocking my chin, I anchored myself in as much courage as possible. "Prove it, Jethro. Prove how cold you are by giving me something I desperately need."

I need to see there is hope. Just a small shred of hope.

"What makes you think I can be manipulated? I don't care about your needs or desires."

"Liar," I whispered. "You *do* care. Otherwise, you wouldn't still be here. You wouldn't be fighting this." I rested my hands on his chest, digging my fingernails into his t-shirt. "You would've struck me and left if you were anything like you portray."

I stood on my tiptoes, reaching for his mouth. "I told you, you're a hypocrite."

He paused, calculation dark in his eyes. "One kiss?"

I nodded. "One kiss."

Jethro's control broke. "Just one fucking kiss? Don't you know what you're asking from me? I don't want to fucking kiss you!"

My heart broke. Was I so repulsive he didn't want his lips anywhere on mine?

I withered in his gaze, falling back to my position of Weaver Whore. But then, I stopped. This was the only time I might get him this undone, this close to snapping. It might be my only hope.

Glaring, I snarled, "Kiss me. Give me one fracture of human company, and I'll never say another word to you again. I'll be whatever you want. Just kiss me!"

His eyes narrowed. "You're an idiot."

"So you keep telling me."

"You're wasting your time."

"So you keep telling me."

"I don't want to kiss you!"

I lashed out. My arms came up. I opened my palm. And I slapped the self-righteous, egotistical arsehole on the cheek.

The moment went from lust-heavy to stagnant with violence. We stared, caught dead centre in war.

"You're a fucking nightmare," he snapped.

"Kiss me."

"You're ruining my life."

"Kiss me."

"You're—"

"Kiss me, Jethro. Kiss me. Just fucking kiss me and give me—"

His body crashed against mine. His hands flew up, grabbing my cheeks and holding me firm. His lips, oh his lips, they bruised mine as his head tilted, and with pure anger, he gave me what I'd wanted for weeks.

He kissed me.

My lungs were empty—he'd stolen all my air, but I no longer

survived on oxygen. I survived on his mouth, his taste, his unbridled energy pouring down my throat.

His tongue tore past my lips, taking me savage and hungry. There was nothing sweet or gentle. This was a punishment. A reminder that I hadn't won. He wasn't kissing me. He was fighting me in every underhanded way.

His hands dropped from my cheeks, cupping my breasts. The violence in his touch throbbed instantly. I arched my back, opening my mouth wider to scream, but he swallowed my cries, kissing me deeper, harder, stealing every inch of sanity I had left.

I thought a kiss would put me on even ground—show him that he did care. That he was human—just like me. I hadn't gambled on being detonated into a billion tiny pieces that had no notion of who I'd been before he'd stolen my soul.

He backed me up, faster and faster to the bed. His breath saturated my lungs. His touch skated from my cheeks, to my breasts, to my waist, to my arse. Jerking me hard against the huge length of arousal in his jeans.

The bed stopped our motion, tumbling us onto the sheets, but nothing, absolutely nothing could unweld our lips.

We were joined, kissing, frantic, *desperate*.

He groaned as I slid my hands beneath his t-shirt, needing to feel his skin against mine.

He was blood and fire and heat.

So different to the glacier he pretended to be.

"Fuck," he grunted as my fingers drifted to his buckle. I thanked my past of making countless pairs of trousers as I ripped through the barrier and dived into his boxer-briefs with eager fingers.

His teeth clamped around my bottom lip as I stroked him. The faint taste of metallic smeared between us as our kiss turned into pure violence.

My vision went black, seeing only white sparks and sensation.

Jethro's hands suddenly went to my waist, rolling off me to shove up my dress and tear my knickers from my hips. He shoved them desperately down my legs.

The world spun faster and faster as we discarded every item in our way and left the rest. Our lips never unglued; our heads twisted and turned as our tongues slipped and glided.

Moans and groans echoed in my ears, but I didn't know who

made them. Fingers bruised my skin, nails scratched my flesh, and our souls grew teeth—snapping and tearing, trying to consume the other before it was too late.

We were furious.

We were wild.

We were completely delirious with lust.

Jethro grabbed my hip, planting me hard against the mattress. My inner thighs tickled with wetness of all-consuming desire. I'd never been so wet. Never been so slick and dying to be taken.

His hand disappeared between my legs, wedging his naked hips between them. The moment he found how much I wanted him, he groaned. "You—fuck—I—"

My heart winged at his incoherency. I loved that he'd given up, given in. Stabbing my fingernails into his lower back, I panted, "Don't stop. I don't want you to stop."

His head flopped forward, his lips capturing mine again in a soul-searing kiss. His five o'clock shadow razored across my sensitive skin, but I loved the burning, loved the assault.

My back arched as one long finger entered me.

"Yes—God…"

His tongue slipped between my open lips, forcing me to kiss him back. I struggled to pay attention to the exhilarating taste of him and the eye-popping sensation of his finger rubbing my inner walls.

The tingly precipice he'd shown me that first day returned; I latched onto it hungrily.

I wiggled closer, needing more…needing something bigger, broader…I needed his cock.

He grunted as he forced a second finger inside me. The garbled noise might've had words strung together, but they poured unheard down my throat.

"Don't stop." I arched my hips, welcoming, imploring him to thrust harder.

I didn't care I wasn't on birth control. I didn't care about anything but driving us out of his nightmarish world and into a new dimension.

"I can't—you don't—" Jethro groaned between kisses.

"Yes, you can. You can't stop. Not now."

His fingers froze.

I refused to let him overthink this. It was my turn to bite his lip. Hard.

He bellowed…then…he went rogue. The final barrier he'd always stayed behind shattered, and he poured his broken soul into my being.

His fingers hooked inside me, making me unbelievably wetter. His lips nibbled and ravaged, leaving me hollow of thoughts and humanity.

His free hand shot to my chest, twisting my nipple beneath the fabric of my dress while his fingers plunged harder, faster inside me.

The invasion blew my mind.

It was too much. *It's not enough.*

I arched in his hold, spreading my legs wider. All thoughts were gone. All worries were dead.

I didn't care how I looked or what would become of me afterward.

I just wanted him.

"Take me. Please."

He stopped kissing me. His lips swollen, red. His eyes frantic with passion and affliction. His jaw tightened, and for a horrible second, I thought he'd refuse. He knew my sexual history; there was no reason to fear taking me bare. I didn't know his, but he was impeccable in all facets of his life. Somehow, I couldn't see him sleeping around. I couldn't see him putting himself in such a vulnerable position.

His lips crashed against mine again, his tongue tearing past my lips. I grabbed the back of his neck, forcing our mouths harder together.

His fingers disappeared from inside me, smearing my wetness onto my thigh as he pushed me ever wider. I let my legs spread shamelessly. I was beyond decency or concern. My body was flushed, acutely sensitive, and entirely feverish.

In a seamless male move, Jethro clamped my hip and pulled himself higher. The relief at *finally* feeling the broad head of his cock against my entrance sent me spiralling into madness.

"Shit, you feel…" His voice was a decadent purr. "You feel like…"

"Like freedom," I breathed, taut and trembling, just waiting for him to enter me.

His eyes flared wide, dazzling me with bronze need. "Yes, exactly."

The moment stretched for far too long, somehow turning this from fucking to something unbearably precious.

With our gazes still locked, he pushed inside me.

A breathless cry escaped me as discomfort blazed. I squirmed beneath him, trying to find relief from the pinching, consuming pressure of him filling me.

I'd been terrified once of taking him. Horrified at his huge size, so sure he would never fit, but inch-by-inch he stretched me, changing my whole perception.

My core rippled around him, welcoming and rebelling against his invasion.

He was perfect.

Utterly perfect.

Our foreheads crashed together as he sank deeper and *deeper*. Only once he was completely sheathed did he close his eyes and kiss me again. Pleasure seeped from the one place where we were joined—the only place we were naked.

It was carnal, lewd, and fit my salacious need better than any position.

I reached up to kiss him back, diving my fingers into his sweat-misted hair. His body radiated heat, trembling above me as I sucked his tongue into my mouth.

He didn't stop me. He didn't try to control me. He gave that part of himself, so gently and sweetly, my heart cracked with unknown joy.

I rocked my hips, grinding myself on his thick cock, seeking the solace from the overbearing need to explode. My mind scrambled with the primitive instinct to fuck, to claim, to drive each other until we burst and this intolerable hunger would be sated.

The rawness of being laid bare, of being full to the brink and taken so thoroughly, pushed me to the edge of an orgasm.

My knuckles turned white as I anchored myself on his waist. My mind swirled with vertigo as the first scrumptious rock annihilated my world.

There was no shame or shyness.

This was beyond that.

This was the first true thing that'd happened to me in my entire life.

My gaze locked with his, unable to look away.

In that moment, he owned me. I'd do anything he wanted. And he knew it.

He rocked again, sending spindles of fireworks in my blood. The smell of our desire laced the room, a seductive mix of wrongness and right.

My nipples pebbled as he drove into me again; my breasts throbbed, heavier than they'd ever been.

This was what I'd wanted, what I'd fought for. Every time we'd duelled, I'd wanted to possess him, to climb on top of him, and impale myself on his aristocratic cock.

"Fuck," Jethro groaned, driving hard, rocking his hips to an uneven rhythm.

His back was granite beneath his t-shirt, his skin a rippling volcano of heat.

I gasped, flexing around him as he thrust once, twice.

"More. Please, more."

Somehow this had turned from war to intimacy. We'd both stepped over the line, and I had no clue how to go back.

His gaze was turbulent as he drove again. I knew he struggled with what I did—sensed he was just as ruined and destroyed as me. We'd been fighting against each other, but ultimately, we'd won and lost.

Eye-to-eye, skin-to-skin, there was no room for bullshit or lies.

And it was perfectly petrifying.

I opened wider, taking more of him.

He sucked in a loud breath, stretching me exquisitely.

There was no way any other man could ever compete with the elegant chilliness of Jethro. He was exactly like the iceberg he favoured, only in different lights, more truth shone. Some bright and light and blinding, others black and deep and terrifying.

But it didn't matter, because in that moment, I was in the heart of the iceberg, and all I found was passion.

Our rhythm lost its sedateness, straining toward a frenzy to mate. To dominate.

His pace picked up, bruising me in all new ways. "Fuck, I want to come."

My neck arched, rising off the mattress. "Then come." Searing pleasure split me in two as he drove explicitly hard.

A gleam of masculine smugness filled his eyes, knowing he had me completely in his control, completely submitting.

He groaned as my core rippled around his cock.

Then, he lost it.

His lips descended fast and hard on mine as his hips surged upward, driving my spine deeper into the mattress.

My mouth popped open as every nerve-ending zeroed to my womb, to the melting liquid coating Jethro as he claimed me.

Then, pain.

Glorious, furious, mind-numbing pain as he thrust harder and harder, faster and faster.

Every inch I screamed with agony. He was too big, too long, too damn much. Even with the slow acclimatization and gentle welcome, I wasn't wide enough, long enough, prepared enough.

I cried out as he drove never-endingly into me.

There were no more walls, no more locks or secrets. This was him. Caught up in lust—both sexual and savage. He gave me what I wanted. He gave me himself with nothing hidden.

His lips opened beneath mine as he thrust again, hitting the entrance of my womb. I couldn't breathe. I couldn't think. His incessant need to take never ceased, his kisses never stopped.

Sweat sprinkled my skin as he drugged me body and soul. The room fogged with the sounds of skin slapping against skin and heavy breathing.

But then, the pain disappeared, switching into exquisite pleasure.

My body deliquesced, adjusting to his huge invasion.

My hips arched to meet his.

His heart thundered against mine.

We drove again and again and again, our grunts and moans and groans plaiting into one angry battle.

I scraped my fingernails down his back, grabbing his behind, driving him harder still.

I didn't think I'd survive it. I worried we'd end up killing each other before we finished.

The pleasure was too much!

The dark promise of finding a satisfying ending seemed an impossible task.

A curling, unfolding orgasm barrelled from nowhere. I tensed, moaning beneath his invasion.

My legs stiffened as he took me ruthlessly, never stopping his angry thrusting.

I couldn't control my body. I didn't want to.

With a scream, I came so fucking hard I almost passed out with vertigo. Ecstatic spasms of bliss undid my world as surely as threads from gossamer. My mind fluttered like a flimsy ghost, deprived of its old home—decimated by euphoria.

The room swam. I felt sick and overjoyed and ruined.

Jethro cupped my throat, linking his fingers through my diamond collar as his eyes shot black. His jaw locked as he witnessed me falling apart. I held his gaze, even though I wanted to look away and hide just how shattered I was.

I was possessed, enraptured.

Another wave of paradise shuddered through my core, making me jerk with spent muscles.

Jethro didn't stop. The minute my pussy stopped clenching around him, he gave himself permission to follow. I moaned as his hips pounded unforgivingly into mine, punishing me with heavenly corruption.

The tip of his cock hit the top of me with every lunge, bruising me, ensuring I would feel the ache of his possession for days afterward.

With every thrust, he grew in size, throbbing hotter, thicker, harder, driving toward the finish he craved. His face etched with danger, his eyes positively beastly. His self-control was non-existent as he hurled himself over the edge.

He orgasmed with a primitive snarl of feral ecstasy, his release splintering him into pieces.

"Shit, shit, shit!" His voice echoed with ferocity and vulnerability at coming completely undone. Pulling out, he grabbed the base of his cock and fisted himself as ribbons of white liquid shot through the air and splattered against my pubic hair and lower belly.

His stomach rippled as spurt after spurt drained him, marking me with musky threads of semen.

Breathing hard, he looked down at the mess he'd made—the evidence of our betrayal to hatred, family, and debts.

We couldn't deny what'd just happened.

It wasn't just sex. It wasn't just lust.

It was something *more*.

I expected him to leave. To hate me.

But he folded over me, planting his slippery cock against my belly, smearing the now translucent mess until we stuck uncomfortably together.

My core cramped and trembled from such abuse, but I'd never felt so languid or tranquil.

Slowly, hesitantly, I brushed my lips across his, comforting him.

He didn't say a word, nor did he kiss me back. His head fell forward, nuzzling his damp face into the curve of my neck.

I froze as his strong arms wrapped around me, crushing me against him.

Tears raced into being as my heart twisted and pulverised. I couldn't handle him holding me like that—especially after what'd happened. I needed him to be cool and aloof if I had any chance at keeping my soul in one piece.

Liar.

It was already shredded, like shards in a breeze.

Jethro's heart hammered against mine, beating hard, slowing its drumming the longer he held me.

We stayed like that for a long time. Too long. Both of us acknowledging wordlessly what we would never be able to do with conversation.

We were stripped. Naked. Exposed.

Woefully defenceless against each other.

With every second that passed, I tried to repair the damage he'd done. I felt him trying to do the same, gathering the pieces of his façade, gluing them unsuccessfully back into place.

Moment by moment, our connection drifted, slipping us further and further away.

My skin turned to goosebumps, exchanging sweaty lust for aftermath regret.

Finally, Jethro pulled away, climbing off me, tainting any illusion of togetherness. Not making eye contact, he whispered, "What just happened can never happen again. If it does, they'll see the truth, and I won't have any power to keep you."

His powerful neck convulsed as he swallowed. "We're fucked, Nila Weaver. Well and truly fucked."

GODDAMMIT.

I needed to get out of there.

I needed to fix myself, find my ice.

I need to destroy the camera footage.

No one must know. *No one.*

Not looking at Nila, I grabbed my jeans off the floor and jerked them on. I couldn't get a grip on my breathing. Everything inside me had switched upside down, and just the thought of walking away from her, after something so life changing, brought me to my fucking knees.

But I had no *choice.*

My mind replayed sinking inside her—hearing her moans, feeling her clench around me as she shattered.

Fuck.

Go.

Before it's too late.

Before she sees.

Before he sees.

Before everyone sees the goddamn truth.

Dragging a hand through my hair, I glanced at her once out of the corner of my eye. She sat dishevelled and used. Her dress bunched around her waist, her broken knickers discarded on the floor, and her lips swollen and red.

I refused to look between her legs and see the sticky evidence of the best orgasm of my life. I thought blowing down her throat was amazing, but it'd been nothing compared to thrusting inside her.

I'd held back at the start, knowing I would be too big for her.

But like everything about Nila, she'd surprised me. She'd been able to take my entire length, and the moment I'd felt her body give and welcome, that was it for me.

I'd fucking lost it.

"Jethro—"

I held up my hand, cursing the tremble in my muscles. "Don't. Stay here for the rest of the day. Do. Not. Tell. Anyone. You hear me?" My eyes narrowed, and I hoped I looked vicious and crazed, rather than unguarded and scared shitless about the consequences of what we'd done.

I knew what they'd do to her if they found out.

She didn't.

It was best to keep it that way.

When Nila didn't respond, I growled, "Promise me. This is our fucking secret. Don't tell anyone. Got it?"

Wrapping her arms around her knees, she looked five years younger than she actually was. Her legs were coltish and long, her grace almost balletic. She was the perfect willowy female, but with soft curves and fragility came danger.

Danger in the form of being so fucking breakable.

"I won't tell anyone, Jethro."

"Good." Stomping to the door, my mind was already on the things I'd have to take care of in order to hide this catastrophe.

Twisting the key, Nila's voice stopped me. "When—when will I see you again? Are you disappearing?" The sheets rustled as she shifted on the bed.

I refused to turn and look at her. I couldn't. I didn't trust myself not to grab her and sink inside her wet, tempting heat again.

"Stop asking questions, Ms. Weaver."

She sighed angrily. "So, we're back to Ms. Weaver again? Stop it. Just stop it. Don't run from me, and call me Nila, for God's sake."

Looking over my shoulder, I tried to ignore her flushed skin, her sated sigh, but most of all, I pretended I didn't see the connection blazing in her eyes. The understanding.

It pissed me off just as much as it made me crave a simpler existence.

"I meant what I said, Ms. Weaver. We're well and truly fucked. So keep that pretty little mouth closed and forget what happened."

Opening the door, I added low so she wouldn't hear, "You've destroyed me, Nila. And now it's my job to make sure they don't destroy you, too."

THE MOMENT JETHRO left, I knew I wouldn't be seeing him again for a while.

Sure enough, a week passed where my life fell into a routine of sketching, reading, and hanging out with Kes and the Black Diamond brothers.

On the seventh day of missing Jethro—of having erotic dreams that made me wake on the echoes of orgasms and of living with a heart tied into so many knots it'd forgotten how to beat properly—I gave up trying to hide my confused sadness and spent the afternoon outside.

The summer had finally given way to autumn, and the air was crisp. The leaves hadn't started to turn yet, but they bristled in the breeze, just waiting for that certain magic to turn them from green to orange.

My latest sketchbook was almost full, and my fingers were chilly as I put last-minute details onto a matching sable coat that would go with my Rainbow Diamond compilation. Over the past few days, I'd created my favourite collection yet. Turned out, I wasn't one of the lucky people who thrived on stress to meet deadlines. I preferred lazy afternoons with birds chirping and insects humming in the shrubbery.

A shadow fell across the paper.

Shielding my eyes with my hand covered in pencil smudges, I looked up into the golden eyes of Kestrel.

"Been looking for you." He smiled. His face was open and scruffy with a five o'clock shadow. He wore blue denim jeans, a black shirt, and a leather jacket.

"I'm hardly hiding." I spanned my arm, encompassing the pretty lounger, lace umbrella, and side table complete with a carafe of tart cranberry juice and sugar crystals.

"No, you're not hiding." His smile fell as he shoved his hands into his pockets. "Have I done something to upset you?"

My heart dropped to hear the distress in his voice. "What? No, of course not."

I waited to see if he would ask why I never messaged him back after his text of wanting to kiss me, but the questions lurking in his eyes suddenly disappeared. "Okay, just checking."

Ever since telling my father off and hearing the passion in Kite's latest text, I hadn't been strong enough to turn my phone on. My past scared me, and I preferred to keep my head in the sand for a little while longer. Not to mention, I'd been distracted with repeating replays of Jethro thrusting between my thighs and an orgasm that seemed to live in my every heartbeat.

Tilting my head, I asked, "Why do you ask?"

Come on. Be honest, so we can get this out in the open once and for all.

Kes cleared his throat. "Well, to be honest, you've seemed...distant the past few days. Even when you're hanging with me in the saloon, your mind is elsewhere."

Yep, it's reliving the best sexual experience of my life. With your brother, no less.

It'd taken a miracle for me to walk normally and not show the world that Jethro had bruised me deeply. I hadn't stopped cramping for hours afterward. But I wouldn't trade the pain for anything. As much as the discomfort drained me, I wouldn't change a thing. Every movement—every clench of muscles shot my mind back to the pure bliss I'd found in his arms.

It wasn't just sex.

I'd repeated that over and over again.

It wasn't just sex, but I had yet to determine what exactly *had* happened between us. Debtee and Debtor were no longer relevant.

"Just had a lot on my mind. I've been worried about the Second Debt."

Not entirely a lie, as the days ticked past, I freaked out wondering how and when I'd be summoned to pay the next one.

Kes sighed, looking chastised. "Shit, yeah of course. Sorry." Running a hand through his hair, he perched on the end of my lounger. The watery sun dappled his face as he hesitantly reached out and touched my knee.

His touch warmed me through the comfy pair of jeans I had on. The grey hoody I usually wore when working at the Weaver headquarters was marked and torn in places, making me look totally underdressed.

"Do you need anything? Want to talk?" he asked. His face was earnest, young—entirely confideable.

Suddenly, I wanted to tell him everything. About my crazy feelings for Jethro, for my regret over not replying to him as Kite. I wanted to purge and get it out of my heart.

What are you thinking?

You can never do that.

I could never confide. Not because I'd slept with his brother. Not because I had no words to confess how much I'd unravelled when Jethro drove deep and dangerous inside me. Not because of the traitorous truth—that in the moment when I'd come around his cock, I'd never felt so alive or so dead.

I could never confide, because my emotions for Kes were simple—I *liked* him. I appreciated his friendship and enjoyed his company. But that wasn't enough for him. He might have gone out of his way to make me feel welcome because of some warped instruction from Cut, but he genuinely liked having me around.

I wasn't inexperienced enough not to understand when another was attracted to me. The tingles of awareness when he looked at me made me blush and glance away.

No matter how much I liked him, though, it wasn't close to what I felt for his brother. Which gave me yet more strength as Kes was the lethal one—to me at least. He had the power to undermine my newfound courage—the snake just waiting to coil around me and asphyxiate me in a hug.

I didn't think he knew how nervous he made me—how anxious I was of his kindness.

"You sure nothing happened? You're completely in your head." Kes nudged my knee again, capturing my attention.

I smiled quickly. "Yes, I'm positive. Nothing's happened, apart from leaving my old life and entering this new Hawk world." I hoped the minor zing would stop him from prying.

Jethro said not to tell a soul about what we did.

I intended to obey him.

And I couldn't do that if Kes kept asking me in his tender voice.

I shifted my knee away from his warm fingers. Sitting cross-legged, I said, "Thanks for the concern, but I'm good. Truly."

He scowled, not believing me. But he let it go.

We sat in silence for a moment as his eyes fell to my sketches. "They're really good."

I stroked the page, thinking how much I'd love to start creating. I missed my studio back home. I never thought I'd admit it, but it was true.

"If you want to start making them, you can place the order for the material and whatever else you need. Bonnie will make sure it gets to you."

"Bonnie?"

He smiled, showing perfect teeth. "My grandmother. She's in charge of expenses for the business and family. If you want something, just tell me, and I'll make sure she orders it."

My mind raced with thoughts of demanding all types of things. How about a compass or a helicopter to find my way to freedom?

"Do you think she'd give me a one-way ticket out of here?" I laughed softly, knowing I could get away with such a joke around Kes. Jethro—never. But Kes…he understood that my captivity was fucked up and was pretty open with what he thought about the Debt Inheritance.

Was that a cleverly played ploy or the truth?

"Believe me, if there was a way, I would."

I froze at his confession.

Awkwardness fell, and I hunted for a different subject before we treaded deeper into forbidden waters.

"Did you need me for something? Is that why you were looking for me?"

My body flushed with panic at the thought of paying another debt so soon. For some reason, I felt at ease, knowing the Hawks meant to keep me for years. Unless they had thousands of debts for me to repay, I had some holiday time between repayments.

Kes looked into the distance, drinking in the view of Hawksridge Hall. No matter how long I resided at this estate, I would never get over the impressive turrets, gleaming windows, or dripping wealth.

"I came as a favour." He narrowed his eyes. "Jethro is looking for you."

I blanched. My heart consumed with both happiness and fear. What did he want? To punish me for what happened between us? Did he hate me so much that he'd blame the incredibleness of what'd happened completely on me?

That wouldn't be fair.

But nothing about Jethro was fair.

He was certifiably crazy.

But...thawing.

"Do you know what he wanted?" I murmured, flicking the cover of my sketchpad closed.

Kes shook his head, spreading his long legs in front of him. "Nope. Where did you guys end up the night of the fireworks, by the way? You missed the grand finale."

I fought to keep a natural smile on my lips and not relive the pang of breaking in his office. "Nowhere. He just wanted to make sure I'd behaved while he'd ignored me for two weeks."

That was another thing I couldn't tell Kes. The Sacramental Pledge Jethro had made me sign was our secret. Another one. *Seems he's dragging you deeper into his secretive world.*

Inch by inch, he was drowning me in his icy existence, making me an accomplice rather than a hostage.

I shifted, sitting higher. Even a week later, I still winced from internal bruising of Jethro's passion.

"You okay?" Kes caressed my arm in concern. My skin warmed beneath his fingertips, but it was nothing like the sharp sting whenever Jethro touched me.

I patted his hand. "Yes, I'm fine. Thanks."

Kes was everything I wanted in a man. Warm, dependable, sweet with a kinky side he only showed in messages. *If that's true, of course.*

God, it hurt my head trying to figure out these men.

Jethro was everything I *never* wanted in a man. Temper, complexities, secrets, and a dominating side that terrified. *Yet I feel safer with him than I do with Kes.* Was that stupid, or was there something instinctual inside that understood more than I did?

Why was I drawn to Jethro? *Why* did I have no hope in hell of ever forgetting about him, even while his younger brother was so much nicer? And *why* did I prefer the man who admitted he would kill me? *You can't be serious?*

I sighed. I was deadly serious. I wasn't in love with Jethro. I didn't think I could ever fall in love with someone who I could never understand, but I couldn't deny I was desperately in lust with him.

So much so, my mouth watered at the barest thought of having him inside me again. My core grew wet at the slightest memory of what we'd done. And my heart fluttered at the very idea of conquering him.

Kes cupped my cheek. "Nila...talk to me. You okay? He didn't hurt you again, did he? I know the First Debt needed to be paid, so I can't get angry about that payment, but anything else outside what is owed is completely uncalled for." Temper made his golden eyes boil with fire. "Tell me—what did he do?"

He made me doubt everything.

He owned me the second he kissed me.

He made me grow claws, and I like it.

"Nothing." I smiled, laughing away the uncomfortableness. It wasn't right to have Kes care so genuinely about my welfare, not when I didn't know if it was true or fake.

If it wasn't real, he was a fabulous actor. My heart raced at the concern in his face, reacting to the compassion in his eyes. It'd been a long time since anyone looked at me with...pity. V and Tex used it more than any other expression, keeping me in my place of uncertain, fumbling daughter.

Now, it just made me angry. So damn angry.

"Hey..." Kes leaned forward, gathering me in a hug. "It's okay. Whatever he's done, we can fix it."

I stiffened in his embrace. Rage bubbled in my blood.

I felt...played.

What is he doing?

The longer he held me, the more my anger boiled, morphing into recklessness. Words tingled my tongue—words I shouldn't say out loud.

What's your purpose?

What do you get if I fall for your tricks?

Then guilt smothered my lividity. What if I had it all wrong and Kite/Kes was the one true person in this slithering cesspool of lies?

Perhaps Kes was right, and I should fear Jethro more.

Maybe I was totally wrong about everything.

I slouched in his arms, giving in to the pounding headache and questions.

Once again, Kes had the uncanny ability to make me doubt. Jethro gave me power, but with one hug, Kes took it all away.

I transformed into Nila—dutiful daughter and fumbling twin sister, not the fierce fighter I was when Jethro called me out to fight.

Even fucking each other had been a fight.

A delicious, incredible, insidious fight.

Kes's arms tensed as he pulled back, holding me firm. My eyes widened as he leaned forward, pressing his dry lips against mine.

Whoa—what?

I locked in place as Kes closed his eyes, licking the seam of my mouth with a questing tongue.

What should I do?

I couldn't move.

His taste slipped through my lips, bringing the richness of coffee and chocolate. His heat was nice but not consuming. His touch was gentle but not devouring. There were no fireworks, no detonation, just sweet...

I whimpered as his tongue speared into my mouth against my approval.

"Kestrel."

My heart galloped at the barely muttered word.

We jumped apart.

Guilt saturated my lungs, even though I had nothing to be guilty about. After all, I'd been told I was to be passed around the Hawks.

So why did Jethro stand rigid and furious above us with his hands fisted by his side? "I see you did as I asked and found her but went against my orders and decided to keep her for yourself."

Oh, shit.

Kes stood up, his body tensing against his brother's wrath. "I could say the same thing about you the other night."

My eyes whipped between the two men. How much did Kes know?

Jethro's eyes flashed, looking over Kes's shoulder directly into mine.

I saw a question and an answer.

Did you fucking tell him?

Because I didn't.

My heart bucked against my ribcage. Subtly, I shook my head, giving him my oath that our secret was still safe.

Jethro relaxed just a little. His gaze landed back on his brother—

the man he now saw as a rival.

"You can't monopolise her all the time, Jet." Kes spoke quietly, keeping his temper in check. I didn't want to come between family, even if it was the worst family on earth who meant to exterminate mine.

Jethro balled his hands. "You're forgetting I'm the firstborn son. She's mine until I tire of her. Only then can she be chased. But until then..." He prowled forward, closing the distance. "She's fucking off limits. Got it?"

Kes stood taller, his arms locked by his sides. He didn't look like he would back down. Seconds ticked past, the late summer sky filling with throbbing testosterone.

I waited for the kindling of a fight to erupt, but Kes rolled his shoulders admitting defeat. "Fine. But I'm not waiting until you tire. Fair's fair, brother. I'll catch you around." Prowling away, he turned to wave goodbye. "See you soon, Nila. Remember, my quarters are always open to you."

The moment he'd disappeared, Jethro rounded on me.

I huddled on my lounger, wishing he wasn't towering above and blotting out the sunshine like the devil incarnate.

If he wanted to berate me for what happened the other night, then so be it, but I wouldn't take his temper without drawing blood of my own.

But just like Kes had shed his animosity, Jethro managed the same.

His face settled from rage into normalcy. Bowing, he held out his hand. "Come. There's something I've been meaning to show you."

My jaw dropped to the floor.

I'd never seen anything so spectacular and perfect and inviting in my entire life.

Is this real? Or am I in a dream?

"What—what is this place?"

Is this what Kestrel meant when he said Jethro had something to show me?

Jethro placed his hand on the small of my back, pushing me forward. The double doors behind him closed. Leaning against them, he never took his eyes from my wonder-filled face.

"It's yours. Your quarters. Your *real* quarters."

"I—I don't understand."

He chuckled softly. "The buzzard room was a stupid idea I had to keep you in line. I've grown up a little since then."

I had so much to ask, but all I could do was drift forward in awe.

The room was huge, completely open plan with arched walkways leading to a sitting room, dressing room, bathroom complete with huge shower and claw-foot bathtub, and a bedroom that looked straight from a Persian souk. Acres of divine beaded material hung in heavy swathes from the teak four-poster bed.

But it was the room we stood in that fascinated me.

It was better than any haberdashery I'd been in.

Far exceeding any priceless material market I'd travelled to with my father and brother on expeditions to find exclusive textiles.

The walls were decorated with floor-to-ceiling racks. Bolts and bolts of every colour fabric imaginable hung enticing and new. Ribbon spools, lace sheaves, threads of every style and width rested on huge tables groaning with scissors, needles, chalk pens, and tape measures.

In the centre of the room stood three sizable busts, two full-size models to design the perfect dress on, and a skylight above, which drenched the space in natural light.

Comfy couches, love-seats, and velour stylish chairs were scattered beside bookcases full of histories of fashion; there was even a fish tank in the corner with tropical fish glowing in pristine turquoise water.

My fingers ached to touch everything at once.

Then my eyes dropped to the carpet.

Deep emerald richness glowed with elegance and the repeating design of W.

"This is the Weaver quarters. They're only shown and offered when the current Weaver fully understands her place."

I couldn't stop my smirk, turning to stare at him. "I haven't learned my place."

His face remained locked of emotion. "No, you haven't. And my father won't be happy that I'm giving you this so soon, but…things changed."

My heart sprung into an irregular beat, waiting for him to continue.

But he didn't.

Moving through the room, he stood out in his black shirt and grey slacks like a spot of ink or a stain on such pretty fabric. He didn't belong.

I followed him. Finally seeing what I should've seen all along.

He doesn't belong in these rooms.

He doesn't belong in this house.

He doesn't belong with this family.

Everything I knew about Jethro was wrong. And despite his task and our fates that were horribly entwined and shadowed with death, I wanted to *know* him.

Following him through the space, I slammed to a stop as he spun to face me.

His face twisted. "I don't want to talk. I don't want to discuss what's happening or even try to fucking understand it."

My stomach flipped over at the lust glowing in his gaze. "Okay…"

Closing the distance between us in one large stride, he captured my cheeks, holding me firm. "I want to fuck you again. So fucking much."

I couldn't breathe.

"You're asking my permission?" I whispered.

His face contorted. "No, I'm not asking for your damn permission."

"Then…just do it."

The air solidified and for a second, I thought he'd throw me away and storm off.

But then his fingers dug into my cheeks and his mouth crashed against mine.

WHAT THE FUCK am I doing?

I'd spent the past week working for my father, having sessions with my sister, and running the latest diamond shipment—not to mention the frantic hour I'd had after fucking her and sneaking into the security room to destroy the camera footage.

I was playing with fire. And instead of getting burned and becoming a puddle of melted ice water, I was stronger, better, firmer in my convictions than I'd been in...well, forever.

I didn't understand how the direct contradiction to my world could improve me rather than destroy me.

I knew I should question it—find answers rather than keep going down a path I didn't understand, but how could I stop when Nila was at the end, beckoning with a corrupting smile, spreading her legs in wanton invitation?

I wasn't a monster, but I wasn't a fucking saint either.

My willpower to stay away had snapped this morning when I'd seen her disappear into the gardens with a hungry haunt in her eyes.

I liked to think that look was for me.

But then she'd kissed my fucking brother.

Nila's hands flew up, her fingers slipping through my hair. She moaned, sucking on my tongue, driving me mad.

My stomach swooped as my cock instantly thickened.

If she was hungry, then I was fucking ravenous.

Her cheeks were pliant beneath my fingertips. Our tongues meshed and parried. Her soft moan echoed in my chest, and I couldn't stop myself from walking her backward to the bed.

Countless evenings Cut had told me how I was to fuck her the first time. A game plan of pain, torture, and no pleasure permitted for her. That was part of the Third Debt—amongst other things.

But here I was again. Disobeying.

Fucking disobeying everything I was, just for one little taste.

My cock wasn't supposed to go anywhere near her for months. How did this happen? How was I so weak when it came to her?

Nila cried out as the back of her legs crashed against the bed. She tumbled from my grip, her cheeks pinpricked with red from where my fingertips had dug into her flesh.

My dick had never been so hard as she clambered onto her knees and looped her arms around my neck, jerking me close.

I should stop this. I should walk out the fucking door and lock it. Better yet, I should strike her and make her cry—instil a healthy dose of fear into the woman who was supposed to be my toy. Not my master.

"Jethro—please...stop thinking. I can hear your thoughts; they're so loud."

I reared back. *"What?"*

That....that was too close to home.

If she could hear my thoughts, why the hell wasn't she running? Couldn't she see the danger? Didn't she understand the nightmare this could turn into?

I not only played with my life but hers, too. Death wouldn't be given lightly if Cut found out. He'd make her beg for it. He'd tear her apart piece by piece for every delicious feeling she invoked in his firstborn son.

Every kiss, every touch—I was sentencing her to worse than any debt she could repay. And all for what? Because I was fucking weak. Weak. *Weak.*

You can have today.

I'd premeditated this—that was how addicted I'd become.

'Someone' had spilled something sticky onto the security hard drive; a new part had to be ordered before the cameras in the Weaver quarters would be operational.

I calculated two days, possibly three, before it was replaced.

Two or three days to fuck her as much as I could, before going cold-turkey and forgetting that this ever happened.

"Kiss me," she murmured, her black eyes glittering with lust.

A smile tugged the corner of my mouth. "Aren't those the two words that got us into this mess?"

She grabbed the front of my shirt, her expert fingers undoing the buttons in record time.

My head fell back as her tiny hands splayed on my chest and tickled their way around to my spine.

She pulled me close, sealing her lips over mine.

The second her taste entered my mouth, I snapped again.

I couldn't help it.

She was a fucking drug.

Grabbing the diamond collar, I shoved her hard. Toppling, her nails scraped my ribcage as she fell backward on the bed. The moment her ballerina legs spread, I pounced.

I couldn't resist anymore—it was futile.

Ripping my shirt off my shoulders, I kneeled on the bed and grabbed her hips to drag her body beneath mine. Pressing myself over her, we both shuddered in delight.

Her belly fluttered like a dying creature; while her heart pounded so hard, it rearranged my own beat.

I'd never enjoyed kissing anyone as much as I enjoyed kissing Nila. I felt her tongue in my mouth but felt it stronger on my cock. I'd never been high on the taste of another person. It wasn't just chemistry sparking between us or the battle of willpowers or even the knowledge of how this would all end.

It was *different*, and I had no urge to put a description on it. The moment I knew what it was, was the moment I would have to run from it.

Her tongue stroked slow and inviting with mine, dancing like liquid silk.

My hand fell between her legs. The jeans she wore were my worst enemy as I attacked the button and zipper.

She giggled against my mouth, shoving my fumbling fingers away to release it with one twist of a single hand. "Now you can get rid of them."

My stomach clenched at the need in her voice. "Thank fuck for that." Rolling off her, I yanked the offending material away and bent my head over her hip to tear at the black lace knickers she wore. Ripping them off, a groan echoed in my chest.

"Hey! You keep doing that and I won't have any underwear left."

My cock lurched at the thought of her spending the rest of her days walking around with nothing on beneath her fancy skirts and dresses. I liked the idea way too much.

An image of her dressed in that gorgeous black and feather gown when I'd stolen her from Milan filled my mind. I wished I'd brought it with us, instead of leaving it on the sidewalk, tattered and dirty. Nila was the type of beauty who deserved to wear decadence every day.

I couldn't deny I liked seeing her in shorts and regular clothing, but there was something overwhelmingly sexy about a woman in corsets and garters.

Fuck, stop thinking about that.

I was hard enough to kill someone with the weapon in my trousers; I didn't want to come before I'd even filled her.

Her hands landed on my belt buckle. I blinked as she magically undid both my belt and jeans. With feisty hands, she shoved them, along with my boxer-briefs, down my thighs.

I groaned as her fingers latched around my cock.

The fire she conjured in me was too fucking strong. My psyche did what it had been trained to do and retreated instantly, protecting itself, hiding the truth.

I went frigid.

Nila paused, panting. "What—what's wrong?"

Everything.

"Nothing." I pulled back, sitting up and swinging my legs over the edge of the bed.

This is so bloody dangerous. You have to stop it.

I sucked in a breath as Nila's graceful arms wrapped around my neck, pressing her now naked breasts against my back. The swell of soft flesh and pinpricks of hard nipples almost undid me.

I curled my hands, drawing blood as I bit hard on my lower lip. "Let me go."

"No."

A small flare of anger shot through my blood. "Christ, woman."

"Nila. My name is Nila." She pressed a kiss on my shoulder. "Try it…it won't kill you."

You're wrong. You're already killing me.

"Jethro—if you're pulling away, then you should know if you walk out that door and leave me for days on end…we're done."

The very word implying I would never be allowed back inside her welcoming body was blasphemy. My anger increased, thickening my blood. "You're forgetting that you're mine to do with as I see fit."

"I'm yours to torment, I agree. But somehow I think your father wouldn't be pleased with us doing this." Her lips grazed my shoulders again. "You can't lie about that. That's why you told me to keep it a secret."

I slumped forward, trying to dislodge her hold.

Silence fell awkwardly between us. I battled with doing the right thing by leaving and the wrong thing by spinning around and thrusting my aching cock inside her.

Nila murmured against my skin. "Sex is meant to strip us back. It's meant to show the truth of what we keep hidden. Don't be afraid of something that could ultimately save you."

My heart froze at the thought of revealing my innermost secrets.

I laughed coldly. "I don't want saving, Ms. Weaver. And sex is the opposite. It's a projection of nothing more than animalistic need."

"You don't believe that. Not what we have."

"What we have is so far out of my comfort range, I'm hanging on by a fucking thread."

What. The. Fuck?

I snapped my lips closed at the awful confession.

Nila stiffened, her heartbeat tapping against my back. "See, you can be honest when you don't censor yourself."

I sighed. "You want honesty? Fine. I'm used to living my life with an iron fist of control. You undermine that control. I can't let that happen. I don't handle things well when I'm not…"

"Cold."

I nodded. "I'll admit that you've gotten under my skin in a way I didn't think was possible. I'm feeling things I've never—" I cut myself off. What the hell was I saying? I sounded like a fucking pussy. "I won't deny, now that I've had you, that I want you again and again and fuck, I doubt I'll ever want to stop, but it *has* to stop."

It has to stop before I do something worse.

Nila pulled away, moving to sit beside me. "Something this good shouldn't have to end, Jethro. Screw family. Screw the debts. We want each other. Let's just give in to that and forget about tomorrow."

If only it was that easy. If only we had unlimited tomorrows.

But we don't.

"What—what do you want from me, Jethro? You've taken everything—either by force or by allowing me small glimpses of who you are. What are you so afraid of?" Her voice lowered to a curse. "What do you *want?*"

I want…I want…

Fuck, I don't know what I want.

My body ached with frustration, confusion, and need. How did this go from sex to revelations?

Everything I'd ever wanted in my life had turned me into this…mess.

Everything I'd ever let myself crave was used against me and taught me to hate rather than love.

It was easier to run from compassion and empathy when they were the very things that had the power to steal everything I'd worked so hard for.

I would continue to fuck Nila, because I was done depriving myself of everything *good.* But I wouldn't let her get inside my head, and I definitely wouldn't let her climb inside my heart.

Bracing myself, I snapped, "I want you to understand that you will never know me. You'll never have any power over me, nor will you have any hold on my loyalties. No matter what goes on between us, I will never release you, never take your side against my family, never bow to any demands you make. Nothing has changed in that respect."

Breathing hard, I finished, "If you can handle that, then I'll fuck you and grant us both some happiness. But if you can't, then I'm walking out that door and won't be back until it's time for the Second Debt."

She cupped my cheek. Her hand was steady; her eyes clear from vertigo or stress. It seemed the truth from me didn't upset her nearly as much as when I locked myself in ice. "I want to keep feeling this. So I'll agree…for now." Her gaze dropped to my lips, anxiousness and passion pinking her cheeks. "Enough talking. Kiss me."

I groaned. I'd never hear the command 'kiss me' again without wanting to devour her.

This was a steep learning curve for both of us. We just had to make sure we didn't fall off the edge and plummet to our deaths.

She fell backward on the bed. My body took over, intolerable need ordering my limbs to follow. Kicking off my jeans from still around my thighs, I planted my elbows by her ears on the mattress and settled between her legs.

My cock twitched, dying to enter her.

Lowering my head, I bit the soft vulnerability of her neck.

My mind ran riot with everything I wanted to do. Resting between her legs was enjoyable...but it wasn't what I wanted. It wasn't what would keep me sane.

If I let myself fuck her again, the next time I took her—it would be very different. It would have to be. I had no choice.

She gasped, writhing beneath me, pushing her hips upward.

She was eager—ridiculously so. And I was damn near desperate to fuck her again. I wanted to pour inside her. I wanted to look into her eyes as I let loose and filled her.

Nila's hands grabbed the back of my neck, guiding my face to hers. Licking my bottom lip, her warm tongue was searing torture.

My stomach clenched.

Kissing her deeply, I stiffened. Pulling back, I drank my fill of her naked body. I'd seen most parts of her—either running, hiding in a tree, or spread-eagled on a table—but her bruised skin and elongated muscles seemed to control my cock completely.

My brain scattered as I followed the hollow path of her belly to her sharp hipbones over silky skin. There wasn't an ounce of fat anywhere on her delicate frame. She had abs that were impressive but cute and a pussy that was tight and hidden demurely by perfect pink lips.

She was pure female—the embodiment of fragility and tenacity that I coveted and fantasised about.

The things I wanted to do to her. The things I'd always locked away bubbled beneath the surface.

I hadn't noticed before, but she had a singular subtle scent of freshness—a comforting perfume that was both an aphrodisiac and intoxicant, making me fall deeper into hell.

I wanted to tell her she was beautiful.

I wanted to tell her what she was doing to me.

But I couldn't.

Grabbing her breast, I pinched her nipple, before bowing my head and sucking it into my mouth.

She moaned, clamping my head to her chest. Every lash of my tongue made my cock ripple with need.

Her hands were insatiable as they slid over my burning shoulders, kneading, stroking, seeming to both calm and drive me wild.

I crawled back up her body.

Her eyes latched onto mine, glowing with things that were too intense and painful. My heart cleaved and lurched, exceeding my realm of ability to function.

Frantically clawing at a small hint of ice, I kissed her deeply.

It should've just been a kiss, but her mouth had a sorcery against my control. Her silent plea for more whispered around us; her body shifted and begged beneath mine, driving me closer to throwing myself into the pit that I'd climbed from and not give a flying fuck about anything anymore.

"I want you inside me, Jethro," she whispered, her breath misting over my skin.

My hand went to her throat, tensing around the tender column. "I've never wanted to fuck someone as badly as I want to fuck you."

She moaned, "Then stop delaying."

"No, I like watching you squirm." I dropped my nose to where I cupped her throat. "After all, you won again, Ms. Weaver—"

"Nila. Please…you can call me Ms. Weaver when we aren't millimetres from claiming each other."

I shook my head. "As I was saying, before you rudely interrupted." I bit her bottom lip, sucking it into my mouth. "You won because I fucked you."

"I think you won on that account, too."

I licked her, tracing the tip of my tongue along her jaw, making her tremble. "You didn't beg though, did you?"

She stiffened, a small moan echoing in her chest. "Don't…don't make me."

A small smile played on my mouth. "Oh, I'll make you, Ms. Weaver." Nuzzling into her throat, I kissed a cold diamond on her collar. "Let's begin, shall we?"

She growled, "Just put it in me, Jethro."

I chuckled. "Just put it in me? That's hardly romantic."

"This isn't romantic. If it was, we'd have candles and rose petals and soft music. This is a means to an end."

I reared up on my elbows. "A means to an end?" I shouldn't be hurt, but goddammit I was.

Nila clenched her stomach, reaching for me. "I want to come. You want to come. Stop prolonging it."

My cock wept at her distress—she'd passed the edge of commonsense. I wanted to give in—fuck, how I wanted to—but I also wanted to win just once. She'd somehow become the victor in all our battles. This one I intended to walk away the vanquisher.

Slamming my hand on her sternum, I pressed her against the mattress and scooted down her body. Every inch I travelled, I nipped and sucked—her nipple, every rib to her naval.

"Jethro…" she panted, her hands once again diving into my hair. My heart did weird things when she held me like that—her fingernails digging into my scalp, her barely restrained lust causing pinpricks of pain that felt better than any pleasure.

"Tell me what I want to hear, Ms. Weaver. Then I'll give you what you want."

"I won't. I won't beg. You'll break before me."

I laughed softly, rimming her belly button with the tip of my tongue. "Are you so sure about that?"

She's right.

My cock hadn't stopped throbbing, and the sticky wetness at the top told me I'd been unsuccessful in stopping my need.

She yanked on my hair, trying to pull me up. Biting her flat stomach, I caught her wrists and pinned them against the mattress. "No more touching, Ms. Weaver. Remember that control I mentioned? Well, I need it." Blowing air on her pussy, which was mouth level and glistening, I murmured, "You have the tightest, wettest, greediest cunt I've ever had the pleasure to taste. And I plan on dining again. Take your time and decide if it's beneath you to beg."

"Bastard," she growled, fighting my hold on her wrists.

"I'm the bastard?" I positioned myself, swiping my wet tongue along her slit. Her back bowed as her breath caught. "I'm the bastard for wanting to give you pleasure instead of pain?"

Stop that.

I hadn't meant to say that. Another slip. Another fucking dangerous slip.

Nila didn't notice as I tongued her again, diving below and dipping quickly and intrusively inside her.

"Ah!"

A violent shiver of lust commandeered my muscles. My ears roared with the need to forget about taunting her and fuck her dirty and wrong.

"Jethro…please…"

"Almost a beg, Ms. Weaver." Without pause, I buried my face in her pussy.

She tried to move, but I kept my fingers locked around her wrists and gave her no room to move as I fucked her with my tongue.

I looked up, following the delicious contours of her stomach. She glared down at me, her eyes full of black flames.

I smiled, licking her harder.

"I won't do it."

I didn't reply, only sucked her clit into my mouth.

She spasmed, shuddering uncontrollably.

"It all ends with one little word, Ms. Weaver."

"I won't. Not until you call me Nila."

My tongue drove into her tight pussy; her muscles clenched viciously around me.

"How about a tr—truce?" Her voice strained as her legs stiffened, toes curling.

"A truce?"

"Two winners."

I breathed hot, drenching her inner thighs with everything boiling inside me. "Fine."

"You go first."

I chuckled, so turned on with need, I rapidly lost the skill for conversation. "No chance. Beg." I pressed my mouth and nose hard against her, inhaling deeply until my lungs were soaked with her smell.

"Jethro!"

My heart raced. My breathing made every word clipped and breathless. "Say it—put us both out of our misery."

Her head twisted to the side, pressing her cheek against the sheets.

"Do it and I'll do what you want. I'll use your name. I'll climb on top of you. I'll spread your legs and drive my cock so deep and fast inside, you won't be able to walk for a week."

We both groaned at the mental image. Fuck, she better beg. Otherwise, she would win another round. I was two seconds away from taking her.

My impressive self-control—the same restraint that had protected me all my life—had disappeared.

Her hips churned as I dragged my tongue through her quivering pussy. "Beg, Ms. Weaver. *Beg*." Her velvet skin against my tongue sent all thoughts of family and consequences far into the stratosphere.

I sucked her clit again, my ears straining for her to give in to me, but *still* she resisted.

I stuck my tongue deep, driving her toward an orgasm. Her cunt convulsed, milking my shallow penetration.

I groaned. Sweat ran down my temples, and my back ached from tension. My hips rocked against the mattress, driving my cock into the surface, seeking relief from the quaking pleasure-pain.

"Beg, damn you!" I hissed against her clit. I couldn't take it anymore.

"Use my name and I will."

Fuck, we wouldn't get anywhere. We were both too strong. Too damn stubborn.

Panting hard, I looked up into her blazing eyes, glassy and intoxicated with desire. "Together." It was the first time I'd conceded a truce. I didn't like it, but if it got me inside her, so be it.

Nila froze, her mouth falling wide. Finally, she nodded. "Together."

Pressing a kiss onto her pussy, I climbed her body and settled between her legs. Locking my fingers in her hair, I held her firm with nowhere to go. My cock twitched, resting against her entrance, imploring to slide inside.

Our hearts matched with racing beats, our breathing just as threadbare and frayed.

Her lips moved; sound spilled. "I'm begging you to fuck me, Jethro Hawk."

My eyes snapped shut as a full body shudder took me hostage. "Again." I swallowed hard. "More, Nila. *Beg.*"

The moment her name fell from my mouth, she let go of everything she'd been holding back. Her hands fell to my arse, digging her nails and drawing her knees up. With a fierce burst of power, she jerked me forward, forcing my tip inside her.

We both moaned. Loudly.

"Fuck me, please. I'm begging. I need it. I need you. I've never needed anything as much as you filling me." She tried to reach up to kiss me, but my hands in her hair kept her open and honest and stripped bare.

"Jethro, I'll die if you don't fuck me this very minute. I'm hungry. I'm starving. I don't know what's wrong with me. I just know I'm itchy and achy and weepy and so damn angry that you won't give me what I want."

"And what do you want…Nila?"

She shivered. "I want your cock. Now."

And you can have it.

I thrust.

There was no gentle easing like last time. My self-control was done. Over. Finite. I sank inside with a barbarous impale.

She screamed.

I groaned.

We both collapsed into one another.

Falling. Falling. Swirling. Swirling. We took each other prisoner. Punishing our bodies, focused on one blistering goal.

"Oh, God, no…stop," she cried. Her hips tried to dislodge my size.

"I can't stop."

"It hurts." Her breath was cool against my fevered flesh.

"Let me in." I thrust again, gritting my teeth as a wash of pleasure shot into my balls.

Her mouth opened to scream again, but I clamped a hand over her lips, silencing her. Her cheekbones were stark, skin stretched with lust. Her eyes were so dark they mirrored my reflection, showing a man I didn't recognise. A man who'd well and truly passed the boundary of right and wrong.

Then a drawn out keen of welcome vibrated in her chest.

My eyes snapped shut as her body gave in to me, stretching, inviting.

Fuck.

My hands fisted harder in her hair. The foreplay had drained us of everything. This would be hard, fast—bloodthirsty.

"I'm going to fuck you now, Nila."

"Yes." Her fingernails sliced deeper into my lower back as I thrust into her. I rammed inside over and over, balls-deep and buried. I wasn't just fucking her body but her mind and soul, too.

She let me in everywhere.

She dropped everything, letting me bulldoze through her defences.

My heart bucked at the preciousness of what I held—the gift in which she gave. It fucking tore my innards out and turned me hollow.

The connection was too acute. Physically, spiritually. I'd never wanted to belong…always been an outcast and outsider, but between the legs of my Weaver Whore, I found….redemption, salvation.

She clamped around me, dragging a ragged groan from my chest. I ground my hips harder, deeper, faster.

We locked eyes.

I shouted at her silently.

Cursed her wordlessly.

You feel me inside you?

You feel me claiming you?

You feel me destroying you?

My muscles went rigid as her eyes recognised my message and shot one of their own.

You feel me around you?

You feel me undermining you?

You feel me making you care?

I slammed forward, drawing a primitive sound from her. "God, you—you feel…"

"What? What do you feel?" I growled.

"Good. Too good. I need—I need to come."

You and me both.

I couldn't do this anymore. I needed it over, so I could run and hide. So I could fix everything that was wrong with me. So I could find the man I'd been for twenty-nine fucking long years.

She made a helpless sound of need, grinding herself on my cock. We dripped with sweat, our skin slipping and slicking against each other, our lungs desperate for air.

Tightening my hold on her hair, I increased my rhythm. Nailing her to the bed, I fucked with wild savagery.

Her orgasm came from nowhere and with no warning. One second she rode me as hard as I rode her, the next she went stiff and taut. Her mouth fell wide. A moan that twisted my heart fell around us as her pussy fisted my cock with strength that tore me into pieces.

My own release percolated like a typhoon, howling and buffeting my every cell.

"Fuck." Grabbing her hip, I tilted her body so she was angled for even deeper punishment.

Tears of delirium trickled from her eyes as I drove my cock further inside her. Her face squeezed tight as I hit the spot where I could go no further. Her body halted any deeper claiming.

The moment she finished coming, I couldn't stop.

Pleasure surged through me with every thrust. I turned to stone as fiery release exploded from my balls and splashed inside her.

Fuck, pull out. Pull out.

Lurching upright, I wrapped my fingers around the base of my dick and fucked my own hand as I shot thread after thread of release onto her belly.

The second it was over, the guilt came back.

The fear.

The anger.

We were now doubly fucked, and I had no clue how to fix it.

Nila looked at her stomach, and in the boldest, sexiest move, ran her fingertip through my release and sucked it into her mouth.

Fuck. Me.

My entire body tingled.

"If sex with you is like that every time, I have a horrible feeling we'll end up fucking each other into an early grave."

An icy gust skittered down my spine. If only she knew how true that sentence was.

She had no clue what I would do to her the next time. She'd had me twice with only skin between us. The next time…shit, I couldn't think about what I'd do without getting hard again.

The joy at what I planned trickled into my double-crossing heart, and I knew this was the beginning of the end.

We would keep on ruining each other.

We would keep on desecrating debts and vows.

And we would keep on fucking up our future until nothing but horror remained.

LIFE HAD TURNED from manic to surreal.

I still lived in a den of beasts, with fear around every corner and dread in my future, but my present had never felt so right.

I had obligations to talk to my father and brother before they appeared with guns blazing.

I had messages to reply to Kite.

I had bridges to mend with Kestrel.

But for some reason, I couldn't bear to leave the insanely comfortable mattress of the Weaver quarters.

The ceiling above was obscured by the bolts of Persian material, and the scent of freshly spun fabric was the best air freshener I'd ever smelled.

I stretched, basking in the echoing pain of being used by Jethro once again.

He'd shown me how much passion was hidden beneath his wintry shell, and I knew he'd only just started to thaw. The thought of more sex, better sex, deeper, soul-blistering sex made me shiver in both excitement and nervousness. I meant what I said about killing ourselves with pleasure. I didn't think I could stand much more. But nothing on earth would stop me from willingly walking to my demise if it meant I could take Jethro with me.

Don't forget the plan.

I froze.

My goal of seducing him had worked. He'd changed and for some reason, had let me worm my way into his affections. But by letting me inside him, he'd stripped me of my defences. The moment when my body stretched around him, letting him take me fully, I'd felt something give inside. More than just an invitation or coy come-hither to destroy him—it had been real, and I'd had no willpower to stop him from invading.

You're playing such a dangerous game.

My heart crawled up my throat at the thought of losing.

What can truly happen, though?

I already lived with a death sentence. So what if I died with a broken heart as well? It wouldn't change my fate. It would only grant fullness to a life while it was still mine to enjoy.

Commonsense didn't like my conclusions, but I switched off my thoughts.

I rolled over, inhaling the scent of his woodland leather from the pillow he'd rested upon.

After we'd crashed back to earth, he'd spent an hour just lying there. Regrouping or thinking or just being himself...once he'd gathered his façade, he'd wordlessly disappeared and not come back.

All my belongings had already been transferred, and I noticed my phone, recharged and no longer in pieces, blinking with incoming mail on the duck-egg-blue bedside table.

Not only had Jethro given me my phone, but he'd left it on and waiting for me to use.

Why did Jethro want me to use it? Wasn't he jealous that I had an affinity with Kes/Kite? *You have to put a stop to that.* It wasn't fair to confuse Kestrel by flirting with him via messages only to pull away in person.

I had too much to juggle with dealing with Jethro; I couldn't enter into another masquerade with his brother.

Grabbing the device, I skimmed through my emails and opened text messages.

There were a few from Vaughn, a couple from my father, and one only an hour old from Kite.

My heart skipped a beat as I read.

Kite007: *I dreamed of kissing you last night.*

I reclined against the pillows. Ordinarily, I would've loved to respond and tease. Now, I felt as if I was cheating on Jethro.

Needle&Thread: *Sorry I haven't been in touch. I—I think...it's time to end this. Don't you? We both know who each other is. It's too complicated to keep pretending.*

I chewed on the inside of my cheek. My heart ached at pushing him away, especially as I'd relied on Kite to be neutral. Giving him up, even though I knew the truth, seemed like I'd pulled away from the last remaining part of my past.

Kite007: *End it? As in the thought of sleeping with me was so abhorrent, you're done?*

Needle&Thread: *I just...I'm sorry.*

Kite007: *Fine.*

Needle&Thread: *We'll still be friends. I'll still see you every day.*

Kite007: *Sometimes, having a relationship entirely based on seeing each other stops us from learning the truth. Sometimes, the only way to see that truth is to block off all other senses but the mind. Goodbye, Needle. Guess you weren't ready to see the truth after all.*

Four hours had passed since Kite's text, and I still hadn't shed the pain inside my soul. What had he meant? And why wouldn't he reply to any of my messages?

I'd frantically sent text after text, asking for forgiveness and an explanation.

But nothing.

It was only hunger that drove me from my room in search of lunch.

I hadn't seen Jethro again, and the burn between my legs was the only reminder that something irreversible had happened between us.

Irreversible and responsible for me hurting Kes and ruining any chance of having another Hawk on my side.

Goosebumps scattered along my arms at the thought of bumping into him and the awkwardness that would follow.

I might've lost Kestrel, but I'd somehow chipped into Jethro's arctic shell. No matter what Cut or the debts did to me, no one would be able to ruin what I'd found with one of their own.

I had no clue what it all meant, but Jethro Hawk was no longer Cut's little plaything. He was mine. And despite the guilt I felt at potentially using Jethro to save my life, I knew I would do it. Eventually, I hoped to bring Jethro deeper into my spell. I would make him protect me. I would somehow survive this Debt Disaster.

We'd started as enemies and still were, but now…now we were enemies with a common goal. A driving need to fuck and devour.

A strange combination of delivering pain and pleasure.

It wasn't ideal. It probably wasn't healthy.

But it was the best damn relationship I'd ever had.

Deciding to make my way to the kitchens, rather than have staff wait on me, I entered the realm of baking and home, inhaling deep the delicious smells of rosemary and garlic.

One of the maids, who I recognised with curly blonde hair, looked up. Her pretty button nose and brown eyes were open and honest. "Hungry, miss?"

I nodded, drifting forward and running a fingertip through the dusting of flour on the countertop. Hawksridge Hall had been updated with every modern convenience imaginable but still managed to retain its heritage. The kitchen was no exception, with a brilliant blend of old world and new. Stainless countertops rested on rickety handmade cupboards. Ancient flues, stained black from coal smoke, loomed over top-of-the-line stovetops and ovens. The massive rotisserie was still used over a large open fire, and a huge black pot dangled on a tripod in the corner. Mortar and pestles lined the windowsill with herbs and flowers drying above.

The maid kindly wrapped up a fresh baguette with a dollop of fresh cream and strawberry jam, and shoved a packet of salt and vinegar crisps into my hand.

A random meal, but I took it with gratitude. "Thank you."

She smiled. "Don't be outside too long today. A storm is coming, according to BBC. The fine weather is over."

Is that a metaphor for my life? That my summer is past and now I have to survive the winter?

Nodding my assurances, I climbed the steps to the main part of the house and exited Hawksridge by the front door.

The maid was right. On the horizon rested heavy clouds, black and ominous. Regardless, I wanted to stretch my legs; fresh air never failed to bring clarity to my world.

And I needed clarity after Kite's message. Every time I thought about it, my heart squeezed in regret.

My jewelled flip-flops, cut-off shorts, and turquoise t-shirt were hardly suitable clothing, especially as small raindrops splashed from above, but I refused to go back inside.

"Nila!" Kes appeared from the side of the house, his boots crunching on the gravel as he jogged closer.

Shit.

As much as I wanted to confront him, I had no clue what to say. Breathing shallowly, I hoped the faint bruises Jethro had left on my upper arms didn't show.

Kes came to a stop, his eyes drifting over me. "Where are you going?"

I frowned, drinking in his face, seeking the hurt that had been in his message. His gaze was blank, locked against any cypher or clues.

How is he hiding what happened between us?

Unable to understand, I shrugged. "Nowhere in particular. Just getting some air."

"Mind if I join you?"

I shrugged again. It was best to clear the air sooner rather than later. "Sure."

Kes fell in step beside me, his gaze rising to the black clouds on the horizon. His silence was heavy, judging.

"Where were you going?" I asked. *Were you running after me?*

His golden eyes landed on mine. My stomach twisted, thinking how fiery Jethro's had been last night as he pushed himself inside me.

"I was just going to the stables. There's a polo match next week—wanted to make sure my horse is shipshape." Kicking a pebble, he added, "Bloody Jet always wins at polo. This time, I'm going to kick his arse." His voice was sharp, completely unlike his usual ease.

I wanted to bring up the message but had no idea how.

Instead, I took a bite of my baguette. Once I swallowed, I mumbled, "I've never watched a polo game. Do you think I'll be allowed to come?"

Please tell me I haven't ruined our friendship. That you'll let me hang out with you still.

If I didn't have Kes's company, I would go bonkers when Jethro disappeared.

God, I was selfish.

Selfish and greedy to try and keep both men, while using them for my gain.

Kes grinned, but it didn't reach his eyes. "Of course. All the staff are given the afternoon off to come and watch." He joked, "Even prisoners are allowed to go."

Before Jethro had shown any signs of caring for me, that would've stabbed me in the heart and fortified my need to run.

Now…it only gave me courage to continue with my plan. And gave me strength to ignore the hurt I felt at pushing Kes away.

Yes, I enjoyed sleeping with Jethro. Yes, I could even admit to developing confusing emotions toward him. But my end game was the same.

I wanted him to fall in love with me.

Only then would he stand up to his family. Only then would he be so blindsided by affection, he wouldn't see the knife when it went into his heart.

Gratefulness filled me. Kes had just reminded me of my goals. I had no time for bruised feelings or misunderstandings. I had to be as manipulative as they were and never waver.

You're just as bad as them.

Good.

I never admitted I would die for them. I would eat their food, play with their toys, and fuck their oldest son, but I wouldn't die. If the Weaver Wailer collar couldn't come off until my death, I planned to wear it until I died in my sleep at a very old age.

Kes and I walked in awkward silence, neither of us willing to go too deep. The Hall grew smaller behind us as we traversed the lawn, heading into the woods.

Silently, I offered him my packet of crisps. With a sideways glance, he took it.

A bird of prey swooped from a tree as we moved further into the forest.

Kes paused. "See that?" Slowly, so as not to spook the animal, he pointed to his bare forearm and the bird tattoo inked into his flesh. "See how similar they are?"

My heart beat faster. I peered into the foliage. The plumage of the bird glistened like fine auburn.

"That's a kite—see him?"

Something twisted inside at the mention of Kite.

I narrowed my eyes. The raptor spread its wings, soaring away. Glancing at Kes's tattoo, I said, "It didn't match the bird on your arm."

He nodded. "That's because mine's a kestrel. They're from the same family, though."

Everything went very still.

Was this it? The admission.

Nerves scattered over my spine as Kes looked at me with tension etching his jaw. "Same family, same genes, just a different name."

I stopped breathing.

He stepped away, popping another crisp into his mouth.

Dammit.

Why didn't he just come out and admit it? I didn't want to have to prompt him, but I was done waiting for the truth.

Wiping my crumb-riddled fingers on my shorts, I asked, "Same family just a different name. Tell me, Kes, do you have another name, or was that a riddle I'm supposed to never figure out?"

He stopped, sucking in a breath. "If you're asking if I have another name, I do."

My knees wobbled, waiting.

Go on…

I waited. And waited. Tension thickened. *Come on. Admit it. Admit that you're Kite.*

Admit that, until recently, you were the man I spoke to every night. The man I relied on for my sanity, even while you were cruel and unpredictable.

My heart bucked in sadness.

I'd been kidding myself. I would miss Kes. I would miss our affinity and dirty conversations. I would miss the strength he gave me and the sexual power that came from talking like a masturbating minx.

Suddenly, I didn't want to give him up.

He was the missing link—the brother so different from Jethro. Maybe I could have them both—have a balance of nasty and sweet.

My eagerness to uncover the truth waned.

Taking a step back, I whispered half-heartedly, "What is it? Your other name?"

Kes shook his head. "I don't want to tell. It sucks."

Kite doesn't suck.

It was rather…sexy. Not Falcon or Eagle or Vulture.

Kite.

A sharp bite of a name. Violent and dangerous, but also whimsical, with its fellow paper-bow-flying counterpart.

I shifted closer, placing my hand over his. "Tell me."

He froze, his eyes filling with uncertainty.

"You can say it," I whispered. "I know I ruined it, but it's best if you tell me."

His forehead furrowed. "Ruined what?"

Before I could reply, he licked his lips and asked, "Promise you'll still like me after I tell you?"

My heart skipped, fluttering faster at the thought of *finally* knowing. I couldn't hide the ugly truth anymore. The lies I'd spun disintegrated. It didn't matter I was Jethro's plaything; I wasn't prepared to give Kes up. Not when faced with all my future held.

I wanted to keep him. I would play two games. One twisting Jethro around my finger and another evolving Kite's and my conversations to something deeper.

I could have both.

I nodded. "Yes."

He sighed, his large shoulders rising and falling. "Fine. It's Angus."

My world screeched to a halt. "What?"

He shifted, his body wary. "I know it's not the greatest name in the world, but it's my given name. People called me Gus as a kid, which I hated. Luckily as a Hawk, we're given nicknames. I demanded everyone use mine from my eighth birthday onward."

My mind wheeled.

Pieces slowly realigned, slotting unwillingly into place.

No. It couldn't be.

Horror filled my heart.

Could Kestrel be using another name or could it be worse…

Could Kite be Daniel? That psychopathic fiend who would die at my hand the moment I had the opportunity.

Holding my chest, I demanded, "What's—what's Daniel's nickname?"

Kes smiled. "He hates it. That's why he sticks to his true name." He ran a hand through his hair. "Can't say I blame him, though."

Stop stalling!

"What is it?" I croaked.

His eyes tightened, staring at my shivering frame. "Buzzard. His nickname is Buzzard."

I couldn't breathe.

It's not him.

Then…

Oh, my God.

The betrayal. The unfairness.

Please, no.

I swayed on my feet as a black gust of vertigo took me prisoner. I fell forward, crashing into Kes's arms. "And Jethro's?" My voice was just a whisper. "What's his nickname?"

My heart roared. I felt sick. I felt suicidal.

Kestrel held me tight, his fingers digging into the bruises his brother left last night. The brother I'd believed was falling for my games.

But all along...was I falling for his?

Alarm at my sudden change of mood widened his eyes. "Nila, it's okay. Sit down and breathe." He tried to gather me close, but I flinched away. Blinking back the nausea and urge to topple, I breathed, "Tell me, Kes. What's Jethro's nickname?"

I waited with bated breath.

I cursed my flying heart.

I overheated with terror.

My sanity hinged on the answer Kestrel gave, but it was too late. I already knew.

Of course, I knew.

Of course, it was true.

Why did I think otherwise?

My instincts blared an answer I didn't want to believe.

The name reverberated with every panicked breath.

Kes placed his large, warm hands—so unlike his older brother's icy ones—on my shoulders. "Jethro? He never goes by it. Never has."

I don't care. Tell me!

I swallowed back my scream. Impatience roared in my blood.

Kes sensed my unravelling. He narrowed his eyes, anger flushing his skin. "It's Kite."

I couldn't do it.

I collapsed, landing in his arms.

He huddled me close, pressing a kiss against my forehead. "His nickname is Kite...but I think—I think you've known that all along."

I wanted to cry, but no tears came.

I wanted to rage, but no sound remained.

Him.

He'd not only stolen my body but my mind and fantasies, too.

He'd infiltrated me when I still believed in princes and fairy tales. He'd corrupted me before he'd come to steal me.

Kite.

Jethro.

Kite is Jethro.

A wail clawed up my throat.

Not only had I given my body to my mortal enemy, but I'd unlocked my heart for him, too.

He'd gotten under my skin. He'd heard my innermost desires.

He was playing me like a master of duplicity.

My ridiculous game at making him fall in love with me pulverised.

I had no chance at winning.

Not when faced with the proficient firstborn Hawk.

My salvation was now my damnation.

Jethro is Kite…

…

And he'd successfully trapped me in an aviary of deceit.

Continues in SECOND DEBT

"I tried to play a game. I tried to wield deceit as perfectly as the Hawks. But when I thought I was winning, I wasn't. Jethro isn't what he seems—he's the master of duplicity. However, I refuse to let him annihilate me further."

Nila Weaver has grown from naïve seamstress to full-blown fighter. Every humdrum object is her arsenal, and sex...sex is her greatest weapon of all.
She's paid the First Debt. She'll probably pay more.
But she has no intention of letting the Hawks win.

Jethro Hawk has found more than a worthy adversary in Nila—he's found the woman who could destroy him. There's a fine line between hatred and love, and an even finer path between fear and respect.
The fate of his house rests on his shoulders, but no matter how much ice lives inside his heart, Nila flames too bright to be extinguished.

THE ENTIRE SERIES IN THE INDEBTED SERIES ARE OUT NOW!

Playlist

Animals by Maroon Five
Fight for my Love by Jack White
Dark Horse by Katie Perry
The Lonely by Christina Perri
Titanium by David Guetta
Bittersweet Symphony by The Verve
Warriors by Imagine Dragons
I know what you did in the dark by Fallout Boys
Budapest by George Ezra
Moth by Hellyeah
Desire by Meg Meyers
Time is Running Out by Muse
Roar by Katie Perry
Human by Christina Perri

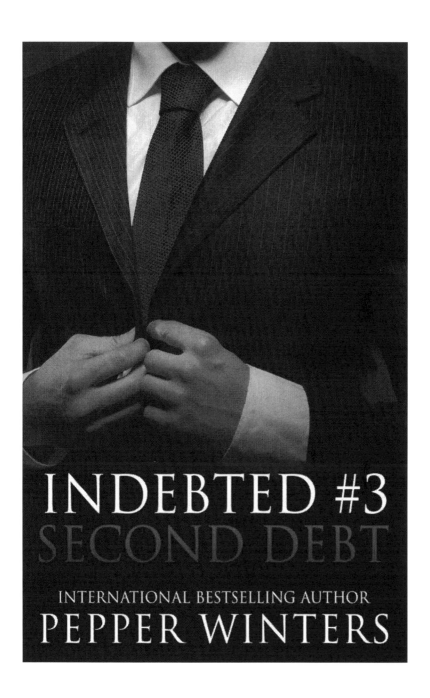

INDEBTED #3

SECOND DEBT

INTERNATIONAL BESTSELLING AUTHOR

PEPPER WINTERS

I'D TAKEN HER, but ultimately, she'd taken me.

I'd tried to destroy her, but serendipitously, she'd destroyed me.

This was the beginning of the end.

Not the end of my feelings for her but the way of my life, my world.

Something would have to change.

Something would have to give…

…

Someone would have to die.

I EXISTED WITH a brain full of betrayal, schemes, and plotting.

Living with the Hawks was utterly exhausting. Every day was a challenge to figure out the truths from the lies. But no matter how hard I worked, I could never seem to unravel reality from fiction.

He'd won.

And with a winner came a loser. One triumphant and one depressed. A trophy over misery.

Two days had passed since Kestrel had granted the truth to one huge mystery. Two days in which I hadn't been able to think of anything else.

I wanted to hate Jethro for duping me—for stringing me along like an idiot.

But whenever my anger boiled over, needing desperately to confront him, I remembered one thing.

One important, vital thing.

He'd initiated contact before he was told.

He'd communicated with me almost as if it were a cry for help, rather than a plot to deceive.

If this were another trick, then so help him, I'd find a way to castrate him.

But, somehow, I didn't think it was.

I had a horrible feeling this was the one way that he would let me in. An avenue of truths that he felt comfortable enough to continue, because a silent written word didn't have as much weight as a loudly spoken one.

Which brought me back to my vitally important conclusion:

Jethro wants to be honest.

He wanted to stop playing charades and show me everything he kept hidden.

He wanted to talk to someone. Perhaps, for the first time in his life, he wasn't satisfied with the hand life dealt him and...

Stop fabricating excuses.

All day, I'd been coming up with theories on why he was how he was and reading too far into things that he'd done.

It could be as simple as: he'd been told to get in touch. Told to initiate contact in a way that could potentially mould me into a more submissive captive, especially if I were to believe he was on my side.

I wanted to believe he'd acted against his father. But no matter how much I wished it, it didn't mean it was true.

How do you explain the knowing then?

I slouched against my pillows in bed. That was true. A part of me just seemed to *know*. Call it either sheer idiocy or feminine intuition. I believed he'd texted me because I was the first outsider permitted into his world—the only one not a Hawk.

My brain hurt.

When we were alone, when we weren't arguing or fighting, there was an enchanting calmness. A *connection*.

Closing my eyes, I let my mind skip back to Kes's unwilling promise. The way his eyes had darkened with secrets as I'd collapsed into his arms from the vertigo spell two days ago.

"Nila?"

A crushing headache appeared from nowhere. It was the most I could do to stay present and not permit my mind to relive every text Jethro had sent to see the hidden agendas now that I knew it was him.

"I'm—I'm okay. You can let me go." I struggled out of Kes's embrace, my skin humming from his touch. I needed some space. I needed a world full of space to get over the treachery and lies.

"You didn't know? You hadn't guessed?" Kes crossed his arms, never taking his golden eyes from mine.

I glowered. "How could I know? I thought the messages were from you!"

He flinched. "Yes, that was the plan. To make you believe it was me, so he could continue on with whatever little mind games he was playing." Leaning closer, he added, "I haven't been privy to any of the messages he sent you or you sent him— so don't feel like I've intruded on details that I shouldn't."

Anger infused my blood. "If you were both in on it—why didn't he show you the messages? Why were you so nice to me? What does all of this mean?"

Kes moved away, reclining against a sapling. "I was nice because that's just who I am. Yes, I come from a family with twisted up morals and I'm loyal to those twisted up morals, but I also did it out of loyalty to my brother. If you're pissed, direct it all on him. Not me."

"Oh, believe me. I'm pissed. Beyond pissed." My hands balled as my mind filled with crazy ideas of retribution and revenge. I would make him pay.

"I'd cool down before you spring it on him. Best to keep it quiet. Cut doesn't know. It was just me who knew Jet had been in touch with you before he was given the go-ahead to collect you in Milan."

I froze. "Why did he initiate conversation with me almost five weeks before he could claim me?"

Kes shook his head. "The day I understand my brother is the day I'll gamble my entire inheritance on the stock market. I can't work him out. The only thing I can do is be there for him. And I only found out 'cause he changed pretty much around the same time he started messaging you. Something was different—we're close. So, I saw it before the others."

My brain throbbed trying to figure out just what had changed in Jethro. He'd seemed the perfect Hawk when he'd come to collect me. Cold as ice and deadly as a sword.

Now that I knew his secret, I had power. And I had no intention of giving that power back. Jethro had been playing me for far too long. He'd successfully screwed with my head. It was time for payback. "Don't tell him that I know."

Kes's eyes popped wide. "Pardon?"

"You heard me. Don't tell Jethro about today. Let him continue to think I'm clueless." My heart frothed with rage and unhappiness. I was so stupid to believe I'd gotten through to him on some level. The sex between us left both of us stripped bare. Something more than family feuds and hatred existed when he slid inside me and sent both of us shattering into dust.

I'd let him inside me. In so many ways. It was my turn to do the same.

"You know I can't do that, Nila. As welcome as you are in our household, and as much as I like hanging out with you, I can't betray Jet. Not after everything he's been through."

I pounced on the small thread of truth about my tormentor. "What has he been through, Kes? Tell me and I'll march back to the Hall right now and tell him myself."

Kes shifted uncomfortably, refusing to meet my eyes. "Slip of the tongue. Forget it."

Crossing my arms, I hissed, "Fine. Seeing as you're so capable of keeping secrets, keep this one for me."

Kes scowled. "Keeping my own flesh and blood's issues hidden isn't the same thing as helping out a Weaver."

My heart raced. If Jethro hadn't taught me how to stand up for myself, I would've cowered at the thought of being so pushy with a full-grown man all alone in a forest. Now, I was raging and fully intended to get my own way. "Give me two weeks. Two weeks before you tell him that I know. Do that and I'll be forever grateful."

His shoulders slumped in defeat. "How can you be forever grateful when forever isn't something anyone has."

Especially me, seeing as my lifespan was destined to be significantly shorter than his.

"Just…please, Kestrel. One favour."

It took him a while to give in. His allegiance to his brother was strong.

Finally, he huffed. "Fine. But it won't save you from his temper when he finds out."

However, I had no intention of suffering Jethro's wrath. I had every right to deceive him after he did it to me. My revelations were safe—for now. I trusted that Kes wouldn't say anything. I didn't know why, but on some level I *did* trust Kes—just enough to use him in my plans. And I was fully committed to tripping Jethro up.

It was his turn to divulge things he might not have if he'd known the truth. Hiding behind the pretence that Kite was Kes had made him softer the past few weeks. I would use that chink to make the crevice I'd been trying to form since I gave him a blowjob after hunting me down.

I couldn't think about anything else. I couldn't focus on sketching, sewing, reading.

Nothing.

My brain was a whirly-gig of Jethro. Kite. Jethro. Kite.

And I'd had enough.

Throwing myself out of bed after another sleepless night, I wrenched back the curtains and glowered at the dismal weather.

The watery dawn did nothing to inspire either anger or contentment. The sky was grey. Fog looked like haunting ghosts, threading its ghoulish tentacles over the lower woodland of the estate. No birds chirped or sun shone.

Summer had truly abandoned us. The bite in the air shouted 'go back to bed where it's warm' but my brain had no such intention.

I hadn't relaxed for two days. I'd stared at my phone, determined to text Jethro and trip him into revealing everything he kept secret, only to stare blankly at an empty message.

Now that I knew it was him, my willingness to show so much had gone. Knowledge was power and he had too much of mine already. How could I dig deeper into his mystery while maintaining all of mine?

The answer—I couldn't. And that made me incredibly nervous. To find out who he truly was, I had to show everything that made me real. And despite the emotional growth spurt I'd endured at the hands of the Hawks, I wasn't ready to evolve again. I'd lost so much of myself already—how much was I prepared to leave behind before I became a perfect stranger?

"Ah!" I dug my fingers into my hair. I needed a reprieve from my racing thoughts, and I knew exactly how to do it.

Mother Nature's sudden urge to switch seasons from summer to winter couldn't stop my itch.

I needed fresh air, and I needed it now.

Racing around my room in the new Weaver quarters where Jethro had made me beg and come apart with his cock deep inside me, I found my black spandex shorts and highlighter pink sports bra. Pulling the clothing on, followed by my trainers, I quickly smoothed my hair into a bun, and shot from the room.

I hadn't worn my exercise gear since the morning of the Milan runway show. I'd sprinted until I'd collapsed off the treadmill at the hotel, hoping I could dispel my anxiety enough to hide my stupid nerves and prevent a vertigo spell in front of the press.

It had worked—mainly. Until Jethro arrived, of course.

The moment when I'd set eyes upon him, I'd been done for. He'd been so dashing with his suit, tie, and diamond pin. So perfectly refined with his elegant haircut, chiselled physique, and sculptured lips. Even though his soul was dark, his body had summoned me.

He'd called to me, and like the stupid Weaver I was, I'd followed him blindly.

Now, it's his turn to follow my whims, my rules.

Jogging down the corridor, my racing mind and temper eased, already reacting to the stress relief I'd sought all my life.

I need him out.

It wasn't fair. I was supposed to seduce him and make him care for *me*—not the other way around. I wasn't supposed to fall for my own games.

Lust was as dangerous as love. Only it was worse because it had the power to make even the worst ideas seem plausible—and even recommended—when a sexual reward was given.

The moment Jethro gave in and kissed me, I'd betrayed more than just myself. I'd betrayed my entire family line and all the Weaver women who'd died before me.

I had feelings for him.

A dangerous softness toward my would-be-killer.

It has to end.

I had to find a way to seduce him…to make him love me, all while I kept my heart frigid and locked away in an ice fortress.

I laughed under my breath. *You sound just like him.*

Only, ice wasn't impervious. Ice melted and succumbed to fire.

I'd proven that over the past month.

The house breathed around me with gentle heartbeats only ancient dwellings could have. Spirits of past generations lived in its walls, revenants danced in the drapery, and figments of long forgotten lovers floated through the tapestries.

A grandfather clock tick-tocked as I jogged past, showing the time at six thirty a.m.

After being privy to the business meetings with Kes and the Black Diamonds, I knew the men never got up this early. They worked late, dealing with shipments and the transportation of stones worth more than any dress I could sew. Darkness was their asset, the sun their foe.

At least I could run and be back before anyone tried to stop me.

I didn't want them to draw the wrong conclusion that I was trying to escape again. I blinked as I ran head first into a horrendous conclusion.

Even if you found the boundary this morning, you wouldn't leave.

My heart thumped harder at the tangled web I lived.

Freedom was something I wanted more than anything. But even if I escaped the Hawks, I would only run back into the trap of pity and vertigo. I wanted more than that. I *deserved* more than that.

If I found the estate edge, I wouldn't disappear. I *couldn't.*

My captivity wasn't just about me anymore. It was about the future. It was about Jethro.

Admit it…

It was about *living.*

The passion, the intensity, the blazing ferocity of existing with enemies and plotting beneath their noses was a much worthier cause than sitting at home sewing for the masses.

This was about me. Me standing up for myself, and for a future I wanted, not a future already planned for me.

This was about so many twisted things.

I yanked open the French doors at the end of the corridor and stumbled into the foggy dawn. Fresh air welcomed me and I found a reprieve from my scrambled thoughts.

I can't forget my ultimate plan.

No matter how Jethro endeared himself to me—giving me glimpses of someone barely coping inside his wintry armor—I wasn't going to forget my goal.

Freedom.

Not just for myself, but for the rest of my legacy. My children and their children and their children's children would never have to go through this. I intended to be the last Weaver stolen.

It's time for a new debt—one that owes us life, not death.

Sucking in lungfuls of crisp air, I steeled myself in what I had to do. In order to win, I had to guard my soul. I had to play along with Jethro's mind games and hope to God I won first.

A cool breeze whistled through the trees, sounding like haunted laments. I shivered, wishing I'd brought a jacket.

You'll be sweating in ten minutes. Ignore it.

Gritting my teeth against the cold, I bent over and stretched my quads. The tug and slow release of muscles was heaven after the stress of the past few days.

My body hummed with the knowledge it was about to run.

And run.

And *run.*

For fun this time, not for survival.

Bouncing on the spot, I rolled my shoulders, eyeing up the sweeping lawn before me. If I went right, I'd loop around the stables. If I went left, I'd cut through the sprawling rose garden and orchards.

Go straight.

Down the meandering path that disappeared over the horizon.

I switched from bouncing to jogging.

"And just where do you think you're going?" a cool voice whispered through the silver fog.

I wrenched to a stop, peering behind me.

No one.

"I thought you'd realised running wasn't a viable option, Ms. Weaver."

His icy voice sent a strange mixture of hot and cold desire down my spine. Jethro morphed into being, seeming to solidify from the mist like a terrible poltergeist. He leaned against one of the pillars holding up the portico, crossing his arms.

My heart collapsed, unable to untangle the maze of hypocrisy between us. My skin begged for his touch. My lips tingled for his. Every inch of me *craved* what he could deliver.

Heat. Passion. An eruption that I felt in every cell.

But none of that was real.

And I refused to believe in trickery any longer.

Mirroring his body language, I crossed my arms. "I realise *escaping* isn't a viable option. But I'm not escaping. I'm running. Running is my *only* option to escape the mess you've made."

His jaw clenched. "The mess *I've* made?"

"Yes." I took a step backward as he advanced. "You're messing me up, and I'm done playing whatever it is that you're doing." I sucked in courage and embraced honesty. It seemed to work around him, and I needed him to see how serious I was. How hurt I was with his deception.

He's Kite.

Bastard.

Baring my teeth, I said, "It seems I have a weakness for you, but I changed my mind. I don't—"

A low growl escaped him. "A weakness? You call what happened between us a fucking weakness?"

My breathing ratcheted as if I'd already run two miles. "The worst kind of weakness."

He smiled, but no mirth entered his gaze. If anything, his golden eyes were luminous with anger. "You're the one who started it…*Nila.*"

I gasped at the delicious decadence of my name on his lips. The sound echoed in his mouth, shooting straight to my core.

Shit.

Jethro advanced again, his body trembling with barely veiled lust. "*You're* the one who created this problem." His hand came up, fingers slinking through my tied-up hair, tightening around the back of my skull. "I can't hear the name Weaver without getting fucking hard. I can't even think of you without boiling with need."

His nose brushed against mine, his lips so damn close to stealing all my scrambled plans and sending me headfirst into a life of debauchery.

"You should never have said those two words, Ms. Weaver. I told you. We're both fucked now."

My mind was blank, every synapse focusing on his fingers in my hair and his mouth only millimetres from mine. "What two words?"

He chuckled. The sound was self-deprecating and almost morbid with dark intensity. "Kiss me."

I shivered in his hold. "You're reminding me of what started this mess, or you're asking me to kiss you?"

Ask me. And I will. God, how I will.

I'd kiss him until I'd stripped him of his arctic armor and destroyed it, I'd lick him until I tasted his truth, and I'd bite him until I'd eaten every morsel of his soul.

I'd do all that so he had nowhere left to hide.

We stood wrapped in foggy silence. The drawn out anticipation of a kiss turned my legs to jelly. If he pressed his mouth to mine, I wouldn't be going for my run. I would climb his body and sink onto his cock.

Fakery be damned.

Kite's messages and deceit be damned.

I just wanted a raw connection—with this man, who made my soul whimper for wrongness.

Jethro's tongue slipped between his lips, hypnotising me. Then…he let me go. "No, I'm not asking you to kiss me. I won't ever ask anything from you."

I flinched as if he'd slapped me. "Why not?"

"Because I own you. Everything I want will be given, not requested."

Double shit.

I should hate him. I should smite him. So, why did his every word seduce me, even while I knew his morals were chauvinistic and heartless?

Forcing my body to obey, I shoved the weakness I had for him as far away as possible. My eyes trailed down his front. He wore tan jodhpurs, black riding boots, and a tweed jacket. The bulge between his legs looked heavy and far too dangerous to be legal.

"You've been riding."

A gentle gust of early morning air blew his scent directly into my nose. I inhaled, soaking my lungs in hay, horse, and all things Jethro.

He nodded, crossing his arms once again. "You run. I ride. Seems we have something else in common."

Something other than being forced into this debt and finding each other irresistible, you mean?

"Oh, what's that?"

Jethro stepped closer, seeming to bring shadows into the smoky light of dawn. "We both need time alone to hide from the things that chase us." He stiffened, his eyes churning with things he refused to voice. A five o' clock shadow decorated his strong jaw, his lips parted while his gaze was pure brimstone.

Swiftly, he cupped my cheek.

Oh, God.

Electricity instantly sparked beneath his fingertips.

Would I always suffer the rhapsody of his touch?

My skin smouldered; pinpricks of light, of fire, of hell, all burnished beneath his hold. I swayed, pressing my face harder into his palm.

He sucked in a breath, his fingers digging harder against my cheekbone.

The chemistry and need to devour each other thickened with every heartbeat.

One beat.

Two beat.

Three.

We stood there, frozen on the stoop of Hawksridge Hall just waiting for the other to move. The moment we did, our clothes would disintegrate and I would willingly let him drag me into a bush and fuck me.

Lust and tension swirled.

I had so many questions and doubts; so many reasons to hate and fear him. But when he touched me...*poof.*

I no longer remembered, nor cared.

We swayed closer, drawn against our will to close the aching distance.

I couldn't breathe.

Kiss me. Please, kiss me.

The moment stretched until it hummed with overwhelming possibilities.

Then, it snapped.

Loudly.

Painfully.

Shattering around our feet.

"You're too fucking dangerous," Jethro muttered, removing his touch and stepping away. Dragging his hand through his hair, he commanded, "Wait here. Don't go anywhere." His hands went to his jacket buttons, undoing them with nimble fingers.

I blinked, struggling to shed myself of heavy need and focus on the true reason why I stood barely dressed in the freezing morning. "I'm not escaping. I'll be back in forty minutes or so."

He shook his head, slipping out of his tweed and revealing a black long-sleeved jumper.

My mouth went dry. Even in clothing, I could make out every ridge of muscle in his stomach, every ripple of energy as he breathed in and out. He was designed straight from my fantasies, and I hated him for being so splendid.

My core clenched, sending flutters of wetness between my legs.

I hadn't seen him in two days, yet I'd panted after him as if he'd been missing my entire life.

If he suspected I knew that he was Kite, he hadn't let on. After Kes had told me the truth, I'd waited for Jethro to barge into my room and swear me to secrecy.

But he hadn't.

He didn't look at me any differently; he gave no outward sign that his lies had begun to unravel. As much as he confounded and frustrated me, I couldn't help admiring his perfection at hiding.

I wanted to be like him. I wanted to protect my secrets so damn well that whatever I did next would come as a surprise.

I wanted to *rule* him.

"I'm coming with you. Don't leave." He disappeared into the house, leaving me abandoned and covered in chills from both the morning air and his departure.

Jogging on the spot, I deliberated ignoring him and leaving.

Just go.

What was the worst that could happen? He'd have to chase me again. My tummy coiled at the thought. I liked that idea way too much.

I liked the thought of what would happen after he found me.

The power I'd felt giving him that blowjob. The awe and attraction that'd glowed in his eyes.

I want that again.

Screw waiting like a good little captive.

Make him hunt.

And then I would make him explode.

I bolted.

OF COURSE, SHE ran.

I fully expected her to.

Unlike last time when I expected her to cower by my feet, I'd had the last month to get to know my charge. Through getting into her mind via text messages, and getting into her body by sheer insane passion, I'd come to understand her—more than she knew.

And unfortunately for her, she'd lost the ability to surprise me.

She'd lost the ability because I'd been inside her body and mind. I'd traded my soul for hers—no matter how much she would deny it. No matter how much *I* would deny it. We were linked.

Connected.

Bound.

Somehow, she'd crept inside my barricaded heart. She'd weakened me—but that weakness worked both ways.

I *felt* her. I heard her fears, tasted her tears, and somehow knew how she would react.

I hadn't permitted anyone to have that control over me since Jasmine. Even Kes and I didn't share such a strong connection.

That strange bond had a name.

I called it my disease.

And it only got worse the more I was around Nila.

I craved her so intensely; I would break both of us before any more debts were paid.

I didn't think she believed me when I said we were well and truly fucked. And not just because of my father and what he would do. But because of what I *was*.

Because of my…condition.

The moment I left her on the porch, I knew she'd go. The knowledge echoed in my bones, making it fact rather than speculation.

In the time it took to jog back to my room and trade my riding attire for all-black workout gear, she'd gone.

Balling my hands in the cool morning air, I smiled. A genuine smile. It'd been forever since I'd let myself relax enough to be genuine about any emotion.

Just like empathy and compassion were banned from my repertoire, so too, was feeling something so purely that it became a spark in my dead heart. I didn't want to be genuine about anything because it could be used against me.

It was best to hate everything and everyone. To hide my true desires even from myself.

The anticipation of another hunt sent my blood flowing thick and hot.

Her tiny footprints led a trail, like enticing crumbs. The dew-damp grass flattened from her path.

I'm coming, Nila.

Just like before, I took off after my prey. But the difference between this chase and the previous one was I *knew* she wanted me to hunt her. I knew she wanted to be found. And I knew she fed off this cat and mouse idiocy as much as I did.

My legs spread into a large stride as I left the Hall behind.

I preferred to perch on the back of Wings when galloping fast and far. I wasn't a jogger. It wasn't quick enough for me. I missed the power of a large beast between my legs, responding to the commands to race and outrun everything that I was.

Every footfall caused me to wince from what I'd done to myself in my last 'fixing' session. The pain radiated up my legs. I supposed I should be grateful for the agony—it helped me in so many ways. And I needed all the help I could get with Nila wreaking havoc on my world.

You know it's no longer working, so why still do it?

That was true.

Pain no longer held the comfort or fortress it used to. Jasmine was right. It was time to start looking at other methods, or, if I was brave enough, let everything that I'd been hiding emerge.

I snorted at the reaction that would get me. Not to mention the complications with my father.

No, I wasn't ready. Not yet. Besides, I had more important things on my mind.

Such as hunting.

Leaping over the rock wall and tearing down the path, I put my head down and ran after my little Weaver.

A pitiful six minutes later, I gained on her.

Her stride and pace were impressive, and I had to appreciate her wily ways of trying to throw me off her trail by cutting across the driveway and disappearing into the woods on the other side.

But I was an experienced hunter.

Her clues littered behind her, leading me directly to my prey.

Her hair bounced, tendrils coming loose from her hair-tie. Her sculptured legs led to the firmest arse I'd ever seen.

My mouth watered.

I wanted to bite it. Bite her. Lick her. Fuck her.

"This seems all too familiar," I muttered, pulling up beside her with a burst of speed.

She jumped, clutching her heart. "Shit, I didn't hear you creeping behind me."

"Creeping? I did nothing of the sort."

She rolled her eyes, settling back into the punishing pace she'd set. I matched my stride to hers. Companionable silence fell as my attention turned inward again, focusing on the agony in my feet.

I really shouldn't have chosen that part of my body—especially if running with her became a frequent occurrence. I'd have to find a new place in which to fix myself. The soles of my feet had been used for years—when I needed the extra buffer. No one could see the marks, no one would know, and the pain was constant whenever I moved.

A perfect place for secrets.

"Do you run?" Nila asked. Her breathing was heavy but even, her fitness level higher than mine.

I shook my head. "No. I prefer exercise where a horse does the hard work, or perhaps a punching bag that takes my fists."

"You do that often?"

"What, ride?"

"No, assault an innocent punching bag." Her dark eyes landed on mine, diving deep into my complexities before I slammed up my walls and prevented her from seeing any more.

"No more than usual," I said, pulling ahead of her.

With a small grunt, she matched me, not letting me disappear. "I know you have issues, Jethro. But I'll keep my speculations to myself…for now." Running for a while, she finally asked, "What time did you wake up today?"

I frowned, gritting my teeth against the pounding pain in my feet. "What?"

"It's dawn, yet you've already been for a ride. Are you an early riser?"

I snorted. *You could say that.* "I'm not good at sleeping. Wings is used to me."

"Wings?"

"My gelding." I threw her a glance. "The horse I was riding when I tracked you. Remember?"

Nila's face shadowed. No doubt thinking of the hunt and the consequential amazing blowjob.

Sexual tension sprang harder between us, itching my skin, making my cock swell.

My voice turned gruff as I added, "Ever since he was broken in, Wings has been used to me sneaking into the stables and going for a ride in the dead of night. He got a small sleep in today. I didn't saddle him up until four a.m."

Nila nodded, soaking up my confession as if I'd announced the epicentre of why I was fucked up.

"You didn't have any shipments to take care of?"

I narrowed my eyes. "How do you—" I cut myself off. Kestrel. Of course. The weeks they'd spent together meant she would probably have a good idea of the sort of wealth we smuggled and the amount of shipments completed since she'd arrived at Hawksridge.

"Why can't you sleep?" she asked. We ran side-by-side, leaving the gloom of the forest and trading mud for the gravel of a pathway.

I looked up. My heart clamoured.

Shit, we're on the wrong track.

I didn't want her to see what was up ahead. Not yet. I was sure my father had some sick agenda to show her when she fell out of his good graces, but I didn't want to break her again. Not so soon.

I'd avoided the place most of my life. It held only terror. So why the fuck were we running toward it? It was almost as if she'd been summoned by forces outside my comprehension.

A chill darted down my back at the thought. I slowed my pace.

Nila looked back, decreasing her steps to match mine. "Are you going to answer me?"

What, why can't I sleep?

"No."

I had no intention of answering. There was no easy response, and she knew far too much about me already. Trying to distract her, I said, "Why do you have to run?"

She ran a hand over her forehead, wiping away glistening sweat. "To re-centre myself. At home, it was the only time I had to calm my mind. The deadlines, the demands—it all stole something that I only found again when I was alone with just my frantic heartbeat to keep me company."

Shit.

Her answer was fucking perfect.

I swallowed hard as a glow of more than just lust washed over me.

She understood. She dealt with the same pressures, the same expectations. Only her flaws were visible to everyone, while I hid mine as best I could.

Admit it. The moment you saw her on the catwalk in Milan, you knew.

I fisted my hands, trying to stop the conclusion from forming.

But it was no use. My mind delivered the crushing knowledge with fanfare and barely hidden relief.

She's the same as you. You could tell her.

No fucking way would I ever tell her.

I didn't want to feel anything for her, but I did care. Enough to stop her from seeing what existed ahead. I might not want her in my brain, but I didn't want her in pieces, either.

I slammed to a halt. "Nila. Stop."

Locking her knees, she bounced in place and turned to face me. Her chest rose quickly, panting for breath. "What? Why?"

My eyes involuntarily went to the break in the trees up ahead. Damn sunshine broke through the fog at the exact same moment, spotlighting the one place I didn't want her to see.

Nila followed my gaze. Her shoulders hunched, feeding off my nerves. "What's up there, Jethro?"

"Nothing."

"If it's nothing, then why are you determined not to let me see?"

My temper fed off her nervousness, creating a sick sensation in my gut. "Because it's time to get back. You've wasted enough of the day doing something as pointless as running." I snapped my fingers. "Let's go. Now."

Her eyes filled with rebellion. She looked back to the hill, chewing her lip.

I moved forward, ready to pounce and drag her back to the Hall. "Ms. Weaver—" I inched closer.

Hesitation flittered over her face.

I tried to grab her. But I was too late.

Darting away from me, she said, "I want to see what you're hiding," then bolted down the path.

"Fuck!"

Her hair flew free from her hair-tie as she sprinted faster up the gravel and onto the moor that I wished didn't exist.

Shit, she's fast.

I tore after her, wishing I had Bolly and the foxhounds to swoop in and cut her off before she reached the crest.

My feet burned and my socks became slippery as old wounds opened. My lungs were pathetic in delivering enough oxygen as I sprinted the final distance and skidded to a halt.

She'd turned from super-sonic to a statue, staring dumbfounded at what existed before her.

Goddammit, why did she have to be so determined to uncover what I wanted to keep hidden? The truth never helped—it only made things worse.

Her hands flew into her black hair, fisting tightly. "Oh, my God..."

I sucked air, hating the sensation of trespassing on such a sacred site. I wasn't welcome here. None of my family was welcome, and if I were superstitious, I would admit there was a stagnant force that howled with hatred and pain.

"No!" she whispered. Her strong legs that'd sent her flying into hell suddenly collapsed from beneath her.

Her fingers dove into the dirt, clutching at grass and mud. "This can't be real. It can't."

She bowed with disbelief, kneeling on the grave of her mother.

Her anguish joined the storm of revulsion that never seemed to leave this place. Goosebumps darted down my arms as a gale whipped her hair into a frenzied mess.

"Ms. Weaver—" I moved forward, fully intending to pluck her from the earth and hurl her over my shoulder. I couldn't be here another fucking second.

Goddammit, this isn't supposed to happen.

Her eyes met mine, but they didn't swim with tears—black hate glittered instead. "Is this true? All along, my father said she'd run off. All along, he told us stories of her leaving us for a better life. My brother understood that meant she was dead, but not once did Tex take us to her grave. After what your father said…about what he'd done, I still held onto those childish stories that she was alive. But this…" Her voice sliced through me. "Is. This. True? All this time my mother has been buried, cold and lonely, in the ground of the men who murdered her?!"

I swallowed, rapidly diving into the safety net of my snow. I couldn't stand there and hear her horror. I couldn't let her grief infect me. I refused to fucking listen.

"I didn't do it."

As if that makes it any easier to bear.

Nila shook her head, staring at me as if I were some grotesque abomination. "*You* didn't do it? Do you think I care if it wasn't your hands who severed her life? It was your family, Jethro. Your bloodline. You're a monster—just like them!"

The cuts on my feet no longer protected me. I was so fucking close to losing control.

I itched with the need to shut down. To hide from everything snowballing inside. "Let's go."

"I'm not going anywhere with you!" Nila spun to face the burial place of her mother.

My eyes rose to read the inscription on the simple marble headstone looming over her trembling form.

In here lies payment for debts now paid.

Rest fitfully Emma Weaver wherein hell you may face another toll.

Nila looked over her shoulder; her eyes widened until they were as black and as soul-sucking as an eclipse. "Jethro—"

The pain and hatred in her voice sliced me better than any cut on my foot. I took a step backward, placing distance between us. "I can't give you what you want."

She shook her head. "You can't or you won't?"

I knew she wanted answers. An explanation. Facts on why her family was buried on Hawk land and how we circumnavigated the law to do things no one else could.

But what could I say? I was bound. Muzzled. Shackled, not just by Hawk blood, but the very condition that made me a reject in my own family.

The truth hurt. Fuck, everything hurt.

Her panic. Her grief. The throbbing pain in my feet.

I had to get away.

This was why I'd remained cold. Why I did what I did.

This was why I never let anyone get close to me and embraced my duties as a son over the cravings of my heart.

My disease meant I couldn't let things like this happen.

I couldn't handle it.

"I told you I didn't want you to see this place but you fucking defied me!" Hot anger gave me somewhere to hide. "I refuse to indulge your feelings of self-pity." Rage coated my veins, granting sanctuary.

I backed away, distancing myself from the raw fury glowing on her face. "Come here. We're leaving." I snapped my fingers again. "Now!"

Nila stood. Her eyes darted to the semicircle of death surrounding us. An unlucky horseshoe of tombs.

Her chest rose as a silent sob escaped her. Waving her hand at the other graves, she shook her head. In one motion, she asked a lifetime of questions.

How could you?

How did you get away with it?

Why has no one stopped you?

I had no answers.

My eyes fell on the graves.

Six in total.

All with a diamond chiselled into the remembrance of their tombstone and the ultimate mockery of all: a hawk perched on the top, its talons dripping blood down the face of the eulogy.

"This—it can't be real. No one could be this diabolical."

You're wrong. The Hawks can.

I pinched the bridge of my nose. "Quiet." Looking back up, I demanded, "Say goodbye. We're leaving, and I doubt you'll be allowed back up here."

Her mouth twisted with black amazement. "You…I don't have any words for what I think about you. How sick you make me."

"Good. I don't want words. I want to leave." Storming forward, I grabbed her elbow, yanking her away from the cemetery.

"No!" she screamed, scratching my hand and backpedalling. A huge wave of anguish buffeted me. Everything she felt poured from her like a tsunami. I stood, unable to move as it drowned me.

Apart from knocking her unconscious and carrying her back to the Hall, I had no way of making her leave. I couldn't handle carrying her kicking and screaming.

I'd break.

She rattled with the pieces of her broken heart, and just once, I wanted to give in to the benevolence that others enjoyed.

But I couldn't.

I couldn't stand there while she grieved.

It just wasn't possible.

Not for a man like me.

Sighing, I said, "Fine. Stay. Pay your respects and worship the dead, but you'll do it alone."

You'll do it alone, so I don't lose the rest of my soul.

This wasn't a good place for a Hawk, but in a way, it was home to a Weaver. She might find whatever she was missing by conversing with her past.

"I'll—I'll leave you alone."

Nila balled her hands, looking as if she wanted to strike me. "Disappear, Mr. Hawk. Run like you always do. Good fucking riddance. Leave. Get the hell away from me and don't come back!"

I paused for a fraction. I should do something about her outburst—teach her that I wouldn't permit her to raise her voice, but I was done here.

Taking another step away, I said, "I'll see you back at the Hall."

She didn't reply.

With a black-laced heart and thundering headache, I backed away, faster and faster. Her arms wrapped around her body and her hair danced in the turbulent breeze. She looked like a witch placing a curse upon my house. Then she collapsed at the base of her mother's tombstone, bowing in the dirt. I left her with only ghosts for company, kneeling on the grave of her ancestors.

Shuddering once, I turned and didn't look back.

I GOT MY wish.

My wish to become as cold and as merciless as Jethro came true as I huddled on my mother's grave. My sweaty skin turned to ice with renewed hatred for the Hawks. I struggled with rage so damn strong I was sure the earth would crack beneath me and swallow me whole.

How could he?

How could they?

How could devils live so blatantly amongst us?

My teeth ached from clenching; my eyes bruised with unshed tears. I breathed revenge. I ate vengeance. All I saw was hate.

I felt invincible with rage, as if I controlled the tectonic plates and had the power to summon a catastrophic earthquake to devour this disease-riddled place forever.

How could any goodness live inside me when all I wanted was four graves—one for each of the Hawk men? How could I believe in right and wrong when all I wanted was their blackened hearts bleeding at my feet?

Morning turned to noon.

Afternoon turned to dusk.

Twilight turned to midnight.

I stayed vigil, moving slowly between the six graves. My bloodless lips whispered as I read aloud their horrific epitaphs.

Farewell to Mary Weaver

Long ye may rest in solitude and reap the havoc in which you sowed

My heart broke at the thought of my grandmother and great-great-grandmother enduring such a life.

Herein rests the soul of Bess Weaver
Her only redemption was paying her debts

The oldest looking tombstone had the simplest carving but the one with the worst desecration of a dead soul.

The corpse of the Wicked Weaver who started it all
Wife to a traitor, mother to a whore

I couldn't forgive. I couldn't forget. I couldn't even comprehend how I could ever set eyes upon the Hawks again without wanting to slaughter them with my bare hands. My rage fed me better than any material sustenance.

I wished I had magic; a potion to strike them all dead.

Every murmur that escaped me, every incantation and promise, worked like a spell.

My whispers wrapped around me like a cocoon—turning my tenderhearted naivety into a chrysalis where I rapidly evolved into a monster as bad as them.

I threw myself into darkness. I traded any goodness I had left for the power to destroy them. And with each chant, I chained myself deeper to my fate—cementing me forever to my task.

I didn't want food or water or shelter.

I didn't need love or understanding or connection.

I wanted retribution.

I wanted *justice*.

No one came to get me. If they cared I was missing, no Hawk came to corral me back to my prison.

In a way, I wished they *would* come. Because then my removal from my dead family would've been a justified struggle. I would've screamed and cursed and fought so hard, I would've drawn their blood.

But they never came.

So, I had to swallow my bitter resentment and plod back to purgatory on my own accord. I couldn't fight. I couldn't scream.

I had to deliver myself willingly back into the devil's clutches.

By the time I entered my quarters, I shook so hard I was sure my teeth were chipped from chattering so badly—from cold and from horror.

I didn't recognise the woman inside me. Something had switched permanently and any facet of the little girl—the twin who'd always believed in fantasies—had died upon that patch of earth.

I'd been destroyed, yet my eyes remained dry. Not one tear had been shed. Not one sob had come forth.

I'd become barren. No longer able to display emotion or find relief from the pounding terror of seeing proof of my ancestor's demise.

The diamond collar around my neck disgusted me and the weight seemed to grow heavier with every breath, sucking me deeper into hell.

Struggling to remove my sweat-dried exercise gear, I barely managed to crawl into the shower. Gradually, I turned my blood from snow to spring—thawing out the phantoms that now lurked within.

I stayed beneath the hot spray for ages, curled upon the floor with my arms wrapped around my knees. Mud and soil from the graves siphoned down the drain, swirling around like dead souls.

So much had happened, so much that would've broken the old Nila.

But this was just another hurdle—another obstacle to clear in my quest for victory. My essence had been infused with the lingering spirits of my ancestors. They lived within me now, wanting the same thing I did.

The clock hanging above the fish tank in my sewing room announced the witching hour as I climbed exhausted into bed.

Three a.m.

The time when ghouls and demons were thought to roam the passageways of homes and terrorize helpless sleepers.

I'd always been superstitious about keeping my wardrobe doors shut against night monsters. Vaughn used to laugh at me, saying beasts and night creatures didn't exist.

But now I knew the truth.

They *did* exist, but they didn't come out when the witching hour opened a portal from their world into ours.

They weren't called werewolves or vampires.

They were called Hawks.

And I lived with them.

The next morning, I woke to a text.

A single message from the crux of my annihilation.

Kite007: *I feel what you feel. Whether it be a kiss or a kick or a killing blow. I wished I didn't, but you're mine, therefore, you are my affliction. So, I will feel what you feel, and I will live what you live. You won't understand what I mean.*

Not yet. But it's my best sacrifice. The only thing I can offer you.

I waited for my heart to spike.

I held my breath for a sparkle of desire.

Jethro had just shown me the truth. In his cryptic, almost poetic message, he'd torn aside the mysterious curtain of who Kite was—fully admitting something that only he would know. There was no way a message like that could come from Kes. I doubted the middle Hawk was deep enough to pen such a complex riddle.

If such a message had come yesterday, I would've tripped from lust into love. I wouldn't have been able to stop my heart from unfurling completely and letting my enemy nest deep inside.

But not now.

Not now that I'd seen the heinous truth.

With steady hands and an even steadier heart, I sent a single message to my brother.

Needle&Thread: *I'm living a nightmare, V. I…I can't do this anymore. I miss you.*

Once it had sent, I deleted Kite's message and turned off my phone.

Jethro

A NEW MORNING, yet I felt older than I'd ever been. Every part of me ached.

I'd left Nila at the cemetery—I'd had no *choice*.

But when she didn't return after dusk, I went back for her.

She'd sat beneath the crescent moon, arms wrapped tight around her ribcage as if to prevent whatever meagre body heat she had from escaping. Her white skin glowed in the darkness, etched in shadow, making her seem part wraith, part woman.

I'd waited in the blackness, obscured by trees. Waited for her to either fall asleep or fret herself into unconsciousness. I wanted to wrap her in warmth and take her back to her chambers where she could find some resemblance of living…with me.

I wanted to kiss her frigid lips and run my fingers down her icy arms. I wanted to be *warm* for her and forget all notions of being a glacier.

But powerful waves of hatred and disgust rolled from her delicate form, lapping through the trees and around my ankles. As much as I wanted to go to her, I couldn't.

For the same reason I needed to see Jasmine so often.

For the same curse I'd lived with my whole life.

So, I'd waited.

I'd sacrificed myself by feeling her pain.

I'd shared the cold with her.

I'd hoped she sensed my presence and it offered a shred of comfort.

And when she'd finally retreated to the Hall, I'd followed

discretely. Shadowing her every step, determined she wouldn't see me.

It wasn't until she'd stumbled from her bathroom in a cloud of steam and wearing a towel that I'd left the security hub and the constantly recording cameras and returned to my own quarters.

As I lay staring at my ceiling, thinking how disastrous my life had become ever since I texted her over two months ago, I felt another stirring inside my broken heart.

One that gave me a small blaze of hope that there might be *some* way to salvage this nightmare.

For the first time in my life, I wanted to talk to someone. Fully confess. And not just to my sister.

I wanted to unload and spill everything to my sworn enemy. To the woman I wanted but could never have.

If I stepped off that ledge and took a leap of faith, I had no doubt I would end up dead when I fell. But I'd left it too long to fix myself and no longer had control over my impulses.

I'd regret it.

Shit, I already did.

But it couldn't stop me.

With a rabbiting heart, I'd messaged her the first shred of truth.

I began the journey that would pulverize me.

Cut looked up from his newspaper, his eyes narrowing. "Where were you yesterday?"

Torturing Nila. Torturing myself.

"Nowhere. Not important." I strode toward the dining table, glaring at Daniel. He was the only other man indulging in breakfast. Everyone else must've eaten and split.

Daniel smirked, smearing butter onto a fresh croissant. Keeping eye contact, he stuffed it into his mouth.

The idea of eating with my two least favourite people turned my hunger into repulsion. Grabbing the back of a chair, I made no move to pull it out. "Where's Kes?"

Cut pursed his lips, folding the newspaper sedately beside him. "How would I know?"

I cocked my head in acknowledgement. Fine. If he wanted to play hard-arse, I could play. Squeezing the back of the chair, I nodded and made my way back to the exit. I had something to discuss with Kes, and wasn't in the mood to deal with my father and his mind manipulation.

Reaching the door, my fingers wrapped around the doorknob, but before I could escape, Cut said, "We haven't finished. Come in. Sit. Eat."

I turned, finding it no hardship to find the snow that protected me. I vibrated with icicles, just waiting to use the glittering tips as weapons. "We have finished. I have things to do."

Daniel snickered. "That's what you think."

"Shut up," I snapped. "Eat your damn food and mind your own fucking business."

Cut raised an eyebrow, pushing back his chair to stand. Moving to the buffet table where Nila had collected the trays to serve the Black Diamond brothers, he used a pair of tongs to place a raspberry Danish and some fresh grapes onto his plate. "I'm not convinced you're coping with the pressure of what is required of you, Jethro."

I swallowed, fisting my hands. "I'm coping just fine."

"Then why have you been making almost daily visits to see Jaz?"

"Oh, someone's been caught sneaking," Daniel chuckled.

I threw him a death stare before focusing the rage on my father. "Jasmine is our flesh and blood. I'm permitted to see family. Or is that against the rules now, too?"

If he took Jaz away from me, I would go fucking rogue.

Cut clucked his tongue, turning to face me. "Your temper and wisecracks have been steadily getting worse for weeks." Tilting his head, he added, "In fact, it's become so bad no amount of bullshit from you can convince me that you're coping. You're losing control, Jet. Losing it all thanks to that little Weaver Whore."

My heart thundered. Words flew and collided in my head.

She's not a fucking whore.

Don't fucking talk about her like that.

Stay the fuck away from her.

But I swallowed every syllable and forced myself to stay stoic.

When I didn't respond, Cut glowered and made his way back to the table. Sitting down, he waved at a chair. "Join us."

"No. Whatever you have to say, say it. I have somewhere to be."

Someone to see.

"I do not like this side of you, Jet. I thought we'd turned a corner with you a few years ago. Don't make me regret what I promised you."

My heart switched from anger to anxiety. I hated that he had such power, such sway over me. "I've done everything you asked."

Cut popped a grape into his mouth. "Ah, see, that's where you're wrong. I know more than you think, and you haven't been following the rules."

Shit.

Sweat dotted my brow at the thought of him seeing me come undone while thrusting into the woman I was meant to treat like filth. "Name one thing."

My father's eyes twinkled.

Shit, I shouldn't have said that.

Cut took a bite of his pastry, never taking his gaze off me.

"You're in fucking trouble," Dan sneered.

My head tore up, locking eyes with my psychotic little brother. I didn't think it was possible to hate someone as much as I hated him. I didn't want to be anywhere near him. He wasn't good for me. *Healthy* for me.

Snapping between clenched teeth, I said, "Watch your tongue, Buzzard."

Daniel growled, "Don't use that nickname, *Kite.*"

"Shut it," I hissed, glaring behind me just in case Nila had arrived for breakfast. I'd given her the truth in my last message, but I wanted her to come to me and ask. I wanted to stare into her eyes as she waged between anger at being tricked and acknowledgement that in some way, she'd known all along.

"Enough. Both of you," Cut ordered, pointing a spoon at us. "Stop being a twat, Dan, and, Jet, he's right. You're in trouble."

I trembled with pent-up aggression. The pressure of competition and testosterone in the room seemed to drip down the damn walls. "Why, exactly?"

My father relaxed into the chair, believing he was in complete control.

And he was. As much as I hated it.

"What didn't you do after the First Debt was paid?"

My mind charged with all sorts of things. There were so many instructions I hadn't kept. I struggled to recall one that he'd caught me out on. Did he know that I hadn't dropped her core temperature before the whipping? Did he know I'd fucked her and in turn fucked myself?

Keeping my face blank and cold—just like I'd been taught—I snarled, "I tended to her injuries, as per the custom, and left her to heal."

Cut sighed. The weight of his disappointment and annoyance crushed me. "You didn't do the tally, though, did you?"

My heart clenched. "Fuck."

He nodded. "Fuck, indeed."

How did I forget that part?

My body filled with thick resentment. "I'll fix it."

"Damn right, you'll fix it." Cut lost his smooth edge, showing his jagged temper beneath. "I don't know what you're playing at, Jethro, but I'm not fucking happy. Get it done. Today. Now, in fact." Grabbing his napkin, he wiped his fingers. "Go grab her and meet us in the solar."

My soul twisted, feeding off his blackness, his darkness. Every moment I spent in his presence, I slipped back into the man he wanted me to be. I became infected with whatever madness lurked within my family tree.

"I'll get it done. I don't need an audience."

They could trust me.

All my life, I'd lived with these men, and all my life, I'd drank their poison. I was one of them. It didn't matter that I'd had a weak moment yesterday. *This* was who I was.

I'm a Hawk.

Before Nila, my family was all the company I had—their morals all I'd been taught.

And up until two months ago, I believed Cut loved me—cared for me—that was why he gave me a system to follow.

Another thing Nila and I had in common: we blindly followed our elders, naively believing they had the answers to our problems.

No matter who Cut groomed me to be, he failed. I might want to obey. I might crave to be happy in the boundaries he'd set, but I never lived up to his expectations.

Cut broke into my thoughts. "You're right, you will get it done. And you'll have witnesses to ensure it happens correctly." His eyes bored into mine. "Unless you'd rather hand Nila over to Kes and spend the month working on your disposition?"

My teeth clenched at the thought. "No. I'm fine."

The spike of possession and desire overrode my frosty heart, showing me once again how thin the ice was that I skated upon. It was no longer solid and strong. The surface was breakable, just waiting for me to step into its trap and drown me.

I'd suspected for years that there might've been another way to 'fix' me. But whenever I attempted to revert to my true nature, Cut would notice and stop me.

I knew what it did to me. I knew how to survive with the sessions, but ever since Nila had arrived, it hadn't been enough.

Nothing was enough anymore.

"You're not fine, Jethro, but I'm willing to give you the benefit of the doubt. One more chance, son. Don't make me regret it." Striding past, he ordered, "Go fetch your Weaver. It's time to fix your mess."

Nila looked up as I entered her quarters.

Her onyx eyes cleaved right through my heart. I slammed to a stop as she glowered. Words flew between us, but none were spoken aloud.

I don't want you here. You disgust me.

I want you to obey. You terrify me.

I understood her temper, but it didn't mean I had to take it. It wasn't me who'd slaughtered and buried her family.

I fumbled for my ice and strode into the room.

Nila looked away, cutting me off from her thoughts. She sat in the middle of the huge oblong table, surrounded by material and brightly coloured pins.

She's sewing.

I didn't know why that comforted me, but it did. She'd returned to her craft because it was a part of her. She'd found a way to stay fundamentally true to her family, all while I drifted further and further from mine. Where I was melting and losing myself, she was forming into a defiantly stronger person.

You're doing that.

It was because of me that she'd grown. Because of who I was and what circumstances we found ourselves in. I shouldn't take such perverse happiness from that, but I did. It wasn't her father or twin who'd made her grow and see her own potential.

It was her sworn enemy.

The man who'd tasted and fucked her.

The man whose heart thumped uncomfortably alive whenever she was near.

I couldn't work out the complex mess inside. One moment, I hated her for dragging me from where I'd existed all my life, but the next, I wanted to kiss her for showing me an alternative to how I'd been living.

My ice couldn't compete with her.

And what was worse, I didn't want it to.

"What are you doing in here?" Suspicion, lust, and anger buffeted me in her stare, turning me to stone.

Before she'd arrived, I'd been a ball of twine—carefully packaged with no loose ends in sight. But Nila, with her needles and scissors, had somehow found a thread and pulled. Every tug undid the tightly wrapped nucleus of who I was, and I battled with fighting against the change or just giving up and letting it happen.

I couldn't remember the last time it got this bad. But it was my own fucking fault. I shouldn't have let myself slide so far from my safety net. Who knew if I could find my way back?

When I didn't move or speak, Nila placed the swatch of turquoise cloth onto the table and narrowed her gaze. "Either speak or leave, I can't be around you right now."

She couldn't be around me? How about *I* couldn't be around *her?*

Silence granted me a reprieve. I stood taller, locking my muscles against the haunting memory of her yesterday.

My eyes fell to her hands. Her index finger had a bright pink plaster on the tip—no doubt from pricking herself with a needle while working.

Needle.

What would she do if I were to suddenly call her Needle? What if I just admitted I was Kite? Would she hate me for the deception or be grateful that she no longer had to pretend?

Why had she not confronted Kestrel? And how much longer would she continue to avoid my text last night?

It fucked me off that I couldn't drop my guard, knowing whatever she felt toward Kite transferred to my brother. He was winning, even while I stripped myself bare in the hopes of achieving the impossible.

Her eyes glinted. "Dammit, say something or go!"

Her voice jolted me back into the present. "I need you to come with me."

"Why?"

"Why? You belong to me, that's why. I don't have to have a reason."

Her knuckles turned white as she fisted the material. "Carry on being delusional, Mr. Hawk, but disappear so I don't have to look at you." She turned around, showing me her back.

Temper frothed in my gut. How dare she turn her back on me? I snapped my fingers, growling, "I won't ask again. Come here."

"You didn't ask the first time. And don't snap your fingers. I'm not a dog and I will not heel." She wore a gypsy cream skirt and black sweater. With her spine ramrod straight, she looked haughty and as chilly as any sovereign.

My mouth watered to kiss her.

My cock twitched to fuck her.

My heart thumped with desire.

An argument brewed between us, gathering force until the curtains twitched with an animosity-storm.

"You're right, you aren't a dog. A dog is much easier to train."

"Believe me, if I was a dog, my fangs would be buried in your arse, and you'd be pleading for mercy. I definitely wouldn't be well-trained."

My hands balled. A stupid flippant comment but it spiralled us deeper into a quarrel.

Just knowing she had the guts to stand up to me made me fucking hot. I wanted to bend her over the table and fuck her, hard and ruthless.

Were all Weavers like her? Strong willed and contentious or was she unique—a once in a lifetime adversary?

"Turn around. Look at me."

If she did, I'd give into the throbbing in my cock and make my father wait.

"No. I don't want to look at a Hawk." Her voice was sharp and cutting. Whatever liveliness she'd had before had disappeared—almost as if she'd left her soul where her family lay on the moor.

Her dismissal and obvious unaffectedness of our pointless argument tensed my muscles.

Didn't my desire for her mean anything? Didn't my text help her see me? The *real* me? Surely, the truth granted me some leeway for forgiveness.

I stepped forward. I wanted to curse her for making me this way. This *weak*. "Last night—" *I gave you more honesty in one text message than I've given anyone.* Who was I kidding? She didn't fucking care. She *shouldn't* fucking care.

Grow a pair, fuckwit, and forget about whatever connection you thought you had.

Nila spun around; her cheeks dotted red with rage. "Last night! You dare talk to me about last night? Where I spent the evening mourning family members that were subjected to the likes of you?"

The weakness she conjured inside switched to fury. I stormed forward, towering over her. "I told you not to go up the path, Ms. Weaver. Whatever you're feeling is your fault, not mine." Moving fast, I snatched her elbow and jerked her from the bench. "Enough. I'm done reliving something I had no part in." Shaking her, I dragged her from the puddle of fabric heading for the exit.

My fingers tingled from touching her. My lungs eagerly inhaled the unique scent of cotton, chalk, and Nila. If I wasn't so damn angry, her smell would've entranced me. It would've granted a tiny oasis from everything else I dealt with.

"Let go of me, you arsehole!" She squirmed in my hold.

"No, not until you learn how to behave."

"How about you learn to behave, you cold-hearted-emotionally-screwed-up-jerk!"

I slammed to a halt. "Careful, Ms. Weaver."

She stabbed me in the chest with her fingertip, a maniacal laugh escaping her perfect lips. "God, you're—I don't know what you are. I think your rule of not letting people call you mad or insane is because it isn't a slur, but the truth. You're bonkers, Jethro Hawk. And you can hit me for saying it—but it's about time someone pointed out the obvious." Her voice dropped to a murmur. "You're a nutcase. Completely cuckoo."

I'd never suffered a barrage of words so fucking painful.

Grabbing her by the diamond collar, I shoved her backward until her spine hit the wall. Dropping my head so my mouth lingered above hers, I whispered, "And you're the Weaver who let a psychotic Hawk between your legs. You're the one who's damned, not me. I have an excuse for what I am. You? You have no excuse but getting wet all over—what did you call me—a nutcase Hawk."

Her lips twisted into a snarl. I tensed for her barrage.

Our eyes locked with fury.

Then something happened.

Something switched.

Fury became desire.

Desire became insanity.

I couldn't withstand the command.

"Fuck this."

I kissed her.

She cried out as my lips slammed down on hers. In a seamless move, I pressed my entire body along Nila's twisting one, pinning her unforgivingly against the wall. My leg jammed between hers, opening her wide, crushing my thigh against her clit.

Her mouth hung slack for a second as her hips involuntarily rocked on my leg. My stomach twisted and everything I'd been trying to hide rose up completely out of control.

Heat.

Wetness.

Hardness.

An ache so fucking brutal in my chest it almost brought tears to my eyes.

Then pain.

I reared back as Nila's sharp teeth punctured my bottom lip. I licked the tender flesh. She'd broken the skin.

Blood.

Metallic.

Life.

Her chest rose and fell; her eyes wild and sending messages that tripped and conflicted. She felt what I did. But she hated me for it.

Too bad. I had to have more.

I grabbed her, smashing our bodies together and reclaiming her mouth. Offering my blood, forcing her to drink my injury and share my bone-deep pain.

She wriggled and fought, but beneath her rage echoed the same mind-crippling desire that turned us from enemies into something *more.*

"Stop—" she moaned before my tongue danced with hers, stealing her curses. In her arms, feeling nothing but heat and passion, I could pretend life was simpler. There were no debts, no arguments, no families, no hatred.

Just us.

Just this.

Nila stopped fighting and kissed me back. She vibrated in my arms, her hands pushing and pulling at once. Her lips opened to scream or beg, but I silenced her by tangling my tongue deeper with hers.

She fought me.

She encouraged me.

She confused the shit out of me.

My mind roared and instinct took over reason. I thrust against her, grinding my aching cock, seeking relief from the annihilating greed to consume her.

Her back arched as I shoved her against the wall—harder and harder. I wanted to crawl inside her. I wanted to own her every thought.

Agony erupted in my balls.

"Fuck!" My stomach swooped and my gut roiled as if to vomit. Stumbling away, I clutched my cock, willing the blistering pain to ebb.

She kneed me!

Over the stupefying pain, I barely noticed Nila encroaching on me. Her breath was ragged, her cheeks flushed, and her eyes blazed with an odd mixture of lust and hate. "Don't touch me, Jethro Hawk. You might have been between my legs. I might've let you inside my body, but I will never let you inside my soul. Not now."

I hissed between my teeth, riding the waves of torrid agony. I couldn't stand straight.

Nila bent over to whisper in my ear. "I might not have fangs, but I do have a sharp knee." With infinitesimal softness, she brushed away the hair that'd flopped over my forehead. Her touch was tender, loving, but beneath it lurked the truth.

Something was missing inside her.

Something that drew me to her and made me believe.

Once again, my family had destroyed any hope of me finding salvation by breaking the one woman who might've been strong enough to help me.

Nila murmured, "I don't kiss men who I find abhorrent. Whatever happened between us is over."

Gritting my teeth, I unfolded. "Quiet!"

She froze.

My outburst sliced through our bullshit, granting a smidgen of clarity. "Don't lie to me. You *will* let me inside you. And you *will* let me own you." Snatching her wrist, I jerked her close. "You will because we don't have a choice. You're inside me. Don't you get it? *You're* inside *me*. And it's only fair that I'm inside you."

Silence.

Breathing hard, I growled, "You know as well as I do the dangerous game we're playing. I won't retaliate from what you just did, but don't push me any further. And don't you dare fucking say it's over." Pressing my nose against hers, I hissed, "Because it's not."

Her eyes flared. "Believe me, it *is* over. I have no intention of ever touching you again."

My temper boiled at the thought of her denying me more of this—whatever this was. I'd tasted her; I refused to believe we were through.

Cupping her jaw, I murmured, "The moment this morning is done, I'll show you how wrong you are. I'll show you how deep I am inside you. How fucked both of us are." I pressed my lips against her cheekbone. "You want to win? What if I told you it would be better if you lost? Better for both of us if you submitted and stopped fighting for a change."

She laughed. "Stop fighting? That's all we have. Don't you see? If I don't fight you—then what am I supposed to do? Am I supposed to be okay with all of this?"

"Yes."

She snorted, anger sharpening her features. "Delusional as well as insane." Shoving me, she demanded, "Tell me why you're here before I knee you in the balls again."

God, I wanted to strike her.

I wanted to antagonise her to the point of giving in just so I could fuck her again. My blood was lava; my cock rock hard.

Trying to get myself under control, I snapped, "I forgot to complete a part of the First Debt. My father just reminded me."

She stiffened. "Didn't I pay enough for that monster? Twenty-one lashings complete with scars that will last a lifetime. Or did he find out you didn't freeze me before making me bleed?"

Resentment radiated on her face.

How could I handle her like this? This belligerent?

"No matter what you think of me, I'm doing my best to protect you. I told you I would be in equal trouble for disobeying. I have no intention of explaining the truth."

Despite herself, some of her temper dispersed, leaving resigned tolerance in her gaze. "If it's not that...then what?"

My fingers curled tighter around her wrist. I winced as something sharp dug into my thumb. Holding up her arm, the glint of metal winked through the black fabric of her jumper. "Are there needles in your cuffs?"

She tried to jerk her arm away. Unsuccessfully.

"Hardly safe, don't you think?"

She looked at the sharp pins as I pulled them free and dropped them onto a side table.

Her lips curled. "A hazard of the occupation. It's convenient to have them there—I misplace them if I'm knee deep in material." Her black eyes met mine. "Careful where you touch me, Jethro. You'll never know if a needle will stab you to death."

I froze. Everything she said came layered with hints and metaphors.

A chill scattered down my spine. "You're beginning to piss me off, Ms. Weaver. If I didn't know any better, I would take that as a threat."

"Maybe you should."

"Maybe you should say what you mean and be done with it."

"Oh, I'm sorry. I thought I just did. I hate you. There, that blatant enough?"

Oh, my fucking God. This woman.

"You don't hate me."

She snarled. "Believe me. I do."

"You don't know me."

"I know more than I need and I don't like what I know."

My heart lurched. "You're just like them. Judging me before you understand me." The moment the words were free, I panicked. *What the fuck?*

My fingers twitched to wrap around her throat, to squeeze the knowledge of my secrets from her ears. She'd cut me out. She didn't deserve to understand.

I moved forward, closing the distance between us, unable to ignore the twinges of cuts on my soles. "Stop punishing me for what happened yesterday."

She laughed coldly. "Yesterday? You think my repulsion of you is from yesterday?"

I frowned. "Of course, it is. Before you saw what was on the moor, you liked me. You kissed me. You wrapped your legs around me while

I fucked—"

"And you fell for it, didn't you?" Her smile was nasty. "I made you kiss me. I made you fuck me to prove a point."

The fire in my blood suddenly snuffed out, leaving my heart blackened and charred and eager for the creeping icicles in the dark. My voice dropped to an emotionless void. "What do you mean?"

You used me.

Same as them.

You lied to me.

Same as them.

"I told you to kiss me to prove you have a soul. You have one. I see that now. But I don't like it." She sucked in a breath, cocking her chin with a haughty dismissal. "I slept with you because I was weak and because I believed you were different. But you're not different. You'll toy with me, hurt me, and ultimately kill me. And then you'll bury me with the rotting corpses of my slain family."

Her blood pumped thickly beneath my touch. A headache brewed from nowhere. I'd only been here for ten minutes, yet it felt like an eternity. An eternity where all my dreams had just vanished, transforming into nightmares. "What do you want from me? An apology? A fucking—"

"That's the thing. I don't want anything from you. All I want is to have nothing to do with you or your bastard kin ever again. I intend to stay in my quarters until each debt must be repaid. I don't care how long it takes or what you do to me, I'm done playing your stupid games."

My muscles locked.

Stupid games?

She thought my texts were stupid games? She thought everything that I was going through was a *fucking game?*

Ice turned to sleet, raining upon my soul. "What are you saying?"

Her eyes glittered with cold-hearted conviction. "I was wrong to think I had any power in this fate. I'm done. Seeing those graves made me grow up."

"So, you're just going to lock yourself away and wait to die?"

She nodded. "Having free roam of this place, receiving gifts, and enjoying people's company undermines my right to feel wronged. I won't play along anymore. I'm a prisoner and I refuse to forget that."

I wanted to slap her. I wanted to throw her onto the bed and fuck her. Whoever this woman was in front of me, she wasn't the Nila who'd made me unravel.

She thought she couldn't change my family? Maybe she was right. But she sure as fuck changed me.

"Everything you just said is bullshit."

She shrugged. "Believe what you want to believe."

I searched her gaze, delving as deep as I could, trying to see the truth. Something about this entire exchange felt fake.

She stared right back, hinting at nothing.

We'd run out of time. Extracting the truth from her would have to come later.

"Enough melodramatics. We're leaving," I muttered. "Time to go."

She scoffed. "Do what you have to do. I'm sure there's a special place reserved for you Hawks in hell."

"Goddammit, Nila!"

She flinched.

I didn't have the strength to have another fight, especially when I needed to concentrate and get through what was about to happen. "Behave. Just once if your fucking life trust without having to understand."

Yanking her forearm, I pulled her toward the exit.

In a magical twist, she somehow dislodged my grip and stalked to the door on her own.

My jaw locked as she threw me a cold glare and disappeared into the corridor.

Bloody woman.

Catching up to her, I captured her hand.

My heart skipped at the simple touch. Up until now, I'd always grabbed her elbow or arm—keeping our roles perfectly clear. So, what was I doing grabbing her hand like an equal?

Her fingers twitched then looped purposely through mine.

My cock hardened and I slammed to a halt. Christ, I wanted her.

Her nails were long and the tips suddenly sliced into the back of my hand.

I hissed between my teeth. The pinpricks of pain sent me reeling into a memory of her clutching my back as I thrust deep inside her.

Her fingers turned white as she tightened her grip. I didn't jolt as two fingernails broke my skin and drew blood. This was a perfect example of her undoing. She didn't understand me. Didn't understand that she'd just given me a gift better than anything. With pain, came relief, and with relief, came snow.

My heart slowed its beat. My temper faded. Any remaining fire dwindled to nothing. "Thank you for reminding me of my role in your life, Ms. Weaver. What just happened won't happen again."

I won't be so weak as to kiss you again.

I won't be so stupid to believe you can see me.

She tilted her chin. "Good."

I slipped into the dutiful firstborn son. "Kindly remove your claws."

A coy smile played with her lips. "My claws?" She blinked innocently. "I don't know what you mean."

Lowering my head, I murmured, "You know exactly what I mean."

Your claws around my fucking heart.

Untangling our fingers, I snagged her elbow. The throb where her nails had punctured helped me focus. I'd been blinded by her. Hypnotised by a promise of more—of a connection I never dared dream of.

It was a lie.

And I was sick of being used.

Striding down the corridor, dragging my prey through the house, I said, "No more, Ms. Weaver. No more games. We're through."

The solar.

A room hidden on the second floor located down twining corridors. Glass cases lined the hallways displaying ancient crochet and needlepoint. Black Diamond brothers and visitors were prohibited from this floor.

It was feminine territory—housing only my grandmother and sister, along with my father's study and private rooms. His bedroom was up another level in one of the turrets. Fortified and armed, ready for a war that never came.

Nila didn't speak as I guided her up the massive spiral stone staircase in the east wing. She'd gone peculiarly obedient but lagged behind me; I practically had to drag her.

"Where are you taking me?" Her eyes darted around the second floor as we stepped onto the landing.

"You'll find out soon enough." Gritting my teeth, I pulled her forward.

"Did a Weaver do those?" she asked, jerking me to a stop to stare at an embroidery of Hawksridge Hall bathed in golden sunlight with wild horses prancing on the front lawn.

"No."

Her eyes met mine. "Who did then?"

"No one you need to know about." We moved in testy silence to the large double doors at the end.

"Is this where you sleep? Upstairs, I mean?"

My head whipped to face her. "You're asking where my quarters are?" Dragging her close, I whispered hotly in her ear. "Why? So you can sneak inside and fuck me? Or perhaps murder is more on your mind."

She vibrated with anger. "Like I would tell you."

My palm itched to strike again. I'd never been a violent person, preferring to intimidate with winter rather than with fists, but goddammit, she made it hard to remember just who I was and what was expected of me.

I'd lost myself.

I'm fucking floundering.

"Stop asking questions." Splaying my hand on the doors, I pushed them open.

Her gaze went wide, sweeping around the large space. The solar was masculine in both use and décor, and frankly, rather drab. Heavy oak panels, with carved hawks and feather wreaths, covered the ceiling. The walls were gold-gilded leather, oppressing the space with dark brown while the carpet was blood red.

Slouchy black couches rested in clusters, some by the huge fireplace, and others by the lead-light window. An oversize coffee table took centre place with thick glass imprisoning the bleached bones of my father's old dog, Wrathbone.

A slow clap filled the space. Daniel smirked, his eyes locking onto Nila. "You didn't get lost after all. Pity, I'd just volunteered to be the search party."

My spine locked. Shit, not only had my father decided to be present for this, but he'd invited Kes and Daniel, too. The thought of Daniel seeing me around Nila both enraged and terrified me.

He'd always seen how different I was and used my flaws to hurt me.

Nila subtly moved closer to me, never taking her gaze off my younger brother.

So, she hates me but still expects me to protect her.

I wanted to pull away and leave her on her own. She deserved it. But no matter what just happened, she was still mine and with ownership came responsibility. Her welfare was my concern.

"About time you two arrived." Cut leaned against one of the embossed walls, his posture relaxed. In his hand was a tumbler of cognac. Not even midday and he had hard liquor in his belly. My father wasn't a drunkard. He would never give up control enough to be under the influence. He just indulged in things he wanted, when he wanted them.

Cut's gaze went to Nila. "Pleasure to see you, my dear. I heard you've recently relocated to the Weaver quarters. How are you finding your new accommodations?"

Her arm jerked beneath my hold, her fingers curling into a fist.

Nila sniffed. "I appreciate a place to work and equipment in which to do it, but if you think I'll find happiness anywhere in your home, you're mistaken."

Cut laughed. "I would suggest you stop lying to yourself. I've seen you smiling. I've witnessed your contentedness these past few weeks."

Nila growled low in her chest. "Yes, that was a mistake. And before I saw what I did yesterday."

Cut pushed off from the wall, throwing back the rest of his cognac. "And what did you see yesterday?" His eyes flickered to mine, glowing with annoyance.

"Nothing to concern you about," Nila snapped.

I glanced at her out of the corner of my eye. She could've told him about the graves. She could've told him all manner of things that I'd sworn her not to tell. If she wanted me punished, my father would ensure I would pay.

My heart thundered, waiting for her to announce my weakness. The secret of what it meant to both of us when I'd slipped inside her and felt her come around my cock.

She felt it, too.

I know it.

I sucked in a breath, holding on to the faint connection still between us—not ready to submit to our fight—to believe that whatever existed was gone.

"Jethro, are you going to permit your charge to speak to her elders so disrespectfully?"

Shit.

My forehead furrowed at the challenge, the command.

If I was anything like the son Cut had taught me to be, I would force Nila to her knees and teach her better manners. I would hurt her, scold her, and deliver her heartbreak at his feet.

But if I did that, she might reveal my darkest secret. The fact that I'd fucked her. And that it'd destroyed me.

Cut grunted, "Jet—"

Embracing the cold, I shifted my hold on Nila and grabbed her around the back of the nape. My fingers dug into the tender column of muscle, holding her firm. "Be polite, Ms. Weaver. Drop the insolence and be grateful for all that my family has given you."

She flinched but didn't try to break my hold. Glaring at Cut, she said, "Forgive me, Mr. Hawk. What I meant to say was thank you for welcoming me so cordially into hell. I'm so happy to live so close to the devil."

"Why you—" Cut grabbed a handful of Nila's long black hair, jerking her from my grip. "I'll make you pay for—"

"Gentlemen, surely there are more interesting things to be done than tormenting the poor little Weaver Whore?" Kestrel inched closer; his ability to guard his emotions and true feelings were a gift. He glowered in my direction, warning me not to move, to obey his unspoken help.

And like so many times in our past, I listened. I forced my heartbeat to regulate and latch onto the projection of calmness he oozed.

Nila hung in Cut's grip. Her tiptoes kept her balanced, but her face screwed up in obvious pain. Despite her agony, she didn't look away from my father's challenge or cry out.

Kestrel sidled up to them. "Father, we have a shipment arriving today and one of the brothers said a rival MC plans to ambush us. Save your wrath for those who deserve it. Not a guest who will be here for a long time to come."

My heart raced. My fists locked.

I closed my eyes so I wouldn't have to see my father holding my woman so possessively.

A moment ticked past. Sometimes Kestrel's reasoning worked. Sometimes it didn't. And if it didn't, it only made Cut worse—making him feel manipulated and eager to prove dominance over his sons.

The room held its breath; the air hovered stagnant and poised.

Then Cut let Nila go, rubbing his hands as if he'd touched something foul. "Next time you address me, my dear, make sure it's with respect, otherwise I won't be so lenient."

"That goes for me, too, Nila," Daniel said. "Don't forget we own your life; best to treat us like gods if you wish to survive longer."

Striding forward, I looped a fist in Nila's long hair, tugging her firmly but not cruelly, reminding her that as long as she obeyed me, she would be safe from other Hawks.

Don't you see I'm bad, but I'm not the worst?

"I'll remember," Nila snapped, moving backward until her shoulder brushed my bicep. That small point of contact sent tendrils of heat licking through my blood.

Kes grinned, hiding the fact that he'd just controlled the situation. "So, are we going to just stand around glaring at each other or what?" He moved forward, nudging me out of the way and slinging an arm over Nila's shoulders.

She sucked in a breath but didn't fight his guidance as he moved her away from me. He pecked her on the cheek and whispered something into her ear.

My jaw clenched as she willingly went with him, drifting away.

I hated their bond. The bond I'd made happen by letting her believe Kite was Kes.

She hated me for what she'd seen at the cemetery. Therefore, she should hate my brother, too. He wasn't innocent. Not by a long shot.

I took a step forward, intending to steal back what was mine. But I stopped as Kes squeezed her and laughed at something he'd said. She didn't respond. Just like she'd shut down around me, she tolerated Kes's touching. But the moment his hold loosened, she ducked from his arm and placed distance between them.

Her attention was divided between the men surrounding her, but mainly, it was turned inward, barely acknowledging her predicament of being in a room full of Hawks.

What had she done? And how did she turn off so successfully? I wanted to know her trick. So I could do it.

Kes beamed, gathering Nila's willowy frame and tucking her firmly against him again as if she'd never left. Raising his voice, he asked, "Where's the party? And when does it start?"

Cut scowled, pouring himself another finger of cognac. "You always were too jovial, Kestrel. Tone it down. You're getting on my nerves."

Kes's gaze met mine for a second.

"Don't want to be on Daddy's nerves now, do you?" Daniel cackled. His attention never left Nila as Kes manhandled her to a black couch and sat down.

Her dark eyes flickered between me and my family—never locking onto one of us for long, hiding her thoughts.

"Enough, Daniel." Waving his now empty glass, Cut added, "Retrieve the box."

Daniel shook his head, inching toward Nila. "In a moment, Pop."

Nila sat up straight, her nostrils flaring in fear and repulsion as Dan squatted before her. "Hello, pretty Weaver. Just say the word and I'll steal you from my brother. I'm sure you're bored of him by now." He placed a hand on her knee, gathering the material of her skirt. "I'm the one you want, admit it."

I couldn't stand by and tolerate this bullshit.

"Fuck off, Dan." I prowled forward, fists clenched. I wanted to throw him across the room. With every step I took, I was exceedingly aware of Cut watching me.

My father said, "Jet, don't interfere."

It took everything to obey, but I ceased and stood still.

Nila didn't flinch, nor look in my direction. Her lips curled in distaste. "Stop touching me, you arsehole." Her voice was just a whisper, but it echoed dangerously in the room. "I'm not yours to toy with so do me a favour and leave."

My mouth twitched.

The atmosphere thickened, fizzing with intensity like a fuse on a bomb.

"I rather like touching you." Daniel's fingers tightened.

I stomped forward, unable to stop myself. "Hands off, Dan." *Don't show too much.* I squeezed my eyes for a second, trying to find some sanity amongst the animosity between us. "She's mine."

Daniel chuckled, making eye contact. "Just 'cause you have a plaything doesn't mean you're better than me. She belongs to *all* of us."

"Not until I say—"

Cut slammed his glass onto the coffee table, rattling the bones of his deceased pet. "Must I mediate every time my sons are in the same fucking room?" Running a hand over his face, he growled, "Kes, seeing as Daniel won't listen, you go get the box. Dan, shut the fuck up. Jet, control yourself and sit down."

Kes gave me a look. I knew what he thought, but now was not the time to discuss our family issues. He rose from the couch and headed toward the sixteenth-century sideboard by the entrance.

Moving forward, I kicked Daniel out of the way and took Kes's spot beside Nila.

Daniel stumbled from my boot before rising in a fit of fury. "One of these days, brother."

I stood up, towering over him—willing him to raise a fist. "One of these days, indeed, *brother.*"

Dan breathed hard through his nose. I waited for him to punch me, but he had enough control to snicker and retreat.

"For God's sake," Cut muttered. "I raised a bunch of idiots."

Dan moved to his father's side. "Only one, Pop. And pity for you, he's the firstborn."

My nostrils flared. Fuck, I wanted to knock him out.

Something warm and soft touched the back of my hand. I jumped, looking down at Nila. Her hair cascaded over her shoulder in a wash of ink. Her eyes wide and gleaming with a silent request.

Sit down.

Do what you're tasked to do.

Protect me.

Her message filtered into my soul, switching my irritation to protection. My legs bent, depositing me beside her. A small gap existed between us, but it didn't stop my skin from prickling with awareness or her chest from rising when I placed my palm next to her hip and touched her once with my pinky finger.

Her eyes shot to mine, holding the fierce whip of connection.

The blackness of her eyes reflected my lighter ones, showing the strain and anger I couldn't contain. These wordless moments seemed to happen frequently between us.

Sucking in a breath, Nila broke eye contact and shifted away.

"Got it," Kes said, moving back toward us.

I risked another glance at Nila. She refused to look at me, her attention split between my father and Kes, who carried a smallish box in his hands.

"What's going to happen?" Nila whispered, her body swaying a little toward me.

Forcing myself not to inhale her scent, I shrugged. "The tally. It should've been done the same day I took the debt."

Kes set the box before us on the coffee table. It clunked into place with the finality of pain.

This would hurt. For both of us.

"I forgot to do it that day."

I'd forgotten because I'd permitted myself to feel her grief and pain while I washed her back and wrapped her in bandages. I'd forgotten because I'd shamed myself by masturbating all over her while she'd hung whipped and bleeding.

Nila's eyes bounced around the Hawks towering over her in a ring of authority. "Do what?"

Could others hear the trace of terror hidden beneath her snappy anger or was I the only one? The only one cursed to listen to her fears and feel her confusion?

No one was laying a hand on her. I didn't care if I had to draw Hawk blood to make that a reality. She would stay mine until the end.

With a smirk, Daniel leaned over and opened the lid of the Tally Box. "Ready, brother?"

I looked at Cut, but he just crossed his arms, watching to see how I would proceed. Bastard.

I swallowed. I would forever wear these marks. When Nila paid the Final Debt and was dead, I would remain alone and without her. Cursed by her presence every time I looked at the tally.

My father wore his from what he did to Nila's mother on his ribcage. I'd seen it over the years—the marks of coming of age—of being a full-blown Hawk worthy of inheriting the legacy.

"Tell him where you want it to go, Nila." Cut looked at my charge.

She trembled with tension. "Want what?"

Daniel shifted closer, his eyes slithering all over her. My skin crawled at the thought of him touching her. Hurting her.

Fucking arsehole.

Closing the distance between Nila and me, I pressed my thigh against hers—hoping she'd understand that we were in this together. Just like I'd told her. Her life was my responsibility and I wouldn't fail.

"I'll pick," I said.

"You aren't allowed, Jet," Cut muttered. "It's Ms. Weaver's decision."

Cut moved around the back of the couch, and ran his hands through Nila's hair. She bit her lip as he kept her still, hemming her inside the barricade of his fingers. "Time to choose, my dear. Where do you want to wear the mark?"

"The mark?"

"The mark of the debts."

WHAT THE HELL is happening?

Ever since I'd crawled out of bed after seeing my ancestors' graves, I'd been different. Remote, cold. To be honest, I didn't recognise myself.

I'd tried to work, to drown my thoughts with patterns and sewing, but I couldn't stop thinking of the past. How did the other Weaver women cope? How did they justify their captivity and pay the debts in full?

In one month, I'd made more progress with Jethro than I'd hoped, yet now, I wanted nothing to do with him. I'd lied when I told him I'd only slept with him to prove he had a soul. I'd lied to myself, hoping I would believe it. But nothing could sway the truth or hide the tingling connection that stitched us together—for better or for worse.

As much as I needed him on my side, I couldn't come to terms with what his family had done.

His text kept repeating inside my head; the words making no sense but somehow holding a promise of understanding if I only gave it time to unriddle.

Somehow, I had to do the impossible by pretending to care all while hating his guts. It was easier said than done when face-to-face with the evidence of his family's crimes.

Seeing the tombstones of my ancestors hurt me deep, terrified me of my future, but worse than that—it showed me just who I'd become.

I was a deserter. A betrayer to the Weaver name.

How could I wield my heart in a battle that I wouldn't win? And how could I ignore the fact that by letting Jethro into my bed, I'd let him turn me into a Hawk?

Cut tugged hard on my hair, snapping my attention back to my current predicament. His alcohol-laced breath sent fumes into my lungs as my scalp burned from his hold. "The marks of the debts must be done. Chose a place. Quickly, my dear."

I squirmed on the black couch. Cut wrapped his fingers deeper into my hair, flaring worse pain. "I don't understand what you want."

I had no idea what they were talking about or what they expected. Being surrounded by four men—all of whom I despised—would've given me a heart attack when I first arrived. Now, I only drew deeper into myself.

Even vertigo had lost its power over me. I'd stumbled a little as Jethro had dragged me up the stairs, but he hadn't noticed. If Vaughn ever saw me again, he wouldn't recognise me.

Daniel tapped the box, its contents shielded by a lid engraved with birds of prey and the Hawk family crest. "Don't have all day, Weaver. Pick."

I tried to shake my head, but Cut's fingers clutched my skull, keeping me prisoner.

"Pick what? I have no idea what you're saying."

Jethro tensed, his body tight and unyielding. "You paid the First Debt. A mark has to be made to acknowledge that fact." His golden eyes landed on mine and for the first time since I'd asked him to kiss me, I didn't give into a flutter or tingle. I'd slipped too many times this morning. When he'd kissed me before, he'd poured so much passion down my throat I couldn't help but respond.

It made me hate myself.

I couldn't deny that I appreciated him beside me. He was my only salvation against his father and younger brother. But I refused to let him manipulate me.

He's Kite.

Liar.

Con artist.

Deceiver.

He swallowed hard, feeding off my refusal to give in to him. His emotions were locked away, sparkling with snowflakes rather than desire. But it didn't stop the lashing of awareness binding us together.

"Choose, Ms. Weaver. Then we can leave," Jethro said.

"I—"

Cut let me go, moving to perch on the couch arm. He loomed above. "You have to select a place to wear the marks. In this decision, you have full control. Each debt that you repay is recorded. On video, in the ledger, and…on skin."

My heart plummeted into my feet. "What?"

Cut snapped his fingers, ordering Daniel to produce whatever was in the box. The carved wooden lid opened, revealing its treasure.

I leaned forward, trying to glimpse what was inside. My mouth hung open at the glint of needles, vials of ink, and alcoholic wipes.

Oh, my God.

"What—" I swallowed. "You can't mean—"

Jethro said, "The tally is a tattoo. Permanent, and for all intent, non-erasable." His black t-shirt and dark jeans made it seem as if he bristled with bleak acceptance. "After every debt, you earn a mark."

My stomach twisted. "So, it's not enough to take pain from me in way of debts—you have to drill me with ink, too?"

Cut replied, "It isn't just you who has to wear the tally." Pointing at Jethro, he added, "My son will wear the mark, too. And it's entirely up to you where it goes on your body. But bear in mind that it will match on Jethro. A mirror image. Like for like."

I shivered. "Excuse me?"

Jethro leaned closer, granting comfort from a body that'd been in mine. "Pick a place, Ms. Weaver. Just pick. I have things to do and want this over."

His sudden temper left my mouth hanging open. Everything he was and pretended to be filled me with rage. "I hate you."

Jethro's jaw twitched. "Doesn't change anything. Now…where do you want it?"

Daniel smirked, gathering the tattoo equipment and installing a small cartridge of black ink into the hand-held gun. "I suggest you pick, or I'll just mark you where I think it would look best." He rubbed his chin. "Your forehead, perhaps."

I sank into the couch, wanting to run from this madman. Kes smiled softly, standing beside his moronic brother. "It doesn't hurt, Nila." He pointed at his bird tattoo on his forearm. "A few stings and then you get used to it. But in your case, the mark will take a few minutes, instead of a few hours."

I stared coldly in his direction. When he'd hugged me before, I'd had the overpowering urge to push him away. To slap him. To scream at him to drop the act and show the truth. If Jethro struggled to hide his true self, then Kestrel was a genius at it.

I had no clue who he was.

The thought that any of these men were on my side or understood what I faced was laughable after seeing my family's graves. I wanted nothing to do with them.

Not anymore.

Instead of seducing Jethro to make him care enough to free me, I now just wanted him dead. I could see the allure of martyrdom. If I had a bomb, I would willingly strap it to my chest and press the trigger if it meant I could take out these men when I died.

Kes lowered his voice. "I've seen the scars on your back. I know the pain you endured from the First Debt. If you can survive that—you can definitely survive this."

I couldn't breathe. Not only had they taken everything, but now they wanted to mark my body—yet another reminder of my fate.

When I didn't respond, Kes tried again. "You don't have to say anything, just point to where you want the mark then you can go."

Go? Go where? Home? To the nearest black market and buy a bazooka to destroy them?

Kes moved closer, crowding me so I had a Hawk in every direction. "It won't hurt. Much."

Jethro snapped.

Soaring upright, he shoved Kes away and snatched the Tally Box from Daniel. "You're fucking suffocating us. Give us some space, for Christ's sake."

My heart twitched.

Jethro's temper was lethal, his position in the family high up the ranking pole, but the passion underlying his command sounded suspiciously like he'd picked my side over them.

I should've been overjoyed.

I should've done everything in my power to thank Jethro and encourage him to fall for me.

But I had nothing left but hate.

Kes chuckled. "Don't worry, Jet. Just trying to make it easier on Nila." He planted his hand on Jethro's shoulder, squeezing tight.

I expected Jethro to shrug him off and punch him. Instead, he relaxed slightly, nodding as silent communication ran between the brothers.

What the hell does Kes know about Jethro? And how does he use it so effortlessly to keep his brother calm?

Daniel stole my hand, running a sharp fingernail along the centre of my palm. I jumped, gasping in pain and surprise. I yanked my hand back, trying to dislodge the crazy creep.

No way did I want him infecting me.

A hand was the one part of a person's body that touched so much. The first point of contact for new experiences. A five-fingered tool to get through life.

"Stop touching me."

Jethro slapped his brother's hand aside, allowing me to tuck my palm between my legs.

Cut growled, "Stop chitchatting and get it done. You have five seconds to decide where the tally will go, Ms. Weaver. Otherwise, I shall decide for you."

Jethro sucked in a harsh breath, watching me from the corner of his eye.

Your fingers.

What? I shook my head at the idea. It was a stupid place for a tattoo.

It makes sense.

My reasoning laid out my conclusion in crystal clarity.

I intend to use my hands to slaughter them in the future.

If my fingers wore their mark—bore the signs of pain extracted at their whim—it was only fair that they extracted pain in return. My hands were currently virgins in murder, but soon they would smother in their blood.

It's only fitting to wear their tally while I steal their lives.

My eyes fell on Jethro.

Even him?

I steeled my heart against whatever desire existed between us.

Even him.

Sitting straight, I announced, "My fingertips."

Jethro scowled. "Out of anywhere on your body, that's where you've chosen?"

I nodded. "Yes." I spread my hands, silently cursing the shake in them. "One fingertip per debt."

I just hope there aren't more than ten to repay.

Daniel smirked again. "Not a place I would've chosen, but it does leave your body open for more marks in the future."

I narrowed my eyes.

"Put your hand on my leg, palm up."

"I'm not touching you."

Lightning quick, Daniel snatched my wrist, twisted my arm until my palm was as he requested, and slammed it against his thigh.

"Keep it there," he ordered.

My skin crawled. I went to pull away, but Cut said quietly, "Do as you're told, Ms. Weaver."

Jethro sucked in air, his ire buffeting me. "This isn't how tradition states." His head shot up to face his father. "Cut, I should be the one—"

Cut's features blackened. "There are a number of things you should be doing, Jethro. Yet you don't do any of them. What makes you so eager to do this one?"

I looked between the men, all the while trying to forget my hand rested on Daniel's thigh. Apprehension bubbled in my chest as he pressed a button on the side of the tattoo gun. Immediately the machine hummed with life.

Vertigo swirled in my blood at the thought of being permanently marked. I'd never had a tattoo, nor did I want one.

Jethro leaned forward. "This is my right."

His eyes met mine.

My tummy twisted.

My skin ached to be touched, to be kissed, to be bruised with lust.

Gritting my teeth, I shoved away those treasonous thoughts. I forced myself to focus on my mother's tombstone. Instantly, every desire fizzled into ash.

Daniel tore open an alcoholic wipe with his teeth, and swiped the disinfectant across the tip of my finger, breaking our connection. He grinned, holding up the buzzing gun. "Ready?"

"Cut!" Jethro growled.

I squeezed my eyes, biting my lip in preparation of the pain.

"Stop."

My eyes tore open at Cut's angry command.

"Enough, Daniel. Make Jethro do it. Can't break tradition, after all."

Daniel threw a disgusted look at his father. "You were never going to let me do it, were you?"

Cut glowered at his youngest offspring. "Watch what you say."

Jethro shifted to the edge of the couch. "Give me the gun."

Daniel ignored him.

His father snapped, "Daniel, give the gun to your brother."

A glaze of inhumanity and insanity flickered across his eyes. Without permission, I stole my hand back, grateful it no longer had to touch his horrible leg.

I'm living in a madhouse.

Jethro snatched the gun. The vibrating equipment settled between his fingers.

Twisting to face me on the couch, he raised an eyebrow, looking between my hand and his leg.

Ugh.

Obediently, I placed my hand on Jethro the exact same way it'd been on Daniel. The moment I touched him, he sucked in a breath. I tried to ignore the awareness snapping between us. I tried to fight the lashing heat.

I no longer wanted it—not after yesterday.

But it seemed Jethro couldn't control it, either. He bowed over my hand, unsuccessfully hiding the thickening hardness between his legs.

Licking his lips, he focused on my hand. His cool fingers imprisoned my index—the one without a Band Aid on from pricking myself while measuring out material—and pressed the tattoo gun against my skin.

Ouch.

I gasped, trying to control my flinch as the tiny teeth tore through my skin, layering me with ink.

"Don't move, unless you want a sloppy tattoo," Jethro muttered. His concentration level hummed along with the gun as it razored across the pad of my finger. I tried to see what mark he drew but his head was in the way.

Kes was right, though.

The pain started sharp but swiftly faded to an intoxicating burn. And no sooner had I relaxed into the metal teeth, it was over.

Five minutes was all it took.

The gun turned off and Jethro reclined, letting me steal my hand.

Nursing my new brand, I eyed up my fingertip. My flesh was slightly swollen and red; a new black sigil glowed like sin.

JKH

This time I couldn't stop my heart from tangling with my stomach. He'd marked me. Owned me. Controlled me.

"Your initials?"

Jethro pursed his lips. His eyes hooded, trying unsuccessfully to hide what he truly wanted to know. If his text wasn't blatant enough, his initials were a slap in the face with honesty.

His gaze shouted it.

Ask me.

Am I Kite?

I looked away, following the flourish of his old-fashioned handwriting. He wanted me to admit it. To confirm what he'd guessed. I had feelings for Kite. Feelings that I thought were safe being given to a nameless stranger, only to find out that nameless stranger was my nemesis who'd charmed both my body and heart.

The ink glowed black, forever etched into my skin. With evidence like that, I no longer had to ask.

Jethro Kite Hawk.

I looked up through my eyelashes, transmitting a silent message of my own.

I already know.

And I hate you for it.

He stiffened, understanding. "Unless you ask, I won't say what the letters stand for."

Secrets shadowed his eyes. Secrets his family weren't privy to but I was. What did that mean? What did any of this mean?

Deciding this wasn't the time nor the place to discuss something that would no doubt end in another fight, I tilted my head and played dumb instead. Taunting Jethro was too rewarding to let it go. "You want me to ask? Fine. What does the K stand for?"

Jethro frowned.

Kes chuckled. So far, he'd honoured my request for him to keep my knowledge a secret. Turned out he didn't need to keep it, after all.

"Your turn." Jethro deliberately avoided the question by handing me the gun.

I took it, my mouth plopping wide. "What do I do with this?"

Jethro unfolded his hand and carefully rested his knuckles on my knee. The submissive position of his hand and the gentleness in which he touched me sent unwanted pinwheels sparking in my blood.

We both gasped at the contact. My vision went grey on the edges as I fought the overwhelming urge to forget what I'd seen yesterday and give in to him. To trust in my original plan that I had the power to make him care. To trust in my heart and permit it to enjoy this blistering lust.

Jethro's voice was low and full of gravel. "You have to mark me in return."

To brand him. Own him. Command him.

It would be a wish come true. Perhaps, if I tattooed him with my name, I could cast a spell over him to become mine, not theirs. To use him once and for all.

Cut jumped in. "Each firstborn involved in the Debt Inheritance must wear the tally. It's been that way for generations. I must say I'm enjoying watching Jethro be so obedient. I thought his unwillingness to be marked by a Weaver would mean I'd have to strap him down."

Jethro threw him a black look.

Waving at Jethro's awaiting hand, Cut added, "Do it, Nila. Mark him with your initials so even when you're no longer with us, he will remember his time with you."

I blinked, unable to stop my heart from squeezing in pain.

No longer here.

When Jethro takes my life.

I wanted to hurl crude threatening insults but held my tongue. We would see who would die by the end of this.

Bending over Jethro's fingers, the very same fingers that had been inside me, I hexed the heat in my cheeks and twisting desire in my core.

Looking up, I caught Jethro's gaze. It glowed with need, mirroring mine. How could I hate this man? Positively hate him for doing what he did to my family, yet still want him so badly?

Bastard.

Even now, even in a room full of his flesh and blood amidst talk of murder and debts, he still managed to invoke uncontrollable need from me.

I wanted to stab him with the tattoo gun, not mark him.

Taking a deep breath, I turned on the button and jumped at the powerful vibration of the tool. "How hard do I press?"

"Just like a pen, Nila. There's no trick. Not for something as simple as this," Kes said. He hadn't stopped standing over us, watching everything, saying nothing.

Brushing wayward hair from my eyes, I leaned further over Jethro's fingers.

The second I pressed the jumping needle against his skin, he locked his muscles. Instead of tensing against the pain though, I sensed he wanted more. He swayed into me, his lungs inhaling deep. I shivered to think he willingly breathed in my smell, imprinting not just my initials but my essence, too.

Biting my lip, I drew on his flesh. My hand shook and sweat dampened my palms. After ten minutes, I sat up and rubbed at the cramp in my lower back.

His index finger held the same torture as mine.

NTW

Subtly, I glanced at my burning tattoo. First, Jethro had made me sign the Sacramental Pledge, and then made me sign his body.

If we hadn't been bound by sin and debts and a lust that refused to be denied, we were now. Locked, joined, and forever linked until one of us died.

It was tragic to think I'd gone my entire life never finding anyone who interested me, only to find such chemistry with a man who I had to kill before he killed me.

Jethro cradled his hand, glaring at the black ink imbedded in his fingertip. He traced the pattern almost reverently. "What's your middle name?" he whispered. His question was too delicate and imploring for the room full of violence and Hawks.

I wanted to slap him and show him how much he'd slipped from the icy son he was supposed to be.

He looked up, waiting for my answer.

My heart panged. It wasn't a middle name. It was more than that. I missed the loving address that my father and brother called me. It was who I was. Who I'd been raised to be.

Threads.

"Doesn't matter."

Turning off the gun, I placed it back in the box.

Cut clapped his hands. "Perfect. I'm so glad the formalities have been completed." Glaring at Jethro, he added, "Don't forget next time, son."

Jethro scowled, climbing to his feet. "Are we dismissed?"

Dismissed? Not only was the word choice like an obedient child seeking approval to leave his elders, but his voice sounded odd. Strained, gruff—an explosive blend that seemed as if he'd detonate at any moment.

"Fine."

Without another word, Jethro stormed out, leaving me alone with Cut, Daniel, and Kes.

What the hell?

I might not like him, but I was his. I needed him to protect me from his bloody family.

Instantly, the atmosphere in the room changed. It rolled thick and heavy: testosterone, possession, vileness. Why didn't I feel it as strongly when Jethro was by my side? And why had he left in such a hurry without me?

Daniel took the opportunity of my stunned state to lean forward and grab my hair. Whispering evilly in my ear, he said, "The way you watch my brother gives away your feelings, Ms. Weaver. I know you want to fuck him. I know you're horny living in a house full of men as powerful as my family. But you won't get to fuck him; not until we've all had our fill. He's the firstborn, but he'll be the last to stick his cock inside that sweet little pussy of yours."

Wrong, you arsehole. He's the only one who will touch me that way.

I struggled, trying to pull away. Cut watched us, neither interfering nor caring.

Daniel's tongue lashed out, licking around my earlobe. "I've seen you wandering around Hawksridge as if you own the place. Next time you're out for a stroll, you might want to worry about who's waiting. Because believe me—I'm not a patient guy. The minute you're alone and I find you—I'm fucking you. I don't care about the rules."

Pulling back, he stood with a horrible smile on his face. "Until then, Ms. Weaver." Tipping his head as if he had a top hat on his greasy black hair, he smiled at his father and Kes then disappeared out the door.

Oh, my God.

My heart was a fluttering mess. I'd been so stupid to believe I was untouchable. Believing the airs and graces of Cut and timelines of tradition.

I supposed I was grateful to the little creep for opening my eyes. I wasn't safe here—from anyone, at any time.

I need a weapon.

I needed some way to protect myself from that psychopath.

Ask Jethro to protect you.

I shook my head. Jethro wasn't the one in charge. Not yet. And besides, he was on my hit list as much as his family. I wasn't loyal to him. I could never be loyal to someone who made me despise myself.

I stood up, hissing as my new tattoo flared. Summoning whatever strength I had remaining, I glared at Cut and Kes. "Tell Daniel if he comes near me again, I'll make him bleed."

Without a backward glance, I left.

A weapon.

Find a weapon.

I could run to the kitchen and steal a knife. Or I could head to the library and swipe a sword hanging from the walls. Or, if I had any musket understanding, I could commandeer a gun and hide it beneath my covers.

What I really needed, however, was something deadly but also transportable. I never intended to be defenceless again. Not in these walls.

Dashing down the corridor, I plotted where I should go. Weapons existed all over Hawksridge Hall. I hadn't bothered to pilfer one because Jethro hadn't given me a reason to fight—other than verbally. Daniel, on the other hand, wouldn't touch me—not without walking away missing a few vital pieces of his anatomy.

The dining room would be my best hope at selecting something sharp and small enough to hide on my person. I'd seen a ruby-handled dirk there last time. It would be perfect and easy to conceal.

A flash of blackness up ahead wrenched my attention from scheming. I narrowed my eyes, moving faster to catch up with the blur that'd disappeared down the corridor.

Thanking the thick white carpet below my bare toes, I tiptoed the final distance and peered down the hallway.

Jethro.

My heart rate picked up as he strode quickly and purposely, his hands balled by his side.

My gaze fell on the hand where he now wore my initials.

I brought my finger up, inspecting his impressive cursive and arrogant flourish of his name. Not only had we slept together, but we'd stamped ownership on each other, too.

Jethro stopped and knocked on a door. A moment later, he turned the brass door handle and disappeared.

The second the door closed, I darted down the corridor and pressed my ear against the ancient wood.

What are you doing?

I didn't know.

Eavesdropping never brought good news, but I refused to be in the dark any longer. Where did he disappear to when he struggled? Who or what did he run to when he slipped from ice to emotion?

A low murmur of voices came through the door.

I couldn't catch any words, but my heart raced at the sound.

Jethro didn't disappear to be on his own. He didn't run to Kestrel or a Black Diamond brother.

Of course, it wasn't that simple.

No, he came here.

He visited a woman.

A woman who spoke with a softly whispered voice.

A woman who'd lived all this time on the second floor of Hawksridge Hall.

"WHAT ARE YOU doing in here, Kite?"

I slouched.

My nickname. The term of endearment that I allowed no one but my sister to use filled me with equal parts relief and annoyance. I should never have used it to message Nila. Now its meaning intertwined with the debts. It would never again just be a simple term of togetherness between Jaz and me.

I'd been so stupid to call myself after James Bond, too. Kite007. What a ridiculous name. It wasn't that I even *liked* James Bond. I just thought he had cool gadgets and deserved his kickass status for always killing evil bastards.

My fingertip burned with licking fire. My knuckles still tingled from resting on Nila's thigh. So many times, I'd had to brace myself so I didn't flip my hand over and slide my touch between her legs.

I'd been achingly hard the entire time I'd tattooed her. I'd wanted to see if she was wet while repaying the favour. There was something primal about knowing the woman who I'd fucked, who intrigued me over all others, was walking around wearing my brand.

A brand that marked her forever as mine.

Shit, perhaps I should've taken care of myself before coming here. The moment I let my thoughts drift to Nila, I grew hard again.

Jasmine smiled, waiting patiently like she always did for me to reply. There was no judging, no annoyance. Only acceptance and quiet companionship.

"I had to come see you."

Every second that ticked past in the solar had dwindled my defences until I had no reserves, no ice, no energy to fight against my family. The instant the tally concluded, I ran. A pussy move, but the only one to keep my sanity.

Jasmine shifted higher in her chair. She sat by the window, her embroidery threads and cross-stitch pattern spread out on the window seat where she had the most light to see.

Her rooms were the epitome of class. Dark grey walls with yellow coloured upholstery and linen. Archangels and fluffy clouds painted the ceiling while her floors drowned in multi-coloured rugs of different sizes and designs.

This was her world.

This was the only place I felt safe to let down my guard.

Jaz patted the window seat, folding up her pattern chart and moving aside some of the threads. "Want to talk about it?"

Did I? Did I want to admit the havoc Nila wreaked on me, or was it best not to talk about it and hope the power she had disappeared?

I shook my head. "Let me just hang here."

She smiled. "No problem. I'll just continue doing what I'm doing."

She knew me so well.

Her jaw-length black hair flicked at the ends in some fashionable haircut she'd recently adopted and her button nose and heart-shaped face was too kind to be around my brothers. Jasmine Hawk looked exactly like our mother. And only eleven months younger than me, she was practically my twin.

I wouldn't admit it to Nila, but I understood her connection with her brother. There was something to be said for finding a kindred soul in a person who'd been there right from the beginning.

I probably wouldn't have survived without Jasmine. I owed her everything.

"Relax, Kite. Let it go." Her small hands smoothed down her pretty woollen dress. She always looked immaculate in old-world fashions, which was utterly depressing as she never stepped foot off the grounds.

I'd tried many times to take her for a ride, on either Wings or my motorbike, but she claimed she was perfectly content looking through a window and watching others enjoy the world.

One of these days I would drag her out and show her how much she missed by playing Rapunzel in her tower.

Picking up her cross-stitch, Jaz gave me one last smile and continued to work on yet another masterpiece of our imposing monolithic home. Considering she didn't fit the Hawk traits like me, she was extremely patriotic to her heritage.

Threading her needle, she said, "Rest, brother. I'll watch over you."

I woke with a chill.

Gloomy dusk had replaced the grey morning. "Damn, what time is it?" I sat up, holding my head as a rush of nausea battered me. It was always the same. The sickness at the end of a long day. Especially if I'd been subjected to my family for long periods of time.

Jasmine was still in her chair, her legs covered in a blanket she'd crocheted. Her fingers flew, drawing a needle with orange thread through the hoop of her recent cross-stitch.

Not bothering to look up, she replied, "You slept through dinner again. But it's okay. I had the servants bring you up some cold cuts." She motioned toward the sideboard by her bed. Resting on the polished surface was a silver dome covering a plate.

I sighed, running both hands through my hair. Chuckling softly, I said, "You know me too well."

Her eyes met mine. "I know what you are but not who you're becoming."

I froze.

It wasn't uncommon for Jasmine to state such poignant weighty things. She was wise—an old soul. Someone who I leaned on far too much.

Knowing she had questions, I stood up wearily and went to retrieve the meal. Returning to my place, I sighed. "Am I supposed to understand that or is it a helpful way to ruin my sleep tonight?"

She giggled softly. "I think you've ruined your sleep by napping here all afternoon."

Even though she watched me with impatience and expectation, I felt nothing from her but love. Unconditional acceptance.

I sat back contentedly.

Finally, I could breathe again.

Nila tangled me into knots, drove flames through my icicle-ridden heart, and forced me to confront parts of my personality I wished were dead. But Jasmine…she soothed me. She granted me strength in her silence and a place to heal in her adoration.

Pulling the silver cover off, I picked up a piece of honey-cured ham and placed it into my mouth.

Jasmine reached for her glass of sour apple. She refused to drink anything else—water and sour apple quenchers—that was it. "So…you ready to talk yet?"

I ignored her, placing another piece of ham on my tongue.

She huffed, wrapping her tiny hands around her glass. Her fingers were almost as delicate as Nila's. They were both proficient at needlepoint and of similar build. Everything inside knew they'd probably get along.

But I wanted to keep the two women of my life separate. I had my reasons.

Nila couldn't know who I truly was and I wouldn't be able to keep my secrets if she met Jasmine.

Jasmine knew the truth. The whole truth. The truth that could potentially cut my lifespan into pieces and steal my inheritance on the eve of it becoming mine.

My phone buzzed in my pocket. Pulling it free, I scowled at the screen. The alert on keywords surrounding my family and the Weavers flashed with new information.

My blood boiled at the latest leak online about our private affairs. I'd been watching him, just waiting for him to do something stupid.

That little shit-stirrer has gone too far this time.

"I have to make a call."

Jasmine shrugged. "I don't mind. Do what you need to do."

Gritting my teeth, I dialled the number and placed the phone against my ear. I did my best not to crush the device in my fingers. I was angry. Fucking pissed. If I had time to drive to London and tell him in person, I would. Only, I would invariably end up using my fists—not my voice.

"Hello?"

My heart thundered viciously.

"Hello, Vaughn."

"Uh, hi…who's this?"

I laughed coldly. "As if you don't know who this is. Listen, whatever you're doing, stop it. This is the only friendly warning you'll get. She's ours now. Not yours. And you can't win against us so don't even fucking try. Got it?"

Deafening silence came down the line.

"Last warning, Mr. Weaver. Tell the press to mind their own business and put a gag on whatever bullshit you're spreading."

Harsh breathing filled my ear. "Listen here, you arsewipe. Nila is my sister. I love her more than fucking anything, and I *will* get her back. She's not happy with you. If you think I'm going to sit back and let her be subjected to you maniacs, you're completely fucking nuts. Soon, everyone will know what you've done. Soon, every law enforcer and newspaper will understand how sick and twisted you are. And then you'll be ruined, and we will have won. Go suck on that, fuckface. Don't call me again."

He hung up.

I threw my phone across the room.

"Shit!"

Not only did I have to deal with my own fucking weaknesses, but now I had to find a way to stop Nila's brother from destroying everything, too. Christ, this day couldn't get any worse.

Jasmine looked at my phone as it bounced against the wall. "Well…I'm guessing that didn't go as you wanted."

"He's determined to kill himself."

"And take both our families' reputations down with him."

I nodded. "Exactly. He has to be stopped."

I didn't relish the thought of killing Nila's brother, but what else could I do? He couldn't be permitted to steal what was mine. He couldn't ruin what I'd found. And he definitely couldn't take the one thing that I needed to make it to my thirtieth birthday.

"Don't be too hard on him. We took his mother and his sister. He's allowed to be—"

"He thinks having a dead mother grants him compensation?"

Jasmine's face fell. "No, of course not. Just like we don't expect anything after what happened to ours."

Colossal pain howled in my chest. Memories of a woman who looked so like Jasmine filled my mind. I never let myself think about her because that one incident had scarred me for life. It didn't make me who I was, but it had taught me death and pain and horror—things I'd never be free of.

"Kite…"

I swallowed my agonising memories, glaring at my sister. "I know,

Jaz. We agreed not to bring up that day."

She nodded. "You came in here to find peace, yet you brought anger and pain instead. Let it go."

I sighed, hanging my head in my hands. "I'm trying. Just…give me some space."

She shook her head. "If you wanted space, you would've taken Wings for a ride. Don't bullshit me. It's getting worse for you, isn't it? All of this…it's too much." She put her empty glass down, leaning forward in her chair. Her cherub cheeks were flushed from the roaring fire that a servant had set in the white marble fireplace. "You slept with her, didn't you?"

I choked. "Excuse me?"

She reclined, shoving aside all thoughts of our mother and focusing once again on my damn issues. "You heard me." Waving a hand in my direction, she added, "You're the worst I've seen you since you were fifteen. You're stressed and angry. You're *hurting*." Her voice softened with worry. "It's been a long time, Jethro, and I hate to see you in pain. But I think…I think you finally need to learn to control it, rather than bury it. It's not helping anymore."

My heart thumped in horror at the thought of being denied freedom from the horrendous disease I battled. If Jasmine couldn't grant a reprieve, how could I get through the next ten months and finally take my place as heir?

It's so fucking close. I'll make it. I have to make it.

"You know that isn't possible, Jaz."

"You don't have a choice. It's eating you alive, and unless you face it, you're going to massacre your feet or lose your mind. Either way, both aren't healthy and both will only bring disaster."

I shoved away the food, no longer hungry. "Then what the fuck do you propose I do?"

Jasmine narrowed her eyes, conclusions and solutions already formed in her gaze. She looked at me as if all of this had an answer. Which it didn't.

After a moment, she murmured, "Use her."

I froze. Blood roared in my veins. "You know I can't do that. I'm risking everything by letting her get this close to me." I bent forward, resting my head in my hands. "I don't know what the hell I'm doing anymore."

I had too much on my shoulders. Worrying about what Vaughn

was doing. Fearing what my father would do. Stressing about my feelings for Nila.

I'm done. Literally about to fucking snap.

Jaz ignored me, diverting my thoughts back to her original statement. "You'll have to. If you've let her in enough to sleep with her—"

My head shot up. "I didn't sleep with her."

Jaz raised an eyebrow, pursing her lips. "Oh, really? You forget I can see through your lies."

My forehead furrowed. "I fucked her, but I didn't sleep with her."

Even as I said it, my subconscious screamed the truth.

If I had fucked her, I wouldn't have let her affect me. It would've been purely physical and nothing more. She wouldn't have this hold over me—this damn fucking power.

"You're lying, Kite." Jasmine sighed, running a hand through her glossy hair. "And until you fess up and see that you're the one ruining the only thing that might work for you, I can't help you."

My blood ran cold. "What do you expect me to do? She's a Weaver!"

She didn't flinch at my outburst—completely used to me. "Doesn't matter. If you have to use her to cure yourself and realise you can be who you are, even after a lifetime of being told you can't, then do it."

Goosebumps broke out over my skin. "What are you saying?"

She stiffened, looking a lot older than her twenty-eight years. "I'm saying you need to find another way. If you don't, you won't survive, and I refuse to live in this family without you." Reaching forward, she took my hand, linking our fingers together. "In another few months all of this will be yours, Jethro. Don't let her destroy you—not when you're so close."

I squeezed her hand, wishing it were that easy. "I can't let her in."

Jaz smiled. "You don't have to. Make her fall in love with you. Do whatever it takes for her to ignore the reality of her circumstances and fall head over heels for you. Then deal with her brother and make peace with who you are.

"Only then will you find your salvation."

MONDAY MORNING.

I stood in the shower, letting warm water cascade over me.

The past few days had disappeared with no event and the weekend was a distant memory. Not that I had any reason to hate Mondays anymore. I had no deadlines, no runway shows to organise, or orders to fill. My new life was a constant holiday, interspersed with fabric sorting and designing that was a passion rather than a chore. Yet I couldn't stop my body from waking up and hurling me into work mode at dawn. I'd never been able to sleep past sunrise—a curse that Vaughn didn't share. He was a night owl where I was the morning starling.

Leaning my head back, I opened my mouth and welcomed water to trail over my lips and across my tongue. It felt good. Almost as warm as Jethro's tongue when he kissed me.

Ever since tattooing each other, everything turned me on. My bra rubbed against my nipples. My knickers whispered across my clit. I ached with the need to release but had no idea how to give myself an orgasm. I needed to come, but there was no way I would sleep with Jethro again.

I couldn't. It was too dangerous.

My finger, with its glowing *JKH*, had scabbed and healed enough for me to bear the itch as my skin acquainted itself with the foreign ink.

What does he think of his tattoo?

After sneaking down the corridor and watching him disappear, I'd battled every night with the need to return to the unknown floor to investigate the unknown room and interrogate the unknown woman.

He'd gone into her room but didn't come out.

I hadn't waited long—I couldn't. After all, cameras watched my every move. But I needed to find answers, and I had a horrible feeling that everything I needed to know was in that boudoir on the second floor.

Just thinking of Jethro sent a spasm of desire through my core.

Dammit, what's happening to me?

A daydream of Jethro slamming to his knees before me and wrenching my legs wide stole my mind. It was so vivid, so real—a trickle of need ran down my inner thigh. I gasped as I imagined his tongue lapping at my clit, his long fingers disappearing inside me—the same finger that I'd tattooed with my name.

Would I come harder knowing he touched me with a finger branded by me? Or would I hold on as tight as I could and make him work for it?

Oh, God.

I needed to get rid of this satanic desire. I needed to be free.

My eyes opened, latching onto the detachable showerhead.

I could do it myself…

My heartbeat whizzed with need. I couldn't fight the churning demand any longer.

Reaching upward, I unhooked the showerhead and turned the water temperature down so as not to burn myself.

Feeling awkward and ridiculous and a hundred times guilty for what I was about to do, I braced my back on the tiled wall and spread my legs a little.

My teeth clamped on my bottom lip as the water pressure tickled my clit.

Oh. My. God.

My eyes rolled back as I grew bolder and pressed the stream of heavenly water harder against my pussy.

Water cascaded down my legs while my torso shivered from sudden cold. My nipples stiffened as I wickedly angled the jet down and down until water shot inside me. Every jet and bubble aroused sensitive flesh, sending my muscles clenching in joy.

I moaned.

Loudly.

My legs trembled as my neck flopped forward and I gave myself over to the exquisite pleasure conjured by an innocuous showerhead.

Starbursts flashed behind my eyelids; Jethro loomed into my mind. I pictured him shrugging out of his black shirt, prowling toward me while unbuckling his belt and unzipping his trousers. I moaned again as my daydream shed his clothing and stood proud and naked before me. He grabbed his cock, pumping himself hard and firm, while his eyes feasted on what I was doing. He didn't say a word, only watched, then crooked his finger and beckoned me closer.

My heartbeat exceeded recommended limits as I forced myself higher and higher, locking my knees against buckling as an orgasm brewed into being. I rocked the showerhead, biting my lip as the pressure spurted over my clit and then inside me. The rhythm I set was exactly like fucking and I daren't overthink how I looked or how depraved I felt getting off this way.

My daydream forced its way past my misgivings. My forehead furrowed as I trembled, both welcoming and fighting an orgasm.

Daydream Jethro crept closer, working his cock, a dangerous glint in his eyes. The moment I was within grabbing distance, he captured my waist. "I need to be inside you, Nila." I put words into Jethro's mouth, but it was his voice I heard in my heart.

I moaned again, angling the showerhead harder against my clit.

"How do you want it?" my fantasy whispered in my ear as he spun me around and pressed me hard against the wall.

I swallowed hard, answering in my mind. "Fast and…"

"Filthy?" Daydream Jethro's nose nuzzled the back of my ear, sending shockwaves down my spine. "I can fuck you filthy."

I couldn't speak. But I didn't have to. My fantasy knew exactly how I needed it. Jethro bit the back of my shoulder, spreading my legs wider with his.

"Fuck me, Jethro Hawk," I whispered.

"Oh, I will. Believe me, I will." Without further warning, he dug his fingers into my hips and slammed inside me.

My fingers went numb as I slid the showerhead from clit to entrance. I cried out as water shot inside at the same time as Jethro thrust into me from behind, sliding deep and fast, stretching me deliciously painfully.

My heart exploded with bliss. An orgasm squeezed every atom, getting ready to hurl me into the stratosphere.

Jethro thrust again and I rode my new friend the showerhead.

"Oh, God. Yes," I hissed, rocking harder. "Yes, *yes…*"

A masculine cough sounded. "You continue to surprise me, Ms. Weaver; at least this time, I rather enjoy it."

Everything crashed into awareness. My daydream shattered, fracturing by my feet like broken glass. I squealed and dropped the showerhead. It turned into a water snake, spewing water left and right, wriggling like some terrible demon.

Jethro snickered. "You're using up the entire Hall's supply of hot water. Are you planning on saving some for the rest of the inhabitants of my home?"

I couldn't. *I can't.* The horror. The shame!

"What the hell are you doing in here!?" Embarrassment painted my cheeks. I wished I could curl into a ball and die. With trembling arms, I tried my best to hide my decency. Slapping one arm across my chest, I positioned a hand between my legs, exceedingly careful not to touch my throbbing pussy.

So close!

I was so close to coming.

So close, in fact, I wanted to scream.

One more stroke and I would've found peace. Now I was even worse—vibrating with tightly strung desire, fogging my every thought.

The showerhead continued to hiss and spurt by my feet, slipping me further into disgraced hell.

This can't be happening. Please don't let this be happening.

Jethro leaned against the doorjamb, his arms crossed, and a smile on his lips. "Don't stop on my account." He waved at my flushed skin. "By all means, finish. I can wait."

My daydream interlinked with reality and all I could think about was pulling Jethro fully clothed into the shower and impaling myself on his cock. I wanted him so damn bad. I wanted to be ridden, taken filthy and wrong.

My head throbbed as mental images of slippery bodies granting pleasure invaded my normally rational mind.

Jethro laughed quietly. "You look in pain, Ms. Weaver." He lowered his head so he watched me beneath hooded eyes. "Do you need help?"

I almost moaned at the thought of him filling me, fucking me. "I—" *Yes, I need help. Get in here and take me. Fix me so I can get over my horrible infatuation with you.*

485

I shook my head.

Dammit, Nila. Get a grip!

Jethro's jaw tightened; joviality disappeared, replaced with thick, thick lust.

My nipples turned from pebbles to diamonds, so hard I swear they would slice anything that touched them. I couldn't move as he continued to drink me in. With every second that ticked past, the air changed until the steam around us shimmered with barely veiled hunger.

Jethro's gaze drifted down my front. "Fuck," he breathed.

I almost puddled to the floor. I didn't trust myself to say anything—not one word. I'd betray everything I'd promised myself over the past few days. I would crash to my knees and beg him to put me out of my misery.

I would never be able to live with myself again.

We stayed silent, devouring each other but making no move to deal with what we wanted. My eyes fell to his trousers and his straining erection. It was so proud, so big.

Wait. He's wearing jodhpurs.

I blinked, trying to make sense in my sex-hazed brain. "Are—are you going somewhere?"

My voice snapped him out of whatever fantasy he'd been having. My scalp tickled as his golden eyes radiated intensity. "Yes. You're coming, too."

My eyes snapped closed.

Coming.

Yes, I'd love to.

He laughed softly. "Perhaps the wrong choice of words." In a rustle of clothing, he pushed off from the doorjamb. "Or the right ones, depending on how the next few minutes go."

A full body clench tore a small pant from my lips.

My eyes flew wide as he grabbed a fluffy towel and stalked toward me.

I pressed myself harder against the tiles. Shaking my head, I squeaked, "Stay there. Don't—don't come any closer."

His face darkened; a flash of temper etched his features. "It's not like I haven't seen what you're hiding, Ms. Weaver. Or are you forgetting that I've stuck my tongue in your cunt and driven my cock deep inside? I've tasted you. Ridden you. Made you moan."

Shit.

My core spasmed, greedily latching onto his words—seeking the final push for the orgasm living in my blood. It would be so simple to let go. To tell him what I truly wanted and to hell with the rest of it.

They're rotting up there while you fuck the oldest son.

Common-sense threw freezing water onto my overheated libido. With all the power I possessed, I ordered myself to ignore the tantalizing release and step back into the real world.

Seemed Jethro had come to the same conclusion as the aching awareness between us solidified into obligation. "Get dressed. We're late."

Swallowing hard and cursing my heavy body, I asked, "Late for what?"

With an unsteady hand, he held out the towel. He had the willpower of a saint or perhaps he was just as crazy as I feared because he didn't move to touch me.

Damn him.

His eyes narrowed as his fingers tightened around the towel. "Polo."

"Polo?" Images of men on horses whacking a ball around a field gave me something else to focus on.

"But…it's Monday."

Jethro cocked his head, chuckling under his breath. "You think the day of the week influences the crowd who play with us?" He shook his head. "If you hadn't have told me it was Monday, I wouldn't have known. Work days and weekends mean nothing when everyone obeys our schedule."

He's so damn arrogant.

Why do I find that so hot?

His eyes fell to my wet body. "Drop your hands."

"No."

"Obey me."

"Why?"

Because you'll end my anguish and give me what I need?

"Do it, Ms. Weaver. I won't ask again."

My tummy twisted. "Just because you've seen me doesn't mean you have the right to see me again."

He pursed his lips. "I can see and touch and do whatever the hell I want to you whenever I want."

Temper slowly overrode my lust. I stood taller, glowering at him. *Fine.*

He was back to being an arsehole. I could be a bitch.

Dropping my hands, I stood proud and defiant. I ignored the hissing showerhead and dared him to say something cruel. "Go on, look." I spread my arms, twirling in place. "Seeing as you control my fate, I might as well walk around naked so you can always drink your fill."

He growled, "Knock it off."

Snatching the towel from him and throwing it to the floor, I snarled, "No."

"What the fuck got into you?"

"What got into me? How about seeing proof of what my future holds."

God, I didn't mean to bring that up again. But if I wasn't thinking of sex with my mortal enemy, I was plotting ways to switch coffins from Weavers to Hawks.

"You knew that's what would happen."

"Knowing and seeing are entirely different things."

Jethro pinched the bridge of his nose, digging the tips of his fingers into his eyes as if seeking release from the rapidly building pressure in the room. "You're driving me mad."

"At least you finally admit it."

His head whipped up.

I froze. Shit, I'd gone too far. Again.

"What did you just say?"

The spurting showerhead faded; the rapid *thump-thump* of my heartbeat faded. Everything faded as I focused on Jethro's golden eyes—but more than that—I focused on his soul. The ragged, tattered soul that looked so completely lost.

Something inside him scared me to death but also called for help. I backed away—or rather, I tried to morph into the tiled wall behind me.

He glared, then...stepped into the shower.

Water instantly splattered his grey t-shirt and black jodhpurs as he stood over the wriggling water demon. His eyelashes sparkled with droplets as he coldly looked me up and down.

His hand came up. His lips twisted. A flash of violence danced across his features.

I did two things at once.

I cowered and suffered a vertigo wave.

Sickness slammed into me as I raised my arm above my head in defence. "Don't hit me!" The room spun and I stumbled against the tiles, desperately trying to grasp something to keep me upright.

My vision shot black and I flinched as harsh fingers captured my elbows, giving me an anchor just like Vaughn used to do so many times when we were children. The moment I had a sanctuary, the vertigo left me, depositing me firmly in Jethro's hold.

His eyes blazed with fury. "You couldn't hurt me any more than you just did, Ms. Weaver."

Why?

It's because you jumped to conclusions.

When I first arrived at Hawksridge, I would've been completely justified to cower and protect myself, but only because I didn't know who Jethro was. Now, I saw what he hid and violence was just a tool to him. A tool he didn't like to use. A tool he'd been made to wield all his life. But beneath his ferocity was pain. Deep, deep pain that spoke of a man far too immersed in this farce.

He won't hit me.

Not now. Not after what we'd shared—even after I'd tried to push him away, we were still intrinsically linked. He'd proven that when he'd remained on my side in the solar.

Shit, this is too messed up.

Blinking away the residual sickness, I tried to change the subject. "Stop using my last name."

He didn't reply, his face unreadable.

Something shadowed his gaze. Was it regret or annoyance? I couldn't tell. My heart lurched regardless. Sighing, I faced the true issue, hoping to grant him peace. "I'm sorry if I hurt you. I didn't mean to."

He let me go. "You thought I was going to hit you. Your fear…your loathing—you can't hide the truth. One flinch and you proved what you thought of me. I'm a fucking idiot to believe there was anything more between us."

Terror erupted in my stomach. Pushing *him* away was one thing. But having him push *me* away was entirely another.

Wait…fear and loathing?

He spoke as if he felt what I did. There was no way he could correctly feel my horror at what'd happened.

Glaring, I said, "What was I supposed to think? You raised your hand and expect me not to protect myself? You've told me time and time again to fear you." I should stop, but I couldn't contain the fire inside. "You should be happy you got your wish."

Jethro's jaw clenched. He stood so still, so regal, completely oblivious to the spurting showerhead by his feet. "I'm not happy with any of this, least of all you trying to provoke me."

"I'm not trying to provoke you."

He snorted. "Now who's the liar, Ms. Weaver? First you lie about the reasons why you slept with me, and now this." His lips twisted. "I'm beginning to think you are as lost as—"

His eyes flared, cutting himself off.

The words dangled between us. I throbbed to speak them. To see his reaction.

...as lost as me...

I was defiant and righteous, but I wasn't cruel. Holding my tongue, I let the moment pass.

Jethro visibly shuddered, holding up his finger. My eyes fell to his perfectly formed digit and my core clenched thinking of him pushing it inside me and granting me a release.

He sighed. "I came here, not to watch you pleasure yourself or to summon you to get ready, but because I wanted to show you something."

My attention flickered between his raised finger and his glowing eyes. "Show me what?"

He sighed. "It's *your* initials that I bear. Your mark. Your brand. I may be born a Hawk, but I've been captured by a Weaver."

My heart exploded.

Jethro leaned closer, pressing his mouth against my damp ear. "You sewed a cage. You somehow managed to fabricate a web that I only seem to fall deeper into. And this mark is proof of that."

My chest rose and fell. Was this a proclamation of his feelings for me? It was too strange, too forward for Jethro.

Slowly, I wrapped my fingers around his raised one, running my thumb over the tattoo. "Proof of what?"

Jethro closed his eyes briefly before murmuring, "Proof that no matter what happened on the moor, and no matter the grief you feel at my family's treatment of you, we are in this together."

Breaking my hold on him, he bent and gathered the showerhead from the floor. His hair tickled my lower belly, his mouth so close to my core. Standing straight, Jethro placed the showerhead back in its cradle and together we stood under a stream of droplets, drenching both of us and thawing out my frozen muscles.

Without a word, he reached for the tap and turned the water off. Silence.

We didn't move, dripping wet in a billow of steam. I was naked while Jethro's powerful form beckoned me closer. His clothes clung to his body in ways that were utterly illegal. His cock was rock hard, his stomach etching his t-shirt with ridges and valleys of muscle.

I swallowed as my need to come bombarded me.

My eyes drifted down his front to the hard length in his jodhpurs. "You can't keep playing games, Jethro."

He ran a hand through his damp hair. "Where is the game or joke in any of this?"

"There isn't any."

"No, there isn't." Grabbing my hand, he pressed his fingertip against my own newly inked one. "This isn't a game—not anymore. The debts bind us together as long as we're alive. You're mine and I told you before not to throw away that gift before knowing what it means."

My heartbeat lived in my blood, stealing strength from my knees, making me wobbly. "I don't want to belong to you."

He shook his head, a few renegade droplets sliding down the locks of salt and pepper hair. His forearms were wide and powerful as he moved to cup my cheek. "It's too late for that."

"It's never too late for the truth."

Bowing his head, he pressed his forehead against mine. "You're right. It's never too late for the truth."

The way he said it sent my soul scattering for the nearest exit. *What is he hiding from me?* "If you say I belong to you, then, by rights, your secrets belong to me. They'd be safe with me."

He sucked in a breath, his eyes trained on my lips. "I know what you're asking."

"What am I asking?"

He smiled sadly. "You want to know why I am the way I am. You want to know where I disappear to when I need space and you want to know how to use my weakness for you against my family."

Yes. I also want to understand why I feel this way. Why, when faced with the graves of my ancestors, do I so quickly forget and seek what I cannot find?

His fingers tightened against my cheek, holding me steadfast. His head tilted, bringing his lips within a feather-frond distance from mine.

My mouth tingled, sparking for contact. The anticipation raised my blood until I needed a cold shower instead of hot.

"Pity for you, I plan on keeping my secrets." His minty breath washed over me, grabbing me by the soul and tearing me into smithereens.

"Why? What's so terrible that you have to hide who you truly are?"

He swallowed, closing the final distance between us and pressing me against the wall. "Quiet."

I gasped as his lips suddenly sealed over mine.

The moment we touched, everything ignited.

The rage I'd nursed waned. My loathing and bitterness abandoned me. Even the images of epitaphs and graves couldn't stop me from betraying my family.

I wanted to drop my walls and bare everything. I wanted to forget about the past month, and pretend he was a simple boy with a simple offer. I wanted to believe he would save me and not ultimately kill me.

He groaned as I threw myself into the kiss, moulding my body along his.

I was already in hell. I couldn't fall any further. Might as well give up, give in, and just admit defeat.

Every dark facet of who I was, every spark and knowledge that made me human, wanted to be seen and understood. I wanted him to see me as his—not because I was a pawn in a game I didn't understand—but because I was a woman who he couldn't live without.

His delicious form pinned me harder against the tiles. His tongue broke the seal of my lips, diving in as if he had perfect right to be there.

And he does.

Over everyone, my body had chosen him.

Just your body?

I couldn't admit my soul might've chosen him, too.

Despite everything, I couldn't win against the truth.

As our tongues danced, my mind skittered from the present to a memory I never knew was there.

"Nila, this is Jethro."

I blinked through my bangs at the tall skinny boy who looked so dapper in a three-piece suit. I found his attire perfect for the beautiful teagarden I sat in with my nanny. She'd told me to dress up in my favourite ensemble—a white four-tiered dress with pink bows and ribbons—and she would take me for my seventh birthday to lunch.

The only stipulation was no one must know. Not even my twin.

My nanny nudged me. "Say hello, Nila."

I looked again at the boy before me. He had black hair, which was combed to the side. Everything about him spoke of stuck-up and resentful but beneath that lurked the same thing I felt.

Obligation.

A small butterfly entered my tummy to think he might feel the same stifling knowledge that we were already destined for a role—regardless if we wanted it or not.

"Do you have a strict daddy, too?" I asked.

"Nila!" My nanny spanked my behind. "Be polite and don't pry."

Jethro narrowed his eyes at my caregiver. He balled his hands and his cheeks turned red from watching her discipline me. I thought he'd run off, his feet shuffled to the teagarden's exit, but then he locked eyes with me. "I have a dad who expects me to be something I'm not."

My childish heart fluttered. "Me, too. I like clothes, but I don't want to be a weaver. I want to be the first girl to prove unicorns exist."

He smirked. "They don't exist."

"Yes, they do."

He shook his head, something cold and hard snapped over his features. "I don't have time for stupid kids." Spinning on his heel, he left me gawking after him. I didn't stop looking until a man with greying hair and black jacket stole his son's hand and disappeared into the sunshine.

We'd met.

How many times had we been introduced? Jethro had said I'd signed something in pink crayon. And now I remembered my seventh birthday luncheon.

Did I feel what I did because he'd been there in my past—like a stain upon my fate? Or was it because some part of me knew the kid I saw that day still existed?

Jethro pulled back, his gaze searching mine. "What? What are you thinking?" His lips were wet from kissing me.

A surge of need took hold of me; I pressed my mouth against his.

He tensed then opened, inviting my tongue to slink into his dark flavour.

I moaned as his hand moved from my cheek to the back of my

skull, holding me firm. The moment he'd imprisoned me, his kiss turned into a meal. I was the main course and he did exactly like he'd said in his text as Kite. He kissed me so deeply I had no choice but to inhale his every taste, ensuring he lived forever in my lungs. He made drunken love to my tongue, driving me higher, higher with every silky wet sweep.

My blood raced with need, sending throbbing desire to my clit.

If he continued to kiss me that way, I might come from that alone.

"Truth does more damage than lies," he murmured between kisses.

I'd lost the ability to reply. My body craved his, and all I wanted to do was tear off his sodden clothes and sink onto his cock. I wanted to forget about hostility and death. "Then stop lying," I breathed.

He pulled away, stealing his heat and passion. "I've lied all my life. There is no other way I know." Tucking wet hair behind my ear, he added with finality, "However, you're a novice. You better become talented in the art of deception if you wish to survive my family."

Without a backward glance, he left.

I balled my hands as I stalked the length of the corridor to the French doors leading outside.

I was riled, pissed, and entirely on edge. The molten desire of my almost-orgasm had switched into blistering annoyance. How dare Jethro come into my room unannounced and see me doing something so private? How dare he make me feel embarrassed but also strangely aroused at being caught? And how dare he tell me I sucked at lying, all while I caught him out on every single one!

After he'd left me to get dressed, my mind had created a few snarky comebacks. If he hadn't have run—like he always did—I would've had the last laugh. I was sure of it.

I repeated my retaliation, committing them to memory so I could hurl them in his face next time we had a fight.

I'm already a better liar than you are.

Are you so stupid to believe I don't see you?

Congratulations on winning the hypocritical award.

It'd been too late to say them, but I wouldn't forget. It was time to tell him that I didn't believe in his icy shell anymore. I was still afraid of him—on some level—but it was nothing compared to the sick terror I felt toward his father and brothers.

Crap, did I put it on?

I was so in my head while dressing in a knee-length black dress with a silver mesh jumper that I didn't know if I'd attached my new favourite item.

My fingers moved fugitively to my outer thigh.

Thank God.

I relaxed when my fingers found the small garter I'd made out of Victorian cream lace and pearl buttons. Tight with elastic, it was used to hold up ladies' pantyhose back in the day.

Now I used it to keep my stolen weapon from sight. The holster I'd made suited dresses and skirts but would be no use if I had to wear trousers. No matter, that was what bras were for.

After trying to eavesdrop on Jethro and the unknown woman, I'd given up and snuck to the dining room. There, I stole the ruby-encrusted dirk and placed a bronze figurine in front of the now empty hooks on the wall. I just hoped no one would notice.

"Nila! He said you were coming. I'm so glad."

I spun around. My heart rate increased as Kes strode toward me. "Morning, Kestrel."

He beamed; the hazy air of the ancient Hall blurred his five o' clock shadow and neatly combed tinsel hair. I found it strange that the Hawks were so young, yet they were greying already. Almost as if time stole their youth in payment for their atrocities.

Kes took my shoulders and kissed first my right cheek then my left. "Pleasure to see you this morning. How's your tattoo?"

I pressed my thumb against my index finger, activating the remaining burn from the needle and ink. "It's good."

Kes held out his hand, waiting until I slipped mine in his. He ran a finger gently over Jethro's initials. "Lucky bastard gets to live on your flawless skin." He grinned. He also wore a t-shirt and jodhpurs. Not that the tight trousers fit him nearly as good as Jethro. Kes was too bulky—too rough for something so…refined.

"Guess it's official now."

"Official?"

Kes nodded. "Just between you and me, I didn't think my brother had it in him. He's not coping—in fact, I'd go as far to say he's the worst I've ever seen him—but he's still managing to win against Cut."

I peered at the small tattoo. "What do you mean?"

Kes laughed, brushing away the topic as if it was nothing. "Cut has watched and re-watched the video of Jethro whipping you for the First Debt. Apart from the footage cutting off before he untied you, Cut was pleasantly surprised at how vicious Jethro delivered the punishment."

My heart skipped a beat remembering the agony I'd been in. "He didn't hold anything back, that's for sure."

"Exactly. Which was the best thing for all. He's proven he can be trusted to carry out the remaining debts and that means he's still in the running for inheriting it all."

I stood gobsmacked to learn there was more than just me and debts at play. What else was Jethro fighting for behind the scenes? "Inherit what?"

Hawksridge?

A holiday house?

The diamond mines?

Kes shook his head, tucking my hand into the crook of his arm. "Nothing. We're late. Better head out there before they send in the stable lads."

He took off at a brisk pace. I had no choice but to trot beside him as we traversed the remaining distance and exited the Hall.

Unlike a few days ago, the sunshine was bright and determined. I squinted, raising a hand to shield my eyes in the glare.

Kes asked, "Where is he?"

"Where's who?" I looked around at the sprawling mayhem before us. Normally the large expanse of gravel at the front of the Hall was empty. Not so this morning.

Two large horse trucks blotted out the garden with their black sides and gold-gilded hawk crest. Three 4WDs dotted around, some with doors opened, others with their boots wide and being filled with equipment by quickly moving staff.

Kes snorted. "Who do you think? That brother of mine."

"Oh, him. I guess he had to change."

"Change?" His eyebrows shot up. Cut and Daniel stood off a little way, both dressed in suits with a black leather jacket. They looked so similar, so removed from the normal human race.

"Why would he have to change?"

"Because I took another shower quite by accident," a masculine voice said behind me.

I bristled, not looking over my shoulder. The hair on the back of my neck stood up having Jethro so close. I might've been able to push away my never-enjoyed orgasm, but I didn't want to be too near. "There, he answered your question."

Twisting my fingers from Kes's hold, I said, "Now, if you'll excuse me, I'll go see if the staff needs any help with that picnic basket." Without waiting for permission, I disappeared down the steps and beelined for the two women in white pinafores struggling with a hamper.

Up close, I noticed the 4WDs were the newest model Land Rovers, and the horse trucks were ridiculously glitzy. How many diamonds did the Hawks smuggle to afford all this?

I jumped as a large hand splayed on my lower back.

Jethro didn't look down, preferring to keep his attention on a stable boy carrying saddle blankets. "Did you finish?"

I flinched, trying to move away from his touch. "That's none of your business."

Jethro moved with me, his fingertips digging into the tense muscles at the base of my spine. "None of my business? I think it is." He lowered his voice, his eyes still avoiding mine. "You see, I need to know if the woman who belongs to me is wet and panting for a release. We'll be in public today, Ms. Weaver. Having someone who's as hungry to come as you were in that shower is a matter of public security."

His lips twisted as he finally bowed his head to look into my eyes. "So, tell me...did you finger yourself until your cunt squeezed, all while fantasising it was my cock riding you—my cock slamming inside you? Or did you pretend you weren't that sort of girl and stop playing with yourself?"

"Shut up," I hissed. My eyes darted to the staff who crunched across the gravel in front of us. Jethro wasn't exactly quiet—anyone could hear if they tried hard enough.

Hard.

God, even innocent words painted lewd pictures inside my head. Images of Jethro's hard cock consumed me, and my heart hurled itself against my ribs. All my efforts at pushing down the ache between my legs was in vain. In a few sentences, Jethro had made me sopping wet and trembling with lust.

Again.

Damn man has super powers.

"Answer me, Ms. Weaver."

My hands balled and I snapped, "No. I didn't. Satisfied? I was too angry at you for saying I suck at lying. You're the one who's terrible." I laughed, adding, "Congratulations on winning the hypocritical award." I mentally patted myself on the back for using my remembered reproach.

Jethro rolled his eyes. "How long have you been waiting to use that?"

Damn him, he stole any joy I might've had from one-upping him. His hand moved to clutch my hip, tugging me closer. "By the way, I believe if there is an award for such a thing, it would go to you."

Don't ask. Do not ask why.

It pained me to hold my chin high and not grab his bait, but I managed it. Just.

Jethro huffed, annoyed that I didn't play along. "Fine…if you're going to be like that." Letting me go, he turned to leave but brushed his lips against my ear. "If I'm rock hard and in pain after fantasising of fucking you; if I can barely see straight from imagining my cock sliding in and out of your heat, I'm sure as hell going to grab my dick and throttle it until I come so hard it looks like fucking snow."

Pressing a chaste kiss on my cheekbone, he murmured, "Think about that next time you're riding a showerhead and just call me. I'll put you out of your misery, but it won't come for free."

My mouth hung open. My womb ached in a way I hadn't felt before—heavy, tender—a call for more than just sex but the primal need to have a man fill me.

Jethro's lips twisted into half a smile, then he left, prowling toward his father and Daniel.

My heartbeat roared in my ears. I stood like an idiot as staff continued to load and look at me with an odd expression. Chagrin painted my cheeks, thinking they probably knew exactly what ailed me.

Sex.

I'd been debased to craving sex all while my life hung in some precarious balance.

Sex.

The monstrous need that made graves and debts and tally marks insubstantial compared to the promise of finding heaven in his arms.

"Nila…you okay?" Kes asked, sidling up to me.

I blew out a breath. I wasn't in the mood to deal with him.

"Yes, I'm fine." Waving my hand at the dwindling chaos, I asked, "What is all this for?"

Kes grinned. "I told you a few days ago. Polo."

For some stupid reason, I thought it would take place on Hawk ground. I looked down at my black dress and thin mesh jumper. The garments weren't enough now the weather had lost its summer warmth and slid straight into autumn chill. "Am I still permitted to come, or—"

"Of course. I told you...staff, prisoners..." He nudged my shoulder in jest. "The more the merrier. Come on, it's time to go." He moved toward his family, leaving me no choice but to follow, regardless that I wanted to move in the opposite direction to Cut Hawk.

Jethro never took his golden eyes off me as I stopped before them. Kes clapped his hands together. "Ready to get this mayhem on the road?"

Cut rubbed his jaw, looking me up and down. "Would you care to ride with me, my dear?" He pulled free a black handkerchief from his pocket, dangling it between his fingers. His smile was cold and sadistic. "I'll have to blindfold you so you won't know the way off the estate, but you're welcome to the luxury of the vehicle."

I hated that he came across so cordial—almost grandfatherly.

Jethro muttered, "She'll be fine with Wings and me."

My eyes widened. "You're travelling with the horse?"

Jethro nodded. "Wings hates being confined. It kills him to be in the dark with no escape."

My heart flipped. How could he say something so caring about an animal, yet be so strange about everything else?

Cut laughed—it held an edge of warning. "I expected you to grow out of that stupid notion, Jet."

Jethro's hands fisted. "Sorry to disappoint."

Cut glared daggers at his oldest son. I stood poised to jump out of the way, just waiting for a fight to break out or some accusation thrown that might hint at whom Jethro truly was. It seemed his entire family knew and constantly used his weakness, condition—whatever he had— as a warning and an aid to heel.

Breaking the tense silence, I said, "I'd rather travel with the horses."

Cut stopped trying to kill his oldest by death stare and turned his blazing eyes on me.

I rushed, "Plus, I won't have to wear a blindfold as the truck doesn't have windows."

The thought of being cooped up in a dark space while weaving and swaying in traffic turned my stomach. The symptoms would be eerily similar to vertigo. But I would rather go with Jethro over Cut any day.

Cut nodded slowly. "Fine. We'll see you at the match."

Daniel shifted closer. "That's a pity." His unhinged soul glimmered in his eyes. His dark hair didn't have any of the silver tinsel that Jethro and Kes had, but all three of the Hawk boys had inherited their colouring from their father. Daniel's hair had thinned, whereas I knew from experience that Jethro's was thick and entirely too enticing.

I know because his head has been between my legs, licking me while I dug my fingers—

Don't think about that.

Once again, I had to shove away the wetness Jethro had conjured and shut down my bodily cravings.

Daniel smirked. His pristine suit, diamond pin just like Jethro's, and polished boots made him seem the perfect catch for any eager woman—until he opened his mouth, of course. "I rather enjoyed our car ride together last time."

A chill flash-froze my system. He meant the car ride onto the estate the night I had arrived. Jethro had drugged me—bastard. And I could still feel Daniel's probing nasty fingers on my core.

Jethro growled, "Enough." Leaving his family, he grabbed my wrist and stomped toward the closest horse truck. "Time to go."

I couldn't stop goosebumps scattering over my arms at the horrible reminder of Daniel's groping.

Silently, Jethro guided me to the side of the truck and opened a small door camouflaged by decals of his family crest. The entire transport was rich and gleaming with money.

As I stepped into the musky warmth of horse and hay, I said, "The night you stole me. Why did you drug me?"

Jethro froze, blotting out the light from the small door and instantly making the large vehicle claustrophobic. "I did it to make it easier."

"On who? You?"

He slammed the door closed, leaving us in gloomy light. "On you. I made it so you wouldn't fight and cause yourself harm."

I crossed my arms, a horrible suspicion filling me. "Wrong. I think you did it for you. So you wouldn't have to face my tears or put up with my panic."

Jethro shoved me out of the way, moving down the gangway between the two stalls. I spun around, following him. Two horses' rumps faced us with food bales secured within grazing distance and hay on the floor.

"Who exactly are you, Jethro Hawk?"

Jethro ran his hand along the horse's ebony side. My stomach fluttered to witness the sudden softness in him and it turned my heart to mush to see the animal's reaction to his master.

Its ears swivelled in welcome while its flank twitched for more. A gentle huffing sound came from velvet nostrils—a sigh of contentment.

"I'm the man who does what he needs to, but you already know that." Giving me a backward glance, he didn't stop until he passed the two horses and entered the small space at the front of the stalls. In the spacious compartment, there were two seats bolted to the floor facing the horses. Saddles, blankets, and bridles hung from hooks. Every wall and space had been utilised to house horsey paraphernalia.

Windows let natural light in from above, along with a skylight, but they were too high to see.

"Let it go, Ms. Weaver." Sitting down, he pointed at the identical seat. "Sit down before you fall down. Can never be too careful with that damn vertigo of yours."

I sneered at him. "Bet it makes you feel stronger knowing I have an ailment that can strike me down at any time."

He sniffed. "You're right. It does." His eyes narrowed. "Now. Sit."

The truck suddenly rumbled and coughed as the engine turned over. The horses behind me nickered. One stomped its metal hoof on the floor.

I turned around and sat quickly, just before the lumbering vehicle shot into gear.

Fumbling with my seatbelt—hoping it would be strong enough to keep me upright if I happened to suffer a bad spell—I yelped when a long grey nose nudged my leg.

Jethro chuckled. "For someone who says she's in-tune with the law of right and wrong, you don't seem to have experience around animals."

He smiled as the black beast in front of him arched its neck, trying

501

to get at his master.

I had no reply and sat very still as the animal in front of me nudged my leg again. In one demanding move, the horse shoved its way into my heart and I slid straight into love with the beautiful dapple grey. Its huge glossy eyes spoke of ancient worlds and kindness, and I had a vivid recall of my love of unicorns when I was younger.

I'd always wanted a pony—as most girls did. But living in central London and being daughter to a man focused only on textiles meant my dreams were directed into more practical things.

My memory of meeting Jethro with my nanny as chaperone came back.

I reached out to stroke the nose of my newfound love. "Unicorns *do* exist."

My heart swelled as the horse snuffled my knee, its forelock flopping over one eye and catching in its thick eyelashes.

Jethro stiffened. "What did you just say?"

I glanced over, never taking my hand from my warm companion. I waited to see if recognition would flare in his eyes. Did he remember that brief meeting, too?

When I didn't answer, he snapped, "Well?"

I shook my head. "Doesn't matter." Bringing the conversation back to a subject he obviously adored, I asked, "What's his name?" I scratched the horse between its eyes, straining against my seatbelt to get closer.

Jethro never took his eyes off me. Something happened…something I couldn't explain. The harshness, the frost in his mannerisms…they seemed to thaw a little. His head tilted, looking less tense and arctic than normal.

Butterflies spawned in my belly to see yet another side of him. Being around these beasts did something. It did more than relax him—it gave him a place to hide. He seemed to feed off the simplistic animal gentleness.

He took his time answering, but when he did, his voice was soft, beguiling. "Not him, her. Her name is Warriors Don't Cry. But her nickname is Moth."

Moth.

Soft-winged and subtly stunning. It was perfect. I wanted to keep her.

"And the other one?"

Jethro sat still, drinking in the black beast before him. "This is Fly Like The Wind. But he's my wings, as I cannot fly, so I call him that."

So, that's Wings.

The one who carried Jethro away when he'd reached all that he could bear. A wash of gratefulness filled me to think that he had something that didn't judge—didn't try to control him with family tradition.

Perhaps, I should learn from Wings. Perhaps, I should look past the hatred and despair and look deeper. There was something redeemable inside Jethro.

I know it.

"When will you let me see?"

Jethro's nostrils flared. "Pardon?"

Silent courage filled me from touching Moth, and for the first time, I laid it out plainly with no anger or resentment. "When will you tell me what the debts mean to your family? What is the point of all of this? How have you gotten away with it for so long—because the Debt Inheritance wouldn't hold up in any court of law. How did your family go from serving my ancestors to owning..." I waved my arm at the horses, encompassing the world outside the truck and Hawksridge.

I should've stopped there, but I had one last question. A burning question that I would give anything to know. "Why can't I hate you for what you are? Why can't I stop myself from wanting you? And why am I still here? Playing these games and believing that in the end, it won't be my head in a basket and you holding an axe, but something entirely different?"

Thick silence fell between us. Only the snuffles of Wings and Moth broke the tension clouding thicker with every breath.

Finally, Jethro murmured, "If I do the job I'm supposed to, you won't earn a single answer to your questions, nor learn anything about me."

"You're not doing a good job then," I whispered. "Because I already know more about you than you think."

He rolled his shoulders. "I have no doubt that in time you'll learn everything you want to know."

"Including your secrets?" I whispered again, filling my voice with feeling. "Will you trust me enough to show me the truth?"

He looked away, tugging the forelock of his horse. "That, Ms. Weaver, is like blindly believing in unicorns. You can't be mad at me, when in the end, you find out they never existed."

I gasped.

He *did* remember.

He murmured beneath his breath, "I suggest you focus on reality and stop looking for magic in a world that only wants to destroy you."

Silence fell like a heavy curtain, slicing between us and putting an end to all connection.

We stayed quiet the remainder of the journey.

POLO WAS THE only contact sport I enjoyed.

Hunting was a solo pastime—something that was both a hobby and a curse. But riding and being around horses had been my one saving grace as a kid.

Still was.

I permitted myself a brief second where I leaned against Wings and breathed in his musky scent. My heart rate hadn't equalized ever since we'd arrived an hour ago.

What the hell had happened in the carrier coming here? Why had Nila chosen that exact moment to bombard me with questions that had every power to skin me alive?

Jasmine had been wrong to say I had to make Nila fall in love with me. I'd tried—I'd spun some concoction in the shower about her fabricating a web and capturing a Hawk. It'd sounded ridiculous and so unlike me that Nila's eyes had widened, noticing my slip.

There would be no seducing her with deception. No winning her with tricks. If I wanted her to fall in love with me—to grant me another way of fixing myself and being able to survive the next ten months until my inheritance took place—I would have to let her inside me.

Allow her free reign to my complications and disease. I would have to let her *see* me. All of me.

And I didn't have the power to do that. Regardless of what Jasmine thought.

Sighing heavily, I looked out over the large grassy field. Polo players were dotted about, tending to their horses beside a mismatch of caravans, floats, and cars. Tyre tracks had squelched through sodden grass, turning green to mud.

A little distance away, the polo arena was pristine and untouched, just waiting for galloping horses to tear it into a brown mess. And just beyond was a movable grandstand taking centre stage—looming over the field, offering fabulous viewpoints of the soon-to-start match.

Men and women milled about, finding their seats in the tiered chairs or making their way to the tents below which housed gourmet snacks and exclusive wines. There were no hotdog stands or cheap beer in plastic cups. These events were for the elite of England—families with a bank balance in excess of ten million pounds. Caviar, foie gras, and salmon mousse were on the finger-menu along with some of Hawksridge's wine and vintage beer.

Nothing inferior was allowed.

I peered harder, trying to spot Nila in her black dress amongst the teaming mass of spectators.

Nothing.

What do you expect?

Kes would've taken her to the reserved tent on the outskirts of the food and grandstand area. We had our own private gazebo where guests were encouraged to socialise. We also offered uncut diamonds at rock bottom prices to all those we trusted.

Not only was polo beneficial for my mind-set, but it was also a brilliant day for our bank account.

When we'd arrived, I'd deliberated on how best to avoid Nila while taking her to where she needed to be. All my worrying was for nothing as Kes had appeared the moment I'd backed Wings down the ramp and hobbled him to the tethering post.

Moth was his horse, but he summoned a stable boy to attend to her while he offered to take Nila to the viewing area.

With a weighty look at me, Nila had nodded and disappeared with my brother. I hated that she went with him so easily, but at the same time, I was happy to see her go. It gave me time to get my head on straight before the match started.

Hopefully, once I'd had a day on the field with the sound of racing hooves in my ears and power in my veins, I would be better.

I would be stronger.

Moth nudged my spine. I twisted to pat the dapple grey. Nila's reaction to the horse hadn't escaped me. She'd melted the moment Moth had demanded attention.

I doubted she'd ever had pets growing up—her father seemed too consumed with his empire, and I wouldn't be surprised if he put his children to work the moment they understood how to wield a pair of scissors.

The Weavers had always been the same—treating their offspring like slave-labour—getting wealthy off the toils of family who were denied a childhood.

My heart suddenly warmed. *Maybe I can give Nila what she's been missing?*

Kes had no affinity with Moth. She was a good horse, came from a prestigious breeder, and the most tolerant of mares. But she was just a tool to Kes.

What would Nila do if I gave her Moth?

Would she open her heart more readily? Would she see I only meant to do what was required of me while trying to protect her from everything in my power?

Standing between the two horses, I scratched each behind their ears.

Moth was soft and kind and reliable. But she was no match for Wings. Where Moth was eager to please and fast to react, Wings had a heart similar to mine—an imposter's heart where obedience was required but breaking the rules was the only way to survive.

Rubbing Wings down, I quickly saddled him and held his head while I fed the bit into his mouth. He stomped, pawing at the ground.

I could've had the stable hands tend to him.

But I wanted to do it.

It relaxed me, and with Nila in my life, I needed all the relaxation I could get.

The sun was out and today could be a good day. If only there was one other person here, it could've been perfect.

Pulling out my phone, I called my sister.

It rang a few times too long and the familiar panic where her safety was concerned came over me.

"Jethro? Why are you calling me—isn't the match about to start?" Her soft voice came down the phone, sliding straight into my ear.

"You really should've come with us, Jaz. The sun is out and the sky is crystal clear."

"Maybe next time."

Maybe next time.

Her favourite expression.

Only thing was there was never a next time because she would refuse to go on that outing, too.

I sighed, running a hand through my hair. "Okay, well I better go. Just wanted to check on you and let you know I'll win again and give you the crystal vase or whatever shit they give us."

Jaz giggled. "Okay. Be safe. And remember what I said. Try to figure out a way to face what you are. No more 'fixing'. Get that woman to love you then you can hide again."

I didn't want to tell her that it'd gotten to the point where I could no longer hide—even from myself.

"Sure, easy done." My tone dripped with sarcasm. Before she could respond, I added, "See you when we get back tonight."

Hanging up, I looked at the screen.

I spotted Kestrel striding back alone across the field. I knew he would've stopped to place a wager on our team in the betting gazebo.

My stomach tensed.

Nila would be on her own. Cut and Daniel would never leave the gambling tent, so I just had to hope to God that whoever was mingling in our private space would leave her alone. She'd be surrounded by Black Diamond brothers peddling illegal stones. She would be untouchable under their protection. Not to mention imprisoned if she had a lunatic idea of running.

Escaping us was never that easy. There was a reason why her ancestors never fled.

My fingers drummed against my phone. Going against all better judgement, I opened a new message and typed:

Kite007: *I'm assuming you haven't replied because of what happened the other day. But perhaps now you're ready to talk. You have questions. Lots of questions. What if I told you it would be easier for me to answer this way than any other?*

My heart rate spiked, hovering my finger over the send button.

What am I doing?

Not only was it a disaster waiting to happen to write things down for anyone to read, but I had no intention of answering any of the questions she'd asked in the truck.

I always knew Nila would eventually find out that I was Kite. Hell, I wasn't exactly subtle—but I'd always planned to let the ruse die a death when she did. It wasn't needed anymore. I'd had enough enlightenment of her thoughts. And having the ability of talking this way only made the connection between us harder to ignore.

It was too dangerous. Secrets were too easily shared when hidden behind closed doors. Things I never intended to say suddenly had the audacity to find their way into a faceless message.

My fingers hovered, tingling with the urge to press send.

Do it.

I did.

"Ready to kit up?" Kes asked, shrugging out of his over-shirt and revealing the team colours below.

My temper flared to think Nila had feelings for him.

Feelings for my damn brother.

Feelings that I'd made happen by letting her chase the wrong path.

"Yes. I'm ready." Depositing my phone into the saddlebag, I unfolded my matching colours and slipped them on.

Another reason I'd wanted to kill off Kite was to give Nila no choice but to be honest to my face. I didn't want her running to Kes. I didn't want him anywhere near her.

She's mine, goddammit.

With a shaky hand, I tied my cravat and shoved Nila Weaver unsuccessfully from my thoughts.

Game time.

It's time to win.

There were very few places where I could be completely free.

In fact, I could count three in total.

One, when I went to see Jasmine.

Two, when I took Wings for a gallop away from cameras and family and obligations of being someone I wasn't.

And three, when I let down every guard on the polo field.

I fed off people's energy. I drank the players' nervousness, revelled in their tingling excitement, and for once, I was grateful for the disease I lived with.

We took our positions.

In my hand, I held my reins and a short braided whip. My cream jodhpurs, polished black knee-high boots, and gold velvet waistcoat over the billowing old-world sleeves of my white shirt made me feel like a knight about to joust for some fair maiden's affection.

Kes grinned, sitting atop Moth and her nineteen hands of elegant muscle. Wings was only eighteen hands high, but he had something Moth didn't. He had ferocity that rippled around him. Other horses felt it. Their nostrils flared, their eyes tracking him wherever he went.

He was an anomaly.

Just like his owner.

The Hawks were well known for hosting polo matches and commandeering the rules of any game we were invited to. Common rules that we broke were: no horses to be higher than sixteen hands, and multiple mounts per player.

I flatly refused to play on any other horse but Wings. Therefore, the rest of the players were forced to follow my lead.

Another rule we tweaked was to have a longer half-time. Instead of the stupid length of ten-minutes, we stipulated an hour—the horses needed it, seeing as we didn't change mounts.

And an hour would be perfect for what I had planned.

I had every intention of seeking out Nila and finishing what she started this morning. What I wanted to do to her would be a fuck-load better than any showerhead.

The umpire cantered onto the pitch. The game we were about to play would be fast, brutal, and mentally draining. Men were known to break legs from an incorrectly wielded hook or concussion from falling mid-flight.

The umpire spun his speech while everyone nodded but didn't listen. We all focused on the hard white ball in his hand.

The moment the ball hit the turf, it would be on.

The horses jostled and pawed, tasting imminent war.

After the umpire had finished his spiel, the other two members of our team came forward. In a close circle, we slapped mallets in a final hurrah before kick-off.

"I got your back," Kes said, his eyes glowing beneath the shadow of his helmet. His matching waistcoat held the number four. His role was to protect the leader, stop others from scoring, and had no restrictions on where he could go on the field.

I nodded, tugging at my cuffs and curling my gloved fingers firmly around my mallet. "First play is offensive. Steal the ball on the throw-in and slam this chukker so we can crush their hopes."

I wore the number three on our team. My role was tactical leader and the best player—it wasn't ego, just simple fact.

My teammates nodded and touched their visors in acknowledgement.

Excitement bubbled in my chest. It was such a foreign elusive emotion that I quickly became drunk on it.

Trotting to our places, I smiled at Kes, "Ready, brother?" Out here there were no his or mine. No firstborn bullshit. No diamond smuggling or family legacy.

Just speed and accuracy.

Kes smirked. "Ready to whoop your ass."

"We're on the same team, moron."

He laughed. "On here we are, but we both know we can still lose even when on the same side."

Wasn't that the God-awful truth?

We were flesh and blood. By right, we should have each other's back—yet we'd been bred to compete against one another. If I were suddenly to 'disappear or have an accident', Kes would take my place and rule.

Not because he wanted it—he already knew I would give him more than our father ever did—but because he was the substitute.

Born as a plan B.

At least there had been some planning in his conception. Daniel, however, was the accident. Not required and definitely not wanted.

Kes held up his mallet. I did the same and we swatted a salute. "Let the best man win."

I nodded. "Best man."

Two minutes later the bugle sounded, the ball flew, and the world ceased to exist as I threw myself into the match.

I'D LIVED A life of privileged upbringing.

I'd been pampered and spoiled; lavished with praise when I followed my father's wishes and began sewing at barely ten-years-old.

Vaughn and I lived a life of decadence and culture.

Theatre productions, pottery classes, language and disposition tutors—even fencing lessons.

Thanks to my upbringing, I had talents I would never use, and a brain cluttered with useless education.

I'd always felt as if I'd been born into the elite. Despite working twelve-hour days and toiling in workshops, I didn't begrudge our family's business from absorbing my life and turning me into yet another cog in the Weaver Empire.

I was rewarded handsomely, earned pleasure from seeing something grow, and never wanted a different life.

However, there were a few times when our wealth made me self-conscious. I found it hard to make genuine friends at school. Stipulations came with any connection, and I became the girl invited to a sleep-over or party, only because I came with a credit card that brought unlimited pizza and drinks.

It was yet another reason why I'd gravitated toward my twin. V had the same problem. He'd been crushed when he fell for a girl, only for her to break it off the moment he bought her the necklace she'd been begging for.

We were both hurt by others and became sheltered because of it. Money was supposed to make life easy but it was more of a curse than a blessing. And I'd never felt it so acutely as I stood on the side-lines of the polo match and watched the man who owned me galloping up and down.

Jethro looked...*free.*

For the first time since I'd met him, he looked...*happy.*

His face was blank of all responsibility.

His body liquid and graceful.

His eyes warm and golden as he leant over the withers of his horse and whacked the ball so hard it skidded like a comet down the field.

Out there he escaped everything he lived with and the hatred I felt toward him—the disgust and despair at finding my family buried on the moor—softened.

I couldn't hate someone who lived in the same cage as I did. I couldn't hate someone for being a simple tool for his father. And I definitely couldn't hate someone who spent his whole life looking for a way out.

Before, when we'd arrived, and sunlight had streamed in as the ramp of the truck opened, I'd suffered a relentless need to run. People and open spaces and cars all waited to help me flee from the Hawks. It would be so easy—wouldn't it? To somehow escape the attention of my guards and dart to a bystander with tales of ludicrous debts and inhumane treatment.

I could be saved.

I could go home.

But I'd paused and asked questions that I doubted I would ever find answers to. Why did my mother, grandmother, and great-grandmother stay? Surely, they would've found opportunities such as this and escaped?

I knew the reasons for my procrastination: I wanted to be the last Weaver taken. But my ancestors...what was their reasoning? Did they perhaps share the same goal I did—did they believe they could change their fate or murder the Hawks instead?

Did they fail?

Am I destined to fail?

The *smack* of the ball resonated like thunder as Kes hooked his stick around an opposing player, giving Jethro time to swoop in and shoot the ball toward the goal.

My heart raced as Jethro's firm legs wrapped around his galloping steed. His gloved hands wielded his stick like a dangerous weapon, while his concentration level sent a flush of wetness between my legs. I wanted to become so precious to him that he looked at me with the same unbarred happiness.

My wonderings of boosting a car and fleeing faded with every heartbeat. Watching Jethro be free gave me the truth I'd been looking for.

I was an idiot to stay. To not take the fateful opportunity.

But I'd come to the conclusion: I would rather be an idiot and win, than a coward and run.

I didn't think I would like polo. I couldn't have been more wrong. I'd never witnessed something so intense, so visceral.

The rumbling earthquakes formed by eight horses thundering past would forever live inside my soul. My dreams would always conjure Jethro how he looked right now—capable, joyous, completely perfect in every way.

Another strike and the ball shot past, followed by a mass of muscle and men. The clatter of sticks colliding and grunts of players fully in the throes of sport sent my tummy frothing with bubbles.

I'd been told to stay in the gazebo under the watchful eye of Flaw. But I grew bored and resentful as Flaw orchestrated a magical event of disappearing diamonds followed by huge sums of cash changing hands.

The moment the bugle had sounded, I'd rushed out to witness the game. And now, watching the sea of sweat-glistening men, I'd found heaven.

Jethro suddenly looked directly at me. His arm jerked, pulling the reins tight and causing Wings to toss his head mid-gallop. My entire body tingled as Jethro just stared. We held eye contact far longer than was safe, and the moment he was too far away, I felt bereaved—as if he'd stolen my heart and taken it flying up the field with him.

I wanted to chase after him. I wanted to steal Moth from Kes and fight *beside* Jethro, rather than against him. I wanted the rush, the fear, the intoxicating knowledge of invincibility. But most of all, I wanted what Jethro had

. . .

freedom.

I wanted to be as happy as him. To be at peace like him.

I wanted to stare into his eyes while he was truly himself—no games, no lies, no debts.

Kes suddenly stood up in his stirrups, high fiving Jethro for effortlessly scoring another goal.

Jethro smiled. He positively glowed. He was resplendent.

Then the bugle trumpeted and the game began anew.

His happiness turned sharp with aggression. He and Wings moved as one—gliding so smoothly it looked almost telepathic—pirouetting mid-gallop to intercept the ball and steal it. Jethro...or should I say Kite...dominated the entire game.

He truly is one of a kind.

Tears came to my eyes as I finally acknowledged what lived beneath my hate.

My lust was slowly evolving, slowly growing. And I wished I had the power to stop it.

But I had as much power as stopping my heart from tripping into love as I did from tearing myself from the match. I fell into disgrace.

By the end of the first half, my knickers were damp and my heart ached. Every muscle hummed as if I'd been beaten, and I couldn't stop the small voice repeating over and over:

You're falling for him.

You're falling for him.

You're falling for him.

I wasn't.

I couldn't.

I'm not!

But no matter how hard I tried, the words enemy, tormentor, and adversary ceased to have meaning.

Other words came instead: ally, accomplice...friend.

When the bugle blared, signalling half-time, I sagged in relief. I needed to find a cool dark place and glue myself back together. I couldn't let anyone—especially Jethro—see me in such broken pieces.

Out of the corner of my eye, I noticed Wings cantering toward me. Jethro sat proud and regal atop him, his golden eyes blazing with passion and need.

My stomach somersaulted.

He wants you.

I shook my head. He couldn't touch me. Not when I was so...delicate. There would be no way I could halt the mess inside and find my way back to sanity if he touched me.

Run.

It's the only way.

Leaving the border of the arena, I darted through the crowds and away from my feelings and the man I couldn't face.

Ladies giggled as the gates were opened to carry on the time-old tradition of stomping on the divots caused by the horse's hooves. Music floated across the sun-drenched field from large speakers.

I left it all behind.

Walking briskly past the Hawk's private gazebo, I caught the eye of Flaw. He crooked his finger, motioning me to go inside. I shook my head and pointed to the perimeter of the grandstand, indicating I needed some space.

He frowned then weaved through customers, who'd no doubt bought a smuggled diamond or two, and made his way toward me.

No, I need time alone.

I broke into a jog.

My ballerina shoes coasted over the thick grass whereas ladies in heels struggled, their pretty shoes sinking into the mud.

Before the match had started, I'd been in my element—drinking in the designs of their gowns and improving on styles that intrigued me. All around, women clustered in beautiful fabrics, laughing beneath hats that dripped with organza and hand-stitched lace flowers.

Now those same fashions were in my way as I wriggled through the dispersing crowd and ducked down the side of the grandstand.

No one disturbed me as I kept my eyes trained on the ground and didn't stop jogging until I rounded the back of the tiered seating and disappeared into the hushed world of scaffolding and churned earth.

The second the shadows claimed me, I breathed a sigh of relief. *Thank God.*

There was no one here apart from stacked chairs and boxes of polo equipment.

I could let go of my iron control and indulge in a moment of self-pity. I was screwed up, and I had to find some way of fixing myself.

You're not falling for him.

You're not.

I found a place to recline and hung my head in my hands. "You can't be, Nila. Think of your family. Think about why you're here. About your promise."

My voice fell around me like the tears I wanted to shed.

You know how wrong all of this is.

You know what he means to do.

I groaned, digging my fingers into my hair and tugging. A single tear rolled down my nose. It hovered on the tip like a jewel, before splashing to the dirt below.

At least I was hidden. Jethro wouldn't find me, and by the time we returned to Hawksridge, I would've torn out my heart and destroyed all notions of having feelings for him.

I would do what was necessary. What was right.

I just hope I have the strength to do it over and over again.

Taking a deep breath, I drifted further into the gloom. I liked my hiding spot. I never wanted to leave.

You can hide from him, but you can't hide from your feelings.

"Shut up," I scolded myself. "Don't think about him. Not anymore."

"If it's me you're thinking about—I command you to ignore your advice."

My heart flew into my mouth. I spun around.

Big mistake.

Jethro stood behind me. Scuffs stained his tan jodhpurs and mud splattered his polished high boots. He'd rolled up the cuffs of his billowy sleeve shirt and removed the velvet waistcoat revealing the shadows of his stomach beneath the translucent fabric. His five o'clock shadow was rough and ragged while the bones of his face spoke of stark desire and even starker emotion.

My entire body stiffened. My lungs refused to operate, suffocating me inch by inch.

His eyes met mine and everything we'd been avoiding crackled with uncontrolled potency. The unseen force was tangible, powerful—almost visible with ribbons of lust that pebbled my nipples and sent a clench of furious desire through my core.

His breathing escalated as we stood locked in place, bound together by the swirling cloud of need. We didn't speak—we *couldn't* speak.

His tongue licked his bottom lip.

Our eyes refused to unlock. The more we stared, the deeper our connection became.

I couldn't look away.

His smell of musk and leather shoved me from my dangerous precipice, and I slid down and down into scandal.

I'm not falling for him.

I've already fallen.

Jethro sucked in a breath, his fingers opening and closing by his sides.

I couldn't go on like this. Feeling this way. Hating and loving this way.

I couldn't *lie* anymore.

My heartbeat drummed in my ears, behind my eyes, in my every fingertip. My tattoo blazed, the diamond collar tightened, and I knew out of everything that had happened, after everything the Hawks had done, this was the moment where I lost.

Right here.

Right now.

This was why I couldn't run.

This desire.

This fate.

I fell in love.

I turned my back on everyone but myself.

I gave up any notion of ever leaving.

I moaned low in my chest.

Such a simple, subtle whisper.

But it was the starting gun to the explosion that was imminent between us.

The air went up in flames, gusts of heat erupted as passion singed my very soul.

Jethro moved.

He propelled himself into me, his large hands capturing my cheeks and holding me prisoner as he walked me backward until I stumbled against the scaffolding.

His touch was a bonfire. His hold was freedom and a cage all at once.

His forehead crashed against mine, his nose kissing my nose, his breath replacing my breath.

In that simple fusion of flavour and souls, we gave up. We gave in. We answered the same pounding conclusion—the same unmentionable dilemma.

We can't do this anymore.

His head tilted and I trembled in his hold as his fingers dug painfully into my cheekbones. I panted for his kiss. I moaned for it. Almost cried for it.

But he paused for an eternity, breathing hard and fast as if he couldn't believe the preciousness of what was occurring.

This was a gift. A charm. A wish come true.

I'd become enraptured by my capturer. My tormentor. My would-be murderer. I only had eyes for him. My heart only beat for him.

Where does that leave me?

What does this mean?

Jethro groaned, his touch trembling as if he'd heard my silent questions.

I should've had more self-control. I should've found a way to stop this.

But I shoved away my fears and willingly slid the final slope into madness.

I arched my chin, grazing my lips against his.

He froze.

Then, he melted.

His fingers slinked from my cheeks to the back of my skull. I cried out as his tongue tore into my mouth and his hands fisted in my hair. With fingers full of my black strands, he tugged my head back, forcing me to open wider, kiss deeper—give him everything.

I'd like to say I retained some resemblance of myself. I'd like to admit that, while I'd fallen, I still knew who I was.

But that would've been a lie.

There was no me without him.

No Nila without Jethro.

No Threads without Kite.

I knew that now.

And it butchered me in ways no threats or torture ever could.

Tears leaked from my eyes as our lips danced and tongues tangoed.

Our murmurs and moans intertwined until the serenade of our desire overshadowed the music from outside and our racing heartbeats. Every sweep of his taste left a glowing fire around my heart, my skin, my soul.

He demanded everything but gave more in return.

In my arms, I held the *real* Jethro. The one I'd seen but never believed was true. He was strong and brilliant and kind.

And he cared for me. So much.

Never untangling our lips, Jethro bent a little and gathered the material of my dress. Shoving it upward, he groaned as I wriggled and helped, forcing the fabric to bunch around my waist.

He froze as he found the lace garter and wickedly sharp dirk. His eyebrow raised; very slowly, he slid the blade from against my flesh and held it in his fingertips.

I tensed, daring him to berate me for such precautions.

His mouth opened to speak then his eyes darkened with approval. "Use this wisely—if you need to." Throwing the blade to jab upright in the dirt, he murmured, "But I'll never give you a reason to use it on me."

We fell together again. Our lips melded into one slippery seal. I conquered his body—running my fingers over every inch of him. His nipples peaked as I stroked them beneath his shirt and his back bowed as I reached down and cupped his hot erection.

Sweat slicked our skin as our finesse perished, turning into fumbling urgency.

With swift hands, Jethro shoved my knickers to my ankles and waited as I kicked them away.

His eyes incinerated me as he grabbed my arse and hoisted me, pinning me in his arms against the scaffolding.

His lips claimed mine again, eating my every moan. I pressed my fingers into his rock hard biceps, relishing in his strength. Then I lowered my touch to undo the button and zipper of his jodhpurs.

His forehead furrowed as my fingers slid inside the dark heat of his boxer-briefs and captured his scalding cock.

"I'm going to fill you," he murmured, thrusting into my hand. "I'm going to give you what I've been told all my life I couldn't give."

I bit my lip as I fumbled with pushing the tight material over his hips. I didn't need to ask what he couldn't give me.

It was obvious.

It wasn't physical or even emotional.

It was more than that.

The catalyst of what made us human.

The ability to adore.

"I want to spill inside you, Nila."

My eyes snapped shut. My body sung with dark music, twisting me, moulding me into some wanton creature. I opened my eyes and kissed him. "What are you waiting for?"

He positioned me so he could hold me with one arm. With his free hand, Jethro cupped my cheek, running a calloused finger across my lips. "Nothing…not anymore."

My blood turned into a river of molten hunger.

With fumbling hands, I freed his cock, running my thumb over his slippery crown.

Jethro threw his head back, rocking into my palm.

My mouth watered to lick at the glistening sweat at the base of his throat.

I stroked him, harder and faster as pleasure hijacked my body.

Jethro shook his head, his eyes squeezed closed. "Stop. I'm too close…too fucking close." His hands clutched at my arse again, spreading me shamelessly, presenting my wet pussy that was so close to his cock.

"Guide me inside you." His eyes flashed. "Please, Nila. Let me fuck you."

Unashamedly, I opened my legs wider.

Jethro breathed in my ear. "Today, you're all mine."

I bit his lobe, clamping my teeth harder than I intended. He flinched as I whispered, "Not just for today."

His body shuddered. His movements became jilted and eager.

Without a sound, I positioned his cock between my legs and lowered a fraction, angling him inside.

Oh, God.

My eyes rolled back as Jethro growled, "Fuck, you feel so right."

The words wrenched me from my stupor, granting me another clue.

I didn't feel good or wet or warm—or any manner of things a man might say to a woman as he entered her.

I felt *right*.

Right to him.

Home to him.

Sucking in a breath, he thrust, sliding inside me.

The friction of the scaffold behind me bruised my spine as Jethro held me firmer in his arms. Instinct made me wrap my legs around his hips as he buried himself deeper and deeper.

He groaned as I rocked on him. My desire stole the pain of his size, twisting it into a heady aphrodisiac that made me cry out with longing.

Every inch of him invaded me—stretching me, claiming me.

Jethro bit my neck, trailing teeth down oversensitive skin. "I belong in you."

I shuddered as his hips pulsed. I couldn't agree more.

His arms tightened as he secured me in his grip; his legs spread further to balance. I knew he was preparing himself for an unrelenting pace, and my unrequited orgasm bloomed into being, eager, aching.

He thrust particularly hard, his muscled stomach kissing mine with every stroke.

My heart twisted deliciously. I hooked my arms around his neck, holding on and presenting myself completely to this man who held my soul.

Then everything else faded.

Hawks, Weavers, and all things twisted between us.

It was just me and Jethro. Heat and need.

He drove into me with powerful strokes, pressing me relentlessly against the scaffolding. My shoulder blades screamed for mercy, but my pussy begged for more.

I wanted punishment for falling for him.

I needed chastising for going against everything I'd believed.

Jethro seemed to understand. Our eyes locked and we drove each other on. Riding each other's body, hard and brutal.

I lost myself in the rhythm, sinking my fingers into his thick hair. Tugging his mouth to mine, I kissed him deep.

Our breaths became one; the ache inside my womb increased until I flamed with urgency to shatter. The pain of riding on the knife-edge of an orgasm layered the pleasure, turning it into a sharp almost unbearable delight.

Jethro dug his fingers into my arse, driving harder. His voice betrayed where his thoughts were. "Only once." He grunted as he increased his rhythm. "Only once can I be this free."

I couldn't think straight. I was entranced, mesmerised.

What does he mean?

A loud groan wrenched from Jethro's chest as his cock thickened inside me. His shoulders bunched as he bounced me faster in his arms.

My muscles tightened as bands of bliss prepared to release.

Jethro growled, capturing my mouth. His tongue pulsed savagely in time with his hips. He stole my thoughts. I lavished in the rushing hotness of my blood. Gushing, pushing into my core.

My heart bucked in my chest; I couldn't get enough oxygen. I moaned, tearing myself from his lips to bite his shoulder. His arms trembled holding my weight. He sucked in a breath. "Fuck, Nila. I can't—I'm gonna…"

I knew where he was. He was in the dark abyss—the depth of pain where he normally lived. Only in the darkness existed stars and comets and lightning bolts just waiting to shatter and shower us with light.

"Give me everything…" My legs curled around his hips, driving him up the final cliff. I impaled myself as hard and as deep as I could.

"Christ." His face tensed. He gave up.

I followed him.

Our rhythm turned frenzied, fucking and rutting and taking everything we could.

"I'm with you," I murmured just as my orgasm stole my voice and hurled me into the cacophony of explosions.

Jethro's eyes opened; we drowned in each other. His golden irises glimmered with everything he couldn't say. The truth was a blazing thing, sharpening the bands of release, twisting my orgasm into something catastrophic.

I screamed.

It was the only thing I could do to expel the pleasure inside.

I was swept away on a galaxy of popping stars. Starburst after starburst, comet after comet. I shattered utterly and completely.

Jethro cried out, pressing his forehead against mine as hotness spilled inside. His body quaked as wave after wave of cum filled me. The tender ache in my womb both calmed and strengthened, welcoming him into my body.

He'd come inside me.

For the first time.

On some basic level, I owned him. He'd mixed himself with me. He could never take that back.

He was mine as much as I was his.

Now and for always.

Something else could be yours for being so stupid.

I could get pregnant.

My heart thudded with panic, but it was overshadowed by lingering waves of pleasure. I would have to deal with that—but not yet.

Not now.

It seemed as if our release went on forever, but it was only a few moments. A few scrumptious moments that healed and broke us.

After the ebbs of orgasm faded, I uncramped my toes and sighed.

Jethro unlocked his arms and withdrew. Wetness slid down my inner thigh as I puddled down his heated body. I could barely stand.

Jethro shivered, tucking his glistening cock back into his boxer-briefs and zipping up his trousers. He was pulling away already. There was no chance I would let him. He couldn't give me what he did and then shut down.

Straightening my dress and scooping my knickers and dirk from the floor, I said, "You know, don't you?"

He stilled. "Know what?"

"What I was thinking about as you found me."

I wasn't prepared for the way his face softened or how his eyes turned into a warm sunrise of caring. "Yes. I know."

My heart pitter-pattered with fear. Would he use it as a tool to hurt me further or would he honour that my feelings were sacred and not to be toyed with?

He ran a hand through his hair before cupping my cheek and smiling sadly. "Thank you, Nila. Thank you for what you've just given me."

With a single kiss and a heavy sigh, he disappeared.

THAT NIGHT I had no urge to see Jasmine.

No urge to fix myself or try to find my ice.

I had no desire to change or hide or do any manner of things I'd done all my life to exist within my household.

I was grateful.

Beyond thankful.

She cares for me.

I'd felt it.

I'd lived it.

She'd poured the truth down my throat and taken all the wrongness inside away.

I'd never been so happy than when I'd slid inside her. Never been so completely content holding her in my arms.

I lay in bed and smiled, just for the beauty of smiling.

I was at peace…for the first time.

The only time.

I was just…*me*.

Jasmine was right.

Nila had the power to cure me.

She held something that after today I doubted I could ever live without.

To be cared for so deeply.

To be wanted so fiercely.

Despite all my faults and downfalls, she welcomed me.

She gave me a sanctuary deep enough and pure enough to hide in.

My eyes burned with thanks. I wanted to shower her with gifts and promises. I relived the intoxicating joy of finding something so treasured.

You came inside her.

My heart skipped at the thought. It was stupid of me to be so reckless, but in that moment, I couldn't care less.

It was perfect. I had to come inside her. I wouldn't change a thing.

Being with Nila today had allowed me to demolish my walls—be strong enough to drop my guard and take her with nothing bared.

I gave her the *truth*.

The truth of who I was.

And in return, she gave me the strength to believe there might be a way after all.

I might not have to continue hiding.

I might finally be free.

MY OLD HEART was broken.

It'd been replaced with something not of flesh and blood but diamond and immortality.

I'd fallen for a smuggler, a biker—a fiend.

I'd fallen for a boy from my past, a man from my future—a friend.

For four days after the polo match, I didn't see Jethro. I didn't try to find him or turn on my phone to message him. We had things to talk about, but I liked the newly blossomed connection too much to overthink it.

I missed him but understood him.

Understood what he'd be going through.

For four days, I spent most of my time sewing and cutting out patterns for a sequence of gowns that would be the headline pieces of my new design. On a daily basis, my mind hurled profanities at me; reminding me that I lived on borrowed time. That the Hawks were not to be trusted. That I should run and never look back.

But my heart argued just as loudly. Encouraging me to believe in what I'd found with Jethro. To trust that I had the power to change our fate. To give us a bit more time.

I didn't know how yet, but there could be a happy ending.

There has to be.

Hawksridge Hall was quiet—more so than normal. Most of the Black Diamond brothers, including the Hawks, were busy with a large shipment that I'd heard held a pink diamond weighing in excess of eighteen carats.

I'd lingered in the dining room long enough to know that such a stone was almost priceless and would fetch untold millions on the black market.

At night, I slept in my luxurious bed and pondered all things Jethro. I became self-absorbed—completely wrapped up in my feelings for him.

A small part of me hated the woman I'd become. The old Nila would never have removed herself so completely from her family—especially Vaughn.

But at the same time—they removed me.

And Jethro had taken me in.

However, there was no denying that my soul was torn and bruised.

Jethro had given me everything beneath the grandstand that day, and by doing so, he robbed me of my hate and the power of injustice that kept me fighting every day.

It wasn't fair.

It wasn't right.

But there was no changing the will of a Weaver's heart.

I was alone now. More so than when I'd first arrived.

I would never be welcomed back with my family, never be able to return home.

Jethro had successfully torn me from my past, stripped me of my mind, and abducted my heart.

I wasn't okay with that.

I couldn't be.

And that was why I had to do the same to him.

I stroked the diamonds around my neck. I'd come here believing I would never be strong enough to fight. But unbeknownst to Cut, he'd brought a disease into his home. Day-by-day, I undermined his foundations, stealing what was his from beneath him.

I had the tools to continue to wreak havoc…*all but one, that is.*

I needed one last thing to make my arsenal complete.

It was time to know where Jethro disappeared to.

It's time to find out what exists behind the door on the second floor.

I looked at the clock above the fish tank in my room. Just past midnight.

I'd heard the men rumble off in a smog of motorcycle smoke an hour ago. If there were any night to investigate—tonight was it.

The corridors would be empty, and Daniel would be far away from delivering his threats of harm.

Resolution filled my veins. I sat up in bed and swung my legs over the side.

It took me two minutes to pull on a pair of yoga pants and slip into an old hoody before collecting my ruby-encrusted dirk and shoving it down my waistband.

With my heart thundering, I slipped out the door and padded down the corridor.

My ears strained for night prowlers. I tiptoed to every corner and dashed quickly past cameras blinking above the large tapestries.

Hawksridge Hall breathed deep and dreamless—vacant of its usual inhabitations, letting me slink beneath the moonlight undisturbed.

I found the spiral staircase where Jethro had dragged me up and scurried to the top as fast as I could. If I stood at the bottom and deliberated, my bravery might desert me.

My fingertip itched, almost as if it knew this was the floor where Jethro had etched his initials into my skin.

I peered above the paintings, locking onto the flashing red lights of yet more cameras. There seemed to be more on this level…protecting something. Protecting what?

I did my best to walk beneath them, to try to stay out of range, but I didn't know the first thing about dodging a security feed.

Jethro would know where I'd been.

He'd be able to watch my every recorded movement. And even though I feared the retribution I might face, it didn't stop me from sneaking to the door he'd knocked on.

The moment I stood outside, my heart switched from pounding to frantic.

What the hell are you doing?

What did I think I would do? Knock and ask politely why Jethro came up here when he ran from me? Did I perhaps think I could turn invisible and snoop around a room while the woman I'd heard slumbered?

You're an idiot.

I stood there dumbstruck. I should never have come.

My lungs stuck together as something rustled on the other side of the door. A soft light seeped through the crack below, bathing the carpet in a warm glow.

I swallowed my yelp as a shadow interrupted the light, pausing the same way I had.

I took a step back. *Stupid. So stupid, Nila.*

No one in this house was safe to go visiting late at night. I wanted to slap myself for being so stupid. I'd put myself in moronic danger.

My fingers reached for my pilfered knife.

I turned to leave, fear dousing my blood with ice.

The sooner I was back in my quarters, the safer I would be.

"You can come in, you know," a quiet feminine voice said.

I froze.

No one spoke, waiting for the other.

A never-ending minute ticked past before the voice came again. "I won't tell and I won't hurt you. I can see you lurking outside my door. I have a camera mounted outside, so unless you want to run and pretend this never happened, I suggest you come in before my brothers or father find you up here."

My stomach rolled; a sickening wave of vertigo crippled me. I stumbled forward, grasping at the wall.

I sucked in large breaths, repeating Vaughn's poem for me.

Find an anchor, hold on tight.

Do that and you'll be alright.

The spell disappeared as quickly as it had arrived. It pissed me off. I thought I'd learned to control them better. Turned out my body was toying with me. Making me believe I had one less problem to worry about, when in reality, it was just biding its time.

"You don't look well. Come in. Please. Let's talk." The soft voice encouraged and seduced and I craved somewhere to sit for a moment.

Gritting my teeth, I pressed down on the door handle and entered the room where Jethro visited.

My eyes darted around the large space. Lemons and greys and colourful carpets. Sweeping fleur-de-lis silver curtains framed a huge wraparound window with a comfy seat big enough for a whole family of bookworms to curl up on and read.

"You must be the new Weaver."

I bit my lip, spinning on the spot. I missed her in the first sweep. She'd been so still, so well hidden in the welcoming décor.

I found her sitting beside her bed in a large chair covered by a coral blanket. "You needn't fear. I'll delete the recording. No one will know you came here."

I should've relaxed in gratitude. Instead, I stiffened.

I stared at the female equivalent of Jethro. Out of all of Jethro's siblings, his sister looked the most like him. Jethro was the diamond—sharp, faceted, and so pristinely perfect he shot rainbows from every angle. This woman was the mirror image. Her dark hair was sliced with precision, hanging like a silk curtain just past her jaw. Her eyes were more bronze than gold while her round cheeks and full lips were the direct contradiction of sweet but sultry.

I drifted forward, stumbling a little as my vertigo played with the outskirts of my vision.

The woman didn't move, just waited for me to go to her.

Her fingers locked together in her lap, her entire lower half covered by the plush blanket.

When I stood awkwardly in front of her, she motioned toward her bed. The covers hadn't been turned down and it didn't look slept in. The crisp yellow of her linen looked like a lemon meringue pie and just as delicious.

"Sit, please."

I sat. Not because of her order, but because my wobbly legs refused to stand any longer. Who was this woman, and why did she look at me as if she knew everything about me?

I blushed.

Everything?

God, I hoped not. How could I face Jethro's sister if she knew how much I wanted him? How could I look her in the eye knowing I'd had her brother inside me, and despite my conflicted emotions, wanted him every second of every damn day?

"Do you talk or did you make a vow of silence before entering my room?" The woman cocked her head, her hair cascading perfectly in glossy heaviness.

Shaking my head, I swallowed. "No. No, vow."

We stared at each other. Her assessing me and me assessing her. Two women of similar age, with a man in the centre polluting our right to be strangers. We'd only just met, but whatever we said would be weighed and found wanting, knowing we weren't on equal footing.

The thought depressed me.

She held a permanent place in Jethro's life. He openly adored her—I could tell just by looking at her.

I was jealous.

I was sad and happy at the same time.

I hadn't come here looking to make a friend, but I hadn't come here expecting to find her, either.

"Should we start simple or would you rather get to the heart of the matter?"

I shifted higher on her bed. "I think starting with the truth would be more beneficial. Don't you?"

A ghost of a smile tilted her lips. "Ah, now I get it."

"Get what?"

She narrowed her eyes. "Why my brother is struggling."

My heart flip-flopped. "Jethro?"

She nodded.

"How is he struggling?" I didn't dare hope for an answer. Could it truly be that easy?

The woman laughed quietly. "You truly do go for the heart."

What does that mean?

Was it a simple turn of phrase playing on her last words or had Jethro said I'd captured his heart? I'd tried to ensnare him with my games of seduction and beguile. But perhaps by giving him my love…I'd stolen his in return?

Could that be true?

Forcing myself to stay present, I asked, "Who are you?"

The woman leaned forward, extending her hand. "I'm Jasmine."

Mirroring her, I looped my fingers around hers, and we shook slowly, still sizing each other up like an untrusted opponent.

"You're his sister," I whispered, breaking our touch and placing my hands in my lap.

"I'm many men's sister."

"You know who I mean."

She leaned back, sighing a little. "Yes, lucky for you, I do know who you mean. Let's get the introductions out of the way, shall we?" Running French-tipped fingernails through her hair, she recited, "I'm second born to Bryan and Rose Hawk. I chased my older brother into the world as soon as possible, and that fact alone makes us closer than my other two siblings. I love him more than I love myself, and I know what he lives with every day with being the firstborn of a family so steeped in tradition and persecution that it's become an unhealthy combination. I know what you've done to him, and as much as I want to hate you for smashing apart his world and making him struggle more than I've ever seen, I can't."

I couldn't breathe properly. Like a drowning person only interested in air, I was only interested in what Jasmine had to say about her brother. "What does he struggle with? And how did my arrival have anything to do with what's happened to him?"

Her forehead furrowed as her hands fisted in her lap. "Don't play coy in my domain, Nila Weaver. Don't come in here and fish for information on my beloved brother in the hope to twist it into a weapon. I don't hate you, but it doesn't mean I won't if you continue to torture him."

Wow, what?

I held up my hands in surrender. "I don't want to hurt him."

Liar.

I wanted to hurt him by manipulating him to go against his family—to choose me above all others. Even his sister.

Did that make me a hateful person? To want to be the one person he loved more than anyone?

"I…I—" *I have feelings for him.*

The truth danced on my tongue, but I couldn't admit it. I'd barely admitted it to myself, let alone a woman who looked at me with curiosity and disdain.

Jasmine waved away my fumble. "Regardless, you've already hurt him. And as much as I would like to stop you, it's your burden now, as much as mine."

"Burden?"

My mind raced, wishing I knew just what we were discussing.

"You're the one who's forced him to face an alternative to the way he's been living. Thanks to you, the other method of coping is no longer working. It's up to you to give him another."

Anger took over my confusion. How dare she layer me with responsibility when I was nothing more than a captive in her home? "I think you're forgetting one important fact. I'm a prisoner of your father's. I'm a toy for your brother. I have no future thanks to your insane family and have no wish to help one of you."

Lying again, Nila.

I just hoped she swallowed my fibs better than her brother did.

Jasmine leaned forward. It was only subtle, a gentle inclining bringing us closer together, yet I felt her encroachment in every cell. This woman rippled with indignation and righteousness when it came to Jethro. Her unwavering devotion was both humbling and terrifying. "Too late. You're the one who coaxed him into your bed. He fought you. But, from woman to woman, he wasn't strong enough for you. And that excites and upsets me."

My shoulders slouched; her riddles made my head hurt. "What exactly is wrong with him? Why does he think he can only live if he surrounds himself in ice and removes himself from any emotion whatsoever?"

Jasmine sniffed. "That's his secret to tell, and I will not break his trust. And you don't understand—there is nothing wrong with him. He's perfect. Just…not perfect for this family."

"You're of the same blood and seem very close. Are you saying you aren't fit for this family, either?"

Jasmine smiled. "Smart. I suppose you could say that. Jethro and I are a different breed. Born and bred to the same parents but we inherited a different kind of madness than the rest of my relations."

I didn't want to hurt her, but I needed to know. In over a month that I'd been a ward of the Hawks, Jasmine was the first woman I'd come across, not counting the maids. Why was that?

"Does your mother live here, too?"

Jasmine pursed her lips. "My mother is of no consequence. Besides, I'm the protégé of Bonnie Hawk. I have more than enough maternal guidance."

That was the second time I'd heard of Bonnie Hawk. Kes had told me she was in charge of the family's expenses—his grandmother.

As much as I wanted to meet this elusive woman who held an entire family of men under her thumb, I wanted to stay under her notice for as long as possible.

We sat in silence for a time, before Jasmine said, "You should go. And don't tell Jethro you came to see me. He wouldn't handle that well."

"Why?"

She stared for a long moment, as if deciding what to divulge. Finally, she said, "Because in his mind, we are both his. Both under his protection and both in our own little pockets of reality where he can cope. If he knew we'd met and discussed him, the pressure of keeping us protected would increase."

I felt like a parrot as I asked again, "Why?"

"Because, Nila Weaver, he's been raised having no one to protect him and living in a world where just the hint of being who he truly was meant he could be gone tomorrow. Ever since he could understand the differences between him and our father, he's lived with the shadow of his own mortality. Cut wouldn't hesitate, you see…"

She swallowed, a sudden flare of pain filling her gaze. "He's lived twenty-nine years hiding, because if he didn't, one day he'd be gone and he'd leave me all alone. Knowing that we had met would only give him something else to fear."

My heart pounded with every word she spoke. "Fear?"

Jasmine hunched, her voice drifting to a fateful whisper. "Fear what we spoke about. Fear how much of his nature came to light. Fear just how much you knew, because ultimately, it's not him who has the power to destroy you—but you who has the power to destroy him."

By the time I crawled into my bed, my head hadn't stopped spinning.

Jasmine was prickly and wise—an enigma who adored her brother and would do anything to protect him.

Her words were an invitation but also a threat to stay away.

Would she soften if she knew I'd fallen for him?

Would she help me understand him—grant me the help I needed to claim Jethro for my own?

She was as confusing as her brother.

And I knew our conversation hadn't ended. I would return. Again and again.

Until I learned the truth.

But I also had other questions—many, many questions.

It hadn't escaped my notice that she sewed. There'd been an in-progress cross-stitch on her bed, along with a paper chart folded haphazardly. Was she like me and enjoyed the simple creation…or…was it more sinister?

Could she be more Weaver than Hawk?

And if she was…what did that mean?

I tossed and turned, unable to shut off the voices inside my head forming outlandish conclusions.

Just as the dawn stole the stars, sleep finally crept over me.

But it wasn't restful.

Yet more questions chased me into dreamland.
Why did Jasmine never come down from her room?
And who truly wielded the power of the Hawks?

Jethro

THE WEEK AFTER the polo match passed uneventfully.

Tuesday, I went for a hunt on Wings.

Wednesday, I saw Nila at breakfast before leaving to hide in my office until sundown.

Thursday, I was out late dealing with a special shipment of pink diamonds already purchased and due for delivery to a private yacht docked for one night in Southhampton.

Friday, I tried one last time to 'fix' myself, but Jasmine was right. The ice no longer worked, no matter what I did.

But I had a better option—a new regimen that Nila had selflessly given me.

Saturday, I spent the afternoon with Kes and the Diamond brothers playing poker in the billiards room of the Hall—deliberately giving my heart time to adjust to the life-shattering change of what'd happened between Nila and me.

I was ready to admit to myself that my world had changed.

It was time to face what I'd been running from all my life.

However, the next day smashed my hopes and dreams and hurled me right back into the darkness where I belonged.

The last day of the week...the day that belonged to love and togetherness, only brought pain and sadness.

Sunday, I received the worst news of all.

"Jethro, come with me, please." Cut popped his head into my

bachelor wing.

I jumped as if I'd been caught red-handed, just like I'd done most of my life whenever he'd appeared out of nowhere. Sliding a pillow over the tiny sharp knife I used to open the old cuts on my soles, I glowered at my unwanted visitor. "Come where?"

Nila had given me hope that soon I could stop hurting myself in such a way, but until I could be sure what she felt for me was irreversible, I had to use something to keep me in check.

Ice wasn't working—pain would have to do.

Cut's gaze fell to my scarred feet. "Do you need a session?"

The concern in his eyes was the key ingredient to how he'd been controlling me for so many years. He made me believe that he was there for me. That he wanted to help me. That I was the chosen one and deserved to inherit all that he had to give.

Of course, it was all bullshit.

Neither of us could erase what had happened between us that night. The night where we used Jasmine so terribly in a fixing session that we'd stepped over an uncrossable line. I'd refused. Over and over and over again.

He'd pushed and pushed and pushed.

I'd snapped.

I'd almost killed him.

And he'd said the words that were a noose around my neck and shackles around my feet for the rest of my days.

"Do you think your life is a gift? Do you think I can't take it away? I've been so fucking close to killing you, boy. A fraction away from ending the embarrassment of knowing what you are. I only hesitate because I believe you can change. You carry my blood. You cannot be such a disgrace. I won't let you be such a disgrace."

I was only alive because he hoped he'd finally cure me. Every year that passed, he hovered over the birthday cake made especially for his firstborn and contemplated killing me with cyanide.

Or a hunting accident.

Or a shipment gone wrong.

So many ways to dispatch me. I lived in constant awareness of traps and mercenaries ready to steal my God-given right to breathe.

All because I didn't conform.

He also told me what would happen if he *did* kill me. What he would do to not just Jasmine but Kestrel, Daniel, and anyone else I held dear—not that there were many. He couldn't care less if it meant he would be left with no heir. He believed he was invincible and lacked the fundamental trait of a father: love.

He didn't love his children. Shit, he didn't even like us.

Therefore, we were disposable if we displeased him.

That sort of panic...that sort of fear...continued to have a hold on me. No matter my age or strength—I'd lived beneath the shadow of death for so long, I didn't know any other way.

I was a fucking idiot.

Placing my feet into a pair of moccasins, I shook my head. "Thank you for your concern. But I'm fine."

Cut cocked his head. "You're a terrible liar."

Gritting my teeth, I stood up and smoothed down my black t-shirt. I wore no colour today—only black. I should've known that the colour would bring only darkness.

"I'm still following your orders. I'm still loyal."

Cut smiled coldly. "For now." He ran his fingers around his mouth, eyeing me up and down. "However, we shall see if you pass the next test."

My heart lurched. Tests weren't new. I'd been made to complete many of them as I grew—to prove that a son like me could become a man like him.

"What did you have in mind?"

Skinning an animal while it's still alive?

Hurting another one of the club whores?

Cut's smile sent shivers down my back. "You'll see."

I hated when he did this. I never knew if he was walking me out like a horse to be shot or if he genuinely wanted to prove to himself and to me that I was getting better.

For a few years, I'd been good. I'd found how to hide myself in blizzards and snow and be everything he wanted me to be.

That was before he informed me that Nila was my twenty-ninth birthday present. There'd been no cake that year—no threat of cyanide.

Only the detonation of my soul in the form of a woman I couldn't deny.

Forcing a smile, I asked, "What about some father and son time? Forget the test. Let's go for a ride. Talk business."

Over the years, he'd schooled me on the running of the empire. Those sessions were the only time he relaxed and enjoyed interacting with me. Although, he wasn't ready to give up his power—I could tell.

Regardless that our customs stated it would be mine soon, I knew it wouldn't be a simple matter of handing over the throne.

"No. I have a much better idea." Cut opened the door wider. "Come on. Let's go."

My knees locked. Something inside told me to refuse. This test would be worse than everything I'd been subjected to.

"Perhaps another time. I have to—"

Go find Nila and indulge in what she feels for me.

What would Jasmine say if she knew I'd achieved the impossible? Nila Weaver liked me...possibly even loved me.

My stomach tangled with my heart. I'd managed to stay away for six days, but I'd reached my limit. I needed to feel her fight, her goodness, her wet hot heat. I needed to forget about my fucked-up existence and live in hers, if only for a moment.

Cut waved his hand. "No. This supersedes whatever you were about to do." Snapping his fingers—a trait I'd adopted—he growled, "Come along. It won't take long."

Hiding my nervousness behind the glacial façade I still managed to invoke around my father, I followed him from my wing.

Wordlessly, we moved through the house. Every step flared the pain in my feet, giving me something to focus on rather than my whirling imagination of what was to come.

The nights were getting longer, encroaching on the sunlight day by day—only seven p.m., yet it was already dusk.

I swallowed my questions as Cut moved purposely out the back door and toward the maintenance barn at the rear of the estate. Most people had a shack that housed a broken lawnmower and a few empty flowerpots.

Not us.

Our shack was the size of a three-bedroom house, resting like a black beetle on the immaculate lawn.

The air temperature bit into my exposed arms as we stalked over the short expanse of grass and disappeared into the musty metallic world of saw-dust shavings and ancient tools.

Along with servants to ensure our daily needs were met, we also had carpenters, electricians, roofers, gardeners, and gamekeepers. Running an estate such as Hawksridge took millions of pounds per year.

The minute we entered, two carpenters who were lathing a chair leg turned off the machine and subtly left the room. Dusk on a Sunday and still the staff worked—our insistence for perfection ran a brutal timeline.

"Good evening, Mr. Hawk," one worker mumbled on his way out. His eyes remained downcast with respect, his shoulders hunched.

Cut wielded a power that made lesser men—including myself—want to run and hide.

When I was in charge, I would change that. I would change many things.

Cut moved deeper into the workshop, peering into the other rooms where paintings waited for restoration. Only once he was sure we were alone did he turn to me to follow.

With unease building in my gut, I did as ordered and moved into the back room where knick-knacks and miscellaneous childhood toys had been dumped.

"What is it that you wanted to discuss?" I asked, standing still in the centre of chaos. Deliberately, I pushed my heel harder against the ground, activating a deeper throb from the new cut. It wasn't that I liked pain. In fact, I hated the stigma and weakness of cutting myself. I didn't get pleasure from it—but I did get relief from my disease by being single-minded and focused.

Cut shrugged out of his leather jacket, placing the embroidered Black Diamond apparel on Jasmine's old nursery cot. His hair was unruly and grey, his jawline sharp and unforgiving.

"Show, not discuss." With a secretive smile, he moved to the large termite-riddled cupboard at the back of the room. He removed an old brass key from his pocket and inserted it into the lock.

As I moved closer, my heart stopped beating.

It couldn't be.

Yet it was.

Cut grabbed the handles of the cupboard and swung the doors wide, revealing what he'd shown me the night of my sixteenth birthday. That same night, he'd made me watch what he did to Emma Weaver. He made me witness video after video of what he'd done to Nila's mother, all while beating me if I ever dared look away.

Sickness rolled in my gut.

My hands balled.

Palms sweated.

Shit. Shit. *Shit.*

Once again, my father had reminded me of my place and how fragile my wants, dreams, and very existence were.

My eyes burned as I drank in the age-old equipment passed down through generations. Shelf after shelf of torturous items used in extracting debts from the Weavers.

Cut's face darkened, motioning me forward when I stayed locked to the floor. "I think it's time you and I had a little chat, Jet." Taking one particular item from the cupboard, I knew what he would make me do.

And I knew whatever love Nila felt for me would vanish like it never existed.

I couldn't move, but it didn't stop Cut from prowling toward me and placing the hated item into my shaking hands. Curling my fingers around the salt shaker, I hated that something so simple could deliver something so unforgivable.

My father murmured, "You have one last chance, Jethro. Use it well."

Ice howled.

Snow fell.

Blizzards blew like fury.

I hung my head and gave in.

Motherfucking shit.

That was yesterday.

A Sunday I would never forget.

Today was Monday.

A Monday that I wished I could erase.

Last Monday had been full of freedom, kisses, and passion; polo and sex and blistering new beginnings.

This Monday was full of mourning and pain. Today was the day I became the true heir to Hawksridge because if I didn't, I doubted I would wake in the morning.

Cut hadn't said as much. But it was what he *didn't* say that made the biggest impression.

Do this or I'll kill you.

Obey me or this is the end.

Cut had seen what I knew he would. He took great pleasure in informing me that he knew I'd fucked Nila. He knew I'd chased after her during half-time at polo, and he knew my allegiances were changing.

It'd been a long fucking night.

After our talk, he'd forced me to go deep, deep inside. He tore away any progress Nila had made with me and filled me with snow once again.

In an odd way, I was grateful.

Grateful because without him tampering with my psyche, there was no way in flying fuck I would've got through today.

I thought I'd had months.

I thought I'd been the one in control of when the next payment would happen, but as always…I was wrong.

Cut had seen my ultimate plan before I'd even finalised the details.

He'd understood my tentative scheming of dragging out the debts until I was thirty. By then, I would've been in charge. By then, I might've found a way to spare Nila's life without losing mine.

I had the Sacramental Pledge over the Debt Inheritance.

I'd put things in place to end this—once and for all.

But none of my forward thinking mattered anymore.

Today was the day Nila paid the Second Debt.

THE MOMENT JETHRO walked into my quarters, I knew.

We'd slept together three times, spent only weeks in each other's company, yet I knew his soul almost as well as I knew my own.

Mystery still shrouded him, still hid so much, but I'd learned to read his body language.

I'd learned how to listen to his heart.

"No," I whispered, clutching the tulle I'd been working on to my chest.

Jethro looked away, his face blank and unfeeling. "Yes."

I didn't need words to tell me what had happened. The truth was far too vivid to ignore.

His father.

His father had shoved him back into the blizzard and slammed the door in his face. He'd done something to him that wedged a canyon between us and left us with only one thing.

The debts.

Our emotions were on hold.

Our connection severed.

My heart sank.

I let the lilac tulle slip through my fingers, destroying the carefully pinned pattern of a ball gown that would be my centre piece of my Rainbow Diamond Collection.

Last night, I'd formulated a few goals. If I intended to stay at Hawksridge, to finish whatever had begun between Jethro and me, I had to give the outside world an explanation.

I had to put an end to the suspicion about what'd happened to me.

People were talking. This morning, I'd turned on my phone and browsed a few websites for what they thought happened to me. Scarily, there were a few very close to the truth—it seemed strange that something so incomprehensible could be guessed at so closely.

Almost as if someone had been telling secrets that they shouldn't.

Vaughn perhaps?

Could he be behind the leaked knowledge? I wanted to ask him but he hadn't replied to my messages. He'd gone completely silent.

Regardless, it didn't matter. I was stuck here, and I had to find some way to deal with what was out there. It was time to announce a new fashion line, and at the same time, put those rumours to rest.

Along with the hunches on my disappearance, I'd also read Jethro's message that he sent the morning of the polo match. His words were sincere but also full of regret. Would his offer to answer my questions via text still stand—even when he looked at me as if he were dead inside?

Pulling extra pins from my cuffs, I shook my head. "Jethro...it's too soon."

I thought I'd have weeks yet...months even. *You didn't think—you hoped.*

If I had known this would happen, I would've gone to him sooner. I would've forced him to face the truth and discuss once and for all what'd happened between us last Monday. Instead, I'd done nothing but work. I didn't wander the premises or go for a run. The constant fear of where Daniel lurked had kept me trapped better than any bars or cage.

Trembles took over my chilled muscles. "Surely there must be a way to stop—"

"Quiet, Ms. Weaver. I have no patience for your begs." Stalking toward me, he growled, "You know what is expected of you."

I searched his gaze for the warmth and golden glow of before.

There was nothing.

Closing the distance, I wrapped my arms around his frigid body. Once again, his extremities were cold. No heat. No liveliness.

"Jethro...please..." Nuzzling into his chest, I willed him to feel my panic, to comprehend how terrified I was of paying another debt.

He balled his hands. "Let me go."

I snuggled closer. "No. Not until you admit that you don't want to do this."

His fingers landed on my shoulders, prying me away from him. "Don't presume to know what I want."

"But it's too soon! The lash marks have barely healed on my back. I need more time."

Time to mentally prepare.

Time to steal you away.

"How do you know the timeline for what will take place?" Leaning forward, he snatched my wrist and dragged me forward. "You don't know a thing about anything, Ms. Weaver. There is no script—no right and wrong when another debt can be taken. It's time."

The cold finality in his voice siphoned into my blood, delivering a vicious vertigo attack. I fell forward as the room flipped upside down.

I cried out as I stumbled, swaying to the side only for Jethro to jerk me upright.

I hated the weakness inside me. I hated that there was no cure.

I would be afflicted all my life.

Is Jethro the same?

Could whatever he suffer be the same as my vertigo? Incurable, unfixable—something accepted as broken and forever unchangeable?

While I swam in sickness, Jethro dragged me over to the ancient armoire where I'd placed my clothes and shoved aside the hangers to reveal the back panel. Pressing hard on the wood, the walnut veneer sprang open, revealing a secret compartment with hanging white calico shifts.

I moaned, trying my damnedest to shove aside the lingering after effects of the attack, and struggled weakly as Jethro turned his attention to my grey blouse.

Without a word, he undid the pearl buttons, quickly and methodically with no hint of sexual interest or burning desire.

My limbs were endlessly heavy. I lamented the unjust fate of my last name as he pushed my stretchy black leggings to the floor.

Leaving me dressed only in a white lace bra and knickers, Jethro snagged a calico shift and dumped it over my head.

I blinked nauseously as he tugged my arms through the holes as if I were a child.

What was going on? Where was the man who'd held me while he came inside me? Where was the softness…the gentleness?

The minute I was dressed, he demanded, "Take off your shoes."

I stared into his gaze, looking for a smidgen of hope. I wanted to reach inside and make him care again.

He stood taller, a flicker of life lighting up his features. "Don't. Just…it's better this way." He sighed heavily. "Please."

I tensed to fight. To argue. But his plea stopped me.

Ironically, I was the one about to be hurt—made to pay a debt I had no notion of—yet he was the one most in pain.

He needed to stay in his shell to remain strong.

Despite my misgivings and terror bubbling faster and faster in my blood, I couldn't take that away from him.

I'd fallen for him. What sort of person would I be if I willingly stripped him bare when he wasn't coping? Even if he'd been tasked to hurt me?

Only a stupid, love-struck one.

Do something, Nila. It's you or him.

Wrong.

Grabbing his hand, I pressed our tattooed indexes together and summoned all my courage. "We're in this together. You told me so yourself."

He tensed; his face twisted with unmentionable emotion. Hanging his head, he nodded. "Together."

"In that case, do what you need to do."

We stood awkwardly, both wanting to say things that would break the fragile bravery of the moment, but neither strong enough.

Finally, he nodded, and pointed at my shoes.

I didn't argue or reply.

Kicking off my jewelled flip-flops, Jethro led me silently out the door and through the Hall.

Every footfall sent my heart higher and higher until every terrified beat clawed at the back of my throat. I'd been scared in my life. I'd bawled my eyes out when Vaughn had almost drowned at the beach. I'd become almost comatose with terror when I knew I'd never see my mother again.

But this…this marching toward the Second Debt turned my blood into tar. I moved as if I were underwater, suffering a terrible dream I couldn't wake from.

I wanted my twin. I wanted him to make it better.

Leaving the Hall behind, Jethro continued to march me over the freshly mowed lawn, past the stables and kennels where Squirrel and a few foxhounds lounged in the autumn sun, and over the hill.

His footsteps were interspersed with an occasional limp—barely noticeable. Was he hurt?

The shift I wore protected me from nothing. The breeze disappeared up the sleeves and howled around my midriff, creating a mini cyclone within my dress.

My trembles ratcheted higher as goosebumps kissed my flesh.

"What—what will happen?" I asked, forcing myself to stay strong and stoic.

Jethro didn't reply, only increased his pace until we crested the small incline. The moment we stood on the ridge, I had the answer to my question.

Before us was the lake where Cut and his sons had fished for trout on his birthday. It was a large manmade creation in the shape of a kidney. Willow trees and rushes graced its banks, weeping their fronds into the murky depths.

It would've been peaceful—a perfect place for a picnic or a lazy afternoon with a book.

But not today.

Today, its shoreline didn't welcome ducks and geese, but an audience all dressed in black.

Cut, Kes, and Daniel waited with unreadable stares as Jethro propelled me down the grassy mound and closer to my fate.

Cut seemed happier than I'd seen him since I'd arrived, and Daniel sucked on a beer as if we were at his favourite ballgame. Kes had the decency to hide his true feelings behind his mysterious secrecy. His face drawn and blank.

Then my eyes fell on the woman before them.

Bonnie Hawk.

The name came to me as surely as if she wore a name tag. This was the elusive grandmother—the ruler of Hawksridge Hall.

Her lips pursed as if my presence offended her. Her papery hands with vivid blue veins remained clutched in her lap. Her white hair glowed as she sat regally, poised better than any young debutant, not an elderly crone. The chair she sat in matched her bearing, looking like a morbid throne with black velvet and twilled claw-foot legs.

A staff member stood beside her with a parasol, drenching the dame in shade from the noonday sunshine.

It hurt to think the sun beamed upon such a place. It didn't pick favourites when casting its golden rays—whether it be innocent or guilty—it shone regardless.

I looked up into the ball of burning gas, singeing my retinas and begging the sun to erase all memory of today.

Bonnie sniffed, raising her chin.

Cut stepped forward, clasping his hands in glee. "Hello, Ms. Weaver. So kind of you to join us."

"I didn't exactly have a choice." I shuddered, no longer able to fight the terror lurking on the outskirts of my mind. Claws of horror sank deep inside me, dragging me further into panic.

Cut grinned, noticing my ashen skin and quaking knees. "No, you didn't. And you have no idea how happy that makes me."

Turning his attention to his son, he said, "Let's begin. Shall we?"

I NODDED.

What else could I do?

If I refused, Kes would step in. If I refused, I would be killed.

My eyes fell on my grandmother. She hoisted her nose higher in the air, waiting for me to start. Cut had deliberately brought Bonnie to watch—to be there if I failed.

I have no intention of failing.

I'd managed to stay cold the moment I stepped into Nila's quarters. Even when she'd looked into my eyes and snuggled into my chest, I hadn't warmed. I intended to remain aloof and removed until it was over.

It was the only way.

Cut stepped back, squeezing his mother's shoulder.

Bonnie Hawk looked up at him, smiling thinly. He was her favourite. But just like her son, she couldn't stand her grandchildren.

Jasmine. She stands Jasmine.

That was true. If there was anyone who'd excelled in this family and played perfectly in the role she'd been given, it was Jaz.

Cut said, "Begin, Jet. Pretend we aren't here if it will make you feel any better."

I held back my snort. I never wanted to forget that they were here. If I did, I'd lose any hope of being icy and slip. I'd find a way to take it easy on Nila and avoid certain parts of this debt—just like I'd done with the First Debt and not freezing her the way I should have.

Today, there would be no leniency. Today, Nila must be strong enough to face the full brunt of what my family would do to her.

Stop avoiding the truth.

What you will do to her. You alone.

In that instant, I wanted to hand the power over to Kes. Make him do it—so Nila would hate him instead of me.

Nila stood quivering beside me. The air was chilly but not cold enough to warrant the chattering of her teeth or blueness of her fingers.

She's petrified.

And for good reason.

"Jethro, I suggest you begin. I'm not getting any younger, boy," Bonnie muttered.

Daniel snickered, gulping down another mouthful of beer. "Snap, snap, old chap."

Kes crossed his arms, locking away his thoughts completely.

I looked to the piece of equipment that had been secured to the pond's banks. It remained covered by a black cape—for now.

Soon, Nila would see what it was, and she would understand what would happen.

But first, I had to be eloquent and deliver the speech I'd been taught to memorize since I'd been told of my role.

Grabbing Nila's arm, I positioned her on the patch of earth that'd been decorated with a thick pouring of salt. I'd done the design. The sunrise had witnessed my artistry as I followed an ancient custom.

Nila's eyes dropped to her feet as I pressed her hard, telling her with actions alone not to move.

"Oh, my God," she murmured, slapping a hand over her mouth.

My wintry ice saved me from feeling anymore of her panic; I locked my muscles as I prepared to recite.

The pentagram she stood in gave a giant hint as to the debt she would be paying.

Her black eyes met mine, her hair whipping around her face, just like it had when she'd found the graves of her ancestors.

It was almost serendipitous that she would pay this debt now—especially after I'd thought that she'd looked like a witch casting a curse on the Hawks.

"As you can see, Ms. Weaver. You stand in a pentacle star. It's well known that the five-pointed star represents the five wounds of Christ. It's been used in the Church for millennia. Yet a reversed pentagram is the symbol of dark magic—a tool wielded by Wiccans and practiced regularly in witchcraft."

My family stared enraptured, even though they knew the tale by heart.

Nila seemed to shrink, her eyes never leaving the thick rivers of salt penning her in a motif of wickedness.

"Your ancestor was found practicing the dark arts, for which she escaped severe punishment. In the 1400's, it was common for poor folk to seek help from those who promised quick riches. They'd be lured into believing a weed would cure boils or a toad would turn them into a prince. Those who had luck with their spell or incantation did more than just seek men or women who practiced magic—they wanted the power for themselves. They became immersed in Wicca and turned their backs on religion.

"Needless to say, they were caught. Their whereabouts would be noted, their stores of dried herbs confiscated, and the sentence no one survived decreed. They were a traitor to their faith, but they would be given a choice—prove their innocence by drowning, or admit to their sins by burning at the stake and returning to the devil they worshiped."

Nila's pasty cheeks shimmered with cascading tears. Her nose went red from cold and she wrapped her arms around herself, partly to ward off the chill but mostly to keep herself from running.

No ropes bound her. She could leave. She could run.

But she also knew we'd catch her and I'd have to add another punishment for her disobedience.

All that I knew. All of it I understood with one look into her glassy eyes.

I even knew she wasn't aware she was crying—completely enthralled and mortified with where my tale would go.

Taking a deep breath, I continued, "All of what I said is true. However, it came with rules—like most things."

Cut nodded as if he'd personally been there and watched the pyres burning.

"Destitute people were caught while those wealthy enough weren't. It didn't mean that women who dined on cakes and tea and employed servants to wash away their crimes didn't dally in potions—far from it. They were the most proficient. They sold their concoctions to other well-to-do housewives and bribed any official who dared to ask questions about their faith."

I made the mistake of looking at Nila again. Her lips parted and a silent word escaped.

Please.

Tearing my gaze away, I forced myself to continue, "Your ancestor was no different, Ms. Weaver. She blatantly did what she wanted. She brewed so-called elixirs and cast so-called curses. And she did it all from the drawing room of the Weaver household—the same household the Hawks cleaned and maintained for her.

"A few years passed where she went undetected, but of course, she made a mistake. She suffered the misfortune of creating a potion for an aristocratic friend's offspring. It didn't work. Her remedy didn't heal the friend's child—it poisoned him."

Nila buried her face in her hands.

"Word got out, and the mayor came knocking. He'd turned a blind eye up until now, but he could no longer ignore her wrongdoings and buckled under the pressure of whispering folk.

"When he arrived to arrest her, Mrs. Weaver announced she'd been doing it under duress. She was a kind, simple woman with no more power in her blood than the next.

"Needless to say, the mayor did not believe her—he'd seen with his own eyes what happened to the boy who'd died from one of her vials. But he was on the Weaver's payroll. If he sent the richest man in town's wife to the stake, he would kiss his extra salary goodbye. But if he didn't bow to the wishes of his parish, he could face the noose in return."

I swallowed, hating the next part. When Bonnie had told me what'd happened, I'd been almost sick with rage. To think that the Weavers got away with such things.

My lips twisted at the ironic truth. Now it was us who got away with murder—right beneath the noses of the law.

"Mrs. Weaver came up with a solution. She promised it would benefit everyone. Everyone but the Hawks, that is."

Nila bowed her head, hunching into herself.

Bonnie snapped, "Listen, girl. Listen to the disgusting actions from the bloodline who birthed you."

Nila's head came up; her shoulders straightened. Her jaw set and she latched her gaze on mine, just waiting for me to continue.

Shoving my fists into my jeans pockets, I said, "She told the mayor a secret...a lie. She said it wasn't *her* practicing, but the hired help's fourteen-year-old daughter. She said she'd caught her red-handed selling potions from the kitchens. She fabricated untruths of how my ancestor's daughter had been swindling and tarnishing the Weavers name for years.

"The mayor was happy with such a tale. He would have someone to answer to the angry mob and at the same time keep his salary. The Weavers gave him a bonus for his loyalty and the poor Hawk daughter was carted away to be thrown into jail to await trial."

Daniel laughed. "Get it, Nila. Do you see where this is going?"

I glowered at him.

Cut snarled, "Shut up, Dan. This is Jet's production. Let him finish."

Daniel sulked, tossing his empty beer bottle into the reeds by his feet.

I sighed; it was almost over.

No, it's not.

I still had to extract the debt.

I hardened my heart, blocking out everything but the next ten minutes. If I sliced up my day and focused on bite-sized pieces, I could get through this.

I *would* get through this.

"For a week, she rotted in the cells with barely food or water. By the time the trial came to pass, she was delirious with hunger and disease. The Hawk daughter pleaded her innocence. She stood before a court of twelve and begged them to see reason. She tore apart every conviction against her and argued her case that any right-minded human would've seen was all Mrs. Weaver's doing. But the truth does not set you free."

Nila twitched as I said it, her eyes flaring with knowledge from our past discussion on the matter.

Looking away, I said, "She was sentenced to burn at the stake at sunrise."

Nila moaned, shaking her head in horror.

Bonnie Hawk muttered, "Now do you see why we hate you so?"

Rushing ahead, I finished, "One saving grace was she was granted a choice. The daughter was told she could prove her innocence or admit her guilt." Moving toward Nila, I wound my fingers in her hair, cursing my heart for tripping as the black strands rippled around my knuckles. "What do you think she chose, Ms. Weaver?" I brushed my nose against her throat, doing my utmost to tame my cock from reacting to her delectable smell. "Fire or water…what would you choose?"

Nila shook harder, her eyes like black orbs of dread. She tried to speak, but a croak came out instead. Licking her lips, she tried again. "Innocence. I would take innocence."

"So, you would prefer to drown by water than be purged by fire?"

Another tear trickled down her cheek. "Yes."

"Yes, what?"

Bracing herself, Nila said loudly, "I would choose water."

I nodded. "Exactly.

"And that's what my ancestor chose as well."

I WAS ABOUT to be drowned.

I was to repent for heinous lies, to prove my innocence from witchcraft that I didn't practice, and perish the way so many innocent girls had done in the past.

In the 1400's, the law system was run by the Church. And the Church had ultimate control. It didn't matter that they sentenced a young girl to death. It didn't matter that she was innocent. Even if she chose trial by water, she would still end up dead.

The proverb from those days came back to haunt me.

Ye innocent will float upon their demise while ye guilty will sink just like their dirty souls.

Both scenarios ended in death.

There was no justice—only a deranged mob looking for entertainment by heckling and ripping a young girl's life apart.

Shaking my head, I tried to rid the images inside my brain.

Jethro vibrated before me, his back to his family, his eyes only for me.

Beneath the golden ice lurked a need for me to understand. To forgive him for what he was about to do.

How could he ask me that when I didn't know if I would survive?

If you do go to your grave today, don't condemn him any more than what he is.

Somehow, I'd gone from martyrdom to just being a martyr—still unable to hurt him—even while he hurt me.

I nodded—or I tried to nod—I was so stiff my body barely moved.

Jethro's nostrils flared. He saw my acknowledgement, my permission to proceed.

You're insane.

Maybe you are a witch.

You seem to believe you're immortal and can't be killed.

That might be true. In that moment, I wished it were true.

With his back straight and legs spread, Jethro asked the question I'd been waiting for. "Do you repent, Ms. Weaver? Do you take ownership of your family's sins and agree to pay the debt?"

I almost collapsed I shook so hard. It was the exact same question Jethro made me answer before extracting the First Debt.

Before I replied, I had a question of my own. Looking directly at Bonnie Hawk, I asked, "When I first arrived, I was told I would be used callously and with no thought. I was told the firstborn son dictated my life and that there would be no rules on what he did with me." My voice wobbled, but I forced myself to go on. "Yet, everything you do follows strict repetition. Re-creating the past over and over again. You're bound by what happened as much as us. Surely you're powerful enough to tear up such guidelines and find it in your hearts to let go."

My hands balled as anger shot fierce and hot. "Let this madness end!"

Bonnie's mouth parted half in amazement, half in joy.

Her hazel eyes twinkled as she leaned forward, pointing a knobbly finger in my direction. "Let's get something straight, young lady. My grandson is bound, as you say, by records kept for hundreds of years. He has to follow each one perfectly. But the rest—anything outside of paying the debts—that is purely at his discretion."

She cocked her chin, looking at Jethro.

He stood frozen.

"*He* is the one who decides if you're to be kept apart or shared. *He* is the one who decides if you deserve leniency for obedience or punishment for insubordination."

Her dry lips pulled back over cavity-riddled teeth. "There is something you don't know, Nila Weaver. And normally I wouldn't tell a guttersnipe like you what conversations go on within my family, but it should make you grateful to know. Do you *want* to know, child?"

The wind stole my hair, snapping it around me like black lightning. Standing in the pentacle seemed to summon powers I didn't have—

transferring ancient magic that should remain dead and buried. The back of my scalp prickled; I inched closer to the edge of the salt, needing to leave. "Yes. I want to know."

Shooting a look at Jethro, I tried to imagine the conversations he had with the people he held most dear. Was there anyone he let himself be free with?

Just his sister.

I knew that from the way Jasmine spoke of him. He lived with a large family yet remained so alone.

Bonnie took a shallow breath. "Jethro came to me a few days after your arrival with a request to keep you to himself."

"Grandmamma—" Jethro began.

Bonnie glared at him. "No. I can tell her. Perhaps she'll obey you better and we can move on before the moon rises."

Jethro's nostrils flared as he nodded, looking over his grandmother's shoulder, removing himself from the conversation.

Bonnie waggled her finger at me once more. "Your arrival was meant to be celebrated. You were a gift for my son and grandsons. You were meant to be shared." Her lips spread broadly. "Do you understand what I'm saying to you, child?"

Sickness rolled in my gut.

Yes, I knew what she referred to. Jethro had said as much when he made me crawl like a dog to the kennels. He'd said I was to be passed around. But it never happened.

My eyes flew to him.

Even then…even when he was so awful, he was protecting me from worse.

The sickness disappeared, replaced with an intolerable ache inside my heart.

"Yes, I understand what you're saying."

Bonnie Hawk sat back, dropping her bony hand. "Good. You'd be wise to remember that. Remember that we have rules but freedom, guidelines but exceptions, but most of all, immunity against whatever we please to do."

Cut cleared his throat, moving forward and stealing the limelight. "Enough." Snapping his fingers at his son, he ordered, "Jethro. Ask the girl the question again."

My back tensed. The breeze died, untangling itself from my hair and letting it drape like a death shroud over my shoulders.

Oh, God.

My feet tingled to be free from the pentagram, but at the same time, I didn't want to move. Perhaps I was safe inside this five-pointed salt etching. Perhaps whatever pathway was conjured could steal me away and protect me from the Second Debt.

She was only fourteen.

The Hawk girl had died to protect my ancestor. She would've been petrified and so betrayed. Why was I any better than her? Why did I deserve to be freed when she was killed for a lie?

I swallowed as Jethro faced me completely. His hands were fisted by his sides, his face blank and cold. "Do you repent, Ms. Weaver? Do you take ownership of your family's sins and agree to pay the debt?"

His voice echoed in my ears. I wished he were asking me anything but that. I fantasised about a different question. So many different questions.

Do you want to run away with me?

Can you forgive my family for what they've done?

Have you fallen for me, like I've fallen for you?

Infinitely better questions. But ones I would never hear.

I'd delayed as much as possible.

I had nothing left to do but get it over with.

Bracing myself, I locked eyes first with Jethro then with each member of his deluded family. He didn't need to ask me twice— regardless of my stalling. I knew my role—my part in these theatrics.

If there was any power at all in the pentacle, I summoned it now. I summoned age-old wizardry and asked for one thing:

Let me endure, so I may pay the sins of my past. But let me survive, so I may put an end to those who hurt me.

The wind howled, fluttering the hem of my shift…almost in answer.

Balling my hands, I said, "Yes." My voice carried loud and clear with a touch of defiance. "Yes, I accept the debt."

Cut's forehead furrowed as if he were pissed with my strength and ownership of something so terrible. He looked robbed. He looked furious.

Jethro, on the other hand, looked stricken. His face went white and he nodded. "In that case, let's begin."

I closed my eyes, taking one last moment to fortify my soul.

You can get through this, Nila.

You can.

They won't kill you. Not yet.

Another bout of shivers overtook me. It could be entirely possible that after this, I would wish they would. I might want them to kill me and put me out of my misery.

Jethro gritted his jaw and moved toward the ominous looking contraption that remained hidden beneath a black cloth. Every time the breeze caught the edge, I tried to see what it was. The brief glimpses of wood and leather gave me no hint.

Wrapping his fist in the fabric, Jethro tore it off with a flourish.

My heart instantly suffocated.

I stepped back, scuffing the salt line and breaking the pentacle boundary. Thunder boomed on the horizon; heavy clouds inched closer.

I'd seen one of those things—a long time ago—in a book called *Fifty Ingenious Ways of Torture*. Vaughn had checked it out from the local library. I'd hated the book so much. He'd chased me around the house with it, flicking pages of blood and gore and absolute pain.

I didn't need water to drown me. My fear did that spectacularly well on its own.

It was a seesaw.

A terrified giggle bubbled in my chest. I liked seesaws. V had double-bounced me more than once as we played on them as children.

But this wasn't just any seesaw.

This one destroyed all happy memories of ever being on one. I would never *ever* go on another.

Not after today.

Not after this.

Jethro didn't look at me, stroking the end closest to him—what looked like a simple tree-trunk. It'd been carved into a smooth post with leather handholds hammered into the wood.

There were four straps in total.

My eyes followed the length of the seesaw, taking in the fulcrum before gritting my teeth and forcing myself to stare at the other end.

That was where I would go.

That end wasn't smooth or basic. It'd been modified. It was...*it's a chair.*

A simple wooden chair with cuffs for wrists and ankles. There were no cushions, no luxury—a prison cell suspended over the deep lake. It faced toward the pond, barring me from seeing what would happen on shore.

It was worse than any whipping post or dungeon.

Jethro leaned on the wooden joist, tilting the pendulum to sway the chair from the glistening water. It moved as if it was possessed, floating effortlessly, swinging toward me as if it knew I was the one destined to sit.

I moved back, tripping over my feet in my rush.

I bumped into something solid and warm. Jumping, I swallowed my squeal as Kes's strong fingers came around my shoulders, rubbing me with his thumbs. "Trust us. We won't let you drown. We know you're innocent of witchcraft and don't need to prove that by taking your life." His voice lowered, barely registering in my ears. "Hold your breath and let your mind wander. Don't fight. Don't struggle."

His circling thumbs made me want to vomit. His kind-heartedness only made this worse. Jerking out of his hold, I stood shivering in my shift. "Don't touch me."

His eyes tightened with hurt, and for some inexplicable reason, I felt as if I owed him an explanation.

I'm so cold.

Fear had stolen everything.

I'd never quivered so badly—never been so terrified. My teeth chattered harder and I bit my tongue accidently. Pain flared, a trickle of blood tainting my mouth.

Jethro came up beside me. He held out his hand. "Ready, Ms. Weaver?"

No.

I'll never be ready for this.

I paused, swallowing blood and every urge to beg.

If we were alone, I would've toppled to my knees and wrapped my arms around his waist. I would've had no decorum or self-control. I would've promised anything, given him everything, if only he put a stop to this.

Please, don't do this.

His eyes narrowed, glinting with anger. His family watched our every move.

That was it, then. There was no way out. He was resigned to this. And so must I.

Dropping my head, letting a curtain of ebony hair block me from this world, I nodded.

"You need to say it," he muttered. "Say it out loud. Admit that you deserve this."

Closing my eyes, I died a little inside. Forcing myself to raise my hand, I presented myself to him.

Jethro stole my wrist; his cold touch seeped like permafrost into my already freezing body.

With a tug, he stole me from the pentagram and dragged me toward the chair. "You still haven't said it, Ms. Weaver."

My panic had become physical, slapping a gag over my mouth. I struggled with the word. One simple little word.

Stepping toward the chair, I whispered, "Yes. Yes, I admit I deserve this."

Jethro made a strangled noise in his chest.

I closed my eyes.

It was done.

TYING HER DOWN was one of the hardest fucking things I've done.

Not because my family were watching and I had no way of fucking up the debt.

And not because my heart dripped with icicles and frost.

And not even because I was so fucking close to snapping and showing everything that I was.

But because I'd promised myself the next time I restrained her, I would be granting her pleasure not pain.

I'd wanted her to writhe beneath my tongue while she was bound. I wanted to taste her as she came apart while suspended. And I wanted her delicious moans to fill my ears while she was trapped.

I wanted her to give in to me. To *trust* me. To give me every single pleasure she could feel.

When I'd fucked her in her quarters that second time, I'd made a vow to take her completely. To take her my way…all the way.

That meant getting inside her head, her heart, her mind. I wasn't satisfied with owning her body. It didn't give me what I craved. Only her complete submission and immeasurable love could do that.

I would've taken days. Days to extract everything she had to give me. The word 'torture' came from the origins *to twist*. I would've twisted Nila's emotions so she'd carry me forever in her heart. I would've made a home inside her so I could be finally fucking free.

She could give me a cure no one else could grant. She could switch every pain I had into something…*more*.

I wanted more.

I wanted everything.

And now, I would have nothing.

Now, she would forever associate being tied up as something to be avoided, especially by me.

Her rapid breath fluttered over my face as I bent over her and pressed her forearm against the armrest.

The white shift didn't hide the ghost of her lingerie, nor the peaking of her nipples. Her skin was cold, her lips growing bluer by the minute.

She hadn't even been in the lake and already she looked hypothermic.

She's as cold as me.

The leather slipped a few times from my grip as I fumbled to feed the buckle. Luckily, my back blocked my motions from my father—otherwise he would see my frost was thawing. He would see the haunting in my eyes of being so close to this woman while she hated me.

Nila was the culprit—my undoing.

She melted me.

She was the fucking sun. And I was about to splash out her heat.

Once her wrists were shackled, I ducked to attend to her ankles. Her legs jostled as her shaking grew worse. Her teeth chittered and chattered, her hair sticking to the cold sweat dotting her brow.

I hesitated a moment too long. Reaching out, I wrapped my fingers around her leg, preparing to fasten the cuff.

She gasped, dragging my eyes to her.

Fuck.

It was a terrible mistake to look at her.

She looked so small. So easily broken. Her eyes were too wide for her face; her skin stretched over bones that might shatter if she became any colder.

I tried to look away.

I tried.

But I couldn't.

Our gazes locked; I groaned under my breath as the connection between us only strengthened. The diamond collar around her neck sparkled even as the clouds above us blotted out the sunshine and gathered dark grey.

Nila stopped shivering, almost as if she found sanctuary in my gaze.

I stopped fighting, almost as if she tamed the insanity inside me.

What was this…this tether? How had she captured me so completely, and how the fuck did I sever it?

The deeper I fell into her, the worse it got.

Her panic siphoned into my soul, twisting my gut until I wanted to vomit. Her flesh turned white as the moon and just as ethereal.

In the starkness of what was about to happen, she'd never been so beautiful, so bewitching, so intense.

My knees wobbled, itching to kneel before her and place my head in her lap. To just rest…and pretend none of this existed. To have her comfort me.

Cut growled under his breath, smashing through our moment, rendering it dead.

Nila sniffed, tears glossing her eyes.

The link between us had been so bright, but now it was back to darkness.

You're running out of time.

Gritting my teeth, I forced myself to work faster. My fingers moved swiftly, securing the buckle around her left ankle.

I looked up one last time. Needing her to know that I'd come to her full of nothing, but now she'd filled me with everything.

She looked into my eyes, then glanced away.

I wanted to tell her I was sorry. I wanted her to see in my gaze what I could never say aloud.

Forgive me.

With a soft moan, she closed her eyes, cutting me off completely.

Her dismissal butchered my heart, dug it out with a dirty blade, and sent it splashing into the pond. The hole left behind filled with algae, water, and bracken. I was a fucking bastard. I should stop this.

But I won't.

I wanted what I'd inherit on my thirtieth birthday. I was selfish, greedy, and vain. I wanted Nila, too. I believed I could have both.

If only I had more time.

You don't have more time. Not today.

Securing her other ankle, I stood.

I waited for her to look at me—to give me some sign she understood that we were in this together. That despite what I did, the tattoos overrode my loyalty to my family and bound me to her.

My Weaver.

Her Hawk.

I waited another second, and another.

But she never opened her eyes. Her forehead furrowed harder, her fists curled tighter, and she withdrew from me until there was no emotion left—just a tiny dying star that once had shone so bright.

Leaving me heartless and bleeding, she gave me nothing else to do.

I slipped into my role as torturer and began.

PLEASE, GRANT ME strength.
Please, grant me power.
Please don't let me scream.

Fettered to the chair, I kept my eyes squeezed as tight as possible—so tight—no light entered, no swirling colours from behind my eyelids. Just pitch black darkness.

When Jethro looked at me with agony in his gaze, I'd pitied him. He held so many secrets in his golden depths. So many rights. So many wrongs.

I could have a lifetime with him and never understand.

But in that moment, I *did* understand, and I both despised and bled for him. He was supposed to give me strength by making me hate him. I wanted to rue him as much as I did the day I found my ancestor's graves. Hate would've kept me warm and alive.

But he'd stolen that by looking destroyed, crippled with conflicting loyalties.

It made me fall harder.

It made me slam to the bottom of my feelings for him.

I wanted to praise him for letting me into his heart. I wanted to tell him I had the capacity to love him in return.

But I didn't.

I couldn't.

He didn't deserve it.

And then, I found my hate again.

I hated him for being too weak and not going against his family.

I cursed him for not having the courage to choose.

Why should he choose me?

He barely even knew me.

But souls were wise things. They always knew before the brain or the heart. There was no discriminating—if you saw your perfect other…you knew—instantly.

There was something there from the beginning.

Just like there had been for us.

And it would remain there until Jethro successfully tore it out and killed it.

Because even though we were linked by this fragile, fluttering thing, it wouldn't take much to ruin. It was already on the brink.

He's sentenced me to pay the Second Debt.

How many more would he carry out?

Did I trust him to be strong enough to end this before my life was stolen?

Looking over my shoulder, his family glowered at me as if I'd killed their loved ones with a barely spoken curse. They watched with trepidation—as if they believed I'd descended from the witch they hated and would turn them to toads at any second.

Superstition perfumed the breeze. Hate bloomed from the roses. And impatience spiced the water lilies.

I missed the intimacy of the First Debt. I missed the throbbing chemistry between Jethro and me even while he did something so wrong. It had just been the two of us. Together.

Now, it was just me against them.

"Do you know what this is, Ms. Weaver?" Jethro asked, stealing my attention.

I pressed my lips together. My neck hurt from straining to look over my shoulder.

When I didn't answer, Jethro recited, his voice silted and cool. "You're sitting in a ducking stool. It was used traditionally as a torture method for women. Its free-moving arm swings over the river to extract truth and confessions by ducking into the freezing cold water."

He looked away from me, pacing between the reeds. "The length of immersion was decided by the operator and the crime of which the woman was accused. It could last for just a few seconds, but in some circumstances, the process was continuously repeated over the course of a day."

He faced me. "Do you know the crimes the ducking stool was used for?"

I didn't answer. I refused.

I made an oath not to scream. I refused to entertain them with my cries.

Kes came forward, answering on behalf of Jethro. "Most common crimes were prostitution and witchcraft. Scolds were also punished by this method." His lips tilted. "Know what a scold is, Nila?"

I couldn't stop my head from shaking.

Shit, I didn't mean to react.

Jethro's eyes narrowed, his chest rising sharply.

"A scold was a gossiper, shrew, or bad tempered woman," Kes said.

Jethro glared at his brother. "Even though I have experience with your temper, Ms. Weaver, I cannot say you are a scold." Running a hand through his hair, he finished, "Regardless, this is to show you how death by water can be one of the most frightening things of all. This is how my ancestor died. This is how you will pay."

Snapping his fingers, Jethro ordered, "Turn your head. Look away."

Another avalanche of fear tumbled through me. I couldn't do this!

"Turn around, girl!" Cut snapped.

I don't know how I did it, but I slowly resettled on the hard wooden seat, and tore my eyes from Jethro. The pond before me twinkled like cold jewels—blue and green and black.

My heart grew bigger and bigger in my chest until it filled every inch. I couldn't breathe. I couldn't think. I couldn't blink.

Noise came from behind me; I had to fight every instinct to look.

Trust in Kes. He said they wouldn't drown me.

Suddenly, the chair swooped upward. It went from being glued in the mud to flying high over the earth. I gasped, smashing my lips together to contain my scream.

No. No, no, no.

My fingers had nothing to hold onto. My wrists kissed the wood, held in place by tight leather. My legs couldn't move. I was well and truly caught.

The ducking stool wobbled as whatever force held me up readjusted to my weight. The breeze was stronger up here, whistling over the water like tiny mournful flutes.

The view would've been idyllic with the weeping willows and ducks preening on the banks. But I was caught in my worst nightmare.

I didn't want to see anymore.

Squeezing my eyes, I wished I'd been blindfolded. I didn't want to witness what was to come.

Don't open your eyes. Don't open them.

Someone's hands brushed against my ankles. A mechanism was locked then another swoop higher and higher sent my stomach splattering to my toes.

I'd been in theme parks before—I'd ridden a rollercoaster once in my life. Once was more than enough, even though V adored the loop de loop. I didn't understand his joy of making himself dizzy when I lived that way every day.

I'd found no thrill in being bound to an uncomfortable ride, listening to the *clack-clack* of the rollercoaster wheels as we clawed our way higher up a mountain of track. Every clatter of the rails sent equal measures of panic and excitement…until we reached the top…and just hovered there.

We'd hovered like a bird, basking in being on top of the world.

That was where I hung now.

Gravity defying—a girl in a white dress suspended above a dark green pond. A girl who would've done anything to have been born a Smith or a Jones or a Kim.

And then the rollercoaster slipped from weightless to bullet, freefalling over the mountain and hurling me into terror.

I promised myself I wouldn't scream.

It was a hard promise to keep.

The chair lost its support, leaving my belly above me as I fell and fell and fell.

Forever I fell, before splashing into frigid wetness.

The moment the water lapped around my ankles, I gave up trying to be brave.

The water slurped and sucked, devouring my legs in an instant.

The human part of me—the girl inside—was shoved aside by instinct and horror.

I squirmed, gasping louder and louder as the ice welcomed me, faster and faster. The wooden chair surrendered to the water, letting it lap its way almost seductively up my legs, over my waist, my breasts, my throat…my…

…mouth.

I arched my neck as best I could. I fought against the pond's embrace.

I managed one last gulp of life.

Then, I disappeared.

I became a prisoner of the lake.

I promised myself I wouldn't scream.

I lied.

The instant the water crashed over my head, I lost it.

Well and truly lost it.

My eyes flew open in the murky gloom and I screamed.

I screamed as if I would die. I screamed as if my body was being torn in two and eaten alive. I screamed as if this was the end.

Bubbles cascaded from my mouth, gifting all my oxygen to a passing trout in a riot of glistening froth.

I promised myself I would stay calm. That I would listen to Kes's advice and get through this with complete trust, knowing that eventually I would be hoisted back up.

That was another lie.

I had no understanding of time.

Seconds were minutes and minutes were years.

I bobbed in a substance that would kill me with no way free.

It was enough to send me into insanity.

I didn't care I could break an arm or leg fighting against the securely buckled straps. I didn't care I could snap my neck by thrashing hopelessly in the chair. And I definitely didn't care I could break my mind by letting the horror of being drowned consume me.

I couldn't stand it.

I'm dying.

I can't fucking stand it!

And then, just like any rollercoaster, another incline halted the fatal swoop and hurled me back into the heavens once again.

The weight of the water pressed down on my skull and shoulders. My eyes burned from rushing water. The pressure. The unrelenting grip the lake had on me. It fought the pull. It didn't want to let me go.

The sodden material of my gown sucked to my skin as my chair was raised and raised until…

Pop.

The water relented, letting me break the skin of the pond and leave a watery death behind.

Thank God—I can breathe!

Up and up I swooped, spluttering and dripping rain from above. I breathed and coughed and choked and sobbed.

I sucked in air as if I only had one purpose in life: to revive myself and regain my sanity.

My heartbeat was frantic—palpating, double beating—far too fast and petrified.

My long hair plastered to my face. Every mouthful of oxygen I sucked, strands smothered my mouth. More panic screeched through my veins. The claustrophobia was more than I could bear.

Through the forest of my hair, I had to see behind me. I had to look at Jethro and let him see how much I'd unravelled. I wouldn't be able to stand another dunk.

I won't.

Quaking, I looked over my shoulder. My hair tugged, plaiting wetly around my throat as I focused on the banks.

Through drips of water, I vaguely noticed the four Hawk men. All four had their elbows locked, pushing down on the pendulum and gripping hard to the leather handholds.

The strength it took to raise and plummet me into the pond exceeded that of one man.

This debt.

This atrocity had become a family affair.

Jethro, Kestrel, Daniel, and Cut.

Together they played roulette with my life, and in a perfect harmony, they shifted as one and began the rollercoaster all over again.

Their side of the seesaw rose; I dropped.

"No!" I screamed, thrashing in the chair.

But they ignored me.

Faster and faster they dropped me until they disappeared; once again, my aquatic grave welcomed me.

The water's kiss devoured my feet, my thighs, my breasts…my head.

I sank quicker.

Like I belonged.

The second time was no better.

If anything, it was worse.

My lungs burned.

They felt as if they bled with my submerged screams.

My heartbeat sent ripples of horror through the water cradling me. Sonic sound waves alerted fish that I would soon be easy prey…that I was moments from slipping from this world and into another.

One that hopefully treated me better.

I struggled harder, bruised deeper, and drove myself quicker into madness.

I screamed again, unable to hold in oxygen. Something scaly swam beneath me, tickling my toes. Fronds of water grasses and quick flashes of movement from frogs all sent my mind twirling into darkness.

Images of Loch Ness monsters and sea creatures with wicked sharp teeth stole the remainders of my rationality.

I want to breathe.

I want to live.

I strained for the lighter green of the surface. Crying and pleading and drinking gallons of pond scum in my struggle to stay alive.

Time played a horrible joke on me. It never ended.

There was no reprieve…no air.

The emerald depth of the water crowded me, closing in tighter and tighter—crushing me like a tin can beneath its gentle waves.

This ducking lasted longer, or maybe I was destroyed already. Perhaps it was shorter, but I'd run out of reserves to hold on.

I wanted to stop fighting.

I wanted to succumb.

How weak I was.

How fragile.

How broken.

My fighting gave way to twitches. My muscles fought on their own, demanding oxygen I didn't have to give.

My hair hovered around me like it was alive, swaying like seaweed, promising an easy existence if I just followed its gentle dance and give in.

Just…give in.

Give in to the gentle lullaby of sleep.

If I died, I won.

The Hawks would lose as I would be free…

My struggling ceased and I hung there as if I was no longer bones and breath, but weightless freedom. My shift billowed like wings around me, sending me deeper into the abyss.

It was quiet down here. Quiet and calm and…drifting.

I drifted…

I faded…

Then the weight began again, folding my chin against my collar, tugging me from the deep. Pounding, pounding pressure as I was wrenched from my emerald tomb and hurled into the clouds again.

Gravity was now my foe, making everything so eternally heavy. My chest was an elephant. My head a bowling ball.

And I was weak.

So weak.

Air trickled down my throat, mixing with water I'd drank, making me retch. As each mouthful registered, my brain awoke, kicking me into survival. I moaned and begged and devoured every drop of oxygen I could.

I couldn't look up. I couldn't look behind me.

All I saw was blackness. But something granted me inhuman strength to twist in my bindings and look, just once, behind.

The clouds were dark and threatening, shadowing the Hawks in sombre gloom.

Jethro's golden eyes burned me from the banks, superseding all distance, glowing like amber or sunlight—or paradise.

Paradise…

I would like to go to paradise.

But then I looked at Cut, Kes, and Daniel.

Their eyes were the same damn colour.

All of them.

Four men. Four wishes and wills—but one pair of identical eyes.

Evil eyes.

Horrendous eyes.

Eyes I never wanted to see again.

Daniel asked, "Have you given up your power, you wicked witch? Are you cured of the infection of magic?"

Jethro shoved him, cursing him beneath his breath.

Then, I fell again.

The men released their hold, shooing me from dryness and gifting me to a wet crypt.

As the water crashed over my head the third time, I gave up.

There was no point in fighting.

I was done.

I lost all track of time.

Up, down, up, down. Wet to dry and back again.

Every ducking I grew weaker…faded faster.

How many times did they raise me, only to drop me a few moments later? I believed Jethro when they said some torture sessions went on all day.

It felt as if this lasted forever.

I couldn't move. I had no energy remaining.

Underwater again, my heartbeat raced until it splintered my ribs, cleaving me open, letting water pour down my throat and slosh into my lungs.

Delusions were no longer something to fear, but to be *embraced*. Delusions brought fantasies to life, soothing me, eradicating monsters from my world.

Down here, unicorns existed. Up there, only beasts.

I opened my mouth wider, slack-jawed and spaced.

Perhaps I had a gift I didn't know of.

Perhaps I was a mermaid and could breathe water better than air.

Perhaps I could transform and swim far, far away from here.

I would try.

Anything was better than this.

The icy ache in my chest as the water filled me like a balloon was foreign and frightening.

But then it grew warmer.

And warmer.

It comforted me.

The pain left.

The panic receded.

I said goodbye to life.

Death slid over me with the sweetest kiss.

I smiled and sighed and gave into the deep.

Jethro

SHE WAS DEAD.

I knew it.

I couldn't explain how I knew.

But I did.

I'd done it.

I'd killed her.

She'd left me.

IT WAS OVER.

I existed in a fog of warm, comforting blackness. I didn't have a conscience or stress or worries.

I was *content*.

This nether world had no stipulations or rules on how to be. I just was. With no thoughts corrupting me.

I liked it here.

I preferred it here.

I sank deeper and deeper into the billowing softness.

I belong here.

Then something tugged on my mind.

I swatted it away, curling into a ball, becoming invisible.

The blackness grew darker, wanting to keep me just as much as I wanted to keep it.

But the tug came again, harder, stronger.

I fought it.

But it was so persistent. It scrabbled at my mind, breaking my happy bond and dragging me unwillingly from the deep.

It wrecked my contentedness.

It broke my happiness.

No!

I turned feral.

You can't take me.

I belong here. Not there.

Here I had a sense of infinity. I wasn't just human, I was so much more.

I didn't want to go.

I like it here.

Here where I don't care or want or fear.

But whatever it was wouldn't listen. It pulled me faster and faster from my sanctuary.

Blackness faded, becoming brighter and brighter.

I had no choice but to hurtle toward the light, breaking in two with sadness.

Then everything disintegrated.

The darkness. The comfort. The gentle kind of warmth.

It all vanished.

I froze, completely lost and vulnerable.

Where am I?

Something brilliant and bright shone into my eyes. I blinked in pain, seeing an echo of the deep yellow sun.

The clouds are gone.

I blinked again. Bringing the world I once knew into focus.

It made me wish I was blind.

With my eyesight came an unfurling of senses as my soul slipped back into a body I no longer wanted, breathing life into limbs that'd turned into a corpse.

There was something I was supposed to do in this world. Something extremely important.

The knowledge slammed into me with wet panic.

Breathe!

I couldn't breathe.

A shadow crossed the blistering sun, pressing soft lips against mine. My nose was pinched then a huge gust of air whistled down my throat, bringing sweet, sweet oxygen.

My chest expanded then deflated.

Not enough.

More. Give me more.

The life-giver understood, once again filling me with breath along with forgiveness, sorrow, and regret.

I retched.

Strong hands flipped me onto my side, patting my back with solid thumps as I vomited up bucket loads of lake.

It hurt.

God, it hurt.

My lungs turned inside out with agony as the overstretched organ gave up trying to survive on water, holding out eager hands for air instead.

With air came life, and with life came the knowledge that I'd died.

Tears sprang to my eyes.

I'd died.

And I preferred it.

I sank into despair.

How had I given up so easily?

Then realization slammed into me of who I was and where.

I was Nila.

This was the Second Debt.

All around me stood Hawks.

Bastard, traitorous Hawks.

Then it didn't matter anymore.

Pain enveloped me in a heavy cloak, squeezing me from all angles. Agony I'd never felt before battered me like a storm. Agony lived in my head, my heart, my bones, my blood.

Everything hurt.

Everything had died.

Coming alive was sheer torture, welcomed by a ring of devils.

"Come back to me, Nila." Jethro breathed into my ear, barely registering above the bone-crippling agony I lived. "I won't let you fucking leave me." He licked a tear leaking from my eye. "Not yet. I won't let you leave, not yet."

I couldn't look at him.

I couldn't listen to him.

So, I focused on the spot on top of the hill—on a black speck spotlighted by the waning sun.

No, not a speck.

A woman.

Dark hair, feminine grace.

Jasmine.

Seeing her stole my tension. I relaxed. My screaming muscles stopped twitching, melting into the mud upon which I lay.

I didn't need to fight anymore.

Jasmine was regal with honour and resplendent with pride— exactly as expected from any Hawk descendant.

I had the strange urge to wave—to have her grant me mercy.

How was it possible someone could wield so much power even while she was as broken as me?

I'd drowned and come back to life.

I'd been fixed.

However, Jasmine never would.

My eyes drifted from her beautiful face to her legs.

I sighed in sympathy for such a plight.

Wheels replaced legs. Footholds instead of shoes.

Jasmine Hawk was paralysed.

Wheelchair bound and reclusive.

It all suddenly made a lot more sense. About Jethro. His father. His sister.

And then it all became too much.

I drifted off into fluffy clouds.

I said goodbye for the second time.

I CARRIED HER unconscious form back to hell.

I turned my back on my father, grandmother, and siblings.

I let them whisper about my downfall and plot my death.

I did all of those things because the moment I'd felt Nila give up, nothing else fucking mattered.

Money, Hawksridge, diamonds—none of it.

It was all bullshit.

And I didn't fucking care.

All I cared about was making sure Nila healed.

I couldn't let her die.

She couldn't leave me alone.

Not now.

Stalking up the hill, across the grounds, and into the Hall, I ignored the Diamond brothers who'd been watching the spectacle with an array of binoculars and telescopes, and stormed to the back of the house.

In the parlour loomed a huge swinging door, disguised as a bookcase.

Years ago, the door had hidden a bunker. A secret entrance into the catacombs below the house. They were there to save my ancestors from war and mutiny.

Now, that bunker had been converted and served a different kind of function, along with an addition found ninety years after the first brick had been laid.

Nila's body was icy and soaking. Her clothing dripped down my front, leaving a trail of droplets wherever we went. Her long wet hair trailed over my arm like kelp. Not for the first time, I fantasised I'd plucked a kelpie from the pond and taken her hostage. My very own water nymph to keep for good luck.

She would make me right.

She had to.

Pulling on a certain book, the mechanism unlocked, swinging the door open.

Nila didn't stir.

She'd stopped shivering, but her lips were a deep indigo that terrified me more than her unconscious whimpers. She teetered on death's door—even now—even though I'd resuscitated her with mouth to mouth and given my soul as well as my air, she still haemorrhaged life.

It was as if she *wanted* to die.

Wanted to leave me.

Her brittle body made me focus on things I wasn't strong enough to face.

I'd grown up.

I'd begun to see.

I'd begun to believe she was it for me. The only one who could save me from myself.

Slinking through the door, I was careful not to bump her head. Her body lay strewn like a fallen angel in my arms—as if I'd caught her mid-plummet to earth. Her lips were parted; her arms dangled by her sides.

I had to get her warm and fast. I knew exactly how to do it.

Locking the door behind me, I descended the spiral staircase. I had no way of clapping to turn on the sound activated lights, so stomped my foot on the stone step, grateful when balls of light lit up one after the other, leading the way in the dark.

Electricity had replaced gas, which in turn had replaced naked flames that used to flicker in the medieval lanterns on the wall.

Moving forward, each bulb guided me further beneath the house, until I travelled beneath my own quarters and the bachelor wing above.

The bunker had been extended far past its original footprint. The crude concrete walls had been meticulously updated with large travertine tiles and top-of-the-line facilities.

Countless contraptions existed that I could use to warm Nila.

We had a steam room, sauna, and spa.

We had everything money could buy.

But none would be good enough.

I needed something bigger, grander…hotter.

I needed something money couldn't buy: the power of nature.

The scent of sulphur enveloped us as I continued down the corridor and into the humid world beneath Hawksridge. The cave had been discovered after the first part of the Hall had been erected. A workman died falling through the hole when setting new foundations—the cave had been stumbled upon by pure fluke.

Natural springs were a fairly common phenomenon in England— closely guarded by those who had them and a public luxury in places like Bath. Ours had remained a family secret for generations.

The sapphire water never dropped below forty degrees centigrade. Ever. It was consistent and somewhere I used to come a lot— somewhere that Jasmine visited almost daily with her maid to ease her atrophied muscles.

Moisture dripped from the earthen walls, plopping quietly back into the pool where it'd come from. A perpetual circle of death and rebirth.

I didn't stop to strip.

I didn't waste a moment.

Holding Nila tight against my chest, I walked down the carved steps and into the shoulder-deep spring. Every wade made my skin tingle and burn. I couldn't handle such warm waters all at once—I had to ease into it, allow the ice inside my soul to melt little by little.

But now all I cared about was raising Nila's body temperature.

I didn't care about my shoes or clothes.

Shit, I didn't even care I had my cell-phone and wallet in my pocket.

Everything was inconsequential; the urge to heal her before it was too late far too strong.

Not only had I scarred her back, but now I'd scarred her with death.

I have to fix this. Quickly.

As the warm liquid lapped around my waist, it stole Nila's weight, almost tugging her from my arms. Unwillingly, I unlocked my grip, letting her float away from me, bobbing buoyantly on the surface.

Her eyes didn't open. She didn't show any awareness that she felt the warmth after being so cold.

With cupped fingers, I poured hot water over her head, trading the iciness of the lake for the welcoming embrace of the spring.

Waterfall after waterfall I poured on her scalp, careful not to let the droplets slide over her nose or mouth.

It took too long.

The only noise was the gentle splash of water as it rained through my fingers.

Every second waiting for her to wake up ruined my every heartbeat.

I lost track of time. My eyes never left her blue, blue lips, and it was only when the deep colour began to fade that I finally relaxed a little.

Her fingertips weren't ice cubes any longer, thawing thanks to the warmth of the water.

When she finally did start to rouse, she began to shiver.

Violently.

Her teeth chattered and her hair tangled on the surface, jerking with every tremble.

Gathering her close, I held her as ripples arched from the epicentre of her body, fanning out to lap against the three metre wide pool.

Every twitch from her resonated in me—I didn't think I'd ever be stable again.

I continued to pour water over her head, cascading it over her frozen ears, willing her cheeks to turn pink.

Her soft moan was the second sign of her being alive. However, if she was aware of what I did, she didn't show it—she refused to open her eyes.

I couldn't blame her.

I wouldn't want to look at the man who'd done this either.

Sighing, I pressed my forehead against hers. No words could convey everything I felt. So I let silence do it for me.

I filled the space with so much fucking regret. Regret for today, for yesterday, for tomorrow. For everything I was and could never be.

I didn't know how long we hovered in the cave beneath my ancestral home, but slowly the silence filled with more than just sorrow and apology. It filled with a need so fierce and cruel, I struggled to breathe.

Pulling back, my eyes met Nila's black ones.

I froze as she slowly stood upright, dropping her legs beneath the water. Her hands moved. Slowly and weakly, she cupped my face.

I stiffened within her hold.

A hitched sigh fell from my lips.

I would permit her to slap me. I would let her take out her rage. After all, I deserved it.

I knew she was angry. The colour in her cheeks and glitter in her eyes hinted at her rage. I felt her temper building as surely as I felt the small eddies of natural thermals in the water.

I nodded, bracing for punishment.

But she didn't move.

We just stared and breathed and tried to understand each other's betrayal.

My lips tingled for hers. My cock wept for her body. And my heart…shit my heart begged to unlock and let her own it.

"I forgive you," she finally whispered, a single tear rolling down her cheek.

That one phrase cleaved me in two, and for the first time in my life, I broke. I wanted to fucking cry over a lifetime of misuse. Over a childhood I'd never been able to enjoy and an adulthood I'd never been able to embrace.

I wanted to fucking kill for what I still had to do and for what I had become.

I should slip beneath the water and take my own life. I was done fighting. Done pretending.

If I could've saved her by ending my struggles, I would have.

I would've sacrificed all I fucking knew to save her.

Licking my bottom lip, my eyes fell to her mouth.

There was just too much to say. Too many hurts to uncover and I didn't have the strength.

Not yet.

Nila floated before me, her breath hitching as I gently captured her hips and dragged her weightless body against mine.

Her eyes flared; her body bowstring tight.

Her fingers dug into my cheeks, holding me at a distance but not struggling to swim away.

My hands burned where I held her. I was grateful she let me touch her at all. But it wasn't enough. I wanted more.

Lowering my head, I tore past her anger and searched for the emotion from the polo match.

I needed to see I hadn't destroyed what I'd witnessed that day. Slowly, it appeared—floating to the surface of her eyes, blazing true.

She still cared for me.

After all that I'd done.

Fuck, I'm a monster.

Guilt crushed my chest, spinning rapidly with body-melting desire.

"Kiss me, Nila," I whispered. "Let me bring you back to life."

The water waked as she jolted. Her hands landed on my chest, tensing to push me away.

I shuddered as her fingertips scrunched my shirt.

Then, instead of pushing me, she pulled me.

Her hand slinked up around my neck, tugging my mouth to hers.

I sucked in a breath.

And she obeyed.

EVERY INCH OF me hurt.

My lungs were battered and bruised; my throat raw and raspy. My head pounded and throbbed. Every time I breathed, it seemed as if my ribcage had one purpose in life: to stab my heart to death.

I was alive…and paying the price.

Drowning wasn't fun.

Being drowned multiple times, even less so.

I never wanted to go near water again.

Yet you're in a pool with Jethro.

You're in a pool kissing *Jethro.*

My mind hurt trying to understand how he'd destroyed me in water, yet healed me in the same substance.

Cruel then comforting.

Murderous then reviving.

Two sides to everything—not evil or good or even aware of its perception. Just a single entity being used in different ways.

Water could be an enemy, but also a lover.

Could the same be true for Jethro?

His lips slid against mine. Wet and warm and gentle.

He didn't force me. He didn't try to control the kiss I'd given him. And for that I was grateful.

I took my time. Tasting him—tasting his regret.

I did my utmost to swim deep into his soul where the truth just waited to be found. I needed to know what he suffered from. I had to find out if I wanted to remain living.

His head twisted, changing the direction of the kiss so our bodies danced closer. The tip of his tongue licked my bottom lip, shooting a ripple of lust into my belly.

I had to trust in him. Trust in *this*. Had to believe. Had to hope.

Opening my mouth, I welcomed his tongue inside. Licking him, encouraging him, giving into the dark and dangerous undercurrent flowing between us.

He groaned, gathering me closer. Pulling back, he clasped my cheeks with his large hands. "I want you to know."

My damaged heart fluttered. I didn't speak, but I knew my question glowed in my eyes.

Know what?

He sighed. His chiselled cheekbones and dark brows made him look guilty and sorrowful all at once. His thick eyelashes shadowed stunning eyes and his lips—they promised to be the perfect drug to make me forget about my pain.

In the hazy steamy world, I saw how tightly reined he was. His soul didn't just have shadows—it had holes. Holes that might never be stitched together again.

He was heir to an empire worth untold millions. He was smart, capable, and strong. In hindsight, it was inevitable that I would fall for him. How could I not? It was almost a relief to admit that I stood no chance against his spell.

But if he'd ensnared me, then I'd ensnared him.

He suffered the same conflict.

Jethro brushed a thumb over my lips, his touch trembling softly. "You make me better even while making me worse."

My throat tightened, triggering the soreness from previous screaming. The tattoo on my fingertip burned as if recognising he was my other half—whether I wanted it or not.

In so many ways, Jethro was old beyond his years, yet so young at the same time.

"You need to tell me," I murmured. "Let me understand."

"Can't you understand that I've been fucked up ever since I first texted you? I'm insane, but you're the only cure for my insanity."

My heart thundered. The first verbal admission that he was Kite.

It was more than he'd given me before, but it wasn't enough.

"I'm listening and not judging." I couldn't stop myself from adding, "And you made me the same way. I'm mad over you, Jethro. You have to give in."

With a blended noise of frustration and grief, he kissed me again, twisting my thoughts with an eager tongue. I wasn't strong enough to stay firm while he was determined to sweep me away. The kiss distracted me from what he'd said, what I wanted him to say. Despite myself, I mirrored him, massaging his tongue with mine, strengthening our desire.

Don't let him hide.

My restraint barely existed, but I couldn't permit him to change the subject—no matter if I preferred the new topic.

Breaking free, I pushed my fingers into his hair, holding him firm. "Tell me, Jethro. Tell me everything."

He breathed hard, his eyes never leaving my mouth. "Isn't it enough to know you've got me by the heart?" He suddenly grabbed my hand, splaying my fingers over his chest. "Can you feel that?"

My lungs stuck together as my heartbeat kicked into a flurry.

Jethro breathed, "It's become so bad, I can barely breathe. For years I've struggled—my whole fucking life."

I tried to take my hand back. I couldn't stomach feeling the irregular thump of his heart beneath my fingertips. Its rhythm was screwed up, confused...lost.

His face held such yearning, such turmoil. Staring at me that way gave me too much power. Too much authority over his soul.

But it also soothed me—proved that having control in my future was right here—in my grasp. I only had to be brave enough to take it.

Curling my fingers on his chest, as if I could carve his heart out and hold it in my hand, I stared into his light coloured eyes. "Tell me."

"I'll tell you what I can...but later."

"No, you won't. Tell me now."

"What more do you want from me, Nila?" he suddenly snarled. "Don't you see? Do you really need to hear it?"

His fear thickened the air.

Yes, I could see something was wrong. I could almost understand it.

But I needed him to admit it.

"You can't hide. Not this time. Not with me."

Silence webbed around us.

Then finally, his head bowed in defeat, but there was relief in his gaze. "I'll tell you. All of it. What I am. What it means. I promise. I'll tell you."

WHAT I AM. What it means.
WHAT I AM. What it means.
The promise echoed in my head.
Why had I promised such a thing?
Why did I think I could?
Because she needs to see the truth. She needed to know so she could forgive me.

I kissed her again—trying to stop her from seeing my fear at being open and true.

Holding her jaw, I pressed my lips harder against hers, signalling that I would keep my promise, but not right now.

Right now, I needed to be inside her.

Right now, I didn't have the strength.

It was selfish of me to take more from her when she'd only just recovered, but something inside me howled for what she could give.

I needed it before I had the capacity to talk about what I was.

Only then would I find the courage.

I'm selfish.

I'm a bastard.

She paused for a second, as if deciding whether to let me drag her from words to actions. Then her tongue met mine, returning my kiss with a greed that sent my cock on fire.

Her arms wrapped around my waist, holding me reverently.

It was more, so much more than I deserved. My breathing hitched.

Slowly, the kiss evolved into an admittance of feelings and longing.

Our breathing accelerated, echoing in the cave.

Needing nothing between us, I pushed Nila away and grabbed the hem of my t-shirt. The water sucked the fabric against my stomach, gluing it in place.

With a tug that sent a wash of droplets raining over Nila, I tore it off and threw it to the side.

Nila stood there, her gaze drifting down my exposed torso. Her dark beauty stole my fucking breath. Her hair hung like wet silk. The shapeless white shift moulded to her curves, thanks to the Velcro-like ability of water.

Wading toward her, I ducked a little and captured her hem below the water's surface. Without a word, I pulled it up over her thighs and hips then hid her face as I pulled it over her head.

Her arms fell to her sides, lethargic and weak from what I'd done.

Leaning forward, I reached behind her and unhooked her bra. I bit my lip as the fabric fell away, exposing what I'd been dying to see for days.

Her nipples were pink and hard, pinpointed with the same desire that existed in my cock.

Never looking away, I captured the lace on her hips and pulled her knickers down her legs. She trembled but didn't stop me. I shouldn't do this. She needed to rest.

But I had no choice.

I had to take her.

It was the only way.

Her touch landed on my shoulder for balance as I removed her underwear. Her gaze darkened before a slight mask slid into place, hiding depths that I needed to see.

I'd done that. I'd made her build walls. I'd made her hide—same as me.

I couldn't permit that.

Throwing away her underwear, she stood before me naked and completely trusting. Giving me everything I demanded so damn selflessly.

"I'll never be able to thank you," I whispered.

"Thank me for what?"

"For caring more about my own welfare than your own." Capturing her face, I breathed, "I can feel you. I know that doesn't make sense, but the moment you give in to me; the moment you let yourself submit…it saves me. I can't explain it, but you heal me, Nila."

Her eyes glistened. A soft smile graced her lips as she pressed her cheek into my palm. "Don't be afraid of me, Jethro. Don't be afraid of what's growing between us."

I kissed her. Her mouth opened, her tongue dancing with mine.

Breaking apart, I said, "I won't. I'm not letting you go. You're mine, do you understand?"

She nodded, shyness pinking her cheeks. "I belong to you."

I shivered with relief, with gratefulness, with every fucking comfort I'd never had.

With fumbling hands, I undid my belt and pushed my jeans and boxer-briefs down my legs. Kicking off my shoes, I stripped. The water made it a trial to discard the unwanted clothing.

Urgency echoed in my limbs, making me rush. She'd admitted she was mine. I had to confirm it.

The hot water flowed around my erection, lapping at my balls—more arousing than air.

I ached to fill her again.

Gathering her close, I pressed my forehead against hers and wrapped my arms around her tiny waist. "I want to make you come. I want to erase what happened today and give you a better memory."

She lifted her face to the natural cave formation above us. "Here?"

I nodded.

I wouldn't be able to walk with the pounding flesh between my legs. I was a fucking saint taking it slow. One touch from her and I'd explode.

Brushing her hair from her neck, I whispered, "I'm going to fuck you…here." Trailing my lips along her jawline, I murmured, "I'm going to make you moan…here." Baring my teeth, I bit her throat, filled with the primal need to mark. "I'm going to make you scream…here."

She shivered, letting her head fall back, surrendering to me.

I bit her again—I couldn't help myself. I nudged her diamond collar higher up her throat and bit hard. I couldn't ignore the instincts demanding me to claim.

I wanted to give her a gift. A gift where I gave her more than just my body but my heart. There would be no pain, debts, or degradation. Only us.

"I want to care for you, Nila. I want to show you how much I value what you've given me."

The driving urge to climb inside her grew with every heartbeat. The anticipation made it all the more sweeter, but I'd reached the end of my self-control.

Dropping my gaze, I followed my hand as I cupped her breast and squeezed. Her back curved, forcing more of her flesh into my fingers. I pinched her nipple then ducked and covered her other breast with my mouth.

She groaned, hugging my head to her, demanding that I lick harder. The erotic sound of her pleasure sent shock-waves through me.

Thank fuck she didn't like sweet and gentle. I'd tried to be soft—for her sake. I'd tried to control myself. I wasn't such a monster to add more injuries, not when she'd been through so much, but I silently thanked her that she needed what I did.

That she wanted me fierce and true. Nothing bared.

My fingertips flexed around her nipple, dragging another soft moan.

I couldn't stand it any longer.

Standing to my full height, I captured her mouth in another kiss. Her beautiful lips met mine, her tongue licking with passion and hunger. As our kiss deepened, I banded an arm around her, pressing her flat stomach against my cock.

She arched into my caress, her fingers flying into the water to wrap around my length.

"Fuck," I groaned as her tight hold sent my mind exploding with lust.

My hips rocked, forcing myself deeper into her palm. The joy of having her touch me—of me touching her—wasn't enough. I needed more.

I need fucking everything.

Picking her up, I waded to the side and spun her around. The moment she faced away from me, I couldn't stop myself from grinding my cock against the crack of her arse.

Her fingers clawed at the earthen side, her head flopping forward as I cupped her breasts from behind and squeezed to the point of pain.

Dropping one hand, I trailed it down her belly, not stopping until I found her slippery cunt. I sucked in air as I found a different kind of moisture.

Her arousal was thicker, silkier than the water around us.

I bit the back of her shoulder, pressing a finger deep inside her.

The way she gave in to me made me soar. The guilt, the hate—it all faded.

She bucked, her mouth falling open. "Ah…"

Her gentle sound of bliss unravelled me faster.

This was what I needed. *Her.* Where had she been all my life? Why had I fumbled for so long without her in my arms?

Never again.

Never fucking again would I be so alone.

Her torso twisted in my arms, her hand cupping my bristle-covered jaw. "I can feel you."

Fuck, she was too perceptive.

I couldn't speak.

Nila's lips tilted into a sensual smile. "I can feel so much when you let go. When you let me in."

I kissed her.

I had no choice.

Her body wriggled against mine as I slipped another finger inside her pussy, rubbing her clit with my thumb.

"You're so fucking gorgeous…so strong." Words spilled from my mouth, disappearing into her hair, down her back, dripping into the water. "I'm so damn hard, I'm in agony. All my life, something was missing. And now I've found it." I rocked my dick against her, making my need so much worse. "I found you. I stole you. I took you from others who didn't appreciate the gift of what you are, and now I'm never letting you go."

She moaned, her eyes blazing with lust.

I thrust again, welcoming the heat and bliss of being naked with this woman. "See what you do to me? See how much I need to crawl inside you and never fucking leave?" I rolled my hips, panting at the delicious friction.

Nila gasped, her spine bowing in invitation. "God, don't stop. Tell me everything. Don't be afraid. If you want me to beg, I'll beg. If you want me to scream, I'll scream. Just…" Her legs spread in the water as she bent over the side, looking at me over her shoulder. "Just never stop being honest with me. This…what you're giving me, Jethro, it makes everything worthwhile. It makes everything I believed *real.*"

Her cheeks glistened as she smiled through her tears. "Nothing could've prepared me for this. Nothing could've taught me to feel this way. I'm ready to forget everything. I'm ready to be selfish and steal you like you stole me."

She cried out as I thrust my fingers deeper inside her, tearing my name from her lips.

"I—I only want you," she groaned. "Only you. Promise me that I can keep you. Promise me."

My heart…shit, my heart.

It unlocked.

The padlock fell free.

Her words were a key. Her forgiveness and love and strength and everything that made her pure stole me from my life of pain.

She changed me.

Right there.

Right then.

I became hers.

Irreversibly.

"I promise," I swore. I needed to climb into her soul and cement everything we'd just confessed. "I'm so messed up over you. I—" I couldn't talk anymore. I was too fucking fragile. Too overwhelmed.

I grabbed her chin, twisting her neck to kiss me. I took her mouth savage and strong. I drove my tongue past her lips and admitted once and for all that I might be a Hawk; I might be a son destined for tragedy, but none of that mattered as long as I had her.

She trembled in my hold as I kissed her deeper, harder. My thumb swirled on her clit, matching the rhythm of my fingers driving in and out of her pussy.

Her hips moved, using me to drive herself to ecstasy.

"Promise me that you'll never cut me out. Promise me that you'll never walk away—no matter how badly I fuck up." I wanted to bind her in this moment—an ironclad agreement that she would never leave—no matter how bad things got.

Because I would fuck it up. She would end up hating me.

I had debts to extract, her brother to dispatch, and an empire to steal.

I wasn't perfect. Her love didn't make me a better man—it just gave me the strength to continue fighting.

Her inner walls fluttered around my touch. My mouth watered to taste her.

"I—I promise." Another cry escaped as her hips rocked harder on my hand. I wrapped my arm tighter around her.

"Oh, God…yes…Jethro…*please*…" Her face flushed, every muscle hummed with the need to release.

She gave me complete control over her body and soul.

I lost it.

"Christ, I want to be inside you." I grabbed my cock, riding my palm. "So much. So fucking much." I jacked off with brutal violence, trying to tame the lust in my blood all while making it worse.

I'd never needed anyone as much as I needed her.

I'd never had the need to draw pain or bite or devour. But now I did. I wanted to *ruin* her. I was out of my mind with fucking desire.

Nila reached behind, steadying my hand. Her breathing was as ragged as mine. "I need it, too." Biting her lip, she guided my pounding erection between her legs and pushed against the side. "Don't hold back. Never again. I can handle what you have to give."

I shivered. "Fuck, Nila."

She wanted everything.

She wanted me. All of me. The twisted parts. The dark parts.

Me.

She was…peace. She was…sanity. She was…*home.*

She wants me.

I clenched my jaw. Her heat beckoned me. I was no longer human but an animal who needed to claim his mate.

Fisting the base of my cock, I bent my knees and thrust.

We both groaned.

It felt so fucking *good.*

Her slipperiness coated me, but it wasn't enough. She was too tight.

A tameless growl echoed in my chest as she pushed back, forcing me to fill her faster.

"Shit," I grunted as she pushed again.

"More. I need more," she begged.

I almost came from the exquisite tightness of her body. Every ripple of her muscles was like a fist around my girth. My balls twitched, preparing to spurt inside this woman—my fucking woman—now that I was rightfully home.

"I have to work you. You're not relaxed enough."

She shook her head, her face twisting with need. "No. Give it to me. Goddammit, Jethro, please…fuck me. I can't…" Her core contracted as I thrust again.

My lips pulled back as I drank in her piercing lust. "You need me inside you?"

"Yes. God, yes."

I drove harder. "You need me to fuck you?"

Her head flew back as I forced my size past her body's limits. "Yes. I need you. All of you."

I was only half-way in. My dick was too much for her. As much as she wanted me, as enticing as her moans were, I refused to hurt her more tonight. Tonight was about pleasure.

"I'm going to fill you."

"Please."

"I'm going to fuck you so hard, you'll stay wet for days just thinking of me taking you in this pool."

Nila bit her lip. "Do it, Jethro. Punish me. Teach me that I belong to you."

Fuck.

I'd never been a talker in sex. Never saw the allure of dirty whispers. But now all I could think about was talking filthy and wrong.

Reaching between her legs, I rubbed her clit—faster and faster with one goal in mind.

"You're going to come for me, little Weaver. You're going to drench my dick and let me inside you." I breathed harder, rocking faster, forcing her higher.

"No, I want—"

"You don't get what you want. This is what *I* want. I want you to know who's fucking you. I want you to know whose cock is taking you. I need you to scream for me, Nila."

I didn't give her any reprieve. I forced her to feel everything. I wanted her orgasm. She owed me her pleasure.

Nila stiffened; her elbows gave out as she flattened against the side. "Stop—wait…"

"No." I thrust with each swirl of my thumb, gradually spreading her—crawling inside. "I'm the one taking you. I'm the one riding you. I'm the one you want. Admit it!"

Her mouth opened as she silently screamed. Her entire focus turned inward.

I thrust harder. "Say it. Admit that you want me. Admit that you like what I'm doing to you."

Her eyes wrenched open, connecting with mine.

My heart fell down a rabbit hole, completely under her spell.

"Yes, I admit it. I feel you. I want you so much! Fuck me. Please...fuck me."

I couldn't deny her.

My hips rocked, my thumb swirled.

"Come. Come on my cock."

Her body rebelled, clamping around me. I struggled to breathe. I groaned as her pussy flexed tighter and tighter. I saw fucking stars.

"Jethro—" Her breathing turned to breathless pants. The muscles along her spine contorted with pressure. She wiggled, trying to dislodge my hold on her clit. "It's too intense—"

I didn't let her move. "You don't know the meaning of intense. I'll show you intense. I'll show you what it's like to live in a world full of fucking intensity." Bowing over her, I bit her ear. "Come, Nila. Come for me. Let me give you pleasure after the pain I've caused."

Her legs gave way; a long moan crawled from her throat.

Then, she detonated.

I caught her as an orgasm ripped through her core, sucking and melting around my cock. "Yes...Oh, my God..."

I clamped a hand over her mouth as she screamed in delirium. My forehead furrowed as incredible waves of pressure milked my cock as her pussy contracted.

I wanted to come. Shit, I wanted to come.

With each wave, her body tried to reject my size, but then...on the final crest of her orgasm, wetness gushed. She welcomed me with perfect rapture.

I groaned.

"I'm taking you now, Ms. Weaver. You're all mine."

Bending over her, I let myself loose.

In one vicious rock, I claimed her. I slid deep, deep inside.

There was no resistance. Nothing barring me from filling her completely. The head of my cock banged against the top of her, tearing a guttural grunt from my chest.

"Christ!" I thrust again, loving how deep I could go. Her liquid heat slicked over me, turning friction into sheer-minded lust.

I could've come right there.

I could've come a hundred fucking times.

But yet again, I needed more. So much *more*.

Nila's hands slapped on the side, her fingers struggling for purchase as I stopped thinking, stopped feeling, and gave into what I needed.

I rode her.

So. Damn. Hard.

I claimed her.

So. Damn. Hard.

I grabbed her hips and punished both of us for finding what we never thought we'd find. I broke myself by shattering my walls and admitting without her…I was nothing.

Nothing.

I fucked her. I loved her.

I gave everything to her.

My teeth sank into the spot between her shoulder and neck as sweat ran down my back. I wanted to puncture her skin. I never wanted to let go.

The diamonds in her collar reflected the sapphire of the water, blinding me.

Her whimpers echoed in my ears as she tilted her head, giving me more authority, more control with my primitive hold. Unable to stop myself, I bit harder, licking her salty skin, relishing in her flinch.

My teeth sank deeper, and only once I tasted the faintest tang of blood did I stand up and fuck her harder. My fingers gripped her hipbones, conveying greed and possession. My entire mind-set became feral, needing to conquer this woman.

My woman.

Nila turned her head, pressing her cheek to the side. A wince knitted her brows, her lips bowed in pain, but I couldn't stop.

Wouldn't stop.

"Yes. More, Jethro. More."

My chest rose and fell with laboured breaths, my muscles spasmed as I sent my body hurtling into euphoria.

Her eyes opened and I lost myself in the dark chasm of mesmerizing love.

She loved me.

She fucking loves me.

The unmistakable vulnerability of such an emotion tore open my heart.

The cuts on my feet bellowed as I dug my toes into the silty bottom and rode her harder, giving her my entire length thrust after thrust after *thrust.*

"Nila—fuck—"

I jerked. My orgasm shot unrestrained from my balls. It exploded up my cock with such intensity, I folded over her back. "Goddammit," I groaned, sucking in her hair as savage streams of cum erupted from my tip.

Her inner muscles demanded more, conjuring every last drop of semen I had to give. The release kept going and going, threatening to burst my heart as my body continued to devour hers. Ecstasy sparkled in every cell as I hit the top of her, spurting one last time as deep as I could go.

"Feel that?" I asked, grunting as a final wave stole my ability to breathe. Sweat ran down my temples, drenching my hair. "You're inside me, Nila Weaver—as surely as I'm inside you."

"You're it for me, Jethro. You've destroyed me." Her voice was soft, dreamy.

I bent to kiss her—the sweetest, gentlest kiss. "You're wrong. You're the one who's destroyed me."

Ending the kiss, Nila just watched me. No words. No questions.

She accepted everything I gave her. She hadn't looked away while I lost myself in her—she'd given me something I'd never had before. She gave me everything—let me witness how true and steadfast it was.

Trust.

Connection.

No lies.

She fucking loved me.

She'd given me a new beginning.

"WHEN WILL YOU tell me?"

Jethro's step faltered, his eyes shooting to mine.

His naked torso was damp and flushed with heat from the cave-springs, a white towel riding low on his hips.

He'd offered to carry me, but I'd chosen to walk—even though I was just as naked with only a towel hiding my modesty.

I was *alive*.

The sooner my body remembered how to move, the better.

Even though hate had killed me, love had revived me.

Jethro had salvaged me and brought me back.

He'd done more than bring me back.

He'd given me a new home—inside him.

I'm alive because of him.

The Second Debt had taken everything from me.

But Jethro had given it back a hundred fold.

We ghosted to a stop outside my bedroom door. Jethro was the perfect suitor, walking me home after the strangest day of all. His hand came up to cup my cheek, a sigh escaping his lips. "I will tell you, but it's not a simple matter of blurting it out."

I turned my head and kissed his palm, never breaking eye contact. "Whatever it is, I'll understand."

He smiled sadly. "That's the thing; you probably won't. To tell you what I am means I'll have to tell you everything. About the debts, the reasoning, my role." He hung his head. "It's a lot."

I shuffled closer, wrapping my arms around his warm body.

"Tomorrow. Meet me after breakfast and take me somewhere far from here. Tell me then."

His nostrils flared. "You want to go off the grounds? Away from Hawksridge?"

The thought excited me. I didn't want to go back to London or seek out my old life—not anymore, but it would be nice to go somewhere just the two of us.

A date.

"You can trust me, Jethro. You know that. I wouldn't run if you took me somewhere public."

A painful shadow crossed his face. "I know you wouldn't. And that's what fucking kills me."

My heart stuttered. "Why?"

He slouched, pushing me against my door so my back kissed the wood and his lips kissed mine. The kiss was fleeting and soft, but the emotion behind it squeezed my chest with an agonising weight.

I didn't know what the weight was. But the pressure built and built with words dying to leap free.

I.

Love.

You.

After what had just happened between us, it was all I could think about. I wanted to scream them. Blare them. Let him know that my caring for him wasn't conditional or cruel.

I loved him. For *him*. For his soul.

His lips skated over mine again—the sweetest connection.

"Jethro," I breathed. "I—I lo—"

He froze, slamming his fingers over my mouth. "Don't say it." Dropping his touch, he shook his head. "Don't say it. Please, Nila."

"But why shouldn't I...when it's the truth." The weight on my heart grew deeper, stronger. I had no choice but to tell him. The words physically suffocated me, needing to be said. "You mean everything to me." Placing my hand over his heart, I whispered. "Kite...I'm in love with you. It doesn't come with conditions or commands. I can't hate you for what you did today or what you might do in the future. I'm scared and lost and absolutely terrified that I'm doing the wrong thing by choosing you over my own life—but...I have no choice."

He sucked in the sharpest breath. "You called me Kite."

My heart bottomed out.

His name bulldozed through the partition I'd managed to keep in place. My feelings toward Kite plaited with my feelings for Jethro.

I slammed deeper into love.

He's mine.

His eyes squeezed closed, pressing his forehead on mine. "Nila…you—you don't know what you're doing to me." He trembled in my arms, his hands bracing himself on the door. "Take it back. I—I can't take so much from you."

"I can't take back something that already belongs to you."

Tears.

I wanted to cry.

I wanted free my terror at falling in love. I wanted to beg him to be strong enough to choose me after stealing everything that I was.

I couldn't compete with what he did to me in the spring. He'd reached inside me and ripped my heart from my chest. I didn't fight it. In fact, I'd carved it out for him.

My hands were bloody from presenting it to him with open arms.

I.

Love.

Him.

Before, I was in a cage.

I wasn't any more.

I could see. I was free. I *believed.*

"Tomorrow." He exhaled shakily. He clasped my jaw, running his thumbs over my cheeks. "You're mine. You deserve to know the man you've chosen—the man you've saved."

A shooting star sliced through my soul. "I saved you?"

A soft smile tugged his lips. "You have no idea, do you?" He kissed my forehead, filling it with overwhelming feeling. "No idea what you've done to me."

His delectable smell wisped around us. I wanted to fall into him and never let go.

He whispered, "Tomorrow, everything that I am becomes yours."

I shivered at the truth in his eyes, the echoing affection. "Tomorrow."

With a barely-there kiss, he transmitted every emotion he couldn't say and backed into the shadows of the corridor. "Tomorrow, I'm taking you away from here. I'll give you what you've selflessly given me. I'll tell you…everything."

Overnight, I'd turned from a supple young woman to arthritic hag.

I didn't sleep. I doubted I'd ever be able to sleep again with the excitement of what today would bring.

Jethro will tell me.

Finally, I would know.

Last night, I'd thought about reading the Weaver Journal to see how my mother and grandmother felt paying the Second Debt. Had they made note of it? Or were they like me and saw what the Journal was—a way to monitor our hearts and minds? I wanted to see if they'd done what I did: fall for their tormentors.

But despite my bouncing mind and infectious energy, my body grew stiffer by the moment.

It ached, it screamed, it needed to rest.

I'd returned from the dead.

Relearning to live again wasn't easy.

I would have days of recovering ahead and it became painfully obvious when I went to stand. My shoulders cried from the simple motion of shoving my sheets away. My legs promptly went on strike as they touched the thick carpet.

I remained vertical for a brief moment, before face planting instead.

I didn't walk anymore, I hobbled.

I didn't talk, I croaked.

I wore bracelets of bruising around my wrists and ankles, and my skin retained its ghostly white, as if I hadn't quite shed death's grip.

No matter how alive I'd been with Jethro last night…today, I was paying for it.

I hadn't wanted him to leave—not when he was blistering open and profound. I would've preferred to fall asleep in his embrace. But I knew that, regardless of our alliance to one another, his family was still in charge. Things had to go on as if nothing had changed—even though everything had.

My stomach rumbled, adding another discomfort on top of all the rest.

I couldn't remember the last time I'd eaten.

After a slow shower and an even slower time of getting dressed, I headed to the door, hissing between my teeth with every step.

I wouldn't permit my body to steal my plans for today. Jethro was taking me away. He would talk. Nothing would destroy that.

Perhaps it could *wait until tomorrow.*

The thought of returning to the softness of my mattress almost made me turn around.

No!

I was just stiff—that was all. As long as I got on with life, I would heal faster.

Gritting my teeth, I forced my aching muscles to slowly propel me toward the dining room.

As I pushed open the double doors and entered the cavernous space with its dripping blood-red walls and excessively big portraits of past Hawks, my attention swooped to the armoury and the empty place that had held my dirk.

That same dirk was now tucked into the waistband of my yoga pants.

The scents of freshly brewed coffee and intoxicating aroma of buttery pastries turned my hunger into a sharp pang.

Cut looked up from his newspaper, a large grin splitting his face. "Ah, Nila! You're awake from the dead." He laughed at his tasteless joke. Folding the paper, he waved to a few free chairs.

The dining room was a busy place this morning. Black Diamond brothers were scattered around the twenty seated table, eating an array of full English breakfasts.

Tugging on the cuffs of my long sleeve baby-blue jumper, I drifted forward, cursing the creak in my joints.

I second-guessed my need for breakfast and hovered by a chair. If I didn't sit down soon, I'd fall, but I didn't think I could tolerate eating with my archenemies.

Where is he?

I needed to make sure Jethro hadn't had second thoughts. That we were still together—still true.

"I see Jet revived you."

Daniel's voice made my head snap up. He sat between two bikers, gnawing on a sausage.

Crap, I hadn't seen him. If I'd known he was here, I would've forgone an entire day of food.

Daniel sneered. "He's such a soft-hearted prick. If it were me, I would've just let you drown."

My fingers curled around the back of a chair. "Lucky for me, you're not firstborn."

Daniel lost his smirk. His face grew black. "Not lucky for you, though, little Weaver."

What did he mean by that?

Then the doors swung wide and Jethro appeared.

The man who'd drugged me, kidnapped me, and stolen my heart strode quickly to my side and took my elbow.

Every atom wanted to sway into his support. Every cell demanded I turn and kiss him.

But I couldn't.

I couldn't let Cut see what'd happened.

It was one thing to be blatant in my hate for Jethro at the beginning, but now it proved a hard task to pretend. I had to openly despise him, all while suffocating my heart from showing the truth.

It took all my willpower, but I sidestepped out of Jethro's hold. "Don't you think you did enough yesterday? Don't touch me."

Jethro sucked in a harsh breath.

Daniel chuckled, smacking his lips. "Seems you're as hated as us now, brother. Congratulations."

Jethro's eyebrows knitted together, his gaze flaring with hurt.

I willed him to understand.

The tightness suddenly faded around his mouth, his forehead smoothing into a perfect mask.

He knows.

His gaze met mine. With a barely noticeable nod, he agreed to our deception. A second later, a cold shield slammed over his face as effortlessly as breathing. He glittered with ice, so pure, so sharp.

If I didn't bear the marks of his teeth and fingertips from loving me so roughly last night, I would've doubted what was real.

I swallowed hard.

It's only a trick.

It's what needs to happen.

It was us against them now. This was the biggest secret of all.

My attention dropped to what he held in his left hand.

The Tally Box.

The room had been fairly silent since I entered, but now hushed anticipation filled the space.

"Glad to see you remembered," Cut said, taking a sip of his coffee. Jethro nodded at his father, pulling out a chair for me. "Sit, Ms. Weaver. There's something we need to do."

Unable to hide my flinch from bending sore joints, I settled into the offered chair.

Only once I sat did Jethro take the seat beside me.

Folding his long legs beneath the table, he shuffled closer. His aftershave and natural scent of woods and leather trickled into my lungs, causing my heart to squeeze.

My mouth popped open as something pressed against my knee.

Jethro refused to meet my eyes, but I knew it was him, touching me…comforting me, granting me strength.

I sucked in a breath as he nudged me harder. The pressure sent combustible lust fizzing through my blood.

The heavy weight from last night settled on my chest. Words I wanted to spill gathered thickly, drowning me. I wanted to talk to him. I wanted to ask questions and hear his answers.

I want to know him.

Every inch.

Jethro continued to lean his leg against mine. He did it so calmly, all the while pretending nothing was different.

"Get on with it, Jet," Cut ordered, his attention locked on us.

Jethro nodded curtly. "Of course. Don't rush me. I think I've proven I'm more than capable of doing what needs to be done."

Cut smashed his lips together.

Jethro's eyes narrowed as he opened the Tally Box.

My heartbeat sped up as he lifted out the apparatus he would need. Keeping my attention on the needle and ink, I rubbed my foot against his ankle.

He tensed, but continued on as if everything was fine.

Last night, he'd given me power over him in the form of his life.

I knew things no one else did.

And after today, I would know everything.

Jethro was mine, and I would help save him, just like he said. We could change our fates from the plague of his family.

"Hold out your hand," Jethro murmured, ignoring the table of onlookers.

My heart raced as he held up the tattoo gun.

Pressing my knuckles against the wood of the table, I bit my lip as he turned on the gun.

His hair had grown longer and it fell over his forehead. My fingers itched to brush it away, to press below his chin and bring his mouth to mine.

The air shimmered between us, growing thicker with lust.

My pussy ached from him taking me so roughly last night, but I wanted more. I wanted it harder, deeper, faster. I doubted I'd ever have enough.

Jethro bristled, fighting against the building heat humming where we touched. When it came to touching in public, we had no armor against the truth.

My gaze shot to Cut. My feelings were far too obvious—he'd see...he'd know. However, his attention zeroed in on his son, his hands steepled before him.

I gasped as the sharp needle bit into my skin. I endured the tiny teeth as they stained me with ink. The burn this time was faintly familiar, filling with memories—becoming part of the design as much as his initials.

It only took a moment.

Jethro reclined, eyeing up his penmanship. There, on the pad of my middle finger, he'd completed another *JKH* .

A debt for a debt.

A tally for a tally.

The residual pain couldn't compete with my other aches and bruises. It was rather refreshing to have a wound that was sharp, rather than bone-deep and throbbing.

Jethro turned off the gun and handed it to me.

Wordlessly, he splayed his beautiful long fingers and never stopped looking at me as I inked my ownership on his mirroring finger.

My lines were straighter this time, more confident. I embraced the marks because now it only bound us tighter together, rather than recorded a new debt.

When I'd finished, he had two branded fingers.

Like for like.

Same for same.

Jethro nudged my foot again, keeping his face blank and almost cruel. I pressed back, never looking up as I turned off the gun and placed it back in its box.

Awareness scattered over my forearms. I couldn't stop a gentle sigh as Jethro deliberately brushed my pinky with his, tucking away the discarded vial and locking the lid.

Cut muttered, "Good to see you learned from your past mistake and things are following accordingly." Waving at the sideboard groaning with food, he added, "Eat, both of you. You have a large schedule."

My throat closed at the thought of what that could mean.

Cut narrowed his eyes. "Jethro, you're in charge of the Carlyle shipment. The stones arrive in a few hours. You know what to do." Turning his cold glare on me, he smiled. "And, Nila, you've been summoned by my mother, Bonnie, for tea in her boudoir."

My heart raced.

Jethro threw me a look.

What about our plans?

He glared at his father. "Ms. Weaver was subjected to enough yesterday." His voice lowered as he spoke through clenched teeth. "Give her a few days, for fuck's sake."

Knives and forks screeched across crockery as the Diamond men turned to see Cut's reaction.

Cut fisted his hands on the table. "Don't you—"

"Um, sir?"

All heads turned to the youngest member of the Black Diamonds, a twenty-year-old man named Facet. His floppy blond hair and kind eyes were a direct contradiction to the leader he now addressed.

Cut's forehead furrowed. Black anger covered his face. "What? What is so fucking important you interrupt me mid-sentence?"

Facet shifted awkwardly. "Sorry, sir. Won't happen again. But, eh…we have company." His eyes flew around the room, looking for someone to help bear the brunt of his leader.

No one moved.

The guy sucked in a breath, reluctantly delivering his news. "I tried to stop them from entering the grounds. We did what you said. But they ignored us." Sweat gleamed on his upper lip. "Even the gatekeeper at the lock house couldn't stop them."

"What the hell are you talking about, boy?!" Cut exploded.

Facet jumped. "They have a warrant, sir. They—they barged past, regardless of our warnings. We reminded them that we own their department—that our brotherhood is beyond their reach." He hung his head. "It didn't do any good."

The entire table sucked in a breath.

Warrant?

Could it be?

Jethro went deathly still beside me. Every connection we shared froze, no longer a two-way street of togetherness and affection. A road block slammed into place, masking his every thought.

I glanced at him from the corner of my eye. My heart squeezed as he stared fiercely at the opposite wall, refusing to look at me.

"Jethro—" I breathed.

His jaw locked; snowflakes flurried around him as he pulled more and more away from me. Goosebumps dotted my flesh.

Cut roared, "Tell those fucking pigs to get off my land. Their warrant means jack-shit."

"Sir, I've told them. But they won't listen. They say—they say they're here for—"

Jethro burst out laughing—a cold, cynical chuckle. "That low life piece of shit. He did this. They're here for her." He looked at the ceiling, his face twisting into nightmares. "Of course, they fucking are."

A warrant could mean many things. It might not have anything to do with me. Yet a screeching, tearing noise echoed in my ears. *It's my soul.* The awful ripping sound was my soul splintering in two. If they had come for me…that meant…

I'm saved.

I'd wished for this very thing to happen.

I'd prayed for this. I'd begged for this.

Escape.

So, why—if it was true—did I wish to run to my quarters and hide?

I don't want to leave him.

I can't *leave him.*

Not after last night.

Jethro balled his hands, his eyes sharp and deadly. He snarled at Facet, "Tell them they can't fucking have her."

My heart squeezed. Pain blazed through me with more agony than I thought possible. He wouldn't give me up. He *couldn't* give me up.

We were one now. It'd been written in the stars and on our very skin.

Escape.

The word slithered through my brain, bringing forth thoughts of London and home. I shook my head, trying to dislodge the steadily building allure.

You could go home.

No, my home is here now.

But you'd be safe again…

My steadfast promise to stay and steal Jethro from his heritage faded…I became *confused…*

I swallowed, lubricating my throat. "Jethro—please…"

I needed him to fight for me. To prove that this was my place, my destiny.

Jethro clenched his jaw, shoving his chair back and standing. "Quiet!" Pointing a finger at Facet, he growled. "Do they, or do they not, have a fucking warrant for what's mine?"

Facet swallowed. "Yes."

"How?" I blurted, causing every man to look in my direction. "How do they have a warrant?"

Facet's mouth fell open, looking to Cut to see if he should reply. Cut glowered at me as if I'd brought the apocalypse to his door. No one spoke.

What did my father do?

How did V find a way to free me?

My heart winged thinking of my twin. He'd promised he would never give up. I should've trusted him.

I should be more grateful.

I wanted to kill him.

He'd ruined it. He'd taken everything I'd worked for and torn it away from me.

I'm alive and going home.

I'm alive and going home.

The words repeated in my head.

I wouldn't be alive if it wasn't for Jethro.

I'm in love with him.

He'd infected me, and no matter how much distance was between us, that would never change. I was his. And he was mine.

Jethro's eyes locked with me—the golden depths burned with despair and scorching agony. "I warned him. I tried to stop…"

He showed too much.

He *felt* too much.

My diamond collar grew heavier, colder.

You said you'd be the last.

You promised you'd end this.

My stomach somersaulted.

If they're here for you. Leave.

You have no choice.

I ached.

"Warned who? What's happened? Jethro…I'm not leaving. Even if they are here for me."

Jethro didn't move. He looked as if the light in his soul had snuffed out. The peace and openness of last night was gone. Disappeared.

"I'll kill him for this," he muttered.

Unfurling my hand, I looked at my inked finger. I needed him to know that what happened last night wasn't a trick. He needed to know that I intended to stay—even though it might be the worst decision in the world.

My stomach clenched at the thought of leaving.

Facet blurted, "Sir, they're here to take Nila Weaver home."

The words fell like bombs, detonating my last hope.

It's true then.

Cut stood up. He spoke slowly and with the blackest temper I'd ever seen. "You're mistaken, boy. I suggest you get out of my sight. Tell whoever threatened you to get off my fucking land."

"They're—they're in the annex, sir. They said if we don't deliver the girl within five minutes, they'll tear apart the place looking for her."

Jethro fisted his hands. "Tell them she's mine and she's not going anywhere."

Daniel stood. "She's our Weaver now."

In a sick twisted way, the men imprisoning me were now on my side. I was no longer just a betrayer to my ancestors but a betrayer to my father and brother, too.

You would rather stay here than go home.

I would rather love and die young than be empty forever.

"What is the meaning of this screeching inside my house?"

All eyes turned to the raspy voice of Bonnie Hawk as she appeared in the doorway.

Facet moved sideways, giving up his audience to the matriarch of this insane family.

"I see the plot has thickened." Bonnie crooked a finger in my direction, a large ruby glinting in the light. "How did you do this?"

"Me?" I glanced from Bonnie to Jethro. "I didn't do it. I wouldn't."

"It wasn't her," Jethro snapped. "Get rid of the police. She's not leaving."

My arms craved to wrap around him. To thank him for keeping me.

Bonnie shuffled closer, her long skirt dragging on the carpet. Her white hair was curled and immaculate. "She's brought scorn and blasphemy to our name." Her eyes bored into mine. "I've seen what you do, little girl. I know what you want. And you won't get it." Pointing at the door, she ordered, "Get out."

Cut punched the table. "No fucking—"

"She's leaving this house." Bonnie interrupted. "Now."

Jethro moved to stand in front of me, blocking my body with his. "She's staying."

Bonnie smiled coldly. "There is no other way. They're here for her. She's going with them." Her eyes narrowed. "Don't make me repeat myself, boy. You know as well as I do what your obligations are."

I grabbed Jethro's arm, unable to hide my emotions. If I hated the Hawks as much as Cut believed, I should've sprinted out the door, skipping with happiness. Instead, Cut would see that something deeper had happened—something that would be severely punished.

But I didn't care.

Because if I didn't fight, this was over. Here and now.

"Let me talk to them—"

Jethro spun to face me, his temper blazing. "You want to *talk* to them? To tell them what, exactly? The truth?"

"Enough!" Cut yelled. Looking at Bonnie, he frowned. "You want her gone?"

Bonnie nodded, her red lipstick smeared on thin lips. "Immediately."

Cut sighed, his leather jacket creaking as anger wisped off him. "Fine," he said sharply. "Nila Weaver, get the fuck out of my house."

My heart crumbled.

Jethro crossed his arms, still shielding me. His ice slid back into place turning him impenetrable. "I'm the firstborn, and I say she isn't fucking leaving."

Cut moved around the table, his fists clenching. "You dare do this here, son? You know you'll lose—"

"Wait!"

A feminine voice whipped through the aching tension in the room.

"Jaz? What the hell are you doing in here?" Jethro asked, his mask slipping as he looked at his wheelchair bound sister.

She rolled into the dining room with the aid of a blonde-curled maid. Jasmine's bronze eyes met Cut's. "She can't go, Father. It's not finished."

Cut breathed hard through his nose, his temper throbbing beneath his frayed self-control. "Don't speak of things you don't understand. Jethro didn't control the situation. This is his mess. He's failed." Cut looked piercingly at Jethro, sending goosebumps and terror down my spine. "It's over. He's done."

The way he spoke…it sounded like a death sentence.

Jethro gasped, true fear coating his face. "It's not over—"

"Shut. Up." Cut sliced the air with his arm, silencing him. Looking at me, he snapped, "Leave, Ms. Weaver. Your time is up. I won't tell you again."

Jasmine's gaze shot to Jethro's. "Don't let her go, Kite."

Kite.

My soul splintered.

Bonnie shuffled forward. "I see what you're doing, girl. Your family have been clever with their tricks and treachery, but I won't let you spin any more of your filth." Her wrinkly skin furrowed deeper with rage. "Get. Out. *Now.*"

"Was this always your plan, Father?" Jethro looked at Cut, panic and rage twisted his face. "You set me up to fail?" The depth of confusion and agony in his voice broke my heart.

My eyes flared wide. I didn't understand.

"Jethro…he doesn't matter. None of them do." I squeezed his arm. "Believe in us. Believe in me."

"Hush, stupid girl," Bonnie snapped. "You're the same as all the rest. Get out." Pointing at the door, she hissed, "Go!"

The other bikers didn't do a thing. Just sat and watched.

Jethro never tore his eyes off his father—they were clouded and strained. He was a trebuchet straining to release his tension.

"Don't do this," I whispered. "Don't let them ruin what we have."

We were damned to our fates, brought together by a ridiculous vendetta. Yet…something right had come out of something so wrong. We'd somehow found the one person we were meant to find.

I can't go.

"You don't understand, Nila. It's not that easy." Jethro looked at me, running his newly inked finger along the inside of my wrist. "Go, before it's too late."

Memories of the way he'd thrust inside me last night filled my mind. I'd meant what I said—I *felt* him—not just inside me, but what he hid inside *him*.

It was more than truth.

It had been gospel in its legitimacy.

"Jethro…it's too late already. I'm meant to stay. With you."

"She's right, Kite. Tell the police to leave. Find a way," Jasmine said.

I looked at Jethro's sister in her navy wool dress and white pashmina in her lap. Her face was pinched and full of concern. What did she know? Why was she fighting on my side?

Cut slammed his fist onto the table with a resounding thump. "Get your hands off my son and get the fuck out!"

Jethro's face darkened. His gaze sent a brutally painful message.

Leave…at least one of us will be free.

My body wound tighter and tighter.

Tears clogged my throat. "I can't. I won't."

I won't be free without you.

Cut suddenly barked, "Daniel, seeing as Ms. Weaver refuses to leave, escort her off the premises."

Daniel chuckled, his eyes glittering as he moved quickly around the table. "With pleasure, Pop."

"Stop! All of you!" Jasmine shouted, but it didn't do any good.

In a flash, Daniel grabbed my elbow, hauling me away from Jethro, from our bond, from the only existence I ever wanted.

"No!"

Daniel's voice licked into my ear. "Fight me and I'll do something un-fucking-forgivable. Do you want me to do that?"

I tried to stomp on his foot. "You're a bastard."

"Thanks for the compliment."

Jethro lunged, grabbing me and punching Daniel in the jaw. "Get your fucking hands off her." Whipping me behind his body, he glowered at Cut. "I'll get rid of her."

Cut breathed hard. "Good. Then I can deal with you."

Jethro jolted, every inch tight and breaking.

Without a word, he dragged me toward the exit. He trembled as if he'd shatter at any moment, buckling under the weight.

I squirmed, fighting my aching body. "Let me go! I'm not going anywhere."

"You're leaving. If it's the last thing I do, at least I can keep you safe."

I struggled harder. "Safe? I don't want to be safe. I want to be with you."

"Quiet," he choked, his face ashen. "It's better this way."

"You're choosing them over me!" I tried to punch him. "Stand up to them. Leave with me. Don't stay here, Jethro."

He clenched his jaw and didn't reply.

He wasn't strong enough to fight for what we had.

He's choosing his family over me.

I rolled my arm, twisting out of his hold. Scurrying from his hands, I turned to face Cut. "I don't know what power you hold over him, but it isn't enough. He's mine, not yours."

"Nila—don't!" Jethro grabbed me, dragging me backward. "You don't know what you're doing. For fuck's sake, don't make this worse than it already is."

Cut grinned broadly. "Congratulations, Nila. You've successfully just changed the future." His eyes fell frigid and evil on Jethro. "I thought there was hope. But you were just too fucking weak."

The men shifted in their seats. Cut never moved. "Get rid of the girl, Jet. You and I have something we need to discuss."

Life seemed to siphon from Jethro's limbs, growing colder by the second.

"No!" Jasmine screeched, rolling forward. "You can't. You promised!" Tears slid from her eyes, looking at her brother. "Stop this, Kite. I'm sorry. I'm so sorry for making you change, for causing—" She stopped, unable to speak through her sobs.

The worst horror I'd ever felt slithered through my blood.

I'm hollow. I'm hurting. What the hell is happening?

Something darker was at work. This wasn't about me anymore. This was about Jethro. His father.

What would they do to him the moment I left?

I *wouldn't* leave him behind.

Linking my fingers with his, I pulled. "Jethro, come with me."

But he just stood there, rooted to the spot. His eyes wild, lips parted.

I hovered…waiting. Waiting for one tiny sign that he was still alive beneath whatever fear had struck him mute.

Bonnie sidled up to me, bringing the sickening scent of rosewater and biscuits. "Goodbye, Ms. Weaver. You've earned your freedom today at the cost of another." Leaning closer, she whispered, "You're free, but this is *far* from over, girl. Mark my words; you'll pay for what your family has done."

I stood taller, ready to fight even if Jethro wouldn't. "Stop it, I'm stay—"

Jethro suddenly yelled, "Go! Just fucking go."

The room froze, all eyes pinned on him.

He pointed at the door, shattering my heart into dust. "Leave."

His eyes screamed the truth.

If you love me at all, you'll go.

I need you to go.

"You can't ask me to do this," I said, wiping away a fallen tear.

"I can and I will." Striding forward, he grabbed my face and kissed me in front of everyone. His hands shook, his lips trembled.

He broke me completely.

"Please, Nila. Do this for me. Let me make this right."

Pushing me gently to the door, he commanded, "Go and don't look back."

My world crumbled.

My legs didn't want to move.

My heart didn't want to beat.

His eyes begged me to obey.

Please…go.

Stumbling, I did the impossible.

I didn't look at Jasmine.

I didn't look at Jethro.

I kept moving.

I would honour him.

I would obey him.

Even though every inch of me bled.

Even though every part of me was dead.

I would go home.

I would find a way to fix this.
It wasn't over.
Two seconds later…
…
I was gone.

Continues in THIRD DEBT

"She healed me. She broke me. I set her free. But we are in this together. We will end this together. The rules of this ancient game can't be broken."

Nila Weaver no longer recognises herself. She's left her lover, her courage, and her promise. Two debts down. Too many to go.

Jethro Hawk no longer recognises himself. He's embraced what he always ran from, and now faces punishment far greater than he feared.
It's almost time. It's demanding to be paid.
The Third Debt will be the ultimate test of all.

THE ENTIRE SERIES IN THE INDEBTED SERIES ARE OUT NOW!

Playlist

My Demons by Starset
Bleeding out by Imagine Dragons
Somebody I used to Know by Gotye
Lost Cause by Imagine Dragons
Monster by Lady Gaga
I like it Rough by Lady Gaga
Point of No Return by Starset
Bad Romance by Lady Gaga
ET by Katy Perry
I Won't Let You Go by Snow Patrol
Run by Snow Patrol
Beating Heart by Ellie Goulding
Silhouettes by Monsters and Men
Weak by Seether
Suffer Well by Depeche Mode
Break Free by Ariana Grande
I like you the way you are by She the Monsters
Angel by Theory of a Deadman
Saving me by Nickelback

About the Author

Pepper Winters is a New York Times, Wall Street Journal, and USA Today International Bestseller. She loves dark romance, star-crossed lovers, and the forbidden taboo. She strives to write a story that makes the reader crave what they shouldn't, and delivers tales with complex plots and unforgettable characters.

After chasing her dreams to become a full-time writer, Pepper has earned recognition with awards for best Dark Romance, best BDSM Series, and best Dark Hero. She's an #1 iBooks bestseller, along with #1 in Erotic Romance, Romantic Suspense, Contemporary, and Erotica Thriller. She's also honoured to wear the IndieReader Badge for being a Top 10 Indie Bestseller, and recently signed a two book deal with Hachette. Represented by Trident Media, her books have garnered foreign and audio interest and are currently being translated into numerous languages. They will be in available in bookstores worldwide.

Her Dark Romance books include (click for buylinks):
Tears of Tess (Monsters in the Dark #1)
Quintessentially Q (Monsters in the Dark #2)
Twisted Together (Monsters in the Dark #3)
Debt Inheritance (Indebted #1)
First Debt (Indebted Series #2)
Second Debt (Indebted Series #3)
Third Debt (Indebted Series #4)
Fourth Debt (Indebted Series #5)

Final Debt (Indebted Series #6)
Indebted Epilogue (Indebted Series #7)

Her Grey Romance books include:
Destroyed
Ruin & Rule (Pure Corruption MC #1)

Upcoming releases are
Indebted Beginnings
Sin & Suffer (Pure Corruption #2)
Je Suis a Toi (Monsters in the Dark Novella)
Unseen Messages (Contemporary Survival Romance)
Super Secret Series to be announced early 2016

To be the first to know of upcoming releases, please
follow her on her website
Pepper Winters

She loves mail of any kind: pepperwinters@gmail.com

Other Books by Pepper

Tears of Tess (Monsters in the Dark #1)
"My life was complete. Happy, content, everything neat and perfect.
Then it all changed.
I was sold."
Buy Now

Quintessentially Q (Monsters in the Dark #2)
"All my life, I battled with the knowledge I was twisted… screwed up
to want something so deliciously dark—wrong on so many levels. But
then slave fifty-eight entered my world. Hissing, fighting, with a core of
iron, she showed me an existence where two wrongs do make a right."
Buy Now

Twisted Together (Monsters in the Dark #3)
"After battling through hell, I brought my esclave back from the brink
of ruin. I sacrificed everything—my heart, my mind, my very desires to
bring her back to life. And for a while, I thought it broke me, that I'd
never be the same. But slowly the beast is growing bolder, and it's
finally time to show Tess how beautiful the dark can be."
Buy Now

Destroyed (Standalone Grey Romance)
She has a secret.
He has a secret.

One secret destroys them.
Buy Now

Ruin & Rule (Pure Corruption MC #1)
"We met in a nightmare. The in-between world where time had no power over reason. We fell in love. We fell hard. But then we woke up. And it was over . . ."
Buy Now

Unseen Messages
"I should've listened, should've paid attention. The messages were there. Warning me. But I didn't see and I paid the price..."
Buy Now

Pennies (Dollar Series #1)
"I had her and I was the richest man alive. But then I lost her and became destitute."
Buy Now

All other titles and updates can be found on her **Goodreads Page.**

Made in United States
Troutdale, OR
11/19/2024

25078187R00348